PRAISE FOR HELENA

"I am happy to say I might have found a new author to enjoy and I will be checking out some of her other books soon."

ONE MORE WORD BOOK BLOG

"Gorgeous setting, difficult decisions."

5* AMAZON

"Helena Halme does an excellent job giving her readers a perfect portrayal of such beautiful wonder when describing the breathtaking views and scenery of Alicia's surroundings."

CHICK LIT CAFE

"I loved many things about this story, but what I liked the most was the setting. I think the author captured the Nordic islands perfectly."

BOOK DUST MAGIC BOOK BLOG

LOVE ON THE ISLAND
BOOKS 1-3

HELENA HALME

Newhurst Press

COPYRIGHT

A FREE STORY!

The Day We Met is a prequel short story
to the *Love on the Island* series.

**This short story is available FREE
only to members of my Readers' Group.**

Go to *helenahalme.com* to sign up to my
Readers' Group and get your free, exclusive, story now!

THE ISLAND AFFAIR

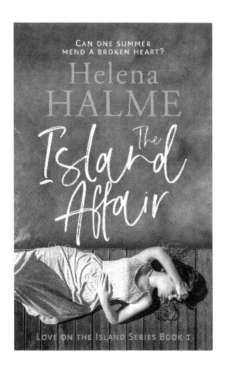

PROLOGUE

Alicia wakes up with a fuzzy head. The curtains to the bay window in the bedroom have been closed, and she hears muffled voices downstairs. She puts her hand on her body and discovers she's wearing a pink dressing gown over the oversized T-shirt she sleeps in. The clock by the bed shows 3.25am. On the small bedside table, she sees a half-empty glass of water and a packet of pills she's never seen before.

Then she remembers, and a horror rises in the pit of her stomach. She gets out of bed and crosses the landing to Stefan's bedroom. The familiar musty smell of her teenage son, her nearly grown-up son, her beautiful boy, hits her as soon as she opens the door, searching the dark room for the bed in the middle of the space. Wanting to see signs of the lanky shape, she looks for a narrow foot peeking out from under the familiar blue and white cover with the cockerel logo of Spurs football club. She prays for the sight of a mop of blond hair on the pillow above the bedcovers. Carefully, slowly, as if still in a dream, she walks over the threshold of the room. When she sees the bed is neatly made up and empty, she falls on her knees and lets out a cry.

She hears rapid steps behind her and feels Liam's hands on her shoulders. He's squeezing her hard, too hard. She can feel tears running down her face and realizes she is weeping. She's making noises she doesn't recognize, animal sounds like a wolf's howling.

ONE

Alicia is standing looking at the vast display of bottles in the ship's tax-free shop when the deck beneath her suddenly shifts and she almost loses her balance. The ferry must be out in the open sea between the islands and Sweden. Liam has gone to sit in one of the 'sleeping chairs'. He's taken a seasickness tablet and feels drowsy. This is the routine they have fallen into over the years, and mostly he is fine, as long as he stays still and keeps his eyes on the horizon. Luckily the quiet compartment has vast windows overlooking the sea.

The Viking Line ferry passes through the small islands between Stockholm and the coast before sailing through the open sea to the Åland archipelago. Usually conditions are calm, but sometimes there's a high wind and the sea is so choppy for an hour or so that the staff close the bars and restaurants.

Alicia tries to listen for any announcement above the clinking sounds of the bottles, but she can't hear anything. Again the ship moves abruptly, and Alicia loses her balance. She suddenly finds herself looking into a pair of piercingly blue eyes.

She had noticed the tall blond man walking along the aisles when she entered the shop. He was difficult to ignore in his trendy jeans, sailor shoes and soft suede jacket. He had an expensive-looking tan and ruffled hair. He's even taller than Liam, Alicia thought, but she didn't spot him standing next to her until she bumped into him.

He takes hold of her arms. His gaze is so direct and suggestive that Alicia gasps.

'Sorry,' she says and the man smiles. The intensely azure eyes and the slightly open mouth surrounded by laughter lines make her instinctively grin too. The sensation on her mouth feels strange; she doesn't remember when she last felt the urge to smile.

Alicia feels the man's strong hands keenly on her elbows. She senses the heat rise into her neck and face. She looks away, embarrassed.

When did she last blush?

'Don't be, I enjoyed it,' the man says, and his smile grows wider at her discomfort.

She straightens up, and the man's hands fall away from her. For a mad moment, Alicia wishes he would put them back and hold her, but she shrugs such thoughts away and gives a short, flustered, laugh.

The man stretches his hand out. 'Patrick Hilden,' he says. He has a very Swedish accent, from Stockholm, Alicia thinks. She tastes the name on her lips.

'Alicia O'Connell.' His hand lingers around Alicia's fingers.

'You're not an islander, are you?' he says.

'Is it that obvious?' Alicia manages to say. She doesn't know how. She's finding it difficult to speak. She's breathless, as if her lungs have been emptied of air.

'It takes one to know one,' the man continues to smile shamelessly into Alicia's eyes.

'I moved with my mum to Åland when I was a baby, but then went away to university and never returned,' Alicia says. She doesn't know why she feels she wants to tell this man her life story.

'Ah, that makes sense. All the best ones leave,' Patrick says.

'And you, you are obviously not from Åland either?'

He laughs. 'Originally from northern Sweden but I now live in Stockholm. One of the unlucky ones.'

Alicia returns the man's laugh. Everybody on the island hates the arrogant *Stockholmare*.

After what seems like minutes, Patrick lets go of Alicia's hand but he's still standing close to her, and his scent of expensive leather and something else, a manly tang, envelops her. She knows she ought to take a step back, but she can't move. She lifts her eyes toward his face and those eyes again.

'You don't sound like a *Norrbotten* Swede,' Alicia says, and then, seeing the man's raised eyebrows, adds laughing awkwardly, 'Sorry, I didn't mean to be rude.' Alicia has forgotten about the many sensibilities surrounding the Scandinavian countries. She's so used to what one can and cannot say about accents in the UK, but she suddenly feels clueless about the similar issues here. She's been living away from home for too long.

The boat shifts again, and Patrick puts his hand out in case Alicia loses her balance.

But this time she's prepared and steadies herself by placing her hand on the edge of the drinks display. 'Not much of a sailor, am I?'

Patrick laughs into her eyes. 'You're over for a holiday?'

'Yes,' Alicia replies simply. His scent and presence are intoxicating. She isn't hearing or seeing anything else but this tall, blue-eyed stranger. It's as if he's mesmerized her, and the old ship's clanging sounds and smells of diesel and paint have disappeared.

'Here you are!' Alicia is woken from her hypnotized state by an almost equally tall and elegant woman, who is striding toward them, speaking loudly in an Åland accent. When she sees Alicia, she looks her up and down and then turns to Patrick. 'Look, they're about to close the shop. There's a storm apparently, so we need to get a move on. Did you find the champagne?'

'This is Alicia O'Connell,' Patrick says, ignoring her urgent question and stretching his arm toward Alicia. He turns to Alicia and says, still smiling, 'And this very rude woman is my wife, Mia.'

The woman looks at Alicia more closely. 'It's you!' Her voice is very shrill and Alicia has a sudden desire to cover her ears with her hands, but instead she smiles. She feels Mia's arms pulling her into a tight embrace.

'Hello, it's been a long time,' Alicia replies from inside the woman's hug. The thin, but muscular arms are holding her tightly.

'So sorry I didn't recognize you!' she says, releasing Alicia.

'You know each other?' Patrick says, his eyebrows raised.

'We went to school together!' Mia shrieks. 'But we have to get on. Alicia, are you going to be on the islands over Midsummer? You must come to our party! Give me your email, will you?'

'Hmm,' Alicia says, not knowing what to reply. She glances over at Patrick, but his face betrays no emotion. He looks bored more than anything else now.

'Oh, don't worry, I've got your mum's address. You must all come. I'll send you the details!'

She drags her husband away. Patrick turns and looks at Alicia. With his right hand, he tips an invisible cap as if in a salute. Alicia stands there with a stupid smile on her face. She watches Mia speak to Patrick rapidly, like a machine gun. Patrick's shoulders are wide and she can see blond hairs curl up at his neck and a tiny, brown patch of skin above his shirt collar. She imagines stroking it, running her fingers along his neck and into his thick hair.

What's happening to me?

TWO

L iam wakes with a start. He checks his watch. He's only been asleep for a matter of minutes—half an hour at most. He wipes his mouth with his thumb; his lips and the side of his cheek are dry. He's paranoid about falling asleep in public and drooling, but all seems to be fine. And then he remembers where he is, on a ferry to the islands, and what has happened. Each time this occurs, each time he lets the knowledge slip from his mind, it's as if a cannon ball hits him in the guts when he remembers. The pain of the realization is intense, and for a moment he struggles to breathe. His heart is beating fast and he closes his eyes again, telling himself that breathing is as natural as living.

Living!

He knows this is just a minor panic attack, a reaction to the death of his son and part of the grieving process. These attacks will lessen and then hopefully disappear. That is what his colleagues at St Mary's Hospital tell him. When it happened the first time, a month or so after the accident, he thought it was his heart and had welcomed the panic and the pain. It would have served him right to die, to follow his son to an early grave. Besides, it would have been a relief.

But to his surprise, after a while his breathing had returned to normal. He remembers how disappointed he had felt, lying in the dark in his bed, next to Alicia, who was gently snoring. She had been on heavy sedatives then, on pills that he had prescribed.

'Acceptance of the facts is the first step,' his psychologist and colleague Constance Bell—a fair-haired older woman—had said. He'd given little credence to her practice before the accident.

'In time you'll be able to celebrate your son's life rather than grieve his death.' Connie, as everyone called her, gave him a half-smile, lifting the corners of her thin lips just a fraction on either side, and nodded her head. That movement meant it was the end of the session. Liam knew the woman was also seeing Alicia, and got the uneasy feeling she was on her side in all of it. He knew that professionally she wasn't taking sides, but after a few sessions, he had detected a coldness in her manner. Now he wonders if, when they're back in London, he should ask to see a different grief counsellor, but he knows changing now would only raise eyebrows in the hospital where they both practice.

Forcing her eyes away from the broad back of the blue-eyed man, Patrick, and her old schoolfriend Mia, Alicia sees Liam walking up and down the aisles. He's carrying a basket and Alicia sees a packet of cigarettes in the bottom. Marlboro Lights. After the accident he started to smoke again.

What is he doing here, especially when there's a storm brewing?

Alicia waves to him several times, and calls his name, soliciting stares from the people around her, until he eventually sees Alicia and walks slowly up to her.

'They're closing the shop,' he says.

Alicia remembers why she is here. Hilda, Alicia's mother, has asked her to bring wine, two bottles of white and two of red, to be precise. 'Something nice,' she had added on the phone, as if Alicia would buy some worthless plonk as a welcome present, or alternatively, as if she was completely unknowledgeable about wine.

'I know,' she says to Liam, and picks up four bottles at random and puts them in Liam's basket.

'We've been invited to a party,' she says over her shoulder, walking toward the tills.

. . .

'You hungry?' Liam asks as they leave the ship's tax-free shop. As they pass the loos, a woman comes out, and the familiar smell of the ferry— a combination of drains, diesel oil and paint—hits Alicia's nostrils. For a moment, she feels a wave of nausea overwhelm her. Perhaps she's suddenly developed sea sickness too?

But she nods to Liam. She wants to follow the old routines on this journey. Veering away from what they always did would be to betray Stefan's memory. Alicia feels his presence strongly now, and she doesn't want to let go of him.

Every summer, Alicia, Liam and Stefan would fly from London to Stockholm and then onto Åland, a group of islands between Finland and Sweden.

Alicia's home.

Usually, Alicia's mother picks them up from the airport and drives them to the *Ålandsfärjan* ferry port in Kapellskär. But this year, Hilda didn't come to meet them in Arlanda. Alicia knows she's scared and wants to postpone the moment when she has to acknowledge Stefan's absence. Instead, she and Liam take a train to *T-Centralen* in Stockholm and a bus to the harbor.

During the hour-long bus journey, Alicia withdrew into her memories of the many times they'd taken this trip together. When Stefan was a baby, they would rent a car, and she'd fuss over the unfamiliar Swedish car seat. How did it work? Was it safe? Alicia would ask all the questions while Liam calmly looked at the instructions and eventually strapped—the usually crying—Stefan into the seat. Alicia looked over at Liam's profile. She was sitting on the aisle seat in the bus, while Liam was asleep, his head resting on his folded jumper by the window. She loved him then; she thought she could never do without him.

In the past, when the seas were heavy Liam got very seasick and had to sit and stare at the horizon close to the bathrooms while Alicia, her mother and Stefan ate and drank in the restaurant, talking about what had happened during the months, or sometimes a full year, since they'd last seen each other. During the meal they admired the breathtakingly beautiful archipelago with its many islands, while Hilda stared besottedly at her grandson, commenting on his taller frame, new haircut or smart jacket.

As the ship picked its way through the small channels, Alicia and Stefan would gawp at the large seaside villas, with their intricate woodwork, built decades ago on the larger islands, or the tiny red houses, with sparkling white window frames, perching on top of small rocky outcrops.

'Can we live there?' Stefan would ask each year, pointing to a particularly beautiful villa, with a boathouse below it and a long jetty jutting out to sea. Even when he was older, they went through this routine, picking out a place they would like to own.

'We already have a cottage on the islands,' Alicia replied.

One year—Alicia cannot remember how old he was—her son said, 'When I'm a grown-up, I'm going to buy that one,' pointing at one particularly grand villa just outside Stockholm.

They had laughed at his naivety—the villas cost a fortune and were rarely even for sale—and Stefan had cried, his dreams crushed by the stupid adults.

'You sure you want to go to the restaurant? It was Stefan who ...' Liam now says, gazing at Alicia, his dark green eyes trying to figure out what is going on in her head. She knows she's shutting him out, pushing him away, but she is too tired to soothe Liam's grief. All her energy is spent on trying to keep herself composed. Trying not to slump down and cry in the middle of the passage, among the holidaymakers, who are laughing, happy at the prospect of a long break on the islands.

Liam is standing in front of her and they are blocking the other passengers, some of whom tut and say '*Ursäkta*', the Swedish for 'Sorry' in a loud voice.

'You OK?' Liam says. He reaches his hand out, about to touch Alicia's arm, but she moves away just in time and Liam's hand flops down.

Alicia looks at Liam. He is definitely a bit green around the gills.

'How are *you* feeling?' she manages to say, even putting an emphasis on the 'you' to show that she cares, even though she doesn't register any kind of feeling for her husband.

'I'm fine—let's risk it. What else is there to do?' Liam says, pulling his mouth into an attempted smile. Alicia looks at her husband. The lines around his eyes have grown deeper in the past few months, and his skin looks pale and sallow. He's got his feet planted wide, but he is ever so slightly stooped, perhaps because he's holding the plastic bag from the tax-free shop. He'll feel better once they enter the Åland archipelago, Alicia thinks, and walks in front of Liam.

Even though Liam knows the layout of the ferry intimately after all these years, Alicia still feels she is the local, and he the foreigner. When the deck below her shifts again, she takes hold of the bannister of the central staircase leading up to the restaurant. She glances behind her and sees that Liam is steady, holding the wall to keep his balance. She nods to him and he follows her up the stairs. As they make their way to the restaurant and are shown to the end of a long table by a large, oval porthole, she remembers how she and Stefan would devour the buffet lunch of gravlax, herring, meatballs in gravy and rye bread and eat too much. She and her son had the same tastes; they both missed proper Finnish food in London. Her lovely, serious boy, who seemed to understand the sacrifice Alicia had made to live away from the islands. He loved the sea, the sauna, the silence of a nightless night at Midsummer when the only sounds were the faint cries of the birds, flying low above the seashore.

Alicia swallows a lump in her throat, trying to control herself. Not that she could cry anymore. There are no tears left, just the pain in her chest, the lump that won't go away however much she cries, or tries to calm down. She makes an effort to concentrate on the familiar, but still stunning, view of the dark wooded islands resting like tufts of carpet on the teal-colored sea. They are entering the calmer seas, thank goodness.

THREE

Hilda has another new car; a red low-slung BMW. Liam's feet almost hug his chin as he settles himself on the back seat. He had insisted Alicia sit next to her mother in the front so that they could chat away in Swedish. It's safer that way. Liam never enjoyed being driven by his mother-in-law. He knows the journey from the ferry port in the capital Mariehamn to his father-in-law's farm in Sjoland takes only 15 minutes—unless the swing bridge over the canal is open—but anything could happen even during the short journey. Hilda's driving is as erratic as her character. If she has to lean back to talk to her daughter, her concentration would suffer even more. Besides, Liam has never learned the language they speak on the islands, a version of Swedish that sounds like Finnish but isn't.

After nearly twenty years of holidaying on the islands, he can understand a little of the Swedish conversation, but Finnish is still incomprehensible to him. Alicia keeps telling him how lucky he is that she and her mother speak Swedish to each other. Alicia never got to learn her mother tongue, because she was just a baby when Hilda moved to the islands.

Liam thinks about Stefan and how fluent he'd been in Swedish, and how much effort Alicia had put into his bilingualism. Although she disliked the Swedes for some curious reason only known to her, for years she had sent Stefan to language lessons at the Swedish Church in Marylebone. When Stefan was fifteen, he'd gone on a week-long confirmation camp in Åland and had fallen in love for the first time. Liam remembers picking his son up from the station in Mariehamn, watching the teenagers spill out from a bus, their heavy bags slung over their shoulders.

Stefan was holding hands with a slim girl with straw-blond hair and bright eyes. Liam could well understand his son's infatuation with her; she had a pale complexion yet was tanned. Her fair eyelashes fluttered as she shook Liam's hand and introduced herself as 'Frida'. Of course, that romance hadn't lasted, but Stefan said they were still friends. Liam had seen her again the previous summer, when the group from the confirmation camp had met up for a drink in Mariehamn. Liam remembers how grown up they had all looked when he'd dropped Stefan off at Torggatan. He'd watched the group of teenagers greet his son with hugs and high-fives through the rear-view mirror as he drove away.

Liam wonders if Stefan's friends have been told. He hopes so, for Alicia's sake. With another pang of guilt, he remembers how Stefan had begun talking about getting a moped; he'd begged and begged to be allowed to ride on the one belonging to Alicia's stepfather, and at last Liam had agreed. Of course, both Alicia and Hilda were against it, so he'd colluded with Uffe to allow Stefan to ride around the farm, and then take a trip on his own into Mariehamn on a day when his mother and grandmother were shopping in Stockholm.

But Liam knew regrets were useless. He made himself concentrate on the road. He would at least try to prevent an accident while in the car with his mother-in-law, and get safely to the farm.

Uffe stands outside the large wood-clad house that he was born in over 65 years ago and watches his stepdaughter and her husband get out of Hilda's car. He decides to let Liam carry the bags; he is young and strong, whereas Uffe's own back has been in spasms all morning. Although he now has enough workers on his farm to do the heavy lifting, he still likes to get involved and has been knee-deep in mud all day. He should have stayed in the fields, overseeing the first crop of potatoes being lifted onto the lorry, but he knows what Hilda's reaction to his absence at the visitors' arrival would be. At a few minutes past five, he hastily got into his Subaru and drove the couple of kilometers home along the road. He had just changed his shirt in the bedroom, when he saw the BMW turn into the drive through the window.

Uffe waves when he sees Alicia walking up to him. Suddenly noticing how dirty his hands are, he places them quickly behind his back.

'Uffe,' his stepdaughter says and buries her head in his chest. Uffe hugs her hard and feels a tightening in his chest as he thinks about the handsome lad, his grandson. Or step-grandson to be precise. (Uffe has never considered Alicia anything but his daughter even if he didn't officially father her.) It's incomprehensible that the young lad would no longer be coming here; that he no longer exists.

Of course, Uffe and Hilda went to the funeral. They stayed in Alicia and Liam's silent house in London and tried to help as much as they could. Alicia seemed distant then, asleep most of the time. Uffe only hugged her once during their two-night stay in the small house in a pleasant suburb. Even when they left, the day after the funeral, Alicia stayed in bed while Liam ordered a taxi to take them to Heathrow. It had been foggy during their stay, and they didn't see the sun once, even though the grass in the nearby park was a lush green, which Uffe marveled at. The landscape in London was so vibrant compared to the gray and brown at home, making a mockery of the reason they had been visiting Alicia.

He and Hilda had spent a lot more time together than they usually did on their visits to London. Normally he'd be stuck with Liam, trying to communicate with his schoolboy English that he'd long since forgotten. While Alicia and her mother shopped in the fancy stores in the West End, Liam usually took Uffe to the pub, or once to see a football match with Stefan. Stefan was a keen supporter, and Uffe had been surprised at the passion he'd displayed when his club, the name of which Uffe now forgets, scored—or missed—a goal. Usually the boy was quiet, a bit like his mother: a thinker.

After Stefan's death, Uffe had been concerned about his stepdaughter; he saw the pills she was taking, but Hilda told him in no uncertain terms that Liam was a doctor and knew how to medicate his own wife. Uffe wasn't so sure. As he now watched his son-in-law struggle with the bags, smiling at Hilda, while glancing furtively back at him, looking for assistance, the older man wondered what it was about Liam that he so disliked. There was just something shifty about his dark eyes, and his unnaturally thick hair. It was as if when he spoke to Alicia, or to Hilda and Uffe, he wasn't fully there, as if he didn't *want* to be there. Uffe had thought that it was something to do with his profession; how could a man deal with death all day without losing his faith in life along the way?

'Would you like a sauna before dinner?' Hilda says as they stand awkwardly in the newly decorated hall. Two years previously, on the advice of their young, female architect, the old steep stairs, which had been in the house since it was built in the 1920s, had been removed and replaced by a set of modern wide steps in light wood. The boxed design with a small landing made the hall look so much cleaner and bigger, even though the new stairs took up more space than the old narrow staircase had. They made Hilda finally feel at home in this, her in-laws, house.

Hilda sees Liam look at Alicia before responding to her query and almost imperceptibly shake his head, but her daughter ignores him and says, smiling, 'Yes please. You'll come with me, won't you, *Mamma?*'

Whenever her daughter uses the Swedish term for 'Mother,' Hilda feels tears well up inside. This has started happening more and more, getting sentimental over silly little things. She must pull herself together, for her daughter's sake, Hilda thinks and nods. She goes into the downstairs bathroom to fill a basket with towels and toiletries. In the large kitchen, which has also been refurbished, she takes a few cans of cold beer from the large American-style fridge.

'Would you like a *Lonkero?*' she asks, turning around to address her daughter.

Alicia is in the middle of what seems like a heated conversation with Liam on the other side of the kitchen island, where Hilda has a collection of fresh herbs neatly arranged under a low white lamp.

Between the plants and the light, she can see Liam shaking his head at Alicia. His lips are in a straight line and his hands are crossed over his chest. Hilda walks around the kitchen island and stands in front of her daughter. 'Everything alright?' she says, feeling her throat constrict, making her voice sound tight and hostile.

Liam looks down at her; he is such a tall young man, or is it that she has shrunk, as happens to so many older women? She straightens her back and extends herself, realizing with relief that she had kicked off her heels when they entered the house and is now in her stockinged feet, whereas both Alicia and Liam are still wearing their outdoor shoes.

'No problem,' Alicia says, putting her arm around Hilda's shoulders. She attempts a smile but all that she manages is a straightening of her mouth. 'Will Uffe want a sauna?' Alicia continues.

Uffe has disappeared. Hilda suspects he's gone into the old milking parlour, which he converted (badly, in Hilda's opinion) into a little farm office just after his mother died. He does all his paperwork there, although how he manages when he doesn't even have a computer, Hilda never understands. Mostly, she suspects, he sits there, reading the paper and listening to the radio. It's his escape from her nagging, she knows. But she doesn't mind, not really. It's good to be rid of his clutter in the house. She avoids the 'office' as much as she can, only glancing in when she goes into the small utility room next door, where there's a large freezer and the washing machine.

'Oh, I'm sure he will,' Hilda says, turning to her son-in-law, 'but it's no problem if you don't want one. Uffe is quite used to going to the sauna on his own.'

FOUR

iam realizes for the first time how much he hates this sauna ritual. He feels awkward having to slip his clothes off in the small dressing room, trying to avoid looking as the naked body of the older man is slowly revealed in front of him. Uffe may be in good shape for his age, if you ignore his pot belly, which seems to grow larger each year, but he still feels awkward with him. But to say 'No' to the first-night sauna would upset everyone, as Alicia said between tight lips to him in the kitchen earlier. Liam doesn't really understand why; all he can think is that it's like refusing a cup of tea when you are guests in the UK. Which, by the way, he is never offered in Åland.

Liam sighs and sits down on the slatted bench.

Uffe is bent over, leaning on his knees, looking out of the small window, at a slice of the sea and the beautiful, cloudless sky above.

I'm definitely refusing a dip in the freezing water.

As the heat seeps into his skin, a sudden image of large full breasts comes into Liam's mind, and he sees her smile, that naughty, raunchy smile Ewa has when she's on top of him. He feels guilt about his son all the time, and now about Ewa, but he's not sure how he would have coped for the past six months without her. Being with the soft-skinned nurse, her body so different from his wife's slim, athletic figure, has given Liam his only respite from grief. He knows he should stop the affair, and that to anyone on the outside, his actions look unforgive-able, to say the least. But he can't help himself. When he is better, when Connie's sessions begin to work, and his mind is clearer, not full of guilt about the moped, then he will stop seeing her.

Liam is rudely brought back to the present when Uffe, before he has time to protest, throws water on the hot stones and a stinging steam hits Liam's face. It catches in his throat and he struggles to breathe, so he ducks, and now the heat is spreading over his shoulders, back, thighs and eventually his legs. How the locals think this torture is pleasurable, he will never understand.

'Hot, hot, hot,' Uffe says in English and gives a short laugh, throwing more water on the stones. His watery eyes, now almost gray, matching the thin wisps of hair that are now damp and stuck to his skull, gaze at Liam. It's as if the old man knows what his son-in-law has been thinking about.

Liam turns his face away from the old man's scrutiny. Sweat drips from his temples into his eyes, stinging them too. Turning back to Uffe, he wipes the corners with his thumbs, and tries to smile at him, but only manages a grimace. It's their joke and the only words that pass between the men during their annual sauna sessions. Liam has often tried to speak to Uffe, but Uffe's English is nonexistent and although he nods enthusiastically, Liam suspects he doesn't understand a word of what he says. Over the years, the two men have settled on a silence that in Liam's mind is all but comfortable. They manage to communi-cate with nods and gestures, like now, when Uffe gets up and moves his head in the direction of the sea to indicate that it's time for a swim. Liam knows from past years that the sea will be bitterly cold this early in the summer, and he wonders what the old man would say—or rather do—if he refused to participate in the ritual. But he doesn't, and the two men walk the few yards toward the jetty. Liam is barefoot and remembers too late the advice Ewa gave him about ticks and Lyme's disease. 'They perch on the blades of grass and just wait to hop on you.'

'Like you,' Liam had said, taking hold of Ewa's waist.

They'd been standing in the basement landing of St Mary's East wing, outside the Chapel, a place they often used if they needed some privacy at work. Ewa was his theater nurse, and Liam had been on his way home, having just finished seeing his private patients. It was nearly 10pm, he'd been running late all day and was exhausted. But he wanted to say goodbye to Ewa. He knew she expected it, and for the first time he felt he would miss her during the two-week holiday with Alicia and her family. He'd seen her more than the usual one evening a week (Wednesdays after his private clinic), and not just for sex, even though that was the main reason Liam couldn't keep away. The sex with Ewa was satisfying. It made Liam forget. Alicia hadn't let him into her bed since Stefan's accident, and even before that their love-making had been—to say the least—sporadic.

'Lyme's disease is very dangerous, you know,' Ewa had said, stroking Liam's cheek.

They were in an embrace, Liam trying to get close to her, to take a piece of her with him to Åland. He kissed her, not caring if someone might open the door to the corridor and see them there. The people using the small room set aside for grieving family and friends of patients, would mostly likely not know Liam, and even if they did, tonight he didn't care.

'I do know, and I will be careful, I promise,' Liam said. 'What time do you finish?' he added, nuzzling her neck, taking in the scent of sandalwood and sweet lipstick.

'Midnight,' Ewa sighed, arching her back and pressing her breasts against Liam's chest.

He knew her neck was her most erogenous zone, and just a few kisses or caresses would be too tempting for her. He thought briefly about his consulting room; it would be empty now and if they were quick, and careful, they could use it again. He wondered if the other consultants had finished their appointments. He decided to take the risk. He'd tell the other nurses he'd forgotten something. Ewa could take the stairs and slip into the room unnoticed, if she was lucky.

'Is this your long break?' Liam said into her eyes, his voice hoarse, his erection hardening in his pants.

'You're impossible,' Ewa laughed, throwing her head back and making her delicious curls shake.

·   ·   ·

The sea, as Liam feared, is extremely cold, and he manages just a few strokes in the water. Uffe on the other hand, swims expertly further away, to the other side of the line of reeds in front of the wooden jetty. Liam gives the old man a wave and walks briskly back to the sauna, holding the towel he's taken to cover himself. He sits on the porch and watches a family of mallards approach the jetty from further along the shore. It's past seven o'clock but the sun is unnaturally high in the sky, bright in a near cloudless sky. There's no wind, and the surface of the sea beyond the band of reeds is still. It is beautiful here, Liam thinks as he watches the mother mallard, ahead of her family of four, take a sharp turn on seeing Uffe's head bob up and down on his way back to the jetty. The pale blue sky, broken only by the cottonwool strips of white clouds, and the three dark green islands on the horizon—one large, two smaller—contrast breathtakingly against the deep marine color of the water. Liam thinks again about Ewa and wishes he could bring her here. But that would never be possible. Liam inspects his feet and toes for ticks and decides that what he needs to do is be braver.

FIVE

Alicia feels pleasantly tired. She's had far more to drink than usual. In the sauna she had two cans of *Lonkero*, the gin drink she'd liked when she was underage in the park in Mariehamn, and later when visiting the islands from Uppsala, where she'd gone to university. It was the drink of her youth. Her mother always remembered to buy some when Alicia was back home. Although sweet, the *Lonkero* tasted delicious after the sauna, as she and her mother sat outside on the porch, watching the calm sea. Alicia had also had wine during the excellent meal her mother had prepared. They had eaten venison, shot by Uffe the previous fall, with lingonberries, a creamy mushroom sauce and new potatoes grown by Uffe. Alicia ate heartily, more than she had since. *Since.* She could see Liam look at her approvingly; he was always telling her she was too thin.

Now up in the attic bedroom that Hilda always prepared for them, Alicia fights back tears when she thinks how much Stefan would have loved the perfectly cooked game prepared by his grandmother, bloody in the middle just as he liked it. Instead, Alicia forces a smile, undresses in the narrow en-suite bathroom, and thinks about Uffe's description of Liam in the sauna. How he was like a baby deer, with his thick hair turning curly and his large eyes fixed on Uffe in horror as he poured more water on the stones.

Alicia translated what her stepfather had said, wanting Liam to laugh too. It was an annual joke of theirs, how Liam hated the sauna but suffered it in silence. Usually he took the Mickey out of himself and got drunk on the vodka schnapps Uffe poured for the two men, but tonight he didn't join in. All through dinner Liam was quiet, hardly saying a word even to Alicia, or Hilda, who always made an effort to speak English to him. *He is hurting,* Alicia thinks. *Or, was he missing her?*

Liam is in bed reading the *The Telegraph* on his iPad. He tries to get himself comfortable on the two lumpy pillows, but fails. What is it about these Nordic types that they can't make proper pillows? They were either as thin as anything or lumpy as hell. Once again he curses himself for not stuffing his Canadian goose pillow into the suitcase. Now he has to look forward to two weeks of bad sleep; just what he needs before going back to his hectic schedule at the hospital.

Alicia slips in beside him. She's wearing a long T-shirt, and her legs look thin and muscular beneath it.

A moment after she's settled down to read, slowly turning the pages of her book, Liam hears a low buzzing noise. He tries to ignore the mosquito, hoping Alicia will get up and kill it. She is a local after all, and expert at it. The mozzy does a low fly-pass over Alicia's nose, but she waves a hand absentmindedly and continues reading.

'You're not going to kill it?' Liam says in disbelief.

Alicia puts down her book and looks at him. 'No.'

There's silence while Liam tries to get back to an article about Brexit. Liam is enraged; all the lies, like the increased funding for the NHS, touted by the Brexiteers during the campaign make him furious. The knowledge that the health service will struggle without the easily available workforce from Europe, or the funding for medical research, makes him fearful for the future. Liam knows he's had too much beer and wine, and that he is probably a bit drunk, but the sense that his life is going in the wrong directing seems suddenly terribly clear to him. His country is going to the dogs; he's lost his wonderful son; his wife is now a cold, skinny woman whom he doesn't love anymore, and he is on holiday on some islands in the middle of the Baltic, where he doesn't want to be, with her.

There, he's said it.

The quiet is broken by the sound of more insects, the sole mosquito has been joined by his friends. Liam throws down his iPad on the bed and climbs indiscriminately across his wife's body. The bed is situated against one wall in the attic bedroom, under the sloping roof. He gets up so abruptly that he bangs his head against a thick beam.

'Fuck!' he exclaims.

Alicia stifles a laugh. Liam looks at his wife in disbelief. Her face is hidden by the book with a bright blue and yellow cover. One of her romance books, he thinks. What is the matter with the woman? Is she drunk? Alicia knows that he suffers badly from mosquito bites; more than anyone else in the family. Even Stefan had a built-in immunity to them, but Liam gets huge swollen, itchy patches on his skin each time one of the little devils gets to him. Liam turns on the main light in the bedroom and stares at the ceiling, holding a rolled-up magazine he's picked up from the round table by the bed. But now there's no sign of the mosquitoes and there is a silence in the room.

'Oj, that light is very bright!' Alicia says, lowering her book and glaring at him.

The use of the Swedish 'Oj,' which he understands means something close to 'Hey', somehow annoys him. Whenever Liam hears Alicia speak her own language, she sounds like a teenager. A stroppy teenager at that.

Liam turns out the light and returns to bed, being careful not to bang his head again when he climbs over Alicia.

Alicia gives a loud sigh, and Liam suppresses his growing anger.

There's silence again and Liam manages to read two sentences of the article. Then two loud buzzing noises fill the room, and Liam feels a sting in his arm.

'Fucking hell!' he says. 'Now look what's happened, I've been bitten!'

'And how exactly is that my fault?' Alicia says. She's lowered the book and is staring at Liam with those dark eyes. There's a dangerous-sounding calm to her voice, but Liam ignores it. He's had enough. There's blood on his hand where he managed to kill the mosquito, but he knows he'll have a painful and itchy bite on his arm tomorrow. The sting will most probably be inside his skin, which means a more prolonged healing process.

'We wouldn't be here if you hadn't insisted. We could have gone to France, or Italy, or ...'

'Really? And not see my mother and Uffe? You would deny me time with my family now, especially now!' Alicia has raised her voice.

'You could have come on your own!'

Alicia is quiet for a moment and then turns to Liam. 'That would have suited you, wouldn't it?'

Liam looks at his wife's unmade, worn-out face. Her eyes are still the same color of blue they were when they met, but they now have dark circles around them. It was those pale eyes, like shallow lakes, Liam had fallen in love with in Uppsala, at the Swedish university he'd visited as a research fellow. Alicia had been a second-year student, cool and collected for her young age.

'What do you mean?' he now says, looking squarely at her.

'So you can fuck your little nurse while I'm out of the way.' Alicia says the words in a low hiss, so quietly that Liam doesn't think he's heard her right. Her face shows no emotion whatsoever, but her eyes regard Liam coldly. All the warmth from her youth gone.

The buzzing of another mosquito breaks the silence, and Alicia, calmly closing her book, turns around and kills the insect with the palm of her hand against the white wall behind her head.

'Why couldn't you have done that before?' Liam says, trying to smile, to make a joke of it.

Alicia picks up a tissue from a box beside the bed and wipes her hand. She gazes at him with hard eyes, which make Liam turn his head away.

A silence fills the room.

'So you know?' Liam says quietly, looking at the white ceiling between the dark wood beams. He moves his eyes to the foot of the bed where they had folded the dark red quilt that Hilda had proudly shown Alicia. Liam understood it was a new purchase to be admired.

'Yes,' Alicia says. Her voice is low but there's no feeling in it.

'How long?'

'Does it matter?'

'No.'

SIX

'I want a baby.'

The words escape from her mouth before Alicia realizes she's going to say them.

Liam gets up and leans uncomfortably against the wall. He turns toward her.

'What did you say?'

Now she's finally plucked up the courage to tell him, because of the *Lonkero* and wine, and because she knows he must feel guilty about the affair. She must carry on. She also rises from the bed, and picks up a red cushion from the floor to place behind her head. She knows tomorrow morning she'll not be this brave. She takes hold of Liam's arm, but he pulls it away.

'Ouch, that's where the mozzy got me!'

'Sorry,' Alicia says. She sits with her hands in her lap, and continues, 'I'm relatively young, and I know if I begin eating healthily and looking after myself again, I'd be able to ...'

'Stop!' Liam raises his voice. He is staring at Alicia with an incredulous expression in his eyes.

Tears are running down Alicia's cheeks now, but she doesn't want to give up. The thought of having a baby, a new Stefan, has been haunting her for weeks now. It started when she was in the local Waitrose. She'd seen a mother, well into her forties, with gray hair, fuss with her child in a buggy. Alicia, who was laden with bags and trying to leave the shop, couldn't get past them. When the woman turned around, Alicia saw the child, perhaps three or four months old, with a mop of blond hair and blue eyes, just like Stefan. She stood there and gasped, letting the mother and baby slowly move away, out of the shop.

At home, she stood in front of the mirror and remembered what it was like to be pregnant, waiting for the miracle that was a baby to be born. She had loved the feeling of life growing inside her. Even toward the end of her term, when her back ached and she had to pee every five minutes, the baby pressing on her bladder and seemingly kicking her innards to smithereens, she was more satisfied with her life than she had ever been before, or since.

She had never forgotten the elation when little Stefan, so beautiful with his handsome, perfect asymmetric face, little toes and hands, and wide, innocent eyes, had been placed in her arms. She could do it again; she could even have more than one child before it was too late.

'I'm only 38 years old, and nowadays women go on to have children well onto their forties,' she says, wiping her eyes.

'Alicia, we don't share a bed anymore,' Liam says quietly.

'But we could.'

'You want to share a bed with me just in order to have a baby?' Liam has grabbed hold of Alicia's shoulders. He fixes his eyes on hers.

Alicia can't read him. Is he angry with her? Or has he been thinking the same? Or is he no longer in love with her?

'You've fallen in love with your little nurse? Is she going to give you more babies, now is she?'

'You cannot replace a child with another. Stefan was ...' Liam lets his hands drop and looks down at them, seemingly unable to go on.

'How can you say that?' Now Alicia is shouting, not caring if Hilda and Uffe hear them.

'Shh!' Liam says and this infuriates her even more. It's her mother and stepfather who live in the house. If she wishes them to hear, it has nothing to do with Liam.

'Stefan was my life! Nothing, or no one,' Alicia gives Liam a stare, making sure he understands exactly what she means. 'No one can ever replace him.'

'Don't I know it!' Liam says and clambers out of bed, over Alicia. He begins to pace the small space, taking two or three steps toward the door and two steps back again. 'I was nobody to you after Stefan was born.'

Alicia stares at her husband. This man, who is so wise, so competent and has been fucking another woman behind her back, has the temerity to be angry with her?

'You were jealous of your own son?'

Liam sits down on the bed. He places his hands, palms up on the white sheet and spreads his fingers out. She can hear him take slow breaths in and out. *He's trying to compose himself.*

'Of course not. I just knew how close you two were and sometimes I felt a bit left out.' He lifts his eyes toward Alicia. They are now full of sadness. Alicia doesn't know what to say, how to respond. She's still angry, and confused. What is Liam trying to say to her?

'Can you understand that?' Liam adds.

Alicia nods, her fury abating.

They are both quiet for a moment. Alicia can hear the old grandfather clock that Uffe insists on keeping in the lounge in spite of Hilda's repeated pleas to have it removed strike one. She checks her phone and sees it is indeed an hour past midnight. Which makes it eleven o'clock in the UK. Still, it's late.

'Couldn't we start again?' Alicia asks.

Liam looks at her. His eyes are so sad that she feels suddenly bereft. I've lost him, she thinks.

'It's late,' Liam says and lies down on the bed, with his back to Alicia.

It's too late, he means.

After the row, lying awake next to Liam, who eventually falls asleep after tossing and turning for what seems like hours, she waits for a feeling of loss, or anger, or something, but there is nothing. What is her marriage compared to the death of her son anyway? If Liam is not prepared to have a baby with her, then he doesn't love her anymore.

Besides, she cried over Liam enough when she found out about the affair from one of their so-called friends—Susan, a do-gooder who runs a charity cashmere stall at St Mary's hospital, where Liam has his private practice.

Four months ago, on a cold February day, Susan telephoned Alicia and asked to see her for coffee because she had 'something very important' to tell her. Alicia didn't have a clue what the older woman wanted; they'd only become friends because Susan's late husband had worked with Liam at the hospital. Feeling sorry for her after the sudden loss of his friend and colleague to an aggressive form of pancreatic cancer, Liam had convinced Alicia to invite Susan for dinner. Alicia felt guilty for not liking the woman. They had nothing in common. Susan was about 15 years older than Alicia, and was staunchly conservative. She always made a point of asking Alicia about her 'home country', making sure it was understood that Alicia was foreign and didn't belong in Britain. Alicia now suspected she had voted for Brexit. With her cashmere cardigans and pearls, and two children graduated from Oxford, she had the air of being better than Alicia. The dinner had been three years ago, at a time when Stefan's Oxbridge ambitions had been mere dreams, mere possibilities hinted at by his school.

Alicia had met Susan for the occasional coffee since then ('You don't drink tea, do you, dear?' she had said), always at the behest of the older woman. Alicia had even bought a cashmere poncho from her stall; at £105, it wasn't cheap, but Susan had said the purchase was 'a steal.'

The day she told her about Liam, they were at Richoux in St John's Wood, where they always met. The coffee was expensive, but Susan always said she couldn't drink coffee anywhere else. Besides, she said, she only used buses to get into town, because she couldn't abide the underground anymore.

Alicia suspected that contrary to what she liked people to believe, Susan was short of funds, because each time they went for coffee, Alicia somehow ended up paying the check. But she didn't mind that much. In spite of her airs and graces, Alicia was certain Susan was lonely. Her two brilliant children, now grown up, rarely visited her, and she didn't seem to have any other family around. That must be why she was so involved in the St Mary's charities, Alicia had once said to Liam, and he'd nodded, although Alicia could tell he'd not heard a word.

Once they were seated at a table at the back of the café, Susan cocked her head to one side, corrected her gray-blond hairdo and placed her wrinkly manicured hand over Alicia's.

'Now, I'm so sorry for what I am about to tell you.'

She looked kindly at Alicia. Her eyes, which looked as though they'd been heavily made up in a darkened room, had traces of dried mascara under her eyelashes, and eyeliner spread heavily over the upper eyelids.

'What is it?' Alicia was puzzled; usually during their meetings Susan tried to sell her tickets to a charity auction, or once a comedy night, raising funds for the hospital. On several occasions she'd used the excuse of 'something important' to a have coffee with Alicia, only to push her into attending another benefit gala.

'I'm sure it's just a passing fling. Robert had one of those, you know. I did nothing, it was a nurse, just like with your Liam, and it soon passed over. Men are like that you know ...'

Alicia suddenly felt bile rise in her throat, and she thought she might bring up the skinny latte she'd just gulped down. She swallowed hard and leaned over to look at the older woman. 'What are you telling me, Susan?'

'Oh ...' It was as if the old woman had forgotten where she was.

After several tries, Susan had finally told her that she'd seen Liam kiss a nurse in the stairwell at St Mary's.

Alicia had been stunned. They'd just celebrated their 18th wedding anniversary in the spring, and although their love-making wasn't as passionate, or as frequent as it had been in the first few years of their relationship, they still did it. And she thought they both enjoyed it.

'I hope I did the right thing telling you?' Susan had said, her eyes full of concern.

'That's fine,' Alicia had managed to say. 'Sorry,' she said, and she left without paying, rushing out of the café and onto the street. It had started raining while they'd been inside, and Alicia got soaked on her way to the car, which was parked a few streets away. She got inside her VW Golf, and sat looking at the dashboard clock, listening to the heavy drops fall onto the windscreen.

She thought back to how Liam behaved with her; had he changed recently? He was always so busy, what with his surgeries going on until late in the evening.

'Oh my god,' Alicia yelped out loud.

Of course, all those late nights! For some time now he'd come home and go straight upstairs to shower instead of flopping down on the sofa next to her, as he used to do. When had that started? Alicia tried to think hard, but she couldn't remember. She started the engine and drove home to Crouch End. Inside the house, she rushed up the stairs and went into Liam's bedroom. His wardrobe looked tidily arranged, with suits, jackets, trousers and shirts neatly organized into sections. Alicia began with the suit pockets. She found train tickets, a few receipts for coffee and meals and a printed sheet for two cinema tickets. She looked at the date, January 23rd 2018, and the name of the film, *A Woman's Life*. Alicia turned the piece of folded paper over in her hands. The film had shown at the Everyman on Baker Street. She'd heard of the movie, and had wanted to see it herself, but knew Liam wouldn't have wanted to see an historical French film. It wasn't his thing.

Alicia carried on looking through Liam's wardrobe for further evidence of his infidelity. (If the cinema tickets were any evidence.) Of course, he could have bought them for Alicia and himself, and then forgotten about the tickets in his jacket pocket. She felt calm, unusually so, and wondered if she was in some kind of shock. It wasn't until she was looking through Liam's sock draw by his bed that she began to feel faint. At the bottom of the drawer she found a key, an ordinary key with a fob to a security gate. It was the keyring that confirmed Susan's account. It was pink leather and, heart-shaped. Alicia recognized it as an expensive one from Smythson. It had a tiny engraving in gold lettering: 'To my love, Ewa x.'

Alicia had sat down on Liam's bed and cried.

SEVEN

When Alicia comes downstairs the next morning she finds her mother fussing over Liam and his breakfast in the kitchen, just as she used to fuss over Stefan. The surge of pain hits Alicia's chest so hard that she has to hold onto the bannister to steady herself.

'Morning,' Alicia's mother says and comes to hug her daughter. Liam doesn't look up. He is reading something on his iPad, all the while eating cereal out of a bowl. Alicia sees it's the kind he likes, Swedish granola that her mother gets in especially for him.

Alicia goes to sit on a stool in the corner of the new kitchen, diagonally opposite Liam, and begins to chat to Hilda about her clothes shop in town, and about Uffe's potato crop. Her stepfather has left early to supervise the work, her mother tells Alicia, as she pours her a cup of strong coffee. As she sips it, Alicia begins to feel better. From the kitchen window, which overlooks an apple orchard, fields, and the sea beyond, she sees it's a sunny day. The rays glitter on the surface of the water. The kitchen is in the corner of the old house, which is surrounded by fields sloping down to the shore and the sauna cottage. She can just make out the roof and chimney pot.

Uffe owns all the land as far as the eye can see, and for some reason, especially today, this thought of complete privacy, being cut off from the world outside, comforts Alicia. There's another red wood-clad cottage at the edge of the field, where Stefan once stayed with a friend he brought along for the holiday, and another one further down, painted pale yellow. There's a third cottage along the shore, beyond the sauna and the jetty.

Alicia knows Uffe built all the simple square structures himself when his parents were still alive, and his father took care of the farm. He rents the properties out to holidaymakers via the Viking Line ferry company, and has done for thirty years or more.

'Do you have any guests this year?' Alicia asks her mother.

Hilda shakes her head. She's mixing flour with eggs and milk; she's making Liam and Stefan's favorite, oven-baked pancakes. 'The red and the yellow cottages are taken up by farm laborers.'

'Oh?'

She looks at the red cottage again, and sees a window is open. Outside, a striped towel and something looking like a pair of swimming trunks are hanging on a washing line fixed between two birch trees. She's saddened by the fact that she won't be able to wander around the cottages; sometimes she helps Uffe on changeover day, when one set of guests are leaving and another arriving. They clear out the rubbish, sort out sacks of empty beer and vodka bottles, plastic mugs, and crisp packets and take the bags on Uffe's tractor to the dump at the edge of one of the fields.

'Can I talk to you for a minute?' Liam says suddenly. His English sounds wrong here somehow. But he's looking at Alicia, so she nods and gets up.

'Sure.'

Hilda lifts her head and gives Alicia a searching look.

'It's OK,' she says to her mother in Swedish, and follows Liam up the stairs to their bedroom in the attic.

Liam stands with his feet apart in the middle of the small room, on the only spot where he has enough space to stretch out to his full height without knocking his head on the beams on either side.

'I've booked a flight from Stockholm to London for tomorrow.' Liam has his arms crossed over his chest and is looking down at his feet.

Alicia gazes at his face and thinks he looks tired. Neither of them got much sleep after the row last night. They aren't used to sleeping in the same bed anymore, but on holiday they usually manage OK. Nothing about this trip is normal, Alicia knows that. Suddenly she realizes that to her it isn't like a break, but a coming home.

'I might stay on a bit longer than the two weeks,' she says.

Liam lifts his head and now Alicia sees anger in his face. His mouth is in a straight line and his eyes dark. 'So this is it then?'

'Says you! I'm not the one who's cheated,' Alicia says, trying to keep her voice low. 'I want us to start again!'

Knowing her mother, she is certain Hilda will be downstairs in the hall, or even on the stairs, trying to listen to their conversation. Luckily, it's two floors up to the attic, and she isn't sure how much Hilda will understand. She doesn't want her to know why Liam is leaving.

Not yet.

She knows how much it would enrage both Hilda and Uffe to learn of Liam's affair; she can't cope with their emotions now.

She adds in a lower tone, 'I want us to have a baby.'

Liam's face crumbles, and he sits down on the bed. 'I'm not a bad man,' he says. 'I just think that when we are hardly speaking, sleeping in separate beds, having a baby is crazy. Besides, I can't do it. I can't take the risk of losing another child.'

His shoulders shake and he covers his face with his hands.

Alicia has never seen her husband cry. Not even during the awful weeks after the accident, or at the funeral. Her memory of those times is hazy, and she is grateful for Liam for taking care of her then, making sure she was medicated just the right amount, so that she could cope with the pain, but not so much that she would become dependent on the pills. Perhaps while she was out cold, he cried alone? She could imagine him at the pine kitchen table in the home in Crouch End, with his head in his hands, but she couldn't imagine any tears. Of course, he might have cried in the arms of Ewa, the Polish nurse. Did he cry while he made love to her, the woman with a beautiful figure and dark curls? Did he break down during her night shifts, no doubt arranged to coincide with Liam's evening surgeries at St Mary's?

Alicia had begun monitoring his movements after the discovery of the keyring, and there was a definite pattern: each Wednesday he would come home late, around midnight, sometimes even one or two in the morning. Alicia could hear the shower being turned on in the bathroom that had been Stefan's—and he would then turn in. The next morning he'd invariably be in a good mood. It was the tenderness with which he kissed Alicia on the cheek when leaving the house that hurt her most. Did he really need the infidelity, the sex with another woman, a woman so different from Alicia, with voluptuous curves, to deal with his grief? Alicia decided he did, so she just accepted this new arrangement. She was not enough for him, so what could she do? If she stopped the affair by making a scene, he'd only find someone else.

After Stefan had gone, nothing seemed to matter anyway. Until the thought of another baby entered her mind. She doesn't know how many times she had tried to talk to Liam about it at home. The time had never seemed to be right. Their individual grief got in the way, Alicia had told herself each time she failed to utter the words she had been brave enough to let pass her lips last night.

Being here, at home with her mother and Uffe, she felt more secure, safe. Even with the memories, the awful gaping hole Stefan had left behind, she is calmer here in Åland than she has been for the past six months in London.

Alicia knows she should go over and sit next to her husband, to comfort him but she isn't able to move. She doesn't seem to have any sympathy left for him.

'I am grateful for everything you did for me after... you know, after.'

Liam looks up at Alicia and nods. His face is drawn, sad. His eyes have red rims and his eyelashes are wet. His whole demeanor is so different from the confident man Alicia knows, and she's suddenly taken aback, forgetting her own pain, or the sense of betrayal she has carried with her for so many months. Even the new, fresh, pain of his refusal to give her another baby.

'Are you OK?' she says and sits next to him.

Liam puts his head on Alicia's shoulder. She places her arms around him and makes soothing sounds. 'It's OK, just let it go.' She hugs him and they rock together on the low bed. Slowly Liam's tears dry up and he straightens his back. He takes hold of Alicia's hands and says, 'You know you are a wonderful woman. And I am sorry.'

'I know.' Alicia looks at Liam's eyes. 'How did it happen? And why?'

Now Liam hangs his head. 'I don't know. I guess you and I weren't, you know, even talking properly and I needed ...'

Alicia thinks back and tries to remember when Liam began sleeping in the guest bedroom. It must be two, three years ago? At first it was because of his late-night surgeries; he'd often stay afterwards to finish the paperwork, and instead of waking Alicia, who liked to be in bed by 10pm, he'd sleep in the guest bedroom. Slowly the occasional night became a permanent arrangement. It's something they'd joke about; they even convinced themselves that sex was better when it wasn't part of a routine.

What a lie that was.

Alicia can remember clearly when they last made passionate love. It was on the August Bank holiday, when Stefan was at a sleepover with some friends. They'd finished a whole bottle of prosecco during a picnic on Hampstead Heath. It was a hot weekend, the last heatwave of the summer, and Liam had been kissing Alicia and covertly touching her breasts and bottom as they lay on a blanket underneath a vast elm. Alicia wore her favorite hot-weather dress: a floaty maxi with tiny flowers on it and a halter-neck fastening. It hugged her slim body and showed off her small breasts. They'd been like teenagers, willing the bus to take them home quicker so that they could devour each other. That weekend they'd made love three times, but as soon as Stefan came home, and the working week began, Liam had returned to the guest bedroom and the passion faded.

'How long has it been going on?' Alicia now asks.

Liam looks at Alicia with alarm.

'Don't worry, I'm not going to do anything. I just want to know.' Alicia is surprised at her own calmness. She knows it's better this way. She doesn't have any feelings left for anyone, she will never love anyone again after Stefan, so it is better that Liam has found someone else. The fact that he hasn't made love to her because he was having sex with the nurse makes Alicia feel better somehow. It isn't her fault their life is coming to an end; it's his.

'Five months.'

Alicia can't help but gasp at Liam's words. 'So it started almost right after ...'

'It isn't as simple as that.'

'No.' Alicia tries to suppress her anger. She stands up and asks, 'What time is your flight from Stockholm tomorrow?'

EIGHT

Early on Sunday morning Liam and Alicia stand facing each other in the kitchen. Liam's luggage is packed and ready by the front door. He glances through the open door at the large grandfather clock, which dominates the back wall of the lounge.

'What time did you say the bridge opens?'

'On the hour and at half past,' Alicia says. She's in her usual spot, perching on a stool next to the window overlooking the fields and the sea. The coffee machine on the other side of the kitchen is making gurgling sounds. Alicia knows Liam is fully aware of the timetable of the canal that runs between Mariehamn and Sjoland, where Uffe's house is, but he's being his English self—making pointless conversation to drown out the silence between them.

The small ferry port isn't busy when Alicia and Liam arrive there twenty minutes later.

Alicia decides to drive him in Hilda's car; it would look odd if she asked her mother to go. The night before, Hilda offered to come along, but Alicia managed to convince her that she wasn't needed.

As usual, they are far too early. The check-in hasn't even opened and the only two desks in the tiny departure hall are empty. Alicia really just wants to leave Liam there, but she feels duty-bound to stay in case something goes wrong with his booking, unlikely though that is. Everyone speaks English, of course, but it doesn't seem right to abandon Liam at an empty ferry terminal.

'Let me know when you get there,' Alicia says and sits down on one of the plastic chairs fixed against the long wall of the waiting hall.

Liam gives her a quick glance, there's surprise in his eyes, but adds, 'Sure.'

Suddenly a door at the far end opens and Alicia sees a familiar, tall shape enter the terminal. Patrick walks confidently in, taking long strides toward the two check-in cubicles and looks up at a screen above them. He checks his phone and turns around to gaze at the large space. His eyes meet Alicia's and his face opens into a smile. In a few moments the man with the blue eyes is standing in front of them.

'We must stop meeting like this,' Patrick says in Swedish.

'Hi,' Alicia says and gives a little laugh. She cannot but return the man's infectious smile.

'Not leaving already?' he says, his gaze moving from Alicia to Liam and back again.

'Sorry, you didn't meet the other day, did you?' Alicia says, switching to English. She assumes Patrick speaks the language and sees that the man nods. She is breathless again.

What is it with this guy that makes her feel like a teenager?

'This is Liam,' she says and then, hesitating just for a moment, adds, 'My husband.'

'Pleased to meet you.' Patrick stretches his hand toward Liam. His face is open, the smile still hovering around his lips.

Liam gets up and the two men shake hands, but while Patrick looks relaxed, saying 'Good morning' in a slightly sing-songy, accented English to her husband, Alicia can see Liam's movements are guarded. With his lips in a straight line, he nods.

'You too.'

There is an awkward silence, magnified by the emptiness of the vast hall.

'Um, I'm collecting some more guests for our party,' Patrick says.

He's speaking to Alicia, who realizes she didn't say why they were here.

'Liam has to go back early due to ... to his work,' Alicia says, trying to sound convincing. She smiles at Patrick. 'But I'm sure my mum and her husband would love to come.'

'And you too, I hope?' Patrick says. His intensely blue eyes are boring into Alicia and she feels herself blush under the man's gaze.

'Yes. I'd love to,' Alicia says, moving her face away from Patrick.

There is a sudden crackle of a tannoy and the arrival of the overnight sailing from Stockholm is announced.

'That's me. Well, nice to meet you. Sorry you have to leave the islands so early. Perhaps see you later this summer?' Patrick says to Liam, and then, turning to Alicia, says in Swedish, 'I'll remind Mia to send your mother the invitation.'

With a wave, he moves toward the other end of the terminal, where a few people are already arriving from the customs hall.

'Party?' Liam says. He's looking at Alicia with a different expression from the one he had before.

'Yeah, his wife, Mia,' Alicia nods at Patrick, who is standing facing the arrivals section, his feet apart and his arms crossed over his suede jacket. 'Mia's dad basically owns Åland. They have a massive house and they like to hold parties. I met them on the ferry coming over and they invited us to their Midsummer bash.'

'And you forgot to tell me about that?'

Alicia looks at Liam.

Is he jealous?

'I forgot about it myself, to be honest,' Alicia replies.

At that point, there is an announcement, in three languages, for passengers to board the *Ålandsfärjan* ferry. They get up and walk together toward the check-in cubicles, one staffed by a woman with pitch-black hair and pale skin.

Liam turns to Alicia. 'Well, this is me.' He's looking down at his phone, the boarding card displayed on its screen, waiting behind two other passengers. He's got the black canvas rucksack that Alicia gave him one Christmas, years ago, slung over his right shoulder.

'Have a good trip,' Alicia says. Suddenly she feels dizzy, and short of breath. Out of habit, she takes hold of Liam's arm to steady herself.

'You OK?' Liam says and grabs her elbow.

Alicia nods, but Liam steps out of the line, still holding her.

'Where does it hurt?'

Alicia wants to laugh. *Where doesn't it hurt?* She's aware of Patrick, who is just leaving with an older couple. He lifts his arm and waves to her, and she nods in reply.

The check-in woman in the glass cubicle is staring at them and listening to their every word. 'I'm OK. I just felt a bit dizzy,' she says and tries to smile. 'I'll be fine.'

Liam gives her his professional doctor's gaze. This was how their relationship began; he advised her about the headaches. She was a student at Uppsala University, studying English and journalism, and he was attending a seminar. They happened to sit at the same table in the cafeteria one wintry afternoon and Liam remarked on the weather. He wasn't used to seeing so much snow, and Alicia said how the cold weather always gave her migraines.

'Do you want me to examine you?' Liam had joked during the evening they spent together, his eyes creasing up at the corners and his full mouth stretched in a delicious smile. Under his direct gaze, Alicia blushed, and lowered her eyes. She was only a student then, and this Englishman was so obviously more experienced, and older than her. But there was something enchanting about his dark eyes and direct flirtation. So Alicia had agreed to a consultation. They had already spent the day together, and they had kissed.

Liam had gazed at Alicia, gently lifting her eyelids to look into her eyes. He then took her pulse and finally listened to her chest with an ear pressed against her breasts. Their proximity ended in another passionate kiss. Then pulling away from her, suddenly serious, Liam said, 'I have to be careful. This could be professional suicide, having relations with a patient.'

'Oh, sorry,' Alicia said, believing him.

Liam laughed, 'You are adorable!'

Liam has that same concern in his eyes now, but without the laughter.

'I'm fine, honestly,' Alicia says, freeing herself from Liam's grip. 'You'll miss the ferry!'

Liam stands facing her for a moment, and then, with a sadness in his face, nods and turns away. Alicia watches him show his boarding pass to the dark-haired woman, walk briskly toward a set of stairs and disappear. He doesn't turn to wave, but Alicia waits until she sees him re-emerge on the high glazed walkway. He looks down at her, stopping for a moment. They look at each other and each lifts a hand in a half-wave at exactly the same time. Liam nods and boards the ferry.

NINE

Liam arrives at the house in Crouch End late at night. It's empty and dark. He's taken a cab from Heathrow, a luxury he decides he needs in the circumstances. Before turning in, he stands outside Stefan's empty bedroom. He can't cry, but when he sees his late son's Spurs duvet cover, a pain fills his chest, making it difficult to breathe. There's a scent in the room, his son's masculine teenage tang, which he has forgotten about until now. Perhaps he didn't notice it before? He wishes he could hold Alicia now. He would like to share his discovery of their son's spirit still alive in their house. He stares at the bedroom, taking in details of Stefan's messy desk, which neither of them has had the heart to tidy. His school rucksack is lying on the floor exactly as he left it, as are two pairs of trainers. Liam can't take any more; he closes the door quietly and goes to their bedroom, the room in which Alicia has slept on her own for the last six months. Or was it a year? Two?

He moves quickly into the room and lies on the bed. Unlike Stefan's room, Alicia's is tidy, with a freshly made bed covered in cream cushions. He catches Alicia's perfume of lavender. He covers his face with one of her pillows and takes a deep breath in. He lies like this, breathing in and out, remembering the contours of Alicia's body, remembering her touch on him. He cannot recall when he has missed her so much.

There's a vintage white dressing table, on which a few bottles are placed attractively. A couple of pieces of jewellery hang from the side of the carved wooden mirror. Liam gets off the bed and sits on the stool with the cream satin cover and touches one of the glass beads. He tries to think when he last saw her wear them. At a charity dinner for the hospital perhaps? Yes, that was it. With shame, he remembers that Ewa was also there, and that they had smiled at each other across the room. Sharing a secret, both visualizing their last love-making. Except it wasn't love. Liam now feels ashamed at the seedy affair. But he was so lonely during those long nights and evenings at the hospital after Stefan's accident. He needed someone to comfort him. He was so empty. He *is* so empty. He catches his own, tired face in the mirror.

How about you stop thinking about yourself for a moment?

All through the long journey from Mariehamn, the extended wait at Stockholm airport, he'd pictured Alicia's face when he left her. She seemed so worried, with dark patches around her eyes. Still, she looked beautiful with her large pale eyes gazing at him. He remembers when he first saw her in Sweden, a young student with long legs and blond hair. Those deep emerald eyes were the first thing to attract him. She was so trusting, almost naive, and he'd reveled in showing her the world. Or his world in England. And look at where he took her? He gave her a son, then took him away, abandoning her to the grief that neither of them has any idea how to handle. He knows he's to blame for Stefan's death whatever his colleague, the grief counsellor, says. Alicia was against it from the start but he thought he knew better. His son needed his independence, and the moped gave him that. Liam puts his head into his hands. What a stupid, stupid man he is.

Alicia blames him too, he knows this. And rightly so. She was immediately so closed in, as if her grief was larger than his. But Liam knows he should have been more understanding. To lose a child for a father is terrible, but for a mother it is unimaginable.

Liam takes his phone out of his back pocket and sends Alicia a short message to let her know that he's arrived in London safely. He waits for a moment, then looks at his watch. It's already past 2am in Åland. Alicia is most probably asleep.

The image of that man, Patrick, at the ferry terminal flashes through his brain. Was he flirting with Alicia? He's married, she said, but that doesn't mean anything, as Liam, to his shame, knows all too well.

Liam undresses and decides to stay in their marital bedroom rather than go back to the spare bedroom. It seems less lonely in the double bed where Alicia usually sleeps. When he lies down he realizes how tired he is. Before sleep takes over, he resolves to fix his marriage. Perhaps a few weeks apart is just what they both need?

TEN

The next morning, a Monday, Hilda drives Alicia to Mariehamn with her. It's the day after Liam's sudden departure, which Alicia explained as a crisis at work. To conjure up an illness of a fellow surgeon at the hospital was Liam's idea. Both Hilda and Uffe exchanged glances and when Hilda and Alicia were in the kitchen washing up after supper on Saturday night Hilda asked her straight up if they'd had a row. Was that why Liam was leaving, she'd asked.

'Of course not,' Alicia said, not looking at her mother and continuing to load the dishwasher. For once, Hilda hadn't pursued the matter.

When Alicia asked if it was alright for her to sleep in the sauna cottage, once again Hilda raised her eyebrows but agreed. 'I need a bit of time alone, to think,' Alicia said, and Hilda nodded.

'You can stay as long as you need,' she said and hugged Alicia.

On Sunday night, Alicia received a message from Liam saying, *'Arrived safely, take care. Liam x'*

She looked at the 'x'. After all these years of marriage, the man still confused her. Hadn't they more or less agreed to separate? You don't send kisses to the woman you are cheating on, don't want to have a baby with, and want to leave, do you?

Alicia decided not to reply, and deleted the message.

The town of Mariehamn is the largest center on the islands, and Alicia remembers how, as a child, she'd thought the central park between Storagatan and Norra Esplanaden the most beautiful place on earth. Now the vast trees had grown, making the central path look majestic, the dappled sunshine reaching between the leaves of the tall elms. When her mother turns into Torggatan and parks the car in a spot reserved for her just outside the shop on Nygatan, Alicia sighs.

'Are you alright, my dear?' Hilda says and places her hand on her daughter's shoulder. Alicia wants to let herself cry then, for Stefan, for the unborn baby she will never have and for her marriage, which is most probably now over. But a knock on the passenger seat window stops her. A man's face, with friendly blue eyes, framed with blond, sunburnt hair, is looking at them through the window. Patrick! Alicia can feel her heart beat a little faster.

'Oh, I forgot,' Hilda says and rushes to get out of the car.

'This is Patrick,' Alicia's mother says when the two women are on the pavement, under the bright sunlight. She takes the man's hand.

'And this is my daughter,' Hilda adds. 'She's also a journalist, from London,' she says, and Alicia sees how she stands a little straighter. Alicia can't help but smile; her mother's evident pride in her daughter's fledgling career as a freelance journalist is endearing. If she only knew how little her articles earn these days, Hilda would advise her to change professions. She doesn't dare look at Patrick.

'How interesting,' Patrick says. Alicia lifts her eyes toward him and notices the blue eyes and the laughter lines around them. Seeing him again, she guesses his age to be around the mid-thirties, perhaps less. Younger than she is, at any rate.

'Yes, we've already met,' Alicia says and takes Patrick's hand. His long fingers touch hers and send currents through her body. Both let go quickly, as if they had burned each other. Alicia turns toward her mother.

Hilda's eyes open wide, 'Oh, really?' she says.

Alicia is glad she decided to wear one of her more flattering dresses this morning. It is a bright, sunny morning, with the promise of a warm summer's day to come.

'This is Mia's husband,' Alicia says to her mother. 'You remember Mia from school? Mia Eriksson?' she adds pointedly. 'Or has she taken your last name?' she asks facing Patrick again.

'No,' he says. The smile has disappeared from his lips and he looks even more embarrassed than Alicia feels.

'Aah,' Hilda says, 'Yes of course, lovely Mia!' she's grasped the significance of the last name, even though Alicia is certain she doesn't remember Mia from school. She was a couple of years below Alicia and they were never friends, but the school in Mariehamn was so small, everyone knew everyone else.

Mia's father owns the largest newspaper on the islands, a major shipping company and a fair amount of property. As well as much more she's certain she doesn't know about. All she's heard is that Mia's father's nickname on the islands is Mr Åland.

Although flustered, Alicia cannot help but be flattered by the covert glances Patrick keeps throwing her as Hilda opens up the shop and directs him and Alicia to the back room, where Hilda has a small office. It's just a cubicle, really, divided from the shop by a pink velvet curtain, matching the drapes across two smaller fitting rooms on the other side of the shop. Alicia knows that when it's busy, Hilda allows customers to use her office to try on the clothes, and to that end, she has a full-length mirror on the far wall. Her mother fills a kettle from a tap in the small sink in the corner of the room and asks if they want coffee, as if both of them are her guests.

'No, that's OK, I've just had breakfast,' Patrick says, and he smiles at Hilda, who says with disappointment in her voice, 'Oh, OK, I'll just make the shop ready to open and we can chat about the article.' She disappears into the main room and Alicia can see lights being switched on and hear Hilda open up the till.

'This is a coincidence, a second pleasant one,' Patrick says. Once again, he's dressed like someone from Östermalm in Stockholm, the area where the upper-class Swedes reside. Today he's sporting a pair of fashionably ripped jeans and a crisp white cotton shirt under the soft suede jacket.

'You a journalist?' Alicia asks.

Sitting opposite each other in the small room, their knees are nearly touching. Hers are bare, and she can see the tanned skin of his legs, and a few stray blond hairs, through the rips in his jeans. This is ridiculous, Alicia tells herself. I am married, at least for now, and so is he. What's more, this is probably all in my imagination. He's just being nice in a very Scandinavian way. But the man's gaze is so direct, and intense, that Alicia has to lower her eyes; is he flirting with her?

'Yeah, I work for *Journalen*. Your mum convinced me to write about her shop. She had a break-in here last week.' His smile disappears, and his eyes look even more fetching with a serious face. I must stop this, Alicia thinks.

'Oh, I didn't know about it. Was anything stolen?'

'Yes. Apparently, they emptied the till. That's all I know, so far.'

'Of course,' Alicia laughs, embarrassed. He's here to find out more about the incident.

'So you're Hilda's daughter?' Patrick asks. He is so tall that Alicia has to look up at him. She can see his taut muscles underneath the white shirt as he leans his upper body toward her. The shirt is open at the neck, revealing a triangle of bronzed skin.

Alicia manages to nod before her mother reappears.

'Right, Alicia, if you wouldn't mind staying on just for half an hour or so, while we chat? You remember how the till works, right?' Alicia's mother stands by the opening to the office, holding back the velvet curtain.

Alicia notices how very smart—and young—her mother looks in her linen trouser suit over a sleeveless silk shirt. Alicia herself is wearing one of her simple Marimekko summer dresses, and just to please her mother, her smart tan sandals with a small wedge heel, which (according to Hilda) make her legs look long and shapely.

'No problem.' Alicia gets up and turns to leave, but as she does so, she stumbles in the damned shoes, and accidentally brushes her shoulder against Patrick. They both give an embarrassed laugh. Alicia can't look at Patrick. The touch of his body against her sends a prickling sensation down her spine. A sensation Alicia knows all too well.

'Thanks, I must stop falling into you,' Alicia says before she knows what she's doing.

What am I saying!

'No problem,' Patrick says again, grinning.

Alicia knows her mother is watching the two of them, but she doesn't dare look at Hilda. Blushing at the sight of Patrick's smiling face so close to her, she walks out into the shop, feeling his eyes burning on her backside. She finds herself hoping her bum doesn't look too saggy. *Talk about making a fool of yourself*, Alicia thinks as she sits behind the till, and sees her mother close the pink curtain behind her.

ELEVEN

For the hour or so that Alicia sits alone at the till, watching the sun rise high in the sky, not one customer comes inside the shop. She sees a few people visit the bank, on the corner of their street and the pedestrian section, diagonally opposite the shop, but there are very few tourists about. It's a Monday morning after all, and the summer season isn't quite here yet. Most tourists arrive for Midsummer, which is four days away. Those few tourists already on the islands must still be asleep, Alicia thinks. It's only just past ten, and to Alicia the center of Mariehamn looks positively deserted. She's got so used to the busyness of London, where even at 4am on a Friday, when she and Liam took the cab to the airport, there had been people about, rushing to work, or home from a night out—or a rave. Did people still go to raves, Alicia wonders, as she listens to the voices from behind the curtain, and the occasional laughter, her mother's trill and Patrick's low, manly tone. Alicia can imagine how her mother's coquettish behavior embarrasses and flatters at the same time. She remembers how Stefan blushed the first time one of her friends from the Pilates class she used to attend became all flirty with him. Stefan had a huge growth spurt during his 14th summer, gaining broad shoulders, just like his father. His jawline became suddenly square, and a few strands of fluffy hair began to sprout from his chin. His new maleness had a strange effect on some women, especially those who didn't know him well. Like her Pilates friends. They'd smile at him, cocking their heads and shifting their bodies. It made Alicia laugh; how shameless they were.

'Meet my son,' she'd say and all at once, the women would become embarrassed, crossing their arms over their chests and rushing out of the door.

Alicia brushes the thoughts of Stefan away; she mustn't brood. This is, after all why she is here, to try to relax.

To avoid her mind wondering, Alicia moves the mouse on the desk and the computer comes to life. She sees her mother's sales report is open. She doesn't want to look, but she can't help herself as she scans the numbers on the screen. She is a financial journalist after all. She's shocked by the lack of sales recorded during the previous week. Only a handful of items were sold the week before that. Quickly she scrolls through the report and sees that since the New Year the shop has barely made 500 Euros a month. The rent on the premises must be that much at least, so how was Hilda able to pay the woman who comes in a few days a week? There must be the heating bill, and electricity, insurance, plus the money Hilda presumably pays herself. Alicia looks through her mother's files and finds a spreadsheet showing the shop's incoming and outgoing expenses. She notices that expenses peak about four times a year when Hilda restocks the shop. The sales look pitifully low compared to the purchases, and as she suspects the rent of the shop is nearly 1,000 Euros per month. But the shop seems to show a profit at the end of the period regardless, and she sees that the simple cashflow Hilda has prepared on a separate tab confirms this; she is over 1,000 Euros in the black. How is that possible when the costs so obviously exceed the income?

Suddenly Alicia hears sounds of movement, and the curtain is pulled to one side. She quickly closes the spreadsheets and lets go of the mouse.

Hilda walks out first, keeping the curtain back for the reporter to walk through. When they reach the till, Alicia's mother thanks Patrick. The man shakes hands with Hilda and turns to Alicia, placing his hand in hers, 'Nice to meet you again. Are you staying on the islands for the whole summer?'

He has long thin fingers and she notices a few pale hairs growing on the back of his hand.

'Not sure,' she says.

'But you'll come to the Midsummer party?'

'Party?' Hilda says, looking from Patrick to Alicia and back again.

Patrick coughs, then adds, 'You haven't got the invite yet? I must remind Mia to send it to you today.'

'That sounds lovely!' Hilda says, her eyes sparkling.

'Unless you have already made arrangements for celebrating Midsummer?' Patrick says, sounding hopeful.

Alicia looks down at her shoes, trying to remove the smile from her face.

'No, no, nothing that couldn't be unarranged!' Hilda says so keenly that it makes Alicia wince.

'Perhaps we'll meet again soon, then,' Patrick says, ignoring Hilda and looking at Alicia for a fraction of a second too long. He drops her hand and takes hold of Hilda's. 'I'll see you both this weekend.'

TWELVE

Alicia meets her mother for lunch at Indigo, one of the new breed of café/restaurant that have sprung up in the town in the past few years. In summer, the place has an outdoor patio area with wooden benches and large canvas umbrellas. The day has turned out windy, so although the sun is out, the umbrellas are down, and flapping noisily against their poles. When Alicia enters the little courtyard, where the tables are set at one end, Hilda is already sitting down with a large glass of white wine.

'Do you want one?' she asks as soon as Alicia sits down next to her.

Alicia has spent the morning wandering around Mariehamn, checking out her old haunts in the little town. Several of her school-friends still live on the islands, but over the years she's lost touch with all of them, not least because when she's here, most of them are on holiday, spending their long summer breaks in the surrounding archipelago. Now she wouldn't dream of getting in touch with any of them; she doesn't want to explain about Stefan.

Or about Liam.

Not yet.

She hasn't touched her Facebook feed since Stefan's accident. She is considering closing her account altogether. There are too many memories there; too many pictures of Stefan and many of him with her, her son with his beautiful, young face and lean body. Alicia shakes her head; she must stop torturing herself. Stefan is gone; as the grief counsellor told her, she must just try to remember the good times and be grateful for the years she had with her son. She was trying to do just that when she stopped for a coffee at Svarta Katten, a café in a little wood-clad townhouse with mismatching old furniture and the best *Ålands pannakaka* in town. It had been Stefan's favorite. Alicia decided against the semolina-filled clafoutis-type cake and sat in a corner reading a book bought from the bookshop at the far end of Torggatan. It is a novel set on the islands, by a recent Finlandia prize-winning author. Alicia decided that she needed to improve her Swedish, and what better way to do it than to read a novel about Åland in the original language?

Alicia now places the book on the table and leans back against the curved wooden bench of the restaurant. She watches the tourists milling around the local artisan shop opposite–a pottery and glass-blower's with various cups, plates and glasses displayed on a table outside. She has several pieces by the same artist at home, colorful glassware that she'd carefully wrapped and transported in her hand-luggage back to London. She decides she ought to buy a couple of new coffee mugs for the sauna cottage as a treat for herself.

'It's only Monday, and aren't you going to drive later?' she says absentmindedly to her mother. The words come out louder and more critically than she had intended.

'Oh, not for hours yet. By then the alcohol will have evaporated to nothing. Besides, you're on holiday!' Hilda smiles and lifts up her glass.

Alicia notices that the smile is somewhat strained, so she nods and asks the waiter, who at just that moment stops in front of their table, for a glass of what her mother is drinking. The waiter is a lanky blond boy, with a long white linen apron over his worn-out jeans that makes him loom even larger over the two women. His serious eyes survey Alicia, 'And food, do you want to order food?'

'In a minute, thank you, Nils.'

Hilda gazes at the boy as he leaves them. He says something to his colleague, a pretty girl with a streak of green in her hair, which makes her laugh. He pours Alicia's glass of wine at the bar.

'They just want to take your money in this place. So rude!' Hilda is speaking too loudly, enough for the boy and girl to hear.

When Nils comes back, Hilda orders the Caesar salad, and Alicia does the same.

Their food arrives. Without looking at either of them, or speaking, the waiter places the bowls down harshly, and a bit of Alicia's lettuce falls onto the table.

'Excuse me!' Hilda says loudly, and stares at the boy.

'Oh, sorry,' he says in a way that shows he's not in the least sorry.

'That's Margaret's son, you know,' Hilda whispers when the boy is out of earshot.

Alicia doesn't know who Margaret is, or she has forgotten, so she sighs and begins to eat. A row with a waiter is the last thing she needs. She gazes at her mother, who is keeping a close eye on the two young-sters, who are still laughing and joking together.

'Wasn't that a nice young man?' Hilda says suddenly.

Alicia looks back at the waiter, who's standing very close to the girl. They look like they are together. The place is almost empty; only a few other tables are occupied.

'Yes, very nice,' she replies.

'No, I don't mean that little rascal! I was talking about Patrick!'

'Oh.'

'His father-in-law owns *Ålandsbladet*.'

'Yes, I know.'

'I bet he could get you a job if you wanted,' Hilda says as she finally begins to pick at her salad.

Alicia stares at her mother, 'What do you mean?'

'On *Ålandsbladet*.'

Has Alicia heard her mother right? 'I live in London, why would I want a job here?'

Hilda's gaze doesn't leave Alicia's face as she carefully places her fork at the side of the large bowl.

'Now, don't be mad, but I got the feeling Liam didn't leave because of work.'

To change the subject, Alicia asks about what Patrick told her.

'Somebody broke into the shop?'

Hilda doesn't look at Alicia, but just waves her hand, which is holding a fork. 'Oh that. Just some kids.'

'But they emptied the till?'

'Yes,' her mother replies.

'Was much taken?'

Now Hilda lifts her eyes. 'Well, it's early in the summer season, so the takings were only just under a hundred Euros. But I might have told Patrick the sum was a bit bigger.' Hilda gives Alicia a guilty smile. 'Any publicity is good publicity.'

'Oh *mamma!*' Alicia is shocked, but she's more worried about the future of mother's business.

'Don't tell Patrick, whatever you do!' Hilda says and grins at Alicia. 'We're not friends, you know. I just happened to see him and Mia on the ferry. And then yesterday, when I was dropping Liam off at the terminal, he was meeting some guests coming to their party.'

At the mention of the Eriksson's Midsummer bash, Hilda's eyes light up and Alicia realizes she's lost the opportunity to ask her more about the shop's finances. It's nothing to do with me anyway, Alicia thinks, and she listens to her mother go on about what they should both wear and how it's too late to find anything unique.

'You need something nice too,' Hilda says and winks at her daughter. 'I saw how that young man looked at you!'

Alicia's cheeks begin to burn at the thought of Patrick's touch on her palm as he said goodbye that morning.

'Mum!' Alicia says. 'I'm married and so is he!' Alicia turns her head away.

Hilda is quiet for a moment. She must have seen the color on Alicia's face change, but, unusually, she doesn't comment on her daughter's embarrassment. Lowering her voice and placing her hand on Alicia's, she says, 'I know, darling. But a little flirtation never harmed anyone. It might be just what you need.' Alicia turns her eyes toward her mother.

Hilda peers at Alicia over her empty salad bowl. 'And being wanted by someone else might just bring that husband of yours running back to the islands too.'

THIRTEEN

When Hilda and Alicia get back to the house in Sjoland a few hours later, they find Uffe at home. He's speaking in an urgent tone on the phone, and when Alicia's mother shouts her usual, 'Hellooo' to the house in general, as if everyone inside the house is deaf, Uffe puts his hand up, his palm open in a gesture for her to be quiet.

'What's happened?' Hilda says in a whisper, her eyes wide. She walks to the other side of the kitchen where their landline, with a long cord, is fixed to the wall.

Uffe turns his back on Hilda and nods, dismissing her and listening to the person on the phone. Finally, he places the receiver back on its hook and sighs heavily, shaking his head. Alicia sees that he's close to tears.

'What is it?' both Alicia and Hilda ask in unison.

'One of the boys, you know the Romanians, had an accident.'

'Oh, them.' Hilda says, and begins to unload the shopping bags.

On the way home, they stopped at the grocery store to get more provisions, even though Alicia couldn't see how her mother could possibly fit anything more into the already packed fridge. But she knew better than to protest.

'We do have to eat. Uffe will have the leftovers,' her mother would say whenever Alicia protested about the amount of food Hilda bought. Hilda would look hurt, and an incident like this could trigger a mood change, which Alicia wanted to avoid at all costs. She now thinks that Hilda is shopping as if she had three more mouths to feed, not one. Has she forgotten that Stefan isn't here, would never again be here, and that Liam left the day before?

Uffe sits down on one of the kitchen chairs and lifts her eyes up to Alicia, 'He's only seventeen.' Uffe looks very gray, with his usually red cheeks drained of color and his eyes pale and watery.

Alicia sits opposite him, while Hilda stops unloading the bags for a moment and turns to gaze at her husband.

'I was on the tractor and the boys were lifting the potatoes. The guy, the one who speaks Swedish, told me that the row had been done. I had to reverse to get more room to turn around, and the boy was behind me. I didn't know he was there!'

'Is he alright?' A dread fills Alicia's gut. Her heart is beating so hard that she has to concentrate on breathing in and out. She thinks she might faint.

'His leg, oh my God, his leg.' Uffe stops for a moment, and runs his palm over his face. 'It went under the wheel, and the first thing I knew was a scream and the guy, the Swedish-speaker, waving his arms madly at me. I looked back from the cabin and saw his body lying there.'

Alicia stares at Uffe, then turns to look at her mother. Tears begin to run down her face. 'No!' she screams.

Hearing her yell, Uffe looks up and takes hold of her wrists. 'He has broken his leg, but he's OK. I was just told on the telephone.'

Alicia frees her arms, sits down and puts a hand to her mouth but she can't stop sobbing.

Uffe is still standing in front of Alicia. 'He's fine,' he repeats a little more quietly.

Hilda comes over and hugs her. 'There, there,' her mother says soothingly.

She lays her head on her mother's lap, inhaling her familiar smell of cooking and perfume. If only she was still a child, still living here in Åland, before she'd given birth and lost a son. From under her mother's arms, which are covering her head, she hears Hilda scold Uffe.

'Look what you've done! You need to think before you speak!'

'But I was upset, it was horrible ...'

'Shush, that's enough from you.'

Hilda lets go of Alicia and hands her a tissue from her pocket. 'I'm sorry you had to hear that. But the boy is OK!'

'Yes,' Alicia manages to say. She blows her nose on the worn-out tissue. She's still concentrating on breathing in and out. The images she carries in her head about the accident have come vividly into her mind. Of Stefan's body lying mangled, covered in blood, his helmet that both she and Liam made him promise to wear, to one side, and his moped, still running and producing oily smoke, lying on its side further away. The policewoman told Liam that Stefan had hit a wall, for no apparent reason, and that he had alcohol in his blood. He'd not strapped his helmet on properly, or had possibly not worn it at all. They couldn't tell. They said it was lucky that when he'd hit the wall between Camden Lock and Chalk Farm Road, no one had been walking on the pavement and no other vehicles were on the road. It had been 9pm, so it was a miracle no one else was hurt. The police couldn't tell Liam why Stefan had slipped; they assumed it was black ice. That November night had been cold and the temperature had dropped to -3°C. Alicia asked Liam over and over whether a lorry, or one of those big 4x4 vehicles, could have nudged him and caused him to lose his balance.

'They have CCTV,' Liam had said, and when Alicia asked if he'd seen it, Liam nodded, with his head hanging, gazing down at the kitchen table, not looking at her. Alicia thought she wanted to see the film too, but Liam persuaded her she shouldn't.

FOURTEEN

Frida parks her bicycle in front of the low-slung red-brick building. She feels clumsy getting off the bar. She is so fat now that people have started giving her sideways glances. She sighs; she needs to think about the future, but not now.

She glances at her phone but there is no reply from him.

It's a beautiful evening, with just a slight wind rattling the empty flagpoles in front of the old people's home. The grass in the front garden has just been cut and gives off the scent of summer. She hears the horns of the ferries in the distance and glances at her watch. Six o'clock exactly. The ships going from the islands to Finland and Sweden are never late.

Frida hopes she can take her mother out to the small garden at the back to have coffee with the butter buns she's bought from *Iwa's Konditori* on Torggatan. The old woman gave them to her half-price because she'd known Sirpa when she was younger and working at *Hotel Arkipelag*. And because Frida lied and said that it was her mother's birthday. It's the end of the month and her funds are running low, mainly because the bastards at the newspaper pay her so little. Besides, Frida is doing Iwa Nygren a favor by buying up the leftovers.

Holding onto the paper bag containing the buns, Frida hesitates for a moment outside the glass doors to *De Gamlas Hem*. Or *Oasis* as it is called now. Which is a bloody joke as far as Frida is concerned. Almost as much of a joke as calling the dementia ward where her mother is, *Solsidan*. The Sunnyside! Frida often wonders if some smart ass had decided it would be funny to name a loony bin for the elderly after the popular Swedish comedy about well-heeled *Stockholmare*, or if it was just a lame coincidence.

She is tired after a day spent researching useless facts about dog tourism to the islands. A Swedish woman has opened a pet hotel in Mariehamn and one of the permanent reporters got Frida to do all the legwork for a feature about the new business. The place would last three months max, Frida knows this, so it was pointless for the newspaper to spend so much time and effort on the article. Correction, it is pointless for *her*, Frida to spend time trying to find out how many dogs visit Åland each year. Now Frida's eyes ache and her brain is fried because of all the useless information she has filled it with. All she wants to do after fixing her eyes on the screen of an office pc for eight hours was to go home, fire up her own brand-new Mac and do her own research.

But that would have to wait. First, she had to see her mum. She just hopes she recognizes her today, or failing that, at least is calm and quiet. Perhaps the butter buns will put her in a good mood.

FIFTEEN

'We must stop meeting like this,' Patrick says. He's wearing the same soft suede jacket, this time over a white polo shirt, with the collar up over his neck. His dark brown leather messenger bag is slung across his broad chest.

Alicia is standing in the open-plan office of *Ålandsbladet* with a woman from personnel, Birgit Sundstrand. She's just been interviewed for a job at the paper, and to her great amazement, has been offered a post as a part-time reporter. The gray-haired woman with half-moon glasses was so impressed by her CV, and especially her work at the *Financial Times*, that she immediately asked Alicia when she could start.

'Today, if you wish!' Alicia replied and the woman smiled, revealing pale yellow teeth with red lipstick marks all over them. Alicia wanted to tell her about the smears, but the woman stood up to shake Alicia's hand before she had a chance.

'I'll email a contract this afternoon. Come and meet everyone!'

The job title, 'Financial Correspondent', is rather grand. It's been open for a while now, Birgit told her, 'waiting for the perfect candidate.' Alicia is still in shock; she only popped into the offices of the one and only newspaper on the islands to see if they had anything for her, anything at all. She has decided to stay on the islands for the summer, perhaps until the end of August, and she needs something to get her out of Hilda and Uffe's way. Besides, she knows her mother will soon start to say how Patrick, and Mia's father, Mr Åland, could get a her a position somewhere in their vast empire. But she wants to get a job on her own merits.

Today, she really didn't think her visit to the paper's offices would get her anywhere. She simply wanted to be able to tell her mother that she had tried. She imagined that a promise to look at her ideas would be the most they would offer, and perhaps the possibility of printing a few articles in the future. Alicia didn't in her wildest dreams imagine she would get a job–even a part-time post.

'You can decide on your hours yourself, all we require is that you turn in an article each week, and a feature once a month. All subjects have to be passed by the editor. I'll introduce you to him now.' Birgit spoke rapidly while walking down the steps. At the bottom of the stairs, at a set of glass doors, she stopped and turned to face Alicia, 'Is that alright?'

Alicia nodded, 'Yes, of course.' She was still trying to get used to the idea of working on *Ålandsbladet* but tried not to show it. She wanted to come across as dynamic and enthusiastic, two of the adjectives she uses to describe herself in her CV, even though she can't remember when she last fulfilled either of those traits.

'Oh, you've met?' Birgit now says. Addressing Patrick, she adds, 'What are you doing here?'

'That's a nice welcome,' Patrick says to the woman while his eyes are on Alicia, who tries hard to keep her professional composure. There's a definite atmosphere between her and the Swedish reporter.

'I was interviewing Alicia's mother last week. About the break-in.' Patrick moves his eyes from Alicia to Birgit.

'Ah, OK,' Birgit says, looking at Patrick and Alicia in turn.

'So why are you here?' Patrick says.

'I ...'

'She's our new Financial Correspondent. Part-time,' Birgit interrupts her, straining her neck toward the end of the large room, which is filled with desks divided by bright blue partition screens. Most of the work stations are unoccupied, Alicia notices, but following Birgit's gaze, she sees an office in the far corner of the room, separated from the main open-plan room by a glass partition. Inside there's a large desk and a couple of tall house plants. A high-backed leather chair is pushed away from the desk, empty.

'I wanted you to meet the editor, but he seems to have popped out.' Birgit glances at her watch, making Alicia do the same. It's 11.15am. Alicia realizes she's been with the personnel manager for just over 30 minutes and she is already a fully-fledged employee of the company.

'Well, well. Congratulations,' Patrick says and reaches his hand out to Alicia. She takes it and once again his touch sends currents through her body.

Pull yourself together.

Patrick sits himself on the edge of a desk, and nods toward the glass box at the end of the room. 'Came to see the old man but he's disappeared.'

Birgit's half-moon glasses move toward Patrick, and suddenly her face brightens.

'Alicia, why don't you tag along with Patrick? He can tell you more about this place at the same time You don't mind, do you, Patrick?'

He looks at the personnel manager, and then smiles at Alicia, revealing his white teeth.

'It'll be my pleasure.'

'What are you working on?' Alicia asks Patrick as soon as they step outside the modern building and the bright sunshine hits their faces. 'Apart from a little break-in at my mother's shop.'

They are standing on the pavement outside the *Ålandsbladet* offices. Patrick rests his hands on his hips, the strap of the leather bag cutting into his wide chest.

'I'm off to lunch.' Patrick says, not answering Alicia's question. 'You want to join me?'

Alicia stares at the man in front of her. He's attractive, she can't pretend otherwise. His blond hair and blue, flirtatious eyes are difficult to look at without smiling.

Alicia tries not to smile in appreciation and keeps her eyes serious.

'Ah, I'm sorry. I didn't realize. When Birgit said I should come along with you I imagined you were going to cover a story.'

Patrick gives a little laugh. 'I don't work here!'

As if she should know the joke, the wide smile stays on his lips. She is standing so close to him that she notices he has cut himself shaving that morning. A tiny speck of blood sits on his chin. Alicia catches herself imagining what his blood tastes like. She licks her lips.

'So, how about it?' Patrick says and Alicia is startled. Has he read her mind?

'Lunch?' Patrick says. 'The Italian by the marketplace is nice.'

'Ah,' Alicia says. 'I'm not sure ...' She makes a show of looking at her watch.

Patrick runs his hand through his hair. 'Look, why don't we have a bite to eat and I can tell you how things work in that madhouse?' He nods with his head toward the building they'd just left.

'I'm not officially employed by the paper, but it's part of the family business, and I occasionally give them a helping hand when I'm here in the summer.'

Alicia doesn't really have a choice. She tells herself: she's just been handed the perfect job, and told by the person who's employed her to go with this man.

'OK,' she says.

Patrick nods and chin points toward the Sitkoff shopping center. They walk through the covered mall, passing a hamburger place where a few youngsters are laughing and jostling with each other, waiting for their unhealthy lunches to be prepared. Alicia thinks of Stefan. Is this where he too spent his time when he took Uffe's moped into town from Sjoland?

Patrick leads the way out of the arcade, past an outdoor café where tourists are having coffees or nursing pints of lager. Everyone is laughing, the sun shining into their faces, their bodies relaxed in a holiday mode.

The sunny Torggatan is much busier, with children running away from their mothers and couples in shorts and summer dresses strolling along the street, looking into shop windows. It's still low season, a few days before Midsummer, but already the ferries are bringing day-trippers from Sweden and Finland to the little island town. Alicia glances across the street, where her mother's boutique is situated. Clothes that Hilda has placed on a rail outside, on the pavement, flutter in the breeze. Alicia quickens her step; she doesn't want to talk to her mother, or for her mother to see her with Patrick. She'd only make a fuss about the job, and the Swedish reporter.

'Do you like Italian food? Have you been to the one in *torg kiosken?*'

'Yeah, that sounds good.' Alicia isn't at all hungry, but she wants to talk to Patrick about the newspaper and her new job. Or that's what she tells herself. She knows that she is immensely attracted to this man. But she also knows he's married. As is she.

They make their way toward the Market Square, where a handful of strawberry sellers and people offering local handicrafts have stalls. As they walk, Alicia is aware that they have matched their steps. Patrick's hand hovers behind her, close to the small of her back, guiding her through the street as if she is a tourist. She can feel the heat of his body next to hers, but tries to ignore the effect his closeness is having.

The restaurant, called Nonna Rina, is bustling. It seems everyone in Mariehamn is here. Suddenly Alicia remembers coming here with Liam and Stefan. Her son was eleven at the time, and he wolfed down a bowl of pasta salad. It was overcast, and cold, the skies above threatening rain. They'd debated whether to wait for a table inside the small café, but Stefan was hungry so they'd opted to eat outdoors. She remembers how they watched the Rockoff festival set-up nearby on the Market Square, and how they debated whether Stefan should be allowed to go there with his island friends. Alicia remembers deciding he was too young to go on his own. Instead, she and Liam had taken turns to accompany their son, much to his embarrassment, over the few days of the festival.

They were always so careful with him, but it had been of no use. Alicia took a deep breath to release the pressure on her chest. This was how Connie had told her to deal with the grief, which so often came out of nowhere, crushing her lungs, making it difficult for her to breathe.

'Just take air in through your nose and release it slowly out of your mouth,' she said.

'You OK?' Patrick asks. They are standing in a line, waiting to be seated.

Alicia nods. She doesn't want to discuss her son with this man she hardly knows. Chances are he already knows about it—her mother isn't the most discreet of people. Alicia guesses she would have told him about Stefan during her interview with Patrick. Or he might have heard about the accident through the wide circle of people Uffe and Hilda know on the islands. Everyone knows everyone else's business here in the small island communities.

SIXTEEN

'I'm sorry about your son.' Patrick's eyes are steady on Alicia. She stares back at him, not knowing what to say. There is an awkward silence between them.

They are now sitting at the table, having paid for their food at the till. The Italian owner of the café brings them two bowls of salad. Patrick seems to know the dark-haired man and the two joke about a football game that Alicia has no interest in. Instead she nods to the man and raises the corners of her lips into a smile.

'Federico, please meet Alicia, a new reporter at *Ålandsbladet*,' Patrick says.

Alicia manages to make some small talk about how lovely Mariehamn is.

'She's a local, though,' Patrick says. His eyes are still on Alicia.

Federico raises his eyebrows and is about to ask Alicia to explain when a woman behind the counter attracts his attention and he excuses himself.

'Federico knows everybody in town,' Patrick says. 'In the summer we play in a five-aside together. He supports AC Milan and I Barcelona.'

'Hmm,' Alicia is munching on a corner of a crispy iceberg lettuce leaf. She isn't really hungry; it's barely 12 o'clock. She's forgotten how early they eat lunch on the islands.

'I'm sorry about before,' Patrick says after they have both finished their food in silence.

Alicia gazes at Patrick's weather-worn face. She wonders if he is or has been a heavy smoker. The lines on his face didn't take away from the rugged attractiveness of the man, but rather added to it.

'It's OK,' she says, and adds, 'Do you have kids?'

Patrick nods, 'Two girls, eight and ten.'

Alicia nods.

'When Sara was three, she had meningitis. We nearly lost her.'

Alicia lifts her eyes and looks at Patrick. His eyes are sad when he begins to tell the story, 'She had a temperature and we thought she just had a cold. It was in the middle of July and we were at the summer place. We had some people over and we'd been drinking. When we went to bed at about 2am, I looked into the girls' bedroom and felt Sara's forehead. She was burning up. I called to Mia and we phoned the doctor. We woke him up, and he told us to look for a rash ... there were red spots all over her body. How I hadn't noticed them when we put the girls into bed, I don't know. We'd both had too much to drink to drive but had no choice. By that stage we both felt pretty sober, though. We decided Mia should stay with Sara's younger sister, Frederica, and that I would drive to the hospital, where the doctor had agreed to meet us. It was the longest night of my life. She was unconscious when I lifted her out of bed and didn't come around until the next day.'

While he's talking, the noise of the café and the people having lunch disappears. Alicia sees how difficult reliving the awful night is for Patrick, and what nearly losing his daughter means to him.

'I'm sorry,' she says.

Patrick is quiet for a moment. 'Don't be. She was OK in the end. Not like ...'

Alicia takes a slow breath in and out. She is not going to cry.

'I'm so sorry,' Patrick says and leans in a little to bring his face closer to Alicia.

She wants to touch him, she wants to put her head on his shoulder. She wishes he'd lean in even closer and kiss her.

What's got into her?

Instead, she gets herself up and says, trying to keep her voice level, 'Would you like a coffee?'

'Anyway,' I'm sorry, it must be hard for you,' Patrick says when Alicia comes back with two cups of hot, black coffee.

Alicia gazes at Patrick's blue eyes and nods. The café is still bustling and two tourists from Sweden are speaking loudly at the counter, demanding gluten-free pizzas and soya milk lattes. Federico lifts his shoulders with his arms stretched out, giving the two a southern European shrug.

Patrick and Alicia follow the ruckus until the two thin women wearing sports clothes and bum bags storm out past their table, incensed that the Italian café didn't have what they wanted.

Their eyes meet and Alicia finds herself returning Patrick's smile. The mood has lifted between them.

'I feel I should say sorry,' Patrick says, laughing.

'You can't be held responsible for the behavior of all the people of your country of birth,' Alicia replies between giggles.

'The whole country? You really don't like Swedes, do you?'

Alicia puts her hand to her mouth to stop her now uncontrollable giggling.

What is going on? She's again behaving like a teenager in this man's company.

Patrick reaches over and puts his hand on hers. 'It's OK, I'm not particularly enamored with you *Ålänningar*. My in-laws can be quite annoying at times.'

Alicia's giggling finally stops and she looks down at Patrick's bony fingers over her own.

Patrick quickly removes his hand, and coughs into it instead.

'I think I need to get back to the office,' Alicia says, getting up. They walk along Torggatan in silence, and only speak once they're back at *Ålandsbladet*.

'Right,' Patrick says and sweeps his hand over the empty open-plan space. 'This is it!'

'Any idea where my desk might be?' Alicia says

Patrick shows her to a space that he says has been vacant for a while and gets the pc working for her. He runs through the intranet, letting her use his access settings, and says it might be best if she reads through the various sections of the paper to see the style of the writing. He briefly runs through who does what.

'You seem to know an awful lot about this place for someone who doesn't work here.' Alicia remarks.

Patrick smiles into her eyes again, 'Well, I'm married to the family, what can I say?'

They have their heads close together over the screen when they hear a door slam.

An older man with totally white hair walks through the door. He has a sizeable belly and wears a gray shirt with worn-out jeans and sandals with stripey socks.

'Harri, meet our newest reporter,' Patrick says, straightening his back.

'This is our editor, Harri Noutiainen,' Patrick says, turning to Alicia.

'Ah, yes, I heard about you.' Harri doesn't take Alicia's outstretched hand, and after an awkward moment, she lets it fall and stands there in silence while the editor peers at her from under his bushy eyebrows. In fact, the three of them stand in silence for what to Alicia seems like several long minutes. Eventually Harri declares, 'I hear you can write about money matters. You worked at the *Financial Times*?'

'Well yes ...' Alicia begins, but Harri interrupts her and says, 'Good, that's agreed then. I look forward to reading your pieces.'

Without waiting for a reply, he turns away and makes his way to the glass-paneled office in the corner of the large space.

SEVENTEEN

Alicia yawns as she opens the door to the offices of *Ålandsbladet*. She couldn't get back to sleep after waking at 4am to full daylight and twittering birds, and now, just before nine, she feels as if she's been awake for half a day already. She decides to just drop off her contract and leave at lunchtime—the job is supposed to be part-time after all.

She sees Birgit come up the stairs and hands her the piece of paper.

'I'm afraid Harri is out today,' the personnel woman says.

'I met him yesterday,' Alicia replies.

'Oh, right,' Birgit says and smiles. There's no lipstick on her teeth this morning. 'But you should come to the editorial meeting on Wednesday morning after Midsummer. I'll send the IT guy to you this morning. He can get you a username, passwords, access to our cloud and that sort of thing.'

'I think Patrick sorted most of that out for me yesterday,' Alicia says

The woman pulls the papers against her chest and starts to walk away. 'You're all set then. Have a good day.' She disappears out of the door.

Alicia nods and smiles at the two other people in the office, a young man and a woman, busy at their desks. She gets similar nods back but neither comes over to say hello. Birgit should have introduced me, Alicia thinks.

Patrick is nowhere to be seen, and why would he be? He was only there the day before to speak with the editor, she reminds herself. She's not sure if she is relieved or disappointed by his absence. It's an odd arrangement, she thinks, but then remembers how things are organized on the islands. Everything is more informal. It's who you know that matters.

Alicia sits down at the desk allotted to her at the entrance to the room. For something to do, she scrolls down her emails. She manages to open her own Webmail inbox and sees there's a message from Liam.

'Dear Alicia,

I just wanted to let you know I got home OK.

Love,

Liam x'

Alicia deletes the message without replying. What is the matter with the man? He acts as if everything is the same as before. He sent her a message on WhatsApp to say he'd arrived home on Sunday, and now this. Alicia wonders if he is now staying with Ewa, if he is in her arms at this very moment. She sees that it's just half past nine, which would make it 7.30 in the UK. He wouldn't still be in bed, if he follows his old routine. He'll now be on his morning run, but would that be in Crouch End or somewhere else, where Ewa lives? Alicia sighs. It's none of her business anymore.

She scans the other emails. There are adverts, messages from companies in London she no longer has any interest in. Alicia closes the page and begins to read the online paper. It's updated twice a day, once in the morning and once around 5pm in the afternoon, Patrick told her the day before. There is nothing interesting there. Alicia wonders how the paper can afford to employ her.

Frida's heart skips a little when she sees the new woman enter the office. What is Stefan's mum doing here at *Ålandsbladet*? With her head down, concealed by the screen that separates her desk from the one opposite, Frida pricks her ears and listens to the conversation between Birgit and Stefan's mum. Pretending to be engrossed with whatever is on her screen, and with her right hand resting on the mouse, Frida takes in the information, trying not to panic. She lifts her eyes slowly up over the screen and toward the end of the room, but neither woman is looking at her. She takes the opportunity to observe Stefan's mum closely. She has the same lanky build as Stefan, and the same tilt of the head when she listens to Birgit. Suddenly Frida feels a pain in her gut again, like she's been stabbed. Her heart is now racing and she has to put her hands under her thighs to stop them from shaking.

It's OK, she doesn't know you.

Frida has seen Stefan's mum from a distance once before, when he'd borrowed his step-grandpa's moped. She was with him when he picked up his mobile, which he'd forgotten at his grandparent's place. Frida was standing by the moped on the side of the road while Stefan ran back to the house. He asked her to come in but Frida didn't want to meet the old folks. She remembers seeing the relief on his face, although he'd tried to hide it, shrugging his wide shoulders and running his long fingers through his blond, shoulder-length hair. He jogged to the house and when he re-emerged from the front door, carrying his mobile, a woman whom he later said was his 'overcurious' mother stepped out behind him. She peered at Frida standing by the road, and Frida turned her back just in time, so that the woman couldn't tell whether she was a boy or a girl. With her short-cropped hair, Dr Martens, leather jacket and loose, ripped jeans, she often passed for a guy. She didn't mind what people thought.

Quickly, Frida now types 'Alicia O'Connell' and the *Financial Times* into the picture search on Google. Her fears are confirmed. The smiling image of the woman now sitting down at one of the free work stations is the one on the screen in front of her. She closes the page down and decides to take the bull by the horns.

EIGHTEEN

'Hi,' Alicia lifts her head and sees a young woman, with short cropped hair, colored pale gray and blue, standing by her desk, with her arm stretched.

'I'm Frida,' she says.

Alicia gets up and takes the hand. It seems a very formal greeting from someone so young. Frida doesn't look any older than Stefan, but her handshake is surprisingly strong.

'I'm the summer intern,' she says and she lifts one side of her mouth into a grin. 'So basically I do everything around here.' Her face is now in a full smile.

'Right,' Alicia says.

'And my mother is an ABBA fan, hence the name.' The girl looks down and kicks the floor with her left boot.

'It's a nice name,' Alicia says.

'Whatever. You smoke?'

'No.'

'OK, well, I'll show you around anyway, yeah?'

'Now?' Alicia asks and glances around the open-plan office and the editor's cubicle at the far end. What more was there to show her?

Frida shifts in her clumpy boots but doesn't say anything. Alicia feels sorry for the girl. She's only trying to be friendly, she thinks and gets up.

'That'll be lovely, thank you,' she says and gives the girl a smile.

Frida takes Alicia out of the office and points at the door to the bathrooms on the landing. 'There's a shower in there if you ever need it,' she says and grins at Alicia. Then she turns back into the main office and leads Alicia to a door on the right. It's a coffee room with a kitchenette and a round table covered in a bright green Marimekko cloth. There are chairs all around the table. At the far end of the narrow space a tall window reaching down to the floor overlooks the Eastern Harbor.

'That's nice,' Alicia says and nods toward the view of the sailing boats rocking in the wind. The sun is high in the sky, its rays reflecting on the rippling surface of the sea.

Frida follows Alicia's gaze. 'Yeah, nice to see the Russian Mafia boats every day.' Her tone has changed, and the smile has disappeared from her lips.

'What do you mean?' Alicia asks. She gazes at the young woman who's wearing a white T-shirt and a pair of tight ripped jeans, revealing slices of the, almost luminous, white skin of her thighs. On her feet she wears a pair of black, heavy Dr Marten's, which look too hot for the warm summer weather. The temperature had already reached 20°C when Alicia left the sauna cottage that morning and got into the car with her mum.

'Oh, nothing, it's a joke.' Frida is standing by the small kitchen area, her face turned away from Alicia. 'Would you like some coffee? I'm making a pot.'

'Yes please.'

While Frida fills the percolator with coffee from a packet she's retrieved from a cupboard above the sink, Alicia admires the scene of the harbor through the tall window. There are a couple of expensive-looking yachts among the many sailing boats.

The East Harbor gets busier each day coming up to Midsummer, when the high season starts. At its peak, there will be no free spots on the jetties. The sailing club, *Club Marin*, which has a restaurant, saunas and restrooms for the yachties will be bustling with families. Alicia regrets that she didn't take Stefan sailing. Neither she nor Liam were particularly interested in boats, she thinks, as she watches Frida turn to look at the view. The coffee percolator has started dripping water loudly into the glass pot.

'You don't like Russians?' Alicia asks.

The girl whips her head around and her eyes are dark with hatred. 'They're bastards, every one of them.'

Alicia is startled by the girl's hostility. Growing up on the islands, which are part of Finland, no one had liked Russians, or Soviet citizens, as they had been some twenty years ago. But there was never this kind of animosity toward the people themselves, only toward those in power. Like Putin, now rumored to own land on the islands.

The girl's demeanor suddenly changes, and a grin returns to her face.

'How do you take your coffee?'

'Oh, black please,' Alicia says, still slightly shocked by the sudden changes in the young woman's mood.

Frida places a mug on the tablecloth in front of Alicia and sits down opposite her. Alicia sees she has tattoos on the inside of her wrist.

'That must have hurt,' she says, nodding to the small image of an angel carved onto the pale skin. It's obvious they need to change the subject.

'Nah, not really,' Frida says, glancing inside her own arm. She lifts her eyes toward Alicia. 'It's in memory of someone very sweet. I believe he's an angel now.'

Alicia stares back at Frida. How does she know that is exactly how Alicia thinks about her own son. Has Frida also lost someone dear to her? The question, 'Who?' hangs in the air, but for some reason Alicia is too afraid to ask.

'Well, I'd better get back to work,' Alicia says instead, and gets up.

'It was nice to meet you and thank you for the coffee,' she says over her shoulder to the girl, who is not looking at her, but staring out of the window. She doesn't reply and Alicia hesitates for a moment by the door. She cannot put her finger on it, but Alicia has a strange feeling that Frida was talking about Stefan, her Stefan, but surely that couldn't be? To stop the train of thought, Alicia throws another glance at the luxury Russian yachts. The East Harbor has more of them each year, flying their wide striped white, blue and red flags. But so what? All they do is bring tourist cash into the small economy, surely?

NINETEEN

'Have you seen this?' Hilda has printed a sheet from her computer and is waving it in front of Alicia. She's sitting on her favorite stool in the corner of the kitchen, waiting for her mother. They're planning to cook dinner together and Hilda has been upstairs changing out of her work clothes. Alicia takes the piece of paper from her mother. Her heart skips a beat when she sees it's from Mia—Patrick's Mia.

'Patrick is true to his word then,' she says, trying to sound nonchalant.

'Of course he is!' Hilda snatches the paper out of Alicia's hands and turns toward the front door, where Uffe has just appeared.

'Have you heard, Uffe, we're invited to the Eriksson's Midsummer party!'

Uffe glances at Alicia and smiles, 'Well, aren't we going up in the world.'

'Oh, my,' Hilda says, her eyes fixed on the piece of paper. 'It was sent on Saturday, that's three days ago and we haven't RSVP'd. That could be seen as rude, you know.'

Alicia rolls her eyes at Hilda, 'Mum, how come you haven't seen the email before?'

Hilda waves her hand over her freshly coiffured blond bob. 'Oh, I don't check my emails more than once a week, if that! It's usually all adverts or messages from people I don't like.'

Alicia has to suppress a smile. She's about to ask how come she doesn't get her emails on her brand-new iPhone, but she doesn't want to get into a long conversation about how the internet does or doesn't work on Hilda's mobile. It's all organized a bit differently in Finland, and she's no expert herself. A few years ago she made the mistake of trying to configure Hilda's first smart phone and managed to delete her settings, so now she doesn't want to touch her mother's phones. Besides, it was always either Liam or Stefan who dealt with the technical things in the family. *I guess I have to learn how to do those things now*, Alicia thinks to herself.

'So we are obviously all going, yes? I know we said we'd spend the evening here, but this is such an opportunity ...' Hilda says, looking at Uffe.

Alicia looks at her mother. 'When is it?'

'What?' Hilda is staring at her daughter. Even Uffe is looking at Alicia. He's standing by the kitchen island, with one of Hilda's cinnamon buns in his hand.

'Don't eat that now,' Hilda snaps at Uffe and he puts the bun down on the kitchen counter. 'It's nearly dinner time!' Hilda gives her husband an angry stare, then turns back to Alicia.

'Midsummer's Eve is this Friday, silly,' she almost shouts. You know, Eriksson's Midsummer parties are the talk of Mariehamn, of Åland! Anyone who's anyone will be there.'

'Sorry, I was miles away. Of course we must go.' Alicia says and takes hold of the piece of paper again. 'Did you open the attachment? I bet there's an invite there with more information.'

'Oh,' Hilda says and turns on her heels. Moments later she's back with another piece of paper. Alicia wonders why she didn't just forward the email to her, but doesn't say anything. It's a stylish invite in black and white with images of dancing couples, champagne glasses and balloons bordering a text, 'Come and celebrate the magic of Midsummer with Family Eriksson'.

The party starts with lunch at 1pm and goes on past midnight, or whenever people want to go home. What a long bash, Alicia thinks and wonders how she can get out of it. When she looks up and sees that her mother's eyes are sparkling, she realizes there's no chance. She will have to go. A faint tingling on her skin tells her she is excited at the prospect of seeing Patrick again too.

'I've never been to the Eriksson's villa,' Hilda says, her voice breathless. 'Of course, like everyone else, I've driven past hundreds of times. They have those heavy iron gates now, so you can't see into the drive or the vast shoreline they own anymore, but ...' she stops abruptly, and exclaims, 'Oh, what will we wear! We'll have to pick something out of my stock and everyone in Mariehamn will have seen it already!' Hilda is staring at her daughter, her eyes wide and with one of her hands splayed over her chest in a dramatic pose. Not this again, Alicia thinks, but then she remembers she hasn't got anything suitable either. As if she's read her mind, her mother comes over and puts her arm over Alicia's shoulders. 'Don't worry, I have just the dress for you.'

On the day of the party, the skies are clear and the sun beams down as Alicia makes her way from the sauna cottage to the main house. Uffe has offered to drive Hilda's freshly washed and polished BMW. Two of his farm hands have given the brand-new soft-top a thorough going over. For over two hours they washed and scrubbed every inch of the exterior and then polished the chassis and the cream leather interior. The car looks brand-new.

So that people won't have to drink and drive, the Eriksson's have invited guests to park their cars overnight on their estate. Hilda is taking full advantage of the offer, and has ordered a taxi to take them home promptly at midnight. This, Alicia thinks, will give her mother another opportunity to make contact with the Eriksson's when they fetch the car the next day. She will be able to see the 'summer place' again. *Don't be so mean and churlish*, Alicia tells herself as she watches the streets of Mariehamn whizz past, full of revellers. The weather has brought everyone out to celebrate Midsummer on the islands.

They drive with the roof up to save Hilda's hair-do. Alicia's sense of being a teenager isn't helped by the fact that she is sitting on the back seat, almost doubled over in the small space, obviously not meant to be used by a fully grown person. Like a child being taken to an adult party, she'd rather be anywhere else right now. She wonders if she might be able to smuggle herself out before the twelve hours of merrymaking are over. She can't imagine she will have any fun among the Åland glitterati, most of whom will be the same age as her mother and Uffe. She brushes away thoughts of Patrick.

Still, it will be interesting to see the 'summer place', as the invitation calls (with false modesty) what Alicia knows is a vast estate at the southern tip of the peninsula. She's met Mia's parents in passing before, but she has never really spoken to them, nor has she ever been invited to their home. Alicia knows that not only is Mia's father a millionaire, but her mother is a famous author. That said, she is not a fan of her books, even though her works are celebrated all over Scandinavia and beyond and have been translated into several languages. To Alicia, Beatrice Eriksson's novels are too full of misery and death. She smiles when she recalls Liam's remark after reading one of her books —'I'm surprised she didn't commit suicide while writing this story.' At the time Alicia was angry with Liam's flippant dismissal of one of the most important books that had come out of Finland in years. The story, which centers on the famine under the Russian rule in the 18th century, won prizes all over Europe. But she had to admit, after reading *Frozen Hunger* she didn't wish to know any of the writer's other books, however much she would have liked to support an author from Åland.

Then there's Patrick. Alicia tries to brush away her stupid infatuation with the man. She knows she's being foolish, and that her feelings probably aren't reciprocated. Patrick is just being flirty; he's that kind of a man.

And what about the other day when they were having lunch? Didn't you share a moment then?

She tells herself to stop fantasizing about a married man and tries to concentrate on her mother's incessant chatter. She's talking about all the good Mr Eriksson has done on Åland, about the funds he's plowing into tourism and the charities he supports.

Alicia tunes out again and looks at the beautiful scenery. They're crossing a long, narrow bridge where the sea opens up on both sides of the road. The sun's rays glitter on the surface of the water and Alicia leans her head against the headrest. It's good to be home.

Soon they join a line of expensive cars, all just as well buffed and polished as Hilda's.

'We're nearly there!' Hilda says, with her voice trembling. 'How do I look?' she asks and pulls down the sun visor to check on her hair and teeth.

'You look fine,' Alicia says when her mother turns around.

They get out of the car and Hilda whispers to Alicia, 'You are stunning. That green color really suits you, and the chiffon fabric flatters your figure. I'm glad I managed to convince you to wear the high-heeled wedges with that dress.'

TWENTY

'Networking, that's what you need to do,' Mia says and gives Patrick a look. He knows she is disappointed that he's not come up to scratch.

'Tonight's your chance,' she tells him as they're getting ready in the converted boathouse on the morning of the party. 'Daddy invited the editor from *Expressen* just for you.'

Expressen is the other large evening paper in Sweden. Patrick has been put on notice of redundancy, something he hasn't shared with his wife. His boss at the paper told him everyone got the same notice, but he knows that's not true. He hasn't had a scoop in years. He doesn't care as much about his career as Mia does. He's fed up with the way *Journalen* sensationalizes the news. There are no standards in journalism anymore. But that doesn't matter to Mia and her parents. Her father, who has his fingers in many pies in Sweden too, just needs her daughter's husband to conform to the upper-class image he had of Patrick when Mia married him. Little did Mr Eriksson know that he was just an ordinary *Norrbotten* Swede, who got lucky with a job in a major Stockholm newspaper. Even after ten years with Mia (and especially now, Patrick thinks) it's important that he has a good independent income.

He's married into a family with standing, with a prize-winning author to boot. Something he's often reminded about.

'All you need to do is to impress him with your ...' Mia looks Patrick up and down. 'Well, try at least to sound intelligent.'

Patrick doesn't say anything. He can't think of an equally suitable slur.

'Where are the girls?' he asks instead.

'In the house.'

Patrick thinks of his daughters in Kurt and Beatrice Eriksson's large house, scrubbed clean, watching a cartoon on TV, or playing on their iPads in one of the upper bedrooms. Mia got them ready hours before the party to give herself plenty of time to preen.

Everything needs to be perfect, that's how Pappa likes it.

Patrick has also been required to get ready in good time and is now standing dressed in his best linen suit in front of the floor-length windows of their converted boathouse, looking at one of the Viking Line ferries on its way toward Sweden. Patrick grabs the binoculars out of habit and surveys the ship through them.

'Are you even listening to me?' Mia says, removing the lenses from Patrick's hand. Her voice is gentle, too gentle, and Patrick looks at his wife. She's slim, but with a shapely body. Her legs, which are long anyway, are further elongated by the white outfit she's wearing.

'Isn't that boiler suit going to get dirty?' Patrick says.

Mia takes a deep breath and exhales slowly, throwing the binoculars on their vast *Hästens* bed, which takes up most of the bedroom. Her face is angular, all straight lines. With her hands on her hips. 'Jump suit, not a boiler suit. I'm not a fucking plumber!'

'All the same, red wine on that thing ...'

Now Mia has a knowing smile on her lips. 'Don't change the subject, darling.' She comes close to Patrick and presses her body against his. The top of the suit is open, almost down to her naval, and he pulls the side of the neckline away from her chest and peers inside. He sees one pink nipple on her pert little breast.

'No bra, eh? Who are you out to impress today?'

Mia lifts her dark brown eyes at him. Her smile has disappeared. 'Don't be nasty.'

'I'm not,' Patrick says, releasing his grip on her suit and taking a couple of steps toward the bed to retrieve the binoculars. Turning around and seeing his wife's shapely rear framed by the calm teal sea beyond the large window, he says, 'I can show you how nice I can be.' He reaches out to place his palm on one of Mia's buttocks, but she moves away just before he can make contact.

'Don't.' The expression on her face is icy cold.

Patrick sighs and continues to peer at the large red ferry. He sees people on the deck, gazing toward the coastline. There's a couple kissing, the woman's dress flapping in the wind. Patrick feels almost jealous of the man next to the smiling woman. He's forgotten how to be happy, he thinks, and resolves to try to appease Mia. Perhaps there's still hope? But when he puts down the binoculars and turns around to say something to her, he finds himself alone in the room.

Alicia sees Patrick almost as soon as she, Hilda and Uffe come around the corner and get the full vista of the magnificent house. Along with all the other well-dressed people, they've abandoned their car keys to a young guy with thick dark hair who directs them down a well-tended path toward a vast, modern building.

Valet parking in Åland, Alicia thinks. She's never even been offered it in London!

Patrick is dressed in a light-colored linen suit, with a T-shirt underneath. Somehow, he looks even more bronzed than he did a few days ago. He has a wide smile on his lips as he greets guests at the top of stairs leading to a wooden deck, which has been stained dark gray to blend into the rock surrounding the house. The place itself is covered in glass. A pair of tall windows facing the sea form the center of the house, with two long wings on either side, and sloping roofs half shading the glass. The house seems to be floating in the sea, which today is calm, blue-green in color. A slight wind is making patterns like fish scales on the surface of the water, and the sun is high up, the sky blindingly blue with just a few fluffy clouds breaking up the perfect impression.

Patrick is wearing aviator-style sunglasses, but Alicia can see from his smile that he has spotted them. He whispers something to a man standing next to him and steps down the stairs to greet them personally. He makes a few apologies as he walks toward Alicia, Uffe and Hilda, and a few eyebrows are raised at the attention they are getting. When he leans down to kiss Hilda's cheek, her mother's face lights up in awe. She moves her shoulders slightly lower down her back and lifts her head toward Patrick.

'How lovely of you to invite us!' she says and Patrick smiles. 'Not at all, it's a privilege to have you here.' As he says this, he glances at Alicia, who is standing behind Hilda and Uffe. Hilda introduces her husband to Patrick and the two men shake hands. And then he is standing opposite Alicia.

'Nice dress,' he says quietly against her ear as he bends down to kiss Alicia's cheek. His hand touches her back and she can feel his fingers through the thin fabric. The garment Hilda chose for her skims her body with three layers of fabric. The hem touches her calves but has slits up to her thighs, so that her legs are momentarily revealed when she walks. Alicia tries not to blush and is glad of the large pair of sunglasses she popped into her handbag at the last minute. She's sure her eyes will betray her emotions, so she keeps her shades on, even when Patrick removes his and gazes at her quietly. Just before the moment becomes embarrassing, Patrick says, 'Come and have a drink!'

As he leads the three of them toward a bar, Hilda and Uffe see someone they know and are pulled into a conversation.

'Just you and me, then,' Patrick laughs.

TWENTY-ONE

Patrick takes Alicia to a small bar set up in the main living rooms inside the house. Most people are staying outside, taking advantage of the brilliant summer weather, and the vast room is empty. Alicia gasps when she steps inside after Patrick. The decor is stunning; pared down with a gray color scheme, with just the occasional pop of color—a red scatter cushion here, or a bright yellow throw there. The floor is slate, and the walls, in which there are two massive fireplaces, are constructed out of gray stone. Patrick asks her if she would like champagne, and Alicia nods. A popping sound brings her attention back to Patrick, who is pouring the Moet into two long flutes.

'Is this where you stay when you're in Åland?' she asks when he hands her a glass. 'Yep,' he replies.

Alicia wishes she could put her sunglasses back on. She can feel his eyes on her, but she fears looking at him in case she betrays the speed of her heartbeat. Every time he comes near her, she wants him to move away, yet come closer at the same time. She can feel the heat of his body too well through the damned dress, which makes her feel naked.

'That really suits you,' Patrick says.

It's too revealing, I knew it.

Alicia lifts her eyes briefly. He isn't smiling anymore, but his lips are slightly parted.

'Shouldn't you be looking after your guests?' she says quickly.

'They're not my guests. Besides, I'm looking after you.'

Alicia sips the drink, glad to have the glass to hide behind, and to have something solid between her and Patrick. She looks up, trying to admire the high-ceilinged space, when she sees a figure leaning on a banister that runs between two oak staircases on either side of the room.

Mia.

'Hello Mia!' Alicia says and lifts her glass toward her old schoolfriend.

Well, not so much a friend.

Mia gives Alicia a quick glance and begins to make her way down one of the staircases. She's wearing an all-white jumpsuit made out of some silky fabric, Alicia notices. A belt made out of the same fabric is tied around her small waist. On her feet, Mia has high-heeled gold sandals, and she wears matching hooped earrings. Her dark curls are tied up in an up-do, with a few strands falling over her shoulders. She has barely any make-up on, just a dab of red color on her full lips. Her body is perfect for the outfit, as is her make-up. When she reaches them, she gives Alicia two air kisses and turns to her husband, 'A glass of that bubbly would be lovely, darling.'

Patrick looks back at the bar and realizes there are no champagne flutes left.

'Umm,' he says and looks at Mia.

She crosses her arms and lifts one eyebrow. 'Well, go and get some then! I'm sure Magda has some in the kitchen.'

'Men,' she smiles at Alicia when Patrick has disappeared through an opening in one of the stone walls.

'Amazing place!' Alicia blurts out. She desperately wants to take another sip out of her glass, but doesn't think it would be polite when her hostess is without a drink.

Mia smiles, but her eyes remain cold and almost hostile. She waves an arm into the room. 'Oh, this is where Mamma and Pappa stay. We're over by the cove. In a converted boathouse. It's tiny compared to this.'

'Right.'

Alicia is relieved to see Patrick re-enter the rooms with a small dark-haired woman wearing an old-fashioned white lace pinny over a dark-colored dress.

These people have servants?

The woman is carrying a silver tray filled with champagne flutes. She puts it down and looks up at Patrick. 'Here, let me, Magda,' he says, dismissing the woman with a friendly smile.

'At last!' Mia says, taking a full glass from Patrick. She gives Alicia another of her unfeeling smiles and then turns to wave at somebody in the garden through the open door.

'Excuse me,' she says to Alicia and turns to Patrick, adding, 'It's the Wikströms!' She floats out of the room, expecting Patrick to follow her.

On his way past, he whispers into Alicia's ear, 'See you later.' His lips almost brush her skin, and for a while Alicia stands still, trying to calm her breathing. She gulps down the rest of her champagne and decides to empty the bottle into her glass.

They can afford it, she thinks.

TWENTY-TWO

As the day wears on and turns into a glorious evening, Alicia's fears are confirmed—none of her friends are at the party. There must be at least a hundred people milling around the vast grounds of the house, but most of the guests are Kurt and Beatrice's friends, it seems. Hilda and Uffe also seem to know absolutely everyone. Her mother introduces Alicia to so many people that she cannot retain any of the names however much she tries. Hilda laughs and chats with everyone, and Uffe appears be in his element too, drinking beer and then red wine and schnapps when the food starts to flow. There's fish roe and sour cream served on tiny blinis, marinated herring with beetroot and pickled cucumbers, lobster tails on rye toast, new potatoes and delicious reindeer steak.

Occasionally Alicia spots Magda peering out from the main house, controlling the younger waiters and waitresses in similar old-fashioned outfits, as they weave in and out of the groups of people, filling glasses and offering food. Small frozen tumblers of different flavored vodka are passed around and men and women throw them down their throats.

Alicia steers clear of any strong drinks, but accepts the seemingly free-flowing champagne when it's offered. She's keeping herself away from Patrick, and clings onto her mother as if she is a child at an adult's party. She cannot trust herself around Patrick sober, let alone tipsy. Besides, she's always been a lightweight. It was Liam who could match Uffe's vodka-drinking, and sometimes Alicia wonders if that is the only thing Uffe admires about her husband. *Her husband.* Was she still strictly married to Liam? Or were they now separated?

Only occasionally does she glimpse Patrick, often in conversation with a group of men. Once she lifts her head and he is looking right at her. She is sure she blushes but hopes Patrick is too far from her to see it.

At around eight o'clock, when the sun approaches the horizon, Mr Eriksson stands up on a stool and gives a speech.

'Dear friends and islanders,' he begins in a low, quiet tone. The guests hush suddenly and all strain to hear their host's words.

'My family and I are delighted that you have been able to come and celebrate Midsummer with us in our small cabin.' Here Kurt Eriksson pauses and looks around the guests, most of whom burst into laughter.

'Small cabin indeed,' Hilda whispers loudly in Alicia's ear. She turns around and returns her mother's smile. But there's something about Kurt Eriksson that Alicia doesn't like. He is a tall man, with a slight paunch. In spite of this, he looks fit and handsome in his white linen trousers and striped blue-pink shirt. Alicia sees his Rolex glint in the sun and spots the almost compulsory footwear for wealthy islanders—Docker shoes. Mr Eriksson's hair is gray-blond and his eyes are pale, as if both have been bleached by a life spent in the sun. He's wearing a pair of expensive-looking sunglasses on top of his head. On the whole, he looks as if he's just stepped off an exclusive sailing yacht, which Alicia guesses he probably has. Alicia remembers her mother saying something about Kurt Eriksson speaking Russian and convincing some oligarch or other to come to the islands for a holiday. Many more followed in his wake, making the islands a prime holiday destination for Russians.

'He's a good man,' Hilda told Alicia.

Alicia is suddenly aware that Mr Eriksson's eyes are on her and she widens the smile on her face. The host nods toward their group, where Alicia stands with her mother and Uffe, a little apart from the other guests.

Turning his head away, Kurt Eriksson scans the lawn where the people are arranged below him. He invites all the guests to come down to the lower level of the garden, where a fully decorated Midsummer pole lies on its side. The Erikssson children, with the help of staff, have attached flowers and paper lanterns to the pole and now it's the job of two men to lift it up. One of them is the young guy who parked Uffe's car. Everyone cheers the lifting of the pole, raising their glasses to sing, 'Hurrah, hurrah', and then Mr Eriksson leads the crowd in the little frog song. When she was a child and living in Åland, it seemed completely natural to sing about frogs at Midsummer, but now it strikes Alicia as very strange. But funny. She smiles as old and young leap up to sing,

'Små grodorna är lustiga att se,
   små grodorna är lustiga att se
   Ej örön, ej örön,
   Ej svansar have de.'

Most people also do the actions, waving their hands around their ears to show a lack of them, and on their backside to show the lack of a tail. Alicia laughs and catches Patrick's eye. He dances with his daughters until the end of the song, when Mia leads the two girls away. Alicia looks toward Uffe and Hilda, who are laughing with a group of their friends—or acquaintances—Alicia has never seen them before. When she looks back to where Patrick had been standing, he has disappeared.

TWENTY-THREE

All through the party, Patrick watches Alicia's slight frame appear from behind a group of people, or around the corner of the house, her pale eyes looking at him from a distance. If only Mia, in her ridiculous white boiler suit, wouldn't keep pulling him further away from her to meet this and that person. He doesn't understand why she still cares.

After the ridiculously overdecorated Midsummer pole is lifted up by the East European boys, and the frog song and dance is over, Mia decides it's time for the girls to go to bed. At first, both Sara and Frederica protest, but their mother is firm. Patrick sees that the girls are over-excited but tired, and he promises to go and kiss them goodnight when the party is over.

'Even if I'm asleep, will you do it, Pappa?' says Frederica, her eight-year-old eyes grave and her blond curls messy after the party.

Patrick kneels down in front of his two daughters and looks from one to the other. 'I promise.' He gives them both a kiss and adds, 'You have to promise to be good for your mother.' The two little girls both nod gravely, and as Mia takes their hands, she gazes at him and gives him an almost kind smile.

. . .

Patrick watches his wife and daughters walk toward their cabin. He suspects Mia will not read the girls a story, or tuck them in. She'll leave all that to the Finnish au pair she has employed for the summer. She's a nice girl and both Sara and Frederica like her. He knows that if he had offered to do the bedtime routine, it would have caused a further row. Deciding to make his escape from the party, he slips down toward the water, where he knows there's a little cove among the rocks that is not visible to anyone. When the girls were little and learning to swim, his father-in-law shipped in a truck full of sand to make a little beach. He also paid a fully trained lifeguard from one of his sports charities to come and give the girls lessons.

Patrick remembers how his own father taught him to swim the summer he turned five, well before anyone else in his neighborhood in Luleå. He and his parents lived in a two-bedroomed flat in a working-class part of the city. They both worked full-time for the city council, and he attended nursery school from the age of one. He was lucky that his granny had a small summer place in Kalix on the coast. It was a little hut with just two small rooms, a tiny kitchen, and an outside toilet, built by his grandfather. But it was close to a beach and that's where Patrick's dad taught him to float for the first time. It was a far cry from a private beach and a qualified private tutor.

Of course, neither girl used the cove beach anymore. The novelty wore off a summer or two ago, and now they liked to dive into the sea from the sauna at the tip of the peninsula, which formed part of the Eriksson family summer place. Or 'cabin'. As if! More like an estate, and the biggest one in Åland, of course.

What a ridiculous man my father-in-law is!

With his hands in his pockets, Patrick makes his way across the lawn, then down some steps and finally to a narrow path on a small triangle of land between two large boulders, where the sea laps onto the imported sand. Patrick kicks off his shoes and pulls his socks off. The cool sand feels good as it spreads through his toes. Toward the end of the day, the clouds had gathered and the sun is now hidden behind them, leaving pink streaks visible between the white, fluffy shapes. Suddenly Patrick gets an urge to jump into the sea. He takes off his jacket and pulls his shirt over his head without bothering to undo more than the first few buttons. He unzips his linen trousers and pulls them off with his boxers.

Running into the water, he ignores the cold. He feels like a boy again when the water reaches his calves, then thighs. There's a bit of shallow water, and then the ground drops dramatically where the artificial beach ends. Patrick dives in and the shock of the chilly water nearly makes him turn back again. It's early summer, and the few days of bright sunshine and temperatures above 20°C haven't yet managed to warm the seawater. Patrick perseveres and swims, taking long, regular strokes in a front crawl like his late father taught him.

TWENTY-FOUR

When the traditional games and singing around the pole have finished Alicia walks away. Even though she was quite young when she and her mother moved to Åland, she still thinks the Midsummer celebrations on the islands are wrong somehow. Her Finnish roots make her want to be by the shore, watching a bonfire being lit, as she must have done as a baby, when her mother and father were together. She didn't know her father at all; all she has is a photograph Hilda gave her when she got married. It's a picture of a man with a serious face in army uniform. Hilda said it had been taken when her father, Klaus, was doing his military service. He was just eighteen.

A year older than Stefan.

Growing up in Åland, Alicia would imagine her father living in the house by the sea in Helsinki in which she was born. She wonders now why Hilda never took her to see her father before it was too late. Hilda never wanted to talk about Klaus; the little Alicia knows has all been extracted with difficulty. When she was seven years old, Hilda took her to *Svarta Katten* café after school and told her gently that Klaus had died. Nothing more was said about Alicia's father. As far as she knew, Hilda didn't even go to the funeral in Finland.

. . .

The light is fading a little now, helped by the shroud of gray clouds. She walks toward the shoreline, down a path to a small cove with a tiny sandy beach. As she gets closer, she spots someone in the water. The person turns around and Alicia sees who it is. Surely it can't be ...?

TWENTY-FIVE

Patrick is swimming back toward the beach. He doesn't spot the woman standing by one of the boulders until he has nearly reached the shallow water by the shore. He stands up and smiles at Alicia. The water comes just above his hips.

'Come in, it's wonderful!' he shouts.

He can't see her face properly, but he thinks she's considering it. Then he can see she's shaking her head. She forms a funnel with her hands and replies, 'Do you have a towel?'

He shakes his head and continues walking toward the shore, aware that he is naked. He wants her to see him, even though he knows the cold water will have diminished his manhood somewhat. As he gets closer, he is holding her gaze, and to his delight he sees she is not shy, but looking at him. He goes to the gym at least three times a week, plays football regularly and knows he's in good shape. Suddenly Alicia, in her thin dress that the slight sea breeze has plastered to her body, revealing a slim but shapely figure, bends down and picks up his shirt.

He walks toward her and she hands him the shirt.

'To preserve your modesty.'

'Thank you,' he says but instead of placing it over his hips, he takes the linen shirt and uses it to dry first his face, then his chest and finally between his legs. All the while Alicia is looking out to sea, but he knows she is trying to keep her gaze away from his body, because just now, when he lowered the shirt from his face, her eyes shifted quickly away from him.

Patrick rushes to pull on his pants, not bothering with underwear, because he can feel a movement in his groin. Looking down, he sees he's just in time, and tucks himself in.

'You missed out,' he says, sitting down next to her on the rock. He means the swim, but knows she will get the double entendre.

And he is rewarded with a smile.

He sees she's taken off her sandals and is burrowing her toes in the sand.

'Did I now?' she says, and her smile reaches her eyes and widens.

Patrick is so close to her that their thighs are touching. He wants to put his arm around her, but is afraid she will bolt.

'How did you find this place?'

'Has the beach always been here?' Alicia and Patrick speak at the same time and both laugh.

'My father-in-law made this for the girls.'

'Ah,' Alicia says. 'Lucky girls.'

'Yeah, not that they appreciated it. Not then, not now. I'm the only one who comes swimming here nowadays. It's my secret place.'

Alicia turns her head and looks at him, 'What are you escaping from?'

For a moment Patrick considers Alicia, noticing the thin lines around her mouth and how her eyes have a sadness etched into them even though she is smiling. He wants to touch the curve of her jaw, pull her face close to his and kiss her.

'Isn't it obvious? All this,' he says instead.

Patrick throws his arm out, pointing toward the house behind the large boulders. They hear faint party noises; someone has put on music. All of it seems far away to him. He feels as if he's sitting on a desert island and the only person who matters is this vulnerable, beautiful woman next to him. 'Besides, you're one to talk about escape. I believe you're on the run as we speak.'

Her large eyes stare at him, and the grief in them fills him with sudden, strong desire. Her lips are slightly parted. An invitation. He needs to kiss those lips now. He bends closer and presses his mouth to hers. He's hungry for her. He puts his left hand onto her neck to pull her close, and his other hand finds the small of her back.

Alicia pulls herself away. She's breathless. She stands and smooths down her dress to disguise how strongly she feels.

'You shouldn't have done that,' she says and picks up her shoes from the sand. She doesn't dare look at Patrick. She loved the taste of his lips on hers; the desire she can feel emanating from his body.

And hers.

Patrick is quiet and Alicia moves her eyes toward him. He's still sitting on the boulder, leaning on his hands, which are placed either side of his body. Alicia can see his muscles flex. His eyes are a darker shade of blue now, and she has to turn her head away to avoid sinking into them.

'I can't wear these!' she laughs, stealing another sideways glance at Patrick. She's banging her wedges against each other, but the wet sand is sticking to the inside and soles.

Alicia sits down next to him again, facing the small beach, where the water laps gently against the sand. The only sounds are from the party beyond the boulders, further up the bank behind them.

'Wear mine,' he says, pushing his shoes toward her feet.

'No thanks,' Alicia says and they both giggle uncontrollably.

I must be very drunk. I don't have any sense of guilt about kissing another man.

'I love champagne, must have just had too many glasses of the stuff,' Alicia says, between bouts of laughter.

'I'll remember that,' Patrick says, then he is suddenly serious. He touches Alicia's cheek. 'I hope this wasn't just too much drink?'

Alicia looks into his brilliant blue eyes. She sees there are specs of brown in the aquamarine and that his eyelashes are unnaturally long and dark for a man.

For a man with blue eyes.

She says nothing but allows Patrick to put his lips on hers, and once more they kiss. This time, Patrick is gentle; he doesn't use his tongue as he did before, but gently presses himself against Alicia. She pulls away again.

'I like you,' Patrick says breathlessly.

Alicia touches his lip, and another cut on the side of his chin.

'You haven't learned to shave yet?' she says and smiles.

But Patrick is serious. He doesn't reply but silently takes hold of her hand and kisses the inside of her palm. Alicia's insides riot. Her head spins in a rush of desire. She glances down at Patrick's linen trousers which clearly reveal his arousal.

A sudden bout of loud laughter makes them both turn their heads toward the party, which they can't see from below the bank, but which is very close. Anyone—Mia, Kurt Eriksson, Alicia's mother, or Uffe—could at any moment walk down and see them sitting like this.

They are both married and Patrick has two little daughters.

Alicia pulls her hand away and gets up. She decides to rinse her feet in the water. When she walks back, Patrick tries to take hold of her hands. But now, shaken awake by the sounds of the party, she turns her head away, acutely aware of the proximity of Patrick's real life. His wife and children are in the boathouse, which she could see lit up in the distance as she walked to wash her feet in the sea. And her parents too—or mother and Uffe—are there, talking to their friends, being pleasant and civilized, unaware of what's going on between Alicia and Patrick. While they have been acting like any good guests of the richest man on the islands, Alicia has been kissing the son-in-law of the benefactor. And what was Patrick doing? How could he behave like that, so close to his wife and children? The children he was leading in a traditional Midsummer dance only moments ago? Or was this what he did all the time? To punish his rich father-in-law?

'You OK?' Patrick now says. His face is serious, his eyes searching, trying to lock onto Alicia's. But she won't look at him, can't look at his face. She must get away and pretend this never happened.

'I have to go,' she says, getting up, and putting her sandals onto her still sandy feet, praying that no one will spot her wet canvas shoes under her flimsy dress. It's all the fault of the dress; she knew it was too sexy, like an invitation to Patrick. Perhaps he'd taken it as a sign that she wanted him.

Oh my God, what have I done?

'Alicia,' Patrick says, but she's not listening.

Alicia bolts off the beach and onto the path. She's slipping in her damp shoes. Only once when she's on the other side of the large boulders does she dare to look back. But Patrick hasn't followed her. She can just spot the top of his blond head framed by the beach and the sea beyond it. For a moment she stops and sees that he's lit a cigarette. She can spot the red burning light of the tip as he sucks on the filter.

TWENTY-SIX

Alicia wakes up to a ping on her phone. She gets up quickly, still used to being on call in case Stefan is in trouble somehow. Her head hurts from the quick movement and as she reaches toward the illuminated screen of her phone, she remembers. She'll never again be called to fetch him from a party after a night bus has failed to arrive, or a friend has let him down.

The screen shows a message.

'You OK? You disappeared and I couldn't find you anywhere. P'

Alicia stares at the words. There's a persistent hammering on her temples. How much did she have to drink last night? She scans the room and spots a packet of painkillers in the corner. Birds are happily twittering outside and the sun, which barely dipped below the horizon last night, is blasting into the room through the large sea-facing window. Alicia swallows two pills with a glass of water and opens the door to the beautiful early morning scene. The sea is calm. A family of mallards is swimming in a long line in the distance, and the reeds covering the shore are gently swaying in the light sea breeze.

You could almost feel content here.

Alicia goes inside and fetches a throw to cover herself; the morning is sunny, but there is a chill in the air. She sits down on the porch, which Uffe, on her mother's instructions, has extended into a deck the same size as the main room in the sauna cottage, where Alicia sleeps on a double sofa bed. She glances at the phone again and finds herself smiling at Patrick's message. She thinks back to last night; the way it took them seconds to attach themselves to each other. How exciting, yet so wrong, it had felt to touch another man's lips. How taut Patrick's body had been when he emerged from the sea. How easily he had lifted up her chin and kissed her. She should not reply to his message. But in spite of herself she taps the phone and writes, 'Good morning. I'm fine. You?'

'Flying. When can I see you again?'

Alicia's heart begins to beat harder. She wants to write, 'We can't do this.' or 'This is wrong, you know that.' Instead she types, 'Monday at the office?'

There's no reply to this message. Alicia waits for a few minutes, then decides to go for a morning swim. That will sort the headache, which is bouncing behind her temples. Inside the cottage, she exchanges the blanket for a towel and walks swiftly toward the jetty a few meters along the shore. She leaves her phone behind on purpose. She wants to play it cool. She'd already made one mistake by replying to him far too soon.

What am I thinking?

This is all wrong. He is married with not just one child but two. And to an old friend of hers. Well, not a friend exactly, but at least an old school mate. And she is still not even separated from Liam. Alicia resolves to reply 'No' to the next message, whatever Patrick asks.

At the jetty, Alicia glances quickly around, but there's no one to be seen. It's just half past eight on Midsummer Day and everyone is still in bed. Alicia pulls the T-shirt she wears as a nightie over her head and lowers herself into the water. The cold hits the skin of her calves and thighs and is a shock, but Alicia walks quickly through the shallow water, almost running into the deeper sea. She doesn't want anyone along the shore to see her naked. She wants to feel the caress of the water on her body. Soon, she's taking long strokes, in a perfect front crawl.

· · ·

Pleasantly tired from her swim, Alicia slowly approaches the sauna cottage, trying to resist the urge to run to her phone to check if Patrick has replied. All through her time in the cold sea, she has not stopped thinking about him, or about what happened last night. She feels guilty but she cannot stop thinking about him, so she shoos away thoughts of Mia and the two little girls. It was Patrick who initiated the kissing; if anyone should be feeling bad it's him, and he obviously doesn't. *Flying*, he had written. Flying because of her, Alicia?

When she gets closer to the cottage, Alicia is surprised to see her mother sitting on one of the chairs on the decking.

'Nice swim?' her mother shouts.

Alicia nods and waves a greeting. From the distance Alicia can't see her phone. She's sure she left it on the table outside. What if Hilda saw Patrick's reply? What if he'd replied with something sexy? Alicia pulls her towel a little tighter around her naked body and bends to kiss her mother on the chin.

'I'm wet, sorry,' she says as a droplet falls on Hilda's crisp white linen shirt.

'That's OK.' Hilda takes a hankie out of her shirt sleeve and blows her nose. Now Alicia sees she has red-rimmed eyes.

'You've been crying?'

Hilda nods. 'It's Uffe.'

Alicia sighs. 'What is he supposed to have done now?' Her words come out harsher than she anticipated, and Hilda lowers her head and puts the hankie to her eyes. 'You always take his side,' she says.

'Look, I've got to get some clothes on. Have you seen my phone?' Alicia says, putting her hand on Hilda's shoulder, trying to sound nonchalant about the phone and caring about her mother at the same time. Hilda doesn't look at her, but nods at the window sill.

The screen is black. Alicia snatches the mobile and runs inside. There it is, a message from Patrick. It doesn't look as if it has been opened, but Hilda could have seen it displayed on the screen.

'I can barely wait. Meet me outside von Knorring on Monday at 12 o'clock?'

. . .

Ten minutes or so later, she's sitting opposite Hilda, her hands holding hers.

'Tell me what happened.'

This is not the first time her mother and stepfather have rowed, but as they've got older, the arguments have become worse and more frequent.

But her mother seems to have changed her mind.

'It's nothing,' she says, affecting a bright tone. She looks at Alicia and takes her hands away.

'Where were you yesterday?'

Alicia is caught short with this sudden change of subject.

'What do you mean?'

'You disappeared during the party.'

Hilda's eyes are sharp, and Alicia very nearly crumbles under her gaze, ready to reveal everything to her mother. But surely Hilda can't have seen Patrick and her together? They were away from the party for only an hour, if that. It was very quick and very passionate, she thinks, and she cannot help a smile forming on her lips.

'What are you not telling me?' Alicia's mother demands.

'Nothing, I was just thinking of the drive home.'

They had taken a taxi home. The driver had been an older man with a huge moustache, which Hilda, after copious glasses of champagne, had found hilarious. Uffe knew the man and it was left to him to try to hold up conversation while Hilda made faces in the back seat. Alicia thought that her mother had behaved really quite badly, but at the time she had also found it funny.

'Is Uffe upset about the taxi driver last night?'

'What?' Hilda says. 'No, it's just money, boring, boring money!'

TWENTY-SEVEN

Alicia forces herself to sit down and have a coffee after Hilda returns to the main house. She's shocked by what her mother has told her. She had no idea her parents had money troubles. Seeing how little Hilda was making at the shop had been a surprise, but she thought Uffe's farm was very profitable—enough to cover Hilda's losses. She had never discussed money with her stepfather; her mother wouldn't entertain it. All issues relating to the support she had as a student had been done through her mother.

Alicia recalls a time at a Midsummer dinner when she had thanked Uffe for everything he had done for both her and her mother. Hilda had risen from the table and come back several minutes later puffy eyed. Later that evening she had argued with Alicia in front of Stefan, who had been just seven at the time. Rows with Hilda were never understated affairs, and Alicia had learned to avoid them, but on that occasion, fueled by too many schnapps and wine during dinner, she had confronted her while helping with the dishes. She had put her arm around Hilda's shoulders and asked what was the matter. Her mother's reaction was explosive; she began shouting how Alicia had never appreciated the efforts she'd made to support her through university, nor since, and did she have any idea how much food cost? Or how many hours she spent scrubbing the house and the sauna cottage to make it ready for Alicia and her family? Or how much time she devoted to looking after Stefan, and cooking breakfast, dinner and supper for them? Alicia was and had always been an obnoxious, ungrateful girl.

That time, Alicia had moved away from her mother, and put her arms over Stefan's narrow shoulders. She was about to turn away, knowing that nothing she could say could make her stop, when, without even a glance at Stefan, Hilda threw a plate at her daughter and left the room. Luckily, her aim was poor and the dish ended up on the kitchen floor between Alicia, Stefan and the sink.

Alicia's heart had been beating hard, but she forced herself to remain calm. She heard her mother stomp up the stairs and slam her bedroom door. Turning to Stefan, who had wrapped his arms around Alicia's waist, burying his head into her lap as he had done as a small child, said, 'Don't worry, *Mormor* is just a bit upset. She will be fine tomorrow.'

The look in the boy's blue eyes nearly broke Alicia's heart. 'It's OK,' she said and hugged him hard.

Alicia sent Stefan to watch cartoons on the TV in the lounge, where she could keep an eye on him, swept up the remains of the broken plate, and finished clearing the table and doing the dishes. As usual, Uffe had gone to his office well before the argument to listen to the late news on the radio, and Hilda's outburst had eluded him. After half an hour, when she hoped her mother had calmed down, Alicia climbed the stairs to her mother's bedroom, determined not to start another argument, but to restore peace for Stefan's sake if no one else's. She knocked on the door.

'Yes?' had come a faint reply.

Alicia opened the door slightly. Seeing her mother lying on the bed on her own, with her face red and swollen from tears but without fury in her eyes, she stepped inside the room. Her mother had remodeled the house Uffe had been born in, adding an attic and extending the master bedroom with a wooden balcony and an en-suite bathroom on the middle floor. Alicia had been inside this room only once before, when Hilda had proudly presented the new interior. The walls of the room were dark, and there was a large wooden bed in the middle. The overhead lamp was off, but Hilda had her bedside light on, which cast a somber glow into the room and over her dramatic facial features.

When Alicia walked slowly toward the bed and looked down at her mother, Hilda brought an arm out from under the blankets and said, in a miserable, small voice, 'Sit down here, Alicia.'

'I'm sorry,' Alicia had said and took her mother's hand. She felt fourteen, or perhaps fifteen years old. Her mother's scent reminded her of the many nights they would stay up late together, watching a romantic film on TV while Uffe was in his office, doing the paperwork for the farm.

'Don't be,' Hilda said and gave a faint smile.

Alicia bent down and hugged her mother.

'Goodnight,' she said and left the room.

After this incident, Alicia was careful not to raise any subject that implied Uffe was supporting her and Hilda. The summer after the outburst, Stefan begged to be left behind in London to stay with a friend for the summer. He was just eight. In the end, Alicia managed to convince him to come, but she'd been careful not to upset her mother since. Talking about money now would, she was certain, cause a similar reaction.

TWENTY-EIGHT

During the first three days back at work, Liam doesn't see Ewa and he is relieved. He is supposed to be on holiday, so there's no contact between them, as planned. But on the Friday afternoon, as he enters the hospital in St John's Wood where he has a private clinic, she's there. Wearing her blue nurse's uniform, and with bright red lips, she looks up at him and smiles.

'Didn't think we'd see you today, Mr O'Connell,' she says with a smile full of meaning.

Liam keeps his face steady. 'Change of plan. I believe you have some patients for me?'

Ewa grabs a clipboard and follows him into the consulting room. Liam puts his briefcase down, but remains standing behind his large desk. He faces Ewa, who closes the door behind her and, with her back straight, showing off her large breasts, straightens her mouth, and with serious, widened eyes asks, 'What happened?'

Liam looks down at his desk.

'Nothing,' he says and stretches his hand out, to indicate he wants Ewa to hand him the files. 'Who do I have today? Any new patients?' he says, sitting down, not looking at her.

Snapping into her professional role, Ewa briefs Liam on who he will see. The day is already filled with patients, even at this short notice. As Liam listens to Ewa rattle off the names and their medical history, he wonders how he can ever be away, even on a short holiday, without people suffering because of his absence. He makes notes, with his head bent. He's suddenly aware that Ewa has stopped speaking. He lifts his head and sees her standing in front of him, with the clipboard pressed against her ample chest, gazing at him with an expression he can't read.

'Are you going to tell me what's going on?'

Ewa's eyes are startlingly dark against her artificially colored blond hair. She always wears bright red lipstick to match her long nails, something Liam used to find irresistible, but now, he thinks, she looks like a painted doll to him. *How can you fall out of love—or lust—so quickly? In a heartbeat?*

'Nothing. I just decided to cut my holiday short. And for good reason, it seems.' Liam lowers his gaze to his papers again, but Ewa isn't shifting.

'I'm not talking about why you are back,' she says, and walks around the desk to stand next to him. He can feel her arm slide along his shoulders and he feels her breast brush the side of his jaw. Her scent of musk and cigarettes is strong and for a moment Liam thinks of her soft belly, of the curve of her back when he makes her climax. Then, his thoughts go to Alicia, his wife, and her eyes, full of sorrow, but also full of love for him.

I hope she still loves me.

I have to be strong.

Liam gets up. His movement forces Ewa to drop her arm.

'Not here, not now,' he says and looks at her.

The woman's eyes are even darker, if that's possible. Great big inky pools, ready to brim over. He feels bad for her, but he never promised her anything. They were always clear on that. No divorce, no declarations of love, just fun. Liam reaches over and takes Ewa's hand. 'Look, we can't carry on. I ... and Alicia, we need to ...' he looks to Ewa for help but the woman is just staring at him with those eyes. She blinks and Liam is afraid a tear will fall from her lashes, but luckily she keeps her composure.

The door to his office opens suddenly and another surgeon, his younger colleague, pops his bald head in. He sees Liam and Ewa standing next to each other, holding hands. 'Sorry, didn't mean to interrupt,' he says and disappears.

Liam drops Ewa's hand and curses under his breath.

Ewa lifts her chin up, then turns on her heels and walks through the door.

Liam sits down again and has only a minute or two to recover before there is another soft knock on the door. Sighing, he says, 'Come in.'

TWENTY-NINE

Patrick looks tall and tanned leaning on the bonnet of his car by a small parking lot opposite *von Knorring*, an old steamer that has been turned into a bar and a restaurant in the East Harbor. His car is just behind a new seafood restaurant on the old concrete jetty. Alicia had spent the morning in the newspaper office, sorting out her next story, about the newly released employment figures on the islands. She could not concentrate on the words, or the figures, and had failed to make any sensible connections that would have provided an interesting thread to the story. Her deadline isn't until the end of the week, so she allows herself to be excited about meeting Patrick. She's wearing a red Marimekko cotton dress that comes just above her knees and a pair of Swedish Hasbeens clogs.

When she was getting dressed at the sauna cottage that morning, she noticed that her daily swim in the sea had made her legs and arms firmer and her skin bronzed. The dress fell attractively over her firm bum, and she had decided to wear her best underwear, bought at an expensive boutique before ... she shook her head to stop her thoughts going to Stefan. Instead she found the matching shoes and made sure she had her phone on. There were no other messages from Patrick and Alicia had only replied to the last one with a thumbs-up emoji.

The Island life suits me, she smiled, looking at herself in the full-length mirror Uffe had installed in the cottage at her mother's behest.

In the car on the way into town, Hilda remarked, 'I like that dress on you.'

Alicia tried to ignore the question in Hilda's voice, and just smiled at her mother.

Alone in the sauna cottage, Alicia had made up her mind to meet Patrick today, nothing more. She wanted to find out why he had kissed her, and whether their connection was real, and not just the result of too much alcohol and the Midsummer spirit. Alicia remembered how as a girl, she and her friends would place wildflowers underneath their pillows on Midsummer Eve. According to old Nordic folktales, if you did this, you would dream of your future lover on that magical night.

What nonsense!

But when Patrick talked about his daughter's near-death, it felt as if he'd been describing the torment she feels over Stefan. Of course, he can't know exactly how it is, because his daughter survived, but ... Alicia feels as if Patrick is the only person who can understand her. She knows seeing him is wrong, but what if they became just friends?

Alicia can see Patrick watching her as she walks along the road running parallel to the harbor. There are a few people milling around, lowering their sails or setting up to leave the jetty. The outside tables in the *Club Marin* café are all taken up by sailors and tourists, enjoying their drinks and talking loudly. There are a few parked cars beside the walkway. The Finns and Russians dock their sailing boats on this side of the Mariehamn peninsula, and the harbor is full. Hoping she doesn't bump into anyone she knows, Alicia quickens her step. She is a few minutes late—on purpose. But now that she is here, she can't wait to see him.

There is a slight wind, which makes the rigging of the sailing boats rattle against the masts. Alicia brushes a few strands of hair away from her face and tries not to run toward the man who is waiting for her. As she gets closer, something about how he moves from one foot to another and fidgets with the leather strap of his bag, indicates that he too is eager to touch her. She can hear the blood pulse in her head, and for a moment feels faint.

She stops two paces from where he is standing. She can smell his scent.

He looks sideways, checking for other people, but no one seems to notice them. The seafood restaurant is full, as is *von Knorring*. Even the old harbor hut, which is now a bicycle hire place, has a line outside. High season in Mariehamn.

'Come here,' Patrick says but he does the opposite, closing the small distance between them and taking Alicia into his arms. He plants his lips on hers and she relaxes into his kiss.

'God, I've missed you,' Patrick says when at last they manage to release each other.

Alicia can't speak. She nods, looking into Patrick's blue eyes, committing them to memory. She now realizes that she could never just be friends with him. This feels right, this is where she wants to be, with this man who understands her pain. She is at peace yet anxious at the same time, certain and doubting, happy and afraid. But not guilty anymore. How can you feel remorse when you have found someone so precious; someone you can find a safe harbor with?

'I have a boat; we can take it out and find a place for a picnic?'

Patrick pulls something out of his shoulder bag and reveals the neck of a bottle of red wine.

'Sounds good,' Alicia says through the hammering of her heart. She is trying to calm her breathing, and to fight the urge to touch Patrick again. But she knows it's dangerous; anyone in the busy harbor could see them. Besides, she knows she mustn't appear needy. But Patrick also seems paralysed; he's just standing in front of her now, smiling.

'It's down there, shall we go? I have an extra wind breaker and a pair of trousers for you onboard if you get cold out on the water.'

'You've thought of everything,' Alicia says. Still she isn't moving.

'I'm delighted to see you,' Patrick says. His expression is soft, but Alicia can see desire in his eyes. She feels color rise to her face.

'Me too.'

Patrick makes a move as if to kiss her again, but Alicia takes a step back and puts a hand up. 'I don't think we should ...'

Patrick's smile disappears for a moment and Alicia wants to take him into her arms. She shouldn't have reminded him of their hopeless situation. Because that's what it surely is, impossible?

And wrong.

But suddenly his lips smile and he guides Alicia toward the wooden boardwalk, which she passed on her way from the newspaper office. 'It's the fourth jetty along from here,' he says.

As they walk toward the rows of boats, Patrick leans on Alicia and whispers in her ear, 'Just wait until we get onboard.'

Desire rises up in Alicia as if an army of ants had begun crawling down her spine. She turns and lifts her eyes to him. 'You have to catch me first,' she says and starts skipping down the wooden walkway. She knows full well he can't follow her at the same pace without it looking as though they are a couple and playing some kind of lovers' game. Alicia doesn't know what excuse he has given Mia for this outing, but she doesn't care. If this afternoon is all they have together, she is going to enjoy every minute of it.

THIRTY

As they pass the first jetty, jutting out of the broad walk, they see a couple wearing matching white sailing jackets having coffee onboard a sailing boat. Alicia nods to them and smiles, and they nod back, unsmiling. 'Finns, why do they always have to be so serious!' She remembers Liam exclaim on more than one occasions. She brushes away any thoughts of her uncaring, cheating husband, and glances at Patrick, who is keeping his head down.

Did he know them?

The islands are small and everybody knows everyone else. What's more, the Erikssons are like celebrities in Åland, but she hopes Patrick isn't as well-known as his wife and father-in-law. Alicia, at least, didn't know him by sight before. And judging by the way she was talking about Patrick before the interview, her mother hadn't been aware of his connection to Mia Eriksson either. Otherwise she would have mentioned it, Alicia is sure. He's from Sweden, after all, and has never lived on the islands. There are no schoolfriends who could pop up from anywhere. As Alicia watches him walk along the second jetty, she wonders why Patrick doesn't seem to be concerned about being seen? It was a risk to kiss by the beach during the Midsummer party, and now, meeting up in the middle of town, where anyone driving past could recognize them, is careless, if not foolhardy. Is he doing this to hurt someone? Mia? His father-in-law?

Oh God, what am I getting myself into?

Patrick's boat is moored about halfway down one of the jetties. To Alicia, 'Mirabella', as it says on the hull, looks like a medium-sized sailing boat. She imagines it was expensive, but then she knows nothing about boats. Having lived most of her life on the islands, she feels slightly embarrassed about her ignorance, so makes no comment about the vessel.

She watches Patrick lean down and step onboard, hoping her body, which is aching to touch him, doesn't betray her desire. When he turns to help her with his hand, the touch of his fingers sends another jolt through her. His hand is warm, and she holds onto it even when she's standing safely on the wooden decking.

Finally, Patrick lets go. 'You can get changed in there.' With a slight movement of his head, he indicates a hole between two seats. The boat has a large steering wheel in the middle of the stern.

'Sure,' Alicia says. 'Where are we going?'

Patrick smiles, 'Not too far, but far enough.'

Alicia is certain she has blushed under Patrick's gaze. Standing so close to him in a confined space is torture. She inhales his particular scent of pine needles and leather.

'The galley is below, and there's also a loo.' Patrick hands her a pile of clothes and picks up a life jacket from a cabinet. Alicia steps through an opening, which takes her below to a cabin with a seating area arranged along the bulkhead. It's clean and tidy without any visible signs of family. As she turns around to perch herself on the leather seat, she sees through another opening a double bunk made up with white sheets. Her heart quickens at the sight of the bed. Although there are no visible signs of anyone ever having been onboard, she wonders if this is where Patrick sleeps with Mia. Her heart is racing.

Calm down, you knew what you were doing when you kissed him on Midsummer's Eve. And when you agreed to meet him again. This is what you want.

Alicia realizes the boat is new; there is a faint scent of furniture polish and the leather on the white seats is hardly worn. No children have been playing here, or eating at the teak table, which has a perfect shine. The woodwork in the hull above the seating and the cabinets is gleaming.

How much does a boat like this cost?

Suddenly Alicia hears the roar of the engine and she can feel the deck below her move. There is a rocking motion and she quickly puts on the sailing jacket Patrick has given her. Ignoring the trousers, which look too large anyway, she adds the life jacket, then climbs the few steps out of the cabin and up into the daylight.

'Sit down,' Patrick says, nodding at the seat on the side of the steering wheel. Not looking at her but concentrating on maneuvering the boat out of the harbor, he points toward a coolbox behind Alicia. 'There's wine and beer in there. I'll have a *Karjala.*'

Holding onto the side of the boat, Alicia sees there's champagne and a rather good Sauvignon Blanc, plus several bottles of beer in the bottom. She smiles. She's certain the champagne is meant for her. He said he'd remember how much she loves the stuff. Alicia opens up two bottles of beer, hands one to Patrick and takes a sip out of the other as she sits back down. She finds a pair of sunglasses in her bag and watches as they pass the *von Knorring* restaurant boat moored at the end of the old concrete jetty, and then on toward the open sea.

'This is nice,' Alicia says, raising her voice above the roar of the engine.

Patrick reaches his hand across the space between them and squeezes her knee. 'I've been thinking of nothing else but you for the last three days.'

'I meant the boat,' Alicia replies with a smile.

Patrick presses her leg once more and also grins, 'Cheeky.' He removes his hand and slows the engine down as they approach the Sjoland canal.

'I didn't know we were coming this way,' Alicia says. 'I think I might need to go down below.'

Patrick looks over to her. 'What do you mean?'

'What if my mum or Uffe, or someone from the farm sees me in your boat?'

Patrick's smile fades. He replies to Alicia in a dry tone, 'Just keep your glasses on, I'm sure you'll be fine.'

They pass the canal in silence, following the three other boats that had been in the line for the swing bridge to open. Alicia wonders why he is annoyed at her. She was trying to protect them both, surely? If their affair—*if that's what this is going to be, an affair?*—came to light, Patrick would be the one to lose the most, wouldn't he? Marriage to the richest family in the islands must have its benefits, surely? So why would he not care if Alicia was seen in his boat. Is she here just to make Mia jealous?

Alicia looks at Patrick's profile. His straw blond hair has been mussed up by the swirling sea breeze and his lips are in a straight line. Paler laughter lines are visible along the side of his mouth. The white polo shirt under a navy sailing jacket brings out his bronzed skin. His chin is clean-shaven, but she can see a few pale hairs pushing through. No cuts today, she notices. She wants to run her fingers along that chin, feeling the rough bristles against her palm.

'That's where I am,' Alicia says when they are on the open sea. Patrick has put the sail up and the boat rocks gently from side to side as they are moved along by the strengthening wind. She points at her sauna cottage and the jetty, from where she takes her morning (and sometimes) afternoon swims. The jetty, with Uffe's rowing boat tied to it, looks tiny from this distance. The green wooden building is barely visible between the reeds in front and the thicket of pine trees behind the building. Uffe and Hilda's white house, standing high beyond the potato fields, is more visible from this far. In the distance, Alicia can see a red tractor working on one of Uffe's fields. She wonders if her stepfather is driving the vehicle. She's sure no one would recognize them at this distance, but she wonders what he *would he say if he knew what she was doing?*

But what does Uffe know? He has no idea what Alicia's life is really like. He's never been a father. He's never lost a son.

'Good, I can drop you off there later,' Patrick says as if it was the most normal thing in the world. Once again Alicia wonders what he's thinking. Wouldn't it look odd to Uffe and Hilda if they saw her being dropped off by Patrick? In a flash sailing boat like this? She looks at him, but he is concentrating on the water and steering. Suddenly he runs along the deck and indicates for Alicia to duck. With great skill he moves the sail to the other side and they change course.

THIRTY-ONE

The little island Patrick chooses for their picnic is uninhabited and looks barely bigger than one of Uffe's potato fields. Patrick drives his boat to a small cove, and after turning off the motor, expertly floats the vessel toward the gently sloping rockface. Before the hull hits anything, he jumps onto land with a rope in his hand. He puts his foot out to soften the blow as the vessel makes contact with the rock, and then moves the boat sideways. There is no mooring as such, but a single ring attached to a pole where Patrick hooks the rope and secures the boat. Alicia is impressed. She's been on the water with friends and Uffe, of course (her mother is afraid of water and doesn't even swim in the sea), but she knows that to maneuver an expensive boat on your own when there are no jetties, is not easy. It requires experience.

'How did you know about this place?' Alicia asks, as she gazes at the cool box that Patrick has brought out.

'It belongs to a friend,' Patrick says.

He places a blanket on the rocks and hands Alicia two glass flutes; he begins opening the bottle of champagne. The pop makes them both laugh, and they down the first two glasses, full of froth, in a few mouthfuls. Patrick refills the flutes and settles himself down beside Alicia. As he stretches out, supporting himself with his elbows, Alicia sees the short sleeves of his polo shirt strain over his muscles.

How many times has he done this? Taken a girl to an island that belongs to a friend?

'Lie down beside me,' Patrick says, reaching out to Alicia with his hand. She can't resist him.

Patrick brushes hair away from her face and looks deeply into her eyes.

'Is this OK?'

Alicia melts, 'It's lovely. You've thought of everything.'

Patrick nods, but he's not listening.

'Can I kiss you?'

Alicia bows her head, already mesmerized by his strong arms, blue eyes and his soft voice. And those velvety strong lips. She wants to melt into them, into him and never leave.

When they come up for air, Patrick says, in a hoarse voice, 'Let's get back onto the boat?'

Alicia smiles into his eyes. Ever since she saw the white sheets of the small cabin below, the image of Patrick's body lying there, naked, has been haunting her. She wants to examine every detail of his strong chest, arms, thighs and legs. She wants to run her fingers along his tummy, to follow the line of hairs on his chest to the place between his legs. The desire in her is making her feel faint.

Patrick practically carries Alicia back over the rocks to the boat. Pulling his jacket and white shirt off, he places one hand on Alicia's neck and uses the other to take off her jacket. He then reaches under her dress and along her thigh to her knickers, which he deftly pulls off. As they tumble onto the bed, Patrick turns Alicia around, saying, hoarsely, 'You'll hit your head.'

He enters her almost as soon as their bodies hit the sheets. Feeling his hardness inside, she gasps and arches her back. He moves in and out, then stops for a moment to remove her dress and pull down her bra. He gazes at her breasts. It feels as if his eyes are caressing her skin. Taking one nipple in his hand, he pushes hard into her. She finds his mouth and they kiss, but then he pulls away to suck on her nipples, one by one. Unable to hold on any longer, she comes. Her pulsating grip makes him groan and he also climaxes.

Afterwards, as they lie between the sheets, Alicia examines the ceiling of the little alcove containing the bed. They are lying with their heads toward the galley, underneath the bow. Alicia smiles as she remembers how Patrick had turned her over and around when they fell onto the bed earlier. She'd felt like a rag doll in his grip.

She cannot remember sex like this. She hadn't thought about anything but Patrick, and how to satisfy and please him. She places her hand on Patrick's flat, hard tummy, and then on his thigh.

'Again?' She can hear a smile in his voice, even though she can't see his face from where she is lying in the crook of his arm. She's fully sated, and although she knows this sense of overwhelming warmth and mellowness will eventually disappear, she is determined to enjoy it to the full. She lifts herself onto her left elbow and glances down at Patrick's erection. 'Do you have time?' she says.

'Now I need something to eat!' Patrick throws his jeans on, leaving his boxers on the floor of the cabin, where he threw them earlier. Alicia hears him clattering on the upper deck and soon he's back with his rucksack. From the bed, she watches him set out red wine, bread, ham and cheese in the galley. Suddenly, she is also ravenous. She slips on her dress and sits down opposite Patrick at the teak table. He pours the wine into two glasses taken from a cabinet over the small sink in the corner.

'We could live on this boat, couldn't we?' Alicia says between bites of her open sandwich.

Patrick looks at her in alarm. His mouth is full of food and he puts a hand over his lips, still gazing at her. His blue eyes seem more piercing somehow.

Alicia is embarrassed. 'I didn't mean ...'

Patrick takes a gulp of wine and looks down at his food.

'Look,' he begins, lifting his eyes again. 'I'm not sure you understand my situation?' He has a serious expression on his face.

Alicia is staring at him.

This is it. He's going to say, 'This was fun', next. And you have no knickers or bra on under your dress because you thought he would want to have sex again after eating.

Patrick bites his lower lip.

Alicia panics. She can't hear this. She gets up and, picking up her pants and bra from the floor, rushes into the tiny toilet in the corner of the cabin.

'Alicia,' Patrick says, but Alicia isn't looking at him. She's trying to get into the small space, but the door won't open.

'Let me,' Patrick says behind her. She can feel his hot breath on her neck, but she ignores it and waits for him to unlock the door. It seems you have to pull it toward you and then turn the handle.

'Thank you,' Alicia mumbles into her hands, which are holding her underwear. Inside, she sits on the toilet seat and puts her head in her hands.

Mustn't cry, mustn't cry.

She takes a deep breath and exhales slowly. What does Connie, her grief counsellor say? 'You can always breathe; it's natural. When you feel overwhelmed, just stop and concentrate on your breathing. Think of nothing else, just air going in and out, in and out.'

After she's calmed down a little, Alicia has a quick pee, washes her hands and face, and puts her underwear on. She struggles in the small space, but finally manages to pull her dress over her bra and knickers and step out of the bathroom.

'You OK?' Patrick says. He's bent over, not able to fully stand in the cabin.

Alicia smiles at him, holding the sides of her mouth up even though all she wants to do is flee the boat and swim to the nearest shore. She knows she needs to keep calm, appear cool, and let Patrick take her home.

'Could you take me all the way back to Mariehamn?' she says, trying to appear calm and collected. She doesn't add, 'As soon as possible,' but Patrick seems to get the message and fusses with ropes and pulleys to make the boat ready, while she clears the galley and puts the food and wine back in the rucksack. When she hears the engine start, she realizes that he intends to take them back with horsepower. Much less romantic than sailing.

This was a big mistake.

THIRTY-TWO

Hilda is in the back room, unpacking two boxes of summer wear that have just arrived from her supplier in Italy. When the door chime sounds, she shouts, 'Just one moment, I'll be with you shortly.'

When she enters the shop, she's surprised to see a man. Men very rarely—if ever—visit her shop unless it's to buy something from her small line of jewellery and handbags as a present for their wife or girlfriend. She can count with the fingers of one hand the number of male customers she's had during the five years she's owned the shop. The man looks foreign, Russian, and immediately she takes a couple steps back. He's wearing a light beige bomber jacket with a pair of cotton trousers and an expensive pair of loafers without socks. There's a single gold stud in one ear and a small, black tattoo on his hand, between his thumb and forefinger. He also wears two rings on his fingers, both heavy, shiny gold. He's a large man, and he fills Hilda's little shop with his bulk.

The man crosses the room and comes to stand close to Hilda. He is so tall, and his chest so broad, that he obscures her view of the street. The man bends down and puts his lips close to Hilda's ear. 'We have a mutual friend,' he says.

Cold shivers run down her spine. She reaches out her hand to support herself on one of the rails of special offer tops in the middle of the shop.

The man is now looking around him. 'Where are your most expensive dresses?'

'Why?' Hilda whispers.

'Our mutual friend needs a small gift for his lady friend.' He continues, his cold eyes on Hilda, 'Because you have been a naughty girl, haven't you?' The man gives a brief grin, but soon this becomes a mock sad face.

'I am going to have a very good month, so I can catch up ...' Hilda stammers.

The man looks around the shop, 'You busy?'

There was no one there. No customers, not even tire-kicking Swedes, who pull the clothes off the rails to hold them up against themselves, glancing briefly in one of the long mirrors on either side of the shop. They never buy, or put the garments back in the right place again.

'It's a slow day today. The week after Midsummer always is, because people are out in the archipelago with their families. But they'll soon get bored of each other and come into town. People argue when they are on holiday and then they need to buy something to make themselves feel better,' Hilda realizes she is talking uncontrollably, but she can't stop herself. 'Tomorrow will be very busy and ...'

He places one fat finger across his lips, interrupting her. 'Shh.' The man bends down so that his face is very close to Hilda's again. He smells of alcohol and cigarettes and very strong aftershave. 'No talking, just doing. We need money next week.'

Hilda nods. 'You will have it, I promise.'

'I said no talking,' the man whispers, and he straightens up. He glances around the shop and his eyes fix on three dresses displayed close to the till.

'But now, a small gift to keep our friend calm, yes?' The man says.

Hilda nods and moves toward the items the man is looking at.

'You like this dress?' she asks, picking out a silver lamé thing she had foolishly bought in three sizes at a Stockholm fashion fair last fall. With a price tag of 495 Euros, it hadn't had any takers in Mariehamn. The one person, a very pretty blond girl from the islands, who liked the dress, lifted it off the rail and exclaimed, 'That's more than my monthly rent!' Hilda's margin on the dress is now just 25 Euros. She should really charge more like 600 Euros for it.

'What size?' she turns around and asks the man.

He looks blankly at her.

'Is she 36, 38 or 40?'

When the Russian doesn't reply, Hilda adds, 'What size is the lady?'

'I take all,' the man says and Hilda gasps.

The Russian grins and says, 'You put them in silk paper, make look nice.'

For a moment, Hilda hesitates. It occurs to her that the cost of the three garments comes to over a thousand Euros and that she should be able to deduct that from what she owes the Russians, but she keeps quiet. Her heart is beating so hard she can hardly hear herself think. With shaking hands, she packs the dresses one by one into her special pink tissue paper and then into one large plastic bag. She should, according to the law, charge the man for the bag, but again she says nothing, just hands the package to him.

'Tell him I will have the money next week.' Hilda says with a dry mouth.

'He know,' the man says, and takes the bag. Again he gives one of his brief grins, and says, 'Nice doing business with you.' Then he walks into the street.

Hilda leans against the counter. She wants to cry, but she lifts herself up and brushes her brand-new Birger et Mikkelsen skirt with her hands to calm herself. She will be fine. She always manages and she will manage this situation too.

Uffe walks along the edge of one of his fields. The earlies are nearly in flower and look healthy. His eyes follow the line of the dark green plants and then stop at his house. The white structure looks magnificent with its new paint and dark copper roof, which gleams in the late afternoon sunshine. He's proud of this house, the home where he was born and which his father built with his friends and relatives from the village. Would his parents, long gone now, approve of all the modernizing Hilda had instigated during the past two decades? Her standards are high, with every detail—a door handle, the color on the walls, kitchen appliances and bathroom fittings—having to be just so. Nothing but perfection will do for Hilda.

Uffe has lost count of the times they've argued about the works. When Hilda greets him at the door with a look like a storm warning, her arms crossed over her chest, he finds it best to say nothing. She will soon tell him how he is at fault. Usually he hasn't seen some minor mistake that the builders made while Hilda was at the shop. He's got tired of pointing out that he could not afford the time away from the farm, especially from supervising his laborers, most of whom spoke no Swedish. But to Hilda, his time in the fields didn't count as any kind of useful excuse, even though the land provided all the money Hilda spent on the house. And everything else.

But this is the limit.

Uffe nods to one of the Romanians standing smoking a cigarette outside the red cottage and then turns away from the house, deciding to take another tour around the fields. He shakes his head. How can Hilda be so stupid as to get into debt? Credit cards were one thing, she'd been there before. Uffe can't remember how many times he has bailed out Hilda from that particular trap. But this; this is different. No amount of money will ever get Hilda out of this bind. To accept a loan from a man like that?

He curses under his breath. He knows this is his fault. He should never have got involved with the man, but he thought Hilda had more sense than to accept money from him. Besides, when and where did that happen? Uffe was too upset to find out the details. He had stormed out of the house when Hilda, tears in her eyes, finished the tale of her latest financial catastrophe.

At first, he had stood in front of her, mouth open, not able to utter a word. She must have seen in his eyes how bad it was. Of course, she had only told him because she had no choice. He is—as always—the last resort. She said that she was three payments late and that there had been threats. She assured him that the article in the *Journalen* by Patrick Hilden would bring in customers from Stockholm, and she could then start the payments again, but frankly, Uffe doubts it. Even though he knows nothing about fashion, something Hilda has repeatedly told him, he knows enough to understand that no woman would come from the capital of Sweden to buy clothes in a tiny shop on the Åland islands. As usual, Hilda is being naive—some might say stupid.

'You are incredible,' was all Uffe said. He couldn't trust himself not to shout at her, which he would never do. It isn't right. His father had never in his life raised his voice to his mother and had taught Uffe to respect women in the same way.

But Hilda is testing his patience to the limit. When he left Hilda standing alone, he heard her shout after him, but he'd ignored her. He knew she wouldn't run after him and make a show of herself in front of the farm workers, but all the same, he turned on his heels as quickly as he could, put his rubber boots on and walked rapidly along the edge of the closest field to the house. He had now walked two rounds, but he's still not calm. He needs more time to think, so he decides to do another round. He knows the two young lads will be watching him from the red cottage, wondering what's up, but he doesn't care.

Hilda is fuming. The one time she reaches out to her husband, who promised to love and honor her, Uffe flees and doesn't say anything. Hilda needs a glass of white wine. It's only 5pm, but she has to have something to calm her nerves. It's an emergency after all. On second thoughts, when she opens the fridge, she decides on something stronger and goes in search of Uffe's drinks cabinet in the 'best' room to pour herself a whisky. The strong liquid warms her throat, and she takes half a glass more. She needs to drive later, so she better not have a third, she thinks, after gulping down the second.

With the alcohol inside her, she can breathe more easily. The nervous anger is slowly dissipating, and she considers her options. If Uffe will not help her, she will need to negotiate with the Russians. But how to get to the main man? The thugs he sends to collect the money don't even speak Swedish properly, so how can she make them understand that she needs more time?

THIRTY-THREE

Alicia is getting ready to leave the newspaper office when Patrick appears next to her cubicle. He has his hand on the bright blue divider, where Alicia has pinned useful information such as the Intranet codes and the staff telephone lists that the personnel woman gave her. There is also a picture of Stefan taken in their garden in Crouch End in London, with him smiling into the camera.

'You off?' Patrick asks.

Alicia is aware of Frida, the only other person left in the office listening in on their conversation. Most people, including the editor, have gone hours ago. Alicia wanted to stay to map out a piece on Russian influence on the islands, but is hitting a brick wall each time she comes close to any useful information. Of course, she knows that there are strict rules on ownership of land and assets by non-Åland residents on the islands, but she also knows that there are ways both wealthy Swedes and Finns get around those rules. Why couldn't Russians do the same?

'Yeah, my mum's giving me a lift home,' Alicia says, not looking at him.

'I emailed her the PDF of the article just now.'

'Thanks, I'll tell her.'

There is a silence. Alicia, having placed her laptop into her backpack, picks up her cotton jumper, tucks her chair under the desk and tries to smile at Patrick. What does he want? Surely the fact that she hasn't answered any of the texts since that disastrous boat trip would be enough to make him understand she doesn't want anything more to do with him.

She feels like she's been played.

Before the boat trip, she thought they meant something to each other, but the way he reacted to her remark about living on his boat—as if she wanted to stay there—showed that all he wanted was a quick summer fling. She's been feeling stupid ever since, especially because Patrick said nothing about it during the journey home. She pretended to be OK, but she didn't let him kiss her when he dropped her off in Mariehamn. All of his previous bravado had been just that, showing off. It was all a game, she decided. A rich man's game to get her into bed. She's done playing games with him.

'Any plans for the weekend?' Patrick says, his blue eyes squarely on Alicia. Suddenly she has an image of his naked body lying on the white sheets of the bunk in the cabin. She can recall the fair hairs on his chest and the thin line reaching down between his legs. Flashes of their love-making—or sex—invade her brain.

She must stay strong.

'Spending it with my family,' Alicia says pointedly, trying to steady her breathing and hoping the words come out without any show of emotion in them. She is aware that Frida is now listening to their conversation.

Patrick turns around and gives a nod to Frida, who smiles briefly then looks at her screen. Gazing back at Alicia with those flirty eyes of his, Patrick says, 'Mia is taking the girls shopping in Stockholm. I thought I might talk to you about the article we're working on?'

Alicia is fighting a smile forming on her lips, but failing.

'But if you can't meet up, I'll walk you out and tell you my theory?' Patrick says. He moves to touch her elbow, but she is quicker and pulls her arm away.

She nods and says, 'OK'. She can hardly say no to a suggestion like that in front of Frida, and he knows it.

'See you Monday,' Alicia says to the intern as she begins to walk toward the door. She can feel Patrick's body behind her, too close. As soon as they're in the stairwell and the door has closed, he takes hold of Alicia's arm and turns her around to face him. 'You're driving me crazy. I need to see you!'

'Not here,' Alicia hisses and glances up the staircase. The space is open to all the offices in the building and Birgit—or anyone—could at any moment step out and see them. When her eyes return to Patrick, she can see his face is full of emotion. His grip on her arm is strong.

'You're hurting me,' Alicia says in a low voice.

Patrick lets go, dropping his arm to the side of his body. Alicia sees now that he is unshaven, and that his clothes are crumpled.

'What happened to you?'

'I need to see you.'

Alicia sighs. 'OK, I'll tell my mother I need to work late.'

A smile forms on Patrick's lips.

'Just for a talk,' Alicia says pointedly and Patrick nods.

'And we go our separate ways. Where shall we meet?'

'I know a place,' Patrick says and begins to tap on his phone.

Alicia goes back inside the newspaper office and tells Frida she's forgotten something. She doesn't want the girl to think that she left with Patrick. She taps a message on her phone, and makes a show of looking for something in her desk drawers. When her mother replies to say she is in the car waiting for her, Alicia assures Hilda that she will make her own way to Sjoland later. She picks up her bags again and goes out via the ladies. She gives herself a wash, just in case, using the shower placed for just that purpose next to the loo. She isn't sure what Patrick is going to say to her, but she thinks it will be good to get things out in the open. Perhaps he isn't playing games after all?

Who am I kidding?

She will be strong and not jump into bed with him. She thinks about the message she's received from Liam where he says he's sorry and that he's finished with Ewa. She hasn't replied. She is so confused. Why has Liam suddenly changed his mind? He has been pleading with her to talk to him, but she is still too angry to do that. Besides, she now feels guilty for sleeping with Patrick, although when she did, she thought her marriage was over.

What a mess.

Trying to think about something else, she remembers her promise to look over her mother's new plans for the garden in Sjoland. Secretly, she is glad she doesn't have to spend another Friday night listening to Uffe and her mother squabbling. Hilda is never satisfied with what Uffe does in the house, or the yard. He hasn't watered the flower beds, or the hanging baskets enough, or he's given them too much water. Or the gravel paths that crisscross the yard between the barns and the main house are, in Hilda's view, neglected and full of weeds. Each time Uffe sits down on the small bench he's placed under the oak tree, Hilda will find him something that needs fixing immediately. Uffe doesn't often complain, but occasionally he will mutter something under his breath, and a small quarrel will ignite between the couple.

Their harmless altercations, which she and Liam once thought endearing, are now beginning to get on Alicia's nerves. Besides, she suspects there's more to it than she's previously imagined. She is afraid they have serious problems with money, and that what her mother told her on Midsummer Day is not an exaggeration. Her stepfather looked more and more morose when he talked to Alicia about the future of the farm, and having seen the accounts in Hilda's shop, Alicia can only conclude that Uffe is pouring cash into the venture to keep her mother happy. She wonders if she should be brave and talk to her mother about it. It isn't right that Hilda is putting the future of the farm in danger.

Looking at herself in the bathroom mirror, Alicia sighs. Who is she to lecture anyone about morality? She's been with a man, a father of two little daughters. And she is breaking her own marriage vows. Not that they matter anymore. Liam broke them first, and now he is full of remorse.

He's too late.

Alicia looks at her phone and sees that Liam sent another message last night. He asks when they can talk (again) but she doesn't intend to reply. Why should she talk to him? Alicia glances at her watch. It's just past 5pm on a Friday night, or 7pm in the UK. *Whatever he says, she bets her husband is in that Polish nurse's arms right now.*

She takes her red lipstick out of her purse and applies a liberal amount to her lips. She tidies her eye make-up and wishes she'd taken mascara and eyeshadow with her to work. Still, she doesn't look bad. The daily swimming and sunbathing have given her skin a healthy glow. Her Swedish Hasbeens clogs make her legs look shapely and she is pleased with the general effect she sees in the mirror. She will not go to bed with Patrick, or not again, but at least she looks presentable. Perhaps she should lighten up a little? It is summer, the sky is clear and the sun is still high in the sky, it's warm, she's back home in Åland, doing a job she loves, and it's Friday night.

THIRTY-FOUR

As Alicia walks onto the street, she gets a message from Patrick.

'We can talk in peace here.'

The address attached is on the western side of town, a bit too far for Alicia to walk so she decides to take a cab. She picks one up from a rank on Norra Esplanaden and steps inside a large Mercedes car. Luckily the driver doesn't say a word during the ten-minute ride.

She cannot help but smile when she sees the new blocks of apartments right by the sea. This area used to be a fishing harbor and she remembers coming here with Stefan to look at the boats and buy fish for supper. Now all that remains are a few red and white huts and a stone jetty to one side of the new development, with a new wooden wharf further along the shore full of expensive-looking yachts. It's still sunny, but the wind has got up and she can see the boats bobbing up and down and the surf rising on the sea.

The block of apartments has around ten floors, making it unusually high-rise for Åland. The façade is covered in balconies, with some facing the sea, the sun glinting off the smoked glass; many have smart wicker furniture. The buildings must be brand-new, she thinks, for there are some building materials under a tarpaulin to the side. She finds the correct block—the nearest one to the sea—and when she enters the number Patrick gave her on the intercom, she hears his voice. He tells her to step inside the elevator but not to touch any of the buttons, and then buzzes her in. When the doors close, the lift begins to move, as if of its own accord. Alicia follows the light that indicates the different floors and when she's at number ten, the doors open straight into a vast penthouse apartment with floor-length windows affording a full vista of the open sea. Involuntarily, Alicia gasps at the view. She is speechless when she steps onto the light parquet flooring.

'Please come in,' Patrick says and she takes a step further inside, dropping her bags on one of two low-slung sofas that face each other. The apartment is furnished tastefully and very understatedly in pale gray and white. A white rug echoes the white of the kitchen units and there's a long table with leather-backed chairs arranged at one end of the huge room. A vast painting of a seascape in grays and blues covers one wall while a balcony, enclosed by sliding glass doors, wraps around one corner of the flat. She recognizes the style from the Eriksson's summer place. Is this Mia and Patrick's apartment? Surely he wouldn't invite her to their home—or one of their homes?

'Come and have a look at the view,' Patrick says, stretching his hand toward Alicia, beckoning her. He opens the sliding balcony doors and indicates for Alicia to step in.

There are no other buildings or blocks of apartments between them and the sea. The ones in view to the right are well below them. Alicia thinks this building must be on a higher elevation, somehow. Or it has an extra floor, not visible from below. She looks at the old red fishing cottages, which seem minute from this far up, like pieces of Lego. Further on, at sea, a yacht is making its way toward the shipping lane, with its sails taut against the wind, the hull creating a V-shaped wash behind it. Alicia is amazed how fast it's moving. To the right there's the new jetty, where the few boats gently rock in the water, and further on the ferry port. One white ship, and a smaller red ferry are moored at the harbor, and unconsciously she checks her watch. It's half past five. One of the two large ferries from Finland and Sweden that dock in Mariehamn twice a day is due in soon. They sail right past this balcony, Alicia thinks. She looks around and sees a basket full of girly toys in the corner of the space. A chill runs through her body and she shivers. She turns around to look at Patrick.

'Is this where you live?' she asks.

Without smiling, Patrick nods.

Alicia, who has been leaning on the balcony railing, moves away from the edge. She doesn't want to touch anything here.

This is Patrick and Mia's family home.

'It was lovely for you to show me where you live, but I'm afraid I have to go now,' Alicia says, stepping out of the balcony. She goes to pick up her bag, but Patrick is beside her, grabbing her arm.

'Don't go, please.'

Alicia is seething. 'You are something, aren't you? Do you have any morals at all? Or is this what the rich boys in Åland do? Take other women to their marital home? How dare you!'

But when Patrick pulls her into his arms and kisses her, Alicia can't resist him. They tumble onto the sofa and continue kissing. It isn't until Patrick puts his hand inside her skirt that she suddenly comes to her senses.

'No,' Alicia manages to say, and as abruptly as they started to make love, they both stop. Panting, Patrick gets up and goes to the open-plan kitchen. Alicia grabs the side of the sofa, gets herself up and, smoothing down her skirt, sits down. She watches Patrick, whose shoulders are moving up and down. His head is bent, as he leans onto the immaculately tidy kitchen counter.

'I'm making coffee, do you want some?' he asks after a short while. He sounds out of breath.

When he doesn't get an answer, he turns around and goes over to where Alicia is sitting. She is fighting tears; how did she get herself into this mess? Faced with Patrick's family situation, she can't continue with the affair. She just can't take a father away from his two little girls.

Patrick is now kneeling down in front of Alicia. He gives her a tissue and puts his hands on Alicia's knees, then seeing her expression removes them. 'Please don't cry,' he says, letting his hands rest between his legs.

'I can't do this,' Alicia sobs. 'You are married. With children.'

Patrick looks at her, his blue eyes sad. He gets up with a sigh and comes and sits next to her on the sofa. 'I don't know what to say. You know we're not happy. Mia ...'

'Stop!' Alicia shouts. 'I don't want to hear any excuses!'

'OK, let's not talk about her. But I have to tell you I've never felt like this before. You ... you make me crazy. I can't stop thinking about you. I need you.'

Alicia realizes these are the words she wanted to hear after they made love on his boat. Why didn't he tell her this before? Why had he let her believe this was just a summer fling? All the way back on the boat, Patrick must have noticed how quiet and upset she was. If he really cared, surely he would have said something then?

She turns her head and lifts her eyes up to Patrick. With the sun suddenly pouring in through the windows, she sees there are dark circles around his eyes. He's wearing his customary white shirt and jeans, and looks tanned, but dishevelled. His blue eyes are as piercing as ever, and his lips, drawn in a straight line, give way to lines around his mouth. Alicia has an overwhelming desire to kiss those lips. She places a hand on Patrick's cheek. 'I need you too.'

Seconds after she's uttered the words, Patrick's mouth is on hers. He lifts her up to sit astride him and presses his body against hers, so she can feel his erection through the jeans. She pulls herself away, but Patrick is holding tightly to her. And it feels good, so very good.

Why should she be responsible for his family?

But an image of Liam and Stefan, when their son was about the same age as Patrick's girls, eleven, comes to her mind. They are messing about in the water by the sauna cottage. Alicia remembers that Uffe had cleared the reeds from the jetty, so that Alicia could see them from the veranda. She had some kind of deadline to meet for the FT, and had her laptop on the small table in front of her. But she wanted to join her boys in the water and couldn't concentrate.

Alicia puts her hands on Patrick's shoulders and firmly pushes herself away from him.

'I can't do this—not here,' she says, panting.

She clambers off Patrick and stands up, smoothing down her skirt again, and buttons up her blouse. Before he has time to react, she grabs her shoes and bag and goes to the elevator. Luckily, it's still on the top floor, and Alicia, now panicking, wanting to get away from this place, steps inside.

THIRTY-FIVE

Alicia walks for what seems like ages to reach a taxi rank. Her feet are aching, and her bag suddenly seems much heavier than it was this morning. Tears are running down her face, but she doesn't know what she's crying about: Stefan, or her futile desire to have another child, or the now certain break-up of her own marriage, or the disastrous affair she's embarked on with Patrick.

She feels so stupid. How did she think that sleeping with someone else, someone who is also married, would make her grief for Stefan, her desire for a baby, or Liam's affair, any better? But she has decided now. No more Patrick, no more sneaking around the islands to meet up. No more telling lies to people like Hilda or Uffe, no more feeling guilty about breaking up a family. She feels awful about what they have already done, but she has to trust Patrick not to breathe a word to Mia and to start repairing his marriage.

Just as she sees a taxi waiting at the rank on *Norra Esplanaden*, her phone pings. Automatically, she reaches for the mobile in her handbag, but when she sees who it's from she hesitates. But there's a sentence on her screen that she cannot ignore.

Mia and I are separating. She's leaving me.

· · ·

Half an hour later, Patrick and Alicia are sitting at the kitchen table, facing each other.

'Thank you for coming back,' Patrick says. His hands are resting on the table, his fingers laced together. Alicia remembers how those long, thin fingers were all over her body moments earlier. He lifts his eyes to Alicia's.

'This is what I wanted to talk to you about.'

Alicia nods. After she read the text, she replied to say how sorry she was. Patrick telephoned her and offered to pick her up from wherever she was. Alicia agreed. She decided she would not go to bed with him, if this was a trick, but she didn't believe it was. He sounded sad, and sincere, on the phone, and thinking back, the news explained a lot of his earlier behavior. The bitterness toward his in-laws at the Midsummer party; his apparent lack of concern about being seen with Alicia; the hesitation on the boat when she made a stupid joke about living on the boat.

Alicia hadn't been in Patrick's car before, but it was no surprise to her that he drove a brand-new black Mercedes soft top with cream leather upholstery.

How is he going to survive without Mia's—or, rather, her father's—money?

'Nobody knows about this. So, I'd appreciate it if you didn't ...'

'Of course not!' Alicia exclaims. She touches Patrick's hands, squeezing his knuckles.

'We want to spend the summer with the girls as normal. Mia is going to move here, her father has a job for her in Mariehamn.'

Alicia watches Patrick's face as he speaks. His eyes are as blue as ever, but there are lines around them and a strain around the corners of his mouth. She now realizes the hurt, pained expression that she sees on him has attracted her. It mirrors her own, she's certain of it.

Patrick's eyes fall down to his hands. He opens his palms and squeezes Alicia's fingers between his own.

'I am considering what to do. I'd like to be close to the girls, so ... perhaps go freelance.'

Again, Alicia wonders what he will do for money. Surely a freelance journalist was just as poorly paid here as in the UK? She guesses he didn't have to worry about maintenance payments.

'We're still working out the details but I'll have this flat, car and the boat. Mia never goes onboard anyway and she spends most of her time in the summer place. Plus they've got other blocks of apartments to choose from closer to the center, where I'm certain Her Ladyship would rather be.'

The bitterness of Patrick's last sentence takes Alicia by surprise. As he utters the word 'Ladyship' his face contorts and shows the anger he obviously feels.

Was she unfaithful? Does he still love her?

'I don't want to pry, but what happened?' Alicia asks carefully. She squeezes Patrick's hand in a show of encouragement and support.

Patrick sighs and removes his hand from Alicia's. He straightens his back and without looking at her says, 'I'm a disappointment, apparently.'

She hears that hostility in the tone of his voice again.

Alicia waits. She tries to control her own feelings. She realizes that he slept with her to punish Mia; it was an act of revenge. She wants to ask whether Mia has slept with someone, and whether he still loves her. But to ask these kinds of questions would show how much she, Alicia, was investing—had already invested—in the relationship. It's clear to her now, clearer than it has been for all of the short time they've known each other, that for him this is about something else. It's about his own marriage, and it is certainly not about Alicia. She could be anybody. Yet Alicia tries to suppress the jealousy and anger that begins to bubble inside her. Besides, isn't she also taking her own frustrations with Liam out in this relationship?

Her reticence is soon rewarded.

Patrick leans back in his chair and rubs his chin with his hand. He is gazing over Alicia's shoulder through the tall windows overlooking the sea.

'She met someone last year. A successful businessman like her father. Not a useless liberal journalist like her husband. They all knew about it long before I did.'

'When did you find out?' Alicia asks, trying to control her voice.

Patrick looks at her again, but doesn't say anything.

And then Alicia knows.

Anger and jealousy again rise inside Alicia and she forces herself to breathe normally. She feels used. She gets up, but Patrick takes hold of her wrist.

'Please, I can explain. You don't understand.'

'No need, it's all clear. You got bad news and decided to take revenge with the first available woman. I'm glad I could be helpful.' She can hear the emotion in her voice and is ashamed. Her voice is trembling, she's sure of it. She has to get out. She moves toward the elevator again, the second time that evening.

'You've got it all wrong!' Patrick says. When Alicia doesn't reply, he continues, 'At least let me drive you home.'

Alicia lets out a dry laugh, 'Please don't feel obliged!'

But when she sees the expression on Patrick's face she once again changes her mind. He looks so drawn, so miserable, that she feels sorry for him. They have both used each other. Why did she allow herself to be kissed on Midsummer Eve? And why did she go willingly with him on a picnic to the archipelago? Wasn't it as much an act of revenge for her as she now knows it was for Patrick?

They ride down the lift in silence, and do not speak during the fifteen-minute drive to Sjoland. As they cross the bridge, Alicia is about to ask Patrick to drop her off a few meters from the sauna cottage so that they won't be seen from Hilda and Uffe's house, but then decides against it. Patrick doesn't care who knows about them, and neither does she. Not now. Besides, this affair isn't going to carry on, so it really doesn't matter. Alicia can always say that Patrick was among the people she'd spent the evening with if her mother or Uffe sees her get out of Patrick's fancy car. She will think of something.

She turns her head to look at Patrick's profile as he drives on the empty road. It's not dark even though it's gone 9pm, and she can see glimpses of the sea on the left-hand side of the road as it dips close to the shore. They are nearly at her sauna cottage.

'Turn left down the track there,' she points to a small turning.

As she gets out of the car, she bends down at the open door and asks, 'Does Mia know about me?'

Patrick looks at her and says, 'You really don't think much of me, do you?'

'Thank you for the ride,' Alicia says and closes the door.

As she walks along the lane toward the sea and the sauna cottage, she can hear the engine of Patrick's car as he reverses up the small bank to the road. She is relieved to see that there are no lights on in the cottage. At least her mother isn't sitting there waiting for her. She gets the key from its hiding place under the flower pot on the decking and unlocks the door. It isn't until she's inside the cottage, lying on her sofa bed, that she relaxes and stretches out. What an evening!

Uffe is still up, sitting in his office, gazing at the sea, when he sees an unfamiliar car turn into the sauna cottage. His guts churn when he sees it's a black Mercedes. Surely Dudnikov wouldn't put the frighteners on his step-daughter too? Moments later, he can see the light in the cottage come on, and the car pull out and head back on the road to Mariehamn. He spots a blond man in the driving seat of the open-top car and feels such relief when he sees it is the Eriksson's son-in-law that he almost laughs out loud.

THIRTY-SIX

The water is cold, but Alicia likes it just so. She dives in, letting the chilling water run over her face, arms and legs. The freezing sea clears her mind and forces her to move her body faster, emptying her head of any other thoughts but the sensation of her heart pumping quicker, making the blood course through her veins. Soon, she feels as one with the water and begins to enjoy her own speed, her own agility. Alicia takes long strokes, and slowly the chill diminishes and disappears. Now the sea around her seems warmly embracing. This is the part she most enjoys; when her body acclimatizes and she feels strong and confident in her own ability in the water. She wonders if she could swim all the way to Finland. Stopping at the many islands on the way, she is sure she could do it. She tries to remember if anyone has attempted such a race, like swimming across the English Channel. Perhaps she could be the first, she thinks, when she finds herself near the shipping lane about a kilometer from the shore. Wonder what Patrick would think if I swam to Finland, she smiles.

Don't think about him!

Alicia turns back and sees the reeds along the shoreline swaying in the wind, either side of the jetty, where Uffe has cut them right down. She's swam farther than she's ever done before but decides to carry on.

She has tons of energy left in her body; she could swim until she reaches a small inlet on the other side of the open water. She could rest there until she has to turn back.

These early morning swims are her favorite hour of the day on the islands. When Stefan was small, this was the only time during the family holidays when she could please herself, stop being mum and just be Alicia.

When Stefan was older, she would slip out of the house, safe in the knowledge that either Liam (if he was there—he often came over for just a day or two during the summer, while Alicia and Stefan spent weeks on the islands) or her mother would occupy Stefan while she was in the sea. She'd walk slowly down to the shore, listening to the birds and slip into the cold water.

As she remembers, the calmness of the morning is suddenly broken by a loud motorboat, and a triangle of wash around and behind it cuts the scenery in half. She sees there's a Russian flag at the stern. Alicia stops and treads water. She realizes she may be in danger if she goes out any further. The boat looks far too close to her and has no intention of changing course.

Suddenly alarmed, Alicia turns around and dives as deep as she can. Holding her breath, she concentrates on moving her legs and arms in a breaststroke just as her swimming teacher on the islands taught her all those years ago. 'It's all about the rhythm,' she had said. 'Keep the strokes strong and use your hands as paddles. Kick hard to propel your body, keeping the arms long. Don't rush and you'll go faster.'

She hears the deep hum of the engines roar above her.

When Alicia surfaces, she turns around and watches the boat make its speedy way toward the Sjoland canal. She can see a lone man at the helm. Didn't he spot her in the water?

She takes a deep breath before making her way back toward the shore.

Back on the wooden jetty, panting, she sits down and wraps a towel around her shoulders. Listening to the sounds of the sea birds all around her, Alicia closes her eyes and lets the sun warm her face. There is now a thin layer of cloud shading the sun, but the rays are still warming on her skin. She realizes she hasn't thought about Stefan for the past few minutes, while concentrating on getting back to the shore. She has also not let Patrick and his problems into her mind.

It's over, she's convinced of it. She is ashamed that she let herself be seduced by someone like that, but she was vulnerable, so she must forgive herself.

Whatever he says, Liam is probably at this very moment back in the arms of his nurse, so why shouldn't she try out another man? But Alicia cannot help but feel dirty and used; more than anything she feels stupid for thinking a man like Patrick would find her attractive and desirable. Images of their love-making—or sex—onboard the boat flash in front of her eyes. It did *seem* as if he was into her, but Alicia's emotions may have been blinded by her own desire. Alicia lifts her legs up and wraps her hands and the towel around her knees. She decides to ignore Patrick from now on. She has enough worries with Hilda and Uffe. How is she going to be able to broach the subject of money with her mother without a huge argument? Perhaps she should talk to Uffe instead?

THIRTY-SEVEN

'I hear you're sleeping with my husband,' Mia stands with her arms crossed outside the newspaper office.

It's a Monday morning, past ten o'clock, and Alicia is running late because her mother has overslept. Reeking of alcohol, Hilda had allowed Alicia to drive. It wasn't Alicia's day in the newspaper office, but her mother should already have been in the shop, especially now that she'd given notice to her assistant to 'save money'. Getting her mother together and on the road was a novelty. As Alicia parked the car and said goodbye to her outside the little boutique, she resolved to talk to Uffe as soon as possible.

That morning when she saw Hilda's red-rimmed eyes she knew she needed to ask her what was going on, but she was preoccupied by a message she'd received from Harri earlier that morning. The body of a boy had been found in the waters around Sjoland, near the sauna cottage, and he needed Alicia to cover the story. She wondered if she should inform him that she had never reported on crime, but Harri was the editor, and she wanted to make a good impression, so she typed 'I'm on my way,' got dressed quickly and ran to the main house to see if Hilda had yet left for work.

Now Alicia, her head already full of concerns for her mother and the story she is required to cover but doesn't know how to write, regards Mia. She's wearing a huge pair of dark sunglasses, red lipstick and a sleek trouser suit. Not exactly summer wear for the islands; more like an office outfit one would wear in Stockholm or London.

'I'm sorry, I'm running late,' Alicia says and she tries to walk around Mia to reach the door to the newspaper office.

Mia steps in front of her again and leans in to speak, close to Alicia's ear, 'I always knew you were a little tart. At school you'd go around with that blond head of yours held high, like a primadonna, as if you were somebody. Which you weren't. And then after you moved to London, you blanked me every time I saw you in town.'

Alicia sees how angry the woman is but she has no time for her now. Besides, she couldn't give a monkeys about Patrick and his little domestic argument. She is well out of it.

'Look, I don't know what's going on, but I need to get to work.'

'Are you, or are you not, sleeping with my husband?' Mia asks. 'I demand an answer.'

Who's being a primadonna now?

Alicia tries to keep calm. Mia has her arms crossed and appears taller than Alicia, and she wonders briefly how come she doesn't remember her being so lanky at school, but then she notices the sky-high heels.

'No,' Alicia replies, trying to look Mia in the eyes through her dark lenses. She knows this is a half-lie, but at the same time, she has no intention of sleeping with Patrick again.

Her reply seems to take Mia aback and she doesn't stop Alicia as she walks around her and into the *Ålandsbladet* building.

'You're a liar,' she hears Mia shriek behind her back, but Alicia quickly runs up the stairs. She hopes the woman will not follow her. A scene with the jealous daughter of the owner in front of the editor is all she needs.

When Alicia enters the open-plan office, the first person she sees through the glass of the editor's office in the far corner is Patrick. He's standing opposite Harri's desk, with the leather satchel slung across his jacket. He's nodding to something Harri is saying. Neither he nor the editor have spotted Alicia yet.

What the hell is he doing here—again?

Alicia steadies herself and walks confidently past Frida and another junior reporter, who are both watching her. She nods to them and opens the door into Harri's glass cubicle.

Patrick doesn't look surprised to see her. He glances at her without smiling and she nearly asks him, *'Do you know your wife is downstairs accosting reporters on their way to work?'* but her thoughts are interrupted when Harri says, 'Oh, good, you're here. Patrick has offered to take you to the crime scene on his boat.'

Alicia meet's Patrick's eyes. His hair is ruffled, which makes him look even more handsome than usual. She notices he has shaved this morning.

When Alicia doesn't say anything, Harri asks, 'Did you read the police report I sent you?' 'Yes,' Alicia replies. She had quickly scanned it while waiting for Hilda to get ready.

'Off you go then,' Harri says. He's gazing at both her and Patrick in turn, and Alicia is sure he's noticed the tension between them. When neither moves, Harri adds, 'Everything OK?'

'Yes,' both Patrick and Alicia say in turn.

'Get a move on then!'

THIRTY-EIGHT

'You OK?' Patrick asks and touches Alicia's elbow.

They are out of the office and walking down the stairs. His touch through the thin fabric of her cotton blouse runs through her body.

How am I to resist this man?

'Sure, but I ran into Mia outside the office,' she says, trying to pour cold water over both his tenderness and her own weakness.

Patrick stops and stares at her, 'What, where?'

'Outside, just now.'

Patrick runs his hand over his face and Alicia notices that he's cut himself shaving again. There is a small nick at the side of his face, and a stream of blood has run down his chin where he has rubbed it.

'You're bleeding...' Alicia says, taking a tissue out of her handbag and, after a moment's hesitation, handing it to Patrick rather than wiping his chin herself. She touches the side of her own face to indicate where the mark is.

'Ah, thanks,' Patrick says and rubs the tissue against his face.

'You OK?' Alicia asks.

'Yeah,' Patrick says. He crunches the napkin in his palm and gazes at Alicia. She sees he too has red-rimmed eyes much like her mother.

Has everyone else on the islands been binge-drinking overnight, Alicia wonders.

'I didn't go home last night—I mean home to the Eriksson's summer place,' Patrick says. His voice is quiet.

'Right,' Alicia says and carries on walking down the stairs, but Patrick stops her, taking hold of her arm again.

'What happened with Mia?'

Alicia is suddenly weary, fed up with being these wealthy people's piggy in the middle.

'Nothing,' she replies and frees herself from Patrick's grip. 'You coming?' she says over her shoulder and hears Patrick following her down the stairs. When they reach street level, she's relieved to see Mia is no longer there.

'The boat is docked in the East Harbor,' Patrick says and he chin nods toward the sea.

'I know,' Alicia replies.

Patrick gives Alicia a quick glance. 'Of course you do,' Patrick says and grins.

Patrick and Alicia hardly say a word to each to other on the way to the harbor. When they get to the moorings, Patrick offers Alicia his hand, but she lowers herself onto the boat without as much as a glance at him. When she's onboard she avoids looking at the ladder leading to the cabin below. She is trying hard not to think about the day they spent in the bunk, wrapped around each other.

Harri has given them a grid reference for the place where the body has been found. At the *Sjoland* canal they see a police boat. Patrick nods to the three shapes onboard the other vessel. As they leave the canal, and speed up toward the open sea, Patrick says to Alicia, 'We can't go as fast, but I know the way.'

Alicia nods. She digs out a hairband from her handbag and ties her hair back to avoid the wind blowing it into her face.

Moments later, they dock on the side of a small rocky island, right next to the police boat. The three police officers are gathering equipment on top of a small hill. Alicia sees one of them walk toward the edge of the island, holding some police tape. His head dips down as he climbs down the bank.

A policewoman turns around as they step off the yacht. 'It's Alicia, isn't it?'

'Hi,' Alicia replies and adds, 'I didn't know you'd moved back to Åland, Ebba?'

'Likewise.'

Alicia walks the few paces along a rocky island and regards the policewoman. She's wearing a midnight-blue police overall and white rubber gloves. She's changed since their schooldays and looks more assured, a little more filled out, although she is still lanky and a head taller than Alicia. Her dark hair is cut short and she isn't wearing any makeup at all, which makes her look freshly scrubbed. When, years ago, she bumped into Ebba in the corridors of Uppsala university and heard that she too was studying there (criminology, while Alicia was studying English), she thought they might become closer friends, but somehow it didn't happen. She heard later that Ebba was working with the Stockholm Police.

Alicia is brought back to the present by Ebba's voice. She's issuing commands to the other policeman. There are two men standing next to her old schoolfriend, one an older man, wearing shorts and carrying a case, and another one, a younger male police officer in an all-blue overall like Ebba's.

'Simon, you help Gustav with the body and take the pictures. I'll deal with the press.'

'Where's the body?' Patrick asks Ebba. He is standing next to Alicia, and she is trying to ignore the effect the closeness of his body has on her. They are facing Ebba, who has her eyes on Alicia and Patrick, regarding them gravely.

'How did you know about this?' Ebba asks.

Patrick smiles, 'Oh, come on, Ebba, we get live police reports.'

'You two know each other?' Alicia asks, glancing at Patrick and then at Ebba.

'Everyone knows everyone else here, surely you know that?' Ebba says drily, and adds, 'But you've made a wasted visit. I can't let you near before we've made our investigations. And definitely no pictures,' she says as she sees Patrick dig his mobile out of his pocket.

'Just for my own reference?' Patrick replies, holding firmly onto his phone.

'You don't want me to confiscate that, do you?' Ebba says and smiles.

'OK,' Patrick replies with a sigh, 'Be like that.' He puts the phone back into his pocket.

As they stand there, the third policeman re-emerges from behind a rock and waves them over.

Without a word, Ebba begins to move toward the sea's edge, followed by an older man carrying the heavy case. Patrick and Alicia look at each other, then start walking behind the two policemen. As they approach the sea, the young policeman points to a shape in the water.

He is lying face down, his limp body tangled in the reeds. His thin, fully clothed shape moves with the gentle waves of the sea wash. Alicia stares down at the torso and sees in her eyes Stefan, or how his lanky figure would have looked in the morgue. She regrets she didn't insist on seeing him; her mind's image of how he looked is far worse. There's blue and white police tape strung across two thin, twisted pine trees sprouting from the rocky ground as if by a miracle. The tape is for show only, Alicia thinks. Who would come to a little outpost like this?

Ebba glances behind her to where Patrick and Alicia are standing, but she doesn't say anything. She moves carefully down the side of the rock that leads down to the water. With one foot on a stone close to the boy's head and another resting on the main rock face, Ebba squats down to take a closer look. Alicia's stomach turns as she sees the swollen state of the corpse. The body is puffed up underneath a dark-colored parka and long shorts. The half-upturned face of the boy looks pasty, bloated and blotchy. Ebba steadies herself on the rock and leans in to take a close look.

Alicia moves closer, stepping over the police tape.

'Stay there!' Ebba shouts, but Alicia replies, 'I think I know him.'

Ebba stares at her and then nods in agreement.

Alicia puts her other hand to her mouth and nose to stop herself from smelling anything as she takes the few steps down the slippery rock. She squats down beside Ebba, who reaches out to steady her. Alicia looks at his legs and sees the plaster cast on his bare left foot. It too is discolored with a greenish yellow hue, but there are still a few scribbles left visible. His friends must have written stuff on the cast.

'He is—was—just a kid,' Alicia says.

THIRTY-NINE

Alicia thinks about her stepfather. How shocked Uffe would be to see the boy in that state. He is a good man, Alicia knows that. He looks after his staff well, too well in her mother's opinion.

'He keeps asking them to come into the house and then I have to feed them!' she's often said to Alicia. When she was growing up there were two farm laborers who came back each summer to work for Uffe. They were both born and bred in the Åland islands, and Uffe had known them since childhood. But when Eastern Europe opened up to the West and cheaper foreign labor became available, Uffe began employing first Estonian boys, then Polish and now Romanian. It has never occurred to Alicia to ask Uffe where he found the temporary labor; she assumed the boys themselves turned up on the doorstep of her stepfather's farmhouse in Sjoland.

'Oh my God,' she hears Patrick say behind her. He's standing on the rock above Alicia. The sun is shining directly into Alicia's eyes so she can't see his expression fully. Taking her hand away from her mouth, she holds onto the rock and straightens herself up. Patrick reaches his hand out to help her up the bank. This time she takes it and he pulls her up.

Alicia looks around the little island where the police and Patrick have moored their motorboats; how has the boy ended up here, on this small rocky outcrop? There are clumps of grass in the middle and around the edges, but mostly it's just a flat, stony surface with patches of moss.

Alicia is shivering even though it's a very warm day, with little wind and silent except for the seabirds and the occasional sound of a motorboat somewhere in the distance. They are just ten minutes or so away from her swimming place in Sjoland. She hears the sound of an engine, but it soon fades and gives way to the twittering or squawking of the birds. There isn't much habitation in the surrounding islands. One jetty juts out from a shoreline, about 500 meters away, and Alicia can make out an old boathouse, and then a large wood-clad villa further up the hill. The water looks shallow between the larger island and the one they are standing on. Alicia wonders if the little outpost is owned by the people with the jetty. In her mind's eye, she can see children swimming from the larger island to the smaller one, laughing and drying themselves in the sun when they reach the other shore.

Her own childhood.

What a deserted, beautiful place it would be if it wasn't for the dead body of a young man floating between the reeds just a few meters away.

The older man with the heavy case edges down toward the body, while Ebba, helped up by the young policeman, comes to stand next to Patrick and Alicia.

'So who is he?' Ebba asks.

'His name is Daniel. He works—worked—for my stepfather.'

Patrick makes a sound. Since the exchange with Ebba about his phone, Patrick has been unusually quiet. Alicia now looks at him. His face is very pale.

'You OK?' Alicia asks. Ebba is regarding them both.

'Yeah, I keep thinking I should take notes, but I don't seem to be able to think straight.'

'Shock,' Alicia says.

Patrick nods.

'You didn't cover anything like this in Stockholm?' she asks him.

Patrick shakes his head. 'No, I was more political and financial crimes.'

Ebba coughs, ending Patrick and Alicia's conversation abruptly. Her face is grave.

'Tell me everything you know about him,' Ebba says, and chin nods back to the other end of the island.

'I haven't really met him, just seen him from afar. He works as a casual laborer for Uffe, and stays in one of the cottages, that's all I know. The plaster cast is from an accident he had with the tractor last week.' Alicia shivers. She pulls her arms around herself. 'I mean, I *think* it's him ...' Suddenly Alicia is afraid she's mistaken.

'OK. I don't want any of this in your paper,' Ebba says.

Patrick nods, again not uttering a word, but Alicia replies, 'Surely we can say that a body has been found here?'

Ebba sighs. 'OK, but no details about his ID until we know more about what's happened and can contact his next of kin.'

'How do you think it happened?' Alicia asks.

Ebba looks at Alicia, but doesn't answer the question.

'Wait here, I may need to ask you more questions,' she says instead and moves toward the police tape to talk to the older man.

Alicia and Patrick are kept on the island for another half an hour, while the police move back and forth between the body and their boat. Eventually, the young policeman fetches a gray plastic body bag. A few minutes later, the three policemen carry the dead body into their boat.

'You can go now,' Ebba says with her head bent over her notebook, not looking at Alicia or Patrick.

They travel back to Mariehamn in silence. Patrick doesn't put the sail up, and the noise of the engine provides Alicia with an excuse not to talk to him.

'What an infuriating woman,' Patrick says as they pull up to the jetty in the East Harbor.

'Yeah, I remember she was a bit of an odd-ball at school,' Alicia replies.

Patrick is standing in the boat, facing her with his hair mussed up by the wind.

'Sorry, I forgot she was a friend of yours,' he says, gazing at Alicia from under his eyebrows.

Alicia climbs onto the jetty, not waiting for Patrick's help. She's holding onto the strap of her canvas handbag, which she'd slung across her body as she got out of the boat.

'You were very quiet out there,' she says, looking closely at Patrick's face. She's standing above him, watching him getting ready to leave the boat.

'Not used to seeing dead bodies, I guess,' he says, lowering the fenders, locking the doors to the cabin and putting away their life-jackets. As he steps out onto the jetty, he leans down and makes sure the fenders are in place to protect his precious boat.

'Right,' Alicia says.

'I'm off then.' Patrick says. But he only stands opposite Alicia, looking down at her.

'Oh, you're not going to write the article?' Alicia says, surprised. She's still not sure what his role at the newspaper is, nor what is expected of her.

'This isn't exactly a story for the finance section,' Alicia says, 'so I assumed ...'

'I told you, I don't work for *Ålandsbladet*.'

'So why were you here today?'

'To give you a lift, of course,' Patrick says, a smile playing on his lips.

Alicia feels stupid. She looks down at her shoes and nods, 'Well, I should thank you then.'

They stand on the jetty facing each other. Alicia isn't looking at him, she can't, because she knows what will happen if she does. Instead, she glances down the jetty and into the restaurant at the far end of the harbor. A few tourists are walking on the path that runs along the wooden jetties, and a cyclist passes them.

Patrick takes her hand, 'Look, can we start again?'

Alicia lifts her head and sees the sincerity in his face. He's standing so close to her now that their bodies are nearly touching. Her breath is caught in her chest and for a moment she can't speak. But then she remembers the anger in Mia's face a few hours before, and the pain in Patrick's when he spoke about their break-up.

Those two aren't finished with each other.

'Look,' Alicia begins. She briefly squeezes Patrick's hand, then lets go and steps backward to put some space between them. 'You need to sort things out with Mia. Perhaps in a few months' time, when ...'

Patrick's face shows no emotion when he says, 'OK, I understand.' There's a pause, then he adds, 'I guess I'll see you around?'

Alicia stands still for a moment and then walks away. At the end of the jetty, she turns around and sees Patrick still looking at her. She nods and makes her way quickly toward the newspaper office.

Harri is so excited about having a scoop with the body of the Romanian boy that he convinces Alicia to write the story up in spite of the promises she made to Ebba.

'I'll clear it with her, don't worry about that. We know the Police Chief, and he'll be fine about it.'

Reluctantly, Alicia writes a brief report about the discovery of the body, leaving out the connection to Uffe, which she hadn't mentioned to the editor. She just quotes 'unnamed sources' saying that the boy was from Romania and had been working as a farm laborer on the islands.

Moments later, she sees it's been uploaded to the paper's online version. As she re-reads her own words, the article strikes her as too simple, as if she's forgotten something. Bloody Patrick, he keeps getting into her thoughts, clouding them. She needs to be a good journalist and to learn new skills to keep the job at *Ålandsbladet*. For now at least. She doesn't know if she's going to stay indefinitely, but at least for now. The money she earns comes in handy.

But she had no idea when she was offered the job by Birgit that it involved working with all the breaking news. When she'd returned from seeing the body Harri had said, 'Everyone turns their hand to anything here.'

He swept his hand across the newsroom, where just two people were sitting, Frida and a younger boy, just as they were when she'd met Patrick there earlier. 'Those two are both interns, they are not ready to tackle an article like this.'

The pieces she wrote for the *Financial Times* were rarely needed quickly. She often had a few days to write a report on a company, or a feature explaining the impact of a possible interest rate rise, or the effects of the fall in the UK pound after the Brexit vote. Only when she worked on the 2008 financial crisis, did she remember having to turn in stories fast. But she's a trained reporter and she knows she can handle anything. Better than Patrick, it seems. Bloody man! Alicia decides enough is enough. She will control her emotions from now on.

FORTY

That evening after the discovery of the boy's body, Alicia convinces her mother that she is too tired for a nightcap after dinner. She wants to collect her thoughts about Patrick, about the boy, and think about Stefan in peace. Seeing the dead Romanian has brought back her own fabricated images of Stefan's body after the accident. She curses Liam, who kept her away from her son. *Think of the positives.* She forces herself to remember how Stefan loved the islands, how he made friends here. Suddenly, she realizes she doesn't know any of the youngsters he used to 'hang out' with as he put it. She resolves to find out from Hilda who they were - surely she would have heard from a friend of a friend who Stefan befriended?

Alicia tries to empty her mind, and uses the techniques her psychologist, Connie, had taught her.

'Notice everything around you, look at the trees, take in the color of the sky, the fluffy clouds. Breathe in and out.'

Alicia sits on the wooden decking outside the sauna cottage and watches the birds dip in and out of the water, picking up insects off the surface, trying to think only about the beautiful nature around her. But her mind wanders and she thinks about the young Romanian man instead. Both Uffe and Hilda were shocked to hear of Daniel's death. Uffe wanted a glass of whisky straight away but then didn't have wine with dinner, whereas Hilda drank several glasses. At the end of the meal her mother was slurring her words and giggling. She acted so inappropriately that Alicia exchanged several glances with Uffe during the meal. Alicia didn't say anything about her drinking, but resolved to talk to Uffe, again, about it, as well as the money worries. The alcohol, the rows and the losses the shop was making must be linked, surely? As soon as the police found out what had happened to the boy, they could move on with their lives.

Again, Alicia forces herself to think about her surroundings. It is a still evening, with the sun hovering over the horizon, and she sits on the decking, trying not to think about anything, and just concentrating on her breathing. She thinks how amazing it is that the sun will only dip down a couple of hours before midnight and emerge again around 4am, leaving a dusk that never gets truly dark. It's now 9pm, and there is no sign of darkness. This is what she has missed in London. The quiet peace where you can really gather your thoughts.

This is her favorite time of the year on the islands. The end of the day, when the wildlife around her is busy calling each other, or feeding their young, is magical. Watching the calm sea in front of her, she spots a pair of birds emerge from the reed bed and dive elegantly, hardly breaking the glinting surface. Alicia holds her breath as she waits for the bird to emerge. She thinks they are Artic loons, which have an amazing ability to stay under water for several minutes, and her suspicion is confirmed when she sees the first bird emerge a couple of meters away from where it entered the water. Alicia wants to clap but is afraid of alarming the wildlife around her.

A noise of a motorboat cuts through the landscape. A wooden rowing boat with an outboard motor attached to the back is heading across the shipping lane toward the island opposite, a young man holding onto the tiller. When the boat disappears around a point, peace is once again restored. Alicia closes her eyes and concentrates on the natural sounds around her: the soft rustling in the trees and the lower sound of the reeds swaying in the breeze. The birds are twittering warnings to each other.

Suddenly a noise she doesn't recognize makes Alicia open her eyes.

'Your mum said I'd find you here.'

Ebba stands with her feet wide apart, her hands in the pockets of her trousers. She isn't in uniform anymore, but she still looks as if she is on duty, with the same waterproof coat she was wearing earlier, now over a plain white shirt bearing the logo of Finnish police force—a gray sword and the head of the Lion of Finland against a blue background. On her feet she wears sensible black, flat shoes, which Alicia suspects are police issue too.

'So what happened to your promise not to write about the body?' Ebba has her eyes on Alicia.

'Sorry, Harri said that you'd be OK with it. Apparently, he knows the Chief of Police.'

'Yeah, the same man who chewed my head off when he saw what you'd written.'

'Sorry,' Alicia says. 'I'm still new at the paper. I couldn't refuse it.' Alicia tries to smile at Ebba. 'Please sit down?'

Ebba plonks herself on a chair next to Alicia.

'Apology accepted. Besides, I knew that would happen, but I thought it'd be Mr Eriksson's son-in-law who would write about it, not you.'

'Me too,' Alicia says, trying to avoid looking at Ebba, and instead studying her hands.

Ebba regards Alicia silently for a moment before speaking. 'We've definitely identified the boy.'

'Oh,' Alicia says, 'that was quick.'

'I've also just spoken with your mum and dad.'

'You mean my mum and Uffe?' Alicia remarks.

Ebba raises an eyebrow and scratches her hair. 'Sorry, yes, your step-dad.'

'That's OK. It's just that I don't, never have, called Uffe "Dad".'

Ebba exhales. 'Let's cut the crap. We didn't know each other that well at school, nor at uni, so I can be excused for not knowing the ins and outs of your family relationships.'

'Sure,' Alicia says. She's surprised at Ebba's tone, but recognizes her direct manner. She was just the same at school and university.

'But what's the issue, what more can I tell you? I came to see the body because of my job and happened to know who it was. That's all,' Alicia says.

'Why didn't you tell me about you and Patrick?' Ebba says, looking straight at Alicia.

'I didn't think it was relevant.' Alicia is hoping Ebba is referring to the fact that she knows Patrick.

'See, that's where I disagree.' Again Ebba lifts her eyebrows. 'It seems a bit of a coincidence that a boy you and your boyfriend both know turns up dead ...'

'Colleague,' Alicia says. 'Look, I've just started at *Alandsbladet* and Patrick, who didn't know Daniel, offered to take me to the island on his boat. That's all.'

Ebba looks at Alicia, raising an eyebrow, 'I bet he offered,' she mumbles and before Alicia has time to reply, continues, 'So you're living here now? You're not registered as living here. We have your home address as ...' Ebba refers to the screen on her phone, 'Crouch End, London?'

Alicia looks down at her hands, 'Yeah. Sorry, I'm not sure what I am going to do.'

Ebba makes a note on her phone and looks at Alicia again. Don't forget you have three months, after which you have to register your move from one EU country to another. The rules still apply until Brexit.'

Alicia sighs, 'OK. Give me a break, will you!' She grins, trying to remind Ebba that even though they weren't the best of friends before, they're not exactly strangers now.

But Ebba isn't having any of it. 'I don't make the rules,' she says, not returning Alicia's smile. 'Going back to my investigation, can you tell me how exactly you and Patrick came to the scene?'

'I told you—we were covering a story. Harri called me into his office this morning and Patrick was there. He offered to give me a lift. Apparently *Ålandsbladet* isn't wealthy enough to own a boat of its own.'

'But I thought you were a financial journalist, not a breaking news reporter,' Ebba says and crosses her arms.

Alicia groans. 'Yes, that was a bit of a surprise to me too. It seems there are no such distinctions here.'

'Right,' Ebba says, and continues. 'Your step-dad filled me in on the unfortunate incident with the tractor, and their working relationship.'

Ebba's glance settles on Alicia once more. 'It's a shame you didn't let me know about the connection before. Any reason why you didn't?'

Alicia bites the inside of her lip. She hadn't mentioned this to Ebba because she wasn't sure whether the farmworkers' work status was above board. She is well aware that Uffe takes on summer staff without worrying too much about permits and taxes. She is almost certain Daniel and his Romanian friends were paid cash in hand, no questions asked.

'I didn't want Uffe, or my mother, to get involved in something that had nothing to do with them. Besides, I wasn't even sure it was him.'

'Hmm,' Ebba says, still keeping her eyes on Alicia. Alicia is beginning to feel uncomfortable, as if her old schoolfriend is accusing *her* of something. Instead of saying this to Ebba, however, Alicia keeps quiet.

'Anything else you'd like to tell me? Any other small details about the boy you have kept to yourself, in case it would get someone else in trouble?'

'No, of course not.'

'Nothing to do with your son, Stefan?'

Alicia stares at Ebba. Suddenly she feels very cold. She can't speak.

Ebba continues, 'We have reason to believe the two youngsters knew each other.'

FORTY-ONE

Alicia can't sleep that night. Images of Stefan involved in some crime on the islands, speeding fast on a motorcycle, or his body being replaced by that of the Romanian boy creep into her dreams and she wakes with a start.

Finally, when she has tossed and turned in bed for what seems like hours, and when she sees the light streaming into the room through the small window and making an oblong pattern on the pine log wall, she gets up. She looks at her phone and sees it's a few minutes past 6am. The birds are already singing outside, noisily making preparations for the day ahead.

Alicia gets out of bed and fills the coffee machine Hilda has brought to the sauna cottage. They already had a small fridge for beer, and Alicia has brought some butter, rye bread and cheese for breakfast. She needs to be more independent of her mother and Uffe.

From now on, she plans to take the bus into town rather than rely on Hilda's lifts to the newspaper office. Her mother's time-keeping is terrible, and her drinking, which Alicia knows she must mention, worries her sick. She plans to leave a note at the house later, or discuss it with Uffe, who's usually awake early. As well as the drinking, Alicia is seriously worried about their money troubles. She needs to speak to Hilda, but has no idea how she will broach the subject.

And she can't do anything until the matter with poor Daniel has been settled.

With a hot, steaming cup of black coffee, and a woollen throw around her shoulders, Alicia goes to sit on the terrace and watches the sun, which is already high over the horizon. It looks like being another bright and hot day, with just some hazy clouds scattered over a deep-blue sky. She can see a row of sailing boats moving slowly around. They are gathered in the shipping lane, waiting for the swing bridge to open so that they can make their way through the Sjoland canal and into Mariehamn's East Harbor. These are early risers, she thinks.

Later, the town will be full of tourists and the restaurants and cafés buzzing. She hopes Hilda's shop will be filled with customers too.

Alicia pulls her knees up and turns her thoughts to what Ebba said about the Romanian boy, Daniel. Alicia feels ashamed that she never even met him. He had just turned eighteen, so he was exactly the same age as Stefan. And Daniel knew Alicia's son.

'Two friends, both dead now,' Ebba said in that serious, level voice of hers. Her intelligent eyes were on Alicia, as if waiting to hear how she could explain it. But, of course, she wasn't able to do that. How could the policewoman imagine she would have an explanation when she didn't even know the two boys were close?

They'd sat in silence for what seemed like hours, on the same terrace where Alicia is now, watching the birds duck in and out of the reeds. 'Look, I'm not sure what you are saying. How do you know that Daniel knew my Stefan?' she asked Ebba.

'There are messages on his phone. And photos of the two of them —and a girl.'

'Who?'

'We don't know yet.' Ebba sighed and stood up. 'Come and see me on Monday at the station. I should have more information by then.'

Alicia nodded.

'Have a good weekend,' Ebba said and disappeared around the corner of the cottage.

Now, sipping her coffee, Alicia resolves to find out who that girl is. Surely there must be something on Stefan's phone or laptop. She needs to ask Liam to look through any images. Alicia picks up her phone and sees the latest messages Liam has sent her, all gone unanswered. She types in a few words, rereads what she has written, and then deletes the word 'sorry'. She realizes she's not sorry for having kept her distance from him. Liam is still her husband, that is true, but as far as she is concerned they are separated.

When, two hours later, Alicia makes her way up to the house, her mother is standing by the kitchen window above the sink, looking over the fields and the sea beyond. She's clutching a cup of coffee.

'Hi,' Alicia says.

Her mother turns around and Alicia goes and hugs her. Hilda's eyes are red again, and she looks so miserable that Alicia has to ask, 'What's the matter?'

Her mother turns back to the window. Alicia sees Uffe walking along the side of one of the fields, and they follow his slow progress to the end of the path until he disappears into the narrow strip of pine trees separating the rest of Uffe's farm from the house.

'Oh, the boy's accident has upset us both,' Hilda says.

'It's terrible,' Alicia agrees. She decided during her morning swim that she will not mention what Ebba told her about Stefan, Daniel, and the unknown girl. Not until she has a chance to find out from the policewoman who the girl is.

'Do you want breakfast?' Hilda asks. Alicia realizes that her mother is still in her dressing gown.

'No.' Alicia tells her mother that she plans to take a bus into town. She sees relief in Hilda's eyes.

'Aren't you going in today?' Alicia asks.

Hilda glances at her daughter. She can see her expression change to a wary one. 'Oh, the summer girl is there today.'

Her mother smiles and turns around, giving her daughter the message that the matter is closed.

Hilda offers Alicia Uffe's old bike, but Alicia decides against the rusty old thing. She plans to buy one in the shops in the fall, when the tourist season is over and prices plummet for things like that.

If she's still on the islands then.

FORTY-TWO

The first person Alicia sees when she enters the newspaper office is Patrick.

Why is he constantly hanging around here?

'There's a meeting with Harri at 9am sharp. You and I are covering the murder case,' he says to Alicia.

She stares at Patrick. She glances at her watch and sees it's nearly 9 o'clock already.

'Murder?'

'Come on,' he says and touches the small of Alicia's back, pushing her toward the glass cubicle where Harri is already sitting, talking to Birgit. The personnel woman is standing with her back to the general office and there is another man sitting down, with only his blond hair visible. When she opens the door, forced by Patrick behind her, Alicia immediately recognizes him. Kurt Eriksson—the majority owner of the newspaper and the most famous man on the islands.

'Where's that girl?' Harri says as soon as Alicia and Patrick enter his fish-bowl of an office.

'Called in sick,' Birgit says. The woman is holding a stack of papers. Did she ever go anywhere without them, Alicia wonders.

'If that's all,' she now says, looking at Harri. The editor nods and Birgit leaves the room, closing the door behind her.

Alicia feels Kurt Eriksson's gaze on her. He coughs. It's just a small sound, barely audible, but it stops Harri in his tracks.

'Ah, and Kurt, please meet Alicia, our newest recruit. From London,' he adds and lifts his chest a little.

If only they knew, Alicia thinks and looks at the famous million-aire, who stands up and extends his hand to her.

'Hello again. We met at Midsummer,' Alicia says and takes his hand.

'Yes, of course,' Kurt Eriksson says and moves his eyes toward Patrick, who is now standing next to Alicia. His face hardens from the polite smile directed toward Alicia just a second before.

'I believe you know my son-in-law?' he says, bringing his face back to Alicia with a false smile on his lips again. Alicia notices his pale eyes have the same, cold, expression in them. His tan has an orange hue, and his artificially blond hair has been professionally styled to look naturally ruffled. Close up, he looks far too young, his skin a little tight and thin across his face. He is wearing a pink striped shirt, tucked into dark navy chinos, revealing a slightly extended but firm stomach, and gives off a scent of expensive aftershave. No tax-free junk from the Viking Line ferries for this guy, Alicia thinks, and she pulls her hand away.

'I hear you've worked for the *Financial Times*?' he says and gives Alicia a smarmy smile.

'Yes,' she replies, and wonders whether to add that she was a free-lance reporter, but decides against it.

There is a silence and Alicia wishes more than anything that she could turn on her heels and leave the room.

'Right, I want you two to go and talk with the police, come back and write a thousand words,' Harri says, ignoring the polite chit chat Kurt Eriksson has started.

'I'm not ...' Alicia says, but Harri puts his right hand up, palm facing Alicia.

'If you want to go full-time for the next few weeks, we've just OK'd it with the shareholder.' Harri nods at Kurt Eriksson, whose smile widens but still doesn't reach his eyes.

· · ·

'What the hell?' Alicia spits at Patrick when they are outside the news-paper office, walking toward the police headquarters a few blocks away along the East Harbor. The wind has got up and the rattle of the sails and rigging in the wind is so loud it's almost deafening. They walk right past the spot where Patrick's boat is moored, where he first invited Alicia onboard.

'What have I done?' Patrick says, stopping in the middle of the path. He is wearing another white shirt (*how many does he own?*), black ripped jeans and his suede jacket.

'What are you even doing here?' Alicia faces Patrick, her hands on her hips. 'You don't work for the paper, and you don't want to be involved in this story.'

Patrick touches Alicia's arm, and in spite of herself, the contact sends a jolt deep inside her. She shrugs Patrick's hand away. 'I'm wait-ing. What is going on?'

Patrick runs his fingers through his hair and Alicia can't help but find the gesture endearing. The breeze catches the blond strands and a few fall back onto his face. Alicia is glad she put her own hair up in a ponytail this morning.

'Look there aren't many suspicious deaths in Åland, so this is big. Plus you aren't experienced in this kind of thing.'

'And you are? When we saw the body you told me you'd never covered crime. I'm a big girl, I can do this!' Alicia almost shouts the words.

Patrick lifts his eyebrows. 'Yeah sure, but we don't have anybody who has written about something like this. So it makes sense if we put our two heads together.' He regards Alicia for a moment and then stretches his arms out in front of her. 'Honestly, that's all it is. Harri just wanted me to help you out.'

'I told you, I don't need any help,' Alicia says, but she is close to being convinced. She turns on her heels and continues walking along the path by the jetty to the police station.

Patrick hurries to catch her up and takes her arm. 'I knew you'd come around.' He grins like a little boy and Alicia shrugs her shoul-ders, detaching herself from him.

'Don't get any ideas,' she says, but she cannot help a smile forming.

FORTY-THREE

They walk along Strandvägen in silence, passing the Hotel Arkipelag and the library. Images of visiting the place with Stefan flood Alicia's brain. She glances over at Patrick and wonders if she should tell him what Ebba said about Stefan knowing Daniel, but decides against it. She will try to speak to Ebba on her own. They cross the main thoroughfare of the town. In the distance, the sun, now high in the sky, is reflected on the surface of the sea. The light bouncing off the shifting water is blinding and Alicia has to shade her eyes. She's forgotten to bring her sunglasses.

The police station is an old 1950s building, clad in dull gray cement. They have to wait for Ebba. Patrick and Alicia sit on green plastic chairs.

'I need to speak to her privately first,' Alicia says, when the door eventually opens and Ebba gestures for them to enter.

Patrick has already stood up.

Alicia turns and looks at him, 'Please?'

For a moment Alicia thinks that Patrick will insist on coming with her, but then he relents and sits back down.

'Before you ask,' says Alicia, 'I have no idea why he's here. Something about crimes against persons being rare on the islands.'

Ebba doesn't say anything. She folds her long legs behind a light pine desk and points Alicia toward one of two chairs set against the table.

'As far as I'm concerned I'm speaking to *Ålandsbladet* when I'm speaking with you.'

Alicia nods in agreement.

Ebba leans across the table and adds, 'But I have to tell you something off the record first.'

She is looking at a screen in front of her and turns it around toward Alicia.

'Or, rather, I have to ask you some questions.'

'OK,' Alicia says. She's got her phone in her hand, with the notes app opened, just in case she needs to jot down some details.

'Do you know this young woman?'

Alicia gasps. The hair color and length are different, and her cheeks are a little less plump but the face is unmistakable. 'Yes,' she replies.

'Thought so.'

'What has Frida got to do with anything?' Alicia asks.

'How do you know Frida Anttila?' Ebba asks.

'She works as an intern at *Ålandsbladet*.'

'And before that?'

Alicia shakes her head, 'I met her for the first time the day after I started at the paper.'

'That's strange,' Ebba says, staring at Alicia, as if trying to determine whether she is speaking the truth.

'What is this? What has Frida got to do with anything.'

'I'm asking myself the same question,' Ebba says. She turns the screen back toward herself and taps it.

There is a silence during which Alicia stares at Ebba, trying to understand what the policewoman is getting at. Eventually she cannot stand it any longer. 'What is it?'

When Ebba still doesn't reply, Alicia gets it. 'She knew Stefan ... and Daniel! She's the girl in your picture?'

Ebba nods and turns toward Alicia, calmly eyeing her. 'That's why I can't quite understand how you didn't know her,' she says.

Alicia sighs. She too, is amazed how she didn't get to know the young people Stefan hung out with during their holidays. Looking back, there was always the conflict between her and Liam getting in the way. He didn't want to spend time on the islands, while Alicia was always desperately trying to make him love her home.

What a waste of time; I wish I'd never tried.

'I don't know, but I just never met his friends here. He didn't have many, you know. We were always here when everyone else was away in their summer places, so Mariehamn was just full of tourists ...'

Ebba puts up her hand as if to stop Alicia speaking.

She leans over the desk again. 'I need to tell you something. But none of this can go into the paper. Or to be known by anyone else. Is that clear?'

Alicia nods.

'We have reason to believe that Frida and the deceased had a very close connection to your son. Several images from security cameras around the city indicate that they spent some time together in central Mariehamn last summer. Plus we have witness statements from a home where Frida's mother, Sirpa Anttila, is being cared for that say they visited her together on several occasions.

'I didn't know,' Alicia says and gets up. She wants to go and talk to Frida. She'll get her home address from Birgit and pay her a visit.

'Sit down, there's more,' Ebba says. Her expression is serious. 'We believe she is pregnant.'

Alicia sits down. Her head is spinning. 'Sorry, what did you say?'

Ebba shrugs her shoulders. 'I'm just telling you so that you know about her condition before you speak with Ms Anttila.' She gets up and adds, 'Of course, we need to speak with Frida ourselves first, but at the moment we cannot get hold of her. So if you do find her, can you ask her to contact us as soon as possible.'

Patrick watches as Alicia storms out of the police detective's room.

'What's going on,' he says and runs after Alicia, onto the street, but she waves him away and starts walking fast toward the bus station. He is confused. If Alicia has got a scoop out of the police she would head toward the newspaper offices and not in the opposite direction, surely?

When Patrick returns to the grim police headquarters, the constable at the desk tells him Ebba has also left. Cursing under his breath and not knowing what to do next, he walks down Hamngatan, where he has left his car in the multistory next to the Hotel Arkipelag. His thoughts turn to Mia and the divorce.

What is he going to do? He knows his career at *Journalen* is over. He's never going to win any prestigious prizes for his writing however much he wants to. What he needs to ensure now is that he is still going to be involved in the upbringing of his two girls.

Kurt Eriksson, his father-in-law, is a rich and powerful man. Patrick knows he has never liked his Swedish son-in-law. Perhaps in the early days when he saw how happy his daughter was. But lately, after Mia's affair, everyone can see the marriage is anything but blissful. Patrick feels the man's disappointment in his fledging career as a journalist. But what would he have him do? Work 12-hour days and let his children be looked after by a paid help?

In Stockholm, Mia is always busy with the Eriksson's estate business. It's mostly Patrick who fetches the children from school and takes them to their ballet and riding lessons. It's becoming easier, now they are older and sometimes take themselves on the bus and *tunnelbana,* but Patrick is overprotective, of his eldest in particular. He will never forget that night when he thought they were going to lose little Sara, and the memory of her limp body in his arms as he carried her to the car in the dead of night. Or how she looked lying on the emergency ward bed with her eyes closed and her damp hair spread either side of her pale head, as if she was a little sleeping princess.

And he's known about Mia's affair for ages. He knows their relationship hasn't been good for years. They haven't had sex for twelve months. The images of Alicia's slim, strong body writhing beneath his own come into his mind. Alicia's got under his skin, he knows, but he's not sure she feels the same. She seems to think that he and Mia aren't over and he doesn't know how to convince her otherwise.

The confirmation that the marriage was at an end came the morning of the Midsummer party. It was long overdue. Patrick had surprised himself at how calm he'd been. He told Mia that he would want to share custody of the girls, and she had nodded. Not in agreement, he knew, but in acknowledgement of his demand.

'I am going to move to Mariehamn. With the girls,' she replied, regarding him with cold eyes. He tried to recall the last time she had looked lovingly at him, but he couldn't remember.

Patrick said nothing. He just nodded. Afterwards, he was proud of himself, because he didn't want an argument, and he didn't want Mia to back him into a corner. She was a brilliant negotiator, a skill learned at her father's knee. And he needed time to think about his own options. What was there for him in Stockholm, really?

Patrick changes his mind and returns to the multistory. He decides to go back to the newspaper offices. Perhaps Alicia has returned by now.

FORTY-FOUR

Frida cannot get out of bed. She knows she needs to go and see her mum, but her limbs are so heavy. She's been crying so hard since she saw the news on the online version of the newspaper the previous day that her eyes are swollen and her head hurts. Perhaps she's coming down with something. She lights another cigarette, although she knows she should stop, and drags herself over to the French doors and the small patio in front of her flat. Or, to be more precise, her mother's flat.

She still misses her mother's presence in the three-roomed apartment. The place is so quiet without the low humming of her mum as she cooked by the stove in the kitchen, or her laughter in the evenings when she watched old Finnish comedies on TV. Although Frida knows her mother will never come out of the home, she still hopes that a miracle may happen and her mum will return to normal.

What if I don't go today, will she even notice?

Frida takes a long drag from her cigarette. She's sitting wrapped up in her duvet on a kitchen chair, blowing the smoke out through the open door. That's when she sees her.

Quickly, Frida puts out the cigarette in a flower pot she uses for that purpose and shuts the door. As she closes the curtains, she sees

Alicia walking toward her with a determined gait. *Fuck, fuck, fuck.* Frida swears and goes back to bed.

The knocking starts almost as soon as she's back in her bedroom.

'Frida, I know you're there. I just want to talk!' The woman shouts through the door.

Shit, she'll alert the neighbors. An old hag who lives next door would love nothing more than to complain about Frida to the council.

'Coming,' she shouts back. Still wrapped up in the blanket, Frida goes to the door and lets Alicia in.

'Thank you,' the woman says politely.

Frida eyes her up, 'Sit down there,' she says indicating a beaten up green velour sofa. 'Let me get some clothes on.'

Alicia surveys the room where Frida lives. It's not exactly dirty, all the surfaces in the kitchen by the living room are clean and there's only a faint smell of smoke. All the furniture is old, though, and the sofa where she's sitting has a frayed head and armrests. There is an expensive-looking oriental rug in the middle of the room, but that also looks worn-out. The walls are lined with dark wooden bookcases, filled with old hardback volumes and the occasional china figurine. This isn't a young woman's home, Alicia thinks, as Frida reappears wearing a loose dress. Looking at her, Alicia can clearly see there is a bump.

Frida sits down opposite her in an armchair belonging to the same suite as the sofa.

'What do you want?'

'You didn't come to work today and no one has been able to get hold of you.'

'So? I called in sick. Besides, you're not my employer.' Frida has crossed her arms over her chest, making the bump even more pronounced. Her face looks blotched and the purple color of her dress clashes with the blue of her hair, making her look as though she is in fancy dress. A clown.

'How far gone are you?' Alicia asks.

That takes Frida aback. She heaves her back straight, and her eyes stare at Alicia. They are very bloodshot.

She's been crying.

For a moment she is afraid that the girl will get up and hit her.

'What's it to you?' Frida says after a while. Still, there is anger, or defiance in her voice.

'Is it Daniel's?'

'No!' she says. Frida is now staring at Alicia.

'Whose then ...?

Suddenly Alicia knows.

'Surely not Stefan?'

Now the girl breaks down. She lowers her head and begins to sob into her hands. Alicia immediately gets up and goes to hug her.

'There, there,' she says and rocks the bulk of the girl back and forth. Finally, her crying subsides.

'Why didn't you tell me? You knew I was Stefan's mother, didn't you?' Alicia asks as Frida wipes her face and blows her nose loudly into some kitchen paper. It was the only thing Alicia could put her hands on when the crying started.

Frida nods, 'But Daniel was going to help me. And I have this apartment, and the job at *Ålandsbladet*.' She blows her nose again and Alicia fetches more paper.

'Why?'

Frida looks up at Alicia. Her eyes, with swollen lids, are large. Alicia sees that she is truly devastated.

'Do you know what happened with Daniel?' Alicia asks gently.

Now Frida's eyes widen, 'No, do you?'

Alicia shakes her head. 'He drowned but there are suspicious circumstances.'

'Yeah, that's what it said online.'

Alicia says, 'I know, I wrote the article.'

Frida smiles for the first time since Alicia stepped inside her apartment. 'Sorry, I'm being dense.'

Alicia squeezes Frida's shoulders. 'No, you're not.'

They are silent for a moment. Alicia wants to ask all sorts of questions about when Frida is due, how she had met Stefan, did he know about the baby, but she tries to hold fire. She doesn't want to scare Frida away. She looks at the girls' bulging tummy and suddenly feels such joy. In there is a precious thing, a part of her beloved Stefan. A part of her. And a part of Liam. Suddenly Frida starts speaking.

'We first met at the summer confirmation camp when we were both really young. But it didn't start properly until last summer. He was so nice, Stefan, you know?'

Alicia looks at her eyes and nods. She feels tears prick behind her eyes but she controls them and waits.

Frida continues, 'When we met again, last year, that was it. We fell in love. My mother had just been taken into hospital and Stefan was so good about it, taking me to see her on his moped.' Frida is playing with the frayed piece of tissue in her hands, and now lifts her eyes to Alicia. 'Or Uffe's.'

Alicia nods. 'Go on.'

'We spent the whole summer together and in the fall I was accepted onto a language course in Brighton. We met there every weekend until ...'

Alicia thinks back to the fall frantically. And then she remembers, Stefan said he had a friend in Brighton, but she doesn't remember that he went there *every* weekend.

'Sometimes I'd come up to London. Stayed in hostels,' Frida says as if she's read Alicia's mind.

'When did you find out?' Alicia asks carefully after Frida has been quiet, in her own thoughts, for a few minutes. She knows this grief well, it takes over and then you are gone to the world. Poor girl, she's now lost two of her close friends.

'November, I'm nearly eight months now.'

Alicia is shocked and sees the packet of cigarettes by the French doors. 'You shouldn't be smoking.'

Frida lowers her head. 'I know. I've cut down to two or three a day.'

Just as well she doesn't look like she's having a baby, Alicia thinks. She's heard of expecting mums being humiliated in public places if they as much as look at a cigarette, or an alcoholic drink.

'It's really dangerous for the baby,' Alicia says, trying to sound gentle. She takes hold of Frida's hand.

The girl nods and says, 'Daniel told me that all the time.' Tears start running down Frida's face again and Alicia puts her arms around the girl and says, 'I'm here now. I'll take care of you.'

. . .

On her way back to the bus stop, Alicia gets a message on her phone.

It's from Ebba, *'Did you get hold of Frida?'*

'No,' Alicia taps in reply. The last thing that girl needs is brusque questioning by Ebba. No. The longer she can stay at home and calm herself down, the better. For Frida—and the baby.

The baby! Alicia stops walking. She's going to be a grandmother! And she's not even forty herself! As this realization hits her, the whole of her heart fills with love toward Frida and the child she is carrying.

Will the baby look like Stefan?

Alicia begins walking again, dreaming about a little boy or girl with Stefan's blond curls and hazel eyes. Of course, Frida is also blond, at least when she hasn't dyed her hair the colors of the rainbow. Alicia smiles to herself. She finds Frida's odd style endearing now. She hasn't felt this happy for months. Not since she lost Stefan. What a wonderful gift this is! She imagines herself being at the birth, supporting Frida through the last stages of her pregnancy, and holding the newborn in her arms.

Another ping from her phone brings Alicia back to the here and now. As she digs out her mobile again, she resolves to stop fantasizing and slow down. Frida might not want her to interfere; she must be careful not to overpower her. She needs this baby more than she has ever needed anything, so she must make sure she will not lose it before the little thing is even born. Frida seems a very independent young woman, and Alicia understands that. She has to respect her wishes above all else. First there is the issue of Daniel's death. She needs to shield Frida from its horrible consequences.

When Alicia's eyes reach the phone, she sees the message is from Liam.

'I can't find anything on Stefan's laptop but I know he knew someone called Frida at the summer camp. I can tell you more if we talk. Please call me?'

It occurs to her that Liam is also going to be a grandparent. Should she tell him now? No, she needs to wait until she has had more time with Frida and has talked through all her options. She deletes his message. She has no desire to talk to Liam.

Alicia knows Frida is seeing a doctor regularly at the health clinic. That is how Ebba found out she was expecting. She is surprised that the police have access to such information, and that Ebba was allowed to tell her, but knowing the islands, she is aware that rules are often ignored. She remembers when she had conjunctivitis as a child, and her mother went to get some drops from the chemist. The woman who served her already knew Alicia was off school with an eye infection. Her class teacher had told the other kids to keep away from her as it was very infectious.

'This island mentality is something else,' she remembers her mother muttering as she applied the lotion to Alicia's eyes. At the time, Alicia didn't understand why Hilda was so upset, but as she got older, she understood how suffocating it could be when everyone knew everyone else's business. It was the reason she eventually left to go to university and never returned.

Until now.

FORTY-FIVE

Patrick sits in the deserted offices of *Ålandsbladet*. He knows that Harri is struggling to make money from the newspaper and that the advertising takings are down, making it necessary to slim down the operation, but it seems there is never anyone around.

It's true that it's the height of summer, and most people are on holiday, but it seems Harri is relying on just Alicia and a couple of interns to produce the paper at the moment. He looks at the editor in his glass cubicle. He's written most of the articles for the latest edition himself, with the ads and announcements coming from two members of staff working alongside the personnel woman on the second floor.

Patrick glances at his watch. It's nearly 2pm. If Alicia doesn't show up, he'll have to produce a piece on the Romanian boy's death on his own and he has absolutely nothing to go on. Yesterday Harri asked him to help Alicia out, but there was no mention of a fee. It is unbelievable how they use him. The only reason he comes to the offices in summer is to make himself useful. This year, there's also Alicia.

Alicia.

He was hoping he could take her out to lunch again, even take her to the flat, but there's no sign of her. Where could she be?

He doesn't want to go back to their summer cottage. Now that negotiations on the divorce settlement have started, the atmosphere at the Eriksson's villa is even more stifling. Even spending time with his daughters is fraught with the possibility of being told how useless he is. Only last week, when he was there for a night, his mother-in-law had stomped into the kitchen to get a glass of water and found him giving the girls ice creams. 'Those will spoil their appetite for dinner,' she had said, not even glancing at Patrick, before floating back to the vast living room.

Magda had been in the kitchen too, preparing dinner, and Patrick had made a conspiratorial face to her behind his mother-in-law's back. They all laughed, including the girls, but Patrick had had enough of his in-laws. When he was rid of them, he would give Sara and Fred-erica as many ice creams as they wanted. So what if they have too many sweet things every now and then? Patrick spent his days helping out at the newspaper to avoid being constantly humiliated. But being near Alicia was also a bonus. He is surprised how quickly he's become infatuated by her. Just the thought of her face near to his makes him smile. The Midsummer night was magical too. He couldn't remember the last time he'd wanted to kiss anyone so badly. He needs to convince her he is serious.

He sees Alicia enter the office before she spots him. He gets up from the desk where he has been waiting and walks toward her.

'What happened to you?' Patrick says. He's trying to keep his voice level, but judging by Alicia's face, his words have too much urgency in them.

Alicia shrugs, but she looks happy, which is strange. Patrick cannot help but smile in return.

'You've had good news?'

Alicia regards Patrick for a moment. She looks over to where the editor is sitting. Patrick knows he has his door open.

'It's complicated,' she says in a low voice.

'Try me,' Patrick replies, moving closer to her. He takes in her scent of flowers and sunshine. It's just the two of them in the vast office, but Patrick knows the editor can hear everything through the open door. 'Let's have a coffee,' he says, indicating with one hand the small kitchen to the side of the office.

Alicia nods.

Inside, Patrick and Alicia sit opposite one another. Alicia, taking a deep breath, begins to talk.

Alicia didn't think she would blurt everything out to Patrick, but she realizes she has a dilemma. The only thing she could write about Daniel would be an interview with Frida on what sort of person her friend Daniel had been. She decides to tell Patrick the truth.

'Wow,' Patrick says when she's finished. 'I thought she was just a bit fat,' he says as if to himself.

Alicia slaps him on the arm, but she can't help the smile that keeps spreading over her face since Frida told her the news.

'Who's the father?' Patrick asks. When he sees Alicia's expression, he opens his mouth, then closes it and nods, 'Of course, I get it now!'

Alicia can't say anything. Talking to Patrick about Frida and the baby has made it even more real to her. Plus she doesn't know if Frida will mind her sharing the news. Although, it will soon be visible to everyone.

She realizes she doesn't care about the paper, the story or anything except protecting the baby. She's close to tears, happy tears, and instead of saying anything more, she bites her lip.

'OK?' Patrick says, leaning back in the chair.

At that very moment, Harri steps into the kitchen.

'This is very cozy,' he says.

'Just talking about the case,' Patrick says and Alicia nods.

After the editor has left, Patrick and Alicia write their thousand words without mentioning anything about Daniel's personality. They decide to simply say that he had friends on the islands and worked on Uffe's farm. The decision to mention Uffe was difficult. In the end, Patrick convinced Alicia that they had to give Harri something.

FORTY-SIX

When Patrick and Alicia walk out into the late afternoon sunshine, they are tired but relieved. It had been hard to convince Harri that the article contained everything they knew about the death of that poor boy. She could tell the editor sensed there was something they weren't telling him.

When they're outside, Patrick takes Alicia's hand. 'Look I know you don't believe me, but Mia and I are over.'

For a moment she doesn't say anything, doesn't even look at him. But she doesn't remove her hand from his either. When, at last, she lifts her pale eyes up to him, he has to fight the urge to kiss her. Instead he says, 'Why don't you let me take you out to dinner? I know a fantastic place.'

She gazes at him and hesitates. 'I don't know. I'm not dressed for going out.'

Seeing his chance, he moves a little closer to her, making sure he doesn't lose eye contact. 'It's a place in the archipelago used by sailors, so no one dresses up to go there. They cook freshly caught fish and have their own smoker for *abborre*.'

He knows most islanders who live abroad miss the local delicacy of wood-smoked perch. The fish taste different here, sweeter than the

European species, because it swims in the brackish waters of the Baltic.

Alicia bites her lower lip and again Patrick has to control himself not to bend down, take her into his arms and press his mouth onto hers. But he has to be patient. He sees she's tempted.

'I'll behave, I promise,' he says and grins.

And that does it.

'OK,' Alicia says.

Alicia is again sitting next to Patrick on his boat. This time she's wearing more suitable clothes, a pair of jeans and one of Patrick's jumpers over her T-shirt. When she saw the Henri Lloyd logo on the navy knit, she smiled, but pulled it over her head anyway. The garment smells of him, and wearing it makes Alicia feel excited and safe at the same time. They've passed Sjoland canal and Uffe's farm, and her sauna cottage. Patrick said it would take about 45 minutes to reach the small Getviken island where the restaurant is. He sends a text to the owner to make a reservation.

'As I thought, Bertil's got freshly caught *abborre* in the smoker,' Patrick told Alicia as he read the reply.

Alicia smiles at Patrick now. They are traveling fast, so there's no point in trying to talk. Instead Alicia enjoys the fresh sea breeze on her face and leans back to catch the rays of the sun.

The restaurant is as remote as Patrick had promised. Five or six tables are set in a small wooden building. The owner, Bertil, a gray-haired, shortish man with a round belly, greets Patrick and Alicia at the jetty with a wide smile. Alicia wonders if he knows Mia and whether everyone on the islands will know about Patrick and her after tonight, but she decides not to care, if Patrick doesn't. Which he doesn't seem to. Instead, he jokes and laughs with Bertil, whose lined, weather-beaten face reflects a life spent fishing in the waters around his island. He takes Alicia and Patrick around the back of the restaurant to the smoker, where the delicious smell of charred fish fills Alicia's nostrils. Suddenly she's famished.

Patrick places his hand protectively around Alicia's waist. 'Alicia here has come back home just because of this.'

Bertil laughs and Alicia explains that she's lived in London for the past eighteen years.

'Oh,' Bertil exclaims. 'Well, you won't get anything like this in England,' he says and adds, 'Now you two, aren't you thirsty after your long journey? Go inside and Miriam will give you something to drink. I'll bring these little fellows in when they're ready.'

Alicia cannot remember when she last enjoyed food so much. Before the *abborre,* which is served with new potatoes covered in chopped dill, Bertil brings them *gravad siik.* The whitefish is marinated in salt, sugar and pepper to perfection and goes perfectly with the sweet rye bread and homemade butter, which Bertil proudly explains is his wife, Miriam's, specialty.

To Alicia's relief, the restaurant is almost full with tourists. There's a large group of men from Finland who've arrived in three sailing boats, which are docked at the small harbor, as well as two other couples. Everyone is served at the same time from a small selection of freshly cooked dishes made from locally sourced fish and meat. The Finns take schnapps and sing drinking songs, and Alicia, Patrick and the other couples occasionally join in.

They sit opposite each other in a corner of the fishing cottage. The table has a small candle in the middle, but the place is shrouded in half-light due to the low ceiling and tiny windows. All evening, Patrick's eyes are fixed on Alicia's. It's impossible not to be affected by the general happy mood of the place, or Patrick's attentions.

As they are served coffee, she wants to ask Patrick so many questions about himself, Mia, and the situation. But she doesn't want to break the mood of the evening. She refuses dessert, but when she hears it's homemade *Åland's Pannkaka,* she gives in and agrees to share a portion with Patrick.

After the meal, which Patrick insists on buying, they step into the pale light of the day's end. Patrick takes her hand and they gaze beyond the small jetty to the sea. Boats rock gently against their moorings and the scenery is even more breathtaking than at home in Sjoland. The sun is going down, suffusing the horizon in flaming orange, red and yellow. The light is reflected on the still water. There is no wind at all, and the sea beyond the cove has a surface like glass.

'Shall we have a swim?' Alicia asks Patrick. It's a spur of the moment suggestion. Really, she wants to talk to Patrick about his marriage, what will happen to his daughters, and about Frida and her pregnancy. But the evening, after such an incredible day with the news of the baby, has been so wonderful that she decides the conversation can wait. Perhaps Patrick will tell her about his future plans of his own accord, when he is ready.

She can see he's surprised by her suggestion, but says, 'Wait here. There's a place around the back that's private.' He walks down to the jetty and disappears inside his boat. A moment later he comes out carrying two large striped towels and a blanket.

Neither has brought swimming costumes.

When they get to the small rocky cove, Patrick spreads the blanket on a little grassy mound between two large rocks. He gives Alicia a grin and takes his shirt off. Following his example, Alicia pulls her jeans down and her T-shirt over her head. She doesn't dare to look at Patrick when she unhooks her bra and slips her knickers off. Instead she runs into the water and shrieks as the cold hits her calves and legs. She should be used to it by now, she thinks, as she lowers herself down and begins to take long strokes, her body relaxing into the cooler temperature of the sea. Suddenly, Patrick pops up from under the water and takes hold of her. They kiss, until breathless.

'We need to swim, it's too cold,' Alicia says.

'You think so?' Patrick says and grins. He's staring at her nipples, which are half-covered by the water. 'I rather like the effect.'

Alicia laughs and splashes water over him. She turns toward the open sea and begins to make strong strokes. As usual, the sensation of the water on her body calms and excites her in equal measure. It's almost too pleasurable.

After the swim, they sit wrapped up in the towels, watching a seagull bullying a flock of smaller birds. The only sounds are the bird calls and some music from the restaurant on the other side of the island. Patrick leans over to kiss Alicia and she lets him. But when he begins to explore her naked body beneath the towel, she stops. 'What if someone sees us?'

'Hmm?' Patrick murmurs, not hearing what she said. He's caressing her left nipple while kissing her neck, his other hand moving downwards from her belly.

Alicia pushes him gently away. 'Let's get dressed and take the boat somewhere more secluded?'

FORTY-SEVEN

Liam drives along the road from Mariehamn to Sjoland, thankful that he doesn't have to stop to wait for the bridge to open. He sees from the dashboard that it's quarter to midnight, yet the horizon is still pale yellow. The nightless nights always take him by surprise. In London it would be pitch-black now—except for the streetlights of course. He's pleased how quickly he'd disembarked. He is sure they got stuck in long lines in the past, though to be honest, he doesn't really remember. Because he didn't plan this trip, he'd ended up paying over the odds for the flight to Stockholm, and for the car at Stockholm airport. He'd got to the ferry port in Kapellskär just as the previous ferry was leaving, so had a long wait for the last transport of the day. For some reason he felt he needed to get onto the islands that same night.

During his long four-hour wait he had time to think as well as sleep. Several times he wondered if he should send Alicia a message, but he resisted the temptation. He knew he had let her down with his earlier behavior, and leaving like he did, so he wasn't sure she would want to see him now. It was best to surprise her, he thought.

He wonders now, as he makes his way along the deserted road toward Hilda and Uffe's place, if—once again—he is being stupid, coming after his wife like this, but he thinks he needs to give it one more chance. He knows he's been a fool, having an affair behind Alicia's back. She is the one he wants. He needs her, especially now.

He's glad to see a light in the sauna cottage as he turns into the little lane. He thinks back to all those summers they spent here, where he never felt at ease, but could see how happy it made Alicia to be home. He could understand her delight in how Stefan took to the islands; almost as if he had been born there. Perhaps Liam was jealous of the close connection between his son and wife? He doesn't know. All he is certain of now is that he was stupid not to see how much Alicia will always mean to him, and how much the islands mean to Alicia. But he is here now. He will even try to enjoy the sauna, if that's what it takes to get Alicia back.

'Do you know that you just had sex with a soon-to-be grandmother?' Alicia says and laughs. She's in Patrick's arms and for the first time since she doesn't remember when she feels almost completely happy. They are in Alicia's sauna cottage, lying on her sofa bed, listening to the evening chorus of the birds outside. After leaving Getviken, Alicia surprised herself by suggesting they drive back to Sjoland. She's fed up with going around worrying what people think. She will tell Uffe and Hilda the truth if they see her with Patrick. She can't wait to tell them about Frida's pregnancy anyway. After the news about Stefan's baby, she's almost giddy with the possibilities for the future. And Patrick could be part of her life here.

Patrick squeezes Alicia closer and kisses the top of her head. Alicia is amazed how quickly they fell back into each other's arms, and how quickly she felt comfortable being naked with a new man. She lifts herself up on her elbows to look at him, to make sure he's real. With the movement, she reveals her breasts and Patrick gives them an approving glance.

Laughing, Alicia takes hold of his chin and says, 'What again?'

'Well, if you insist?'

As they start to kiss, they are interrupted by the sound of an engine outside. Wheels are crunching against the small lane Uffe prepared with hardcore.

FORTY-EIGHT

When Liam knocks on door, he is nervous. There's a blind covering the windows overlooking the decking, but he can make out movements inside. Next, he hears steps on the wooden floorboards of the sauna cottage.

'Who is it?' Alicia says through the door.

'It's me, Liam.'

There is a long silence, and then more commotion inside. Liam doesn't understand. It sounds as if Alicia is talking to someone, but the voices are low and Liam can't hear what is being said. It sounds as if they are speaking in Swedish.

Eventually, Alicia opens the door. The first thing Liam sees is the unmade sofa bed. To one side of it, stands a man, wearing a white shirt, rumpled and unbuttoned, with a pair of chinos, with bare feet. He thinks he recognizes him, but he can't process who he is. Liam turns to Alicia, who is also barefoot, wearing a long striped Marimekko T-shirt. The shirt, or dress, barely covers Alicia's buttocks. Liam notes how bronzed and slender her legs are, and then how ruffled her long hair is. She looks blonder and her face has a healthy tan, like the rest of her body. Is that a blush on her cheeks?

And then it hits him. Suddenly he realizes what he is seeing. As if in slow motion, he notices the man is putting on his shoes, picking up a set of car keys and walking toward Alicia, who is still holding the door open to Liam. The man bends down to kiss her—his wife, for God's sake—on the lips (*lips!*).

'Are you sure you are OK?' the man asks Alicia.

She nods and touches his arm briefly. Intimately.

The man nods to Liam, with a serious face, brushing past Liam's jacket and disappearing out of the door. Bizarrely the first thought that comes to Liam is where this man's car could be, but he ignores his stupid old brain and tries to concentrate on understanding what his eyes are seeing in front of him.

Alicia, his wife, is looking at him. The room is messy, and filled with the sofa bed. The duvet is half on top of the sheets and half on the floor; one of the two pillows is also on the floor. There's a bottle of beer on the floor too, with a glass of wine on the narrow coffee table, which has been pushed to the side of the room. Liam tries to remember when he last saw a scene like this and suddenly realizes he is thinking about his son's bedroom when he'd had friends over. They too had been drinking beer and wine, and there was a similar mess. He remembers telling them off and asking where the alcohol had come from.

'You've turned into a teenager, now, have you?' he asks Alicia.

What a stupid thing to say.

He hears the sarcasm in his voice and tries to calm himself. His thoughts are filled with the image of the man and Alicia in that bed, drinking beer and wine.

'Are you coming in?' Alicia now says. She has her arms crossed over her body, no longer holding onto the door.

Liam realizes he hasn't moved from the threshold of the sauna cottage, so he steps inside the messy room.

Alicia removes some clothing from one of the wood-framed chairs. Liam remembers joking that they must be pre-war, because the woollen fabric was so threadbare. Now his jibe seems childish, or even visceral, a betrayal of his deep resentment against Alicia's close connection to these islands.

Betrayal, that's the word.

. . .

Alicia is sitting on the bed, facing Liam. She's dumbfounded by his sudden appearance. Acutely aware of the shortness of her night-shirt, she tugs at the hem, and then lifts her legs up and tucks them underneath herself. She thinks with horror about the scent of sex that must surely linger in the air of the small cottage and fidgets with her wedding band. She's only aware of this because she sees Liam glance at her finger. She stops and forces herself to speak.

'You should have let me know you were coming.'

'Clearly,' Liam replies in the crisp, cool, sarcastic tone she used to hate.

Alicia regards her husband with what she hopes is a cool gaze. What right does he have to sit there and judge her? Obviously, it would have been better if he hadn't walked in on her and Patrick, but really, she has every right to find someone to comfort her, considering he has been sleeping with another woman for months.

'How's your little nurse?' Alicia asks. She is angry now and wants Liam to understand that she does not feel any shame. Why would she?

She can see her words take him aback. He presses his hair down at the back of his head and looks away from Alicia, toward the small window at the side of the cottage. Alicia sees he's wearing his light wool 'traveling' jacket over a crisp checked shirt, a pair of chinos and his old brown Dockers on his feet. He's not wearing any socks, and Alicia can see a few dark hairs peeking out between the tops of his shoes and trouser legs. He looks younger and slimmer, and she wonders briefly, out of old habit and before she can stop herself, if he's been feeding himself. He looks tired too, with untidy (for him) longish hair that lands on the collar of his jacket and half covers his ears. Alicia's anger subdues a little. How familiar Liam's athletic shape is, as he sits opposite her in the small sauna cottage, where they often slept.

'It's over,' Liam says, lifting his eyes to Alicia.

'That's alright then,' Alicia says. It's her turn to be sarcastic, but she regrets her words as soon as they've come out.

Liam is slumped in the chair. He's holding onto the old wooden arm rests. It's as if what he witnessed as he entered the sauna cottage is only just registering. His eyes are downcast and he looks crestfallen when he says, 'I don't suppose it matters now.'

Alicia then takes a snap decision.

'We're going to be grandparents.'

Liam straightens his back and stares at Alicia.

'What do you mean?'

'It's a miracle, I know. Frida, a girl from Åland, was Stefan's girl-friend and she is about to have his baby.'

Alicia tells Liam about the newspaper office and about Frida, Daniel, and how she found out. When Liam doesn't say anything, Alicia moves toward her husband and squats next to him, taking his hand. 'I know it's a lot to take in and believe me, I was equally shocked. Frida is a lovely girl, a bit different, but a really nice young woman at the bottom of it all. She is eight months gone, so there's not long to wait now. Just imagine, we will have a little Stefan in our lives!'

'You've got yourself a job here? Does that mean you are planning to stay? And leave me?'

Alicia gets up and goes back to the bed again.

'I'm not sure. It's a long story. I literally popped in to enquire about freelance work and they offered me a part-time job.' She is smiling, but seeing Liam's serious face, she adds, 'I didn't know what to do after you left. I didn't want to come back to London, so ... but that's not impor-tant now. We are going to become grandparents. If you wish to be involved, that is.'

Liam brushes his hand over his face. 'Are you sure this isn't some kind of ... hoax, or joke, or something?'

Alicia takes a deep breath.

'Never mind,' she says, trying to control her voice, which has suddenly started trembling. 'You don't need to believe any of it.' Alicia is quiet for a moment while she fights the tears that are welling up inside. 'For me, it's the most wonderful thing that has happened to me since ...' Alicia swallows and manages to keep her composure. 'I will welcome this little miracle into the world and into my life, but I know for certain we can do it without you.'

With this Alicia gets up and goes over to the door. 'And now I think you should leave.'

. . .

Liam sits in his rental car, driving toward Mariehamn. He is numb and shocked by the man he found with Alicia. He just cannot process it in his mind. How could she have begun an affair with someone? And so soon? Liam knows he hasn't got any rights to Alicia, even if she still is his wife, but he is devastated that she has betrayed him.

He is tired and suddenly enormously hungry. As he approaches the junction that will take him into the city, he sees a van selling Finnish meat pastries and hot dogs. He drives over and orders a pie with a sausage. There are a few youngsters, swaying and clearly drunk, eating hot dogs out of greaseproof paper. They watch silently as Liam pays and takes his pie to eat inside the car.

He wonders if his son used to come to this fast-food joint when they were here on holiday, while he and Alicia were sleeping in their bed in the sauna cottage, unaware of his nightly escapes. Could it be true, Liam wonders? Could there really be a girl here who was impregnated by Stefan?

But when?

He knows that the last time Stefan was on the islands was in August last year. Whatever happened must have happened in the late fall. Is this girl (was it the same girl Stefan had fallen in love with when he was fifteen?) claiming that Stefan traveled over just before he was killed? Or did she come over to London? That is more likely, Liam thinks, but he shakes his head at the thought. How easy it is for someone to claim to a grieving mother that her son has miraculously made her pregnant? Surely it must be a cruel sting.

Liam decides that he will not travel back to London on the early morning ferry as planned, but will take a room in one of the hotels in town and find out the truth. He will need help. Perhaps Hilda will help him? She has always had a soft spot for Liam. But first he needs to get some sleep.

As soon as Liam has shut the door behind him, Alicia puts her head in her hands and takes a few deep breaths. She is so angry and also sad that she doesn't know whether to scream, laugh or cry. Instead she gets up and pummels the bed with one of the pillows from the floor. A ping on her phone stops her.

'Are you OK?'

The message is from Patrick. Alicia stares at the words displayed at the top of the screen. She asked Patrick to leave when she discovered it was Liam standing outside the sauna cottage. She now wishes she hadn't. And then she realizes that she wouldn't talk to him about how she is feeling even if he was there. What is she feeling? She is so confused that she doesn't know her own mind.

Patrick will not understand the connection she has with Liam. In spite of everything, their marriage has been a good one. Liam was a good father, he is kind, generous and intelligent. And even funny. Or, at least they used to laugh a lot together before. Before Stefan was taken away from them.

She knows the affair with the nurse is partly her fault. She drove him away, not letting him into her own grief. Or comfort him in his. All she could do was keep herself breathing through the first days, weeks and months after the accident. Connie always says during their sessions that breathing is natural, but Alicia never feels she can take the air flowing through her body for granted. It's getting easier now, but only since she's been here, at home on the islands.

What about Liam? Is he telling the truth about the nurse? Is it finished? And why was he so skeptical about Stefan's baby? Now her anger has abated, she hopes Liam's reaction to the news about Frida and her pregnancy was simply shock, and that with time he'll come around. He would be a wonderful grandfather, as he was a father, Alicia is sure of it. And turning up like he did tonight must mean that he wants their marriage to work.

Alicia puts her head in her hands and takes deep breaths. She goes over to the small sink and fills a glass with water. When she gets back to the bed, she sees her phone. She wants to give Liam one more chance. Alicia finds his number on her phone and types in a message. But when she's done, a message pings.

'I'm out of town during the day tomorrow, but I need to see you. Meet me 6pm at the jetty in East Harbor. Kisses, Patrick.'

Alicia looks at the message and shakes her head. How can he think that they will continue seeing each other while Liam, who is still her husband, is in town? She can't decide what to say, so she resolves to get some sleep and reply in the morning. She turns the lights off. In the semi-dark, listening to the wildfowl calling to each other, she wonders how her life has got so complicated. Then when she remembers the shape of Frida's round belly, she thinks about the baby, and how wonderful it will be to hold a small version of Stefan in her arms. She has been given a new chance at life and she is going to take it. If she has to carry on alone, without Liam, or Patrick, so be it.

FORTY-NINE

Svarta Katten used to be Stefan's favorite café in Mariehamn when he was little. He grew out of the place when he hit his teens, but Alicia is certain he still had a soft spot for the *Ålands pannkaka*, the oven-baked semolina pudding with jam that the little café was famous for. As she climbs the stone steps to what is really just a sand-rendered residential house, she remembers the last time they visited the place together. She smiles as she recalls that Stefan wanted coffee instead of Fanta with his pudding, and how this simple request made Alicia realize her boy was growing into a young man. Alicia takes a deep breath and selects an open cheese and salad sandwich from the glass cabinet.

Inside the café, she sees that Frida is already sitting at one of the sofas in the largest of the small rooms that make up *Svarta Katten*. The interior is a little like a grandmother's house, with several tiny parlors leading into one another, with mis-matching sofas, comfy chairs and tables scattered through the small spaces. Lace curtains hang from the wood-framed windows, increasing the sense of being in someone's home rather than a café.

Alicia had the idea to meet here last night. She knew Liam would know the place and she wanted him to remember how much Stefan loved the islands.

'How are you feeling?' Alicia says as she sits down opposite Frida. She pushes the sandwich toward the girl. 'In case you didn't have time for breakfast.'

She wants to kiss Frida on the cheek, but she's afraid she may be appearing too familiar, or oppressive. They don't know each other well, after all. The sandwich is enough of a risk, she thinks, but Frida accepts it without a word. Although they have the large belly, now visibly a baby bump, very much in common, they only met a few weeks ago.

Frida doesn't smile when she nods and says, 'Yeah, OK.' She does, however, add, 'Thanks,' as she takes the sandwich.

She's wearing a green dress with black capri-length leggings underneath. She has large yellow hoops in her ears and her signature Doc Martens on her feet. This time they are red. With her blue hair, she is not unlike a human kaleidoscope. Alicia smiles at Frida. It seems she is no longer trying to hide her pregnancy, which Alicia takes as a good sign.

'Have the police been in touch?' Alicia asks, but Frida shakes her head.

'I've decided to go round there after I've had this,' Frida says, tucking into the open sandwich.

'That's a good idea. They just want to find out when you last saw Daniel and that kind of stuff. If you want, I can come with you?'

Frida regards Alicia for a moment, but before she has time to reply Liam appears in the doorway, carrying a tray with coffee and a plate of *Ålands Pannkaka*.

He looks unshaven and dishevelled, with red eyes, but Alicia realizes she is glad to see him. She's glad to have his support with Frida.

Liam can't believe what he sees in front of him. He smiles at Alicia and nods to the girl, who seems to be wearing every color of the rainbow—including in her hair. And this person is supposed to have had a loving relationship—or a relationship at least—with his son? No way, he thinks, and sits down next to Alicia.

'This is Stefan's father, Liam,' Alicia says in English, and the girl stares at him. Her round face doesn't betray much, although perhaps there's mistrust around the corners of her eyes? Liam is amazed how somebody like that could have fooled Alicia. She is an astute journalist. Even if she hasn't been a full-time investigative journalist since Stefan's death, she's still very aware of what is going on in the world. How can she be so gullible? Thank goodness Liam came over before any more damage could be done, or any money has changed hands.

'So you knew our son?' Liam asks, trying to take the edge out of his voice.

'What's this?' Frida's English is only slightly broken. She doesn't look at either of them but lifts a canvas holdall from under the table and gets up. It's a difficult maneuver because of her extended belly, which has got trapped between the curved back velour sofa and the coffee table.

'Frida,' Alicia gets up too and tries to take the girl's hand. She speaks in Swedish, 'Don't go! Liam came over last night and I thought you two should meet.'

Frida wrangles her arm out of Alicia's grip and continues to make her way out of the café. Now a pair of young tourists have got wind of their situation, and the English being spoken, and are staring at Liam and Alicia. They say something in Swedish to the girl, but she shakes her head and almost runs out of the room.

'For goodness sake!' Alicia says to Liam and runs after the girl.

The two youngsters, two lads about Stefan's age, continue to stare at Liam, who sips his coffee and cuts a slice of the sickly pudding. He tries to smile at the boys reassuringly. 'Nothing to worry about.' They go back to their own conversation, and Liam puts down his fork. He bought the *Ålands Pannkaka* for Alicia's sake, to show her he remembered it was Stefan's favorite, but it's no use to him now. It's far too sweet for him. Like so many things in this place, he just doesn't get it. How could anyone think the milky desert, something between a rice pudding and a French clafoutis, but with a skin as thick as a rhino's, could be considered a delicacy?

Liam waits for ten minutes, aware of the glances from his young neighbors. It's embarrassing being left like that in a café, not eating his *pannkaka,* he thinks. After another five minutes, he decides to make a dignified exit.

FIFTY

Although the sun is blazing down from a cloudless sky, the wind has got up when Alicia comes out of the *Ålandsbladet* office that afternoon. 'Alicia!'

Squinting against the sun, Liam is standing a few paces away, across the small road, by the corner of Arkipelag Hotel. Is that where he is staying, Alicia wonders. He's still wearing the same chinos he had on that morning, and is holding the same jacket in his hand, but he's changed into a dark green T-shirt. The shirt shows off Liam's muscular arms, something she used to find attractive. It was Alicia's favorite shirt. Is that why he's wearing it now?

'What are you doing here?' Alicia asks when she reaches him.

They are standing facing each other. Alicia glances around; she's afraid Patrick will pop out from somewhere. He's been bombarding her with messages all day. She managed to reply evasively to one of them, while also fending off the editor's requests for news of the investigation into the Romanian boy's death. Harri also asked after Patrick, who didn't turn up at the paper that day. Alicia and the editor had been the only reporters there. Frida had called in sick again, and Alicia wondered if the girl had come clean about her situation, because Harri didn't seem to worry about her absence as much as he did about Patrick's. It was the strangest situation Alicia had come across: Patrick, who didn't even work for the paper seemed to be held more accountable than the permanent staff.

So much for my part-time post, Alicia thinks, but she doesn't say anything to Harri. She needs the job in Åland more than ever now, if she is to stay and support Frida with the baby on her own. Liam's performance in *Svarta Katten* that morning had been appalling. And infuriating.

'I would like to talk with you,' Liam says. He glances at his watch. It's just past 4pm. 'We could have a beer?'

Alicia looks up at Liam. She's forgotten how tall he is, and how comfortable she feels with him. Although she's still angry at the bloody man for frightening Frida. But she understands that Liam has a lot to cope with suddenly. And she feels guilty. She should have at least told him she was moving on with the job. And Patrick. Possibly.

As it is, he's had a completely wasted journey to the islands. Unless he wants to see Frida again, that is.

'I was planning to see if my mother can give me a lift home, and then call Frida,' Alicia says. After the morning's meeting with the girl, Alicia has decided against pressurizing her with messages during the day. But she needs to find out if Frida has been to see the police, and how she is feeling. And if she has told Harri about the baby.

'It's Frida I wanted to talk to you about,' Liam says. His voice is calm and he looks serious, but his expression is open and his eyes have lines of concern around them. He seems different from how he'd been that morning. Perhaps he's getting used to the idea of Stefan's baby?

'Ok, I'll message Hilda to say I don't need a lift.'

'It's already done, I spoke to her earlier in the shop,' Liam says, and he takes hold of Alicia's elbow to lead her across the little garden and down the steps toward the East Harbor. *As if she is one of his patients.*

'What, you saw my mum?' Alicia is flabbergasted. Liam and Hilda have always got on well, but seeing his mother-in-law without Alicia would have been awkward in the circumstances. Of course, neither Hilda nor Uffe knew about her involvement with Patrick, but at least Hilda was aware (and Alicia assumed she had told Uffe) that Liam had left the islands because of a row, and that their marriage was in trouble. But neither knew about the baby.

If there was one thing Liam hated more than anything else, it was an awkward situation. A face-to-face conversation with Hilda today would rank as very uncomfortable in Liam's mind, she's sure of it.

'Is that OK?' Liam asks, not answering Alicia's question and pointing toward the floating restaurant, *von Knorring*. Liam and Alicia had often gone for a drink in the pub on the top deck during their holidays here.

Alicia glances toward the jetties and spots Patrick's boat. It seems to be empty and locked up. She lets out a sigh of relief. A confrontation between the two men is the last thing she needs now.

'Shall we go up to the top?' Liam is behaving very strangely, Alicia thinks, but she nods in agreement and they ascend the wooden steps to the upper deck of the old steamer. The ship is all shiny mahogany, with tilting wooden decks, round brass portholes, and tables made out of barrels. While Alicia selects a seat at the stern, which is covered and a little more private, Liam heads for the bar. Before he goes, he asks Alicia, 'What will you have? White wine or *Lonkero*?'

Alicia smiles. She's touched that Liam remembers the Finnish bitter lemon and gin drink.

'OK, I'll have a *Lonkero*,' she says and smiles.

'Cheers!' Liam says as he sits down. He is sounding far too cheerful for the circumstances. What on earth has got into him?

But Alicia doesn't want to say anything. She nods and pours her drink into a glass. She takes a sip of the drink. Boy, it tastes good. It's carbonated, bitter and sweet at the same time. She hasn't had a *Lonkero* since the first sauna evening. Usually Hilda buys cans and cans of it for her, but this year she seems to have forgotten. As has Alicia.

'How are you?' Liam asks. He looks deeply into Alicia's eyes in a way she cannot remember him doing for a long time. There's concern in his eyes again and suddenly Alicia wishes she could just lean her head on Liam's shoulder and tell him all her troubles. And share her excitement for Stefan's baby.

'You haven't asked me how I am—and meant it—for a long time,' she says instead. She is speaking in a low voice, and Liam pushes his upper body over the solid wooden table to hear her better. Their eyes meet again, closer this time. Alicia can see Liam hasn't shaved. There are prickly dark hairs all over his chin and some on his neck. His lips look dry, but it's his eyes that have changed. Although she can see he's tired, there's an honesty, a clarity to the green pupils that she hasn't seen for months. He is really looking at Alicia, truly seeing her.

Alicia moves her face away. Guilt, which she thought she didn't possess, suddenly rises and she has an uncomfortable, constricting sensation in her chest. She can't breathe. *Don't think about Patrick. He's not important. Stefan's baby is.*

'You don't believe Frida, do you?' Alicia says when she lifts her eyes to Liam again.

Liam shifts on his seat and moves away from her. He takes a swig of his beer.

He's buying time.

'It is rather surprising, isn't it?' Liam says after a few moments have passed.

'I knew it,' Alicia says and feels a new anger rise inside her. It hits her head like a wave. 'But I don't care what you think.' Alicia gets up, but Liam takes her hand and pulls her gently back down.

'We need to talk about this, don't we?' he says equitably.

Alicia exhales. How can she not agree to his reasonableness? She sits down again, but folds her arms over her chest, refusing to look at her husband.

'C'mon.' Liam tries to calm her down by leaning into her again and forcing her to look into his eyes. 'It's a shock, that's all,' he says in his reassuring doctor voice.

Alicia remembers how she used to love that confident, low tone that Liam used if Stefan was ill with a simple cold, or when he had chicken pox at the age of ten and Alicia had been beside herself with worry. When the rash first appeared, she'd been sure it was meningitis, but Liam convinced her that they should monitor him through the night, taking turns to take his temperature and peer into his eyes. The poor boy was exhausted the next day, when the first blisters developed and Liam could diagnose him with certainty. He'd also used that voice when he'd 'treated' her migraines when they first met, and many times since. That voice was one of the reasons Alicia fell in love with Liam.

'Just imagine if it had been the other way around? You would not have believed me if I said I'd found someone who was carrying our late son's baby without first looking into it properly? Your journalistic brain would want to analyse it and search for evidence first, right?'

Alicia knew Liam had a point.

'But we won't know the truth until the baby is born, and then we'd have to ask Frida to do a DNA test. I'm not convinced she'll be prepared to do that.'

Liam finishes his beer and nods at Alicia's bottle.

'One more?'

Alicia agrees to have another drink, and when she watches Liam at the bar, his familiar, muscular, shape leaning on the mahogany ledge, she wonders if he is right to be skeptical about Frida. He is, of course, right. Alicia had not looked for any evidence of Frida's claim. It *could* be a cruel con, of course. Perhaps the father was the Romanian boy, something impossible to prove without a test on the baby. The police will have Daniel's DNA, but could she convince Ebba to share that information with them? No, it would be better to compare the tests with her and Liam's DNA.

Suddenly Alicia remembers the envelope containing Stefan's hair that Liam had handed her the morning of Stefan's funeral. Alicia had spent that day in a daze, medicated up to her eyeballs with the pills Liam had prescribed her, but the one event she recalls clearly is when Liam came into their bedroom, dressed in a dark suit with a white shirt and black tie. The sight of him took Alicia's breath away. When he handed her the brown envelope and she looked inside and saw the blond strands of hair resting at the bottom of the envelope, she flung herself at him and they'd held each other close for a long time.

Alicia is brought back to the present by Liam sitting down in front of her. He places the drink on the table and takes Alicia's hand. 'Can we start again? My flight back to London isn't until next week, so I have a few days to sort things out.'

Alicia is surprised: Liam never takes time off at short notice. His foremost concern is his patients, often to the detriment of his family. Is that what Alicia has always felt? Second best to Liam's patients? Alicia shakes her head; no, she loves the passion he has for his profession. It is something she wishes she could have had too. An important career would have helped her after they lost Stefan.

'You staying at the Arkipelag?' Alicia asks.

Liam nods. He's looking down at his beer, still holding Alicia's fingers in his hand. His expression is serious when he lifts his head up. 'I want you back.' Liam looks deeply into Alicia's eyes. She can see he is holding his breath. Again she is taken aback by the new honesty, a fresh directness in his gaze.

'I'm not sure,' Alicia begins, but Liam interrupts her. 'I don't want you to make a decision now. I just wanted you to know how I feel.' Liam lets go of her hand and smiles at her.

'I don't know what to say.' Alicia takes a sip of her *Lonkero*.

Liam gives a little cough, and glancing at the silver Rolex watch he'd bought when he got his first consultant's job, says in a stronger, more practical voice, 'I thought we could eat here tonight? It'll give us some more time to talk?'

FIFTY-ONE

Patrick is standing on the jetty. The wind has turned to a northerly and he zips up his windbreaker. He scans the people walking on the wooden boardwalk, at the same time keeping an eye out for the steps that run down by the Arkipelag and the newspaper offices. He thinks about the meeting with his lawyers in Stockholm that day, but his mind goes back to Alicia and her body pressed against his.

There is something about her fragility when he touches her. The pale, soft skin on her belly, her inner thighs and her pert, small breasts. She reacts to him in a way that he's never experienced with a woman before. Patrick shifts position as he feels himself getting aroused. Where is she? He checks his watch and sees it's nearly quarter past. He pulls out his phone and checks WhatsApp. Alicia still hasn't answered his messages. He sent one on the ferry back from Stockholm, telling her how much he was looking forward to seeing her later. He didn't think the lack of a reply meant anything; he saw she'd read them and assumed she just didn't get a chance to message him back.

And then he sees them.

He spots Alicia first and then, just before he raises his hand to wave at her, very close behind, Liam emerges from the depths of the von Knorring restaurant. They are walking along the ship's dark wooden deck, side by side. They are laughing, and as they come to the small gangway connecting the boat to the old stone jetty Liam takes hold of Alicia's arm and helps her safely to the other side. On the jetty, he puts Alicia's hand in the crock of his arm. They proceed like this, like the married couple they are, toward Arkipelag Hotel and after a brief conversation at the door, go inside.

Patrick doesn't know what to do. Naturally, he knew Alicia would need to talk to Liam, after he turned up last night and saw them together. Earlier that evening, she'd told him how Liam had been unfaithful, just like Mia. She cried when she recounted how she had found out, through some woman working as a volunteer at the hospital. And that the affair had started after their son was so tragically killed. From how she behaved, and from her words, he assumed she would not want anything to do with the man. Yet here she was walking arm in arm, laughing—*laughing*—with him. Could she be that fickle? Or had he completely misread her?

Patrick starts to walk toward the hotel but is stopped by a sudden surge of traffic. He glances at his watch and realizes the last ferry of the day has arrived. He curses under his breath as he watches the cars speed along the coastal road. Most contain holidaymakers from Sweden, their vehicles laden with bags and luggage. Patrick thinks he's already sick of this bloody place after only a few weeks.

His thoughts return to his meeting in Stockholm that morning. Mia's family have offered him a handsome settlement, but they want him to leave the islands. He can keep his boat, and the flat in Mariehamn, but he's only to use it for eight weeks a year. They want him to stay in Stockholm, ideally. His lawyer, Harriet Wisktrand, told him that the settlement was very generous. But Patrick told the woman that he wanted to stay in Mariehamn. He wants shared custody of the girls.

Harriet had sighed at Patrick's comment. She'd told Patrick before that the Eriksson's counsel was a famous man, reputed to be one of the best divorce lawyers in Sweden.

'It's up to you, but I would say this is an unusually good offer,' she'd said, closing the file of papers. 'It depends how quickly you want this to be over, and how much you want to pay in legal fees,' she added.

That morning, leaving the lawyer's offices in Hammarby, a new area where high-rise offices overlooked the straits separating the southern part of Stockholm, Patrick went straight to see his boss at *Journalen*.

'I'm making it easy for you,' he told the balding editor.

'What?' he said, finally looking up from his computer screen. For the whole time Patrick had been standing in his office the man had been tapping at his keyboard. 'Sit down,' he said and he rolled his chair to face Patrick.

But his old editor had not managed to convince Patrick to stay. Patrick would never get to write that prize-worthy article, so he might as well take the redundancy money and run. It was time he moved on.

FIFTY-TWO

E bba stands in the doorway to the large newspaper office. She's leaning casually against the frame, looking at Alicia as if judging her. Alicia wonders how long she's been there, then gets up smartly and walks toward the police detective.

'So I hear you're going to be a grandmother,' Ebba says as she sits down at the round kitchen table.

'Coffee?' Alicia asks. She smiles at Ebba and nods, although having spent yesterday in Liam's company, she is less sure that the baby Frida is carrying is actually Stefan's.

'Any news on the Romanian boy, Daniel?' she asks Ebba as she sits down at the other side of the table from her old schoolfriend.

'Do you believe Frida is carrying your son's baby?' Ebba asks instead, and Alicia tries to suppress her annoyance at the woman's habit of answering a question with one of her own. And of interfering in her life.

'I guess so,' Alicia says, but seeing Ebba raise an eyebrow, she adds, 'Yes, I do,' trying to sound more assertive.

'Hmm,' Ebba says. She regards Alicia and takes a sip from her mug of coffee. Her eyes do not leave Alicia's and once again Alicia feels she's the one under suspicion.

'The pregnancy and your son's fatherhood seem very convenient now you're back on the islands and your son no longer ...' Ebba stops mid-sentence as someone opens the door to the kitchen.

The policewoman, who's seated with her back to the window, facing the entrance to the small kitchen, raises her eyebrows, as if she is conducting an interview in her own office. But when she sees who it is, she says, rather gently after what Alicia thinks she's just inferred, 'Ah, Frida, how are you?'

Frida walks into the room. She nods, and says in a surly, teenage voice, 'OK.' She gives Alicia a glance, not catching her eye. Still pissed at me then, Alicia thinks and smiles. That tone reminds her so strongly of Stefan, but she's surprised at her overwhelming feeling of pleasure at the memory, rather than sadness. She recalls Stefan standing in their kitchen in London with his back to her, unwilling to accept something, or not wanting to show he agreed with her, or concede that she, his mother, had been right all along. The recollection is so strong and warm, that it catches her breath.

Ebba, as usual, notices something is going on. 'You OK there?'

Alicia nods and smiles at the policewoman, who's now gazing up at Frida. Alicia senses that the two have agreed on something, or that they have come to some kind of conclusion or resolution, but she doesn't wish to rock the boat with Frida by asking questions. Last night she made Liam promise that if she can convince Frida to meet with them before he leaves the islands, he will listen to Frida and not say a word.

Briefly, Alicia's thoughts go back to the previous night. It was good to spend time with Liam. He was attentive, listening to her talk about Stefan and Frida, and her worries about her mother's finances and rows with Uffe. And she'd been able to tell Liam about seeing the Romanian boy's body, and how it had brought back her grief, and her regret that she hadn't visited Stefan at the morgue.

'There was nothing to see,' Liam had said. His eyes had been sad and he'd taken Alicia's hands into his. They were in Liam's hotel room, sitting opposite each other in two armchairs. The room overlooked the East Harbor, where Alicia knew Patrick's boat was moored, but she didn't look toward the jetty where she knew Patrick would be waiting for her. She and Liam had decided to go upstairs when they saw the Arkipelag restaurant was hosting a karaoke evening. It was too loud for them to hear each other shout, let alone talk.

'I was protecting you,' Liam continued, leaning closer to Alicia.

Alicia lifted her eyes, which had been fixed on her fingers as they rested inside Liam's palms. How many times had they sat like this, but it had felt different, as if it was the first time Alicia had been held by Liam. She had examined his bony fingers, looking at the hairs growing on his hands. She had always loved his hands, the hands that had saved so many patients. The hands that had not, however, been able to save their son.

'But that was a decision I should have made myself,' Alicia whispered in a low tone. She wasn't going to cry, even if talking about Stefan, with Liam particularly, brought a lump to her throat. But there were no tears. Perhaps she had finished crying and there was nothing left in her?

Liam's eyes were sad too, and Alicia could see there were tears welling up behind them.

'I'm sorry,' he had said, and for the first time in months, years, Alicia believed that he really, truly, was sorry.

All evening Liam had acted like the man she married all those years ago.

It was after 11pm when Liam put Alicia into a taxi outside the hotel. There had been a strong wind, and the riggings of the many boats in the harbor opposite had rattled against the masts. Alicia pushed away thoughts of Patrick's proximity. As she stood facing Liam, she wondered if he would try to kiss her goodbye; a gesture they had made hundreds, thousands of times during their marriage, but Liam had just squeezed her arms with his hands. When Alicia didn't resist his touch, he pulled her toward him and hugged her. She had promised to meet him for lunch at *Svarta Katten* the next day, today at one o'clock.

Suddenly the kettle comes to a boil, bringing Alicia back to the kitchen in the newspaper office. Nobody speaks a word while Frida prepares a herbal tea for herself. With a quick glance at Alicia and Ebba leaning over the small table, Frida then leaves the room.

Immediately after they hear the door close, Ebba turns to Alicia.

'We've solved the case, thought you might like to know.'

'Is this an official statement?'

'The police chief will give a press conference in about an hour,' Ebba glances at her watch, a large manly one that seems unnecessarily complicated for just time-keeping. Perhaps she's a diver, Alicia wonders.

'I might as well save you a trip to the HQ.'

Alicia scrambles to get her phone out; she didn't expect this. Everything is done so differently in Åland. She cannot imagine any police in London, or Stockholm for that matter, would permit an official press conference to be bypassed like this.

'Can I record you?' she asks when she has unlocked her phone.

Ebba nods. Alicia gazes at the policewoman's face, and realizes she looks triumphant.

'It was a simple accident.' The police woman says, crossing her arms over her chest.

After Ebba has left the newspaper office, Alicia puts her earphones in and listens to the policewoman's account of Daniel's accident. According to Ebba, the boy had been in a rowing boat on his own, fishing, when his rod had got stuck in the reeds around the little island where his body was found. They assumed he'd lost his balance and, with the weight of his cast, drowned. The breakthrough came when they found the rod floating above the line and discovered the deserted rowing boat in a cove a few kilometers away, where it had drifted. There was Daniel's DNA all over the vessel, and some marks from the cast on his leg. Frida had confirmed that the boy used to go fishing alone in the evenings, because he didn't have a local permit. According to Frida, he earned so little on Uffe's farm that he had to fish for food, but he also sold some of his catch to a few locals.

Alicia takes her headphones out and wonders if these locals included her stepfather. Poor lad, Alicia thinks, and wishes she could have helped him when he was still alive. She resolves to talk to Uffe; surely he must know he pays the boys too little?

At that moment Harri, the editor, walks past and seeing Alicia says, 'What are you doing here? There's a press conference at the police station!'

Alicia fills him in and plays Ebba's statement.

'This is the headline. On my desk in an hour?'

Alicia nods, replaces her headphones and starts transcribing Ebba's words.

FIFTY-THREE

Liam is sitting in the restaurant *Club Marin* overlooking the jetties of the East Harbor. He is scanning the boats, tied to the ten or so wooden piers, wondering which one belongs to Patrick. He's nursing a beer, at eleven o'clock in the morning. Stepping onto the decking of the sailing club, he had remembered the many times he'd come here with Alicia while Hilda babysat Stefan. He remembers the time when there was a live band, playing old Finnish classics and he had made a complete fool of himself trying to lead Alicia in a tango. She had laughed, pulling her head back, letting her long, blond curls fall down her back. Suddenly no longer minding his awkwardness on the dance floor, he'd taken hold of Alicia and spun her around the space.

Later, when Stefan was old enough, he and Stefan would come here together to admire the boats, leaving Alicia and Hilda to do their shopping. Those holidays had been good, and Liam knows he should have appreciated them more instead of complaining about the food, the rudeness of the locals, and the Finnish and Swedish tourists, or the high prices in the restaurants. He realizes that he didn't even notice how much his beer cost today.

His thoughts about the past come to a halt when he spots the man walking along the jetty. His gait is a confident one, reinforced by his tall and impressive stature. Patrick is slim, with wide shoulders and a rugged look that comes from his sun- and sea-bleached hair. Liam can see why any woman would fall for this guy. But Alicia? She is intelligent and Liam is surprised that she would go for looks alone. *Perhaps the bloke is an Einstein too, although looks and brains rarely go together,* Liam thinks, as he drowns the dregs of his beer.

Patrick doesn't spot Liam until he's standing next to him on the jetty. He can't help the sarcastic smile that forms on his lips; a jealous ex is just what he needs now!

'Can I talk to you?' Alicia's husband says in English. Patrick notices the man firming his foothold on the moving pier. He's standing with his feet artificially wide apart, with his chest pushed forward, as if he's preening for a fight.

Patrick nods and stretches out his hand, replying also in English, 'What about?'

The man ignores his hand and says, 'You know perfectly well.'

Patrick sighs.

'I want to talk to you about Alicia,' the man says after a short silence.

Patrick gestures toward his boat. They're standing right by *Mirabella*. Patrick steps onboard and begins to uncover the cockpit seats. 'I promise we won't leave the jetty,' he says glancing back at Liam.

I can spot a non-sailor a mile off.

After a while Liam steps uncertainly onto the deck and resumes his legs-wide-apart stance. He goes to take hold of the gunwale, but sees him watching, so sits down instead. Patrick smiles and opens the fridge. He pulls out two cans of beer and hands one of them to the man. He opens the tin and takes a swig.

'So, what is it? You left your woman and now you want her back, that it?'

Liam holds the unopened can, looking down at his feet. He's wearing a pair of Dockers at least, Patrick thinks.

Trying to blend in and look the part. But anyone can see he's not from the islands by his tidy checked shirt tucked into his pristine chinos.

'We've been married for 18 years,' Liam says in a quiet, calm voice, looking directly at Patrick. When he doesn't reply, the man continues, 'And we were happy—very happy—until,' here he pauses for a moment. 'Until we lost Stefan.'

Patrick holds Liam's gaze. He can't but feel sorry for him. He read somewhere in a magazine article that *there are no words, not in English, Spanish, Arabic, or Hebrew, that have been invented to explain what it's like to lose a child.* How true, he thought, and the most overwhelming sense of gratitude, an almost spiritual experience, for having escaped that inexplicable grief, overwhelms him. He remembers how happy he and Mia had been at their luck. Of course, he now thinks bitterly, he didn't then know about their doomed future together. That reminds him of what he knows about Liam.

'So happy that you had have an affair?'

The expression on Liam's face tightens.

'You don't understand anything,' he says, getting up. His movement makes the boat shift, and he takes hold of the edge of the seat to keep his balance.

Patrick puts his can down and opens up his palms. 'Look, if Alicia had been happy, she wouldn't have turned to me,' he says. He has no desire to fight with the guy. 'She's her own woman.'

'That she certainly is,' Liam says and steps off onto the jetty. But instead of walking away, he turns back toward Patrick. 'She's been through a lot. I just don't want her to get hurt again. What I really wanted to ask you is how well do you know Frida Anttila?'

The sun is in Patrick's eyes and he lifts his hand to shade them in order to see the man's face. Liam is standing slightly above him.

'She's a good kid.'

'Would she lie about the baby's father?'

Patrick thinks for a moment, 'No, I don't think so. Why would she?'

Liam sighs and says, 'Money, of course.'

'She doesn't need money! Her dad is loaded.'

Liam stares at Patrick for a moment. 'Thank you for your time.'

'No worries,' Patrick says, but Liam doesn't hear him because he's already striding along the jetty toward the road and the low buildings in the center of Mariehamn.

FIFTY-FOUR

Hilda is shivering inside the shop in spite of the sun blazing down from a clear sky outside. It's one of those early July days when it was possible to imagine she was somewhere completely different, like Estepona in Spain, where Uffe had taken her during their first year together.

Hilda sighs. Before their marriage, when Uffe was attentive, booking the best table at the Arkipelag, they'd dance the night away. They would often be the last ones in their group of friends to go home.

Uffe has lived on the islands all his life, so knows almost everyone, and in those days they had a large social circle. Slowly, this circle had disappeared. One of the couples now lives in Spain half of the year, several have since divorced and moved to Finland or Sweden. The rest are such miserable company that Hilda refuses to go out with them. Uffe has the odd beer out with his old classmates in town, but that's it.

The lack of a social life, however, is not the reason Hilda is out of sorts this morning. Naturally the death of the Romanian boy has upset both of them, as has pressure to repay her loan to the Russians, which Uffe eventually agreed to foot. But it's the news that her son-in-law delivered yesterday afternoon that is playing on Hilda's mind. Hilda's English isn't as good as it used to be, but she got the main points of Liam's revelations, she's sure of that.

Hilda can't believe that her wonderful grandson would have associated himself with someone like Frida Anttila. She hasn't spoken to the girl much but has seen her around. She would be difficult to miss with her awful spiky hair and strange clothes. What is it with young women these days, Hilda wonders, and she shakes her head. She looks around her shop, at the beautiful things she has filled it with, none of which the girls in the town want to buy, it seems.

Uffe's ultimatum to shut the shop down at the end of the summer if her sales don't improve plays on her mind briefly, but the prospect of having a great-grandchild by that awful girl consumes her. She knows her mother of course.

Sirpa Anttila worked at Arkipelag as a waitress for years and years. She's from Finland like Hilda, but more than ten years younger. She had Frida at a late age and Hilda remembers the rumors about who the father was, fueled when she suddenly moved into one of the expensive new apartments in the center of town. A rich Russian oligarch, they said, but neither Hilda or Uffe ever saw her with anyone. She brought up Frida alone.

The poor woman became an alcoholic, although no one knew until one day she had a stroke right in the middle of the Arkipelag restaurant. Uffe had taken Hilda for a rare night out just before Christmas a couple of years ago, when they heard the most awful noise. The tray of empty glasses and bottles that Sirpa had been carrying clattered to the floor and the woman fell down like a marionette whose strings had been cut. Frida, who had been in Stockholm Gymnasium studying for her Baccalaureate exams at the time, immediately came home to take care of her, but couldn't cope in the end. Sirpa Anttila was now in the old people's home in town. Hilda heard from one of Uffe's friends that the girl visits her mother every day and that the bills for the home are paid by an unknown benefactor.

Frida's Russian father?

Hilda pulls her sand-colored cashmere shawl tighter around her shoulders and thinks about the awful possibility that her great-grandchild may have Russian blood. And that's not all. Hilda is nowhere near old enough to become a great-grandmother! Alicia herself is only 38!

No, the whole affair cannot be true, Hilda thinks. Where is the evidence that Stefan had been with the girl? Hilda, nor Uffe, had ever seen them together. Plus, they were so young! Hilda suddenly remembers that she herself fell pregnant with Alicia at the age of seventeen. She gave birth two weeks after her eighteenth birthday.

But times were different then, she thinks. At least Alicia's father did the right thing and married her. That he then left when Alicia was only a baby is another matter. Good riddance, Hilda had thought at the time. He was a selfish pig of a man and Hilda is glad she kept him away from Alicia all these years. In the beginning, it hadn't been hard, but when Alicia began to grow up and start asking questions, Hilda had decided to tell her he was dead. It was as good as true, anyway. She had hidden all the letters that her old landlady in Finland had forwarded.

In those days it was so much easier, without all this internet activity. Luckily, in the end he gave up when she moved to Åland and married Uffe and was able to change her and Alicia's surname without him knowing.

But what to do about Frida and the baby? Liam had given Hilda quite a shock when he walked into the shop yesterday. She didn't know he'd come back to the islands, but she was glad. Alicia would be foolish to let such a good man go. A surgeon! But Liam hadn't wanted to talk about Alicia. No, he just said that there was no problem, that he and Alicia would be staying at the Arkipelag for a few days, to 'talk'. Imagine Hilda's surprise when she saw her daughter on Uffe's old bicycle in Sjoland, riding fast toward Mariehamn that same morning. She'd turned her nose up at that same bike only days before. She had a good mind to send a text to her daughter asking what an earth was going on, but Uffe convinced her not to interfere.

'Let them sort it out themselves,' he said over the rim of his breakfast coffee.

Uffe was a man of few words, so when he did speak, Hilda usually took notice, even if this particular dilemma had nothing to do with Uffe, strictly speaking.

In any case, when Liam had dropped the baby bomb in this same shop twenty-four hours earlier, she forgot all about her daughter's marital worries. She was so shocked she didn't ask many questions.

'Can you try to convince your daughter that this is not a cut and dried thing?' Liam said.

Hilda nodded, 'You think Frida's lying?'

Her son-in-law nodded, 'Most certainly.'

'But why?' Hilda had spluttered. Even if she isn't particularly fond of the idea, she couldn't for the life of her think why Frida Anttila would feel the need to lie about it.

'I don't know.' Liam had crossed his arms over his chest. He'd been wearing nice clothes, Hilda had noticed. *To impress Alicia?* His striped shirt looked expensive, as had the dark brown chinos. On his feet he'd been wearing his brown Dockers.

A thought now enters Hilda's mind. There was something very different about Liam yesterday. He seemed more confident, more approachable. Not happier, but more settled in himself and more assertive.

Perhaps he's got another woman already?

As the owner of a fashion shop, Hilda knew that the first thing a woman changes in a man is his appearance. Perhaps that's why he is staying at the Arkipelag rather than in the sauna cottage with Alicia? Hilda puts her hand over her mouth and decides she must do something. Whatever Uffe said last night. Neither of them understood the severity of the situation then. She goes over to the door to turn the 'Sorry, we're shut' sign on. She glances at her watch and sees that it is nearly 10am. She locks the door of the shop behind her, and with a determined gait, crosses the road and heads toward the *Ålandsbladet* offices.

Alicia is typing furiously at her computer when Liam enters the newspaper office.

'What are you doing here,' she says before she has time to think how rude this sounds. *I'm already going back to being a Finn*, she thinks, and adds, 'Sorry.'

She gets up and steps closer to Liam. Out of old habit she slips her hand around his waist and brushes her lips over his.

Liam stands as if frozen into place. He touches his lips and says, 'Can you talk?' He glances sideways at the other two people working in the open-plan office. One of them is Frida, who is pretending she didn't see Liam enter, and isn't covertly watching him and Alicia. But Alicia notices the glance and says, 'Frida, would you join us for a coffee?'

'Let's go into the kitchen,' Alicia adds and stretches her hand toward the door at the side. Frida rolls her eyes but gets up and walks into the kitchen. She's wearing a bright yellow dress over a pair of see-through black leggings and her red Doc Martens. Her tummy is very visible now, and as Alicia glances toward the editor in his glass cubicle, she wonders if Frida has finally told their boss about her condition. Alicia sees that Harri is watching them. 'I'll just have a word here,' she says in a quiet voice to Liam, nodding toward the glass office. 'Be nice!' she adds, widening her eyes at Liam.

Liam nods and follows Frida.

FIFTY-FIVE

Patrick has been sitting in his boat for the last half-hour, thinking about why Liam came to see him. He's decided it wasn't to do with Alicia, but with Frida and the baby. The man seemed fairly confident about his relationship with Alicia. Is the baby the only reason, or has he managed to worm his way back into Alicia's good books? What happened to her the other day? Did she sleep with her husband?

Patrick doesn't understand how Alicia could possibly forgive Liam for his affair. He knows how it hurts to think about someone you love —loved—with another person. The images of Mia with someone else keep flashing in front of his eyes. He hasn't met the guy yet, but he knows exactly who it is from his internet searches. Good-looking, muscular, a little shorter than Patrick, but a successful property developer. Patrick doesn't care about Mia any longer, but he knows how he felt when he first found out about the affair. Even now, twelve months later, it sometimes hurts when she doesn't look at him the way she used to.

Patrick sighs. Just as he thought he had found someone else, the ex comes flying in (literally). Well, this time he isn't going to give up without a fight. Patrick gets up, locks the cabin door in the boat and steps onto the jetty. He knows Alicia cannot resist him if he gets her on his own. It's worth a try at least, he thinks.

When Alicia opens the door to the kitchen, she is faced with a silence. Frida is standing by the window, looking at the boats bobbing gently up and down in the East Harbor. The wind had been strong last night, before a band of rain swept through the islands in the small hours. Alicia had been up worrying about Liam and Frida and the baby. Now the sun is out and the temperature is in the twenties. Alicia looks at Liam, who's sitting down. The only sound is the burbling of the percolator on the kitchen top.

Alicia takes a deep breath, but just as she is about to speak, the door opens and Hilda bursts in.

'Here you are!' she says looking from Alicia to Liam. When she spots Frida, who's turned away from the window, she opens her mouth and blurts out, 'Ah, Frida.' Even just saying her name, Hilda sounds disapproving and formal. Alicia doesn't know what to do. Should she ask her mother to leave?

'This is nice—the whole family together!' Frida says with such sarcasm in her voice that Alicia feels the heavy weight of the difficult conversation they are about to have. She sits down at the table. She might as well let her mother weigh in too; they will all have to get used being one family.

Frida remains standing, with her arms crossed over her now quite considerable belly, as does Hilda, who seems to be unable to move.

Liam is the first one to speak.

'Look, Frida, you must understand our shock over your news. We are all delighted, of course, if ...' Liam looks from Frida to Alicia to Hilda.

Alicia notices that he's chosen his words carefully, so that he is understood in English.

'Why don't you sit down, Hilda. And Frida?' Alicia says in Swedish.

The older woman sits down first, next to Alicia, taking her hand and squeezing it, as if Alicia is ill. Alicia gives her mother a 'be nice' look, and Hilda smiles and nods at her. Alicia returns the smile and takes her hand away.

'Please, Frida, can we now talk about this?' she says, pleading with the girl. Alicia has switched to English. 'Liam — and I — would very much like to know about you and our son.'

Frida pauses, looks at them and shrugs. Dropping her arms by her side, she walks to the round table and sits on the other side of Alicia.

Liam places his arms on the table and knits his fingers together. Again he speaks.

'Thank you, Frida. As you know, Alicia and I—and the whole family—were devastated when we lost Stefan.'

'As was I!' Frida says. Her voice is loud, but shaky, and Alicia sees she's near to breaking down. She puts her arm around the girl and is surprised when she doesn't shrug it away. 'It's OK. We just want to help and understand, you know?'

Frida nods. She lowers her eyes and leans in toward Alicia.

Both Hilda and Liam are looking at Alicia and Frida. Alicia raises her eyebrows at them. She wants her mother to remain calm and to make Liam understand that Hilda's involvement will only make matters worse.

'OK, Frida, you have no idea what wonderful news it is that you are having our son's baby,' Liam says, at which Frida lifts her eyes toward him.

Alicia watches her mother.

So she already knows!

'But,' Liam continues, and Frida says, 'I knew it!' But she stays seated, letting Alicia hold her.

'You must understand that we are puzzled. We never saw you together, and nor did Hilda,' Liam nods to Alicia's mother and continues, 'So to hear that you were, hmm, that close, is a surprise to us. A wonderful surprise, but perhaps you could tell us more about what— and how—well, perhaps not how, but when did you meet, and where, and that sort of thing?'

Frida is fiddling with a ring on her finger and mutters, 'I already told Alicia.'

'Yes, but we need to hear it too. Hilda will be a great-grandmother and I will be a grandfather.' At the last word Liam suddenly stops. Alicia sees that the news has finally hit him.

He's beginning to believe it.

'And we will have something of what we lost with our dear son,' he continues, more quietly now. Alicia stretches out her other hand and puts it over Liam's fingers, which are still laced together on the table. He gives her a grateful smile and continues in a more steady tone.

'I would love to hear all of it.'

Liam looks around the table and adds, 'As I am sure we all would.'

FIFTY-SIX

'At first we were just friends, but then we fell in love.'

When Frida begins to talk, it's in a low, barely audible voice at first, but slowly she begins to gain confidence. Alicia can hear the joy and love she shared with Stefan. Frida tells them how she first met Stefan at a summer camp years ago, and then fell in love at the reunion last summer. How Stefan had made her laugh, and how they'd agreed to see each other again. The day after the reunion they met in Mariehamn, mostly in the English Park, just talking until Alicia came to collect Stefan.

'He was going home the next day but we kept in touch online,' Frida says and looks at Liam, whose face is now softer. He nods and Frida continues her story.

'We were desperate to see each other again, I was able to come over to England last year, and we spent the rest of the summer together.'

Alicia is fighting tears, because she recognizes her son, her gentle, loving son. But also because she wishes Stefan had been able to confide in her and bring Frida home to meet her and Liam. Frida's eyes shine as she tells them how, once she returned home, Stefan messaged her several times a day and how they talked every night.

'He wouldn't let me go to sleep until I told him I loved him,' Frida says, and tears begin to run down her face. 'I miss him so much.'

Alicia puts her arms around Frida and wipes her make-up smeared cheeks with a tissue. The girl's body is at last non-resistant in her embrace and her shoulders have lost their stiffness.

Liam is staring at Frida, not saying a word, and Hilda is looking down at her hands.

'Well, this is wonderful news,' Hilda says suddenly, in Swedish, and everyone around the table turns to look at the older woman. Alicia notices that her mother's eyes are dampened by tears, but she is smiling. 'We will have something of Stefan in our lives again.'

Even though Liam doesn't understand Swedish, Alicia can see he gets what Hilda is saying. That her mother has accepted the news and believes Frida's side of the story.

Suddenly everyone's faces brighten up with smiles; even Liam's has a wide grin. That's when the door to the kitchen opens and Patrick walks in.

'Well, isn't this cozy,' Patrick says. 'A family reunion, is it?'

Alicia is surprised at the sarcasm in his voice. He's speaking in English, with a very Swedish accent. She can feel her face getting hot with embarrassment. Her mother doesn't know anything about her affair with Patrick, and neither does Frida. The last thing she wants is for this delicate relationship between her and the mother of her grandson to be pushed off balance so quickly.

Alicia gets up and faces Patrick. With her back to everyone, she searches Patrick's eyes and in a low voice in Swedish says, 'Can I talk with you outside?'

'Sure, wouldn't want to disturb this little gathering,' Patrick replies, his eyes dark with anger. Alicia takes the few steps past him and opens the door, but Patrick isn't moving.

'So, Liam, all onboard with the baby now, are we?' He's still facing the room, rather than Alicia, who says, quietly, 'Patrick.'

Hilda's eyes dart from Alicia to Patrick and Alicia sees she's putting one and one together. *Damn, you, Patrick!*

Alicia glances at Frida, but the girl is still wiping her eyes, and hasn't noticed the changed atmosphere in the room. Now Liam, too, gets up and says, 'I should be going. Let you get back to work. He places a hand over Frida's elbow and says, 'Are you going to be OK?'

Frida nods and they exchange smiles.

Liam turns to Hilda, who's still staring at Alicia and Patrick in turn. 'Shall we?'

'Oh, yes,' Hilda says and she too gets up.

After Liam and Hilda have left the room, Alicia repeats Patrick's name once more, and finally the man turns around and follows Alicia out of the kitchen.

'Frida, take a minute, OK?' Alicia says as she closes the door behind her.

'I'll see you later at home,' she says to her mother and hugs her.

Liam faces Alicia and, taking her hand, says, 'We need to talk.'

Alicia nods. She's aware of Patrick's eyes boring into her.

'See you at the hotel later?'

'I don't know ...' Alicia says.

Liam gives Alicia a hug, which she responds to, holding onto her husband for a moment longer than she intended. She can see Patrick over Liam's shoulder and closes her eyes. She doesn't want to see his expression.

'I'll be waiting,' Liam says, and taking Hilda's arm, he leaves the newspaper office.

Patrick and Alicia are standing alone in the middle of the open-plan office.

'Alicia, where are my words?' Harri shouts through the open door to his glass office.

'Nearly there,' Alicia shouts back and she looks up to Patrick. His blue eyes are fixed on hers and she has to swallow in order to speak.

'It's all got very complicated,' she says.

'Has it?' Patrick says. His voice is gentle now. He lifts his hand as if to touch Alicia's cheek, but notices Harri is staring at them, so drops his hand. 'It doesn't need to be.'

'No?' Alicia says. Her heart is racing, beating so hard against her summer dress that she has difficulty breathing.

But this is wrong.

Patrick shakes his head and lifts one side of his mouth. 'Meet me later on the boat. When you finish here.'

Alicia doesn't reply. She glances at the door to the kitchen. If Frida comes out now, she will see them together and guess what Hilda has already worked out.

'Is this an editorial meeting?' Harry is suddenly standing next to them.

'Sort of,' Patrick replies. 'But it's finished now.' He nods to Alicia and turns. She watches his long, lean body disappear out of the door and down the staircase. Just before he is out of sight, he turns and smiles at Alicia.

FIFTY-SEVEN

Alicia just makes the deadline for her story about Daniel's accident, which gets her a 'Well done,' from Harri. As she's about to leave his office, he asks her to sit down.

'I don't wish to interfere in your affairs, and I know you're a big girl, but take it from someone who knows. The Erikssons are a powerful family in this town.'

Alicia shifts in her seat and looks straight at Harri. 'I know that.'

'And you know Patrick is on his way out of that family. He will be what some might call "a persona non-grata" soon?'

Stunned by these words, Alicia stares at the editor. *How does he know about Patrick's impending divorce?*

Harri gives a short chuckle at Alicia's expression. 'Oh, my dear, I know everything that goes on around here. Plus Kurt is a good friend of mine, as well as the owner of this paper. So, if you want to be part of this little set up here, I'd keep my nose clean vis à vis the Erikssons. Kurt and his lovely daughter in particular.'

For the second time in two days, Patrick is standing on the jetty, waiting for Alicia. It's a pleasant afternoon, with very little wind, and just a few persistent clouds. The harbor is busy, with boats arriving in batches as they're let through the Sjoland canal. It's the height of the tourist season and Patrick smiles as he watches families, mainly Finnish, emerge from their boats, windswept and tanned. Some men are sporting jaunty navy caps, with bright shorts and worn-out Docker shoes.

Patrick thinks back to when he bought the boat (OK, when Mia bought the boat for him) and his plans for trips out to the archipelago with Mia and the girls. Foolishly, he thought he could cure Mia of her dislike of boating; the woman was born on the islands, for goodness sake. He envisaged all of them taking a long trip past the outer islands like Kumlinge and Brändö all the way to Kustavi, and even perhaps visiting Turku before turning back. They would dock at all the harbors on the way, overnighting onboard but eating in the marina restaurants. What could be better? Instead, Mia had refused to step onboard *Mirabella*, calling it his 'toy'. Their mother's reluctance had led the girls to reject the idea too, so Patrick had been left to take a few day trips here and there on his own.

As Patrick watches a slim, attractive woman competently deal with the rigging of one of the larger sailing boats that has just arrived in the harbor, exchanging shouted instructions with a man at the tiller, his thoughts turn back to Alicia.

As soon as he stood close to her in the newspaper office, he regretted his earlier sarcasm in the kitchen. But walking into that happy family scene made his temper flare. How could she want to be back with Liam now? What had changed? Frida's baby? Surely that is not enough to wipe out past hurts? Patrick needs to see her to convince her that she has already moved on from her husband, that he is no good, that he has been unfaithful to her. That he has betrayed her just like Mia has betrayed him.

Patrick has read Alicia's article on the Romanian boy's death online on his phone, so he knows her work is done. She should be emerging from the newspaper office at any moment. He wants to go and stand outside the office, to catch Alicia as she comes out but he can't bring himself to appear that desperate. He's certain she will turn up to see him this time. The way she looked at him, with her eyes soft and loving, she definitely still feels something for him.

Alicia wants him, there's no doubt about it. But would the pull of a safe future with Liam, now they are both going to be grandparents, be enough to make her go back to him? The way the two of them looked the previous night was as though they had never been apart. But appearances can be misleading, as Patrick knows all too well. He's been keeping up appearances with Mia for twelve months now, and as far as he knows no one apart from Mia's parents, Mia and the lawyers are aware of their marital problems even now.

Patrick imagines how wonderful it will be to spend the rest of the summer with Alicia. He will look after her. After he left Alicia, he went over to the ALKO store and bought a bottle of pink champagne to celebrate the news of the baby again. He hopes the baby is what they were all discussing in the *Ålandsbladet* kitchen, and not Liam's return to the marital bed. Patrick pulls out his phone and begins tapping on it.

Alicia sits at her desk and stares at the article she has just posted online. It has a catchy title, it's well-written, and with just a few edits by Harri, most of her own work. She sees that the post has already received ten shares after just a few minutes. She has a sense of achievement that she hasn't really experienced since Stefan's death. She had more or less given up chasing commissions from *The Financial Times*. She's forgotten how good it feels to have something you have created read by others.

Alicia moves the mouse and closes the window and the computer. A black screen is facing her when her phone pings.

Are you coming over?

Alicia sighs and gets up. She waves to Harri, who's still sitting at his desk, staring at his screen. The man doesn't see her, so Alicia pops her head around his doorway and says goodbye.

'Good work,' he says and adds, 'And remember what I said. Don't want to lose you.'

Sounds very much like a threat, Alicia wants to reply. Instead, she just nods, 'Yes, thank you. See you tomorrow.'

She walks past Frida's desk, which is empty. Alicia heard Frida tell Harri she wasn't feeling very well soon after their talk in the kitchen. When Alicia asked her if she was OK Frida smiled and said, 'Don't worry. I'm just taking care of myself.' She had her hand over her tummy and Alicia hugged her.

'Let me know if you need anything,' she said, to which Frida smiled and nodded.

Alicia walks slowly down the stairs and opens the glass-paneled door onto the street. She crosses the little garden and makes her way down toward the sea. The sun emerges from a thin white cloud, and the steel riggings and white hulls of boats in the harbor in front of her gleam in the bright sunshine.

Alicia doesn't know what to do.

If she turns left and walks along Strandvägen toward the entrance to Arkipelag, she is sure she is going to find Liam, and possibly Hilda, there. She will be welcomed into the old, safe family life that she knows. Although changed by the tragic loss of their son, there is hope that they can begin to support each other and accept life without Stefan, while they wait for the wonder of an unexpected grandchild. But has Liam really changed? And is the affair really over? And what about Patrick?

All she has to do is turn right, skirt the parking lot, and she will come to the harbor and Patrick, who is waiting to speak to her. But will he just want to speak? Can Alicia trust herself to tell Patrick face-to-face it's over? Does she want it to be over with him? If she goes to Patrick now, she will have to tell Liam. She doesn't want to see the same pain on his face that she witnessed when she opened the door of the sauna cottage to him. She wants to forget the way he looked, pale and drawn, like he had seen a ghost. Even though she was angry with him, she hated seeing him hurt. The more she thinks back to that night, the more shame she feels. The guilt about what she has been doing is suddenly so raw and real that she has to catch her breath.

She taps a message, 'Sorry,' on her phone and presses send.

She begins to walk, quickly placing one foot in front of another. She has made her decision, she doesn't want to linger and change her mind now.

FIFTY-EIGHT

After leaving the newspaper office, Liam managed to convince Hilda that she should go back to her shop. He and Alicia would talk soon, he said. They were standing in the middle of the busy Torggatan, having walked in silence through the *Sitkoff* shopping center.

'You go to her, yes?' Hilda had made him promise. He had taken hold of her arms and given her a reassuring squeeze. He then watched her walk over the road and enter her shop.

Now he is sitting in the outdoor café of the hotel, watching children messing around in the pool. Opposite him is the East Harbor, with its large yachts and the *von Knorring* steamer in the distance. He is keeping an eye on the road leading from Alicia's office, but he is glad that the *Club Marin* obstructs his view of the part of the jetty where Patrick's boat is moored. He wouldn't be able to stomach seeing Patrick with Alicia. Not again.

What if Alicia doesn't appear?

Liam is on his second beer when at last he sees his wife's blond hair appear on the pedestrian walkway between the hotel and the harbor. He holds his breath as he sees her walk determinedly, without smiling — such a Scandinavian trait of hers — toward the Hotel Arkipelag. He sighs with relief.

. . .

The first thing Liam asks her is if she's OK.

'I'm fine,' Alicia says and smiles. Now she's made her decision, the relief is palpable.

Liam reaches out and places his hand over hers on the table. 'That's good,' he says and returns her smile.

They both sit for a while, watching the children in the pool.

'Do you remember when we used to bring Stefan here and he never wanted to get out, even when his skin was wrinkled and his lips blue from the cold?' Alicia asks.

'Yes,' Liam nods.

'I hope we can bring the baby here too,' Alicia continues. She gazes at Liam. She needs to know he is fully onboard with Frida's pregnancy. He looked as if he accepted her story earlier, but she wants to make sure.

'I look forward to that,' he replies.

Alicia watches his face. It looks less drawn than it has done in the past two days. She wishes with all her heart that she hadn't brought such pain to him. But at least he seems to be happy about Frida's baby.

Alicia shifts on her seat and takes a sip out of her glass, removing her hand from under Liam's. It is only 4PM, but with the day she's had, it feels as if it should already be evening.

'I want to stay here,' Alicia says. Again, she is keeping an eye on Liam.

He lifts his head in surprise.

'I see.'

Now it's Alicia's turn to take hold of Liam's hand. The familiar feel of his slender, but strong, fingers under her own reminds her how much they have in common. The long marriage, Stefan, and now a future grandchild.

'But I also want to save our marriage,' she says.

Liam is quiet. He's not looking at her and suddenly Alicia feels cold. She shivers and brings her arms around her body.

What if he doesn't want me anymore?

'I can't give up my job. My patients rely on me,' he says quietly, lifting his now serious eyes to Alicia's.

Again she reaches out to him, this time taking his hands into hers.

'I know. And I don't want to give up seeing our grandchild being born and growing up. And I love my job at *Ålandsbladet*.'

'What do you want me to do?' Liam says.

'I don't know. But I do know that we can make it work. Until the baby is born, I'd like to stay here. You can see if you can get more holiday, and come and stay for long weekends, and then for a few more days when the baby is born? I can come over to London for weekends too. I know it's not going to be easy, but we often don't see each other for days even when I'm in London, not when you are working all hours. Especially not since ...'

Alicia lets go of Liam, but he pulls her back toward him.

'That's over, I told you. You must trust me,' he says and peers closely at Alicia. 'As I must trust you, if we are to live in two different countries from now on.'

Alicia nods. She pushes the feeling of guilt away. 'It won't be easy, but I can't leave Frida. You can see that, can't you? Her mother is not well enough to look after her and she has literally no one else now Daniel is gone.'

'I can see that,' Liam says and after a moment's hesitation continues, 'I love you Alicia. I never stopped loving you and I will do anything to make you happy. I am here until the end of the week, and when I go back I'll see how I can arrange my schedule to get more time off in longer blocks.'

Alicia is so relieved, she wants to jump up and shout out, 'Yes!' It's as if her old Liam, her loving husband, has come back to her.

At that moment, he leans over and whispers in Alicia's ear, 'Can I kiss you now?'

She nods and Liam places his hands on either side of her face, and gently, so gently, presses his lips onto Alicia's.

The effect of his touch, so familiar, yet so exciting, pulses through Alicia's body. Yet, she thinks, it's too soon, so she pulls herself away from Liam and takes another sip of her wine.

'You will be the sexiest grandmother in the world,' he says in a low voice.

Alicia laughs. They are both silent for a moment, gazing at each other. Alicia can't quite believe how far they have come and how much has changed in just a matter of weeks and days. Suddenly she remembers her mother.

'I think we should go over to Sjoland for dinner. Hilda will be driving Uffe mad otherwise.'

'OK,' Liam says and smiles.

EPILOGUE

L ittle Anne Sofie is born at the Mariehamn Hospital at twenty minutes past midnight on September 1st. Alicia and Liam are in attendance. Liam had flown in from London the week before, while Alicia had been staying in Frida's flat for the previous two weeks. Several selfies are taken, and when the baby is asleep in the cot beside her mother, and Frida closes her eyes, Alicia and Liam tiptoe out of the room and hug each other for a long time in the hospital corridor.

As they walk arm in arm into the empty parking lot, the cold fall air hits Alicia. There's a harsh northerly wind and leaves are swirling beside the tarmac, where a line of birches dips down toward the sea.

'You're not going to work today, are you?' Liam asks as they reach Alicia's new car. She had bought a used Volvo a couple of weeks ago, so that she had transportation when the time came for the birth.

'No!' Alicia says and turns to Liam, smiling.

'Well, in that case, perhaps we should wet the baby's head?'

Alicia nods and they drive the short distance to the Hotel Arkipelag parking lot. 'You go on and order, I'm just going to let others know the good news,' she says.

Liam stays in the passenger seat for a moment, looking down at his hands. Alicia can guess Liam wonders if Patrick is one of the people she will contact, but she doesn't want to discuss him with Liam. Not today when her heart is filled with love for the wonderful new little person in her life. Alicia hasn't seen anything as beautiful as Anne Sofie. Her tiny fists tightly closed against her little body and the show of determination in her rosy little mouth. When Alicia first held her, tears began running down her cheeks and they all laughed. She cannot remember being so happy.

'Don't be long,' Liam says eventually, brushing his lips against her cheek.

As Alicia watches Liam walk toward the hotel entrance, shielding himself against the wind with his hand, she thinks how happy she was to see him when he stepped off the plane at Mariehamn airport. He'd decided to fly, to save time. He had to go via Helsinki, but he still arrived about half a day earlier than he would have done by sea.

Their relationship is in a good place now.

Alicia is still living in the sauna cottage and Liam in London, but they have plans for Liam to move to the islands. Alicia keeps in touch with Patrick too, but only as a friend. In the small town of Mariehamn, with the tourists gone, it would be impossible not to see each other. Besides, now Patrick's divorce is official, Alicia is happy to help him by simply listening. As she has got to know him better, her attraction toward him has begun to diminish. Perhaps because she has moved on with her life? Frida and the baby have been Alicia's priority for months now, and she guesses it will be the case for months, perhaps years, to come. And that is exactly how it should be.

AN ISLAND CHRISTMAS

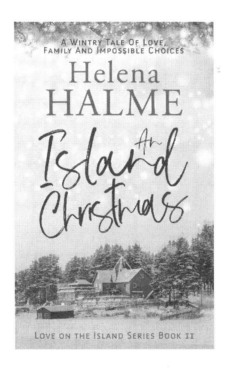

A WINTRY TALE OF LOVE,
FAMILY AND IMPOSSIBLE CHOICES

Helena
HALME

An
Island
Christmas

LOVE ON THE ISLAND SERIES BOOK II

ONE

On Alicia's first winter back home, snow arrives late on the Åland islands. It's the last weekend before Christmas and finally, overnight, a heavy fall covers everything with a pure white blanket. Alicia loves the dramatically altered scenery of the islands, when the sea is frozen over and the teal color of the shipping lanes by the West Harbor is highlighted by the brilliant landscape. Gone are the dull brown fields and the gray buildings, made even more drab by the wind and rain that are the theme of fall.

As she sits in her mother's kitchen, drinking a hot cup of coffee, surveying the coastal view through the window, she smiles to herself. The virgin layer of snow makes the distant sea seem like an extension of the white fields, drawing a straight line between the ice and the blue skies above. It's as if the weather gods have heard her prayers and granted her greatest wish.

This Christmas, her first on the islands since she made a surprise move back to her home six months ago, is going to be perfect. Not only is it her first Christmas here in at least ten years, but it is also her granddaughter's very first Yuletide. How she looks forward to seeing what the little girl will make of the traditional Christmas tree, lit with real candles, at her great-grandmother's house.

Alicia remembers when her son, Stefan, saw the tree, as tall as the room, for the first time. It was Christmas Eve and they were about to sit down for their midday porridge, another tradition her mother, Hilda, insisted on. Stefan, just turned one, had clapped his hands and uttered his first word, *"Ljus"—candle*—in Swedish. He had said the word with such clarity that it had brought tears of joy into Hilda's eyes. The candles on the tree were lit just twice each day of the holidays, once for lunch and once for dinner. Uffe had the task of going around the branches, carefully bringing a match to each candle, while making sure the old candleholders were securely clamped onto a thick branch, and that there was enough space above the flame.

Alicia's thoughts turn to her granddaughter. She thinks of little Anne Sofie as a wonderful surprise gift awarded to her nearly four months ago, when life hadn't seemed worth living. Each breath she took during that dark period had been weighed down by the memory of how her son had perished in a motorcycle accident back in London. She had felt so abandoned and lonely, until she returned to the islands.

And met Patrick.

Alicia thinks of England, where she had lived for nearly twenty years. She remembers what pandemonium a heavy snowfall caused. London would stop in its tracks and everyone would be amazed by this strange natural phenomenon. During all the time Alicia lived in England, there had been at least one chaotic snow day every year. She always marveled at the surprise on people's faces when buses didn't run or trains froze to a standstill.

'This happens to you every time!' she wanted to shout, but of course she didn't. She was a good immigrant, always conforming, always modifying her behavior to the customs of her adopted country.

She took another sip of the hot, warming liquid. How liberating it was not to have to bite her tongue anymore. Or worry that she'd said the wrong thing, or hadn't understood some veiled criticism.

It took Alicia years to get used to living in the UK. She'd been so in love with Liam that nothing–not even her struggles to adapt to her new country–stopped her from wanting to be with him. And then, of course, when Stefan was born, she slowly began to feel at home in London. Alicia shakes her head to banish the dull ache and sadness that overwhelms her each time she thinks of her lovely boy, who didn't get to see his eighteenth birthday. Instead, she turns her thoughts to Anne Sofie, her new grandchild. She finds her phone and looks at the latest picture Frida, Stefan's girlfriend and the baby's mother, has posted on their private online app. The little girl is the most beautiful baby Alicia has ever seen. But she would think that, wouldn't she?

When Frida had dropped the bombshell of her pregnancy in the summer, it had taken Alicia–and especially Liam–quite a while to get used to the idea that their dead 17-year-old son had fathered a child. But when Alicia saw the baby in Frida's arms in the hospital a few weeks later, she wasn't prepared for the absolute love she felt for the new little person. She hadn't expected the joy she experienced at Frida's bedside. When she held Anne Sofie, she sensed a connection like no other. It wasn't the overwhelming adoration mingled with a massive weight of responsibility that she had felt when she first held Stefan. No, this was something much purer, much simpler, and far, far more enjoyable. The first time she saw her little granddaughter, with her eyes firmly shut and her little rosy mouth making sucking noises, searching for her mother's breast, the tiny amount of doubt that Alicia still carried about the baby's paternity disappeared like a puff of smoke.

Alicia is shaken out of her thoughts by the arrival of Patrick. He's standing at the front door wearing a shiny, thick padded coat. Alicia spots the round Moncler logo on the sleeve and smiles. The divorce from Mia Eriksson hasn't altered his shopping habits, it seems. He's stamping his boots against the thick mat that Hilda has placed at the front door for just such a purpose.

'At your service,' he says, grinning.

'Coffee before you start?' Alicia says.

'That'd be nice. Any of Hilda's cinnamon buns going?'

He takes off his boots and jacket.

Alicia shakes her head and laughs. 'I'll have a look. I bet she made a batch before they left.'

She finds them neatly bagged in the freezer and takes two sweet buns out and puts them in the oven.

'So, how are you?' Patrick says. He's standing on the other side of the kitchen island, a safe distance from Alicia. This is the routine they have settled on. No touching, no closeness, and definitely no flirting.

'It's very kind of you to offer to shift the snow. I'm so out of practice, I don't think I'd know where to start.'

Last night, the snow didn't stop falling and the lane has a thick layer over it. Alicia's car is safely in the barn, which Hilda and Uffe use as a garage. She's not sure what she would have done if Patrick hadn't responded to her message earlier that morning and agreed to come and help.

Patrick shrugs his wide shoulders. He's wearing a bottle-green jumper with a zip at the collar. Somehow the color makes his blue eyes more intense, or perhaps it's the ruddiness of his cheeks, caused by the chill outside.

'Mia is in Stockholm with the girls, so I have a free weekend.'

'Even so, I'm grateful. Hilda and Uffe are coming back on the morning sailing, so they'll be here at 3pm at the latest. I don't want Uffe to have to start digging his way into the house as soon as he's home from sunny Spain.'

Alicia hears the ping from the oven and turns around. She can feel the heat of his body even with a solid piece of kitchen furniture between them. It's the intense gaze in those damn eyes of his.

Why did I accept his offer to help with the snow? Did I really think I was over him? Stupid, stupid woman.

After taking the tractor fitted with a snow plow up and down the lane to Uffe and Hilda's house, Patrick comes back in, his boots clattering in the hallway. Alicia has decided to offer him lunch, it's the least she can do to repay him for the favor. She tries to convince herself that this is the reason, but she knows she wants to extend the time she spends with him outside of their work.

'Would you like something to eat?' she asks when he sits down on one of the kitchen chairs.

Patrick looks up, surprised.

'Or at least a beer? You must be tired after all that physical exercise?'

His ruddy face looks even more attractive, if possible, and Alicia has to turn her eyes away from him.

'Beer would be great,' Patrick says. He lifts his eyes up to her and adds, 'Look, Alicia, I'm really glad to help you out, but I wanted to talk to you.'

'Sandwiches OK?' Alicia interrupts him. She doesn't want to have this conversation now. She still doesn't know how she feels.

Patrick sighs. 'OK,' he replies simply.

TWO

Brit gazes at the ship as she waits for one of the car deck guys to open the gate. The vast ferry looks almost threatening. The bow, as yet empty of vehicles, is agape, resembling the mouth of a huge whale or a fantastical monster. Staring at the large red Marie Line logo on the hull, she wonders if she has made a mistake. Why didn't she choose the Caribbean cruise she'd been offered instead of hankering after Christmas at home? She'd told herself she would miss the cold and the snow. It looked like God had answered her prayers a little too enthusiastically: there was a snow storm brewing. A lot of the white stuff had already fallen. Brit can't remember a December like it. Apart from the shipping lane, a channel of dark water, the sea is covered with ice. A faint sun plays on the surface, making it glint as if it is covered with small precious stones. Involuntarily, Brit touches the ring finger of her left hand with her thumb. She needs to be honest with herself. She's on the run, fleeing a bad relationship, plain and simple. She shakes her head. She's done with men for the foreseeable future. She's going to make the best of this job, whatever. Working on the Stockholm ferries may be a step back from her managerial job with Royal Caribbean, but at least here she will be able to visit her father on the islands more often.

It's 7am and Brit shivers. She is cold in spite of the warm padded coat she'd bought at NK as soon as she got back. She realizes her new gloves are in one of the boxes stacked in the car. This, her 10-year-old red VW Golf, which has been waiting for her patiently at a garage in Stockholm, contains the whole of her life. During the week spent in an Airbnb near Slussen, now a trendy area in southern Stockholm, she'd gone through the storage unit she'd rented since she began working on the cruisers twenty years ago. Many times during the long hours spent sifting through her old books, photographs, and the silly ornaments she'd collected on her travels to ports around the world, she'd been tempted to just sit on the cold floor of the unit and weep. Weep for the kitchen table and chairs she'd kept in the expectation that she and Nico would one day settle down and have a home, and even perhaps a family.

Don't think about The Rat!

Brit glances at the ship again. Her new career onboard MS *Sabrina* seems an utterly foolish idea now. She'd worked on the ferries between Finland and Sweden in her youth, but she'd been in her teens then, not in her late thirties, with failure already etched onto her face.

Now, as one of the more senior members of the Marie Line crew, it was a different proposition altogether. Not just a summer job that she can take or leave. She would have to make this new position a success. And why wouldn't she? Just because she'd had to flee her old job on account of the bastard she thought she would spend the rest of her life with, didn't mean she was a failure, did it? Brit would show him, show everybody, all his friends (and some of hers), that she was strong and could manage on her own.

Feeling desperately nervous about the prospect of meeting her new colleagues on the monster of a ferry in front of her, Brit glances at her face in the rear-view mirror. She checks there's no lipstick on her teeth and puffs up her hair with her fingers. Pushing the mirror down, she lifts her chin up and gives the old guy in the bright orange vest who's waving her into the belly of the ship a wide smile.

Jukka likes to come onto the bridge well before they are due to sail, when it's still empty. After an overnight docking in Stockholm, this morning MS *Sabrina* would be heading back to Helsinki in Finland across Ålands Hav via Mariehamn, where most of the day-trippers would change ferries. Jukka doesn't expect a difficult sailing. The shipping lanes have been cleared and although the passengers will no doubt be in festive mood so close to Christmas, the ferry is only about three-quarters full.

As he checks the monitors to the decks below him, to make sure the staff are getting into position by the open bow doors, he sees a good-looking woman step out of a red Golf on the car deck area reserved for employees. For a fraction of a second, he thinks she looks directly at him. But she can't know about the cameras at the side of the deck. Or can she?

Jukka sees she has a good figure, her shapely curves hugged by a tight skirt and boots with high heels, visible under an open padded coat. Her hair is long and dark and her face looks friendly, but her expression appears vulnerable. Jukka follows the woman as she pulls a suitcase toward the bow of the ship. He sighs as she disappears inside.

He shakes his head and tells himself to concentrate on the task in hand, yet he can't help wonder who the woman is. After he's made the regulatory checks, and seen that the car deck is populated by the correct number of crew, Jukka allows himself a glance at the staffing sheets. And there it is. A new restaurant manager is starting onboard today. 'Britt Svensson,' he reads out loud, deciding that he needs to go and say hello to the woman. It's his duty as Captain of the ship after all. There's nothing else to it, just business and professionalism, Jukka tells himself as he makes his way to his cabin.

Brit is shown around the staff quarters by an older woman, who says she's the assistant restaurant manager, 'Or acting manager until today.' She introduces herself as Kerstin Eklund. Brit glances at her uniform and sees there are two stripes at the cuffs. Kerstin has a few years on Brit, with a thin, wiry frame and short brown hair. She has a long face with very narrow lips painted bright red, and Brit longs to tell her that some of the lipstick has run at the side of her mouth, but is unsure if she should. Perhaps later, after she has officially met all of her staff, she can take Kerstin to one side and point it out. Brit is so preoccupied by Kerstin's lipstick that she doesn't notice a tall man with light brown hair, who stands in front of her as they step inside the passenger area of the ship.

'Welcome onboard MS *Sabrina!*' Jukka cringes inwardly at the cliché. Kerstin gives him a look that says, *I know your game.* Why does he always feel so intimidated by the older, female, members of the crew?

'Thank you Kerstin, I can take it from here,' he says, trying to sound authoritative.

The woman nods and scuttles along the corridor toward the staff quarters. He should have reminded her that, as acting restaurant manager, it was still her job to make sure the bar was fully stocked, and that the staff had gathered to welcome the new manager, but he lets it pass. Glancing at his watch he sees that there is more than half an hour until boarding begins. Plenty of time to go through the motions. He turns toward Brit Svensson.

'I'm Jukka Markusson, the Captain.'

The woman smiles, nodding at his uniform. 'I gathered that.'

This makes Jukka cough. The woman is even more good-looking at close hand. She's got striking green eyes, and her dark hair has a chestnut tinge to it. Briefly, he wonders if she is wearing colored contact lenses and whether she has dyed her hair, but then realizes how inappropriate his thoughts are.

Be professional.

It was his infatuation with a woman onboard that nearly cost him his career a few years back, something which the older members of the crew, particularly Kerstin, never let him forget. Although no one actually mentions the affair anymore–at least not in front of him.

'You've met Kerstin, the acting manager. She will show you the ropes during this first passage to Helsinki. Then, for the return leg, you can take over. As you know, we will dock at Mariehamn at 14.10, and sail onward to Finland proper when the island passengers and day-trippers have disembarked,' Here Jukka glances at his list, which shows that the majority of the passengers would leave the ship. He knows that most of the passengers on these cruises are blind drunk by the time they disembark in Mariehamn. Same goes for those who come onboard from the sister ferry to *Sabrina.*

He tries not to get involved in the messy antics of the Finns and Swedes onboard, but he is sometimes called to attend to the more serious incidents, such as fights, or an injury caused by drunken brawling between young men. These days, women also get themselves embroiled in dangerous cat fights. Once, he had to confiscate a knuckleduster from a 16-year-old girl who'd used it to cut the face of another teenager. Both looked as if butter wouldn't melt when Jukka handed them over to the police in Helsinki Harbor.

The most serious incident of all was a man overboard. When a snowstorm was pending, as it was today, with chill winds and the temperature of the sea barely above freezing, anyone falling into the shipping lane would lose their life instantly. And most probably never be found.

But he's used to dealing with drunks. At least he's more at home in his role as the ship's policeman than he is as the head of staff, most of whom are female.

Jukka lifts his gaze toward the woman, who is looking at him attentively.

Goodness, those eyes really are something else.

Jukka coughs again in an effort to keep his thoughts from wandering.

'This time of the year, we will be able to depart Mariehamn within fifteen minutes. We only have just over 800 passengers onboard today. Our ETA in Helsinki is 19.50. The restaurant and bars will be busy this close to Christmas, so you should be vigilant for any trouble. You will be on call for the whole of the journey. Any questions?'

The woman smiles again. She has a knowing expression on her face and Jukka wonders if Kerstin has already spilled the beans about his old misadventure. He straightens his back and corrects his cap.

Brit doesn't say anything, just gazes at him, the smile reaching all the way into those green eyes, and making his heart beat even harder against his uniform.

THREE

W hile she waits for Uffe and Hilda's car to appear in the lane, Alicia is once again alone in the kitchen of their large house. She's been housesitting during her mother and stepfather's two-week holiday. Not that there is any chance of a burglary being committed—she can't remember when such a thing last happened on the islands, if it ever had. For some reason, however, Hilda is convinced that something will happen to the three-story building if is left empty.

The light has begun to fade already, although the snow makes the landscape appear more luminous. The skies are clear too and after the faint winter sunshine of the day, the horizon is lit with reds and oranges. Alicia wonders why she ever wished to leave this place. But in her teens she had felt stranded on these islands, cut off from the real world. Now being isolated seems more attractive, but more than that, Alicia feels a sense of belonging that she never felt in England. She's not prepared to give that up.

Her thoughts turn to Liam, who is due to arrive two days before Christmas. He's been taking more time off from his busy surgery schedule lately. How, Alicia can't fathom. During their last Skype call, he'd said he had *some significant news*.

Alicia has gone back to their house in London only once since her surprise move to the islands. She spent a week doing things that she can't do over the internet, like seeing her doctor and dentist. She will handle all those things here, on the islands, as soon as she and Liam have decided what to do about the house and their marriage. She expected the trip back to London to be more emotional, but it seemed, in her mind, she had already moved back home to Åland. Toward the end of the trip, she was counting the days and hours until she would be back on the Marie Line ferry, crossing the Ålands Hav from Stockholm to the islands.

'Have you lost weight?' Hilda says as soon as she's given Alicia a hug. 'You're just skin and bones!'

'Hello to you too,' Alicia says, glancing at Uffe, who winks at her. 'Did you have a nice time?'

Her mother is wearing a pair of red kitten-heel boots, most unsuitable for the weather. They both look tanned, although there is a slightly worried, harassed air about Hilda.

'Are you OK?' Alicia asks her mother.

'Not really! We nearly had an accident by the swing bridge,' she says, sitting down.

'Didn't we?' She addresses this to Uffe, who's looking down at his hands. He's seated at the kitchen table while Alicia perches on her favorite stool by the window. Eventually Uffe nods, and so her mother turns toward Alicia and carries on talking, barely drawing breath.

'A Russian, in one of those enormous Jeeps, they're called Cherokee, or something aren't they?'

Alicia knows nothing about cars, but she replies. 'Yes, I think so. But what happened?'

Alicia glances over to Uffe to see if he can make sense of what her mother is saying, but her stepfather has his head bent, his eyes firmly set on his hands, which hang between his legs.

'Well, he nearly rammed us over!' Hilda says, her voice rising. There's panic in her red-rimmed eyes. On close inspection, there's something new in her mother's demeanor. Perhaps she had one too many glasses of wine on the flight back from Alicante.

At Hilda's outburst, Uffe gets up. Before turning to go out of the door, he says quietly, 'It was nothing. He was just trying to overtake us, wanting to get to the bridge before it goes up.'

Alicia watches her mother purse her lips, but she doesn't contradict her husband. Both women watch Uffe pick up the post that Alicia has arranged on the table and leave the house for his office, a converted milking parlor just across the yard.

It occurs to Alicia that the swing bridge doesn't go up now the sea has frozen over. There are no sailing boats using the canal between Sjoland and Mariehamn. Why did Uffe say it did?

Hilda wraps her arms around her body and turns toward Alicia.

'It was awful. We were this close from ending up in the freezing water!'

She lifts her hand up and indicates with her thumb and finger a minuscule distance. Alicia considers whether this is another case of exaggeration on her mother's part or whether something quite sinister has occurred.

'What happened then?'

'What do you mean?'

'To the man in the Jeep? Did he stop to see if you were alright?'

Hilda shakes her head. 'No, he just carried on. The thing is, he could have overtaken us easily without trying to ram us! There was no one coming from the other direction, and you know how slowly Uffe drives these days. With all this fresh snow, he was even more careful.'

Alicia nods. Uffe's overly cautious driving has become a concern to her almost as much as her mother's speeding. She wonders if he can't see that well anymore, because he seems to go everywhere at about 30 kilometers per hour. Luckily there isn't that much traffic on the islands, and there are many older drivers who are equally dawdling, and they don't mind.

It could just be that whoever was in the Jeep got frustrated following Uffe.

Still.

Alicia thinks for a moment. She's confused by Uffe's obvious lie about the swing bridge. Perhaps the two of them have had another of their rows and that's why he didn't try to calm Hilda down? Or refute her dramatic tale?

Suddenly her mother's mood changes.

'The house looks wonderful! And you've managed to clear the lane and the paths. That must have been hard? Fresh snow can be really heavy and you haven't done that in years!'

'Oh, Patrick helped out,' the words come out of Alicia's mouth before she has time to think.

'He did!' Hilda exclaims. Her eyebrows shoot up and she looks inquiringly at Alicia.

'As a favor to a friend. We were in the office yesterday afternoon when it started snowing and he offered, in case I needed help this morning.' Alicia is trying to keep her voice steady.

'Uh, uh,' Hilda says, giving Alicia a look that she knows far too well. The brief affair she had with her now work colleague–and boss, to be precise–is still a little raw, and her mother is one of the few people on the islands who suspects that they had a relationship.

'Nothing's going on,' she says, and trying to change the subject, adds, 'Did this Jeep scratch your car? And how did you know the driver was Russian?'

'He's a business associate of Uffe's.'

Alicia can hardly believe her ears.

'Really?'

'Yes, he's had some dealings with him, but that's all done now, so I'm not sure why he didn't even acknowledge us–or Uffe. And our car is fine. Uffe steered out of his way just in time.'

Alicia is staring at her mother.

'What are you telling me?'

Hilda bends down, unzips her boots, and pulls them off her feet. 'That's better,' she exclaims.

'These are so uncomfortable, but they look pretty, don't they? Very trendy someone told me in Spain.'

Her mother gives Alicia a coquettish look.

'There was this man who was so lovely. If I had my time again.' Hilda's eyes take on a dreamy quality. 'We had a fantastic time, sun and Sangria all the way!'

'That's nice,' Alicia replies, but her mind is racing. Why would her mother and stepfather have anything to do with a Russian driving a Cherokee? Those people were rumored to be part of the mafia, something Alicia has been quietly researching since she started working at the local newspaper, *Ålandsbladet*, last summer. She's seen some pretty awful accusations in local blogs and Facebook groups, but nothing that she could actually substantiate enough to write about. She hasn't even told Patrick, who's now the news editor, about her private investigations.

FOUR

Four days after she first stepped onboard MS *Sabrina* Brit is met at the apartment in Mariehamn by her old schoolfriend, Mia Eriksson. Wearing a pair of camel colored Sorel snow boots with a long, white Moncler padded coat, Mia looks for all the world like the heiress that she is. Her father, Kurt Eriksson, owns the local newspaper, *Ålandsbladet*, half the islands and much of Finland and Sweden too. Including the block of apartments in Mariehamn overlooking the sounds where the ferries pass on their way in and out of Mariehamn West Harbor, and where the two women are now standing.

Brit gazes at the magnificent view over the icy sea. 'Seeing the ships pass won't remind you too much of work, will it? On your days off, I mean?' Mia asks her.

Mia has thrown her coat on one of the pale gray sofas that face each other in the large living room.

Brit nearly laughs. This view commands a premium price on the islands, and Mia thinks it'll bother her to look at it?

'That's so sweet of you to worry about me!' she exclaims instead. 'I am very grateful, you know. You must thank your Dad.'

Mia's expression hardens for a moment, then she comes and gives Brit one of her tight hugs. Her thin but strong arms envelop Brit.

Pulling away, she adds, almost as an aside, 'I run the property side of the business now so I don't need to consult him.'

Brit realizes her mistake and says, quickly, 'Of course, sorry. You did say! I'm still a bit tired and jet-lagged.'

When she sees Mia's sideways smile from where she has gone to stand by the large windows again, Brit adds, 'You know, I've had so much going on, since being back.'

Mia's expression changes and, with more kindness in her voice, she says, 'You must be exhausted after your first shift. And here I am keeping you. Don't mind me, I'm off. Send me a message when you want to meet up. Lunch tomorrow, perhaps?'

With that Mia picks up her coat and is gone.

Brit sits down and looks around the luxurious place she will now call home. It's fully furnished with expensive-looking sofas and chairs. There's a kitchen separated from the living room by an island, topped with gray marble. All the equipment is new, as are the beds, linen, and fittings in the other two rooms, leading off from the small hallway. The apartment is nine floors up, affording an amazing view of Ålands Hav.

Brit gets up and opens the fridge door. She puts her hand over her mouth and gives out a short laugh. It seems her friend has stocked up with the essentials. Well, essentials as far as Mia is concerned. There's a bottle of Sancerre, one of Moët and two bottles of San Pellegrino water. A further investigation reveals a packet of sliced cheese, a carton of milk, a couple of tomatoes, a packet of gravlax and a quinoa salad inside a plastic container. There are six eggs in a box and tubs of both butter and olive spread. Brit goes into the larder and finds rye bread, sliced sourdough, Fazer chocolate, coffee capsules for the Nespresso machine standing on the counter, some fancy brown and white sugar sticks, and expensive looking ginger biscuits.

Brit grabs her phone and sends a thank you message with a heart emoji to Mia. She then opens the bottle of white and, finding a Riedel wine glass in a cupboard above the sink, pours herself a few mouthfuls and a sends a selfie to Mia too.

She sinks down on the sofa and wonders what the price of all this luxury will be. Is Mia simply in need of a friend? At school they didn't really mix, but after meeting up again a few months ago, they started to follow each other on Instagram and send the odd message back and forth. When Brit told Mia she was planning to come back to the islands, she offered her use of the apartment. Brit knows she's paying far below the going rate in rent, and now all these goodies just for her. She takes another sip from her glass and presses the bridge of her nose between her eyes.

She's tired.

Brit's first shift onboard wasn't a complete disaster. Apart from Kerstin, who seemed to take a dislike to her from the get go, most of the other restaurant staff are friendly and efficient. As is the Captain. Brit smiles at the memory of her first meeting with Jukka. She's sworn not to fall for a man ever again, but what's the harm in having a little flirtation? Jukka Markusson is handsome, about her age, and seemingly unattached. That much she was able to glean from that sour puss Kerstin. Brit enjoyed seeing the Captain's surprise when she looked straight into his eyes. Over the years she'd been engaged to an Italian Casanova, she had developed a few tricks of her own. Now all she had to do was wait for Jukka to come to her. Which he was certainly doing. During the first three sailings between the islands and Finland and Sweden, he had found a reason to call on Brit, or 'accidentally' bump into her, a total of ten times.

Brit has to admit that she's attracted to him. With his tall frame, wide smile and pale blue eyes, Jukka is nothing like Nico. He has none of the Italian's natural charm, but then it was time for a change! On the last leg, an early morning sailing from Stockholm, Brit had found an excuse to join Jukka on the bridge well before the start of her shift. She'd heard from the other staff that the Captain had a habit of being there well before anyone else had got out of their bunks.

Jukka was surprised but clearly delighted at her sudden appearance and willingly showed Brit the equipment, explaining with great patience the working of the satellite navigation, steering, and various cameras. Once, when they had been leaning over some control panel, heads close, their eyes met, and Brit had made out the darker rings inside Jukka's pale irises, as well as the perfectly formed light brown eyebrows and the specks of closely shaven hairs on his square jaw. His lips were slightly open, his breathing coming in shallow, short bursts. Just as Brit was thinking their proximity was lasting longer than was necessary, an alarm sounded somewhere and they'd both straightened themselves up.

'It's just the bow door checks,' Jukka said and gave a brief cough. Without looking at her, he began talking into an intercom, saying something Brit couldn't quite comprehend.

'I'll let you get on,' she said and smiled at Jukka, who turned to wave goodbye.

'Another time, I'll give you a more comprehensive tour of the controls, and even the engine room, if you wish.'

Brit nodded and widened her smile.'

'If it interests you, that is,' Jukka said uncertainly. 'Sorry, I get carried away with this stuff sometimes.'

Brit took a step toward him, and placed her hand on the Captain's arm, just above the epaulettes, the golden stripes stitched onto his uniform jacket.

Keeping her eyes steady on Jukka, she said, 'I'd like that very much.'

FIVE

On Monday, the skies are blue and the sun is low but surprisingly strong. It's blinding when the rays hit the snow boulders gathered on the sides of the road. The white fields that Alicia passes as she drives her old Volvo into town are glinting as if with a sprinkling of tiny diamonds. She has to lower the sun visor to shade her eyes.

Alicia had decided to stay overnight with Hilda and Uffe in the main house, rather than go back to the sauna cottage. During the two weeks they were away, she had slept in the house. With the snow and the low temperatures, it was more comfortable than her little cottage. Besides, she hadn't asked Patrick to shovel the snow from her own small driveway. It was awkward enough to have him in the main house. He hadn't been back to Alicia's sauna cottage since he left in a hurry when Liam surprised them in a most compromising situation last July. Alicia doesn't wish to relive that moment.

Uffe had got up early that morning, and by the time Alicia was having her morning coffee, he had already cleared the path so Alicia could drive the Volvo down to the cottage and set the wood burner going for the day. By the evening she will be able to return to her own space.

The sauna cottage is really only meant for summer living, and

Alicia knows she needs to make a decision about her future on the islands, something Liam keeps asking her about. She knows she wants to stay, she feels she belongs here, but what about Liam and their marriage?

As Alicia drives over the Sjoland canal bridge, she sees the slow-flowing, freezing water, and shrugs away thoughts of her mother and Uffe in that fatally icy water, trying to scramble out of their low sports car with their aging limbs. There's no way they would have survived that, she thinks and shivers. Then she thinks about her grief counsellor in London who had told her that she mustn't always picture the worst scenario. Alicia turns her mind toward her own complicated life instead. As if that would bring her more peace!

She thinks back to her whirlwind romance with her husband, which had started nearly twenty years ago, at Uppsala University. Alicia was studying English and Liam was a newly qualified doctor, attending a medical conference there. Since then, both Liam and Alicia had broken their marriage vows. Alicia always feels his infidelity was worse than hers. Liam's liaison with a nurse from the hospital where he has a private clinic had been carrying on for months, while Alicia and Patrick's affair was just a matter of weeks.

A few crazy weeks.

There's no way Liam will want to leave his clinic in London. That's not the 'changes' he was talking about, Alicia is sure of that. He loves his job as a surgeon, and will under no circumstances want to leave London. Would they be able to carry on a relationship while living so far apart? Sometimes Alicia thinks that the physical distance is the least difficult part of their current marital problems. It's far harder to overcome the sudden loss of their son, or what happened after Stefan's death, or rather what Liam had been up to with his nurse. And then last summer, Alicia herself was unfaithful with Patrick. Their relationship is now totally professional and platonic. They have both moved on, so Patrick isn't causing a problem in her marriage. Not as far as Alicia is concerned, anyhow.

The image of Patrick standing in the doorway, looking tall, rugged and so blond, enters Alicia's mind, but she shrugs off the attraction she still feels toward him. She's sure it's natural. After such an explosive affair, her body is bound to react to his closeness.

The elation of the birth of their granddaughter, something neither Alicia or Liam had imagined could happen after losing their son at the tender age of seventeen, had wiped out the importance of their infidelities.

But slowly, over the fall months, Alicia's belief in a future with her husband has started to wane. It isn't that she wants to get back with Patrick. She can't imagine they will ever be good for each other. Patrick's marriage is over, but he still has two daughters who need him and an ex who is more than demanding. Not to mention her family, the wealthy Erikssons. It's far too complicated, and her feelings for the man have changed, she's sure of that. They are just friends and work colleagues now. Alicia shrugs off thoughts of how handsome Patrick looked on Sunday morning. She has a new life now, with a new granddaughter and she doesn't need men.

The road veers toward the left and climbs a small hill. In the distance, on her left, she spots the low buildings of Mariehamn, the capital city of the Åland islands, its lights reflected in the white landscape. The rising sun is low behind Hotel Arkipelag and its wide 70's style windows look dark and empty.

The West Harbor in front of the hotel is now void of sailing boats and there's a thick layer of snow on the jetties that jut out into the ice-covered water. She shrugs away her summer memories of spending a day on Patrick's yacht. She can still picture his body. Sometimes, the desire to touch him is overwhelming when he's standing close to her. But she's managed to keep a distance and remain true to her promise to try to settle things with Liam. Working together with a former lover isn't ideal, but they have managed to forge some kind of professional relationship since the summer and the birth of her and Liam's granddaughter.

Thoughts of little Anne Sofie bring a smile to Alicia's lips. Set against her love for the child, the problems she has with the men in her life pale into insignificance, though Anne Sofie is one of the reasons she's trying to work things out with Liam. Poor Frida, now completely on her own after her mother passed away last month, needs help and that is what Alicia intends to provide—a support network to catch the gorgeous baby and her mother if they fall. Wouldn't any grandmother, but especially one whose only son is dead, do the same?

This Christmas–the baby's first–will be one where the family will truly come together. Hilda has already planned a feast for them all on Christmas Eve, when the main celebration takes place. Liam is arriving two days before this, and Alicia has a list of foodstuffs to be bought and prepared, as well as a few last-minute gifts she needs to get in Mariehamn in the coming days. She's lucky that her job at *Ålandsbladet* is far from demanding. She can nip out during her long lunch hour, and leave early whenever she wishes. In theory, she's still a part-timer, but she finds it better to keep to a Monday to Friday routine, only taking the occasional day off. And it has nothing to do with being with Patrick every day, which was something Liam had suggested when she mentioned his name in passing during a video call. Alicia was annoyed with Liam at first, then found it funny. Sticking to a routine had nothing to do with Patrick. But when she saw Liam's expression, she wondered if there could be some truth in it. No, there really wasn't. Patrick and Alicia are work colleagues, and perhaps could be called friends. That's all.

SIX

When Alicia enters the newspaper office she glances around the open space. There are three other reporters there, their eyes trained on their screens, though they lift them momentarily to nod a hello to her. Patrick, who now officially works at the paper as the news editor, hasn't yet arrived. She is relieved. He sits opposite her, behind a screen. If she lifts her head, she can see the top of his blond head and his bright blue eyes. She's thought about moving desks, but that in itself would show that it bothers her to sit so close to him every day. Which it doesn't, usually.

But on Sunday she had felt that Patrick was about to say something personal to her. She shouldn't have accepted his offer to clear the snow. He's featured far too heavily in her thoughts during the drive into Mariehamn, too, something she wouldn't have been able to hide from him if he had been there. Relief, mixed with a sense of disappointment, washes over her.

Alicia opens her email program and tries to banish thoughts of Patrick. Scrolling down her emails, she sees that there has been an accident on one of the ferryboats connecting the other islands to Mariehamn. That in itself is unusual and she's relieved she'll have something a little more engaging to write about that morning. But when she reads on, her interest is further piqued.

A black Jeep Cherokee collided with another car as it disembarked at Föglö.

There was no driver's name or any other details.

Alicia taps a number on her phone.

'Ebba, Alicia here. Do you have time to talk?'

'Yes,' The police chief says in her habitual curt way.

'The collision in Föglö. Can you tell me anything about it?'

There is a silence at the other end of the telephone. Alicia waits. She is now used to her old schoolfriend's manner, and she knows that if she tries to rush Ebba, she'll get even less information from her.

'What do you want to know? And why?'

Alicia tries to keep her voice level as she replies, 'Name, address, that sort of thing. It's a slow news day so anything is welcome. Give me all the information you have. Or *can* give me.'

Alicia just remembers to add the last sentence. She knows how seriously her friend takes her duties as the new police chief on the islands.

Ebba gives Alicia the names of the drivers, and Alicia gasps when she hears the name of the Cherokee driver. A Russian!

'The driver of the Mazda doesn't want to press charges, but we'll still investigate. On behalf of the state, since the incident occurred on a public highway.'

With these words in her official, dry voice, Ebba ends the call.

After she's put down the phone Alicia gets to work on finding a photograph of Sergei Dudnikov, the Cherokee driver. She is certain this is the same man who caused such commotion between Uffe and Hilda that morning. The timings work perfectly. If the man in the car that had tried to ram into her mother and stepfather's car had driven at speed through Sjoland to the ferryboat that runs between the smaller islands, he would just have made the 3.40 sailing, which arrives on the island of Föglö at 4.10 pm. Besides, these kinds of cars aren't very common in Åland. What are the chances that two black Jeeps of exactly the same model would be traveling over the Sjoland swing bridge? Ebba had said that it had been quite a smash, with damage to the bumper, a broken headlight, and scratches to the driver's door of the other vehicle–a small Mazda. The image of the large American

SUV ramming a small Japanese passenger car to smithereens makes Alicia shiver.

She peers toward the glazed office at the end of the open-plan space and sees it's unoccupied. The black leather chair of the editor, a man of few words, Harri Noutiainen, is empty inside the glass cubicle. She goes over to a new intern called Kim.

'I'm off, following up on a story.'

Kim, who has strawberry blonde hair that sticks out in all directions and a long face, matching his lanky frame, nods. Alicia smiles as she turns to leave the office. She hasn't got more than a handful of words out of Kim since he started in September. The boy is painfully shy. A deep blush covers his freckles if Alicia tries to engage him in any kind of conversation, so she mostly lets him be. He does his job well, and has a very precise writing style. As long as he overcomes his shyness, he'll make a great reporter.

SEVEN

After a morning spent hauling the boxes containing her possessions from the underground parking lot up to her apartment, Brit drives her Golf east out of Mariehamn. In the night she'd woken with alarm, not knowing where she was, but when she saw the white headboard of the bed, she remembered she was in Mia Eriksson's luxurious apartment. In the small hours, she realized this was her first night back in Åland for over six months.

Too long to be away from home.

She now needs to catch a ferry to Föglö, but by the time she's driving over the Sjoland bridge, something that was a slight snowfall when she left Mariehamn is turning into a full-blown snowstorm.

Tiny white flecks are swirling in front of her, nearly obscuring the road ahead. Briefly, she considers turning back, but decides that she'll make her way slowly to the small ferry port, which is some twenty minutes away. If the ferry is cancelled due to the bad weather, she will turn around and telephone her father from the apartment. She feels she needs to see him as soon as possible–it's been too long since her last visit.

To Brit's surprise when she arrives at the port, there's another car waiting on the tarmac. In the distance, she can just make out that something is approaching the small jetty. Through the blizzard, the shape of the car ferry slowly becomes more recognizable, and suddenly it's in front of her. After a single car gets out of the belly of the boat, Brit and the driver of the other car are able to drive onboard.

Brit's father lives in an old wooden house on the outer edges of the small island of Föglö. He will tell anyone who wants to hear that he built the wooden red house with a steel roof himself in the early sixties, before Brit was born. After her mother had succumbed to cancer when Brit was still a teenager, many of her father's friends advised him to move to an apartment in Mariehamn to make it easier for Brit to attend school and for him to cope without his beloved Angelica. But Rolf had built the house when he was a young man, newly in love with the prettiest girl he'd ever set eyes on, so he stayed.

As Brit approaches the house along the long drive lined with high banks of snow, cleared by Rolf's old tractor, Brit wonders if it might be time to broach the subject of a move to Mariehamn again, now he is in his mid-seventies. She has traveled the world, never staying in one place for too long, and cannot imagine a whole life lived in the same small community on an island, often cut off from Fasta Aland, the main island. She remembers many a day when she couldn't make it to school because the ferries were cancelled on account of stormy weather.

When Rolf Svensson opens the door, Brit is taken aback by how old and thin he looks.

'Are you eating regularly?' Brit asks when they are sitting at the kitchen table, drinking coffee out of old faded china cups, part of her parents' wedding gifts, that were used only for "best."

Her father laughs.

'I'm fine, don't you worry about me.'

Looking at his wrinkled face, with his sad droopy eyes, visibly filled with cataracts, Brit places her manicured hand over her father's bony thin one.

'Still no man then?' Rolf says, lifting his eyes, which wrinkle at the corners as he smiles.

This is their game. Every time Brit comes back to the islands, he asks about a boyfriend.

'Nearly got there with a Rat of an Italian,' Brit says, surprising herself. She feels a lump in her throat and looks away from her father's direct gaze.

Rolf pulls his hand from underneath hers and pats it. 'You're beautiful and clever, any man would be a fool not to see that.'

'Oh, *Pappa,* I've missed you!' Brit says, tears pricking her eyes. She gets up and hugs her dad, noting how thin and fragile his frame is. Again, she wonders if she should mention a move to some kind of sheltered accommodation in town. Now that she is in Mariehamn, she would be able to visit him even more frequently if he was close by. Sitting back down and accepting another cup of coffee, Brit decides to leave the matter until her next visit.

'So you are living in one of Eriksson's apartments?'

'Yes. Do you remember Mia was a class below me in the Lyceum?'

Rolf nods and pours some cream into his coffee.

'Well, she came on one of the cruises with her husband and we sort of became friends. So she helped me get the apartment.

Rolf lifts one busy eyebrow. 'I hear they've divorced?'

Now it's Brit's turn to lift her lips into a smile. 'Not much gets past you.'

'It was in the *World Sheet.'*

'Really? Mia didn't tell me that,' Brit says. Then she laughs, 'You still call *Ålandsbladet* that?'

There's a glint in her father's eyes, and his smile widens briefly. Then he says, 'You managing the rent? I hear they are worth a lot of money those new monstrosities.'

Brit crosses her arms. Typical of her father to think anything new is a monstrosity. Again Brit pats her father's hand. 'I'm all grown-up now, *Pappa.'*

Brit says goodbye to her father, who in spite of her protests, stands outside in the chill wind to wave her off as she walks along the path to her car. Even though she is alarmed to think how a strong gust could whisk Rolf off, a sense of great peace descends on her as she leaves the house where she was born. She knows she should have visited Åland and her father more often, but now–at last–she is here permanently.

She'll be able to see him once a week, if not more often. Although he looked frail, Brit could see he had chopped wood for the burner in the lounge. The logs were stacked outside the house, covered with tarpaulin and a thick layer of snow, a small corner showing where her father had picked up a few logs each day. She knows that his neighbors, a Finnish couple who moved into the house about twenty years ago, help Rolf with tasks and looked in on him when there was bad weather, or if he hadn't been seen for a day or so. Perhaps they helped her father chop the logs?

They were a nice couple but Brit always had the sense that they didn't approve of her lifestyle, which kept her away from her father for months at a time.

Brit sighs with satisfaction when she looks in her rear-view mirror and sees her father go inside and close the door. From now on she would be here to help and Rolf's neighbors would have nothing to reproach her for.

EIGHT

Patrick sits in the kitchen of his apartment on the tenth floor of a new development overlooking the frozen sea. That morning's cruise ferries have just passed by his window, making their way toward the shipping lanes, cutting the ice beyond the East Harbor in half. There's a sharp wind, with snow flurries swirling up and down and settling on the bannister of his balcony outside. The skies are dark and there's a threat of a full-blown snow storm in the air.

He has just put the phone down to his former boss, the editor of *Journalen* in Stockholm. He smiles to himself, pleased with the decision he's made. Now all he needs to do is convince Alicia to come with him. Once again, he gazes out of the vast floor-to-ceiling windows, which wrap around the kitchen and living area of the apartment. He will not even miss this view. He will not regret leaving Mariehamn behind, or the rows with Mia, or the Eriksson family, whose influence is everywhere on the islands. He fought hard to get his two daughters, Sara and Alexandra, for two weekends a month, and he knows they will be delighted to spend those in Stockholm. Already nearly teenagers, they will revel in being in a capital city rather than in this small provincial island town.

He'd much rather be sitting overlooking Kungsholmen over the water from the buzzy Södermalm part of Stockholm. How he misses the trendy restaurants and cafés, which serve his morning lattes just perfectly. Where *not everyone* knows who he is, and watches his every move.

Patrick has spent his summers in this quirky island community ever since he married Mia over ten years ago, and he has grown to love Åland in his way. But he'd never spent a long fall and winter on the islands until now. And he's never worked on a small newspaper like the *Ålandsbladet* before, where a theft of a flower pot is considered a newsworthy item. He misses the hustling he had to do while working at the *Journalen*. He isn't ashamed to admit that he enjoys the thrill of chasing a real news story, whether it's a senseless knifing of a teenager, or a calculated murder of a loved (or previously loved) partner. He also enjoyed the interaction with the hardened Stockholm police officers, who didn't want to give him any information unless it was in their interest to let the criminals know what they knew. And he has to admit it to himself, winning a prize for his journalism had always been a dream. It wasn't too late, he was only thirty-seven, a full eight years younger than the previous year's winner of Sweden's Journalist of the Year.

That's never going to happen if you stay here in this tiny group of islands in the middle of the Baltic Sea!

Patrick's thoughts return to Alicia. Again, if he is truthful, the reason he has stayed in Åland is to a large extent because of her presence. Of course, being close to his daughters has been a large motivation to stay too, but the journey to Stockholm is so short, four hours on the ferry, and Sara and Alexandra can hop over the Ålands Hav any time they want.

What Patrick needs to do is to convince Alicia to come with him to Stockholm. Since their brief affair last summer, he hasn't stopped thinking about her. And he knows that she and Liam are hardly getting on. He's only been to see her a couple of times since the summer, and Patrick can tell from Alicia's face and her body language that they're not sleeping together. At least he thinks they're not. The thought makes his heart beat fast and he notices that he's formed fists with his hands, so he decides not to think about it.

He's just not got over her. Which has really surprised him. He's tried seeing other women in Stockholm, not here in the gossip-ridden small circles of Mariehamn, but to no avail. However blonde, leggy, and pretty, they just haven't interested him enough to warrant a second date.

When Alicia sent him a message yesterday, accepting his offer of help with the snow at the Ulsson's place, he was certain she wanted something else too. But when he hinted at wanting to talk about more than the mundane, she had clammed up.

He's got to get her on his own soon and talk to her properly.

NINE

Alicia drives her old Volvo back over the swing bridge into Sjoland. She passes Hilda and Uffe's house and her own temporary home, the sauna cottage, as she makes her way toward the small ferry port at the end of the island. It's now snowing heavily, the sunshine of the morning but a memory. Momentarily Alicia's mind drifts to the forthcoming Christmas celebrations. A thick covering of snow over the landscape is perfect for her plans to create a wonderful *Jul*.

Alicia turns her thoughts to her destination. She's taken this car ferry many times to the outer islands whether on an excursion with school, or when invited to the birthday parties of friends who lived in the outer archipelago. Föglö is one of the larger outcrops, which has a permanent population. It's part of the complicated ferry traffic that criss-cross the Åland islands. From memory, she pictures a restaurant overlooking the water, which is a popular venue for summer parties. But in the winter the ferry is mainly used by locals, which makes Alicia wonder if the Russian has a place somewhere in Föglö or farther on. Perhaps he lives here permanently? She ponders the various possibilities as she arrives in the port and sees the ferry making its slow progress toward her.

The falling snow is now dense and the wind has got up. Alicia can just make out the water in the shipping lane, which is the color of steel and moves slowly, like thick oil, at the bow of the ship. Alicia pulls her coat closer when she sees from her phone that the temperature has plummeted. She's glad of her long, warm padded parka, which Hilda had given her from the leftover stock of her shop.

Briefly, Alicia wonders how much money her mother and Uffe lost when they decided to close the fashion boutique. The space is now taken up by a men's hairdressers. When Alicia saw the new sign, 'Gentlemen's Barber Shop' written in an old-fashioned curvaceous font, she thought no one in Åland would pay through the nose for a shave or a haircut. It had seemed far too trendy for the islands. But the shop is still there, and even in winter there's always someone in a red leather chair, having their faces lathered with foam. She has heard rumors that the enterprise is being financed by Russian mafia, but as usual, when it comes to this kind of talk on the islands, her research into the money side has borne no fruit.

Alicia's is the only car waiting to board, and when the bow of the ship opens, she sees just two vehicles emerge and drive past her toward Mariehamn. Once onboard, Alicia makes her way to the upper deck where the passengers sit. There are three other people already there, one couple and a lone female foot passenger, looking out to sea. The snow and chill wind nearly convince Alicia to turn back when, moments later, she climbs the outer stairs from the forehead deck to the bridge. She wants to talk to the staff onboard.

'Didn't see it,' the First Mate says. He's standing half in, half out of the bridge, while holding the door to the gangway open with one foot. He's smoking a roll-up cigarette and he smells of diesel oil and the sea.

'But who reported the accident to the police?' Alicia asks. She's also trying to engage the Captain in the discussion, but he glances only briefly in her direction. He's by the control panel, his eyes trained on the horizon, where the teal-blue sea of the shipping lane meets the now dim, white sky. The visibility is poor and Alicia wonders if the ferry is on autopilot. It's past 2pm and it will be dusk in an hour or so. The Captain, who wears a worn-looking jacket with dirty gold braid on the sleeves, has sandy colored hair and dark eyes, the exact shade of the sea in the shipping lane. Both men are tall and look weather-beaten, with unshaven chins and calloused hands: archetypical sailors.

The First Mate shrugs and flicks his cigarette out over the rail and into the water. Alicia wonders about the safety of smoking onboard. Surely it must be illegal, but she says nothing.

'Close that damn door,' the Captain bellows suddenly, and the First Mate nods to Alicia. He lifts his foot away and the coils on the door spring into action, closing it quickly.

'Wait,' Alicia says and takes hold of the door handle and slips inside the bridge. It's a large space, almost entirely taken up by the control panel at the front. Alicia's coat and hair are wet, she feels like a drowned cat.

She hears the Captain take a deep breath. 'We didn't see anything,' he now says, turning his head fully toward Alicia.

'Take over, will you?' he says to the First Mate and comes to stand close to her. 'It happened before we docked. So there's nothing we can tell you.'

'But,' Alicia begins, but the Captain opens the door behind her and a gust of wind lifts Alicia's hair up, blowing snow and strands of wet hair into her face. She tries to wipe her face and scrape the hair behind her ear. 'The police chief told me the Jeep Cherokee drove into the Mazda when it was boarding the ship,' she says, holding onto her hair, trying to control it.

'Look, lady, we're at sea, and no one is allowed on the bridge while the ferry in in transit. I told you we didn't see the accident and that's that. You're not police, so bugger off.'

When the ferry arrives at Föglö, Alicia can see both men looking at her through the wide glass on the high bridge.

If I've ever seen anyone lie badly, those two did today.

TEN

Ebba has sent her the full details of the other person involved in the rear-ender. He's the manager of the K-Market. Alicia is relieved to see that it's a convenience store right in the center of Föglö. Lars Mortenson turns out of be a youngish man with a large belly hanging over his jeans, and an untidy wispy beard covering his double chin. His mousy hair is short, and he wears small glasses, making his head seem large and round. He walks slowly toward Alicia along the central aisle of the grocery store. Alicia stands by the tills, eyed suspiciously by the young girl with pink hair, who called Lars over the tannoy.

'Who are you?' Lars Mortenson says in response to Alicia's question about the accident.

'Alicia O'Connell from *Ålandsbladet*,' she replies with a smile, but Lars doesn't take her outstretched hand.

He turns away. 'Nothing to tell you. An accident, pure and simple.'

'Not what the police tell me,' Alicia says, following the man along the shop floor to the back where the chilled goods are. The man turns left and opens a door marked *Private*.

'I have nothing to say to you!' Lars Mortenson bangs the door in Alicia's face.

While she's been in the store, the snow has been falling heavily and there's a thick blanket on her car. She can hardly distinguish the land from the sea, or make out the port, even though she knows it's less than a kilometer along the shore.

Visibility on the road is dreadful as Alicia turns carefully out of the parking lot. At the junction to the main road of the island, she's grateful that all of Föglö has decided to stay at home. She prays the ferry traffic isn't affected by the sudden turn in the weather. The last thing she needs is to get stuck on the other side of water. She tries to think if she knows anyone on the island, but only comes up with the father of a friend who works abroad. She doesn't know how old he is, or if he's even still alive. Besides, he may not even remember Alicia.

The summer restaurant has a few rooms to rent, but that will be shut now. She tries to stop herself from panicking and tells herself that the ferries operate in all sorts of weather conditions. There's still 30 minutes until the sailing, and she's glad to spot the outline of a red hut, used as a waiting room, next to the small port.

At that very moment, a car drives toward her at speed. All she has time to register is a large black lump, surrounded by clouds of white.

ELEVEN

Everything is a blur. Alicia turns the steering wheel and ends up hitting one of the snowy boulders on the side of the road. She hears the roar of an engine as the vehicle passes her and then silence. She glances in her rear-view mirror. Through the falling snow she sees the clear outline of a Jeep Cherokee, its engine running empty in the middle of the road. After a moment, it begins to reverse.

'Do you need help?' a man about Alicia's age, with large pale eyes, is gazing down at her through the driver's window of the elevated SUV. He's speaking English with a soft Russian accent.

'You tried to hit me,' Alicia blurts out. This must be the same man who tried to run her mother and Uffe off the road and who'd driven into the manager of the K-Market.

For a moment, a small smile plays on the lips of the man in the car, but it's so fleeting that Alicia later wonders if she'd imagined it.

'I lost control of the steering for a while. I'm so sorry. May I help you out of the ditch? I have some ropes in the car.'

There is absolutely no one about and the ferry that is supposed to take her back home to Sjoland is still nowhere to be seen. Alicia nods and the man gets out of the car.

'You're Alicia, Uffe's daughter, aren't you?' he says after he's managed to pull Alicia's old Volvo back onto the road. The man is now standing next to her car, with the snow falling onto his thin, fair hair. His ears are red from the cold, but he doesn't make any effort to pull up the collar of his thick, expensive-looking down coat. Instead, he takes off a leather glove and offers Alicia his hand.

'Alexander Dudnikov,' he says.

For a moment Alicia considers ignoring the man and just driving off, but her journalistic training kicks in and she takes Dudnikov's hand. His grip around her fingers is strong and warm.

'You can call me Alex,' he says. The lines around his eyes deepen as his mouth lifts into a smile.

'So what happened back there? Why did you drive into me? Can't be the same reason you nearly destroyed Lars Mortenson's Mazda yesterday?'

The Russian stands in front of Alicia. The snow is falling, with gusts of wind occasionally making the landscape around them disappear into a soft, white haze.

'Yes, of course, you work for Kurt's paper, don't you?' Dudnikov says after a long while. Although there are no threatening words in his question, there's something sinister in his voice.

'And you know everybody,' Alicia says, her eyes steady on the man standing by the side of her car. She has to look up at him, giving her a disadvantage, but she's trying to ignore the obvious power he has over her. There's no one around, and the visibility is so bad, with white flurries dancing around them, that even if there was someone inside the red hut at the side of the port, waiting for the ferry, through the small windows they wouldn't be able to discern more than the shape of the two cars and perhaps those of Alicia and the Russian standing by the side of the road.

Dudnikov smiles at Alicia, but doesn't speak, so Alicia adds, 'You may be interested to know that I have already talked to Lars Mortenson. Perhaps you'd like to make a statement now.'

'I'm a very bad driver, I'm afraid,' Dudnikov says, with a widening smile. His gaze stays on Alicia when he adds, 'I believe your ferry will soon be here. If I were you, I'd forget about stories of silly little bumps and return home. You don't want to get stuck on this island all on your own. Have a good day.'

Dudnikov turns to open the door to his Jeep. Inside, he winds down his window. 'I'm sure we'll meet again soon.'

Once inside the car, Alicia shivers in her seat. She starts the engine of the Volvo, which purrs with a comforting sound. Before she moves, she looks through the open window and sees the shape of the black Jeep fade as it moves away from her.

TWELVE

While she's been with her father, the storm has abated a little. Still, it's difficult to see the road ahead through the intermittent flurries of drifting snow, so Brit takes it easy on her way toward the small Föglö ferry port. On a good day she can make it from her father's house in less than ten minutes, but today she's left much more time for the short drive.

At the port, Brit is suddenly aware of a black shape in the middle of the road. She sees a large black American SUV–a rare sight in Mariehamn, let alone on the smaller islands–swerve in front of her, forcing her to break hard. Just before the two cars collide, the SUV corrects its course and drives past Brit. Blowing air out of her cheeks, Brit pulls onto the side of the road and checks her mirror. As the vehicle disappears from view, she sees that the car is a Cherokee, but she can't make out the number plates, only that a largish man is driving without a backward glance to see if she's OK.

Another bastard in a hurry, she thinks and puts her Golf into gear. Only a few meters farther on she sees a Volvo on the side of the road, with a woman inside. She turns, and Brit cannot believe her eyes. Quickly, she parks behind the car and gets out.

'Alicia!'

'Brit!'

. . .

'What are you doing here?' Alicia says. She thinks her eyes are failing her, but here, on the road in Föglö, exposed to the dreadful weather stands her best and oldest schoolfriend. She climbs out of the car and stretches her arms out to give Brit a hug.

'I could ask you the same thing!' Brit says and takes hold of Alicia's shoulders. Brit is a little taller than Alicia. She suddenly remembers how she'd begged her mom for a pair of high-heeled boots just so that she'd be the same height as her friend. But Hilda hadn't budged. 'You'll fall and break your neck. And how would Madam get to classes then, eh?'

'That's a long story,' Alicia says, but her words are swallowed by a sudden snow flurry. The wind is whipping at their bodies, threatening to blow the two women away, so they decide to sit in the car.

'This weather! I've missed the snow but this!' Brit says sitting next to Alicia. She brushes flakes off her shoulders. She's wearing a brand-new padded coat over tight black jeans and fashionable looking snow-boots.

Alicia starts to laugh and soon they are both giggling, and they hug again awkwardly over the gearshift. Alicia sees that there are still snowflakes on top of Brit's dark hair and she wipes them off with her hand.

'I didn't know you're here? You've been to see your dad, I presume? I was just thinking about you and him.'

Brit nods. She tells Alicia about her new job at Marie Line and the apartment in Mariehamn. When she mentions the block and where it is, Alicia's heart stops for a moment.

'That's owned by the Eriksson family,' she says.

Brit nods, but before Alicia has time to ask any more about her friend's new home, Brit takes Alicia's hands into hers and says, 'I heard about Stefan. I'm so sorry.'

Alicia lifts her eyes toward her friend and nods. She's used to hearing condolences from people she knew when she was young on the islands, but to hear it from this particular friend takes the wind out of her lungs. When Alicia doesn't reply, Brit adds, 'Look, I know I should have come over to London, called you, or something, but I couldn't get away.' Brit bites her lip and adds, 'You know me. I'm a coward.'

'Oh, don't say that!' Alicia looks at her friend and squeezes the hands holding hers.

'I've only just surfaced from, you know. I wasn't myself for a long time. If that makes any sense.'

Brit nods. Alicia feels tears welling up inside her, so she changes the subject.

'Did you see that maniac? He nearly ran me off the road. All because,' Suddenly Alicia thinks it best not to divulge what she knows about the Russian until she's found out more and discussed her thoughts with the editor at *Ålandsbladet*.

'He did what?'

'Oh, just driving recklessly. You nearly came a cropper in the Golf, didn't you?'

Brit gazes at her friend, 'Hmm, I did.'

'But let's forget about that bastard. Are you here on holiday, or what?'

It takes so long for Alicia to tell her friend about what has happened to her in the past six months that halfway through, they spot the car ferry making its way toward the little port. They decide to drive on and carry on talking over a coffee onboard.

THIRTEEN

'Mia is nice now, honestly she's not at all as nasty as she used to be at school,' Brit says. Her manicured hands are hugging a white mug of hot, steaming coffee.

'Really?' Alicia says and adds, 'She doesn't much like me.'

'Why not?'

The boat rocks from side to side, and Alicia looks out of the window. The snow storm has rendered the view almost completely white. You cannot even make out the small outcrops that are scattered along this little crossing between Föglö and Sjoland.

Alicia turns her face back to her friend. 'How come you kept in touch with Mia Eriksson after school?' she asks. She feels a small prick of jealousy that Brit hasn't contacted her more than once or twice in all the years she was living in London. She's just reconnected with her best friend who is living back on the islands at exactly the same time as she is, and she's best friends with the person who probably considers Alicia to be Public Enemy Number One on Åland. Brit must have seen it in her face, or heard it in the tone of her voice, because she stretches her hand out and touches Alicia. 'Don't be like that. We'll never be best of pals, not really.' She glances at Alicia and adds, 'At least not like you and me.'

'I didn't mean that. God, we're not at school anymore!' Alicia says, and they both laugh, knowing that there really is no difference. To Alicia, seeing her friend feels as if she's been transported back to the small Mariehamn classroom, where boys threw paper planes at the girls they liked, and girls whispered amongst themselves about the boys they fancied. And the girls they disliked. Mia was always popular–she was thin and had the latest Spice Girls T-shirts and pencil cases.

It transpires that Mia and Patrick and the girls had been on a cruise boat that Brit worked on. 'It was amazing to see someone from the islands out there–hundreds of miles away.'

Brit tells Alicia that it was Mia who sought Brit's company each evening after her shift ended because Patrick wanted to go to bed early.

They must have already been fighting then, Alicia thinks.

'The guy is a complete loser,' Brit says.

'Oh?'

'Yeah, have you met him? Patrick?'

'Actually, I have. I work with him at *Ålandsbladet*.'

'My God, yes. He's an editor there now, isn't he? Mia told me it was part of the divorce settlement, to give him something to do.' Brit laughs and Alicia hears Mia's words coming out of her friend's mouth.

Brit studies her friend. Aware of this, Alicia tries to keep her face expressionless.

'Oh my God, you like him?'

'Patrick is a friend and colleague, that's all.'

'Oh, yeah?'

Alicia sees in her friend's green eyes that she knows Alicia is lying. It's strange that even though she hasn't seen Brit for over twenty years, it's as if they have spoken to each other every day since leaving school. Nothing has changed, apart from a few wrinkles around their eyes. Well, possibly Alicia's schoolfriend has gained a pound or two, but that's made her womanly shape even more attractive.

Alicia remembers that Brit had been the first one of all the girls in their year to have proper breasts. Suddenly, on the first day back from the summer holiday, when they were getting undressed before sports, she'd noticed Brit had an extra garment under her shirt. She remembers how nobody had commented on Brit's new bra, which was white with tiny pink roses, but how they had looked on in awe as she expertly unhooked it and revealed perfectly round mounds with pink nipples standing proud in the middle. They had all looked quickly away, but Alicia had seen from the corner of her eye that Brit had straightened her back ever so slightly. Then she had pulled out a white crop top from her sports bag. This, she later told Alicia, was her sports bra.

Brit was the more outgoing of the two friends, and was always dreaming of travel to exotic places. Her father was a sea captain–now retired, Alicia knew from her mother. It hadn't been a surprise to anyone when Brit had begun a career onboard luxury cruise ships rather than going to university in Sweden, like Alicia.

'So, spill the beans!' Brit now says, hers eyes wide, with a meaning-ful, demanding look.

Alicia tells Brit the whole sorry saga of her and Liam's break-up after she'd discovered his affair with a nurse at the hospital where he worked as a surgeon.

'It started after we lost Stefan.'

Alicia bites her lip. She feels the threat of tears, but takes a deep breath and continues. 'We'd been drifting apart for years without me noticing. When we came here for our usual holiday, things just got worse, so he went back home early and I decided to stay.'

'You decided to move back here from London–just like that?' Brit asks, her eyes even wider now.

'Look who's speaking!'

To this Brit gives one of her loud, cackling laughs that she was famous for at school. The teachers used to say they could hear her across the water between Föglö and Mariehamn.

'Fair point,' Brit says through giggles.

'You know what my mother is like,' Alicia begins and Brit, now quiet again, nods. Hilda wasn't like all the other mothers at school. She had great plans for Alicia's future and always demanded top marks at every exam she ever took. The other Åland parents were happy if their kids just passed each year without too many black marks on their record, but for Hilda nothing but top of the class was good enough.

'When I decided to stay on, she began talking about getting me a job with the newspapers, so I decided to get one myself before she had time to interfere.'

'You met Patrick at *Ålandsbladet*?'

Alicia is quiet for a moment. She's not sure how much of their relationship she should reveal to her old friend who, by all accounts, is now best friends with Mia, Patrick's ex.

'I met Mia and Patrick on the ferry on our way here. That was just before they split up.'

'And?' Brit says, 'I can tell there's more!'

'We had a very brief fling.' As soon as the words come out of Alicia's mouth she regrets them. Being caught in the snow storm and the accident with the Russian must have messed with her head.

'What?' Brit's eyes are wide and her mouth stays open.

'If I tell you everything, you must promise not to say anything to anyone–especially Mia!'

'Who do you take me for!' Brit exclaims.

'OK, so you know I was under the impression that Liam and I had split up, and Mia had told Patrick about the other guy, so basically we were both free agents. It didn't work out that way, but at the time, I thought it might.'

Alicia looks at her friend. She doesn't know how Brit will react to an affair between two married people. When they last saw each other, Alicia had just met Liam and was madly in love. Brit was about to start her first job with a British cruise liner and they talked about meeting up in London, but the plan never materialized. Alicia was already pregnant–without knowing it–and about to head into the whirlwind that motherhood brings.

'Go on, I want all the details!' Brit now says, smiling. 'I can then tell you about The Rat of an Italian that I thought was the love of my life. And the new guy I met recently.'

'What? You've met someone? Where? When?' Alicia is desperate to change the subject. Normally Brit would be delighted to talk about herself, but this time, Alicia isn't so lucky.

'You first.' Brit says determinedly with a wicked grin on her face.

Alicia gives in and tells her friend how Patrick and Mia had invited her and Uffe and Hilda to the prestigious Eriksson Midsummer Party and how, by chance, the two of them had ended up on a beach that Patrick used to escape from his influential in-laws (and Mia). How he'd been swimming naked, how Alicia had had too much champagne, and how they'd ended up kissing.

When, a few days later, Patrick had asked Alicia to go sailing on his boat, she had succumbed to him. And then she had found out that her beloved son had got a local girl pregnant. She'd been so delighted by this news that she had even envisaged a future on the islands with Patrick, and the new granddaughter.

'Suddenly everything fell into place,' Alicia says.

Brit is quiet for a moment, then asks, 'Do you love him?'

Alicia hasn't really allowed herself to think whether she fell in love with Patrick last summer or not. Or how she really feels about him now. After Liam's protestations of love and his desire to try again, and the birth of little Anne Sofie, she hadn't even considered a future with Patrick. She wanted to keep her family together, and this now consisted of Liam, Frida, Ann Sofie and, of course, her parents. The only problem is Liam, who was still in London with no plans to move to the islands. And their relationship, which is another complication in itself.

Besides, Patrick's life was complicated too. With the divorce, and his fights with Mia over access to his daughters, it was easier to keep their relationship on a purely professional level. Alicia thinks back to the Sunday morning at Hilda and Uffe's house, when Patrick had wanted to talk to Alicia about something personal. But she must resist any return to last summer's craziness. She must keep her family together for the sake of her granddaughter.

'No, I don't think so,' Alicia says, and for the first time since the previous July, she feels she's speaking the truth. To Brit and to herself.

'Now it's your turn!' Alicia says and Brit bites her lip.

'Oh, I don't know. Perhaps it's all going too fast.'

'Tell me more!' Alicia is so relieved that she doesn't have to talk about Patrick anymore that she milks all the information she can from Brit—who this Jukka character is, how they met, what he said, and what he's like.

'He sounds really nice,' Alicia says and squeezes her friend's hand across the table.

She casts her eyes over to the window and sees they are close to Sjoland. The tannoy comes alive with a crackle and the senior deck-hand of the ferry asks all drivers to return to their cars.

Alicia gets up. 'Look, I've got to get back to work. But we have to have lunch or something.'

'Yes, we need a proper catch-up. Come to my place soon?' Brit scribbles an address on the back of a receipt and hands it to Alicia.

Alicia looks at the number of the building and her fears are confirmed. It seems Brit lives just one floor down from Patrick in the exact same block.

FOURTEEN

Patrick watches Alicia enter the newspaper office. She looks a little disheveled, he thinks. She's obviously been out in the snow storm, but where? The underground parking lot is available for the staff of *Ålandsbladet* and there's a direct internal lift straight to the office, so there is no need to walk outside.

'You OK?' Patrick asks when Alicia sits down opposite him, half concealed behind a bright blue screen that divides the desks in the open-plan office.

She gives him a quick glance, nods, and without saying a word begins typing.

Patrick pretends to be working, or interested in the preliminary layout of tomorrow's paper which has just been sent to him.

After his divorce, Kurt Eriksson, his former father-in-law, had made him news editor, a title that hadn't existed before. Kurt said it was so he 'wouldn't be a jobless embarrassment to the family.' But what can a news editor do when there is no news to report? Today, for example, his main task is to decide whether to lead with the local school Christmas drawing competitions or the slight delays to the ferry service due to weather conditions. How he aches for a proper story, a snow storm so severe that the island is cut off for days, for example. He didn't want anyone to be hurt, of course not, but oh, for proper news!

After six months, he is so bored and frustrated that he can hardly wait till the end of December, when he can move back to Stockholm.

Patrick smiles to himself as he gazes at Alicia. He sees her turn around and peer at the glass cubicle. Noticing the empty chair of the editor, her eyes move toward Patrick. He can't help himself and grins, which he immediately realizes is a mistake. Alicia's face quickly returns to her screen. She lifts her fingers and begins to type furiously. Patrick sighs and pushes himself up from his chair.

Patrick knows how much it hurt Kurt to give him this job and therefore the chance to stay on the islands. Although nothing to do with Kurt, he had squirmed over Patrick's right to arrange set times to see the girls too. By that point, four months ago, Mia had been desperate to make the relationship with her lover official, so the family had accepted nearly every one of Patrick's demands. Now that he has decided to go back to Stockholm after all, he knows the family will be overjoyed. But he still has Christmas to get over. Perhaps there would be a big story, and he could leave the paper on a high. How sweet it would be to make Kurt Eriksson plead with him to stay on at *Ålandsbladet*.

Patrick decides to forget about his in-laws for a moment and find out what Alicia is up to. Perhaps she is following a story with an international slant that he would be able to sell worldwide? Something like the case of the oldest champagne in the world, which was found in the sea near Föglö a few years ago.

That would do nicely.

Convincing himself that his only motive is professional, he lifts his head and addresses her.

'The snow suits you.'

Alicia looks startled. She touches her hair, and tries to smooth it down.

That was too personal. The deal is: work chat only.

Patrick rubs his hands together and adds, trying to make the conversation sound general and impersonal, 'It's awful weather out there.'

'What do you want, Patrick?'

If looks could kill.

'Wow, steady on! What have I done?'

Alicia leans back on her office chair.

'Sorry, it's been a challenging day.'

'Care to tell me about it?' Patrick glances briefly around at the five other people in the office and nods in the direction of the glass cubicle.

Alicia's shoulders slump and suddenly she reminds him of his eldest daughter, who at the age of 10 is going on 15. When he was young, there was no such thing as a 'pre-teen.' Just like Sara, Alicia gets up slowly, and shuffles behind Patrick, making her reluctance clear.

FIFTEEN

'So, how are you?'

Alicia glares at Patrick. As the news editor, he can use the glass cubicle for private discussions. He's asked Alicia to sit on a chair next to the editor's vast leather one at the side of Harri's desk. She knows this area is less visible from the main office, but Alicia doesn't care if she's seen by the other reporters. Her relationship with Patrick is purely professional and as far as she knows no one at the newspaper knows about what happened the previous summer.

'What is this? Editorial control? By you?'

Patrick sits back and rubs his chin. Alicia sees that he's cut himself shaving again and tries to stop herself from smiling. It's as if the man is a teenager the way he can't shave properly. Like Stefan, she thinks fondly, remembering her son at the breakfast table, his skin covered with pieces of tissue stuck to the bleeding bits.

Her face must have betrayed a mood change, because Patrick leans over and suddenly takes her hands in his.

'I can't stop thinking about you.'

Alicia is taken aback but sits still, gazing at Patrick's strong fingers around her own. These fingers had ignited something animal in her last summer, when she couldn't get enough of him. She doesn't dare look up at him, fearing she will show that she is missing their physical closeness. She knows that if she gives in even a little bit they will be back in that vortex of passion, hurting everybody, including themselves, with their actions.

Without lifting her eyes to him, Alicia says, slowly and deliberately, 'Patrick, we agreed.'

But she's not allowed to finish her sentence before Patrick interrupts her.

'I know what we said, or rather, what you decided should happen in the future, but I am now divorced, Frida and the baby are doing well, and Liam is still in London.'

At the mention of Liam, Alicia looks at the blue eyes that made her wild with desire just a few months ago.

She says, 'But I am still married to him.'

Patrick inches closer with his leather chair. 'Do you love him?'

When Alicia says nothing, Patrick continues, 'Your silence speaks volumes, Alicia. Besides, how can you love a man who you never see? How many times in the last six months has he visited the islands to see you and his granddaughter? Two, three times?'

'He has a very important and demanding job. A surgeon can't just leave his patients,' Alicia says. She can hear her voice betray the doubts she herself has battled with since she decided to stay in Åland. She knows she will never want to go back to London, even though Liam pleads with her every time they see each other, as well as during their occasional video calls.

'They are more important than his wife and family?' Patrick says, releasing her hands. Alicia can see the contempt for Liam in Patrick's face.

'You don't understand,' Alicia says, moving her eyes back to her lap. She glances briefly toward the general office to see if anyone is paying attention to the two of them in the corner of the room. The staff are all sitting at the other end of the open-plan space, where they cannot see Patrick and Alicia, unless they move and openly stare at them. That's something, Alicia thinks and she gazes back at Patrick.

He's looking at the desk, deep in thought, it seems. He's wearing his customary white T-shirt, this time under a blue and white checked shirt. His jeans aren't ripped, but still reveal his strong thigh muscles. Alicia moves her eyes toward his arms where she can clearly make out his biceps. Suddenly an image of his body over hers comes to her mind and she suppresses a quick intake of breath.

Seeming to read her thoughts, he turns his head toward her again and, leaning over, puts his hands on the seat, either side of her thighs, his thumbs under her legs. His touch is burning into Alicia's flesh, sending currents through her muscles and into her center.

Suddenly she's being pulled into the corner of the office. Patrick is holding onto her, and pushing himself against her. He finds her mouth and his lips are soft and probing at first, then hot and demanding. His tongue finds hers and Alicia forgets where she is, or who she is, and just savors Patrick's touch, the taste of his lips, and the passion they ignite in her body. She abandons herself to Patrick's touch, his hands slipping inside her jumper, against her bare back, pulling at the front of her bra. When his fingers find her left nipple, a short yelp escapes Alicia's lips. With that, she wakes up from the trance Patrick has sent her into. Panting, she pulls away from his embrace and says, 'What are you doing?'

Patrick is also breathless. 'You drive me crazy. I can't resist you.

'You know how much you mean to me, Alicia,' he adds, more seriously now, his voice hoarse. Alicia can feel the hunger for her emanating from his body. All she wants to do is close the gap between them and let him fold her into his arms again. Involuntarily, she glances down and sees Patrick's jeans are straining at the front. Oh, my God, how she still desires this man! But she knows that giving into Patrick now is the wrong decision. She is a grandmother and needs to make sure Liam stays committed to Frida and little Anne Sofie. They are a family and families must stay together.

'No, Patrick, I can't.'

Alicia looks pleadingly at Patrick, who goes back to the editor's chair, staring at the computer screen.

When he doesn't say anything, or even look up at Alicia, she adds, 'You know the situation, Patrick.'

Now the man stands up again and his blue eyes meet Alicia's.

'No, frankly, I don't understand what the problem is. I wanted to tell you that I am moving back to Stockholm in the New Year. The apartment in Mariehamn will soon go on the market and I'm getting one in Södermalm. I'm going back to work for *Journalen*. Please say you'll come with me!'

Alicia can't believe her ears.

'Patrick, you know even if I could ...'

But he won't let her speak. He puts one finger over her lips. 'I know how you really feel about me. I don't need an answer now. But I will convince you to come. Stockholm isn't as far as London!'

Alicia shakes her head, but her mind is running wild.

'Look. Think about it,' Patrick says and gives her a quick kiss.

SIXTEEN

Alicia returns to her desk and tries to concentrate on researching the angry Russian driver. But it's difficult to find out anything about him. There aren't even images on Google that match the man she met earlier in Föglö.

She sighs and looks up at the glass cubicle where Patrick has remained after their earlier tête-à-tête.

Why does he have to be such a good kisser?

Alicia can't believe that in one second, a single moment, all the self-control she has been practicing over the last few months fell away. Just like that.

Does this mean I am in love with Patrick?

Surely not? Surely that was just her body reacting to being starved of intimacy, even if it is of her own volition?

Alicia resists the temptation to put her head in her hands. Instead she gets up. She gives a quick glance toward the Editor's glass cubicle, where Patrick is gazing at the computer screen. She slips quickly off her seat, pulling her coat from the back of her chair and grabbing her red bag, and then leaves the office.

The light outside is fading, even though it's just 4pm. Alicia makes her way through the Sittkoff shopping center and decides to stop at the Bagarstugan café on Lilla Torget. The snow storm has left the landscape virgin white. Christmas decorations hang from lampposts and criss-cross the street overhead. Put up for the traditional Christmas Market in early December, they stretch the length of Torggatan from Sittkoff's to the Market Square. Stars are strung through the bare trees growing in tubs along the pedestrianized part of the street, and there's a vast Christmas tree, decked with fairy lights and massive white baubles, in a small square at the end.

The little town is busy with last-minute shoppers, in spite of the freezing temperatures. Alicia sees from the digital display above the shopping center that it's -3°C. Not too bad, she thinks, and she pulls a woolly hat she found in her desk drawer down over her ears. Her hair is still a little damp from her excursion to Föglö. What a day she has already had! With the Russian, then meeting Brit, her oldest friend. It was so strange the way the years just fell away as they talked. She is pleased that her friend is considering a new relationship, despite being cheated on by her Italian boyfriend. And that she's now living in Åland permanently. Both of them back home at the same time.

Inside the warm café, she lets herself think about what just happened in the newspaper office, and what Patrick said to her.

Patrick is moving to Stockholm!

Because she was so taken aback by the news, as well as the passionate kiss, and the invitation to move to the Swedish capital with him, she hadn't thought about how she will miss him. If, as she now suspects, her feelings for him are stronger than she realized, how would she cope with not seeing him every day? They have become good friends, confidants, even, in spite of the constant sexual tension between them—a frisson she has convinced herself is just playfulness, the remnants of what once was. After what had just happened, she knows that neither of them had got over the affair.

Alicia takes a sip of her large cup of coffee and wonders why her overwhelming feeling is one of pure happiness.

You know how much you mean to me, Alicia.

Patrick's words repeat themselves in her head and she feels like a teenager.

He loves me. He loves me.

She must admit that working in the same office, and often together on a story, has been difficult at times. She was the one who had insisted on being professional, rejecting any closeness instigated by Patrick. On occasion, if they were both leaning toward a computer screen, her long blonde hair nearly touching his head, she would catch his familiar scent, or see the stubble on his chin, and have the most overpowering desire to touch him. She would always pull away and sometimes get up and move away on some pretext or other. Did Patrick notice her emotional turmoil on these occasions?

At least she now knows how *he* feels about her. He wants to take her with him!

Pull yourself together! You have a family who depend on you.

She has always loved Stockholm, but she's made her life here on the islands now. There's no way she's going to move away from Anne Sofie. But living an uncomplicated life away from the small island community has suddenly become attractive. She has to admit to herself that she's still hung up on Patrick. But how much?

And what about Liam? What if Liam is planning to give up work and move to Åland after all? Her feelings toward her estranged husband (is that what he is?) are even more complicated than they are toward Patrick. She wishes she could decide what to do once and for all.

After accepting that Stefan was the baby's father, Liam's tenderness toward Frida took Alicia completely by surprise. It was as if her old Liam was back. She was certain that, with time, she'd be able to love him as she had done before Stefan's death.

No, her relationship with Liam had been on the rocks well before that. Over the months since they have been living in different countries, Alicia has come to realize that she fell out of love with him long before they lost their son. Even before she found out about his affair. At the time, when a 'friendly' acquaintance told her about Liam's 'indiscretion', she had been upset, but not really as devastated as she *should* have been. Thinking back, she can't remember when they grew apart. Perhaps it was after Liam decided he should sleep in the spare bedroom. He had used the pretext of not wanting to disturb Alicia when he got home in the middle of the night after a particularly difficult operation. An occasional night away from Alicia's bed had gradually become the norm, and their lovemaking had become even more infrequent. Why hadn't Alicia protested? Or invited Liam back to their bed?

Alicia suspects there had been other women before the Polish nurse, but Liam had sworn she was the first and only one.

Alicia is brought back to the present by a tall young woman in a red and white checked apron, who is going around the small café clearing the tables. She picks up Alicia's empty cup and asks if she'd like anything else, another coffee or perhaps a cinnamon roll, but Alicia shakes her head. She checks her watch and realizes its nearly 5pm. Only five days till Christmas! She's forgotten to pick up the fish for gravlax. If it is to be ready for Christmas Eve, she and Hilda need to put it into the salt and dill marinade today. She picks up her woolly hat and bag and rushes out of the café.

SEVENTEEN

When Frida wakes up, her breasts are aching. They are painfully full with milk. It must be time for a feed, she thinks, looking at the baby monitor next to her. She sees that her daughter is awake. It's just before 6am and Anne Sofie is gurgling to herself, lifting up her long legs inside her pink and white sleep bag.

A gift from Alicia.

Frida tiptoes to the next room, where she has placed the white cot bought by Alicia at IKEA last summer. She opens the black-out curtains and turns around to see a sweet smile light up her daughter's face. As Frida lifts up her little baby girl, Anne Sofie starts making sucking sounds, smelling the milk on her mother.

'Let's just get you changed first, girly,' Frida says and carries Anne Sofie to the living room where she's set up a changing station against one of the walls. Alicia advised her to put it next to the cot, but Frida decided to leave it in the living room, where she spends most of her time with the baby.

She sighs as she thinks about Alicia. As she removes the soiled diaper from the baby, wipes her clean, and quickly replaces the soft cotton and plastic garment, she wonders how the first months of her baby's life would have been without Alicia.

Her cheeks redden when she thinks about the time and money Alicia has devoted to the baby–and her. Of course, Frida is grateful, but.

Frida makes herself comfortable and places Anne Sofie on her lap. The baby quickly finds the nipple Frida offers and starts sucking in steady, satisfying pulls. Frida relaxes her muscles: the relief is palpable. She looks down at the baby's eyes, firmly fixed on her own. She wonders–once again–what goes through that small brain while she feeds. Probably nothing, just pleasure.

How wonderful it must be to be so innocent and new!

Frida thinks over the last five months and to her rash decision to say something she knew was wrong. Why did she do it? Was she hormonally unbalanced?

She's heard of temporary insanity during pregnancy. The death of both Stefan in November, just as she'd found out about the baby, and then later in the summer, of her friend Daniel, who'd had an accident at sea, would surely have made anyone go a bit crazy? Losing someone you were so in love with, and then her best friend so soon after, had been a shock. And then her poor mother. Although that had been a relief for her mother, Frida is sure of it.

As she moves the baby from one breast to the other, Frida thinks how her mother would have loved little Anne Sofie, if she had known who the little baby was! When Frida introduced the baby to her grandmother, Sirpa had looked blankly at the small bundle in Frida's arms. By that stage, her mother had been asleep most of the time and didn't even recognize her own daughter, let alone a new grandchild. The staff at the care home had woken Sirpa to meet Anne Sofie, which meant she was groggy from sleep as well.

Frida would give anything to have that moment again. She would wait for as long as it took for her mother to have a lucid moment, something that still occasionally happened, even then. She's sure her mother would have recognized that the baby was the spitting image of her grandmother–her real grandmother that is. Instead, she left when the baby began to stir, telling the staff she needed to feed her. She'd been upset, still hormonal after the birth. She'd put the baby in her pram, and when she got back to her apartment, she had wept.

She hadn't realized it was the last time she would see her mother alive.

A day later, her mother fell asleep and never woke up again. The doctor said she'd had another massive stroke, but had assured Frida that she hadn't suffered.

Suddenly, a sadness overwhelms Frida. Tears run down her cheeks, landing on the baby's arms. She wipes them away and takes a deep breath. She needs to sort out her mother's affairs. If only she could have talked to her mother one more time, to clear her mind from the thick fog that had enveloped it for over a year now. Frida wanted to ask Sirpa so many questions about herself as a baby, about how she found bringing up a child on her own, about her father.

The day after her mother's death, when Frida was talking to the head of the home about funeral arrangements, a man approached her and handed over his card.

'Keith Karlsson, your mother's lawyer.'

Baby Anne Sofie was in a sling, snuggled up against Frida's breasts. She looked over to the *Solsidan* manager, who had just smiled and nodded to Mr Karlsson.

'I think we are all done here?' She touched Frida's arm and left the little room with its small sofa and two matching armchairs. Frida knew this was a space for bereaved and upset family members. She'd often seen people with their heads bent speaking with one of the carers or the manager there.

Anne Sofie gave a soft cooing sound, and Frida adjusted herself slightly, making sure the baby was comfortable, and that her small head was supported by the sling.

She looked across at Keith Karlsson, a man with thick gray hair, cut short into an American-style crewcut. He wore a suit with a shirt and tie and a large gold watch on his wrist. He was tan with tidy hands and nails as if he'd just had them manicured that morning. Which he might well have done.

'May I?' he said, indicating the seat the manager had just vacated.

Frida nodded. She couldn't understand how her mother could

afford the services of this wealthy looking lawyer. Or why she'd need someone like this anyway?

Frida had never before set eyes on him but Mr Karlsson seemed to know all about her.

'Please come and see me. We need to deal with your mother's affairs.'

EIGHTEEN

Mr Karlsson's offices are right in the center of town, on Torggatan. There's a small entrance next to the bank and stairs up to the third floor where a brass plaque on the door says *Karlsson & Co.*

Frida feels totally exhausted. Anne Sofie had refused to settle for a proper nap all morning. It wasn't until after her midday feed that the baby wanted to sleep. Just as it was time for Frida to come into town for this meeting.

The snow storm has left Mariehamn looking fresh and clean under a white blanket of snow. The afternoon is already turning into dusk, but the Christmas lights strung across Torggatan, and the decorations in the shops, make the center of town look magical.

Little Anne Sofie is now fast asleep in the sling, but Frida has had to drag herself into town, wrapping herself and the baby under layers and layers of clothing, rather than taking a well-deserved rest.

Frida nearly put this meeting off again, but she knew she had to deal with her mother's affairs. It had been two months since her death and she keeps getting messages from Mr Karlsson's office. Besides, she has been living hand to mouth on state maternity pay and relying too heavily on Alicia and Liam's kindness. She has no idea how the rent on the apartment is paid for. She probably needs to transfer the rental agreement to herself. Unless that can't be done, in which case she needs to be rehoused by Mariehamn Council? She's ashamed of her incompetence when it comes to practical matters. It's as if during her pregnancy, and after Anne Sofie birth, she hasn't been able to think straight. Her mind doesn't have enough room to deal with money as well. Especially after her mother's death, nothing but Anne Sofie's well-being seemed to matter.

The lawyer opens the door immediately when Frida rings the bell. He smiles broadly at Frida, and when she reveals the bundle under her thick coat, gently removing Anne Sofie's woolly hat, he admires the sleeping child. Frida's heart melts a little when Mr Karlsson comments on the blonde curls and calls Anne Sofie 'an angel.'

Mr Karlsson ushers Frida into his office, which overlooks the streets below. At two o'clock, the town is busy with shoppers, not put off by the chilly temperatures and snow. Everyone is getting ready for Christmas, Frida thinks to herself.

In a weak moment, she had agreed to spend Christmas Eve with Alicia at Hilda and Uffe's house. She's determined to stay only one night. Of course, Alicia has insisted she should spend the whole holiday in Sjoland, but for now, Frida has managed to stay firm. Alicia could be quite insistent.

Frida sighs.

Since Anna Sofia's birth, her life hasn't been her own anymore. Of course, the baby's demands are paramount, but Frida hadn't counted on such strong interference from Stefan's family. Although his father, Liam, was rarely on the islands, preferring to stay and work in London, Alicia was more than enough on her own.

'We'd better get on with it, don't you think?' Mr Karlsson says, arousing Frida from her thoughts.

Frida nods.

'From my memory, babies have a knack of waking up at the most inconvenient moments,' Mr Karlsson adds as he opens a file on the desk. He hands it to Frida saying, 'Your mother's will.'

Frida is still surprised this wealthy man would know anything about her mother's affairs, let alone looking after babies, but she smiles and takes the folder from the lawyer.

She reads the legal text telling her that she, Frida Anttila, is her mother's sole beneficiary. But when she spots the final estimate of her mother's estate, she takes a quick intake of breath and puts her hand across her mouth.

The baby stirs against her body, and Frida tries to steady her breathing as she hands the folder back to Mr Karlsson. She places a palm on the sling and strokes Anne Sofie's back, trying to calm herself.

'I don't understand.'

'It's good news, my dear,' Mr Karlsson says, smiling broadly.

Frida tries to control her annoyance at the lawyer's patronizing attitude. She's a grown woman, a mother, and a grieving daughter! She may only be eighteen, but that means she is an adult and should be treated as such and not like some little school girl.

'Please explain,' she says, keeping her mouth straight and her voice cool.

Mr Karlsson's smile disappears, and he gives a brief cough.

'As I am sure you can ascertain, there are 998,525 Euros in your mother's savings account. On top of that, a regular sum of 5,000 is deposited to her current account each month.' The lawyer clears his throat once again, and continues. 'This monthly sum more than paid for the nursing home fees, the running costs on the property she owned and other incidentals. Nearly half of it was usually left over. I was instructed to transfer these sums into the savings account at the end of each month.'

Frida is stunned. She knows her mother's salary from Arkipelag wasn't anywhere near 5,000 Euros a month. Besides, since her fall and stroke, her mother wouldn't have been receiving anything apart from some sick pay at most. And nearly a million in savings! There is no way Sirpa would have been able to save that amount of money.

'You mentioned a property?'

'Yes, the one you are living in. Are there any others?'

Frida shakes her head and stares at the man.

While Frida listens in silence, Mr Karlsson tells her that she is now a rich woman and won't need to worry about money, providing she takes investment advice.

'His, presumably', Frida thinks.

He hands her a pile of papers, including 'Ms Anttila's', as he calls Frida's mother, latest bank statements. As if to prove that the previous documents were correct.

'Who makes the monthly deposits?' Frida asks

The lawyer leans back in his chair. 'I'm afraid I can't divulge that information.'

'What? Why not?'

'Client confidentiality.'

'But I'm her daughter, surely if anyone, I am allowed to know this information.'

'I mean the other party.'

Frida narrows her eyes. 'You mean the person who pays in the money?'

The lawyer closes a folder he has been looking into. A copy of what he has given Frida, she supposes.

'I'm afraid I have other clients to attend to. Please let me know if you would like me to continue to look after your affairs. It would be a privilege to do so. Of course, there is no rush, after Christmas is fine. The process will take some time to go through. In the meantime, if you would like, I can transfer a sum, say 10,000 Euros, to your account?'

Frida gazes at the lawyer. The whole of this affair stinks to her. As does this man, his office, his gold watch, tan, and the money. But she can't believe her mother would be involved in something shady. She was a lowly waitress at Arkipelag, how can she have so much money stashed away? Where did she get it? Surely her mother hadn't been a criminal?

'Look, I've looked after your mother's affairs for over seventeen years. Christmas is coming. Please let me make it easier for you and the baby. Just let me have your bank details and the amount will be deposited to your account by tomorrow.'

Mr Karlsson is looking at Frida, waiting for her reply. When she isn't forthcoming, he sighs.

'Your mother had a benefactor. Someone she knew years ago who wanted to make her–and your–life easier. This person just wishes to remain anonymous. There is nothing unusual about that.'

'There is something usual about having nearly a million on a deposit account while working as a waitress, isn't there?'

The lawyer smiles, 'Your mother was an unusual person.'

NINETEEN

Discovering Sirpa Anttila was rich comes as a total shock to Frida. She's always been under the impression that the apartment they had shared, and in which Frida now lives with the baby, was rented and owned by Mariehamn council. She's never seen the bills, but her mother told her before she fell ill that all of it was taken care of by a direct debit.

Now Frida feels stupid that she hadn't looked into her mother's affairs while she was at the *Solsidan* home. Or confronted the manager about where the fees came from. She had been preoccupied with her own problems. The pregnancy, and grieving for Stefan and Daniel, as well as the worry about Alicia's sudden appearance in Mariehamn had distracted her.

'You don't have to worry about a thing,' Sirpa had told her the day Frida came back from Stockholm, where she had been studying for her Baccalaureate exams. Her mother was still in hospital then, with tubes attached to her hand and nostrils. Her voice was weak and croaky, and she looked thin and pale in her white hospital gown.

A week later, when Sirpa was brought back home, she had already become confused, forgetting to ask to go to the toilet and just wanting to stay in bed all day long. Frida cared for her mother at home for just over four weeks. An exhausting and awful time. Every night, Sirpa would soil the bedsheets, and occasionally during the day. She woke up many times each night, calling for Frida, and for someone with a Russian name. When Frida asked her mother who she was talking about, her mother's watery blue eyes would shoot up. 'No one you need worry about,' she'd mutter. Or she would grow hostile and angry, and shout at Frida to leave her alone.

Those weeks Frida tried to care for her mother were the hardest time of her life. Even harder than losing Stefan and Daniel. It was as if she was suddenly sharing her apartment–and her life–with someone else: a stranger. A stranger who would occasionally become her mother again, the quiet, kind woman whom Frida had known all her life. The mother who, when Frida was at the Gymnasium in Stockholm, would text her every day asking how she was, and always ending the message with, 'Don't forget I love you, my darling girl.'

The extent of her mother's drinking was a complete surprise to Frida too. During those awful four weeks at home, Sirpa insisted on having a bottle of vodka by her bedside, 'for nighttime emergencies.' When Frida tried to remove the bottle, her mother became angry and once even hit Frida across her legs.

When Frida read Sirpa's medical records, she found that she'd been treated for various conditions 'indicative of high alcohol consumption.' She saw that there had been other hospital visits when Sirpa's alcohol levels had been sky high.

Of course, Frida knew her mother liked a drink or two. She worked in a restaurant, surrounded by alcohol and drinkers, after all. But she had no idea that her mother was an alcoholic.

It was a health visitor, an overweight woman, speaking with heavily accented Swedish who'd said it was time to move her mother to the *Solsidan* home. She was the same woman who had phoned the school in Stockholm and left a message about Sirpa's fall and stroke at the Arkipelag restaurant.

'She'll be well looked after at the home,' she'd said.

'What about the cost?' Frida had asked. She knew they were barely making ends meet with Sirpa's wages from waitressing. If Frida hadn't received a grant from the Åland Department of Education toward her fees, living costs, and travel to Stockholm, she'd never have been able to go to the Gymnasium.

But the woman just smiled and told Frida 'Not to worry, you will manage.'

When, after the first week, Frida had again asked the manager about the fees, the woman had looked at her computer screen and told Frida it was all taken care of. 'It comes from your mother's bank account by direct debit,' she had said.

How could Frida not think there was something strange going on when the manager made a similar comment about the funeral costs?

'It's all been taken care of. Your mother organized it all before she became confused,' the manager said and touched Frida's arm.

It takes Frida a full 24 hours to come to terms with what Mr Karlsson told her. She sends him an email with her bank details and an hour later, she sees the 10,000 Euros in her account. She's decided to enjoy the money–that's what her mother would have wanted, she's sure of it. She will think more about what to do after Christmas.

That night, Frida wakes suddenly. She gazes at the baby monitor, but Anne Sofie is fast asleep. Frida had been dreaming. In the dream, she'd been living in one of those beautiful villas on Solbacken, the most expensive real estate in Åland. She was sitting in a trendy wicker chair, attached to the ceiling, above a carpet of gold. She'd been rocking Anne Sofie wrapped in an expensive cashmere shawl. An older man had been humming and preparing some kind of food on a white kitchen island behind her. But she had woken up before she could see the man's face.

Frida shakes her head and looks at the clock next to her. It's just gone 12am. The baby will soon wake for her night feed, and as if roused by the power of her mind, the baby begins to murmur.

Now fully awake, waiting for the sounds from the monitor to become louder, the thought suddenly comes to Frida as clear as the virgin snow glittering outside her window. It must be her father who's been paying money into her mother's bank account.

Frida has no idea who the man is. Sirpa never mentioned him, just told Frida he was a foreign sailor who made her pregnant but never returned.

Now that Frida has discovered the money, she's not sure if she wants to know who this rich man is. He must have known about her mother's condition all along, as well as her exact whereabouts. He could have visited her at any time and got to know Frida. He obviously doesn't want anything to do with his family, so she doesn't want to know him either. She'll take the money, however. Why wouldn't she?

As long as she can remember, it's just been her and her mother. They didn't need anybody, but now, with a baby herself, Frida knows how much having the baby's father around would mean to her. Whatever the reason her own father didn't want to know her, it seems cruel to Frida.

Anne Sofie is now in full cry mode, so Frida gets up and goes to her. She decides to forget about the man–her father–and enjoy her newly acquired wealth.

TWENTY

Brit decides to use a bicycle with winter tires that Mia has offered her to get to the West Harbor from the apartment. The distance isn't that far, and with a push she could walk it, or she could drive, but she prefers the exercise that the bicycle provides. There is a walkway along the coast that is beautiful even in the freezing weather. The tires are amazingly good, making Brit enjoy the ride even more.

She also knows that the ruddy cheeks outside exercise gives her is flattering. She wants Jukka to see her at her best when she arrives for her second shift on MS *Sabrina*.

As soon as she has got off the bicycle and put it on the rack outside the terminal building, she sees Jukka driving past and parking his car. It's a sleek black Mercedes and Brit cannot help but be impressed.

She lingers on, pretending to have some trouble with the lock, when Jukka comes to stand very close to her.

'Can I help you with that?' Jukka says over her shoulder.

Brit pretends not to have seen him.

'Oh, hello!' she says and turns around. 'I'm fine,' she adds and smiles.

'Good to hear. Wouldn't want you to be a damsel in distress.' His eyes are wrinkled at the corners and she can see his warm breath turn to condensation. It's a bright, cold afternoon, with the sun low in the sky.

'Here she comes!' Jukka says and points at the horizon where a red dot can be seen moving toward them. He glances at a vast watch on his wrist and mutters, 'But where's MS *Diane*?'

For a moment they both gaze ahead, looking for signs of *Sabrina*'s sister ship in the wide shipping lane, which narrows as it gets further away and then divides in two. The right lane takes the ships to Sweden, the left to Finland. Suddenly, as the first red dot begins to take the shape of a ferry, another small object, like a speck of brick dust against the white ice, appears beyond MS *Sabrina*.

'Ah, there she is!' Jukka says and puts his hand on Brit's back. 'Let's get inside, out of this damn cold?'

Later, when Brit is on the ship, stationed at the door with the Second Mate, a young man in his twenties with a wide smile, ready to welcome day-trippers from *Sabrina*'s sister ship as well as those passengers embarking from Mariehamn, Brit can still feel Jukka's touch against her lower back. Even through the padded jacket, her jumper, a silky slip that she wore over her best bra today, his hand burned through to her skin.

During her first shift, she had found out that Jukka lived just outside Mariehamn. She'd also learned from Kerstin that he had been married before, information she'd delivered with a disapproving sneer.

'Ladies' man, that one,' she'd added.

That suits Brit just fine. She isn't after a serious relationship, just some fun to keep her mind off the Rat who broke her heart.

Getting ready at home, she was excited at the prospect of spending two nights in Jukka's company. She is planning to sneak into his cabin after her shift tonight, unless he makes a move first.

'I cannot be messing about at my age,' she'd told Alicia on the ferry back from seeing her dad.

'You never did,' Alicia said and giggled.

Brit smiles at the memory, nodding at a blond couple with two equally blond children walking through the sliding door of the ferry.

Spending the short ferry journey with her old friend had felt like being sixteen again, talking about the boys at school. Alicia never did anything about her infatuations (at school at least), whereas she usually took the first step. She'd lost her virginity in the back of a farm truck, after the school's year-end party. Brit knows that that particular boy, called Olaf, is now happily married with another girl in their class. They live somewhere in the suburbs outside Stockholm and have a string of kids, cats, and dogs. His Facebook page is full of pictures of outdoor activities, sailing in the summer and skiing in winter. The children look fat and unsmiling.

Lucky escape there.

Jukka has been busy all afternoon and early evening. There'd been a children's Christmas karaoke in the bar, which he'd been persuaded– by Brit–to judge. It wasn't something he usually got involved in but he just couldn't say no to her. Kerstin lifted her eyebrows when he passed her in the gangway on his way to the bar, but he ignored her. The ferry company was always encouraging him to be 'more visible' on the cruises. Apparently seeing the Captain about the ship made the passengers feel more secure. Plus, as one marketing woman put it, 'The Captain's visible presence is romantic.' As if he didn't have anything better to do!

But today, Brit's invitation was just too tempting. Unfortunately, there'd been a lot of people around so he couldn't ask her what he'd planned to.

Now, at 10pm, they should both be less busy. Most of the passengers had eaten already and the three à la carte restaurants and the self-service buffet are closed. There are three bars and a night club, but those are usually looked after by the nightshift and the two bar managers.

He knows Brit will either be in the staff quarters below deck or having something to eat in the canteen, but he doesn't want to go there. Too public, and he knows Kerstin is on duty today. He definitely does not want the old woman to see him making overtures to Brit. Would it be too forward to send Brit a message? He knows her mobile number, but only because he has access to her personal records. Perhaps it would be overstepping the mark. Yes, if he was planning to see her for personal reasons, but there is nothing to stop him from contacting her professionally.

Jukka gets out his phone and taps a message. He's on the bridge of the ship, sitting at the back while his First Mate, an experienced officer, is at the controls, keeping one eye on the ship's progress. Jukka trusts Oskar Brun implicitly. The younger man, who has a thick crop of brown hair, is only a year or so from attaining his Captain's stripes and Jukka will be sorry to see him go. They work well together and Oskar knows *Sabrina* as well as Jukka does, if not better.

It's pitch black outside. They're on the return leg back from Helsinki and are due to dock at Mariehamn just after 1am, so there are a few hours when Jukka can relax. With Brit, he hopes.

'I'm off, but you know where to find me?' Jukka says, addressing Oskar, and the young man nods in reply. There is no 'Aye, aye Captain,' from Oskar. The crew onboard rarely salute him, unless it's a very serious matter, or for show for the passengers. Marie Line, the shipping company, is 'a modern, progressive employer where each member of staff is valued.' Apparently this means that usual seafaring customs do not always need to be followed. He was still the commander of MS *Sabrina*, but it seems no one is required to show it anymore. Unless he is required to play a pantomime character for the passengers, that is.

Although a little weary, Jukka doesn't go straight to his cabin. Instead, he makes his way to the top deck, an area that is not visible from the bridge. It's bitterly cold as he steps outside, but there's not too much wind. The sky is filled with stars, a sight that nearly takes his breath away. He leans over the railing and lowers his eyes to the bow of the ship, checking that their course is a safe distance from the edge of the shipping lane and the thick ice. Which it is, of course.

This winter has turned very harsh. Only three weeks ago, the sea was cold and there was a thin layer of ice here and there, but there hadn't been any need for the ice-breakers. He inhales the night air and is about to turn back when he hears the door open behind him.

Brit sees Jukka's wide back as he rests his arms on the railing through the window of the door leading to the upper deck. The night sky is black against the white of his Captain's cap. Even from behind, he looks good in his uniform—tall, with a slim but muscular body. Brit cannot but wonder if Kerstin's assessment of him is correct: He could have any woman he so much as glances at.

Jukka isn't wearing an overcoat, but he doesn't look as if he's cold. Hot blooded, Brit thinks, and she almost laughs at her own corniness. Is she really so desperate that she needs to go to bed with Jukka, the first candidate since you-know-who, to prove that she's still attractive? Even though she only fancies him a tiny bit?

Don't think about it. You need to get back on the horse as soon as possible.

Luckily Brit has had the foresight to grab her long padded coat from her cabin. On her feet, she's wearing her high-heeled courts that she wears for work. She's not short by any means, but the added height gives her more authority over the staff, which is especially important in a new job. She looks down at the deck and wonders how slippery it is. Perhaps she should fake a fall, straight into Jukka's arms?

TWENTY-ONE

Jukka's cabin is on the top deck, behind a heavy locked door, which slides when he touches it with a keycard. They've taken a route through the crew quarters. When in the public areas, two women stopped Jukka to ask something obviously trivial that they already knew the answers to. The taller of the two wanted to know when they were arriving in Mariehamn, and the other asked what time they kept onboard, Swedish or Finnish? Both women were a bit older, perhaps in their fifties.

'These women want him too,' Brit thought to herself.

The taller, who was more forward, gave Brit a sideways glance as she stood next to Jukka, not too close, but near enough for it to seem they were together. Of course, if any staff saw them, they wouldn't have realized that there was anything going on. Or at least that's what Brit hoped, as she fixed her eyes on the two women.

Of course, nothing *was* going on–yet.

But Brit was delighted Jukka had initiated this meeting. A few moments ago, when Brit opened the door to the deck and Jukka saw her, he'd immediately smiled.

'You got my message?'

Brit nodded and took a couple of careful steps toward him, making them both laugh at the silliness of her shoes.

'You'd think I'd be a bit more sensible with my footwear. I've been working on ships for years!'

'Why don't we go somewhere warmer and more comfortable to talk?' Jukka said. His eyes were locked on hers, and although she was shivering under her warm coat, she could sense the heat inside her rise.

'Good idea.'

'What about my cabin? I could make you a proper coffee? I have a Nespresso machine,' Jukka said.

Brit knew exactly what she was agreeing to when she smiled and nodded. Jukka helped her back inside.

'Shall I show you the way?' Jukka said, removing his cap and smoothing his thick hair into place.

Inside his quarters, which include two rooms, Brit is speechless at the sight that greets her. In the lounge area, there's a sofa and two armchairs, a vast plasma TV screen, and angled rectangular portholes that almost cover one bulkhead. She can imagine what the view must be like in daytime. Now all she can see is blackness. Brit peers to her right, where a massive bed made up with pristine white sheets dominates the cabin area.

Jukka takes off his cap and coat and hangs them up in a small closet. He stretches out his hand and Brit lets him take her padded coat, which she's been carrying in her arms all the way through the ship.

Jukka loosens his tie and turns to Brit, who's still standing by the door, taking in the luxury of the Captain's accommodation. 'Please sit down, those heels must be killing you.' He gives her a wicked grin and Brit feels herself blush as his eyes travel from her shoes to her legs and up the length of her body to her eyes.

What's this? I don't blush!

'How do you take your coffee?' Jukka asks

'As strong as you can make it. Espresso, please, if you have some capsules for that?'

As she watches him stand over and operate the machine, Brit suddenly realizes why she is so drawn to this man. He's the spitting image of George Clooney! She better not tell him she can see a like-ness to the dishy American actor she's been daydreaming about for years. 'Perhaps sometime in the future,' she thinks and smiles.

'What's so funny?' Jukka asks. He places a small cup on a low wooden table in front of her and comes to sit next to Brit on the sofa.

'Nothing,' she says, and she coyly crosses her legs. She's made sure her skirt is just short enough to show the lacy tops of her black thigh-highs.

Although Brit seems completely up for it, even teasing him with her body gestures, crossing her legs and smiling at him sweetly, never taking her eyes off him, Jukka is still not sure if he can risk making an advance. They are in his cabin, having coffee, to which she had will-ingly agreed. How much clearer could she be, without actually uttering the words, that she wants him?

Yet.

Of course, he would like nothing better than to run his hands over those legs, touching the lace on her stocking tops, but what if he's misjudged the situation after all?

Again.

Brit has only just started at Marie Line. This is only her second shift on *Sabrina*. Wouldn't it be wiser–given his history–to just talk to her tonight, find out a little more about her and then, if, say, next time they are on shift together, go the whole way?

'So, tell me, how are you finding life back on the islands? I believe you have been working on the Caribbean Cruises for a few years now? Surely,' Jukka says, sweeping his hand out over the cabin, 'this must be a lot less glamorous. For a woman like you.'

Jukka couldn't stop himself from adding that last remark. As he says it, he feasts his eyes on Brit's perfect figure. Her eyes, which seem more aquamarine tonight, are sparkling and her skin dewy and glow-ing. Her legs are slim and long, and he can just make out the contours of a lacy black bra underneath a silky blouse.

Brit leans ever so slightly toward him and replies, 'On the contrary, I've never seen a more luxurious sleeping quarters.'

When she pronounces the word, 'sleeping' she does it slowly, deliberately articulating each syllable. Jukka thinks, I'm going to kiss her, but then checks himself just in time and instead, gives a small cough. He adjusts his seating position a little, so that he's a fraction farther away from the woman. And temptation.

'Really,' he says, trying to keep his voice deep and calm.

'Uh, huh.' Brit replies. It's as though she's purring at him. How is he going to get out of this situation, that he himself has created, without offending her? Or worse, without her ever wanting to set eyes on him or his cabin ever again?

'Look, Brit, I really like you.'

Again Jukka hesitates. Even that could be misconstrued to be too forward and personal. 'I mean you seem to have fitted in very well.'

Just as he is thinking what on earth he has to do or say to resolve the situation, his intercom buzzes. He takes a quick look at the screen and says, 'I'm sorry, I'm needed on the bridge.'

TWENTY-TWO

Brit wakes up with an inexplicable headache. She's only had about four hours' sleep, if that, but she's well used to doing long shifts with little rest in between. So it's not that. She looks at the screen of her phone and sees it's gone half past four. If she doesn't get a move on, she will be late for the start of 'Sea Breakfast' at 5.30am. Most of the passengers, she knows, will be bleary eyed, but it doesn't do for the staff to look hungover—especially the restaurant manager. She hadn't had a drop to drink last night, but her sleep was disturbed by her encounter with Jukka.

The man was blowing hot and cold on her and she didn't understand why. The electricity between them can't just be in her imagination, can it?

As Brit takes a swift shower in the small cubicle in her cabin, she remembers how, when they were sitting in Jukka's cabin, she thought he was going to lean over and kiss her, stopping himself just before it happened. What is wrong with him? Or is it her? Doesn't he fancy her after all?

Brit dries herself and puts on a new white uniform blouse, although it's cotton this time, rather than the silky number she wore last night. She was relieved to discover on her first day that the Marie Line crew could wear their own blouses and (black) shoes as long as they donned the company uniform jacket and skirt (or trousers, but Brit prefers a skirt). This gives her the opportunity to feel sexy, even at work. Besides, she's learned over the years that the shirts provided are often made out of scratchy polyester, which easily makes your armpits smell foul.

Surprised by the number of passengers who've booked for breakfast, Brit sets about inspecting the buffet, and makes sure that everyone who is supposed to be on duty has got out of their bunks. She makes a quick round of the galley and sees all is in order

It's now quarter past five and there's already a small line outside the glazed doors that lead to the large restaurant. Kerstin is on Maitre'D duty with a junior member of staff—a young dark-haired woman who looks a bit frightened. Brit nods to the two women standing with their backs to the locked doors, and they let in the first passengers. She stands to one side and smiles at the couple who are first in the line. And then she sees him, Jukka, hovering behind the passengers, gazing at her. He touches his cap as if in salute and Brit cannot help but beam at him.

Jukka is on the other side of the door, seemingly in no hurry to enter the restaurant. The passengers are wary of him, leaving an empty circle around the Captain.

No flirtatious ladies this morning.

As is the custom, there is a Captain's table in every restaurant on the ship. It's usually the best table, with the most uninterrupted view of the sea, and only given to passengers if the Captain explicitly lets the staff know that he will not be eating there.

The space reserved for Jukka at the Buffet Restaurant (the only one of the four eating places onboard that opens for breakfast) is no exception. Brit now goes over to the table to ensure it's laid out correctly and that there is a 'Captain's Table' sign on it. It's covered with a white linen cloth and set for six people, in front of two large windows. The sun is far from rising, but there is a faint light on the horizon and Brit can see the outlines of the small islands of the Helsinki archipelago they are sailing through.

She's startled by Jukka's voice behind her, 'Won't you join me for breakfast?'

Brit turns around, and gives him one of her most charming smiles. 'Is that an order, Sir?'

Jukka laughs. 'No one even salutes me on this ship. But if you like, let's say I need to discuss something with you.'

Brit glances behind her, at the staff at the door. Kerstin is gazing at them. She's certainly clocked that they are having a light-hearted conversation even though she couldn't possibly hear what they are saying. She leans toward her colleague and says something. About her and Jukka, Brit is pretty certain.

Let them gossip away.

'In that case, I'd love to,' she says.

'So what was it you wanted to talk to me about?' Brit says after they have ordered their breakfast from a tall male waiter. Brit couldn't remember his name and had to ask him. She finds out that Olli has a stutter, and has only been a member of MS *Sabrina* crew for a few months. Although the breakfast is self-service, the Captain is given table service. Brit wonders why Kerstin, who is the most senior after herself, didn't come and look after them, but decided not to challenge her this time, in spite of the clear snub. Besides, Olli seemed perfectly competent, although terribly nervous, in his duties. In a way, Brit was glad they were not confronted by Kerstin's lopsided, insincere smile.

Jukka sets his eyes on Brit's and pushes his hand forward on the table, nearly touching her fingers, but then thinks better of it and retracts it, opening his linen napkin and placing it in his lap instead.

'I wanted to apologize for last night. I'm afraid there was an incident.'

'Really, what happened?' Although Brit has been bristling over the previous evening's events all night and morning, she's intrigued by what could have happened onboard that she hasn't yet found out about.

'We thought we had a jumper, but it turned out to be a prank.'

'How awful!' Brit is truly horrified. She knows that there have been suicides on the ferries between Finland and Sweden, but she hasn't heard of any for a long while. Perhaps they don't get reported?

'Yes, a YouTuber thought it'd be a good idea to film himself climbing the railings on deck 7. He jumped down to the level below, and it looked like he'd perished, so they called me in. Luckily, the guy is OK, although it could have gone very badly indeed for him.'

Olli interrupts their conversation with a plate of salmon and scrambled eggs for two, plus a steaming pot of coffee.

'I hope you confiscated the video?'

Jukka put his knife and fork down, swallowing a piece of salmon. 'Unfortunately, he managed to post it online before we got to him. I gave him a good talking to, but not sure if it did any good. The company lawyers will deal with it all now.'

He gazes intently at Brit and adds, 'I was quite mad at him. Especially as I had completely different plans for last night.'

TWENTY-THREE

Hilda is so bored. At first after they closed the fashion boutique, the relief she felt was enormous. It was as if a nightmare had ended, and at last she was able to sleep at night, and even have the occasional lie-in in the mornings if she wished. And she didn't have to make up any more stories for Uffe and Alicia about how many clients she'd served on any given day, or how many garments she'd sold.

On so many days she'd sit in that shop, watching the clock on the wall of the bank opposite, visible through the tall windows overlooking the street. The bank was always busy, people going in and out, staff staring at their screens, tapping away and occasionally listening to a client sitting in a chair on the other side of the desk. Hilda could only see the back of the person, but the bank clerk would have their head bent, and nod occasionally. None of those clients would ever cross the road and venture into her shop. Even people who knew her or Uffe–everyone on the islands knew her husband–only waved a greeting, making themselves look busy so they didn't have to come in and spend some of the money they'd just pulled out of their bank accounts.

But now she even misses those disingenuous so-called friends. And she misses the thrill of going to fashion shows in Milan, Paris, and Stockholm. She never attended the main events, that's true, but the buzz of the lower tier shows was enough to make her feel alive. Making decisions on what might sell in her small shop in Mariehamn, how daring she could afford to be, was always such a boost to her confidence. To think that she, a poor Finnish girl, who had hardly been able to pass her maths exams at the Kallio Lyceum at the age of sixteen, was now making calculations in her head about wholesale and retail prices and profit margins?

'For you, marrying a man who can look after you is the best option in life,' was what everyone had said, from her mother and father to her teachers. The general opinion was that she had no talent for study, but thank goodness she had her looks.

When she had to tell Uffe that she'd only been able to keep the shop going because of the loan she'd taken out with the Russian, Alexander Dudnikov, he was furious at first, but eventually he agreed to pay off the debt. To Hilda's horror, this had doubled in the few months since she'd taken the loan.

'What about the payments I made?' she asked Uffe. But he just shook his head.

'Promise me you will never have anything to do with that man ever again?' he said, and she gladly gave a vow. Dudnikov was clearly a crook, and his henchmen were terrible thugs. Goodness knows what kind of criminal organization he ran. What they did on the island, Hilda could only imagine. Drugs, people trafficking, money laundering, and whatever else was illegal. Uffe had told her that he met Dudnikov through one of his old friends, someone he occasionally met for a beer in Mariehamn.

'He begged me to give a job to a laborer, who'd had to flee his own country. I thought he was a good guy,' he said.

When the Russian popped into Hilda's shop a few days later, she didn't think anything of it. The summer before had been a particularly slow June and July, and Hilda dreaded having to tell Uffe how much she owed the bank opposite. The clothes she'd bought in the shows were all hanging on the rails, stuffed to bursting point. She'd calculated that even if she put the stock on a half-price sale, she would still not pay off the loan.

Dudnikov had been a savior. On that first day, he'd bought so much stock–he told Hilda he had a large family, 'A lot of sisters, cousins, and aunts'–that Hilda thought she might even survive until the next season. Two days after that the Russian was back.

'My girls love your style,' he said and smiled broadly. Hilda noticed a gold filling at the back of his mouth and thought, 'How predictable,' but she forced herself to like the man. He was her only hope. All through spring, Dudnikov came into her shop and bought outfit after outfit. At the end of May, he said, 'I your only customer?' He had an accent, and his Swedish was far from perfect, but up till then, he'd been pleasant enough. Now his voice sounded harsh, his accent and demeanor, she decided, were more Russian.

All through her childhood, Hilda had been told never to trust a Russian. Her father had fought the Russians in Karelia, and her mother blamed his alcoholism and eventual death for the mental scars he'd received fighting the Soviets in the Winter War. When her father was out drinking at the weekends—he managed to hold down a job at the railways during the week–her mother would shout 'Don't trust the Russians!' at the grainy black and white television whenever she saw Kekkonen, the Finnish president, shaking hands with the Russian dictators—first Khrushchev, then Brezhnev.

Of course, now, Russians were everywhere. They had money and everyone wanted their custom. Gone were the rare vodka-smelling tourists of her youth, with yellowing teeth, bad crewcuts, and unfashionable clothing. The modern Russians wore Gucci and Louis Vuitton.

In the shop that day, Hilda had laughed nervously at Dudnikov, 'No, not at all.'

The truth was, during the days when the Russian wasn't in, Hilda sold one or two items at most. Without Dudnikov, she would have had to go to Uffe for money weeks ago.

The Russian had smiled and taken a step closer to Hilda. She had been forced to lean against a rail of discounted summer jumpers. They were striped Musto sailing pullovers, which she didn't usually stock, but she'd hoped they might bring a new set of clients into the shop. She'd not sold one. Not even Dudnikov had touched them.

The Russian had made her an offer. He liked the shop, he said, and he wanted Hilda to continue. 'Perhaps I help a little with cash-flow, yes?'

Oh, how Hilda now wishes, she'd been brave and told Uffe about the losses the shop was making. But over the twenty-four hours Dudnikov had given her to 'think it over,' she had calculated she would be able to pay back the loan—if the Russian carried on spending 500 Euros per week, as he had been doing, and began telling his wealthy Russian friends about her shop. Being in business meant you had take risks, she'd thought. But, of course, after he'd given her the money in a brown paper envelope (a loan in cash should have rung alarm bells!), the Russian stopped coming, and Hilda was back to long days watching the bank customers coming and going right past her shop.

The 20,000 Euros Hilda ended up owing Dudnikov was a vast amount. Uffe had to sell a piece of land he owned two fields away from his farm.

'It overlooks the sea and I always hoped we might build our own place there for retirement,' Uffe said and that made Hilda cry.

When they went to the bank to withdraw the money so that they could give Dudnikov his cash in a brown envelope, Hilda glanced over to the shop, which was being refitted. 'Barber Shop opening here soon,' said the notice on the door. She wondered if there was anyone inside, looking out at the two of them as they sat opposite the bank clerk. Someone worrying about their business, just as she had done. Most likely not, Hilda decided, turning her head back toward the woman, who, it transpired, had been in the same class as Uffe at junior school. Hilda hoped their lie about why they needed the money in cash—to buy a boat from a Finn on the mainland—was accepted by the woman, but it all seemed to be OK. She smiled at Uffe and Hilda as she counted the notes in front of them.

'I hope you are happy with your new boat!' the woman, who was wearing large black-framed glasses, said.

Hilda glanced nervously at her husband. 'I'm sure we will,' he said, returning the woman's smile. Hilda took a deep breath.

Uffe made the payment to Dudnikov alone.

'I want to see the whites of his eyes when I repay him. I don't want any comeback from that man.'

Hilda was glad; she didn't want to see the Russian ever again.

That was last August, over four months ago. Since then, they hadn't heard a word from Dudnikov. Until yesterday. Or was that man really Alexander Dudnikov, and had he really tried to run them off the road? The way Uffe reacted and didn't want to talk about it frightened Hilda all over again.

Hilda gets up and decides not to think about the Russian. Not today. Christmas is nearly here and she still has so much to do.

She reaches for her telephone and sends a message to her daughter.

'Don't forget the salmon!'

She gets up and climbs the steps to the attic where, in the back of the wardrobe, she finds a box of tree decorations. Some of them look a bit worn out, but she knows Alicia will want everything to be just as it was before, so she will resist an impulse to buy a new set from a shop selling stylish homeware that has just opened in town. Putting aside all the old candleholders, Hilda carefully untangles the silver-colored tinsel and checks that the ancient baubles are all intact. She then counts the number of candles left over from last year; there are enough for the first lighting of the tree.

She can't wait to see what little Anne Sofie thinks of the tree. She remembers as if it was yesterday Stefan's bright eyes when he saw it for the first time. A tear falls down Hilda's cheek and she wipes it away.

Stop being so sentimental. I won't have it from others, so I cannot succumb to it myself.

TWENTY-FOUR

'Did you get the dill?'

'Yes, and more salt, just in case,' Alicia says, giving her mother a quick hug.

The two women begin working on the fish. Hilda tuts as she runs her hand across the two fillets laid out on the kitchen counter.

'So many bones left. You'd better get the fish tweezers and get them all out. *Så slarvigt!*'

Alicia smiles at her mother's words. She thinks everyone else is lazy and careless, and most of the service you get in shops is shoddy these days.

'I know the fishmongers aren't up to your standard, but they were really busy. Just as well you ordered the fish, they'd run out,' she says and puts her arms around Hilda briefly.

Hilda straightens her back and Alicia smiles. Her mother is a formidable woman but the loss of her shop has taken some of the sparkle and fight that Alicia has come to love and dread in equal measure out of her eyes. She knows the prospect of having everyone here to celebrate Christmas has made her mother happy. It's given her something to arrange and look forward to.

'Guess who I bumped into the other day?' Alicia says as she starts to remove bones from the fish fillets.

· · ·

Hilda leaves Alicia alone in the kitchen to go and tell Uffe who, as usual, is sitting in his office across the yard, about the return to the islands of Alicia's old friend. Alone with the fish, Alicia suddenly thinks back to the previous Christmas, which they had been planning to celebrate with Hilda and Uffe in London. They were going to have the traditional Christmas Eve supper-a large roast ham, vegetable bakes, meatballs, marinated herring–the peculiar mixture of Finnish and Swedish traditions that the islanders adhered to. On Christmas Day, they'd have a British Christmas with turkey and all the trimmings. She remembers how Stefan hated turkey, and would always have leftover ham from Christmas Eve instead.

Last year, Hilda and Uffe journeyed to London weeks earlier in late November. Instead of celebrating Christmas, they attended Stefan's funeral. Hilda wanted to stay for the whole of December, until the New Year, but Alicia couldn't bear the thought of having everyone assembled around the Christmas table without Stefan. She wanted to forget that the holidays were coming. She wanted to forget everything and just sleep.

And sleep she had. Liam had administered various pills that allowed her to rest and feel detached from the world.

In the end, Liam booked them into a hotel in the center of town for Christmas. She didn't want to be among the strangers in the dining room, eating the stupidly expensive lunch, or listening to the other, happy, laughing, diners cheerfully wish each other Happy Christmas. And the weather was awful, with cold drizzle falling on both days. Walking along the cold streets, they had to duck into pubs, where the other customers were in the same high spirits as the hotel guests they'd tried to escape. On Boxing Day, in spite of the rain, they walked along the South Bank of the Thames to visit the seasonal outdoor market. But when she looked into the dark, fast-flowing river, Alicia had yearned to be there on her own. She wanted to walk across the brightly-lit Waterloo Bridge and jump into the Thames. But she knew Liam would stop her.

Those dark thoughts frightened her and the next working day she contacted Connie, her grief counsellor, to book an emergency session.

Alicia shudders at the memory now and decides that this coming Christmas will be better. Much, much better. She'll make sure of it.

Breathe and come back to the present.

Alicia removes the fish bones one by one, and arranges the sugar and salt mixture, followed by the cut herbs, on top of the salmon fillets. She's closely supervised by her mother, back from Uffe's office across the yard. Hilda makes the final adjustments to the salmon.

'We'll look at it tomorrow and turn it over the day before Christmas Eve. Now, how about a glass of mulled wine? I've got the special edition *Blossa Glögg*. It tastes like limoncello this year!' Hilda shows Alicia a yellow bottle.

Alicia glances at the large clock on the other side of the kitchen wall. It's just coming up to five o'clock, but she nods to her mother, 'Why not?'

Over the past six months, Alicia has been trying to get used to the different drinking times–or lack of them–on the islands. With Liam in London, they had kept to strict times. Nothing until 6pm on weekdays, and only the occasional glass of wine at lunch on the weekends. She'd forgotten it was a British custom based on the old pub opening times, but after nearly twenty years in the UK, it was hard for her to get used to being offered an alcoholic drink at all hours of the day.

She's also worried about her mother's drinking. There isn't a day when Hilda doesn't have a tipple, be it a glass of beer or wine. Alicia hasn't seen her mother actually drunk, not more than a little tipsy on special occasions such as a meal when Liam is visiting from London, but there's rarely a time when Hilda doesn't have a glass of wine in her hand.

Alicia usually refuses a drink when her mother offers one, because she doesn't want to encourage any more alcohol consumption. But today, it's nearly Christmas, and after the day she's had—being nearly driven off the road by that unpleasant Russian, meeting her old friend, and then kissed and offered a new life by Patrick—she needs a drink herself.

• • •

After they've wrapped the marinated fish up and placed it under some weights on the bottom shelf of the refrigerator, Alicia and Hilda sit down at the kitchen table with their glasses of mulled wine, *glögg*. Hilda looks at two pieces of paper, one covered with Christmas menus and the other a shopping list, with some items crossed out and more added, some in black ink, and some in blue and red.

'I think we'll invite Rolf and Brit over for Christmas, what do you say?' Hilda asks. 'Uffe thinks it's a brilliant idea,' she adds.

Alicia smiles, 'Really?' She doubts her stepfather put it quite like that.

'Yes, Rolf is quite frail and on his own, so I think it's perfect. There's enough room for them to stay over. If Liam and you can stay in the sauna cottage?' Hilda gives Alicia a careful glance.

'Yes, that's fine,' Alicia says quickly. Her mother hadn't commented on the sleeping arrangements during Liam's previous visits in the fall. This is uncharacteristic, but Alicia is grateful that her mother hasn't interfered.

'Now, tomorrow I will fetch the turkey from *Kantarellen*, unless you're in town? What do you think we should get for little Anne Sofie?' her mother continues.

'You sure we want to do the British Christmas as well? Isn't it just too much this year, with so many mouths to feed?'

Hilda takes a large swig out of her glass and goes around to the stove, where she's heated the *glögg* in her traditional copper pan, to pour some more for herself and to top up Alicia's glass, although she's only had time to take a sip. Hilda uses little silver spoons resting in a pair of a small decorative pots to add the traditional slivered almonds and raisins to her mulled wine.

'You know, I wasn't sure if these would go with this year's special edition wine, but they do, don't they?'

She looks up at Alicia and smiles.

'Don't change the subject. It's just too much. There's going to be, what, eight of us, including Brit and her father, who you really don't need to invite, you know!'

Hilda places her hand on Alicia's. 'I think it's perfect to have a full house this Christmas, don't you?'

TWENTY-FIVE

As soon as Hilda heard that Brit Svensson was back on the islands, she had the idea of inviting the girl and her father, Rolf, whom Uffe knew way back in school, to celebrate Christmas with them.

She now looks at her daughter, sitting at the kitchen table, inspecting Hilda's long Christmas list. She's got her mussed blonde hair in a bun, which highlights her angular face, where her weight loss shows the most. Her cheek bones are high and there are some fine lines around her pretty pale eyes. It's been a terrible year for her, and Hilda knows Christmas without Stefan will be challenging for Alicia, as it will be for all of them. Hilda will make sure the festivities go smoothly. The more people there are, and the less like a family occasion it is, the better Alicia will be able to cope.

Suddenly her daughter lifts her face up to Hilda. 'Mom, that Russian that you nearly collided with. Do you know him?'

Hilda's eyebrows shoot up. She curses herself for making the mistake of telling Alicia that they recognized the driver of the Cherokee on their way back from the airport. She'd had too many miniature gin and tonics on the flight and wasn't thinking straight. Uffe was so angry with her that night. Even then, he wouldn't say why Dudnikov did it, though.

'It's nothing for you to concern yourself with,' he said and turned over in bed.

Hilda can now feel a faint blush rising her cheeks.

'No, of course not. Whatever gave you that idea?'

She can see her daughter knows she is lying, but can't challenge her. Or doesn't want to, perhaps?

'A man tried to run me off the road and I think it's the same Russian.'

'What? Are you alright?' Hilda takes Alicia's hands in her own. She glances down at her empty glass. She's finished her second glass of *glögg*. She should have added a slug of vodka to it, but she knows Alicia would have declined and then she would have looked like some kind of alcoholic. Which she isn't, of course.

Suddenly she can't take the lying anymore. She releases Alicia and covers her head with her hands instead. Alicia gets up and puts her arms around her.

'Tell me what's going on?'

Hilda can feel the strands of her daughter's blonde hair against her fingers, but she can't get the words out. The whole affair with that monster is so awful, and she's been so stupid, she really can't bring herself to tell Alicia.

'It's, it's nothing,' she manages to utter.

Alicia lowers herself to her knees and gently pulls her hands away. She peers at Hilda's face. 'This doesn't look like nothing,' she says gently. 'You can tell me. I might even be able to help.'

Hilda gazes at her daughter's face. She can now see the lines that weren't there twelve months ago more clearly, around her mouth and on her forehead. Alicia doesn't need any other worries, she tells herself, but at the same time Hilda is so tired of the secrets she's been keeping.

Hilda digs a tissue from the pocket of her Christmas-themed apron and dries her eyes and blows her nose.

Her mother is buying time and Alicia knows it. So she waits, perched next to the older woman. Eventually, after Hilda has had a good wipe of her face and blown her nose again, she inhales and exhales through her nose. 'It's all about money and my stupidity, really.'

TWENTY-SIX

The flight to Mariehamn is delayed by a further hour and Liam swears under his breath. He has Christmas off, but doesn't want to spend any more time in an airport than he has to. Truth be told, he's not a good traveler. He gets seasick on ferries and uneasy before a flight. The trip he's just taken from London to Helsinki was fairly uneventful until they began to descend. The captain informed the passengers that there was a snowstorm over southern Finland, but that they were going to attempt to land as usual.

Attempt to land!?

Luckily, Liam now travels in business class and the Finnair staff were understanding of his need for an additional double whisky to cope with these new circumstances. And they made it down without incident, but that doesn't do anything to allay his fears about the next leg of his journey. In another twenty minutes he's due to board a much smaller plane that will take him back in the direction he's come from, back over the Baltic toward the Åland islands.

Liam sips his drink–he's switched to gin and tonic–in the business lounge and thinks about his complicated life. Only twelve months ago, he was fairly happy with his lot. He loved his work as a respected surgeon at St Mary's Hospital in St John's Wood, North London. He was seeing another woman, but he still loved Alicia. He was close to finishing it with Ewa, the Polish nurse with the red lips and soft, willing body, when the worst happened. Alicia and Liam's wonderful, talented, beautiful boy, went out on his moped on a frosty night with icy roads and ended up hitting a wall. Not to have been able to live his life, to be killed even before he reached adulthood, is the cruelest fate. And Liam has to live with that. As well as the knowledge that it was he who persuaded Alicia that Stefan was sufficiently responsible to own and ride a bike at the age of seventeen. As if having an affair with another woman wasn't bad enough, Liam also carried the guilt of being responsible for the death of his own son, denying his wife the pleasure of seeing her child grow into a man.

Liam finishes his drink and goes to the bar to pour another one.

On his way back to his seat, he sees that the flight is at last boarding, so he downs the contents of the glass in one and makes his way toward the gate.

While he tries to ignore the bumpy ride back over the Baltic, he thinks about the surprise grandparenthood he and Alicia are now experiencing. Frida is a strange girl, with her rainbow colored hair and tattoos, but she has proved to be a good mother. There is no doubt that Anne Sofie is the most beautiful, thriving baby girl he's ever set eyes on. And it's clear the birth of a granddaughter, as well as the close friendship she shares with Frida has given Alicia a new reason to live. Without those two, Alicia would no doubt have returned to London by now, and possibly found some other way to cope. Perhaps by involving herself in some of the charities that he supports?

But, seriously, Liam can't see Alicia hosting charity galas or organizing a bunch of women to raise money for worthwhile causes. In the months after Stefan's death, when she surfaced from the depths of her grief, she would have left him if she'd stayed in London, there's no doubt in Liam's mind about that. There'd be another man–just look how quickly that arrogant Swedish reporter had lured her into his bed. But in the end she chose her husband, after Liam had made it clear how much he loved her and how sorry he was about his past actions. He didn't lie when he said Ewa meant nothing to him–it was just the sex.

Don't think about her.

Alicia and Liam are still not on those kinds of terms, which is making Liam crabby, but he knows he has to give her time. He needs to convince her to come back to London, where their marriage will have a fighting chance. This is why he's done what he has done. He thinks about the report emailed to him yesterday. At first, when he saw the results, he was jubilant. It was exactly what he had suspected from the very beginning, and it would give Alicia good reason to come home to the UK. But now, when the moment is nearly here, when he has to share the news with Alicia, he's beginning to doubt his own reasoning. To him, back in London that same morning, it had seemed clear. If Anne Sofie isn't their granddaughter, there is no reason for Alicia to stay on the islands. But what if Alicia feels differently?

Liam shakes his head–no, this is just his own fear of flying making him draw these irrational conclusions. Of course Alicia will see sense. Liam thinks he needs to be ready for the anger she will no doubt feel toward Frida. Having considered it carefully, Liam doesn't think she has led them to the wrong conclusion regarding the baby's paternity on purpose. No, he's sure she *thought*–even wished–Stefan was the father. It's clear that the girl was in love with their son, but sadly for her, the baby is somebody else's. The DNA test cannot be refuted: it's as clear as day that Anne Sofie is not the daughter of Alicia and Liam's dead son.

When Liam finally steps out of the plane at the small airport in Mariehamn, he spots Alicia standing behind the wire fence, smiling and waving. How he deserves this woman's love–or even friendship (because he's not sure she still does love him) he doesn't know. Dusk has fallen while he's been in the air, making the falling snowflakes quite pretty. He must learn to love this place. Everything would be so much simpler if he did.

'Good flight?' Alicia asks and brushes his chin with her lips.

Liam, possibly spurred on by the amount of alcohol he has drunk during the long journey, takes his wife into his arms and pushes his lips onto hers. For a moment, Alicia doesn't react, but then she pushes him gently away.

'Long wait in Helsinki?' she says and grins at him. 'C'mon let's get you home. Hilda is waiting with your favorite reindeer steak and a chanterelle sauce.'

Liam sets his suitcase inside the trunk of the old Volvo and sits next to Alicia. He grins and squeezes her thigh.

Alicia looks at his hand. 'Sorry,' he says, 'I've had a few, but it isn't just that. I've missed you. And you look so good in that outfit. Those jeans,' he says, slurring slightly.

Alicia smiles sweetly at him and removes the hand from her lap.

'Alright, let's get going, eh?'

TWENTY-SEVEN

Alicia cannot stop thinking about Patrick and the taste of his lips. Here she is, sitting in the car with her husband, obsessing about another man. The kissing in the office released something inside Alicia and all she wants to do is to dump Liam in Sjoland, turn around, and go to Patrick. But, of course, she won't do that. Especially now she knows about Dudnikov. She needs to keep her family together, she needs to protect them from the Russian. As soon as she's at work, she will find out where the man is, and do some serious research into his illegal activities. She'll hand all the information to Ebba rather than write about it for the paper. Which is another reason why she needs to keep away from Patrick. He would love a juicy criminal story like this, but Alicia wants the man caught. Her journalistic ambitions must be put aside for the safety of her family.

'How have you been?' Liam says. He's looking at her across the darkened car, but Alicia stares straight ahead.

'Fine,' she replies and increases the speed.

'Don't be like that,' Liam says and stretches his hand toward Alicia once more, but she prevents another squeeze of her thigh by touching the gearshift between them.

'Sorry,' Alicia says and tries to smile at Liam. 'It's been a busy day.'

Liam sighs heavily and leans back in his seat, looking out into the darkness.

'There's a lot of snow,' he says.

TWENTY-EIGHT

'You've done what?' Alicia's pale eyes are almost black. While she has been reading the email on Liam's iPhone, he has been waiting patiently. Waiting for her reaction.

They're just back from the main house–Alicia's parents' place–and are about to set up the bed in the sauna cottage, when Liam decides it's a good time to tell Alicia the news.

It's past eleven in the evening and Liam is tired, but he thinks the sooner he tells Alicia, the better. But his early start from London, the delay at Helsinki, and the choppy flight into Mariehamn have taken their toll on him. The compulsory meal Hilda cooked in Liam's honor included some kind of game in a creamy mushroom sauce and copious amounts of red wine, all which now rests heavily in his stomach. Luckily, they had decided before he arrived that they wouldn't insist on a sauna. Apparently, they would light one tomorrow. He calculates that if he'd been forced to endure an evening in a hot room, silently sweating with Uffe, his father-in-law, who speaks no English, his first evening on the islands would have stretched well past midnight.

'There'll be plenty of opportunity to have one before you go back to London,' Alicia had said with a wink as they sat in her old Volvo on their way from the airport to Sjoland. She knew how much Liam hated the sauna bathing ritual, and only suffered it because he didn't wish to offend Uffe or Hilda.

Alicia had been in a good mood when she picked him up. When they first set eyes on each other, she'd even replied to his kiss with enthusiasm, abandoning her mouth to his lips for much longer than she usually did. It gave Liam hope that she had finally come round to committing fully to their relationship.

Liam was further encouraged by the news that he was to sleep with Alicia in the sauna cottage. This was the first time since their brief separation last summer that he had not been banished to the attic room of the main house.

'Frida and little Anne Sofie are coming over for the holidays and I promised she could stay in the main house. It's much warmer and better with the baby. So you'll have to camp out in the sauna cottage with me.' Alicia grinned at Liam and her eyes had the playfulness they had before.

Before Liam ruined her life.

But he believed he was in the process of making good his mistakes, so he smiled back at her and placed his hand tentatively across the gearshift and onto her thigh. She didn't resist and let his hand rest there until she turned into the roundabout, which took them to Sjoland.

'I did it for you!' Liam now says. He doesn't understand her reaction. 'I thought that when you know the truth, you will see more clearly.'

The phone flew toward Liam at such speed that he barely managed to duck in time.

Alicia is staring at the man that she thought she knew. Liam is standing in front of her, holding the telephone she threw at him. It landed on the floor with a loud crack. She can see it has a deep slash across the screen. As if she cares! She's trying to understand how and why Liam has–against her clearly expressed objections–obtained a DNA test of little Anne Sofie.

'How?' Alicia now says.

Liam looks up from his phone and appears baffled for a moment, then his face brightens and he says, 'I know someone who runs a company doing these kinds of tests. It's the best one there is, so I am absolutely certain that these are correct. I can get you to talk to Steve.'

'I mean how did you get a sample from little Anne Sofie?' Alicia is trying to control her voice but her words come out almost as a growl.

'Oh, I took a strand from her hair. It didn't hurt her. She's got such a mop. And as you know, we have Stefan's.'

'You used the locks I kept from his hair?'

Liam looks at his hands. 'I had no choice.'

There's a silence. Alicia doesn't know what to say. Anger surges up, and she tries to concentrate on her breathing to try to calm down. She glances at the sofa bed, which they were about to open up. To think she had been considering sleeping with Liam tonight! She made the decision that day while making Christmas preparations with her mother. The way Patrick had ignited her desire might simply be because she missed intimacy, she'd reasoned; perhaps she will react in the same way with her husband? But now, she can't even imagine touching Liam.

There are so many things rushing through her mind. The violation of poor little Anne Sofie. When did Liam pull a hair out of her head? Did the baby notice? Cry? Oh, Alicia is so angry she has to hold herself to stop her from lashing out at Liam. And then there is the envelope of Stefan's hair that she had kept in the drawer of her dressing table in the bedroom in London. When she was there in the fall, she'd considered taking it with her, but she thought it belonged at home. Stefan's home. If they came to sell the house, she would then decide what to do with it. But for Liam to help himself and send her little boy's blond curls to some laboratory. It was just inconceivable!

'I know you're fond of both Frida and Anne Sofie.'

'Fond!' Alicia shouts.

Liam puts up his hands. One is holding the phone. Alicia notices that the screen is broken in two, but that the light is still on. She has to fight the temptation to snatch the device out of his hand and jump on it with both feet. But what would that achieve?

'Please, let me explain?' Liam says. 'Why don't we sit down?' he adds, trying to take hold of Alicia's arm and guide her to the sofa bed.

But Alicia turns her body away and sits in one of the chairs set opposite the coffee table instead.

Suddenly Alicia thinks of her mother. With yesterday's revelations about the Russian loan shark, which haven't quite sunk in yet, this would just be too much for her mother to bear. Or would it? Last summer, when Alicia found out about Frida's pregnancy and the baby's paternity, Hilda hadn't exactly been convinced by it all. She didn't have to say it, but Alicia knows Hilda would rather not be related to Frida's late mother, Sirpa Anttila. She was only a waitress, after all.

Alicia puts her head in her hands. The snobbery on this island!

Liam is looking out of the darkened window.

Alicia follows his gaze. It's pitch-black beyond the snow bank outside the window and the icy sea farther on. In the summer, it never gets dark but in the winter it never seems to get fully light, even with fresh snow on the ground.

'Go on,' Alicia says. She can't take in the news Liam has told her, nor can she understand why he would do such a thing. She can't believe that after everything that has happened he is trying to take away the thing that is most precious to her.

'You know I always had my doubts about the baby,' Liam says.

Alicia wants to scream that 'the baby' he's talking about is the most important human being in her life, but through enormous effort, she manages to keep her mouth shut. So she nods instead, and lets Liam carry on.

'So last time I was here, I noticed the little nail scissors Frida has in her changing bag and when you two left me alone with Anne Sofie, I simply cut a tiny bit of hair from her head. Honestly, she didn't feel a thing.'

'When did you get the results?' Alicia asks. Again she manages to keep her voice level, even though she wants to get up and shout in Liam's ear. And pound her fists into his chest.

'About a week ago. I didn't want to tell you over the phone.'

There is a silence. Alicia wonders how she can tell Liam the extent of the devastation he has caused with his actions, how violated she feels on behalf of herself and little Anne Sofie. And Frida.

'I'd throw you out but I know you won't be able to get a cab into

Mariehamn at this hour. Not in mid-winter. But tomorrow, you're on your own,' Alicia says. She gets up and yanks at the sofa bed.

With her back to Liam, she pulls open the chest of drawers where she keeps her bedding. 'The chair is yours,' she adds and throws a woolen blanket toward him.

TWENTY-NINE

Alicia doesn't fall sleep until the early hours. She keeps looking over at Liam, who is slumped in the chair, with his head resting backward uncomfortably. Still, he is fast asleep, gently snoring. Does the man have any feelings at all? Does he not know that her world has fallen apart. Again? And if he knows, which surely he must by now, how can he sleep so soundly?

She can't believe that the wonderful, now fully smiling, gurgling baby girl that she fell in love with the first time she held her, isn't related to her by blood. Nor to Stefan. She looks so much like him, with her combination of blonde curls and blue eyes. Of course, there's some of Frida in her too, particularly in the curve of her chin, but Alicia can't believe she would have imagined all the similarities to Stefan.

Anne Sofie has his long limbs and body. Even as a baby her son looked like the thin, gangly teenager he so soon became. Just like Stefan, Anne Sofie didn't have any of the rolls of fat most babies have in their thighs and arms. Instead, she has lean arms and strong legs, which she kicks, trying to grab them at every opportunity.

Alicia cannot help a smile forming on her lips and she reaches out to her phone to look at the most recent pictures of the baby. She is so beautiful, with a mischievous smile and a glint in her eyes, as if she knows she's got everyone wrapped around her little finger.

Everyone apart from Liam, it seems.

Toward the early hours of the morning, after a night mainly spent trying to sleep, and an awful dream in which Liam took Anne Sofie to the police station and told Ebba, the Chief of Police, that she was an imposter, Alicia realizes something. It doesn't matter to her if Anne Sofie really is Stefan's daughter or not.

She knows the test is probably right, and that Frida has unwittingly (or on purpose) misled her, and that she will have to ask her about it at some point in the future. But for now, Alicia *feels* like Anne Sofie's grandmother, so that is what she will be. With the death of Frida's mother, the poor little mite has no one else, so why shouldn't she help out? Frida obviously also believes that Stefan is the father, so what harm can there be in forgetting about the stupid test and carrying on as before?

If it's finally over with Liam, she can examine her feelings toward Patrick. From the kiss she knows her body still hankers after his touch. But is she one of those women (like Brit, she cannot help but think) who jump from man to man with speed and without so much as a glance back?

In the small hours, as she listens to Liam's snoring (how can the man sleep?), she aches for Patrick. She hasn't seen or heard from him since he kissed her and asked her to move to Stockholm with him. She has a great temptation to send him a message, but she manages to stop herself. What would Patrick think of a message in the middle of the night? It's like being a teenager again, sending covert declarations of love to each other. Besides, he knows Liam is back on the islands, so he'd know she was thinking of him while she is with her husband. Alicia cannot let him know that.

Suddenly the desire to leave all of this—the DNA test, her marriage, Hilda and Uffe and their problems with the Russian—is too great. Could she do it?

Alicia decides she can't think about that now, not when she needs to arrange the first family Christmas on the islands for years. She resolves to face it all in the New Year with a clear head.

THIRTY

The text from Frida takes Alicia by surprise. It's short and just says, '*Can you come and see us this lunchtime?*'

'*Of course! Just before 12 noon?*' Alicia adds three heart emojis to her reply. It's unusual for Frida to contact her, it's normally her who gets in touch first. Asking how the baby is doing, and if Frida needs any help. Often the reply is a 'No,' so Alicia has to invent reasons to visit mother and baby.

Alicia has got used to Frida's rather abrupt demeanor and she totally understands that having anyone, let alone your 'mother-in-law' around when the baby is small can be a little overwhelming. Besides, she has just lost her mother, which must be just dreadful for her.

Yet when Alicia thinks back to when Stefan was newborn and a toddler, she would have done almost anything to have an older woman around. Liam's parents had died when he was at university, and Hilda could only stay with her a week or two at a time. How she had longed to be able to call someone at short notice, or to ask someone to babysit, so she could have an hour or so of uninterrupted sleep. But, Alicia muses, baby Anne Sofie is very good at sleeping. Already at nearly four months, she needs just one feed at night and has two (regular) good naps during the day. Oh, what Alicia would have given for that! Stefan didn't like to sleep at night, during the day, or ever, really. For at least six months after his birth, Alicia went about the house in a sleepless trance, rocking the crying Stefan, who had suffered from terrible colic, night and day. Liam had started at a new hospital and had crazy hours.

Alicia sits herself down at her desk in the newspaper office and looks at the time on her mobile. She has two hours to write an article about holiday opening hours on the islands. She's looked at last year's piece, which Harri, the editor attached to his email telling her to *'Just copy & paste.'* There has been absolutely no 'real' news on the islands for days now. Everyone is busy getting ready for Christmas. Most of the Christmas parties, which provided some fodder with their disturbances and complaints from residents in the center of town, are over and people are just gathering with their families and loved ones to eat gingerbread biscuits and drink mulled wine while preparing for the Christmas Eve feast.

She should really be trying to find out more about Dudnikov, but she's found nothing at all so far. A virtual brick wall seems to surround the man.

She sighs, perhaps this paper and this town are too provincial for her?

Whereas Stockholm ...

After what Liam has done, she cannot see herself ever being able to forgive him. She left him at the house with Hilda that morning. He offered to come with her into town, but Alicia just gave him a short 'No,' and kissed her mother goodbye. Hilda was standing at the sink with her back to both of them, so Alicia hopes she didn't notice the chilly atmosphere between them.

'Let's all have lunch in town!' Hilda said, just as Alicia was at the door, thinking she'd escaped.

Alicia muttered something about work, and it being the last day before the holidays, but Hilda ignored her and arranged to meet in town at noon.

Alicia quickly gets her phone out and sends Liam a message.'Can't come to lunch, work thing.' She sends a similar but a little more wordy message to Hilda.

After she's posted the article on shopping hours to the intranet for the editor to approve and publish, Alicia goes into the little kitchen in the newspaper office and pours herself some coffee. Someone has brought in homemade Christmas stars, traditional flaky pastries shaped like stars with prune filling in the middle. Alicia picks one up, and just as she's biting into it, Kim comes into the kitchen.

Alicia nods to the lad, who doesn't blush as he usually does, but smiles.

'Are they good? My mom made them.'

'Very,' Alicia replies. She places the half-eaten tart on a piece of kitchen paper and starts to head past Kim out of the door.

'Hmm, I hope you don't mind, but I noticed you were looking for information about a person called Alexander Dudnikov?'

Alicia regards the young intern, who is wearing a freshly pressed blue shirt and neat dark jeans.

'Yeah, why?'

'If you want, I think I can help you with that.'

Frida opens the door to her ground-floor apartment. Alicia notices that the living room is in turmoil, there is a packet of diapers open on the floor, next to wet wipes and a tube of cream. A pile of baby clothes sits in one corner of the room and as she glances into the kitchen, Alicia sees a stack of dirty dishes in and around the sink.

She gives Frida a hug, moves a pair of torn jeans and a hoodie from the sofa, and sits down.

'Baby asleep?' she asks when Frida, clearing a space for herself on an armchair opposite, sits down and pulls her bare feet under her legs. She's wearing black leggings and a long black and red checked shirt. Her hair has grown a little, and is no longer the color of a rainbow, but pale brown. Her toenails are bright blue, though, so the girl hasn't lost all of her quirkiness through motherhood. Looking at Frida's still cropped head, Alicia absentmindedly thinks again that Anne Sofie must have got her blonde locks from Stefan.

And then she remembers.

Stefan is not the baby's father and I am not the grandmother.

Frida nods. She hesitates for a moment, and then says, 'I've read my mother's will.'

'Really?' Alicia can't quite understand how Sirpa Anttila, a waitress, would have needed to write a will. She was under the impression that her mother's–and now Frida's–small apartment was a rental and that she had no property, or savings. Or perhaps she did?

'Yeah, and it seems I am now quite rich.'

Alicia doesn't say anything. After a while she's aware that her mouth is open, and has been for some time. She closes it and sees that Frida is smirking.

'She left me just under a million Euros and this apartment, so you don't have to worry about me anymore. There's no need for you and Liam to help me so much.'

'How?'

At Alicia's simple question, Frida appears a little discombobulated.

'It seems she had a benefactor.'

Alicia thinks for a moment.

'But you know we'll always want to make sure you're OK. It's not a question of money,' she says.

Frida gazes at her with an expression Alicia finds difficult to inter-pret. Has Liam spoken to her? Surely he wouldn't dare?

'In any case, I thought you'd like to know,' Frida says finally.

THIRTY-ONE

Hilda is looking through her various Christmas lists in the kitchen. She has so much to do. She has to cook the vegetable bakes and check on the various marinated herring dishes she's been making in the week leading up to the holidays, as well as the gravlax that Alicia prepared. And she has to remind her daughter to fetch the ham. It needs to go in the oven tonight, so that it's ready for tomorrow.

Liam is already here and she has no idea what to do with him. Alicia has gone off to work, and left the poor man alone. There was a definite atmosphere between the two earlier that morning, so even if they shared the sauna cottage last night, Hilda very much doubts that they slept together. How can a married couple live thousands of miles away from each other and still have a sex life? Besides, she's seen how Alicia acts when she talks about Patrick. And now he's divorced from Mia Eriksson, leaving the coast clear for another woman. She's tried to find out from Uffe what the gossip about the Eriksson girl is, but he says they're all tight-lipped about it. It's at times like these that Hilda regrets not having the boutique. Even though there weren't that many customers, the old village gossips would pop in and update her on what was happening on the islands. Now she's completely in the dark.

Perhaps she should take Uffe's advice and join the local women's club, the Lionesses? A suggestion Hilda laughed at when Uffe made it.

'Me, a member of that knitting circle? Please!' she'd said, and that was the end of that conversation.

As she enters the lounge to ask if the men want another cup of coffee, she sees her husband is fast asleep in an armchair. His mouth is open and he's snoring gently, his gray mustache quivering slightly at each breath. Hilda stands above Uffe for a moment. She wonders what secrets he is withholding from her. What does he know about Dudnikov that he hasn't told her?

Although it had been a frightening incident, the run-in with the Russian provided her with some excitement.

Forget about that terrible man!

No, Hilda needs to concentrate on the family Christmas. They will want for nothing. She goes over to the other chair, on the opposite side of the lounge, where Liam is reading on his iPad.

'More coffee?'

Her son-in-law smiles at her but shakes his head.

So Hilda goes back to her lists, which she has carried with her everywhere since they returned from Spain. Suddenly she sees something on it and remembers that she needs to look into the linen. Does she have enough Christmas napkins? And are the matching tablecloths that she will need for Liam's week-long visit all pressed and spotless? How can she have forgotten such an important detail!

Hilda hurries to the far end of the lounge, where she keeps the linen in an old cabinet. It's not until she's by the large window overlooking the fields that she notices the change in weather. It's sunny, the rays shining down to the whitened ground. The view is breathtaking.

How wonderful, it's going to be a special Christmas!

THIRTY-TWO

While she's been with Frida, Alicia has received several messages from Hilda and Liam. She sees Liam has asked why they can't meet for lunch, but hasn't sent anything after the first text. Her mother, on the other hand, has reminded her to pick up the ham, more dill and butter, adding Christmas wrapping paper in a second message and festive name tags in a third. Alicia doesn't understand why she hasn't driven into town herself until she listens to a voicemail from Hilda.

'Look, can you call? We can't get hold of you anywhere. Harri at the newspaper says you left just after noon and he hasn't heard from you since!' There's a pause and then, Hilda says in a lower voice, 'I'm here with Liam. I think it would be rude to leave him alone, and he hasn't wanted to do anything since you blew us off at lunchtime. Ring as soon as you get this!'

Alicia glances at her watch: it's just gone half past two. Her mother's voice sounded as if she has been away for weeks rather than a few hours. She sighs and dials Hilda's number.

'There you are! I was getting really worried.'

Alicia cuts her mother short, 'I need to go back to work, but I'll pop over to the store on my way home. It's open late tonight, isn't it? I'm not sure if I can get away early today.'

'Oh,' Hilda says. 'What's going on? Where have you been? There can't be any big news stories this close to Christmas!'

Alicia laughs out loud. 'Yes, Mother, the world shuts down for the Christian festivities although only a third of its population is Christian.'

'Don't be clever with me. And don't change the subject!' Hilda tuts. And again, lowering her voice, she says, 'Your husband is here. He's been waiting all day for you.'

'Well, he knows I work so he'll just have to wait a little longer. Take him shopping!' Alicia says, hoping that her mother will take the bait.

'You better talk to him,' she says instead, and without hearing Alicia's protests, she hands the phone to Liam.

After a few moments, during which there's a stilted conversation between her husband and mother, she hears Liam's voice.

'Alicia?'

'Look, I'm not going to be back until late tonight, so you might as well go shopping with Hilda.'

'Erm, I,' Liam starts, but Alicia interrupts him.

'I've got to go.' She disconnects the line and leans back on her chair. She looks up and sees Kim's eyes upon her.

'Sorry I didn't have time to talk to you before. I needed to be somewhere. You said you could help me track down Dudnikov?'

Kim blushes again, but says in a confident voice, 'It's not really the done thing, but I can access Stockholm police files. I came across someone of the same name, Alexander Dudnikov, right?'

Alicia nods. She's thinking about how illegal all of this is, but decides it's probably OK for now. Until she acts upon this information, nothing will have been unlawful, will it?

Kim starts to speak quickly now.

'I've been doing some private research into Eastern European crime on Åland and I came across the guy. Then I saw that a search for him had already been made from this office and that it was you.'

Alicia sits down beside Kim. They are the only two reporters in the room, apart from the editor, who's sitting at his desk in his fishbowl office. Alicia nodded a hello to him when she entered the office. Luckily Harri isn't the talkative sort, so he didn't bother to pick her up about Hilda's earlier call. It wasn't the first time her mother rang her at work. She must speak to her about it. Alicia is nearly forty and not a child anymore!

'Is there a mugshot?'

Kim smiles, and, for the first time, seems relaxed talking to her.

'Ta-da!' He flicks the mouse and an image of the man that nearly ran into her a couple of days ago in Föglö fills the screen.

'That's him.'

'He's got a record in Stockholm and is on the run as we speak. Convicted for extortion, with suspicions of money laundering and people trafficking, although they didn't have enough evidence to get him on those two more serious charges.'

'And he's here in Åland, lording over everyone!' Alicia exclaims.

'What do you mean? Have you got some evidence of his activities here?' Kim's face is turned toward Alicia, with an eager expression in his eyes.

Her instincts about Kim were correct, Alicia thinks briefly. He's going to make a brilliant reporter.

'Yes, but nothing concrete. There's also,' she hesitates for a moment, but decides that she can trust this young man.

'He may have been using banks here to launder funds.'

'Really! Can you prove it?'

'No,' Alicia says and adds, 'This is between you and me.'

Kim nods.

'Besides, we can't very well report things that we found illegally by hacking into another country's police files without having any other proof, can we?' Alicia adds, knowing full well that there are ways in which that can be done. By simply quoting 'unknown sources,' for example. Although it would be risky, all the same. Her words seem to have the desired effect and Kim returns to his desk. Alicia ponders what she should do. It's tempting to go to Harri this minute with all the information, and ask if she can write a long piece on Dudnikov. But wouldn't that just make him more determined to scare Hilda and Uffe even more? He could do anything, Alicia is convinced of that. Goodness knows what kind of organization he is part of, or even heads. He can't be running this scam on his own, she's sure of it.

THIRTY-THREE

It wasn't until they were disembarking that afternoon that Brit sees Jukka again. It was a busy morning crossing from Helsinki, with half of the crew changing over. There were members of staff Brit hadn't yet met and she needed to speak with them. Luckily this was the last shift that Brit would do with Kerstin. The woman obviously didn't like her. Whether it was jealousy over her being Kerstin's boss, Brit didn't know, but every time she saw her, the older woman either didn't speak to her or visibly sneered at her comments. At one point, when the lunch time rush in the buffet restaurant was at its worst, and Brit had taken the decision to let the next lot of passengers wait for fifteen minutes before being seated, Kerstin actually snorted. Brit gave her a stern look, but decided that since they wouldn't be working together anymore, she'd let it pass.

Light snow fell as they pulled away from Helsinki Harbor, only an hour and a half after they'd docked. While supervising the second breakfast sitting for the freshly arrived passengers, Brit caught a glimpse of the view through the vast windows. The city, dominated by the Cathedral with its large green dome surrounded by smaller domes and neoclassical columns, looked spectacular. It wasn't yet fully light, but the Cathedral clock shone through the snowflakes, as did the round old-fashioned streetlights outside the Presidential Palace and Town Hall by the water's edge. The ice and snow in the harbor had been broken up by the ferry traffic from the larger ships like *Sabrina* and the smaller boats taking passengers to the Helsinki archipelago. The frozen sea had a luminous bluish color. It moved in slow motion, like a vast bath overfilled with bath salts.

Suddenly, as she steps out of the terminal building in Mariehamn, Brit feels dog tired. She glances toward her bike standing under a shelter, and sees that this hasn't protected it from sidewinds. There is a thick layer of snow on top of the seat. Brit swears under her breath as she undoes the frozen lock on the front wheel.

'Hello!'

Brit turns around abruptly, sending the tiny key into the air.

'Damn!' she exclaims. She's lost the key in the thick layer of snow. She glances toward the parking lot behind her. Jukka is standing by his car, one leg inside, shouting something to her, but his words are caught in the wind.

'What?'

Even before Brit can begin to start looking for the key, he's next to her.

'Come on, I'll drive you home.'

'I lost the key. It's somewhere on the ground,' She points to the thick bank of snow. It'll be impossible to find anything underneath it. Brit swears under her breath once again.

'Listen, you can come and get it when the weather improves?'

The man's eyes look sincere, but Brit has had enough of his toing and froing. Besides, all she wants is a warm shower, a glass of wine, something to eat, and a romcom on TV.

'No, it's OK,' she says, dropping to her knees to try to find the key.

But Jukka stops her before she hits the ground. He takes her arm. 'Look, it's just a lift!'

Brit glances down at the snow. There's absolutely no sign of anything on the brilliant white surface.

She looks up at Jukka's eyes. They are friendly and the beginnings of a smile is dancing on his lips. She realizes that she's being stupidly stubborn.

Damn you.

Brit gives in. She lets herself be led by one arm to Jukka's car. Inside she revels in its warmth. The seats are heated, and a blast of warm air is coming from the vents either side of the panel in front of her. She didn't realize how cold she was.

'Sorry,' she says to Jukka, who is maneuvering the car out of the parking lot and into the main road leading to the center of Mariehamn.

'I really didn't want to leave the bike behind.'

Brit doesn't know what to say next.

And since I don't know what you want from me, I don't want to spend more time with you.

'No worries,' Jukka says and adds, 'Where can I take you?'

'Oh, the apartment is in the old fishing port.'

Jukka whistles, 'Not bad.'

They are soon at the crossroads at Ålandsvägen where Jukka takes a right. While he drives, Brit considers his profile for a moment. He has a strong nose, and a straight, firm jaw.

As they are making their way south, Brit says, 'I hope I'm not taking you too much out of your way?'

Jukka turns briefly to gaze at Brit, and again that look of pleasure is hovering on his face.

'It doesn't matter. I couldn't leave a colleague out in this weather.'

A colleague.

Brit doesn't reply to this. Instead she turns her face toward the window. The landscape looks beautiful. The low-slung wooden villas in this part of the city are decorated for the season. Some have paper lanterns in the shape of stars shining out of the windows, and small Christmas trees strung with fairy lights twinkle in the front gardens. Soon they are in a wooded area, and then Brit can see the old block of apartments on her left. She remembers that another schoolfriend lived in one of the blocks, but she cannot for the life of her remember her name now.

Brit is stirred from her thoughts by a coughing sound.

'It's here?' he says as they near the turning to the old fishing port.

'Yes.'

Brit directs him to her block and after thanking him for the ride, she goes to open the door on her side. But before she can do that, Jukka stops her by placing a hand on her arm.

'Can I send you a message later?'

THIRTY-FOUR

Jukka drives home through the snowy landscape. Apart from a few years in Gothenburg after he finished his Sea Captain's Degree at Chalmers University, he has never lived anywhere else but on the islands. But rarely has the scenery appeared so stunning to him. As he drives along the East Harbor and sees the lights on a small strip of land that juts out of the largest landmass in Åland, across the water, he thinks what a lucky man he is. The dimness of the early afternoon adds an unreal quality to the scenery in front of him. Although he is tired, he decides he'll stay up with a cup of coffee when he gets home, simply to appreciate the view from his apartment in Solberg.

He bought the place, which has uninterrupted views over Slemmern toward the city, after his divorce from Leila was completed two years ago. He doesn't want to think about his ex, or the acrimonious divorce, which has left him estranged not only from his wife of over fifteen years but also from his teenage daughter, Silja. Jukka sighs and parks his car in the heated carport under the block of six apartments. He has the uppermost floor, which he paid over the odds for just to get the view. He still finds it funny that the locals call this admittedly expensive development consisting of terraced, semi-detached and detached villas, plus a handful of small luxury blocks of apartments,

Gräddhyllan-Cream Shelf. But he's more than happy to be considered entitled: he's worked hard for what he's achieved. Jukka didn't have a rich family to rely on when he was growing up. His father was a seafaring man like himself, but unlike Jukka, he was never at home. He worked on freight vessels all over the world, wherever he could get onto the crew, and occasionally, perhaps for Christmas and Easter, he'd honor his family with his presence.

Which wasn't wanted.

Jukka's father, Ville Markusson was an alcoholic, and a violent one at that. Jukka, as the only child, soon learned to duck and hide while his old man was at home. His poor mother bore the brunt of his father's alcohol-induced mirth. When Jukka was old enough to speak his mind, he begged his mother, Pirkko, to leave him.

'But what are we going to do for money?'

Pirkko, who had married Jukka's father when they'd met in Turku, worked as a cleaner for the offices in town and was always scrimping and saving. Her Swedish wasn't very good. She'd never learned it properly. She'd left school at sixteen and started to work on the Stockholm ferries. By eighteen, she was pregnant with Jukka and Ville did the honorable thing and married her, even though he'd only spent a handful of nights with her. He brought his new bride home to Åland and promptly went away to sea, leaving her alone in a council property.

The only good that came out of his father was the monthly payment he deposited into Pirkko's bank account. When the payments suddenly stopped, when Jukka was at university in Gothenburg, he received a panicked call from his mother. Before he had time to travel home (with an emergency grant from the student's union), a letter had arrived telling Pirkko that her husband had died following an accident in the ship's machine room.

Jukka was sure his mother never loved the violent man—she'd spent her life fearing his returns to the family home—but after his small funeral, it took only six months for Pirkko to perish too. Never more than skin and bones, she seemed to become tired of living.

· · ·

Jukka shakes his head, and makes himself a coffee. He needs to halt these dark thoughts now. But he can't stop thinking about his mother's funeral, which was an even smaller affair than Ville's, if that is possible. Jukka, who was on the largest grant possible from the education panel in the islands, as well as a scholarship from the prestigious university he was attending, Chalmers, had managed to pay for the casket and the service out of the savings he'd put aside when he'd worked as a waiter in a posh restaurant in Gothenburg. His aunt, Sirpa's only sister had traveled from Turku and had organized some food and drinks to be served in the small apartment in Jomala. Looking at the coffin being lowered into the ground, Jukka had promised himself that he would never be poor, and that he would make better use of his life than either his mother or father had.

So this is it.

A better life.

Jukka leans back in his Artek designer chair that he bought five years ago when the divorce from Leila was absolute. It was the first piece of furniture he'd got for his new apartment after they'd sold the large family house.

He decided to keep the style of the new place simple with natural tones. All the furniture was black, including the woven leather seat he was reclining in. The floors were pale wood as was his kitchen table (also from Artek), which sat six people. Not that he'd ever hosted such a large dinner party.

There were Venetian blinds on all the large windows, so he just needed thin drapes either end, which didn't even have to meet in the middle. That's what the woman in the shop in Mariehamn told him when he went in to inquire about window coverings. It was the fashion nowadays, she'd told him. Jukka decided on a pale gray fabric and the woman organized the rest, even coming over to fit them. She stood in front of the wide window in the living room, where he was now sitting, admiring the view.

'I can now see why they charge so much for these houses,' she said and turned to Jukka. He just shrugged. With his wife and daughter out of the picture, there was no one making demands on his salary, although he did pay a sum into his daughter's account every month.

. . .

The coffee on the small table next to his chair has gone cold and it's grown dark. The view out of Jukka's window now resembles something out of a picture book or a travel website. The water in front of him is snow covered ice, the color of the palest of blues. In front of him, the city of Mariehamn opens up. He can see the lights of the small red wooden buildings, their roofs covered in thick virgin snow, straight to the right, and beyond that the flickering lights of the city itself. He can just make out St George Church spire in the distance. He remembers how, when young, and so in love, he and Leila tied the knot there. The church had seemed too large for the two families, especially as Jukka only had his aunt in attendance, but he insisted.

'You always had ideas above your station.'

Leila spat the words out during a heated row toward the end of the marriage. He can't even remember what they were arguing about now. Leila was a good wife and a mother, but in the end he just grew apart from her. It was just as well she found out about Sia. Otherwise he might still be living a double life, which wasn't healthy for anyone.

THIRTY-FIVE

'*How about a drink tonight. Meet me at Arkipelag bar 6pm?*'
Brit stares at the message on her phone. She'd just stopped for a cappuccino in town when the cold eventually got to her, freezing her right to the bone. She'd been dragging herself through the shops all afternoon in search of last minute presents for Alicia's family. She has no idea what Hilda would like, let alone Uffe or Liam. In the end she opts for an Amaryllis just in bud, potted into a glass vase for Alicia's mother, and a bottle of cognac each for Uffe and Liam. She bought three bottles from the ferry, together with a case of champagne, some of which she will take over on Christmas Eve.

It's so kind of Hilda to invite her and her father over to the house in Sjoland. They have even offered to put them up for the night, even though Rolf had insisted they should drive home.

'The last ferry to Föglö goes at 7pm, and we're probably not going to sit down to eat before six!' Brit told her father over the phone, so eventually he agreed to the arrangement.

Brit glances at the text again. Earlier that day she was annoyed with the man, but now she has calmed down. She's more of less done with her shopping. She's already got Alicia's present from the ferry's tax-free shop, which to her amazement was well stocked with the latest brands. She's sure Alicia will appreciate the soft fur-lined leather gloves. Rubbing her hands together, Brit regrets that she didn't get a pair for herself too. Perhaps she will next time she's on duty. She got something for Mia too (an expensive cashmere and silk scarf, also from the ferry's shop), although she's apparently not going to be on the islands for Christmas. Mia sent her a message in the week, with an image of herself and the two girls on skis. The whole Eriksson family is spending the holidays in their mountain lodge in the Swedish ski resort of Åre.

Brit lets her mind wander while she decides what to do about Jukka. In any case, he can wait for a reply. Instead of messaging Jukka, Brit finds Alicia's number in her phone and presses 'ring.'

The call goes straight to voice mail. She tries again after a few minutes, but no luck. She must be working, Brit thinks and glances down at her outfit. She's wearing a pair of tight black jeans and a loose jumper with a see-through v-section at the front, which rather attractively shows off her cleavage, and has her lace-up boots on. Although low-heeled, they are quite sexy in a biker-girl kind of way.

This'll do.

Brit taps a message onto her phone.

'Sorry can't tonight, but in town now. Meet me at A in 15?'

Jukka spots Brit immediately in the darkened bar. She's sipping a glass of champagne (what else?) and chatting animatedly with the barman, who's very tall and handsome and at least ten years younger than Brit.

And him.

He stalls for time while he takes in her body. Tight jeans, black boots and a jumper that somehow, although loose, shows off her skin at the back. When he walks toward her, and places his hand proprietarily around her waist, he can see the top is partly sheer at the back and the front.

She is gorgeous, what are you waiting for?

'Hello,' he says and brushes her on the cheek with his lips, as close to her red-painted mouth as he can without actually kissing her.

'Hi,' Brit says. She gazes at him, but doesn't say anything else.

Jukka tears his eyes away from her and orders a beer. When the dark, curly-haired barman hands Jukka the drink, he nods to a sofa farther into the bar and asks Brit if she'd like to move to sit somewhere more comfortable.

The place is heaving with party-goers even this early in the afternoon, but then it's nearly Christmas. There's seasonal music playing and large, red, gold and silver baubles hanging from the ceiling.

'So,' he utters, struggling to know what to say. Brit is so good-looking that suddenly he wonders if she's above his league. Her cheeks are a little flushed and the red lipstick is really flattering, as is her outfit. Her legs seem to go on forever in those jeans. His glance moves down to her boots. What he'd give to unlace them later.

'So,' she replies, and gives a small laugh. 'Have you seen something you like?'

Brit stretches a hand toward the low table between them and grabs her glass. She leans back again and takes a sip of her champagne.

'I'm sorry. I'm rather stunned at how beautiful you are looking tonight.'

Now Brit laughs out loud.

'Isn't that a song?'

Jukka laughs with her. 'Might be. Still true.'

This is good, I'm making her laugh.

Leaning in to him, revealing even more of her delicious cleavage, and wearing a coquettish expression, Brit says, 'What is it you want, Captain Markusson?'

'I want to take you to bed.'

THIRTY-SIX

Ebba Torstensson sits with her hands crossed over the almost empty desk. It's immaculately tidy in the police chief's office. No piles of case papers, no images of criminals, or even pictures of family. Alicia regards her old schoolfriend. Tall, slim, and always straight-talking to the point of being rude, Ebba was always a bit of a loner at school. Alicia only really got to know her better the previous summer, even though they'd studied at Uppsala University outside Stockholm at the same time. But Alicia was on a journalism course, while Ebba had her head deep in thick volumes of criminology. Alicia would sometimes spot her in the university library, and nod a greeting, but she doesn't remember ever going for a drink with her.

In the summer, however, when Alicia, together with Patrick, investigated the death of Daniel, the Romanian boy, who turned out to be a friend of both her late son Stefan as well as Frida, Alicia relied on her police friend for information about the investigation. In the end, it turned out to be a tragic accident. But Ebba and Alicia became friends, or at least professionally connected. Alicia now wonders if the police chief has any close friends at all.

'So let me get this right. You want me to ask for information from the Swedish police on a known–wanted–Russian criminal?'

'Yes, I'd do it myself but I think coming from you, it would be better.'

'And you think he is here, in Åland?'

'Yes.' Alicia bends her head and looks at her hands. She's sitting on the other side of the immaculate desk. She knows what's coming next.

'And exactly how do you know about all this?'

Alicia sighs and lifts her eyes toward Ebba.

'I can't reveal my sources.'

'How did I know you'd say that?' Ebba's inquisitive eyes are steadily gazing at Alicia.

'Look,' she says, leaning toward her old schoolfriend. 'Just think, if it is him, and you arrest him and hand him over to Stockholm, you'll be recognized for the capture both over there and here. Plus you would have stopped the criminal activities of a loan shark, money launderer and goodness knows what other illegal activities Dudnikov is engaged in.'

'Hmm.' Ebba looks unconvinced.

'I believe he has been laundering money through a person you and I know.'

This is Alicia's trump card, and she is rewarded by a look of interest in the police chief's eyes.

'A crime here, on the islands?'

'Plus extortion.'

'Wait here.' Ebba gets up and once again Alicia is surprised at the woman's height. She must be nearly two meters tall! The police chief walks past Alicia without saying another word and closes the door behind her.

Alicia is fidgeting. The heating in Ebba's office is on full blast and she is sweltering under her padded coat. It's already gone past 5:30pm and she still needs to get the ham from the supermarket. Ebba has been out of the room for fifteen minutes now, and there's no sign of her, so Alicia removes her coat and goes to stand by the window over-looking the parking lot of the police headquarters. And there, she spots the police chief stepping into a car, together with two policemen. They drive off, sirens blaring.

What the hell?

Alicia swears under her breath. She picks up her coat from the back of the chair and darts down the stairs, but by the time the cold air hits her body, the police car is too far away for her to catch up with it. She can see its flickering lights and hear the siren in the dusk. It's driving at top speed out of the city on the main thoroughfare skimming the East Harbor.

Alicia sends a message to Ebba.

'What's going on?'

She stands outside, shivering in the late afternoon chill, then realizes she hasn't put her coat on. No message from the police chief, not that Alicia was expecting one. Again, she curses silently into the deserted parking lot in front of the police headquarters. This area is illuminated by bright streetlights and the few dark patches where parked cars have melted the snow make the space look like a huge checkerboard. Alicia decides to go back inside to see if anyone can tell her why and where Ebba took off, but naturally, as expected, the policeman at the front desk is more than tight-lipped about her schoolfriend's movements.

She's trying to decide what to do—go after Ebba in the hope she'll find the police car somewhere along the four roads that lead off the main intersection. Or go home via the supermarket? She's sure Hilda is having kittens by now, and Liam will be bored out of his skull in Sjoland.

That's when she gets a message from Frida.

'Ring me, I have some major news.'

Frida's phone rings for several minutes with no answer.

Alicia sits in her car. She decides to head off into the Kantarellen shop to pick up the ham and try Frida again when she's there. She ends a quick message to her mother, asking if there's anything else she needs to get. Alicia isn't looking forward to the inevitable Christmas rush in the shop, but she can't avoid it. She knows Hilda needs to cook the ham tonight for it to be ready in time for the festivities. Just as she's indicating left on the coastal road, she gets a message back from her mother.

'We've been to the shops with Liam and ham is already in the oven. We're waiting for you to have the champagne. Come home!'

Alicia has no desire to celebrate, but she mustn't let her mother know that. She thinks for a moment and decides to pen a reply, saying she has some last-minute Christmas shopping to do. Turning left, she and heads back into town again. She might as well go and see Frida to hear what other news the girl has. Perhaps this time little Anne Sofie is awake and Alicia can have a cuddle with her. She's come to depend on the love she feels for the baby, and the baby's affection for her, and she's not about to give that up. Whatever the stupid DNA test shows— and her cruel husband thinks she should do—she's still, at least in name only, Anne Sofie's grandma.

THIRTY-SEVEN

When Frida opens the door to Alicia, she is filled with the delicious smells of Christmas baking. There's cinnamon, cloves, and the irresistible scent of butterscotch. Frida's got one hand inside a red Marimekko oven glove and with the other, she's gesturing Alicia to step in.

'I'm baking gingerbread cookies and making *knäck*!'

Hence the delicious smell of burnt sugar and butter, Alicia thinks. She can't remember when she last had the Swedish Christmas sweets, and follows Frida into her small kitchen. What greets her is something close to chaos, in the middle of which is the gurgling and smiling Anne Sofie. She's sitting in a bouncing chair on the kitchen table, surrounded by packets of flour, sugar and spices, and two trays of biscuits. There seems to be flour everywhere, including on Anna Sofie's red and white striped onesie.

'Hello, sweetheart!' Alicia says, letting the baby take hold of her little finger. She's just learned to play with her feet, an activity that seems to keep her occupied for hours.

'Isn't she good?' Alicia says.

'Yeah, well, when she's like this. You should have heard her scream blue murder earlier when I deigned to change madam's nappy.' Frida comes over and kisses the baby's forehead, before returning to the stove, where she is stirring the butterscotch mixture.

'This burns easily, I saw on the Youtube video, so if she kicks off, can you pick her up? There's a bottle in the fridge that you can warm in the micro and give her if need be. I'm trying to get her weaned off these.' Frida glances down at her chest.

'Really, already? Isn't it better for the baby to have at least six months of breastmilk?'

Frida doesn't say anything, but Alicia can tell she's—once again—overstepped the boundaries of her grand-motherhood. She sighs.

Have I turned into an interfering mother-in-law now?

Alicia is fighting the urge to pick up the baby straight away, but she fears that might elicit more silent disapproval from Frida, so instead she sits at the table and just gazes at the beautiful child. Her eyes are so clear blue and her hair so blonde, Alicia cannot believe she doesn't have Stefan's genes.

'You said you had some news?' she asks Frida. She's still talking to her back, while Bing Crosby is singing 'White Christmas' next door in the living room. A song very apt at the moment. Outside Frida's kitchen, there's a snowbank that's nearly halfway up the darkened window.

While all the time stirring the pan, Frida says, 'Yeah, I found out that someone called Alexander Dudnikov is the guy making all those payments into my mom's account. So I guess he must be my father.'

'What?' Alicia cannot believe what she has just heard.

'Did you say, *Alexander Dudnikov?*'

Now Frida turns round, the wooden spoon in her hand covered in the thick, brown candy mixture. 'Yeah, why?'

'How did you find out!'

'Just a minute,' Frida says and turns off the electric plate under the *knäck* mixture. 'I think this is ready, so I can pour it out. Could you hand me that tray?'

Finally, when the butterscotch mixture is cooling on a tray covered with parchment paper, Frida sits at the kitchen table opposite Alicia. She begins to talk, her words being carefully observed by little Anne Sofie, who has grown still and quiet in the bouncy chair between them.

'I got to thinking that it's really unfair for me not to know who's paying me all this money, or has been supporting my mom and me all this time. And I thought it must be illegal to keep me in the dark. And that I must have some right to the information?

'So I went online, had a look at the laws and whatnot and decided to lay it on a bit thick with old Mr Karlsson. And, of course, he cracked and told me everything he knew. Or at least I think he did.' Frida looks up from the baby, whose fair hair she's been stroking.

'He's a bit of a slippery number, that one,' she adds.

'What do you know about this Dudnikov?' Alicia's heart is racing. She isn't sure if she should tell Frida what she knows of the Russian. How he was wanted by the Swedish police and how he'd been intimidating Hilda, and possibly Uffe, and how he tried to run both her parents and Alicia off the icy roads. And goodness knows what other illegal and horrible deeds he was responsible for. And that Ebba, the police chief, was at this minute perhaps arresting Dudnikov and putting him on the next available flight to Stockholm and prison. All because she, Alicia, had told Ebba all about the Russian.

Frida's father and little Anne Sofie's grandfather.

Frida gives Alicia a smile.

'I've known for a while that my father is a Russian. You know what the rumor mill is like on the islands?'

Alicia nods.

'So last year, when mom was taken into the home and I found out I was up the, you know, I decided to find out once and for all. He was going to be a grandad, you know? But there was just nothing. Nothing in mom's paperwork, nothing online. I tried to ask mom, but when she had one of her clear days, she clammed up. Then, on one of her really bad days, she called out to a 'Sasha.' She kept repeating the name over and over, and got quite agitated, so I had to summon the nurses, who would give her something to make her sleep. It was awful.' Frida pulls at her apron, which is covered in flour and blotches of the yellow-brown spices, and dabs the corners of her eyes.

'Of course, I knew that Sasha is a nickname for someone called Alexander, so I went online and looked for anyone with that name who lived–or had lived–in Åland. But again, I drew a blank. It was so weird. Of course, I didn't know about Mr Karlsson and his role in keeping it all from me. Why I wasn't allowed to meet my dad, I still don't know. Especially as he's obviously not short of a penny or two and has supported us all these years!'

Alicia listens intently to Frida. The background music changes to a Finnish Christmas hymn.

'But that's all going to change now.' Frida bends down to kiss Anne Sofie's cheek and continues, 'He's going to get to know this little one as well as me.'

Alicia is alarmed, 'What do you mean? Have you been in touch with him?'

Frida lifts her eyes. Alicia can see the girl's eyes flash dark.

'You haven't got a monopoly over us, you know.'

THIRTY-EIGHT

Alicia's head is spinning. After Frida's revelation about her father, little Anne Sofie started to fuss and Frida made it clear that Alicia wasn't helping the situation.

'She's probably got colic,' Alicia suggested. 'There's no such thing,' Frida replied, over the cries of the baby, who was refusing Frida's attempts to feed her a bottle.

Anne Sofie was displaying all the signs of distress associated with the common baby complaint, pulling her little legs up to her tummy and getting red in the face. But when Frida turned away from Alicia and went into the small living room, trying to rock the baby to calm her down, Alicia decided that it was best for her to leave the new mother to it.

'Call me if you need anything, won't you?' Alicia spoke to Frida's back and gave both mother and baby a quick hug.

Now sitting in her car on her way home–at last–Alicia cannot believe that horrible individual, Alexander Dudnikov, is little Anne Sofie's grandfather. She, as well as Frida, had heard the rumors about Frida's mother's Russian lover, but she didn't take them seriously. When Hilda told her last summer, Alicia was convinced that the woman had got pregnant and then invented a Russian to brush over the fact that she most likely didn't know who the father was. It was quite common in such a small community to blame any kinds of passing travelers for sudden pregnancies. And everything else.

That's mean–I didn't even know Frida's mother!

While she's been working at the paper, Alicia hasn't come across many petty crime stories where the culprit isn't from Sweden, Finland, or occasionally Russia. A recent–although rare–street mugging on a dark night in Mariehamn city center was put down to a Finnish national who (conveniently in Alicia's mind) managed to get on the ferry back to Finland before being arrested and was never heard of again.

Not that she thinks Ebba isn't good at her job–on the contrary–she's very conscientious, but Alicia suspects the islanders rarely drop each other into difficulties. They protect each other, unless something really bad happens, that is.

Alicia drives through the darkened roads back to Sjoland, her mind working hard on what she should do next. She's just ratted on little Anne Sofie's grandfather to the police! Alicia takes a quick glance at her phone but there's nothing from Ebba. She parks her car on the side of the road and dials the number of the police headquarters, but this time the officer at reception is even more abrupt and impolite.

'There is nothing we can tell the press at this stage. We will notify you as soon as we have anything. Please don't call again. You are wasting police time.'

Listening to the empty line, Alicia ends the call and throws her phone onto the passenger seat. Then she sends another message to Ebba, but once again, by the time she's nearing the swing bridge into Sjoland, there's still no reply.

Perhaps she should contact her editor, Harri, but by now he'll be at his summer cottage in the far archipelago and will not want to be disturbed. She's been told that the editor takes a full two weeks off over Christmas.

Besides, this has nothing to do with the paper as such. Harri would only tell her to write up everything she knows about Dudnikov and publish it. Whether it would hurt her family or not.

Alicia decides to contact the one person she knows will help her.

She parks on the side of the canal, where a stand sells ice cream in summer. She dials Patrick's number.

'Hello gorgeous,' he says and Alicia wonders if he's been drinking.

Then she decides to stop being so judgmental. It is the last working day before Christmas after all, and past six o'clock, so even by her stuck-up English drinking time rules, it wouldn't be a crime to be a bit tipsy tonight.

'Patrick, I need your help.'

THIRTY-NINE

For the second time that day, Brit is in Jukka's car, this time driving north, toward Sjoland.

'Where do you live?' Brit asks as she watches the landscape becoming more and more dreamlike. After leaving Mariehamn behind, the snow envelopes them on all sides. Vast pillows of white cover the fields and hang off the occasional rows of pine trees.

'Oh, Gräddhyllan, I believe the area is generally called.'

Brit laughs; this is the expression Swedes give to any expensive seats at a sports match or an exclusive area of housing. Not something in Åland.

'I've never heard of that.'

'Solberg isn't much better,' Jukka says. Brit can't see his face fully in the dim light of the car, but she can hear the smile in his voice. And Brit agrees, 'Sunny Mountain' doesn't exactly suit these craggy islands either.

But she changes her mind as soon she steps inside Jukka's third-floor apartment. The view is even more impressive than the one she enjoys from her apartment. The sun has long since set, so it can't be called 'sunny,' but she sees how this place can be called exclusive. In the distance, she sees Mariehamn open out in front of her. With the freshly fallen snow covering the rooftops and the twinkling lights from

Christmas decorations and buildings, it looks like a picture postcard. Jukka's block is right at the top of the 'Sunny Mountain'–more of a hill–and has uninterrupted views of the city, the frozen sea, and some of the small islands outside Mariehamn.

'How do you get anything done?' Brit glances around and realizes that Jukka is standing right behind her.

Instead of replying, he takes hold of her waist and bends down to kiss her neck. The touch of his lips against her skin sends a signal down Brit's spine and she lets out an involuntary sigh.

She turns and lifts her face up to him.

The kiss is even better than she could have imagined. Brit loses herself in Jukka's arms and lets her body relax. He presses his lips against hers and begins to probe her mouth with his tongue. It's gentle at first, but then urgent, until they part, both panting.

'There's a great view from my bedroom too,' Jukka says hoarsely.

Brit cannot speak. Her desire has overtaken her body, rendering her unable to do anything but nod. Taking Jukka's proffered hand, she follows his tall shape into the bedroom beyond the darkened kitchen.

The bed is wide and covered in a fake fur throw. Jukka pushes Brit gently down into a sitting position and kneels in front of her for another kiss. Gently pushing her legs apart, he presses his body tight against hers. Brit touches his face, his hair, and neck, while Jukka places his hand on her breasts over the thin jumper. Again Brit cannot help but moan. Keeping his lips on hers, he quickly moves his hands to her back and finds the bra fastening. Swiftly, he unhooks the clasp, and leaning back slightly, pulls her jumper up and slowly, oh, so slowly, lowers each strap of her bra so that her upper body is naked. Jukka gazes at her erect nipples. 'You're beautiful,' he says, looking up at her eyes.

Brit is trembling. She wants Jukka to caress her so badly. Reaching out for his hand, she places it on her left breast and leans in for another kiss. Then, bringing Jukka with her, she gets up and begins to undo his jeans. He's already hard, and Brit wants to touch him.

Naked, they tumble onto the bed.

· · ·

Afterward, when Brit is lying next to him on the bed, exhausted from their passion, he lifts himself up on his elbow and moves a strand of her hair behind her ear.

'I want to do this again?'

Brit smiles, 'What now?'

Jukka gazes down his naked body. He's certainly not ready yet, but Brit is so exciting, why not?

He says laughing, 'Not sure I can, but there's no harm in trying!'

Jukka bends down and begins to kiss her, but she stops him, 'I was joking!'

'You've got me going now,' he says and nods at the area between his legs, where some movement is beginning to show.

They make love again, a little less hurried this time. Jukka has time to explore Brit's body more closely, which she seems to enjoy. He cannot remember when he's become so easily aroused by a woman. There is something strong, yet vulnerable about Brit. Her curvy body, firm breasts with their pink nipples, the partly shaved part between her legs, and her flat tummy and round buttocks would make any man go wild. But it's the way she occasionally takes charge during love-making, while moaning in his arms and waiting for him to act at other times, that raises his desire to an uncontrollable level. She's very good at giving him pleasure and her occasional whispers of 'Faster, faster,' reveal her enjoyment and spur him on.

After Jukka has taken Brit into his walk-in shower and gently soaped her whole body, they sit in front of the view again, with glasses of a rather good red wine. Jukka has given Brit the leather chair and pulled one of the seats that matches the gray settee in the lounge next to hers.

It makes Brit feel sad, but reassured, somehow, to see that there's just that one seat, with the matching small table made of light wood, facing the windows. All of Kerstin's snide remarks and hints about Jukka being a womanizer seem completely wrong.

Jukka gets up and walks the few steps into the kitchen, separated from the lounge by a half-wall. A narrow space, it's between Jukka's bedroom and the bathroom and sauna at the other end of the apartment. When Jukka took her into the shower, she had noticed that there was another bedroom facing the road. It had a neatly made up bed with a large, brown teddy bear sitting on it. She didn't want to ask, but she wondered if Jukka had children? Even though they had spent the early evening in bed, making love twice, it still seemed too personal a question. Or was it?

Brit glances toward Jukka, who is preparing spaghetti carbonara.

'My specialty,' he'd told her when he asked if she was hungry.

He's now standing at the stove, in bare feet, wearing a pair of jeans and a loose T-shirt over his wide shoulders. His hair is messy, which makes him look even more attractive.

I'm really falling for this guy.

Brit is starving, and the wine is making her even hungrier, so when Jukka returns with a large bowl of pasta and a fork, she thanks him and starts eating immediately. She tries to remain ladylike, but all the physical activity has given her a huge appetite.

FORTY

atrick is wearing a white T-shirt with a pair of ripped blue jeans. His strong bare arms are still tanned from the summer, and covered in a thin layer of blond hair. He has his back to Alicia when she emerges from the elevator, which opens straight into his penthouse apartment. Alicia hasn't been inside his place since last August, when she was still reeling from their brief affair.

The apartment hasn't changed. There's still the incredible view across the sea from the open-plan living room, the same stylish pale gray sofas, the white kitchen and dining table at the back, and the vast seascape on the opposite wall, which almost matches the view from the windows. If the sea had been stormy rather than icy. Briefly, Alicia wonders how much the painting is worth, but puts aside such thoughts.

Patrick comes over and gives her an awkward one-armed hug, keeping his body inches away from her.

Alicia drinks in his scent, something expensive and subtle. She has a sudden desire just to lean into his strong body and let go. Just stay there and forget about Frida, the baby, Dudnikov, Ebba, her mother and Uffe–and Liam. But she resists and pulls herself away.

He regards her briefly, but Alicia is trying to escape his scrutiny. She doesn't dare look at him and moves into the center of the room, where the two vast sofas face each other. She decides to sit down, then changes her mind and goes over to stand by the window.

Patrick goes back into the kitchen and returns with a wine glass.

'Red or white?'

'This isn't a social call,' Alicia says and places the glass on the smoked glass coffee table set on the white rug between the two sofas. She keeps her face straight.

Patrick sighs and sits down. She sees there's a glass of red wine on the table in front of him. She notices that his hair is wet. He looks as if he's just stepped out of the shower. He takes a sip of his drink and pulls the corners of his mouth into a smile. 'And here I was, hoping you'd decided to give the small island the heave ho and come with me to the big lights of Stockholm.'

'I need you to help with something, but if you won't ...'

'Don't be like that. I'm impatient, that's all,' Patrick says and he comes to stand next to Alicia. He takes her hand and says, 'What's the problem?'

Alicia hesitates. She pulls her hand away from Patrick's. 'Perhaps I'll have that wine after all. I'm driving, so just the one glass. Red, please.'

'Coming up!'

While Patrick goes into the kitchen to fetch the bottle, Alicia sits down. She tries to decide how much she should tell him about Frida, the DNA test, Frida's mother, Sirpa Anttila's riches, and the Russian, Alexander Dudnikov. What does she really want him to do? Why is she really here?

She realizes that she wants to tell Patrick everything, and for him to help her make sense of it all. Should she tell him that Frida didn't have a baby with Stefan after all? A ping from her phone stops her train of thought. She reads the text displayed on the screen.

'*Where are you?*'

Alicia ignores her mother's message. She will have to deal with Hilda later. What will she say when she hears Anne Sofie is related to Dudnikov? And why is he still terrorizing them if he knows–which he must–that Frida's baby is his granddaughter? Alicia accepts the wine from Patrick, who sits next to her.

'So what's up?'

She looks him straight in the eyes. 'If I tell you something, you must promise not to use it to your own purposes.'

Patrick is quiet for a moment and then replies with a serious expression, 'Of course.'

'OK,' Alicia blows the air out of her lungs and says, 'I've just found out that Sirpa Anttila, Frida's mother, was wealthy.'

'Yeah I knew that.'

'What?'

'As did your lovely husband. I told him last summer when he came in asking whether Frida was after money.'

Before Alicia can take in what Patrick has just told her, her phone rings. She glances at it, expecting it to be Hilda. Alicia knows her mother was never going to let her messages go unanswered. But when she sees the name, Ebba, on her screen, she quickly presses the button to accept the call.

'Did you warn him off?'

Ebba sounds angry. Alicia can hear that she's somewhere windy, with loud engine noise in the background, and she immediately thinks, 'The airport'.

'Of course not!'

'Well, someone did.'

'What happened?' Alicia asks, adding quickly, 'I'm asking as a private person, not a journalist.'

Patrick's eyes shoot up when he hears Alicia's words.

'Hold on a moment,' Ebba says, and Alicia can hear the police chief talking to someone. She can't catch what they are saying.

'What's happening?' he mouths, but Alicia shakes her head and puts her hand up to silence him. She rises from the sofa and moves toward the vast windows, now overlooking a darkened sea. She can see lights, what she presumes is a vessel gliding slowly between sheets of ice in the shipping lane.

'Dudnikov boarded a private plane about an hour ago. According to air traffic control, the destination is Russia. St Petersburg to be more precise.'

Ebba pauses for a moment. 'So I ask you again, did you warn him off?'

'No,' Alicia replies. 'Why would I be sitting in your office at the

Police Headquarters telling you everything I knew if I didn't want him to be caught?'

There's a silence at the other end, and then in a tired voice, Ebba replies, 'Stranger things have happened. Anyway, I'm not able to do anything now. I'll pass all the information you supplied–such as it is, without accompanying evidence–to the Stockholm police. They can take it on from there. But you do know, don't you, that to get anyone extradited from Russia is a futile task?'

'Yes. I am aware. But how did you know where to find him?'

Ebba seems to hesitate for a moment, then says, 'I get the traffic movements to and from the islands in my routine reports each morning. A private plane traveling to Russia is always exceptional. I just put two and two together.' The police chief disconnects without saying another word and Alicia presses her forehead against the cool of the window pane. She hears Patrick moving behind her. Next, she feels his arms around her, and she hasn't got the strength to resist.

'Patrick,' she starts, but before she has time to utter the words, Patrick's mouth is on hers and she's again swept into his embrace, into the world that she thought she had left behind. His hands are on her hips and she can feel his hardness as he pulls her against him. Desire spreads through her body like wildfire, setting everything alight from between her legs to the tips of her fingers and toes.

FORTY-ONE

When, later that night, Brit is sitting in a taxi, on her way home, she checks her watch to see if it's too late to contact Alicia. She needs to tell someone about Jukka and the wonderful evening she's had with him.

'*Guess where I've just been?*'

When there's no reply, Brit hesitates for a moment, but decides to try phoning her friend. She feels like a teenager who's had sex for the first time and just has to confess–OK, brag!–about it. But after several rings, there's no reply. Instead she leaves a message on Alicia's answerphone.

'*Ring me!*'

It's not until the cab has pulled up outside her block of apartments that she gets a reply.

'*Can't talk now, sorry.*'

Brit is composing a reply while waiting for the elevator to her apartment, but when the doors open, she stops dead.

In the elevator, facing her stands Alicia. She looks just as surprised as Brit.

'I was just, what are you doing here?' Brit stammers.

Alicia is staring at her.

She looks guilty.

'Where have you been?'

Brit thinks back and realizes the panel had shown that the elevator was coming from the tenth floor, the penthouse apartment.

'Um, I was in the area and thought you might be at home. Your message sounded urgent.'

Brit harrumphs, raising a skeptical eyebrow and says, 'We both know that's not true.' She crosses her arms and when the elevator doors ping and begin to shut, she steps inside and presses the number of her own floor.

'Why don't you come in for a drink? It's nearly Christmas and I'm in love!'

Alicia sits at the kitchen table in Brit's apartment and holds her head in her hands. Brit, who was briefly annoyed when she stepped inside the lift, softened after Alicia told her about her eventful day. Besides, she's so happy herself that she's not capable of thinking badly of anyone.

'I've made such a mess of things!' Alicia lifts her head and Brit sees there are tears in her eyes.

'No you haven't. None of this is your fault,' Brit says and rubs her friends back. She's resting on her knees, next to her friend.

'I'll make you some coffee.'

'Thanks,' Alicia says and smiles sadly. 'Sleeping with Patrick is totally my fault. As was investigating the Russian. I should have just left it alone!'

'But the guy is a maniac. He tried to run your parents off the road and into the icy canal, remember? And you and me in Föglö. What was that but intimidation, pure and simple!'

'Yeah, I'm not sure if that was his way of introducing himself to his new family.'

Alicia lets out a short laugh and Brit, too, smiles at her words.

Brit puts a mug of hot, steaming coffee in front of Alicia, who takes a sip. 'I don't suppose you have anything stronger? It's been quite a day.'

'Now you're talking.'

While Brit goes to fetch a bottle of wine and glasses, Alicia glances at her phone. There are four more messages from her mother. She takes a deep breath and dials Hilda's number. She gets up and says to Brit, 'Just letting my mother know that I'm still alive.'

To say Hilda wasn't happy is an understatement. But Alicia reminds herself that she is a grown-up, a mother and a grandmother (or perhaps not?). But her mother was right about one thing. She needs to call Liam.

'Hi, I'm afraid I'm not going to make it back to Sjoland until much later,' Alicia says.

'I see,' Liam says. Alicia can hear anger in his voice.

He's got a nerve!

'Well, I just thought I'd let you know.'

'Look, Alicia, I am going nuts in here. Your mother is fussing over me constantly, and there's no internet. I'm using 4G, which is so slow.'

'Look, you're grown-up. Call a cab and go into town, or go back to London. Frankly, I don't care what you do anymore.'

Alicia rings off. Hearing Liam whining about her mother has made her furious. Although thinking about it, she has completely abandoned him.

And he has betrayed me!

'Here's your wine,' Brit says, smiling. 'Everything alright at home?'

'Not really. But I don't care,' Alicia says and clinks glasses with her friend.

'I don't suppose you could let me stay tonight?'

The two friends drink wine and talk into the night. Brit tells Alicia about Jukka, his incredible apartment, and their love-making.

'It was just amazing.'

Alicia takes her friend's hand and says, 'I'm so glad for you. You deserve a good man after, you-know-who.'

'Don't say his name! I don't want to think about him,' Brit interrupts her.

Alicia tells Brit everything. She recounts how Liam had stolen a piece of hair from little Anne Sofie, as well as from the envelope where Alicia had saved her son's locks. And how he thought that the DNA test result would be a relief to her.

'He actually thinks that I don't want to be Anne Sofie's grandmother!'

'So that's why you slept with Patrick tonight?' Brit asks.

Her friend's question takes Alicia by surprise. Is that what she was doing?

'No!' she says, but she isn't sure if her friend hasn't just put her finger on it. Is she using Patrick?

Again?

When he'd asked her whether she had thought about Stockholm, she'd been evasive. Truthfully, she replied that she hadn't had time, but she knew, really, that she hadn't considered the move as a serious proposal. Why? Because she is fairly certain she wants to stay on the islands.

Brit puts her hands up. 'You are a free woman. Believe me, men don't mind why you have sex with them. As long as you do.'

They both laugh, but afterward both sink into their own thoughts, looking out of the windows at the empty blackness. The two friends are sitting on a plush sofa. Brit's apartment is the same layout as Patrick's upstairs, with the same views.

Alicia isn't sure whether what Brit just said applies to Patrick. Or Liam, for that matter.

FORTY-TWO

Driving home in the dim light of the morning, Alicia feels terrible. The landscape around her is stunning, with snow banks on either side of the road and hanging heavy on the pine trees. There are no vehicles on the road; it's not even seven o'clock on Christmas Eve. The shops in the center of town will open for just a couple of hours this morning and the offices have already shut their doors for the holidays.

When she comes to the road running along East Harbor, she thinks how dramatically different it looks with snow and the frozen water. The East Harbor doesn't lead straight to the open waters, but is protected by a piece of land jutting out—Sjoland. Smaller vessels from mainland Finland enter from this side of the islands, but they must first cross the Sjoland Canal, which shuts during icy winters.

As Alicia nears the swing bridge, she finds herself hoping Uffe has cleared the fresh snow from the drive down to her sauna cottage. She wants to creep in unnoticed. She needs a large cup of coffee and some time to think.

What am I going to do?

She's had a number of messages from Patrick, asking for her to call him. But she can't. She feels she's betrayed both Liam and Patrick with her actions last night. But she struggles to ignore the warm feeling she has inside. Patrick's touch, his body, the way she melted into his arms, made her the happiest she's been since the previous summer, at the beginning of their affair. Then, Patrick ignited something inside Alicia, something that she cannot ignore. But is that just carnal passion? Just sex, not love? Is this what Liam felt for the Polish nurse? A relationship he ended and now says he can forget?

Whatever Brit says about men, she has the feeling that Patrick isn't like that. Perhaps he was once, but not anymore. Besides, she wouldn't want to be with a man who doesn't think going to bed with a woman means anything more but just the act. Or does she?

Alicia slept badly at Brit's place. She dreamed about Anne Sofie being taken by a faceless man. Frida had been there but she'd just smiled at Alicia and said, 'It's for the best, you know it is.'

During the night she decided she would never tell Frida that she was aware of Dudnikov's disappearance. Or that she knew him. She knows it wasn't her fault that Dudnikov left the islands. The permissions for the private plane to fly from Mariehamn to St Petersburg had been sought well before Alicia went to see Ebba. The police's sudden dash after Dudnikov hadn't make him flee the islands. That proves it had nothing to do with Alicia. Still, her aim was to get the Russian behind bars. Thinking about everything she has done and been through during the last few days makes her mouth go dry. And there's a headache building between her eyes.

She's relieved to see the road down to the cottage has been cleared and the lights in the house are off, apart from Hilda's Christmas star lanterns, which shine brightly out of the dark panes of the downstairs windows and reflect on the snow outside.

When Alicia unlocks the door to the cottage, she can see there's a shape in her bed. Liam's feet are peeking out of the duvet. His legs are too long for the small sofa bed in the cottage. His dark hair is in stark contrast to the white of the sheets, but Alicia can't see his face because he's got his back toward her.

She closes the door behind her silently, and tiptoes around the lightless room. She doesn't want a confrontation with Liam until she's had time to think, and calm down, but she has nowhere else to go. Being challenged by Hilda would be worse, so going up to the main house isn't an option. Besides, if Hilda is awake, she'll have seen

Alicia's car drive down to the cottage and will be in touch immediately.

Alicia seats herself in one of the chairs facing the small window. It's still dark, the sun isn't going to come up for another two hours, but there's a faintest of lights on the horizon behind the pine trees, which are heavy with snow. It's from one of the small islands opposite. It amazes Alicia what a difference the snowfall has made to the light even at night. She's forgotten how it illuminates the landscape. It's as if the sun plants lightbulbs in the snow during the day only to be switched on as twilight settles over the country. 'Solar powered snow,' Alicia thinks to herself and lets out a small chuckle. It's chilly in the room, and Alicia thinks she needs to relight the fire in the wood burner in the corner of the room.

Over in the bed, Liam stirs, and immediately Alicia regrets making a sound. She gazes over Liam's tall shape underneath the covers, and as her eyes wander toward his head, she sees he's awake and watching her. For a moment both stare at each other. Liam's eyes are sleepy, and his hair is ruffled. Self-consciously, he runs his hand through it.

'Good morning,' he says and his voice sounds hoarse.

'Hi,' Alicia replies.

Neither move for what seems like a very long time to Alicia.

Finally, she decides to break the silence and asks, 'Coffee?'

Liam is regretting his stupid decision to go to bed naked. He was drunk last night and planned on seducing Alicia as soon as she came home. But then he fell asleep and now, on waking, he sees from the large clock fixed to the little kitchenette in the corner of the room that it's already nearly eight in the morning. Although it's still dark outside. Why do people want to live in this harsh climate? Or more particularly, why does Alicia want to live here? Surely the knowledge that she's not Anne Sofie's grandmother after all, and the experience of her first cold, dark winter on these godforsaken islands in nearly twenty years, is enough to make her realize that her home is in London?

Liam is dying for a pee, but in order to reach the loo, he has to walk across the room, right past Alicia, who's measuring coffee into a percolator. And all his clothes are in a pile on one of the chairs at the end of the bed. Too far to walk without Alicia seeing the state of him.

The sight of Alicia, who's standing in her tight jeans with her back to him, with her round buttocks at eye level, doesn't do anything to reduce his morning glory.

'I thought you might sleep in the main house?' Alicia says, not turning toward him. Is there an accusation in the remark, or is she making general conversation? Liam can't tell, but fears it's the former. She's now bending down in front of the log burner, crunching news-paper into balls and laying logs on top of them. She lights the fire with matches and stands up, gazing at him.

She doesn't want me here.

'Look, Alicia. Can we talk?' he says.

Alicia sighs. She's standing in front of the now blazing fire. She looks tired and somehow disheveled and suddenly Liam knows where she's spent the night. No, surely she wouldn't? Not when her husband is actually here, on the islands? When in London, rattling around the large house in Crouch End on his own, his jealousy sometimes takes such a firm hold in the night that he has to fight the urge to phone Alicia, just to check she's not in bed with him, that self-satisfied Swede. Liam thinks he would be able to tell just from hearing her voice, without having to lose his dignity and actually ask her.

'Sure,' she says wearily.

Liam's fury is mounting, but he tries to calm himself. It may not be what he thinks. He has been wrong before. Plus he is hungover, so his mental faculties aren't in peak condition. At least the thought of Alicia in bed with Patrick enables him to get out of bed without embar-rassment.

Alicia gasps, surprised by his naked body, but now Liam doesn't care. He's her husband after all! And he's perfectly flaccid, and it's not as if she's never seen him naked before. Although it's several years since they shared a bedroom. Even last year when they slept in the attic room in Hilda's house, he remembers how they both undressed in the bathroom.

· · ·

What is he playing at, Alicia wonders. She gets that he didn't want to arouse Hilda's suspicions by asking to stay in the main house, although that's what she had hoped for, but his nakedness speaks another truth.

Alicia remembers when their sex life was still normal, one of the ways they would indicate that they wanted to make love was to go to bed naked. If she did this and Liam was working late, which he often was, he would wake her up, if she'd fallen asleep, by kissing her neck. Liam would do the same, if on a rare occasion a news story took Alicia out in the evening and he was in bed before her.

While she's watching Liam pull his boxer shorts and jeans on, she realizes that when she was swamped by work, he wanted to make love to her all the time. Her independence and passion for journalism turned him on. But she wasn't happiest then. Yes, she liked working for a large busy newspaper, but she also found it immensely stressful. She hated being away from Stefan and not being there when he came home from school. Motherhood to her was the best job in the world. It wasn't what the modern woman was supposed to want, but it was what she adored.

Liam turns around. He's found an old T-shirt to wear, and his hands are on his hips. His expression is fierce, something Alicia hasn't seen before.

'Did you sleep with him last night?'

Liam's question feels like a slap across her face.

'That's none of your business,' she says.

Liam is staring at her. He's still standing across the room from her, framed by the dimmed window behind him. His eyes are black, like the sky outside. Suddenly Alicia feels an anger emanating from him that makes her want to flee the cottage.

'In other words, you did. How could you? When I'm actually here!' Liam has raised his voice. He takes a step toward Alicia, who wraps her arms around her body. The gesture makes Liam stop and he sits down in the chair where moments ago his clothes were in a messy heap. He puts his head in his hands.

Alicia doesn't know what to do. She turns back to the log burner. The fire is steady, so she closes the doors and briefly warms her hands against the stove. The coffee percolator makes its final gurgling sounds and stops. With shaking hands, Alicia takes two mugs from the hooks

Uffe has fixed onto the wall above the little sink and pours coffee for both of them.

She goes over to where Liam is sitting and places the cups on a table between the two comfy chairs and then lowers herself into one of them. The armrests are worn. All the furniture in the cottage is from the seventies. The chairs are angular and the table has legs that inconveniently jut out beyond the wooden top. It's a style that is coming back into fashion, but Alicia has always loved it. It reminds her of her childhood. The cottage has been the same ever since she can remember and she wouldn't change it for anything. It's a wonder Hilda has let it be, Alicia thinks, and a smile forms on her lips.

'Funny, is it?' Liam says.

He picks up his mug of coffee and takes a swig. Almost immediately he splutters, 'Shit!'

'It's hot,' Alicia says.

Liam gives her a murderous look.

'For your information I was thinking how this cottage hasn't changed in forty years, and how strange that is, given my mother's love of renewing and remodeling everything.'

Now Liam is staring at her.

'You're unbelievable.'

'Sorry, I'm really tired. And so much has happened I can't quite keep my head straight.'

'You think?' Liam says in his most sarcastic tone.

Alicia sighs again and gets up, holding onto her coffee.

'If you are interested in what is happening in my life, rather than just worried about your male pride, we can have a conversation. You and I haven't been married–in its true sense–for years now, have we?'

Liam is looking down at the floor, but then lifts his head. 'OK. I agree, but I love you, Alicia. Isn't that clear? I'm here, aren't I?'

Alicia walks back to the chair and sits down. It's true, Liam is here, he is making an effort. But what for? To get her back to London at all costs?

She places a hand over Liam's. His long fingers with the neat, manicured fingernails and the dark hairs growing between the knuckles are so familiar, yet touching him now seems weird, different somehow. She looks at his face, the contours of which she knows intimately. Perhaps there are a few more wrinkles around his eyes and mouth, but his face and dark eyes with the long lashes are so familiar that she wonders how it can be that she finds him so distant now.

'Yes, you are here now. But you are not taking into consideration what I want. Just what *you* want from me,' Alicia says softly.

She's keeping her eyes on Liam's eyes and continues, 'If you are willing to listen, I can tell you what that is.'

FORTY-THREE

Brit is frustrated. All the previous evening, Alicia talked about her life, which Brit has to agree, is more than complicated at the moment, but her preoccupation meant that she didn't have a chance to tell her much about Jukka. And this morning, her friend dashed off before waking her, only leaving a note to say she needed to get back to Sjoland. Brit wanted so desperately to tell someone how incredibly, deliriously happy Jukka is making her.

Brit is now enjoying a leisurely breakfast, while wondering what Jukka is doing. Buying last-minute Christmas presents, no doubt. Brit is all ready, she just needs to do a bit of wrapping, take a cab into town to collect her car, and drive to Föglö to fetch her father. They are due at the Ulssons' house at 5pm, so she has plenty of time.

During a brief moment when she and Alicia were not discussing Alicia's life last night, Brit said that she feared Jukka was going to be alone for the holidays. Alicia had immediately said he was welcome at Hilda and Uffe's.

'It's a bit early for spending Christmas together,' Brit had replied, but now she thinks it might be a brilliant idea. She knows Jukka is on call with Marie Line, but he can always drive to Sjoland and then take a cab home if need be.

Although their relationship is very new, she already knows how she feels about him. She's more serious about him than she expected. Even when he was driving her to his home yesterday—and she knew what was to happen when they arrived in Solbacken—she'd considered it to be casual. But, unlike the other brief affairs she's had, the love-making with Jukka had been real somehow, better. Their bodies were in perfect sync, and the way he acted afterward, all gentle and considerate, cooking her a meal and making sure she was safe in the cab afterward, spoke to her more than words. He's also smitten with her, she's fairly sure of it.

Brit lifts her arms above her head and stretches.

How wonderful it is to be in love again.

Brit's happy thoughts are interrupted by a buzzing sound. Her telephone next to the coffee cup lights up with an incoming call. The display shows, 'Unknown number,' but Brit picks up anyway. It may be Jukka's home phone. Perhaps they are so in tune already, she muses, that when she thinks about him, he also has her in his mind.

'Hi Brit, this is Kerstin Eklund,' the voice at the other end says.

For a moment Brit has to think who on earth it is, but then she realizes.

'Hi, what can I do for you?' Brit asks, trying to sound professional and not showing her annoyance. Doesn't the woman know it's not the done thing to telephone a member of the crew when they are not on duty? On Christmas Eve? Brit isn't even on call like Jukka.

There is a brief silence at the other end and Brit thinks they've lost the connection.

'Hello?' she says and hears the woman clear her throat.

'You need to know something.'

Brit listens for more, but when the woman is quiet, she replies, 'Yes,' again, trying not to show her irritation.

'Our Captain Jukka Markusson has a murky past. Before you two get all loved up, I think it's only fair someone should warn you.'

Brit has stopped breathing. What is this woman talking about?

'Hello, are you there?' she hears Kerstin say.

'Yes,' Brit manages to reply.

'Look him up on the internet. Especially stories from two years back.'

The line goes dead.

. . .

Brit paces up and down her apartment. She knows Kerstin doesn't like Jukka, or her for that matter. It was perfectly clear from day one when she stepped onboard the ship and was shown around by the older woman. But surely she can't be jealous? Kerstin is nearly at retirement age, past sixty, some twenty years older than Jukka. No, the animosity must stem from something else. Perhaps she's just one of those bitter women who blame what they lack in life on others? But if there is nothing to worry about, Brit will find nothing bad about Jukka on the web, surely?

She opens her laptop and puts Jukka's name in the search box. Why she hasn't done this before, is beyond her. Surely she should have searched the web well before now. Her heart is pounding when she sees the first page on the listing, which is the Marie Line's official website. An image of him wearing freshly pressed uniform and cap fills the screen when she taps on the link. There is nothing there, just an article from a five-year-old annual statement regarding career progression.

Brit goes back to the page listing all the sites containing Jukka's name and finds an article from two years ago that has the caption, 'Captain investigated for sexual harassment onboard a Marie Line ferry.'

Brit scans the article from *Ålandsbladet* quickly.

There is an internal investigation taking place inside one of the island's premier ferry operators, Marie Line, against Captain Jukka Markusson, who has been accused of sexual harassment by an employee, Ms Sia Eklund. Ms Eklund claims that Captain Markusson touched her inappropriately on several occasions and made sexual advances while she worked as a cabin attendant onboard MS Viking. No criminal charges have been brought against Markusson, but Ms Eklund tells Ålandsbladet, 'If nothing comes out of this investigation, I will take the matter up with the police.'

. . .

Brit starts to look frantically for any further reports, but finds only one small item, in the same paper:

The Marie Line investigation on sexual harassment charges brought by Ms Eklund have been completed.

There is no mention of Jukka, nor what the outcome was. Then it hits her. Ms Eklund. Is that Kerstin's daughter? Brit tries to wrack her brain. Did the older woman mention having a daughter?

Brit finds herself shaking.

FORTY-FOUR

Patrick is restless. He's sent two messages to Alicia but she hasn't replied to either of them. She fled in such a hurry last night that Patrick doesn't know what she is thinking. And he knows that her husband is in Sjoland, waiting to pounce on her with his news about Frida's baby and his conviction that she should go back to London with him. He cannot let that happen. He's already been in limbo with Alicia for six months now and he cannot take anymore.

At first, he thought he could manage to be just friends with her; he could wait. But over the months, weeks and days they shared the same office, her close presence became more and more torturous to him. He kept dreaming about having her in his arms, about their lovemaking, which was always so thrilling, so all-consuming. When she asked him to go and clear the snow from Hilda and Uffe's house, he thought that was some kind of change in their relationship. That she wanted to see him out of the office, as much as he longed to be with her.

And then last night–surely what happened changes everything?

With Mia and the girls away for Christmas, Patrick was planning to spend the holidays in front of the telly, eating the lobster he'd bought at the fish market yesterday morning. He has a magnum bottle of vintage champagne, and planned to get himself anesthetized until the festivities were over.

But now, he can't bring himself to even open the bottle, nor can he concentrate on anything, not even the new PlayStation games he got for the two days he would be spending on his own. (He had used the excuse that the girls would love to play with him on their return from their skiing holiday to Sweden.)

Patrick makes a decision. He glances at his watch. He has a couple of hours before the shops close. He puts on his jacket and rushes out of the door.

FORTY-FIVE

'So what is it you want?' Liam says and runs his palm across his face. His eyes are full of sleep and Alicia thinks he looks at least as weary as she feels, if not more.

'First, can I tell you what's been going on?'

Liam nods and Alicia tells him about Dudnikov, how he's been terrorizing Hilda, and how he nearly ran her parents and her off the road.

Liam leans over the small table. He puts a hand on Alicia's thigh.

'Why didn't you tell me any of this? You must have been frightened.'

Suddenly Alicia feels tearful. How easy it would be to let Liam comfort her. Let him take charge of everything again just as he did after they lost Stefan, and almost from the start, when they met in Uppsala all those years ago.

But then she remembers how he, stubbornly, has been driving his own agenda. How he betrayed her for months with that nurse, leaving her alone in their bed at night while he slept in the spare bedroom. She knows she was to blame too, a little at least. She's surprised to find that she no longer feels anger toward Liam. Just sadness that it's now all over.

'It's OK,' she says. And looking at Liam's concerned face. 'The complication in all this is that I also found out yesterday that Dudnikov is Frida's father.'

Liam leans back in his chair, removing his hand and blowing air out of his mouth.

There's an emptiness where his touch was, but the sensation comes almost as a relief to Alicia.

'Right,' Liam says and glances at her.

She knows exactly what he's thinking.

'He's also been supporting Frida's mother, Sirpa, all these years and there's a bit of a nest egg left over for Frida and Anne Sofie.'

Liam nods, still keeping his eyes on Alicia. She remembers that Patrick told her Liam knew Frida's mother was wealthy.

'But then you knew that, didn't you?'

Liam's eyes widen.

'All I knew was that Frida wasn't poor, your know-it-all Swedish boyfriend told me that,' he says.

Alicia ignores Liam's jibe. Instead, she explains how she felt she needed to tell the police chief about Dudnikov, to protect Hilda and Uffe, but that she doesn't want Frida to know.

'Or anyone else, for that matter.'

'Sure, I can see that,' Liam says.

They agree that they will not mention any of this over Christmas.

'How does Patrick fit into all of this?' Liam spits out his name although he speaks quietly, calm now.

'He doesn't,' Alicia says. 'And I don't know what to think about him—or me,' she adds, looking down at her hands.

While they have been sitting in the sauna cottage talking, the light has changed in the room. Suddenly a ray of sunshine penetrates through the small panes of glass, and Alicia peers out, almost blinded by the sight.

'Look at that!'

Liam turns his head toward the window behind him.

'What about Anne Sofie?' he asks softly, not looking at Alicia.

'I haven't told Frida about your little test, if that's what you mean,' Alicia says, trying to keep her anger at bay. She still cannot understand how Liam thought it would help her to know that the baby isn't Stefan's. But it doesn't matter now.

'But both Frida and the baby are OK? Financially speaking, I mean?' Liam asks.

'It's not all about money,' Alicia says drily.

'Of course not, but having it helps,' Liam replies quickly.

Alicia nods. She gets up and, looking toward the bed, says, 'Perhaps it would be better if you sleep in the main house tonight.'

Liam widens his eyes, 'Alone, you mean?'

Alicia sits down on top of the rumbled bedsheets. 'Liam, I'm sorry, but I think we've come to the end of the road. Don't you?'

'Is this because of the DNA test?' Liam asks. He's trying to keep himself calm, even though he can feel his pulse is sky high. Just as well he has low cholesterol levels and a good, strong heart.

Clinically speaking, that is.

He's still wearing yesterday's underwear, jeans, and the old T-shirt he usually sleeps in. He longs for a shower, a good breakfast (what he would give for a full English, bacon and eggs and all the works, at this moment). But more than that, what he really wants to do is take Alicia into his arms and make love to her. Unwittingly, he glances at the bed, unmade and messy, in front of him. He sees from the corner of his eye that Alicia has seen where his gaze has landed.

She sighs and says, in that new, cold voice that he has come to know well over the past six months, 'Liam, you know we haven't been a proper couple for years.'

And there it is.

His own mistake is what has got him here.

'You know I've forgiven you for what happened last summer.' Liam stops when he hears the pathetic pleading in his voice. He feels like a dying man who's trying to get a last-minute reprieve. But before Alicia has time to interrupt, he carries on, trying to make his voice sound stronger and more confident. 'I know I am the one who made the biggest mistake. And I am truly sorry. I don't know why I did it. It was stupid and unforgivable. But to throw away eighteen years of marriage, isn't there something out of those wonderful times together that we can salvage?'

Alicia is gazing at him and he can see that she has tears in her eyes.

Liam stands and goes to kneel before her. Taking her hands into his, he says, 'Please, Alicia, don't give up on us yet.'

'I want a divorce.'

Liam is staring at Alicia, but his face looks resigned.

'I see,' he says quietly and looks away from Alicia. He fidgets with his empty coffee mug, but says nothing more.

There is a long silence, which Alicia is tempted to break on several occasions. She looks at his familiar shape, his chin where a stubble is growing. His long, bare feet and his strong arms and legs.

On one level she still loves Liam more than she can let him know now, but the love is more like that for a brother, perhaps. Having never had siblings, she doesn't know how that feels but she imagines this is what it's like. He can be infuriating, and she is still angry with him over the baby's DNA test, but she finds now that she has forgiven him.

Seeing his empty coffee cup, she wants to ask him if he'd like more, but she stays quiet. She knows she has to let Liam take in her statement in his own time and on his own terms.

Finally, Liam lifts his face up and asks, 'Do you want me to leave today?'

'No, goodness, no!' Alicia says, almost too emphatically. 'Besides, there are no flights or ferries to the mainland today, I'm fairly sure of it.'

'OK,' Liam says simply.

Relieved that he's taken the news so calmly, Alicia adds, 'Do you want some more coffee?'

Alicia picks up some clothes from a rail she's put up in one corner of the cottage and gets changed in the shower room. She can hear Liam taking up the sofa-bed and moving furniture. She wants to go and hug him, but she doesn't want to send the wrong signals. She's surprised how calm Liam was when she told him she didn't want to be married to him anymore. There was none of the drama from last year, when he'd turned up unannounced and caught Patrick and Alicia in bed in this very same cottage—one of the reasons she'd been so surprised to find him sleeping there naked this morning.

He must have been quite drunk.

But that's all over now. She has finally made the decision that she should have made months ago, perhaps even years ago. The relief she feels is such that she actually finds herself smiling. She pulls out her phone and sees Patrick's messages. She types a reply, and begins to think about Christmas dinner. Hilda must be going frantic with all the last-minute preparations without her. Alicia rushes out of the bathroom, but finds the sauna cottage empty. From a small side window, she sees her soon to be ex-husband walking toward the main house, taking long strides across the snow.

FORTY-SIX

When she walks up to the main house, the view could be from a Hans Andersen fairy tale. The sun is low on the horizon, behind a layer of clouds, giving the landscape a yellow hue. The strange light makes Hilda's minimal decorations of the house, with the star lanterns in the windows and the pine tree strung with fairy lights in the yard, look wonderful. Alicia begins to get the Christmas feeling she thought she would never again experience after Stefan. How he would have loved this family celebration!

As soon as Alicia steps into the main house, she hugs her mother and wishes her *God Jul*.

'Happy Christmas to you too!' Hilda is smiling but Alicia can hear that that her voice is strained. She's stressed over the day.

'What can I do?' Alicia says and the two women begin to go over Hilda's lists, with the day's meals and activities, including when to light the real candles on the indoor tree. Alicia looks over to the lounge, where an enormous spruce is standing, its tip almost touching the ceiling.

'Will you decorate it later?' Hilda asks before they begin going through Hilda's Christmas agenda.

'Of course. It's all going to be wonderful,' Alicia says and she squeezes her mother's hand. 'You've done so much already!'

Hilda beams. After the two women have decided what still needs to be done and by whom, Alicia's mother glances over at Liam, who's sitting in the lounge, his eyes fixed on the screen of his reading device.

'Everything OK?' she asks Alicia in a low voice. Her eyes are full of concern and Alicia wonders how much she knows, or has guessed, about her and Liam's relationship.

'Don't worry, all is well,' Alicia says.

'In that case, I think it's time for a drink!'

Sitting around the kitchen table, beautifully dressed with a red linen cloth and four Advent candles in a holder decorated with reindeer moss and red berries, Hilda, Uffe, Liam and Alicia eat rice pudding, the traditional Christmas Eve lunch. Hilda cuts up some ham and they discuss whether it's too salty, or perhaps not salty enough? It's what happens every year. Uffe offers Liam a beer, but he refuses.

Alicia smiles at him and says, 'Peaked a bit too early, did you?'

Liam gives a short laugh, and nods to Uffe. 'I think I will have one after all.'

Uffe gets his meaning without Alicia having to translate the English, and opens a bottle for him.

In the middle of the meal, Alicia gets a call from Brit.

'Can I pop over on my way to get my dad from Föglö? I need to talk to you about something urgently.'

'Come to the sauna cottage, we can talk better there,' Alicia says.

Hilda gives Alicia a look, and Alicia mouths, 'Brit,' to her.

Half an hour later Brit gets out of her car and waves to Alicia, who opens the door. She's in her padded coat and snow boots, but she still manages to look glamorous. How does she do it, Alicia wonders. Brit has bright red lipstick, which matches the bobble on her woolly hat, as well as her nails. Her face is made up, although in an understated way, apart from her lips.

'You look nice,' Alicia says and hugs her friend. 'And thank you for last night, I don't know what I would have done without you!'

Brit extracts herself from Alicia's arms and waves her manicured hand, 'My pleasure. It's so nice to have you living so close. Now we can have these girly nights in!'

Alicia smiles and asks, 'Coffee?'

'Please! It's started snowing again. When will it ever stop?'

'Don't knock it, it's wonderful to have a white Christmas.'

Brit nods and sits down on the sofa.

'Listen, I've seen something awful about Jukka online.'

Alicia examines the articles Brit shows her on her mobile phone. 'That's what, two years ago?'

'Yes, but look what he's been accused of? And then there's nothing to say what happened. Did he do it, or what? I don't know what to think. I've been going crazy at home. At first I thought I'd phone him, but then I didn't know what to say. How am I going to tell him that the woman, Kerstin, shopped him to me? How would I know about it otherwise? And they work together. I don't want him to think that I've been stalking him online! But I think the woman who was accusing him may have been her daughter.' Brit's eyes are wide and she is speaking so quickly that Alicia has to concentrate hard to understand her.

'Slow down, who told you about this?'

Finally, Alicia gets all the facts straight. She fetches her laptop and checks *Ålandsbladet's* archives, but finds nothing more than what Brit already saw online.

'I think you need to talk to him,' Alicia says.

'That's what I think too, but I don't want to do it over the phone. And now it's Christmas Eve and I'm late picking Dad up already.' Brit glances at Alicia and adds, 'Plus I don't trust myself with men anymore. What if he swears there was nothing to it, and I believe him. And then the next thing that happens is that he turns into–or turns out to be–a total rat?'

Alicia doesn't know what to say. She wants to tell Brit that, with only two serious relationships in her life, she's hardly one to give advice on how to tell if a lover is truthful or not.

But Brit doesn't seem to want her to respond. Instead she says, 'I wondered,' here she hesitates for a moment, bites her lower lip, and then continues, 'Jukka is on call this Christmas, but because none of the ferries start operating until the 26th, he's basically off for the whole holiday. He's on his own in Solbacken, so I wondered if your mother and Uffe might be able to invite him over tonight after all?'

Alicia is again speechless. She knows her mother would certainly not mind having another guest. Her motto for any celebration is, 'The more the merrier.' And there's so much food, they could feed the five thousand. Adding a sea captain to the guest lists would certainly please Hilda.

When she doesn't reply, Brit goes on, 'The thing is, you and your mother, who I know is an excellent judge of character, could check him out and tell me what you think!' Brit is smiling now, 'Please, will you have him?'

Alicia returns her friend's smile. 'I'm sure it'll be fine. He might have to get a cab home, though. We're running out of rooms!'

Brit flings her arms around Alicia and thanks her so many times that Alicia has to tell her to stop. She waves Brit goodbye from the side window, and shaking her head, checks on the fire in the cottage, and follows her out, shutting the door behind her. She can't wait to tell Hilda the good news.

FORTY-SEVEN

'Markusson,' Uffe says rubbing his chin. 'That name rings a bell.'

Hilda and Alicia are standing in the kitchen, waiting. Uffe knows everybody on the islands, something her mother and Alicia often laugh about. When he doesn't say anything else, and picks up a paper, Alicia assumes Jukka's family isn't known to him after all.

'Anyway, he's welcome! The more the merrier and he can talk to Liam in English and keep him company.'

Hearing his name being mentioned, Liam looks up from his iPad.

He's got no problems getting on the internet today.

'We've got yet another guest for supper tonight, and Hilda thinks he'll be good company for you,' Alicia translates for Liam.

He nods and goes back to his iPad.

Alicia smiles at her mother, who is always worrying about Liam. She puts her arm around Hilda and says, 'That's true, but you mustn't worry about him. He'll be fine.'

Hilda's eyes meet hers, 'Well, he's still a guest in this house.'

Alicia checks if Liam has heard her, or understood the Swedish, which she knows he hasn't. Sometimes, however, he has a sixth sense about what's being said. But Liam has his head bent over the device. Suddenly, Uffe's voice booms over the house.

'I've got it!' her stepfather says, putting one finger up in the air. 'Ville Markusson was a nasty piece of work. A sailor and a drunk. He was never at home, but when he deigned to see his family, he knocked his wife about something awful. She was a Finn. Pirkko, I think she was called. Everybody, including old Pirkko, were pretty relieved when he kicked the bucket somewhere abroad. But the old girl died soon after, probably tired of life, leaving young Jukka alone. I think he's a sea captain now?'

'That's a terrible story,' Hilda exclaims. 'Not something we want to talk about on Christmas Eve!'

Now Liam is looking at the three of them. He's worked out that they're talking about something serious. Alicia puts her hand up to Liam and moves closer to Uffe, who's sitting at the opposite end of the room from Liam, in one of the many armchairs in the large lounge.

'Are you sure it's the same family?' she asks Uffe, who's gone back to his paper.

He lowers his reading glasses and looks over them. 'Yes, I'm fairly sure. If the boy is a sea captain?'

'He is. On Marie Line.'

'That's the right family then.'

'How do you know them?' Alicia asks.

Uffe folds his paper and balances it on one of his knees. He takes off his glasses and regards Alicia, as if to consider whether he should tell her the story. Alicia waits.

Uffe sighs.

'Well, I knew Ville at school. He was a little bully then. A year or two younger than me, but still, he tried to land one on me. I gave him what for and he didn't bother me after that. But I believe he beat up the pupils in the classes below him. Often in trouble with the teachers. A naughty boy who grew into a nasty man.'

'Stop talking about such unpleasant matters.' Hilda comes over to where Alicia is standing. She's wearing her red and white Christmas apron with rows of snowflakes and reindeer interspersed with hearts. Brandishing a wooden mixing spoon, she adds, 'He's welcome here to celebrate with us. I've got plenty of food. But mind, don't be talking about his family when he's here. We don't want to embarrass the poor boy.' Hilda points the spoon at Uffe, who harrumphs, opens the paper, and pulls it up to cover his face.

Alicia wonders how domestic violence can be more 'embarrassing' than tragic.

'Surely you mean, you don't want to upset him?' she cannot help commenting on her mother's words.

'Yes, yes, whatever.' Hilda waves her hand at Alicia.

'Now, we'd better get on if we are to have anything ready by 5pm for all this crowd to eat!'

'Wait,' Alicia says. She follows Hilda into the kitchen, and in a low voice says, 'I wanted to tell you that Dudnikov won't be bothering you two anymore.'

'What do you mean?' Hilda says, so loudly that Alicia is afraid Uffe will hear. She hasn't spoken directly with Uffe about the Russians and she doesn't want to start now. The less she knows about what has been going on between her stepfather and Dudnikov, the better. She doesn't want to have to lie to Ebba, who might wish to investigate the Russian's activities on the islands further. She hopes that the police chief doesn't know that her parents, or at least her mother, was a victim of that man. It would just complicate everything.

'Shh,' Alicia says, putting her finger to her lips. She points with the head to the lounge, where the two men are reading.

'Aah,' Hilda says and leans toward Alicia.

'He fled the islands in a private plane to St Petersburg yesterday. That was one of the reasons why I was so busy.'

Hilda's eyes widen, 'Good riddance!' she says, again raising her voice. 'You're not writing about him, are you,' Hilda says more quietly now.

Alicia shakes her head. She looks into the lounge through the little serving hatch Hilda installed when she remodeled the house, but both men remain engrossed in their reading, so she continues, 'No, of course not. I don't want anything more to do with him.'

Hilda has tears in her eyes and puts her arms around Alicia.

'You're a good girl,' she says.

FORTY-EIGHT

Jukka arrives carrying a massive bouquet of flowers. They are bright red roses.

'Where did you get all of these?' Hilda exclaims, clearly delighted with the gift.

Jukka gives a short laugh. He glances at Brit, who is standing in the hall behind Hilda. Brit has left her father with Uffe. The two know each other from years back, but don't move in the same circles anymore. They have a lot to catch up on.

'I think I emptied out the City Blommor on Torggatan.'

'I should think so,' Hilda says, her head half-buried behind the greenery. 'Lilly would have made sure she didn't have any stock remaining over the two-day holiday, so you were lucky.'

'Hello,' Jukka says and moves closer to Brit for an embrace. But before his mouth touches Brit's lips, she shifts her head sideways, so that his kiss lands on her cheek. She didn't plan to do it, but suddenly, she couldn't face such intimacy with him.

Before she'd left Alicia in Sjoland to make her way to the Föglö ferry, she messaged Jukka to ask if he'd like to join the Ulsson family for Christmas Eve. He took a long time to reply, but when she was disembarking in Föglö, her phone showed an incoming call from him.

Brit did feel bad about lying to him, pretending that her only motive was that she didn't want him to be alone in his apartment, however wonderful the view was. The result justifies the means, she thought. And then, to her huge surprise, he agreed.

Now she feels like she's hatched some kind of trap for him. When the three women saw his car pull up the drive, Hilda said, conspiratorially, 'Alicia, you stay here, and Brit and I will go and meet him in the hall.' She undid her red apron and fluffed up her hair. 'I'll just nip into the bathroom to check my makeup.'

'Your mother's not going to overdo it, is she?' Brit whispered to Alicia when Hilda was out of earshot.

'I'm sure she'll be cool,' Alicia said, though she didn't look at all certain.

'Come and meet the others,' Brit now says and takes Jukka's hand. She's jumpy, but he presumes she's nervous about introducing him to her friends and father. Truthfully, on the drive toward Sjoland, Jukka, too, wondered if he made the right decision–a rash one at that–to celebrate Christmas with virtual strangers. Not that he doesn't know, or at least know of, most people on the islands, especially such an old family as the Ulsson's. He's aware that Uffe and his father and grandfather before him have farmed this area of Sjoland for decades, if not centuries. He also knows Hilda by sight, and knows she used to own a women's clothes shop in the center of Mariehamn. But he has never been inside the house. He's only seen it from the road, standing on a hill above the neatly laid out fields.

Inside, the smell of *glögg* and Christmas food is irresistible, as is the sight of Brit in her slinky outfit. Hilda, too, seems pleased with his presence and very welcoming. Thank goodness he had the foresight to get the flowers.

But then there's Brit's father. Jukka is no longer a teenager meeting the girlfriend's parents, but it feels strange to have such an encounter on Christmas Eve of all days. He straightens his back as Brit leads him by the hand into the living room.

Four men, all holding a small glass of mulled wine, stand in front of a huge Christmas tree. The tree is decorated simply with silver baubles and old-fashioned narrow tinsel, which looks like it's lost some of its silvery shine. But the most striking feature is the live candles, flickering against the darkened windows. The lights are low in the room, making the space look very festive.

Jukka watches Brit go over to the shortest man in the room. 'Dad, let me introduce you to Jukka. He is,' here Brit glances at Jukka and bites her lower lip, 'my friend from the ship.'

Rolf Svensson isn't as short as Jukka first thought, but he has a considerable stoop. His handshake is firm, however, even if his eyes are gray and his frame slight.

'I knew your father,' Rolf says. The words of greeting Jukka was about to utter get caught in his throat. When he doesn't say anything, Brit's father turns toward Mr Ulsson, who is also standing in the small circle. 'You remember him, Uffe, don't you? A real tough guy.'

Jukka can see Brit's face is crumbling, but the situation is saved by Hilda who sweeps into the room with a flourish. 'This is my husband, Uffe.'

The man with gray hair and beard, with a rounded farmer's physique, takes Jukka's hand and pumps it for a long time. His hands are calloused, but his face is warm and friendly.

'Welcome, welcome! And Happy Christmas!'

Before he has time to return the season's good wishes, Hilda touches his arm.

'Why don't you come into the kitchen and meet my daughter, Alicia. She's Brit's best friend from school, did you know that?'

Jukka glances behind him at Brit, who sees his look and decides to follow him.

'Now you do eat everything, don't you? Alicia, would you be an angel and get Jukka a drink?' Hilda is talking non-stop.

Jukka takes a glass of beer, grateful to have escaped the talk about his father.

'Nice to meet you,' Alicia says, looking at Brit. 'I've heard so much about you.'

'As have I!' Hilda says. 'You are a sea captain?' she adds, 'I want you to tell me all about the ships. I use them so often but I have never met one of the captains.'

The older woman leads Jukka back into the living room, where she dominates the discussions, not letting Brit's father or Uffe Ulsson get a word in. Jukka is grateful and he begins to tell Hilda all about how he took the entrance exams to the Swedish University in Malmö, and how he ended up working on Marie Line.

'Best job I've ever had,' he says.

While is talking, Brit walks back in and stands next to him. He takes in her scent and is momentarily stunned into silence by her intoxicating presence.

Gazing from Brit to Jukka, Hilda squeezes Jukka's arm. 'Please excuse me, I'd better see to the supper.'

Jukka is so grateful to Hilda for rescuing him from talk of his father that he takes her hand and kisses the back of it in the old-fashioned way.

'I can't wait to eat the food you have cooked. It smells delicious.'

Hilda beams at him and leaves them standing in the back of the large lounge.

'What a charmer,' Brit says. Her voice has an edge to it, which Jukka doesn't understand. He puts an arm around her waist and leans close to her. 'I've missed you,' he whispers in her ear.

'Where is that girl?' Hilda says later, while she's checking all the items on the smorgasbord that has been assembled on the kitchen table. She and Alicia decided that it was best to set the cold fish course here, and then serve the hot main course, and the pudding, directly in the dining room. Silently, she's ticking everything off a list in her hand.

Herring in mustard, tick. Herring in curry sauce, tick. Herring with onion and dill, tick. Cold smoked salmon, tick. Gravlax, tick. New potatoes, home cured gherkins, beetroot Rosolli salad, dill sauce, soured cream sauce, two types of rye bread, rye crackers, homemade butter.

'Oh,' Alicia says, looking down at her phone.

'What is it?'

'She's not coming,' Alicia says silently. She's still staring at the screen and Hilda can see tears forming in her eyes.

Hilda folds her list into the pocket of her apron and puts her arm around Alicia's shoulders.

'What does she say?'

But Alicia is already moving away from her, the phone pressed against her ear.

Hilda's just thinking that she needs to remove a place from the table, and wonders how it will all work without Frida there. She was warned by Alicia that the baby may disturb dinner (as if she didn't know that already!), still with eight diners, it would have been perfect with Uffe and Hilda at the ends of the table and three guests either side. Now it's going to be all lopsided. Naturally, Hilda is sorry not to spend Christmas with Frida and her new great-grandchild, but the baby will be too young to appreciate the gifts or the general seasonal merriment, so it's not really that much of a big deal that she isn't coming. Hilda can see Alicia talking in a low tone on the phone. She's holding the handset tightly against her ear, while gesticulating with her other hand.

She's trying to convince Frida to come.

Hilda sighs. She can hear laughter from the lounge. She picks up her glass and tops it up with white wine. She has a spot by the serving hatch between the kitchen and the lounge where she leaves her glass, so that she can always locate and retrieve it.

She peers out of the opening and sees Jukka telling a story, which is amusing everyone. She's glad to see Rolf and Uffe have stopped talking about the poor boy's parents. She just about rescued the situation. Her impression of Jukka is favorable. She smiles to herself when she thinks how the girls came to her for advice on Brit's new man. She knows she's good at spotting unsuitable boyfriends, not that she ever had much chance to use her skills with her own daughter. She was never allowed to say anything to *her*. When she brought Liam home for the first time, there was no discussion about the relationship not going forward. Alicia was already pregnant by then, so even if she'd had doubts about Liam, there would have been no point in voicing them.

As if he knew she was thinking about him, Liam turns his head toward Hilda and she smiles and raises her glass. Liam has been very subdued all day, and Hilda suspects something has happened between husband and wife. But Alicia, as usual, will tell Hilda what's going on when she's ready, and there is no point in trying to dig it out of her. She just hopes her daughter will see what a good man Liam is and let him look after her. What woman wouldn't be pleased to be married to a surgeon? And to live in London without a care in the world. If she chooses, she doesn't even have to work!

Hilda knows how terrible losing Stefan was and how it knocked them both sideways. As it did Uffe and Hilda, too. Those wounds will never heal, but at the same time they are so young! Hilda wants to tell Liam and Alicia that there is no point in dwelling on what you have lost; you had to look to the future and see what you have.

Just then, a set of headlights appear in the driveway and Hilda shouts to Alicia, 'She's here after all!'

FORTY-NINE

Patrick turns into the Ulsson's drive and parks the car next to a VW Golf. He turns off his lights and stays in the car for a moment. On the passenger seat is a paper bag filled with Christmas presents wrapped up expertly by one of the assistants at the fashionable interior design shop in town. They are beautifully understated, in white paper with wide red ribbons.

There's also the large box containing a magnum of vintage champagne resting on the floor of the car. He wonders if that is overkill. Should he perhaps leave the bottle behind and fetch it later, if he gets a good reception from Alicia?

He gazes up to the house, shining brightly in the dark afternoon light, the downstairs windows decorated with large star lanterns. The freshly fallen snow has formed a blanket over the sloping roof and the landscape. With the large pine draped with white lights, the whole scene looks serene and festive, like a TV advert.

Damn it, be brave.

Hilda will appreciate the champagne, he's sure, so he picks up the box, takes hold of the paper bag, slams the door of his car, and makes his way up to the house.

. . .

Alicia cannot believe her eyes. Responding to her mother's call, she moves into the kitchen and watches as Patrick gets out of the car, picking something up from the passenger seat. She has her phone against her ear, still talking to Frida. The baby is crying in the background.

'Can I ring you later?' Alicia says and ends the call.

'Is that who I think it is?' Hilda says, her mouth open, forming an 'o.'

'What the hell does he think he's doing?' Alicia says and hurries to the door.

But Patrick is quicker than she is, and by the time she opens the door, he is already standing there, a wide grin filling his face. He's carrying a bag full of presents and a large box.

'Surprise!' he says.

Alicia stands there, dumbfounded. She cannot speak.

'Can I come in?' Patrick asks. 'It's bloody cold out here.'

'Patrick, what a lovely surprise!' Hilda says. She's standing behind Alicia, who's unable to move or speak. At her mother's words, she turns to scowl at Hilda.

Hilda widens her eyes at her daughter. 'Come now, let the poor man in. He must be freezing.'

Patrick smiles at Hilda and steps past Alicia, who is still holding onto the door handle. Alicia gets a waft of his perfume and the smell of the crisp outside. She tries not to let his rousing presence affect her judgment.

What is he playing at? He must know Liam is here?

'Alicia, close that door before we all catch our death,' Hilda says.

'*God Jul*,' Patrick says and hugs Hilda. He hands her the box he's holding and, when she sees what it is, she exclaims, 'Oh, my goodness. Thank you and Merry Christmas to you too!'

'I'm sorry I've come unannounced, but I thought I'd drop my presents off. I didn't get a chance to do it before today, but I won't keep you.'

With that, he hands the large paper bag to Hilda and turns around.

'Happy Christmas, Alicia.' His voice is soft and he bends down to give her a kiss on the cheek while grabbing the door handle, ready to go back outside.

'Patrick, you can't leave without at least having a drink with us!' Hilda exclaims.

'I couldn't possibly, it's a family occasion,' Patrick says.

Alicia rolls her eyes at him, but he either doesn't see her or ignores her on purpose and, smiling at Hilda, continues, 'If you're sure?'

FIFTY

L iam has been trying to follow the conversation with the help of the newcomer, Jukka, who is translating bits of it for him. They're talking about Brexit, a subject that he wishes Uffe hadn't brought up. But the sea captain is quietly spoken and is constantly glancing toward Brit, who when she arrived, had introduced herself as Alicia's oldest friend.

'I remember you from the wedding,' Liam said, a comment that produced a trickle of laughter from the woman. She was dressed in a red jumpsuit and open-toed shoes with matching red toes peeping out from the flared hems, and was perfectly made up with a deep tan and unnaturally white teeth.

Now, standing on the other side of the room, next to her elderly father, she looks jittery, somehow. Liam thinks it's to do with Jukka, who's standing next to her. They keep exchanging what they think are covert glances, but Liam finds them revealing. He can't quite understand why they don't just stand next to each other, rather than play this cat and mouse game. Seeing the romance unfold in front of him, he feels old.

'They're asking how you feel about Europe,' Jukka says.

But before Liam can answer, they all hear a commotion in the hall.

The door from the lounge is open toward the front door, but no one can quite see what is going on.

'Excuse me,' says Uffe and he moves toward the hallway.

When Patrick enters the room, smiling broadly and closely followed by Uffe, Hilda, and Alicia, Liam nearly drops his glass of red wine.

'What would you like to drink? I have some mulled wine, a rather lovely Rioja, or a South African Sauvignon?' says Hilda, fussing over the newest guest.

Patrick chooses the red wine, and goes around the room to shake everyone's hand.

Brit giggles when she says hello to him. 'I've heard so much about you!'

Liam glances at Alicia, who is standing in the doorway to the lounge. She's motionless, as if she's been struck dumb. He moves quickly behind Patrick, nodding to him briefly, and goes over to Alicia. He puts his hand under her elbow.

'You OK?'

'What?' Alicia says, looking at him as if she's just remembered that he is here, in this room with all these people who don't belong here. It's as if all the waifs and strays from the islands have decided to crash Uffe and Hilda's Christmas.

'You're shaking,' he says looking into her face for any signs of a serious health problem.

But Alicia lifts her arm away and says irritably, 'I'm fine. I'm not one of your patients.'

Liam is taken aback by her sudden aggression. Didn't they agree not to spoil Christmas? He wants to say something to that effect, but Patrick is now standing in front of them, gazing at Alicia.

Reluctantly, it seems, Patrick takes his eyes off Alicia and looks in Liam's direction. 'When did you arrive?'

'Merry Christmas to you too,' Liam says and hears the sarcasm in his own voice. He immediately regrets it, and from the corner of his eye he can see Alicia staring at him. With an exasperated expression, no doubt. He doesn't need to turn toward her to know that.

Patrick gives a short, embarrassed laugh. Embarrassment, which is entirely his.

'I'm sorry if I'm spoiling your party. I'll just have this drink and then go.'

Hilda must have heard and understood Patrick's words because she pipes up, 'No, no, Patrick, you stay!'

Patrick gives Liam a wide smile and, switching to Swedish, begins a mock argument with Hilda.

'My mother is saying that we have a spare place because Frida and the baby aren't coming,' Alicia says to Liam.

'What brilliant luck for Patrick,' he replies.

Alicia turns toward him and says in a low voice so that the others can't hear, 'I didn't plan this. I had no idea.'

She moves to the kitchen and leaves Liam standing there, watching the spectacle of the Swede commanding the room. He's telling some story or other about his days as a reporter in Stockholm, in Swedish. Liam doesn't understand a word, something that the man is obviously enjoying immensely, judging by the occasional victorious glances he throws in Liam's direction. The room erupts in laughter as the story comes to an end.

Liam follows Alicia into the kitchen. He can't take any more of Patrick.

In the kitchen Alicia is speaking in low tones to her mother. They are both standing with their back to Liam, bent over the stove. When Hilda spots him, she says, 'Ah, Liam, would you like another drink?'

Alicia says something to her mother in Swedish, and then turns to Liam. 'Can I talk to you for a moment?'

Alicia leads him up the stairs to the attic room, which is pristine, the bed made up with white linen. Once she's closed the door Alicia turns to Liam.

'I'm so sorry,' she says, wringing her hands.

Liam gazes at his wife. He sees a woman he hasn't known in years. Her cheeks are burning, her eyes shining, and her lips are soft and red. She looks extremely attractive. Suddenly, he realizes all this change has happened since the Swede walked into the house.

'But you're glad he's here,' Liam says, sitting down on the bed.

. . .

Her heart is beating ten to a dozen. She needs to calm down but doesn't know how. Liam is sitting on the bed, while Alicia paces up and down the small attic room.

'No, I'm *not* glad here's here,' she almost shouts, but seeing Liam's expression, she stops.

'Sit down,' Liam says.

How he can be so calm, Alicia has no idea, but she joins Liam on the bed, a little distance away. Liam turns toward her and lifts her chin, bringing her face to eye level with him.

'Alicia, I know you very well. As much as I'd like to pretend otherwise, I can see how much he means to you. It's far from ideal to have him here for Christmas of all times, but if I can deal with it, so should you. Just make sure your mother sits me as far away from him as possible, eh?'

'Thank you,' Alicia says, now a lot calmer. She removes Liam's hand and squeezes it.

'You're a good man,' she says. She can feel tears well inside her eyelids, but she resists them and gets up instead.

'I'll go down and make sure the table arrangements are OK,' she says and forces a smile.

Liam doesn't say anything but nods to Alicia with a sad expression on his face.

FIFTY-ONE

'Alicia,' Patrick is standing on the second floor landing when, much later, she comes up the stairs. It's dark up there, outside Hilda and Uffe's bedroom, and Alicia doesn't spot him until he is standing in front of her. She's on her way to the loo, forced to come up to Hilda's en-suite bathroom because someone was already using the downstairs cloakroom.

'What are you doing here?'

Patrick doesn't answer her question but presses his lips on her mouth. For a moment she relaxes into his kiss. She's been wanting to be touched by him all evening, resisting the temptation to respond to the pressure of his thigh next to hers under the table. Once he even placed his hand on her arm, but when she looked across the table, she saw Liam's eyes burning into the two of them. Remembering how unfair all of this is on Liam, she now pushes herself away.

'Stop it!'

'Come on, I've missed you!'

'Since yesterday?'

'Yes,' Patrick says and grins. 'I'm in love with you.' He pulls her close to him again and kisses her neck.

Once again, with great effort, because her body just wants to be caressed by this man, Alicia removes herself from Patrick's embrace.

She cannot help but return his smile when she says, 'You are terrible. And drunk.'

'It's Christmas Eve!'

'Yes, it is and my husband is downstairs. This is not fair on him.'

Patrick looks down at his hands. 'I know.'

'You shouldn't have come.'

'Perhaps,' Patrick says. He takes Alicia's hands in his. 'I'll get a cab home as soon as Hilda serves coffee. But you have to promise to see me tomorrow.'

'Oh, Patrick, I can't tomorrow. Liam doesn't leave until Boxing Day.'

'I can wait if you'll stay the night this time? The girls aren't back until Sunday so we'll have two glorious days together.'

Alicia nods. She can't imagine spending 48 hours–guilt-free–with Patrick. The prospect just seems too good to be true. She smiles and nods at him.

Patrick gives her another hasty kiss, and before turning toward the staircase, he adds, 'I've saved your present for when we are together again, so don't let me down.'

FIFTY-TWO

There is an atmosphere around the table. Alicia's husband is not saying a word, while Alicia is talking too much. Sitting next to one another, Alicia and Patrick already look like a couple and Liam cannot take his eyes off them. Brit thinks there's going to be an almighty row any second, but then halfway through the main course, Patrick starts to talk about his daughters. He tells them how his eldest, Sara, had meningitis when she was just three years old. He's making a great effort to translate everything into English for Liam's benefit, which Alicia's ex seems to appreciate.

'We nearly lost her,' he says and looks over the table at Liam.

And just like that something passes between the men and Liam replies, 'I'm so sorry to hear that.'

'Don't be. She's fine now but I will never take either of my daughters for granted. Ever.'

'You must miss them, especially now at Christmas time,' Hilda says and she places a hand on Patrick's forearm resting on the table.

'I do,' but I see them every other weekend, and sometimes more often. 'I'm hoping that once I'm in Stockholm, they will want to stay with me for longer. They're nearly teenagers after all, so I think living in the city will appeal to them.'

Liam stares at Patrick and suddenly he smiles.

'You're leaving the islands?' he asks.

He doesn't notice that Alicia is looking down at her hands, biting her lower lip.

'Yes, I'm going back to the bright lights. To my old job at *Journalen*. I love it on the islands,' Patrick pauses for a moment and glances first at Alicia and then at Hilda, 'but I am a *Stockholmare* at heart.'

'Really, is that so?' Alicia says teasingly, but seems to check herself and quickly adds, 'When are you going?'

'As soon as possible. January 2nd is my first day back.'

A look passes between Patrick and Alicia, and suddenly Brit knows what's going on. He wants her to move to Stockholm with him!

Oh, no, just when we've become friends again!

But Liam doesn't seem to have seen or understood the glances between Alicia and Patrick and he lifts his glass, 'Well, good luck in your new job!'

They all clink their long-stemmed crystal glasses. Rolf and Liam, who are sitting at the far sides of the oval table, get up to ensure they touch each and everyone's drinks.

Brit can almost hear a collective sigh of relief around the table when they are all seated again and Hilda offers more of her excellent vegetable bakes and ham for a second round.

People chat about the food, praising Hilda's cooking, about Stockholm, and the snowy weather, and everyone is in good cheer.

Jukka places a hand over Brit's fingers and whispers, 'I'm so happy to spend Christmas with you.'

Brit gazes at Jukka. His blue eyes are sincere, but can she trust this man? She wants to, with all her heart, but what if he turns out to be another womanizer? Or worse, a predator who thinks touching people up is OK if you're their boss?

She removes her hand from under his grip to take a sip of red wine. It tastes good and since she and her father are staying over at Hilda and Uffe's, and she doesn't need to drive, she can drink as much as she wants. She is stalling, she knows, and wonders if Jukka has noticed. But she is saved by Hilda, who begins to remove plates from the table. Brit and Alicia get up to help. Patrick and Liam, too, rise from their chairs, but Hilda tells them in no uncertain terms to sit back down.

'It's OK, equality hasn't reached Sjoland yet,' Alicia says with a grin, addressing the men.

'Alicia,' her mother reprimands her, but they both laugh. 'They are guests and you are family.' Turning to Brit, who is holding her and Jukka's plates, Hilda says, 'You too, Brit, please stay seated. But Patrick, on second thoughts, perhaps you'd like to open that huge bottle of champagne? I thought we'd have that with the dessert?'

'With pleasure,' he says and follows the women into the kitchen. Liam, too, gets up, heading toward the bathroom.

Brit's father begins to chat to Uffe about his farm, and Jukka once again takes Brit's hand in his. He has turned in his seat so that he is fully facing her. Brit glances toward her father and Uffe and sees that they are deep in conversation at the other end of the table.

'Is something the matter?' Jukka says. 'Have I upset you for some reason?'

Brit looks hard at Jukka and says, as quietly as she can, 'I had a call from Kerstin.'

Jukka's eyes widen, but he doesn't say anything, so Brit continues, 'She told me about Sia Eklund.'

Jukka drops her hand and leans back in his chair. He runs his fingers over his light brown hair and sighs. He leans toward Brit again and says in a serious tone, while keeping his eyes firmly on hers, 'There was nothing to it. I misread her signals. Besides, she had her own agenda. Did you know she's Kerstin's daughter?'

Brit nods.

When she doesn't say anything, Jukka carries on. 'The company would have sacked me if there'd been any truth to any of it!'

He has raised his voice and Brit is suddenly aware of a hush in the room. Everyone is staring at him. Her father and Uffe, sitting at the table have turned their heads. Alicia and Patrick are standing behind them, also gazing at Brit and Jukka.

Hilda is at the other end of table, carrying a silver tray of champagne glasses, all filled to the brim. She puts it down and in a falsely joyous tone says, 'Bubbles, anyone?'

FIFTY-THREE

On Christmas Day Alicia drives to Mariehamn with Liam. The weather has turned colder, but it's sunny, making the snow-covered fields and the snowy pillows hanging off pine trees and roofs sparkle.

'I'm so sorry about Patrick last night,' Alicia says.

She glances briefly at Liam who is sitting in the passenger seat of her Volvo, wearing his padded coat fully zipped up. Something has happened to the heating in the old car and they can both see their breath vaporize in front of their faces.

'It's OK,' Liam says.

She'd been aware of Liam's discomfort all evening. While they were sitting at the table eating the delicious dishes that Hilda served after the overflowing smorgasbord starter, she'd begun to feel sorry for him. Luckily, she managed to get her mother to seat the two men at opposite ends of the table. But she hadn't realized that this meant Patrick would be next to her. By the time she'd seen where she was sitting, after everybody had found their places, she couldn't ask anyone to move without an explanation. She wonders now if Hilda had done that on purpose? Perhaps her mother thought, if Liam was lost, Patrick was a good second-best? Alicia wouldn't put it past her mother.

She was sure that Liam must have seen Patrick's attempts to touch Alicia all evening. It had been painful, not the joyous family Christmas Alicia had hoped for. And yet, she was happy to sit next to Patrick, and to share the evening with him, and the rest of the people: family, friends, old and new–and Liam.

Liam has hardly said a word to her since Patrick's surprise appearance and their conversation in the attic room. Apart from thanking her for his present, a woolly jumper, and saying goodnight with a brief kiss on her cheek. He had only nodded when Alicia came over to hug him to say thank you for the beautiful gold necklace he had given her.

'It's too much,' she'd whispered into his ear, but he had just smiled and let go of her, almost pushing her away.

Liam stayed behind in the main house, sleeping in the attic room that Hilda had prepared for Frida. Surprisingly, she didn't bat an eyelid when Alicia discreetly asked her if she could find him a bed in the house.

'Of course. You'll be in the sauna cottage, I presume?'

Alicia nodded.

'OK, lovely,' Hilda had said, hugging Alicia. She was stunned that her mother didn't make a fuss, or demand an explanation, or even worse, tell her what a brilliant man Liam was and how she was foolish to let him go. This was a lecture she had heard at least dozen times during the last few months. Alicia wonders now if Hilda had seen the way they were together and concluded that their marriage couldn't be saved.

'I used to go out every Christmas Day,' Frida says, hushing the baby, who is crying at full volume. She's speaking English, for Liam's benefit. Something for which Alicia is grateful.

'Really?' Liam says.

'Yes, it's a tradition here. Christmas Eve is for family and Christmas Day for partying,' Alicia says, adding to Frida, 'Do you want me to take her?'

Frida hands Anne Sofie to Alicia and she begins rocking the baby just as she used to do with Stefan. Liam is gazing at the two of them and Alicia can see tears in his eyes. He turns away quickly and asks Frida for a glass of water.

'Oh My God, I haven't even offered you a drink!' the young woman says and goes into the small kitchen. 'What would you like, tea or coffee, or mulled wine?'

'Coffee, please,' both Liam and Alicia say in unison. Liam smiles at Alicia and the baby, who has calmed down and is blinking slowly in her arms. She returns his smile and looks at little Anne Sofie, who has now closed her eyes completely. Gingerly, she steps inside the kitchen and, mouthing to Frida 'She's asleep,' goes to put the baby down in her cot.

When she's tucked the baby in, she comes into the living room, where Frida and Liam sit facing each other across a low table covered with baby clothes, packets of baby wipes, and one of diapers.

'I'm glad you came over. I'm sorry about last night. She's been so restless for a couple of days now that I didn't think it was a good idea to take her out. Besides, I'm exhausted. I went to bed at six o'clock, just after I put her down last night.' Frida runs her hand across her forehead. Her hair is standing almost upright. The tips have a faint hue of blue, otherwise the color looks almost normal. She's wearing a pair of ripped black tights and a bright red dress.

Alicia sits next to her and gives the girl a hug.

'That's OK. You did the right thing,' she says, letting go of Frida.

She glances toward Liam, who opens his mouth to speak, but Frida speaks first.

'The thing is, I feel a bit of a fraud.

Both Alicia and Liam stare at Frida, who's gazing down at her hands, crossing and uncrossing them.

Alicia touches her arm and asks, 'What do you mean?'

'I'm so sorry!' Frida says and bursts into tears.

Alicia puts her arms around the girl again and looks over at Liam. He widens his eyes in a question, to which Alicia shakes her head.

'What is it? This can't be about last night?' she says to Frida, who has buried her head in Alicia's chest.

'I'm a terrible person. You'll hate me forever,' Frida sobs.

'It's OK, Frida. We already know Stefan isn't Anne Sofie's dad,' Liam says in a matter-of-fact voice.

Frida lifts her head up and stares at him.

'How?' She asks.

Alicia puts her hand up to stop Liam saying anything more. Speaking in Swedish, she says, 'Without telling me, Liam took a hair out of Anne Sofie's head and together with something I had from Stefan, was able to do a DNA test. And it proved conclusively negative.' She lets this information sink in for a moment, and then adds, 'But it doesn't matter to me. I am still Anne Sofie's grandmother.'

Frida is quiet, then she gets up and starts walking up and down the living room, from the bookcase overfilled with old volumes and her mother's trinkets to the window overlooking the apartments next door.

'How long have you known?' Speaking in English, she gazes at Liam and Alicia in turn.

'A few days. Liam told me the day he arrived,' Alicia replies.

Again Frida paces up and down the living room. Liam moves on his seat and opens his mouth, but Frida stops him once more. 'And when were you going to tell me?'

'Today. Now,' Liam replies.

Frida nods.

'Sit down, Frida. Can I ask why you let us believe Stefan was Anne Sofie's dad?' Alicia says as gently as she can.

Frida lowers herself on the sofa and blows air out of her mouth.

'We were in love. So much in love.' She looks pleadingly at Alicia.

'I know,' she says.

Liam gets up. Looking at both Alicia and Frida, he says, 'Do you want me to wait in the car?'

'What?' Alicia says.

'No, Liam, you have a right to know what happened,' Frida says decisively in English.

'Stefan and I met just as I told you in Mariehamn and then again in Brighton when I was there on a language course. But we didn't do anything. There was nowhere, to, you know,' here Frida looks at Liam and then Alicia. 'Besides, we wanted to wait.'

Alicia puts her hand on Frida's and squeezes it.

'So who?'

'Who's Anne Sofie's father?'

'Yes,' Alicia says.

'Daniel,' the girl says so quietly that Alicia and Liam have to lean forward to hear her.

'It was right after Stefan's accident. I was so sad, and he was there and we got very drunk one night and I don't even remember much of it. I felt so awful afterwards. I'd been unfaithful to Stefan with Daniel of all people, and then I found out I was pregnant. Well, I kept thinking and hoping it would be Stefan's. But, of course, it couldn't have been. I'm such a fool.'

'Did Daniel know, before he perished?'

Frida nods. She's not looking at either Alicia or Liam.

There is an awkward silence, which is interrupted by a baby crying.

Frida leaves the room and they hear her talking softly to Anne Sofie, who gurgles in reply. Alicia looks at Liam.

'Do you think we should leave her to it?' Liam says and gets up.

Alicia nods and hands the car keys to Liam, 'You go on, I'll just say goodbye to Frida.'

FIFTY-FOUR

'She lied to us. Just as,' Liam says, but Alicia stops him.

'Yes, I was there, I heard her. What are you going to say now, "I told you so?"'

Liam takes a deep breath and Alicia can see his chest rise and fall next to her in the car, but he doesn't reply to her. They are driving back along the empty streets, with just the occasional vehicle coming in the other direction in the center of town.

'You'll have to tell Uffe and Hilda,' Liam says after a while. They've just crossed over the swing bridge in Sjoland and are nearing Alicia's home.

Hilda is in the kitchen, preparing another feast for the evening. Uffe is at the sink, peeling potatoes. His back is to them when Alicia and Liam step into the room. It's warm inside, with candles flickering on the table in a wooden red and white candelabra.

'There they are!' Hilda exclaims, making Uffe turn around. He lifts his wet hands out of the sink and says, 'More food to be prepared.' He's grinning widely and nods toward Hilda. 'Mind you, we have enough to last till next Christmas!'

'Nonsense,' Hilda replies and smacks Uffe's back with a tea towel.

'Can we do anything to help?' Alicia asks, but Hilda says, 'No, we're not going to eat until much later. How was Frida and the little baby?' she adds.

'Fine,' Alicia says.

'Have you had anything to eat?' Hilda asks next, a question that makes Alicia and Liam, after she's translated what her mother has said, smile.

'No.'

'Oh, in that case, let's all have some coffee. I've got some wonderful Karelian pies I bought from the market and cinnamon buns. And there are Christmas stars.'

After the table is set with the rye-crust rice-filled pies, sweet pastries, and cinnamon buns, and everyone has eaten far too much again, Alicia says, 'Mom and Uffe, we have something to tell you.'

Her serious tone stops Hilda in her tracks. She puts down her cup of coffee and gazes at her daughter.

'I think I know what's coming,' she says, glancing sideways at Liam.

'We have two things to tell you,' Alicia says. She looks at Liam, who is sitting next to her, and says to him in English, 'I'll tell them, and then I'll translate. OK?'

Liam nods and Alicia continues, 'Liam did a DNA test on the baby.'

Both Uffe and Hilda gasp. Her mother puts a hand to her mouth. 'She's not ours!' she exclaims.

'Now, now, don't jump to conclusions,' Uffe says, patting Hilda's hand.

But she takes no notice of her husband and says instead, 'I knew it, I knew it all along!'

'Mom, yes, you are right. But that doesn't mean that Frida didn't love Stefan. And Stefan most certainly was in love with her.'

Alicia tells Hilda and Uffe everything Frida has told them. About how she slept with Daniel, Stefan's friend, the Romanian boy who'd worked on Uffe's farm and so tragically died last summer.

Then she adds, 'I also found out who Frida's father is.'

FIFTY-FIVE

'Y ou know that she is a vindictive woman?' Jukka says.

'Yes, but there must have been something to it. And this Sia, I mean she can't have been very old,' Brit replies.

Jukka sighs. 'Yes, I admit, I was stupid and it was totally wrong of me in that sense. She was coming onto me and I thought she wanted it.'

'When you say "it", what do you mean exactly? What happened?' Brit now demands.

They are sitting in Brit's apartment, on one of the light-colored sofas. The night before, Jukka had left Hilda and Uffe's place a few moments after they'd toasted the season with Patrick's expensive champagne. Jukka wasn't drinking because he was on call, and because he was driving back home after the festivities. He also didn't take any presents, something he felt pretty bad about, and he'd decided to leave before the traditional exchange of gifts.

'We had sex, but only once.'

'As if that would make any of it better!'

'But it was two years ago! And it has nothing to do with you.'

Brit sighs. Jukka is right, of course. His previous sexual escapades have nothing to do with her. If she pursues this, she could come across as needy and spoil her chances with Jukka altogether. They've only had sex once and are by no means an item. Except, he agreed to come and spend Christmas with her best friend's family–and meet her father. So she must mean something more to him than just what happened in Solbacken two days ago?

'Look,' Jukka takes her hands in his. 'I am falling for you. When I was with Sia, it was to do with my wife, my ex, and I wasn't myself.'

Jukka lets go of Brit and leans back on the sofa.

'I don't know what to tell you, except that it won't happen again,' he says, looking out across the wintry view out of his window.

'Really?' Brit bites her lip after she's made the sarcastic comment.

Stop being so needy!

'Yes, really. Why do you think it took me so long to ask you for a drink?'

Now Brit thinks back to their last shift together on MS *Sabrina*. She was confused about his behavior. He *was* blowing hot and cold and she couldn't understand what he was playing at. She looks at him, sitting upright on the sofa next to her. His hands are knitted together, resting on his thighs. He's wearing a striped shirt but the strong muscles in his arms are flexed and showing underneath the clothing.

Why does he have to be so good-looking?

Brit wants to sit across his lap and have those strong arms around her waist. She wants to see how quickly she can make him hard. She gazes down at her outfit. Luckily, when Jukka phoned and asked if he could come over and talk to her just after midday, just as she was getting ready to go and spend the Christmas Day evening with her dad, she'd had time to change into a slinky black dress and some sexy underwear.

A girl can never be too prepared.

But what if he is a complete rat, and this is the way he gets over the women he plays?

'You look very nice, by the way. I've been wanting to take you in my arms all night.'

Brit leans over and brings her lips toward Jukka. He takes hold of her waist and pulls her onto his lap. They start kissing and tumble onto the sofa.

FIFTY-SIX

'What about the two of you?' Hilda asks.

Liam has understood her question, Hilda thinks. He exchanges a look with her daughter and immediately looks down at his empty coffee cup on the table. And Hilda understands. Alicia has decided to leave him. Of course, Hilda suspected that already. Seeing Alicia with Patrick yesterday confirmed her suspicions about those two too.

'Mom, I'm sorry, but Liam is leaving tomorrow and we've decided to separate.'

No one says anything. Uffe is looking out into the snow-covered fields across the window at the far end of the kitchen. He hasn't said a word while Alicia has been speaking, as if none of it has anything to do with him. Mostly, he appears embarrassed. As usual, he's leaving everything to her.

I bet he wishes he was hiding in his study now.

'I'm sorry to hear that,' Hilda says in English and then, addressing her daughter in Swedish, 'I guess you're going to go swanning off to Stockholm with Patrick?'

That gets everyone's attention, even Uffe is back in the room.

'What did you say?' he asks.

'Mom!' Alicia says and gets up. Like a teenager, she runs out of the room and up the stairs.

Liam is staring at Hilda and she suspects that once again, Liam has managed to understand Swedish.

'Go after her,' Hilda says and Liam rushes toward the staircase.

'What?' Hilda exclaims when she sees Uffe's expression. 'It's about time she made up her mind which one of them she wants,' she says.

'A bit cruel, don't you think?' Uffe says quietly.

Hilda sighs. He's probably right, but what is she supposed to think, or do? After all the surprises she's had to contend with today, and in the last year, she just wants to get back to normal.

'She was always the same as a girl. Couldn't make a decision to save her life,' she says and starts clearing the table.

FIFTY-SEVEN

U p on the third floor of the house, Liam sees that the door to the attic room is shut. He stands outside for a moment, listening to any sounds coming from inside, but since it all seems completely still in there, he gives the door a gentle knock.

'Yes?' he hears Alicia say.

'It's me,' Liam replies.

When there's nothing more from Alicia, Liam opens the door.

Alicia is sitting on the bed, with a tissue in her hand. She looks vulnerable in her loose blue jeans and thin, red cashmere jumper, which has gold glitter at the wrists and along the high collar. He thinks she must have lost weight again since he last visited. He hasn't noticed it on this trip before, but seeing her now, with her back resting against the wall with her legs pulled up and hands wrapped around her knees, she looks thin and fragile.

Liam sits on the far edge of the bed. 'You OK?'

Alicia nods.

'It's been quite a Christmas,' Liam says.

Alicia lifts her eyes up at him and gives him a sad smile.

'Yes.'

'Not quite how you'd planned it?'

Alicia laughs. A short snort, really, but Liam takes it as a good sign.

'Can I ask you something?'

'It's OK, Liam. I'm not going to move to Stockholm with him,' Alicia says. She's looking at him, but now Liam doesn't know what to say.

'But our marriage is over,' Alicia adds.

'OK,' Liam says. 'OK,' he repeats, and then, knowing he shouldn't but unable to help himself, he asks, 'So you and him aren't an item?'

Alicia gazes at Liam for a long time, and he doesn't know what she is thinking. He's dying to say something but is certain that he has already said too much. Or that whatever he says now will spoil it for him forever.

'Liam, it really isn't any of your business. I'm truly sorry, but I know that I haven't felt what I used to feel for you for some years now. Stefan, well, Stefan in a way was the catalyst. I don't love you anymore. And if there is someone else, that's for me to tell you. If and when I wish to share that information. You lost the right to know when you decided to break our marriage vows.'

'And Frida and Anne Sofie?' Liam says.

'I don't know about that. I'll see how it all goes. I love that little baby girl and her mother more than I thought I could love anyone new, and I can't just turn that love off. You do understand that, don't you?' Alicia says. Now there are tears in her eyes.

'I'm so sorry, I thought I was doing the right thing with the test. I thought you'd want to know. I've been such a fool!' Liam shuffles over to where Alicia is sitting at the other end of the bed. He lays a hand over Alicia's wrist, and adds, 'Can you forgive me?'

'Yes, Liam, I do know you were just thinking of what the best thing for everyone would be. Besides, it doesn't much matter now anyway. It seems the truth had been torturing Frida too, so she would have told me sooner or later. It was almost better coming from you. At least I was prepared when she told me.'

'All the same, I'm so sorry,' Liam says.

Alicia moves off the bed and kneels in front of Liam. She puts her arms around him.

'Let's try to be friends, eh?'

Liam nods inside Alicia's embrace. Her scent of roses and jasmine, so feminine and so familiar, is pulling at his heart and he feels tears–he never cries!–pricking his eyes.

Liam gently pushes Alicia away and says, 'I better pack before the re-run of food and drink fest tonight. I was quite worse for wear last night.'

She gives him a last squeeze and steps off the bed. At the door, Alicia stops and turns around, 'You are a kind man. I'm not saying anything to the contrary, you know that, don't you?' And with those words Alicia, his lovely Scandinavian wife, walks out of his life forever.

FIFTY-EIGHT

On Boxing Day, Alicia gets a message from Patrick. He's been unusually quiet since they parted under the full gaze of everyone on Christmas Eve, and Alicia hasn't wanted to be the first to contact him, even though they decided to spend the rest of the holidays together. She doesn't know what she's going to tell him.

Are you coming over?

Alicia regards the text and smiles. What is she going to do?

Let's have coffee in town. Bagarstugan?

Half an hour later, when Alicia steps into the small coffee place, busy with shoppers who are in the little town for post-Christmas bargains. Patrick is in the back of the rammed room, at a small table with two chairs on either side.

'I got you a cappuccino,' he says. He gets up to give her a kiss and she cannot resist it, but lets his lips touch hers for far longer than is wise in front of all these people. There is bound to be someone that either she, or more likely, Patrick, knows. Or someone who recognizes one of them. Apart from Patrick's dubious reputation as the former son-in-law of the richest man on the islands, both their images are plastered over *Ålandsbladet* and its internet edition, which is read by about three times as many people as the paper version.

'How are you?' Patrick leans over and now, as if the kiss wasn't enough for the many eyes Alicia feels sure are boring into her back, he takes Alicia's hands in his.

'I'm fine,' she replies, and adds in a low voice, 'Isn't this a bit too public?'

'Your choice,' Patrick says and leans back in his chair. He's grinning from ear to ear.

'You're impossible. Let me take a couple of sips and we'll go over to yours.'

'Suits me,' Patrick says and finishes his black coffee in one gulp.

'I can't leave the islands. Not now. Frida and Anne Sofie, my mother and Uffe, and now Brit, are here,' Alicia says. They are sitting opposite each other at Patrick's white table, drinking wine.

'But things have changed, haven't they?'

'If you mean that I am no longer Anne Sofie's grandmother and that Dudnikov is her grandfather and that Frida is fine, financially speaking, yes. But I still love that little girl. And Frida, of course. I can't turn my feelings off just like that.'

'No, neither can I, and that is just what you've been asking me to do for these past four months,' Patrick doesn't sound annoyed, even though Alicia can see that she has been indecisive. Not being able to choose between the two men, and her two lives, in London and on the islands, has left both in limbo.

'I've been very confused, I'm sorry,' Alicia says.

She gazes at Patrick who is wearing a white T-shirt as usual, revealing his strong chest and arms. His blond hair has grown longer, and his chin is clean shaven, and for once, there are no shaving cuts. Alicia wants to joke about the lack of scars, but it doesn't seem right to do that now.

Patrick nods slowly.

'The thing is, while you've not been able to decide, I've had to think for myself. And I want to do something more than report on stolen flower pots and delayed ferries.' Patrick looks intently at Alicia.

'At the *Journalen* I can make a difference. Report and investigate real issues, real stories.'

Alicia sighs. She, too, is bored with *Ålandsbladet*. She craves a good story, a corruption case or just a good, old-fashioned financial crisis.

'Stockholm isn't that far! You can get over to Mariehamn in four hours,' Patrick says and he grabs Alicia's' hands.

'That's right, it isn't that far. We can see each other almost every weekend. I can come over to you, or you come over here. Surely you'll have to do that for the girls anyway?'

Patrick throws his arms up in the air.

'You are the most frustrating woman I've ever met!' Biting the inside of his cheek and keeping his eyes firmly on Alicia, he continues, 'The girls will come to me in Stockholm every other weekend. I'll only be coming over here during the summer. Besides, the job at *Journalen* is pretty full-on.'

'Mia has agreed to this?'

Now Patrick looks annoyed, 'Yes, anything to get me off these golden islands.'

She shouldn't have mentioned Mia, Alicia thinks.

But then Patrick's face softens, 'I didn't tell you this before, because I didn't want to make you mad. Or to think that I was taking you for granted,' Patrick pauses for a moment to laugh, 'which is such a joke!'

'What?' Alicia asks, suddenly interested in spite of herself.

'I know one of the guys working on *Dagens Finans* and he says there's a post open there. You know, it's a very similar paper to the *Financial Times*. It's just a maternity cover for a year, or maybe only six months, if you wish, but my mate says you'll definitely get it if you apply.'

Alicia is staring at Patrick. Suddenly she imagines herself working in Stockholm, writing relevant stories, not just about lost pets or shop opening times.

She could be going out to lunches with Patrick, not having to worry about who will see them or what stories will get back to her mother and Uffe. And she would still be able to come and see everyone here in Åland every weekend if she wanted to. Or at least every other weekend, when Patrick has her daughters over. And it could just be a trial. Six months, a year, to see how it goes?

'If you don't like me or Stockholm after a year, you can just move back to the islands,' Patrick says as if he's read her mind.

He's giving her his most charming smile.

Why not? I can do what I want for the first time in my life.

'OK, you win, if I get that job, I'll try Stockholm out for six months,' Alicia says and grins at Patrick.

'Really?' he says and jumps up from his chair. In a second, he's got his arms around Alicia and he's kissing her.

'I can't believe I've finally got you!'

EPILOGUE

In late January, Patrick moves into his new penthouse property. The two-bedroom apartment overlooks Kungsholmen island across the Riddarfjärden channel. He is in his favorite part of town, Söder. His daughters have already visited him for one weekend and they love that they can walk into the most fashionable shops and cafés in the trendy part of town. His eldest, Sara, had her hair cut into a short pixie, and spent Saturday morning in the area's popular secondhand shops. Both his daughters are into sustainability and avid followers of Greta Thunberg, much to their mother's annoyance.

On the Sunday morning, after he's handed Sara and Frederica back to Mia, at the Marie Line ferry port, Patrick looks at the pretty pale yellow and red brick houses, with their jagged roofs topped with layers of snow, on the other side of the water from his new apartment. The sea is iced over, with a narrow shipping lane cutting it in half. A small tug boat is making its way through the channel. The sun is out and the view is making Patrick feel better about the sudden emptiness of the apartment. Unlike in Mariehamn, where the view was of open sea, void of any signs of habitation, and with only the twice-daily ferry traffic, Patrick can feel the pulsating life of a city, even if he can't make out the people on the streets. He cannot wait to share this view and show the city off to Alicia. She's coming over on Wednesday for an interview, which Patrick has been reliably informed is just a formality, with *Dagens Finans*. Initially, Alicia will work for the paper for six months, starting in February, but she has insisted that she will look for a rental as soon as possible. Patrick is confident that once she's shared his bed for a few weeks, she will forget about finding her own place. Besides, getting a rental in Stockholm is notoriously difficult. But Patrick has decided not to push her. They have agreed that her stay in Stockholm, and particularly with him, is strictly a temporary measure, and that's fine with Patrick—for now.

Alicia is packing up the sauna cottage. She's decided to stay in Stockholm with Patrick for the week, coming back to the islands on the last ferry on Sunday. Irrespective of how the interview with Swedish newspaper goes, she will move in with Patrick on the first Monday in February. In the meantime, Hilda and Alicia have decided to shut up the cottage for winter. She was surprised at how well her mother took the news of her plans.

'You are young,' Hilda said, wiping a tear from the corner of her eye. 'And you must start living your life again. Stockholm is only a skip and a hop away.'

Alicia hugged her mother and promised she would come and see her every other weekend, when Patrick's daughters were in town.

'You mustn't worry about me,' Hilda says, pulling away from her daughter's embrace. 'Surely you will need to get to know the girls if your relationship with Patrick is serious?'

Alicia looked down at her hands. This was one issue she hadn't dared think about. Having only ever had a son, she has no idea how to deal with pre-teen girls. Plus, she knows Mia isn't exactly thrilled about Alicia and Patrick's plans.

That morning, as she looks at her scarce possessions, which fit into one suitcase and two large IKEA bags, one of which is filled with Hilda's linen used in the cottage, she thinks back to the past six months in this small space. So much has happened that she would never forget. She's found out that she has strengths that she never thought she possessed, and that she has the ability to love again. Thinking of love, the image of little Anne Sofie comes to her mind.

Frida, too, understood and was glad about Alicia's decision. Much like Hilda, she mentioned the short distance between the Swedish capital and Mariehamn.

'You do know that some people commute each week back and forth?' Frida said and laughed. 'So you can come and see your granddaughter whenever the fancy takes you.' The young mother had handed Alicia the baby as soon as she stepped inside the door, and when Alicia heard Frida call Anne Sofie her granddaughter, tears pooled in eyes, but she wiped them away and smiled.

'I know,' she said.

'But I have to say, you're a bit of a dark horse! Patrick Hilden, no less.'

At those words, Alicia blushed. She turned away from Frida and sat down with the baby, who was wriggling to get out of her grasp. Lately, all she wanted to do was stand up on her knees, and as Alicia held Anne Sofie by her little hands, the girl pushed herself up and gave a self-satisfied giggle.

'She is so lovely, I will miss her terribly!'

Frida looked down at Alicia and came to sit next to her on the sofa. She wrapped her hands around Alicia and her daughter, who immediately began to protest. Both Alicia and Frida laughed, which produced a fresh gurgle from the baby.

'You'll see her almost as often as before. And I will come and check out Patrick's posh pad in Stockholm too. You never know, once this little one is a bit older, I might move there myself!' Frida said and bent down to give the top of Anne Sofie's head a kiss.

Alicia gazed at the young woman who had become such a good mother. The apartment, as always, was in a chaotic state, but Frida's disorganization didn't seem to affect the baby's or her own well-being. With the money Frida had access to, which couldn't, as far as Alicia understood, be traced to Dudnikov, and therefore would never be under investigation, both she and her daughter were guaranteed a safe and prosperous future. Alicia didn't want to ask Frida what she was planning to do with all the money, but she was glad to hear the young woman was thinking about the future.

The future, Alicia thinks to herself. What will it hold for any of them? All she knows is that she loves Patrick and she wants to be with him. If they can't stand to live with each other, so be it. Now it feels good to have a nice place to stay in Stockholm (Patrick's descriptions and the photos he's sent her are amazing), with the possibility of a prestigious job to boot.

At that moment, her phone pings and she sees it's a message from Liam.

Good luck with your job interview. xx

She smiles at the message and pens a 'Thank you' reply. Typical of Liam not to know when the interview is, but she's glad that he's happy for her. He always wanted her to build up her career again.

Liam and Alicia have agreed to put the house in Crouch End on the market in the spring, and perhaps by then Alicia will know whether Stockholm and living with Patrick suit her, and him. Her share of the proceeds from the house would buy a comfortable apartment either in Sweden or on the islands, and if the job in Stockholm works out, and is made permanent, she might even be able to take out a loan to get a bigger, or better located place. But these are all decisions she will make later, much later. Now she needs to finish sorting out the cottage. Hilda has promised a celebration brunch at the main house, after which she will drive Alicia to Mariehamn.

Brit hasn't told Alicia she will be at the ferry port to wave her goodbye. The two friends have already had their farewell dinner in town, after which they went to Brit's apartment where Alicia stayed the night and they talked and talked through most of it. Brit will miss Alicia, especially now that they have only recently rekindled their friendship, but as Alicia pointed out, they will see each other in Stockholm almost as often as they now do on the islands.

It's a bitterly cold day, with no sun and gray skies giving only a faint light to the early afternoon. Brit is waiting outside the terminal building, keeping an eye out for Hilda's red BMW. A few other passengers are dropped off outside the double doors; Brit knows the 12:45 Sunday sailing to Stockholm is a popular one with weekly commuters to the city. Brit herself will step onboard MS *Sabrina* a couple of hours later that same afternoon. She's still sharing her shifts with Jukka, although they haven't yet made their relationship official with Marie Line. Brit smiles when she thinks about Jukka that morning. She stayed over in his apartment in Solbacken and he brought her breakfast in bed. Afterward they made love and he told her that he loved her.

Is it possible to be this happy? Surely something will go wrong soon?

As Hilda's car comes into view, it takes just minutes for it to stop in front of Brit. Hilda has always driven too fast, but in this icy weather, her speeding looks positively dangerous.

'I couldn't let you go without another hug,' Brit says to Alicia, who, looking a little pale, steps out of the low-slung sports car.

'We just about made it in one piece,' Alicia says to Brit under her breath, and laughs.

'Brit, what a lovely surprise,' Hilda says, locking the car remotely with a flourish.

Alicia is wearing her padded coat and a pair of shiny boots. With the color returning to her cheeks, she looks positively beaming. Brit hugs her and says, 'Let me know how the interview goes. I'll be in Stockholm in two days' time, if you have time for a quick drink?'

'That would be lovely,' Alicia says and smiles.

'Come on, let's get you checked in,' Hilda says, to which Alicia rolls her eyes and Brit raises her eyebrows. There's more than half an hour until sailing, so there's plenty of time.

'I've got to get going,' Brit says and puts her arms around Alicia one more time. 'I've got to pack and change before work, but promise to let me know as soon as you know about the job? Ring me or message whenever, yes?'

'Ok,' Alicia replies and Brit can see there are tears in her eyes. She squeezes her friend one more time and says, 'We'll see each other in a couple of days, so this isn't exactly goodbye!'

Hilda is immensely proud of her daughter. She's beautiful and strong. As she watches her speak with the check-in clerk inside the ferry terminal, she can see and hear how assured she is. Patrick, it seems, has been able to win her over, something which surprised Hilda at first, and Uffe. Of course, both of them knew something had been going on with those two ever since the Midsummer party at the Eriks-son's house last summer. It made both of them laugh. How ignorant the youngsters think old people are.

'It's as if we've never been in love,' Hilda said to Uffe, who just shook his head and gave a small chuckle.

Hilda herself cannot even remember the number of times she's been infatuated with a man. What's more it still keeps happening, even now. She knows Uffe notices her little affairs of the heart, which she never (not lately, at least) does anything about.

Hilda thinks the new generations are far too serious about life. It's short, so you might as well enjoy it as much as you can. That's her motto, and now her earnest daughter seems to have understood this too. Of course, she's sad to see her leave the islands, but Alicia has been living in London all these years, a place much farther afield, with another language to cope with too. And Hilda just loves Stockholm, so she's looking forward to visiting Alicia as often as possible.

'This is me, I think I'll go through,' Alicia now says. She's standing in front of Hilda with her boarding documents in her hand. Her eyes are full of tears, which makes Hilda fill up too. She puts her arms around her daughter.

'I love you, darling, and I think you are making the right decision,' Hilda says, trying to keep her voice level. 'It's only across the water,' Hilda adds, letting go of Alicia.

'So it is,' her daughter replies and turning to go, adds, 'I love you too, mom.'

THE ISLAND DAUGHTER

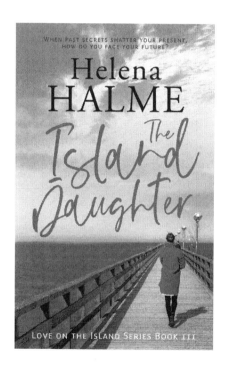

ONE

'Did you forget your keys again?' Alicia shouts as she runs to the front door of the three-bedroomed apartment overlooking the Riddarfjärden water in Stockholm.

When she opens up, she gives an involuntary gasp. On the other side stands Mia, her lover's ex-wife.

'What are you doing here?' Mia asks.

Mia is dressed in her signatory off-white. Underneath her pale, close-fitting overcoat are white slacks and a silky blouse. On her feet, she's wearing a pair of high-heeled tan boots. Her voice is as spiky as her footwear.

Alicia feels drab and unkempt in her old gray jogging pants and a worn-out T-shirt with a hole in one of the armpits. It's as if her home is being invaded by this rich woman, who has not only hurt her boyfriend but has made it as difficult as possible for him to see his two daughters. What right does she have to come to her and Patrick's new place? Or question Alicia's presence here?

'I could ask you the same thing?' Alicia says and lifts her chin. Her dirty hair is in a ponytail, and more than anything now, she wishes she'd showered before Patrick came back from dropping off his daughters. It suddenly occurs to her why this woman is here.

'Is everything OK?' Alicia says, concerned that something has happened to Patrick. She glances at her watch and sees that it's just gone 6pm—more than half an hour before Mia and Patrick are due to do the handover.

'Don't just stand there. Let me in!' Mia says, impatiently readjusting her oversized designer handbag as she pushes past her.

'It's a nice place you have here,' Mia says, looking around.

Alicia stands in the hall, blocking her way into the lounge and the bedrooms. The last thing she wants is to give Patrick's ex a tour of their home. Mia shrugs her shoulders and walks into the newly remodeled, bespoke kitchen. She runs her hand over the shiny gray work surface and admires the cabinets.

'Do you like living here?' she asks.

'Yes,' Alicia says, wondering what on earth the woman wants with her.

Alicia decides to make coffee. Perhaps if she can get Mia to sit down with a hot drink, she can find out.

A few moments later, as they sit facing each other across the kitchen table, cups of coffee in their hands, Mia finally says that Patrick asked her to fetch the girls from the apartment.

'I don't believe you,' Alicia says.

She's sure Patrick would have told her of the change of plan, as well as warn her about Mia's visit. Alicia hasn't set eyes on Patrick's ex-wife since the previous summer. Mia had accosted Alicia outside the *Ålandsbladet* newspaper offices, where she and Patrick were working at the time, and accused her of sleeping with her husband. The fact that Mia was already involved with another man, and her wealthy family, the Erikssons, were negotiating a divorce settlement, didn't seem to matter to Mia. After that unpleasant incident, Alicia had tried to steer clear of her. This wasn't as difficult on the small Åland islands as it might have seemed. Mia was often jetting off to remote locations, with or without her two daughters.

'Whatever,' Mia says.

'What are you really doing here, Mia?' Alicia asks.

But instead of replying to her, Mia touches the leaf of a cactus plant that Alicia had placed with two others on the wide windowsill.

'Do you pay Patrick rent? I mean in money, not just *in kind*?'

Her eyes are as cold as ice. As is her voice.

'What's it to you?' Alicia manages to say. She tries to control herself, but her voice is high-pitched.

'Well, I am the landlord after all.' Mia says, raising her gaze to meet Alicia's.

'What?' Alicia utters the question before she has time to think. *You should be playing this cool.*

'This whole block is owned by Eriksson Holdings, a company I am the Chief Executive of, so in theory—well, not even in theory, but in reality—I am Patrick's landlord, and now *yours*. And he doesn't pay any rent, so...'

Alicia stares at Mia. She wants to shout at her, or get up and yank the woman's hair, but she controls herself. Several times since moving in four months ago, Alicia has asked Patrick how much she should contribute toward the rent. This is an expensive area and the apartment is beautifully done up with oak flooring throughout. On one occasion, Alicia even told Patrick how lucky he was to find the place, and that it must have cost him a small fortune.

Patrick had just taken her into his arms and said he rented it through a friend. Which, Alicia now knows, is a lie. There is no way Patrick would call Mia 'a friend'.

'I'm glad you like the decor. I chose everything myself,' Mia says, letting her eyes travel from one end of the kitchen to the other.

'I even ordered all the furniture,' she adds.

Alicia stares at the woman. Did Patrick know this?

Mia leans closer to her. 'Including the bed. I particularly loved the oak-framed bed. I thought it would suit Patrick perfectly.'

Alicia's mind is briefly cast back to when she first met Patrick and (she can now admit to herself) fell instantly in love with him. She was returning to the islands where she was raised, for a holiday with her British husband, Liam. She bumped into Patrick, literally, when the ferry suddenly rocked in rough seas. His blonde hair, blue eyes and strong arms had ignited a fire in Alicia that she thought had been extinguished by grief for her 17-year-old son and her husband's infidelity.

Alicia can't take anymore of Mia's snarky comments. Her head is spinning, but she gets up. Looking down at Mia, she says, 'At this very moment, Patrick is probably driving toward the ferry port where you were supposed to meet.'

Mia glances at her large and expensive Cartier watch. 'Oh dear, I must have misunderstood.' She gets up, having not touched her coffee.

'I'll be on my way then. Just a piece of advice. Patrick is fickle. He'll soon get tired of you, just as he did of me,' she adds as she floats out of the apartment.

TWO

W hen Patrick opens the door to the apartment, all he wants to do is to wrap his arms around Alicia and take her to bed. He's still frozen from the forty minutes spent waiting with Sara and Frederica outside the Marie Line ferry terminal. The early April day was unusually chilly. He thought he spotted some tiny flakes of snow swirling in the wind.

He'd wanted to go inside the terminal building. There were large windows overlooking the parking lot, and Mia's car would be fully visible, but his youngest, 10-year-old Frederica, had insisted on waiting outside so they wouldn't miss their mother. The girls wanted to board the ferry inside the car with their mother rather than make their way along the covered walkway alone, something Patrick fully understood. He wouldn't have let them do it anyway, but they could have waited inside. He'd hugged his two girls close, pretending to keep them both warm, but he also wanted to feel their closeness. He'd miss them during the two weeks until their next visit to Stockholm.

Mia was late, as usual. By the time her brand-new white Jaguar Land Rover turned the corner, there were only five minutes left to board the ship. Patrick held his tongue. He didn't want to start an argument with Mia. He handed the girls' rucksacks to their mother and hugged Sara and Frederica tightly one more time.

He hurried to the Tunnelbana station at Ropsten, taking the stone steps from the harbor to the underground platform two at a time. The emptiness he felt each time he said goodbye to his daughters was tearing his chest in two, but as the train speeded toward Mariatorget, his thoughts turned to Alicia more and more and her warm body waiting for him at home.

As soon as Patrick steps inside the apartment, he throws his coat on a hook and goes to find Alicia. She's standing against the sink, putting something away in the cupboard above. She's wearing a pair of cotton shorts and a camisole under a long, soft dressing gown, which he'd given her as a moving-in present. The tips of her breasts are visible under the thin cotton, and when he cups her buttocks in his hand, he can feel her soft, rounded flesh. She's not wearing knickers underneath. Her hair is wet from the shower and she smells wonderful.

'You've cleared up!' he says and hugs Alicia close.

'Mia was here,' Alicia says, moving away from him and sitting down at the kitchen table.

THREE

Patrick sits opposite Alicia, in the chair Mia sat in only an hour ago. He lifts his eyes, and once again Alicia is taken aback by how blue they are. But instead of the openness they normally convey, there's something else. When he lowers his head to look at his hands and makes no comment, Alicia knows Mia was right.

'What is it?' Alicia asks, trying not to sound accusatory.

Now Patrick replies quickly, too quickly, 'Nothing.'

His eyes meet Alicia's once again.

'She told me the family own this apartment. Is that true?'

Patrick shifts on the seat. Alicia waits. Involuntarily, she's crossed her arms over her chest, but now she lets them drop on her lap.

'Technically, yes,' Patrick finally replies.

'I can't believe it!'

Alicia has raised her voice and she immediately regrets it.

Patrick reaches over and touches her arm.

'Look, it was part of the divorce settlement. They own this whole block, so it made sense for me to live here.'

Alicia sits back in the chair. She can't comprehend what's happening. When Patrick and Alicia got together, Mia told her in no uncertain terms what she thought of Alicia. It wasn't a surprise. Alicia had known since school that she and her Finnish mother, not to mention her farmer stepfather, weren't good enough for the Erikssons. And now Alicia is living in Mia's apartment rent-free! With furniture that Mia chose.

'I was never part of that settlement, was I?' She's trying to keep calm but she also wants to confront Patrick. She cannot understand why he would lie to her when he knows how she feels about the Eriksson family.

Mia's father also owns the local newspaper, where Alicia and Patrick worked together last year. On the few occasions when she'd met Kurt in the editorial office, she'd disliked him. She could tell from his perma-tan, expensive designer clothes, and abrupt manner that he didn't think her good enough for his former son-in-law. The son-in-law whom he also despised.

And Mia's mother, Beatrice, a prize-winning author, who didn't say two words to her or her parents when they'd met at the Midsummer party last year, is just as aloof. All of them, except the two girls, are just the kind of entitled, self-satisfied rich people that Alicia loathes. And now she is beholden to this family.

'No,' Patrick says quietly.

'Right, I'm moving out as soon as I can,' Alicia says.

'But I love you,' Patrick says in a low voice.

These three words, so simple, are powerful.

She nods and replies, 'Me too.'

'We can work this out, can't we?' Patrick says.

His eyes are on Alicia and she can feel herself melt.

Patrick gets up and places his lips on her mouth.

'We'll both move out, if that makes you happy,' he murmurs in her ear and lifts her up. He half carries, half guides her toward their bedroom at the back of the apartment, while Alicia begins to undo his flies. Before they make it to the bedroom, she's lifted up her top, removed her shorts and guided him inside her.

'I thought I was going burst on the Tunnelbana,' Patrick says afterward, grinning.

'If that's what two days without sex does to you, what will you be

like in the summer when you'll have the girls over for two weeks?'
Alicia says, smiling.

Her tone is light, but she is serious. This had been the first time
Sara and Frederica had stayed with Patrick and Alicia. The plan had
been that Alicia would go back to the islands to visit her mother and
stepfather on the weekends the girls visited, but at the last minute
Patrick had begged Alicia to stay.

And Alicia had loved being with the two girls. She cast her mind
back to when Stefan was that age. She never thought she'd have
another chance to play a part in bringing up children, however small
that part might be.

But now after Mia's unwanted visit, she isn't sure of anything.

FOUR

Since moving to Stockholm and sharing her life and an apartment with Patrick, Alicia has often thought about Mia. This was a surprise to her, because while she'd been deciding whether to leave the Åland Islands behind, she'd hardly thought about Mia. Patrick had convinced her that his ex was history, and that Alicia would never have to interact with her, even though she was Sara and Frederica's mother.

After meeting Patrick's daughters, Alicia thought she ought to give Mia the benefit of the doubt. The girls were well-behaved and lovely, so surely a mother of such daughters couldn't be all bad? Alicia knew that divorce brings the very worst out of people.

This now seems to have been an utterly naive attitude. But what did Mia want? Surely she's too busy with her new relationship and her position in the Eriksson family business? Patrick said that she was now heading the property side of the enterprises, which, as far as Alicia could tell, included everything from a large real estate portfolio to digital startups. Plus, she was the primary carer for the girls—they only came to visit Patrick every other weekend. Times when Alicia usually went back to Sjoland, on the islands, to visit her mother, Hilda, and step-dad Uffe. On these occasions, she often thought about Mia and the girls crossing the Ålandshav in the opposite direction.

Patrick is always a little detached after these visits from the girls, although it never affects their lovemaking. If possible, he's more passionate on those Sunday afternoons after he's waved his daughters goodbye. Although Patrick had—financially speaking—a good divorce settlement, he'd had to give up time with Sara and Frederica.

Alicia's conscience is clear. The divorce had nothing to do with her. When she first set eyes on the blonde Swede on the ferry, Mia was already seeing another man.

Patrick was heartbroken, he told her later, even if the marriage had been a mistake from the very start.

Kurt Eriksson, Mia's father, had never accepted a lowly reporter as his son-in-law, and Mia's infatuation with him soon waned after the children were born. Alicia, who was still grieving for her son, couldn't understand how, according to Patrick, Mia was at times uninterested in her children. As soon as she was able, she went back to work as a realtor, leaving Patrick in charge of childcare. It was only the previous spring, when Mia confessed to her affair with Max von Rosengard, a well-heeled Swedish businessman, that she'd decided to move back to Åland and bring the girls fully into the Eriksson family fold. Before this, they had lived in Östermalm, the most swanky part of Stockholm.

Mia and Alicia had never really been friends when they were growing up, even though Mariehamn was a small place and everyone knew each other. Alicia was a year above Mia at school, but it was impossible not to be aware of Mia. Wearing the latest fashion—even then—Mia had expensive bikes, was driven to school in winter in her father's Jaguar (then the only one on the islands), and threw the most sought-after birthday parties.

Alicia had not been invited to any of the Eriksson family functions until last summer, when Patrick had persuaded her mother, Hilda, to bring her and Uffe along to their Midsummer Party, the highlight of the islands' summer calendar. Hilda jumped at the chance to mingle with Åland's high society. Alicia wanted to stay at home, but it became too impolite to do so. Besides, her mother would never have forgiven her.

It was during the party that Patrick and Alicia had kissed for the first time, on a beach built by Kurt Eriksson for his grandchildren. Alicia often wonders what would have happened if she had stuck to her guns and not gone to the party. Would Patrick and Alicia have had the tumultuous affair that had consumed them last summer? The affair that Alicia had ended after discovering that her son had made Frida, a local girl, pregnant. She'd wanted to try to make her own marriage work for the sake of her new family.

In the end, Liam and Alicia had grown too much apart to save their marriage. Liam was committed to his work as a consultant in a busy London hospital and Alicia didn't want to go back to the UK. When it turned out that little Anne Sofia wasn't their granddaughter after all, they had nothing left in common.

Alicia turns toward Patrick and sees that he's closed his eyes. It's been a busy weekend, and they'd both been tense, wishing it to go as well as possible with the girls. She decides to let Patrick sleep and gets out of bed.

Walking through the lounge, she gazes at the turquoise velvet sofa, with the fluffy pillows, and the vast rug with a swirly pattern. She looks at the white bookcase against one wall, filled with pot plants and trendy publications, and then at the two pale lounge chairs with wooden armrests placed opposite the sofa. She examines the chairs more closely. They're made of pleated leather webbing and much more expensive than she'd thought when she first saw them.

Now she can see Mia's touch everywhere.

Even the bed, where she and Patrick just made love, and had done so many times before, is in Mia's style. Did she buy the white linen bedding as well?

Alicia's immediate reaction is to flee the place and never touch anything in the apartment again, but she knows that's impractical. What does it matter if Mia chose the interior?

If she did.

It is possible that Mia is twisting the truth. Alicia needs to ask Patrick, but she doesn't want to wake him up and start another argument tonight.

Alicia sinks into the trendy sofa and puts her head into her hands. She's fooling herself. She'll never feel happy here again.

FIVE

The place is one of the trendy, buzzy restaurants that surrounds Södermalm, the southern part of the city, close to Patrick's apartment. While Alicia has been getting used to living in Stockholm, they've eaten out nearly every night. And it's often Patrick who picks up the bill, something that bothers Alicia more than she thought it might. She's sensitive about the balance of their relationship, especially today, after the fight they had yesterday.

All night she'd been thinking about Mia. Why, if she'd known all along that Alicia was living with Patrick, did Mia want to see her now? Perhaps it was to do with the girls? It had been the first time Alicia had stayed in Stockholm on one of Patrick's weekends with the children. It had gone reasonably well. The oldest, Sara, had been a little cool to begin with on the Friday Patrick brought them home, but she had warmed up when they'd found a trendy new store selling reclaimed clothes on Ringvägen. The girl was a great fan of Greta Thunberg, something Alicia found encouraging.

Money had been one of the things she'd thought would never come between her and Patrick, but here it was. And so soon in their relationship. They'd only been living together for a matter of months!

But she has no choice but to stay put with Patrick in Mia's apartment for now. Her salary from her new journalism job at *Dagens Finans* is a pittance and Stockholm is an expensive city. Just buying the season ticket for the commute to the offices in town takes nearly a quarter of her earnings. Plus she needed smart clothes (mostly bought secondhand, though) for her role on the financial daily. There is still no sign of her own divorce settlement, which will largely consist of half of the proceeds from the sale of the house that she shared with Liam for nearly twenty years. The house had been on the market since the middle of January, but was not attracting viewings.

'You can blame Brexit for that,' Liam told her over the phone the previous day.

'You sure we can't just get a pizza to take home?' Alicia now asks Patrick.

They are waiting in line to be seated and she can see the mouth of a vast oven. Two men wearing chef's whites are removing delicious-looking pizzas with long peels.

Patrick places his arm around Alicia's waist and bends down to kiss her cheek.

'Don't be silly. I don't want to do any dish washing, do you? You must be fed up with housework after clearing up the mess the girls made at the weekend.'

'I guess,' Alicia replies.

She's got absolutely no willpower around Patrick. She doesn't understand what has happened to her. When she was married to Liam, she'd constantly felt the need to assert her own will and her own opinions on matters, whether it was the color of a lampshade or where to go on holiday. As far as Stefan, their son, was concerned, Alicia was in sole charge. Until a few months before the accident, when she'd made the mistake of letting Liam talk her into giving him a moped.

'He's a young man and needs his independence,' he'd said.

Alicia takes a deep breath and tries to stop thinking about her dead son. She is living a new life, apparently with a new personality. She glances over at Patrick. With his tall frame, sun-bleached hair and piercing eyes, he's rarely ignored by female or male admirers. He's also a good dresser: today he's sporting a matte black padded coat over pale blue jeans (the color of his eyes) and a white T-shirt under a heavy cotton shirt. Whether he notices the covert glances, Alicia doesn't know. Up till now at least, he only has eyes for her. She's still not sure how she is this lucky. For one, she is nearly two years older than Patrick, and although she considers herself good-looking (in the right light), she's never thought of herself as a catch. Perhaps it's to do with the sex, which is intoxicating. Now living together, they have gelled even more, becoming adventurous and exploring every part of each other.

'Varsågod,' a thin young woman with a short pixie haircut says, indicating with her hand for Patrick and Alicia to follow her. She's speaking exclusively to Patrick, with a sweet smile on her lips, but he ignores her and turns around to take Alicia's hand.

That's when Alicia sees Ebba, the Åland police chief. As they are making their way across the narrow, crowded room, she spots her sitting at a table next to a brick wall. She's leaning over a massive plate of half-eaten pizza, talking to a woman, whose hand she is holding. The other woman is a little younger than Ebba, in her mid-twenties perhaps. She's dark-skinned, with a thick mop of black hair pinned away from her face with a pair of mother-of-pearl clips. Her eyelashes are painted bright blue and her pink lips are pulled into a smile. The sight of Ebba, with her long, slim frame and short hair, against the younger woman's dramatic makeup and features is striking.

'Hello, Ebba!' Alicia says, but the police woman's reaction is startling. Usually calm and precise with her language and movements, Alicia's old schoolfriend lets go of the young woman's hand and knocks over a glass of red wine, which smashes onto the floor, covering Alicia and two diners at a nearby tables in red blotches.

'I'm so, so sorry...' Ebba stutters, not looking at Alicia but at the other diners and at the young waitress who's come to stand next to Alicia.

'Can you get a cloth or something?' Alicia asks the waiter, who then turns on her heels and heads for the open kitchen with the large pizza oven.

Moments later, Patrick and Alicia are seated at the far end of the restaurant, from where Alicia can just about make out Ebba and the young woman, whom Ebba eventually introduced as 'my friend and colleague' Jabulani. After the waiter mopped the floor, removing shards of glass, and wiped the table clean, Ebba offered to pay the laundry bills of Alicia and the two diners. Everyone declined, and Ebba sat back down with a sigh.

Now the two women are no longer holding hands and are preparing to leave. Alicia feels bad about scaring Ebba. Although they went to school together, and even attended the same university in Uppsala, in Sweden, she and Ebba had never been close.

The previous summer, when Alicia began working for the small local newspaper, she formed what she thought was a friendship with the police chief. Through her profession, Ebba was often pivotal in various news stories that Alicia was investigating. Not that much happened on the islands, but when it did, Ebba was Alicia's first point of call.

'I'm going to go and say goodbye to them,' Alicia says.

Patrick raises his head from behind the menu. They are sitting at a table for four, next to the open kitchen. It occurs to Alicia that it's one of the best tables in the cozy restaurant. He lifts his eyebrows, a smile playing on his lips. 'You think it's wise? You caused havoc last time.'

Alicia leans in and whispers, 'I'm not sure why she's acting like that. If she prefers women, so what?'

Patrick shrugs.

'Perhaps she's old school. You know what the islands are like. Stuck in the Dark Ages. All the same, I'd let her be.'

Alicia thinks back to their brief conversation after the hubbub of the wine and broken glass had subsided. Ebba told her, in her usual terse manner, that she was in Stockholm for a week-long conference. Alicia suggested a coffee or wine after work, to which Ebba replied, 'Sure.'

Alicia now realizes that even though she's only been in Stockholm for a matter of months, she's already missing Åland. And bumping into Ebba, especially after yesterday's encounter with Mia, has rekindled her connection with the islands.

Alicia and Patrick are looking over at the police chief and her friend, when they both turn and wave. Alicia raises her hand and makes the gesture of a phone against her ear. Ebba nods and, guiding her friend in front of her, quickly walks out. Watching them go, both wearing short jackets—Ebba's a beige Burberry check and Jabulani's a bright blue, matching her eyelashes—Alicia notes once again her friend's unusually tall shape. The smaller woman almost disappears into Ebba's shadow.

SIX

O n her way to her new job the following day, Alicia wonders
why she hasn't confronted Patrick about Mia. She just
didn't find the right moment after their passionate love-
making. Or the next day, when they'd gone straight out to eat after
getting home from work. Patrick had suggested going out, saying he
was starving, and Alicia agreed. By then she didn't want to spoil the
evening with talk of money.

Alicia finds herself blushing when she thinks about the desire that
Patrick rouses in her. Surely something like that cannot last? What's
more, they are both in their late thirties, not kids anymore.

She can't remember ever feeling the same way with Liam. Sex
with him was good, but nothing like she's experienced with Patrick.
Besides, she fell pregnant so quickly after she met Liam, there was no
time to consider whether their relationship was perfect or not. She
was so young, barely twenty-one, that she didn't know what a good
relationship was. But she'd been in love; there was no doubt about
that. What she's learned is that there can be several kinds of love.
When Stefan was born her love for Liam intensified, because he had
given her such a beautiful boy.

The train comes to a stop at T-Centralen and people start rushing
out of the door. Alicia also gets up and glances at her watch. She's half

an hour early for work. She cannot get used to how short her new commute is. In London going almost anywhere would take an hour, whereas here, she barely needs thirty minutes door to door.

The office, as usual, is busy. It's an open-plan arrangement, but unlike at *Ålandsbladet* on the islands, the desks are smoky glass and the dividers a stylish pale gray. The matching chairs are ergonomically designed to support each part of your back while you write.

The Editor, Gunnel Nordsten, who has an office to the side of the large space, with windows overlooking the other editors and reporters, is a wiry, gray-haired woman whose reading glasses hang off leopard print straps. She holds an editorial meeting each morning at 1 o am.

Alicia has only been invited to one so far, the day after she started, 'To introduce her to the team.' It was a scary occasion, especially as she was introduced as an '*Ålänning* who's come to us via London and the *Financial Times*'. Once again, she wanted to point out that her stint at the FT was very short and that she was never on staff but always 'just a freelancer'. But, 'Please call me Gunnel,' as the Editor introduced herself, knew all this, because Alicia made it clear during her interview. Although she'd boasted about Alicia's credentials at the meeting, Gunnel hadn't yet given Alicia any significant assignments. She wasn't even asked to write about Brexit, a subject she knew intimately, although she hadn't kept up with the news as closely as she had in London. So far, all she had written for the paper were articles on the low interest rates, consumer credit levels, and the annual reports of minor industrial companies. Hardly anything that would set the world on fire. Alicia wonders, as she enters the office, twenty-five minutes early, if her job on Sweden's major financial newspaper will turn out to be less stimulating than her work on the islands.

SEVEN

J ust before lunch, Alicia receives a call from Ebba. She's in the middle of writing copy on another company's results, this time a small retail firm that owns a string of secondhand shops in Stockholm, and is glad of the interruption.

'You wanted to meet up?' Ebba says.

'Oh, yes,' Alicia replies. It's surprising that the police chief has got in touch first, because Alicia got the impression that meeting up was the last thing Ebba wanted.

'Lunch?' Alicia's friend says next.

'OK,' Alicia replies. She glances at the large clock at the back of the office and sees it is just coming up to noon. Many of the other reporters have already left for their breaks. Alicia is still not used to the early lunchtimes in Scandinavia after nearly twenty years in the UK.

'You're on Vasagatan, near T-Centralen, aren't you?' Ebba now says. 'I'm at Folkets Hus, so just around the corner. We could go over to Hötorget?'

It's another cold April day, with a northerly wind whipping along the central streets of the city. The spring seems to have stalled. Alicia is wrapped inside her long padded jacket, but even so she's glad to step inside the old Hötorget food hall. Outside, the vegetable and fruit sellers stand behind their colorful displays, clapping their hands together to keep warm. Could be worse, Alicia thinks, at least I work inside a warm office.

Ebba and Alicia agreed to meet in a place called Kajsas Fisk, one of the oldest restaurants in the market hall. Alicia remembers the place from her trips to the city as a student in the nearby university town of Uppsala.

The fish restaurant looks exactly the same as it did then, with dark wooden tables, one black leather sofa, French chairs with curbed backs, and white tiles on the walls. On one side of the room, mirrors reflect a line of spider plants hanging from the roof in front of them, making the space look like a Parisian bistro.

Ebba is already there, seated at the back of the bustling restaurant, reading the menu. She hasn't yet spotted Alicia, which is unusual for the highly perceptive police woman. But what surprises Alicia even more than this, or the earlier unexpected call, is the fact that Ebba is drinking a glass of red wine as she reads the menu. Didn't she say she was in Stockholm to attend a conference?

Many times when Alicia has met up with Ebba on the islands, whether in a café or once when the police chief came to see Alicia in Sjoland, she would refuse an alcoholic drink on the grounds of being on duty. Didn't attending a professional conference count as being on duty too?

'Hello,' Alicia says, standing in front of the police chief.

'It's strange to see you here in Stockholm,' Alicia says after she's sat down and they've both ordered the specialty: fish soup. Alicia asks for water, while Ebba indicates to the male waiter that she wants a top up.

'Hmm,' the police chief says and continues, 'I'm here almost every weekend, but now I'm on holiday.' She indicates her empty glass.

They are interrupted by a different waiter who places a large glass of wine in front of Ebba and removes the old one.

'Well, it's nice to see you,' Alicia says.

Ebba takes a large gulp of her drink and leans toward Alicia.

'This is a bit awkward,' the police woman says.

'Oh?'

'Well, you met my, um, friend, Jabulani, last night?'

'Yes?'

Ebba takes a deep intake of breath and says, 'She's my girlfriend.'

'I guessed as much,' Alicia says.

Ebba's eyes widen.

'You knew?' she says.

Alicia smiles and nods.

'It makes no difference to me. I'm just glad to see you happy.'

Ebba takes another large mouthful of wine.

'Well, the thing is, it's quite a new relationship and I'd appreciate if you didn't mention it to others.'

Alicia is taken aback. Now that she's told her, it makes perfect sense that Ebba is gay. She can't recall Ebba having any boyfriends, or even being in any way flirty with boys at school, or at university. She thought it was Ebba's tall stature that made her feel awkward around boys, most of whom were shorter than her. But why does she feel the need to keep it quiet?

'My family, you know they're quite old-fashioned...I haven't come out to them yet.'

'OK. No worries, I'm not much of a gossip anyway,' Alicia says.

'Yeah.' Ebba says and fiddles with the stem of her wine glass. She adds, 'But you are a journalist. And my colleagues in Mariehamn don't know either. Not that it has anything to do with them or is relevant to my work. Still, it's a small community out in Åland.'

Alicia stretches her hand across and touches her friend's fingers.

'Look, I know it's none of my business, and absolutely, I won't tell a soul.'

Alicia catches Ebba's eyes across the table.

'Keeping a secret like this is hard. Take it from me, when you love someone you want to tell everyone about it.'

Ebba's face crumbles and for the first time since Alicia has known her, the police chief looks as if she's about to cry.

Alicia squeezes her fingers and adds, 'You can talk to me any time.'

Ebba nods.

'Thank you.'

. . .

Back in the newspaper office, Alicia sits down at her desk and thinks about her friend. She feels sorry for Ebba and hopes she can soon find the strength to tell her family and colleagues who she really is. It seems crazy that in 2019 a woman should find it difficult to tell her nearest and dearest that she's gay, but Ebba is right, the island community can be narrow-minded.

She remembers Ebba's parents being highly religious. Not part of any sect, but they went to church every Sunday. She recalls how Ebba once told her at school that her family said a prayer before every meal. But the Lutheran Church didn't have a problem with homosexuality, nor did the Finnish police force, so Alicia hopes Ebba will find the strength within herself to come out soon.

Remembering the islands, Alicia's thoughts turn to little Anne Sofia. Alicia takes out her phone and scrolls down the latest pictures Frida has loaded onto the family app. Even though she's not related to the baby by blood, she feels connected to her. Frida has promised that Alicia will still be her grandmother, and the love she has for the little girl hasn't faded since she found out who the real father was.

EIGHT

Mia is sitting in the à la carte restaurant on the ferry, watching Sara, her eldest daughter, pick at her plate of limp lettuce and a mixture of, frankly, tired-looking vegetables. Since she became infatuated with the climate activist, Greta Thunberg, she's become vegan and Mia worries that she's not getting enough nutrients. Before, her favorite food was meatballs, burgers, and pasta bolognese.

'Are you going to eat that?' Mia snaps, immediately regretting the sharp tone of her voice.

Sara gives her mother an icy look and drops her fork loudly onto the plate. A few people in the restaurant glance at the woman and two girls sitting at the round table in the middle of the small space. Mia tries to ignore them, but can feel the eyes of the other diners boring into her. They'll all know who she is, and probably that she's just fetched her two daughters from their father's place in Stockholm. The gossip mill on the islands is even more unbearable than Mia remembered. Although they can largely control what's written about the Eriksson family in the main paper, since it's owned by her father, there's still the online stuff.

Once, in a weak moment right after the divorce, Mia scanned the various Facebook groups and found that many of them were full of detailed information about her life. They knew that her new boyfriend was Max von Rosengard, the son of a titled family in Stockholm, and that he was 'stinking rich', as one of the contributors put it. There were even pictures, taken covertly while Mia and Max had been out in Mariehamn. This kind of stuff just didn't happen in Stockholm. When Mia had last lived permanently on the islands, she'd been too young for the gossip columns. Besides, Facebook and social media hadn't existed back then.

Mia tries not to groan when she sees Sara has now picked up her phone and is frantically tapping at it. Most likely writing a message about her 'lame mother' to friends, or posting on Instagram, or whatever site is popular among the young nowadays.

'Look Mom, I've eaten it all,' Frederica says, showing Mia her empty plate.

Two and a half years younger than Sara, Frederica, her blonde and blue-eyed nine-year-old daughter, is an angel in comparison, always the one trying to keep the peace. Mia knows she doesn't give her enough attention. She reaches her hand out and strokes Frederica's back.

'Good girl,' she says. 'Would you like a dessert?'

'I'll have the vegan ice-cream,' Sara pipes up without looking at her mother.

Her eyes are still fixed on her phone, and her fingers don't stop tapping for a moment.

'Didn't we agree no phones at the dinner table?' Mia says, again too sharply.

She knows she should refuse to buy Sara dessert since she didn't even try to eat her main course, but she can't risk the girl embarrassing her.

Sara exhales loudly, but puts her phone inside the 'I'm with Greta' canvas bag that she now insists on carrying everywhere. She's vowed never to wear animal products and insists on all her clothes being made out of recycled material or bought from a secondhand shop. Mia can see her point, and even agrees with the girl, but it's costing her a fortune to source things that are now acceptable to her.

'It's good for the young to be passionate and principled about something,' Patrick had said to her when she complained about Sara's behavior.

Of course, Patrick wouldn't understand. Now that the girls are living with Mia on the islands, Patrick gets to be the cool parent. The one the girls have fun with. He doesn't have to worry about the sports kit that definitely does not come in organic, recycled cotton, or have to decide what to do with all of Sara's designer clothes. Some of which have never been worn.

Patrick.

Mia's thoughts return to her ex and that woman. Even at school, Alicia had been aloof, as if she considered herself to be better than anyone else. Mia's father was the richest man on the islands. What did Alicia have? A Finnish mother who'd managed to catch herself a well-to-do farmer and a father whom no one knew anything about. She could be part gypsy for all anyone knew. Or Russian.

Oh, how Mia misses being with someone. She's not suited to a single life. But she doesn't want to think about Max. He was all over her when she was still married, telling her he loved her and wanted to move to the islands and 'be a family'. Fat chance! Only two weeks after the divorce was done, Max started to stay in Stockholm for extended periods, citing work commitments. He'd say he needed to go for a day and then stay overnight at the last minute. One night a week became two, then five and eventually, just before the text he'd sent telling her 'it was all too much' for him, he'd stayed away a whole week.

Mia found out later that he'd started seeing another woman, a Russian model of all people, as early as September.

So that was that.

When Mia told her mother and father, she could see they were surprised. But they'd kept their mouths shut, thank goodness. Mia and Max had been living with her parents, in the large Villa Havis in the center of Mariehamn. The family hadn't even had time to find a suitable place for the four of them before Max decided he'd had enough of the islands.

'Plenty more fish in the sea,' Kurt had said, giving Mia a hug.

Her mother, Beatrice, had said nothing. Mia knew she thought she'd made a mistake getting rid of Patrick so quickly.

'Marriage isn't always easy,' she'd said to Mia when she'd started talking about the difficulties she and Patrick were having. That was about a year ago. Mia had already met Max by then and was falling for him. The sex was out of this world, but now Mia wonders if that was because the passion had been illicit? The secret meetings, the coded messages, the phone calls late at night when Patrick and the children were already asleep.

She remembers standing on the balcony of her and Patrick's penthouse in Östermalm, talking to Max on her cell. It had been a late May evening and the skies were clear over the sea. Max was whispering sweet nothings into her ear while she was sitting on a wicker chair, wrapped up in a blanket against the chilly spring night. They'd been talking about how much they missed each other and how they needed to share their lives. Mia had wished Patrick would just disappear at that moment so that Max could jump in a cab and be with her.

What a bastard Max turned out to be. Mia now wonders how she was so stupid to believe everything he told her.

As it is, Max is still married, 'trying to fix his relationship with Justina'. Justina, who is from an upper-class Swedish family like him, with several properties in Stockholm, an estate in southern Sweden, and a chateau in France. It was the money that convinced Max to work on his marriage to the sickly thin, cold-hearted bimbo, Mia is certain of it. What was it with blondes that made men go weak at the knees? No, Max was not in love with Justina. It wasn't her looks that won him over. He was in love with her family's money and influence. If the rumor mill in Stockholm was anything to go by, he was already seeing the Russian model on the side.

Justina's father is a member of the Swedish Nobel Academy and her aunt a well-known crime novelist, whose books are translated into 30 different languages, with a Netflix series due to start streaming next year. The books are nothing but trash, but they make money, turning Anna af Friesen into a world-renowned author.

Unlike Mia's own mother, who writes serious historical novels about famine in Finland. She won the Finlandia Prize some years earlier, but no one from a US film or TV company had come knocking. And never would, Mia is certain of it. Plus the Erikssons, although wealthy by island standards, had neither the kind of money the af Friesens had nor the title. Mia's father, as he reminds Mia on an almost daily basis, is the son of a simple farmer. Max wanted to stay with his own kind, that was the long and short of it.

Mia thinks back to when she told her father about Max. In spite of Albeit Kurt's humble background—or possibly because of it—he was impressed by the family name. Mia knew her father had never really got on with Patrick. They saw life through completely different lenses. Patrick preferred being at home with Sara and Frederica to putting the hours in at *Journalen*. Kurt knew the owner of the Swedish paper and kept an eye on his progress, reading all his articles and always commenting on Patrick's lack of headline stories. It drove Patrick mad, but he bore the insinuated insults for the sake of Mia, and later the girls. For Patrick, family was more important than being a celebrated journalist.

Mia looks out of the window of the restaurant and scans the seascape. The ships pass bare, lonely outcrops in the steel-gray sea. This starkly beautiful archipelago is her home; this is who she is. And Patrick had accepted that. A good father, he could also be a prize-winning reporter if only he concentrated on his work instead of getting sidetracked by other things.

Like love.

In the beginning they had been so happy. Even her parents had liked Patrick. Mia understood that Kurt had seen a little of himself in Patrick. Patrick also came from a humble background, his father a steel worker up in northern Sweden, but he'd made his way up to a staff journalist in the largest newspaper in Sweden. And what did Mia see in him?

She looks at her daughters, now both eating ice cream. Frederica is the spitting image of her father, blonde and blue-eyed, while Sara has Mia's dark hair and slim face, as well as her determination. Mia knows it's because they are so alike, that they often clash, but she can't help getting agitated by her eldest daughter. She must be more patient, she thinks, as she touches the sleeve of Sara's secondhand organic cotton hoodie.

'Is the ice-cream nice?'

But Sara moves her arm away as if her mother had burned it with her touch.

'Get off,' she says and gives Mia a murderous look.

'Excuse me for trying to be nice,' Mia says and, seeing the girls have finished their food, adds, 'If you want to get up, I'll get the bill. Meet you in the tax-free shop?'

'I'm not buying anything. Shops like that are there just to encourage excessive consumerism,' Sara says, getting up anyway.

'Where will you be in that case?' Mia asks, ignoring another thinly veiled criticism of her lifestyle. Mia uses these regular trips to Sweden to top up her drinks cabinet. Wine and champagne, especially, is often much cheaper on board. She buys other things, too, that she doesn't strictly need. Like cashmere scarves and makeup. She sighs. There was a time very recently when both girls loved shopping with their mother.

'Come with me,' Frederica pleads with her sister. 'You don't have to buy anything. Pleeeease,' the girl adds, lengthening her vowels the way Sara usually speaks. Mia finds it annoying, but she forces her lips into a smile. She's not going to give her eldest the satisfaction of knowing how much it gets to her to see Frederica pick up Sara's habits.

The plea softens her sister.

'OK. I'll show you which are the worst single-use plastic products, which you should absolutely boycott,' Sara says, marching out of the restaurant, closely followed by her little sister.

'I'll see you there, don't go anywhere else!' Mia shouts after them.

NINE

Patrick is trying not to get riled by Mia's antics, which he knows are intended to provoke him. Why is she acting this way? He thinks back to the evening when they met in Stockholm nearly fifteen years ago.

He was drinking a beer on a late August evening on the outdoor terrace of Sturehov, a posh restaurant, with a colleague who frequented those kinds of places. Adam was a few years younger than him and a trainee at the newspaper. Being from a wealthy family, with a private income, the young man didn't need to work, but he had a passion for journalism and was a good kid. Patrick and Adam had struck up a friendship and after a particularly exciting day when the two had been working on a story on political intrigue inside the government, Adam had insisted on buying Patrick a drink.

When he saw Mia, a tall woman with long dark hair and bright red lips, turn toward the restaurant, Patrick couldn't take his eyes off her. At the time, he was recovering from a relationship with a fellow reporter, who had moved to New York to work on the *Washington Post*. Patrick knew that if he'd had an offer like that, he would have been tempted too, but he'd foolishly thought they were in love. They'd been living together in a small apartment in Södermalm, the south side of the city, for nearly two years. They'd been talking about having children when Emma received a surprise offer from the other side of the world. At the time when Patrick met Mia, Emma had been away for three months. At first, she'd messaged him daily, but nearly a month followed without hearing from her. He assumed she'd found someone new to love, and he decided he needed to move on.

And there, suddenly, was Mia standing over their table, talking to Adam. It seemed they knew each other. Patrick heard her Finnish accent, something that he immediately found sexy. When Patrick introduced himself, Mia set her dark eyes on him and smiled.

'Please join us,' Patrick said, keeping his gaze on this amazing woman.

Mia had briefly glanced over the busy terrace and inside the restaurant, as if to see whether there was a better offer. She slid into the seat next to Patrick and smiled. 'I can't stay long. I'm meeting someone.'

Of course she's seeing someone, Patrick thought, and asked if she'd like a glass of champagne.

At his words, Adam's eyes shot up, and when Mia nodded, Patrick indicated to one of the waiters, leaning against the doorframe by the entrance. The guy, wearing a long white apron, moved slowly toward them. It was the arrogance of the staff, as well as the cost of drinks, that kept Patrick away from places like this. But now he was pleased he had accepted Adam's offer.

He was mesmerized by both Mia's appearance and her accent. She radiated confidence when she talked to him about Åland.

'What brings you to Stockholm?' Patrick asked.

Mia set her beautiful eyes on Patrick and delayed her reply by sipping the glass of champagne.

'Oh, Daddy has some business interests here and I have a seat on the Board, so I needed to attend a meeting.'

Patrick nodded and glanced briefly in Adam's direction. He was sitting on the other side of Mia, opposite Patrick. Adam's expression didn't change, but then he was used to mingling with the Swedish upper classes, Patrick reminded himself.

He thought back to Åland. The Finnish islands were a popular tourist destination for the masses. Not a place for wealthy Finns or Swedes. He himself had visited the islands only a couple of times, on a

Marie Line cruise, and had only once spent any time ashore. He and Emma had rented a cottage by the sea the first summer they were together. He fondly recalled the sauna, swimming naked in the sea and catching fish for dinner. Their cottage was beautiful and homely, but it was not luxurious.

Patrick cannot resist a smile when he remembers how Mia had got Adam and Patrick an invitation to a party that night and how he'd ended up kissing her on a deserted street in Gamla Stan, the old part of town.

Mia's friends were all rich, it was obvious, even though no one mentioned money. And no one seemed to have a proper job either. They were impressed by Patrick's position at the *Journalen*. At the time, he'd just been promoted to Copy Editor, and he was immensely proud. Who would have thought that a poor boy from a small town in northern Sweden would be rising up the ranks of one of the major newspapers in Sweden? He'd still been ambitious, then.

Now Patrick sighs and looks around the newspaper office. It's a busy open-plan space, with windows overlooking the wide city streets below. Faint sunlight is streaming in, and the tall pot plants scattered here and there are turned toward the light. It's spring, a time for hope and renewal.

Patrick nods at Adam, who is now a firm feature in the office. He's turned out to be a solid reporter, showing great promise in both his writing ability and his talent for getting the truth out of difficult, slippery politicians. His wealthy background helps him pin down even the most reclusive public figures. The other reporters are either concentrating on their screens or chatting with each other over a coffee.

Just as surprising as his early success at the paper is the fact that the editor agreed to give him his old job back at *Journalen*. When he resigned, after it became clear that Mia was going to divorce him, he had given up all hope of a celebrated career in journalism. He had wanted to retire (at the age of thirty-six!) and look after the girls full-time. He was the natural choice, since he was the hands-on parent. He had already been doing most of the parenting, ferrying the girls to and from school, taking them to their weekend dancing lessons, cooking them dinner. Mia didn't have it in her to mother anyone—even her own daughters. Which is why her behavior now is so out of character.

Surely Mia can't be jealous of Alicia? It was Mia after all who had the affair, who wanted a divorce as quickly as possible. And she wanted him to move away from the islands, back to Stockholm, while Patrick had wanted to stay close to Sara and Frederica.

And Alicia.

When Mia wouldn't budge, he had decided to ask for his job back and persuade Alicia to join him in Stockholm. He couldn't believe his luck when Alicia finally agreed. The only downside now is seeing his daughters so rarely, but he hopes this will change as they grow older. Soon, they'll be able to take the ferry between Åland and Stockholm on their own.

He understands now that he was naive in underestimating his own need for a recognized and inspiring job, and the complications that living in a small island community would bring. Especially when those islands were more or less owned by the family of your ex. And the girls need him much less these days. Now that they're nearly teenagers, being seen with Dad is mostly an embarrassment. While he knows Sara and Frederica love him dearly, it's clear they are becoming independent young women. Which is what he wants.

Moving back to Sweden and his old role as managing editor at *Journalen* was a good decision. The icing on the cake was Alicia agreeing to move with him to Stockholm. It exceeded all his wildest dreams, so why is he still feeling unsettled?

TEN

Leo Tuomainen hasn't visited the Åland Islands since he was in his late teens, or was it early twenties? As he scans the vast sea beyond the shipping lane from his cozy vantage point in the ship's bar, he remembers a tall, slim, smiling man full of hope for the future, like the promise of oblivion that an unopened bottle of Koskenkorva now brings him. He was going to be a famous artist, perform in the coolest venues across the world, not just in Helsinki, or even Stockholm and Copenhagen. No, his music and guitar solos would be enjoyed by screaming fans across Europe, the US, even Japan. 'Big in Japan' had rung in his ears as he led his first band, *The Three Lions* (named after Leo), formed with Jari and Juha, on a support gig for Kirka, then the top Finnish solo artist.

The ship's only bar is almost full, mostly with groups having their office parties. Occasionally, they sing along to the pop songs piped out of the invisible speakers. When a song by *Wham!* comes on a loud cheer goes up and Leo decides to give into his need for nicotine. He's got to brave the upper deck to take a few drags of Marlboro Lights, before the wind and rain become too much for even the most ardent smoker. You wouldn't believe it's April. The spring is a long time coming this year.

As he returns to the bar, he brings with him a strong draught of cold air. The barman looks up and nods, indicating the nearly empty glass he'd left behind on the bar. Leo nods in reply, and the waiter turns around to fill a new pint.

Back in Helsinki, he'd decided that he would stay sober on this journey. Just a pint or two in the bar after the free drinks with his meal in the 'Marie Line's world famous sea buffet'. The one being poured is his second—and his last. A man has to keep himself occupied on such an important quest, right? The second beer is sliding down well and brings him close to the melancholy that too little alcohol often causes. He'll need another pint to get rid of that, he thinks.

What else but regret has brought him back to the islands? Leo digs into his coat pocket and reads the email with an address in Sjoland, which he'd printed out just in case. It's a short taxi ride from the main city, Mariehamn, he'd learned while gazing at the map of Åland on his ancient Dell laptop. He also learned that he could take a bus into town from the ferry terminal. More investigations showed him that there was also a bus to his final destination and the reason for his trip. Briefly, he considers taking the bus immediately on arrival, but then thinks better of it: there would only be a confrontation with *her*. She would only call him names and throw him out into the bitterly cold day, as she did from the apartment in Helsinki all those years ago.

'You need to get up, we've docked in Mariehamn!'

Leo wakes up to loud banging and realizes someone is outside his cabin. He glances at his watch and swears under his breath.

'Alright!' Leo shouts and opens the door.

He's in his underpants. A young woman, wearing a head scarf, takes a step back. He sees she looks frightened and feels ashamed of the state he's in. He has no idea how many drinks he had in the bar in the end. Judging by a painful pounding in his head, it was more than five pints. A faint recollection of Jägermeister chasers enters his mind and he groans. The woman takes two further steps back, hitting the wall of the narrow corridor where the cheap cabins are situated.

Leo raises his hand and says, 'How much time do I have?'

The woman glances at her watch. 'Three minutes.'

Leo just makes it to Deck Four before the two uniformed men

shut the doors behind him. The air outside is cold and he wraps his old leather coat tightly around his body.

This was a terrible idea. I've managed to live without her for three, nearly four decades. Surely I can live till the end of my days without seeing her again?

Outside the small terminal building in Mariehamn, in the faint light of a spring afternoon, he finds the bus waiting and steps inside. He lets the heating of the interior warm his bones. As he walks along the aisle to the row of seats at the back, where he thinks he might continue to sleep the drink off, he nods to the other passengers, who stare at him. He's kept them all waiting, but he doesn't care. He can hear an older woman tut as he passes.

Leo curls his fingers around the piece of paper in his pocket. It has the address of the hostel he'd managed to book online with his limited knowledge of both Swedish and the workings of the internet. It wasn't cheap, but it was close enough to the center where he can take the bus to Sjoland. But that is later today. First he would sleep the hangover away and think about what to do when he feels better. He resists the thought of a cold beer and how that would immediately cure him. He thinks about what the doctor told him. And that question, 'Do you have any close family you should tell?'

It was those words about a family uttered by the hospital physician, a young man with wisps of blond strands resting on the collar of his white jacket, that rang in his ears.

'If you don't stop drinking, your body will give up. As it is, your kidneys and liver aren't functioning properly, and your diabetes— untreated as it is—can lead to a stroke, or even heart failure. To be honest, Mr. Tuomainen, I'm surprised you're presenting as fit as you are.'

This was after he'd been admitted, after he'd fallen on the Boulevard and just missed being run over by a tram. Some bystander had called the police, mainly because he'd been drunk and reeking of alcohol. But the constable thought it was more serious and took him to the hospital in Malmi. Apparently he was concussed, but he couldn't remember any of it. The events were all recounted to him by a particularly unpleasant nurse when he'd woken up some twelve hours later.

It was this nurse that had first asked him if there was anyone they should call to inform of his whereabouts. Leo had just shaken his head. 'Shaken' was the word that came to mind to describe the way he'd been feeling after this incident.

Thinking back to earlier that evening, he remembered meeting up with his drinking pal, Simo, in Punavuoren Ahven to have a few beers to celebrate the end of the month and his receipt of the latest interest payment, which came as regularly as clockwork. Getting paid to do nothing had been a revelation to Leo. Since his expenses amounted to rent, a little food, a few tram fares into town from his apartment in Kallio, much of the money was left over for beer. At the end of the month, when his investment yields dropped into his account, he raised a glass to toast his parents.

Who would have thought that a steel worker and a housewife could amass such a fortune in shares over their short lifetimes? After they died within two months of each other, and the stony-faced solicitor told him about their secret riches, Leo had vowed to leave the capital untouched. He would pass it on to his own daughter.

It was the least he could do.

When he was released from hospital, he rang Simo and went on another three-day bender. Finally, when they'd both run out of money, the words of the nurse and the doctor rang in his ears. He decided to sober up and look up Alicia.

She was his daughter after all.

Leo gazes through the window at the bleak scene in front of him. Åland was supposed to be a summer island, or at least the climate was rumored to be more clement than on the Finnish mainland. So what was this storm all about?

At least the room he is renting is warm, and clean. There is even a small fridge, where he stacked a few cans of the beer, and the bottle of Koskenkorva vodka he'd bought on the ferry. In the corner stands a small stove with a coffee maker next to it. Leo needs to find a supermarket, or a cheap cafe for breakfast, so he decides to brave the weather. For warmth, he takes a swig out of the vodka bottle and heads out of the door.

Once outside, he walks along the main street and finds a cafe that serves breakfast and alcohol. He's promised himself not to drink too much, but the bloody storm has changed his mind. If he is to meet his long-lost daughter, he needs to keep his strength up.

Leo steps inside Marie Bar and sees immediately he's in the right place. Inside the dimmed, sparsely decorated interior a couple of lonely men sit at separate tables, drinking pints of beer. He nods to both of them and goes to the counter. He tries to speak Finnish, but the woman with graying roots in her thin black hair, shakes her head. He tries English, to which the woman gives a loud grunt. Her face is pallid and her eye makeup at least two days old.

Leo points at a ham and cheese roll, sitting on a plate inside a glass cabinet, and at a coffee machine behind the woman.

'Kaffe och en morgonroll? Annat?' the woman says in a loud voice, and understanding that she'd got the order right, Leo nods. He then touches a beer tap in front of him. The woman gets a tall pint glass from behind the counter and shows it to him.

'Morgongöl också?'

Leo somehow understands that the woman means a morning beer, and he smiles.

She pulls her lips upward, revealing a set of yellowing teeth.

The sum displays on the till. Leo pays and finds a space in the furthest corner of the cafe. The woman sits back down at a chair she's set for herself behind the counter and begins leafing through a magazine. There is not a sound in the place, no piped music, for which Leo is glad.

There is nothing worse than some modern, American trash playing when you are trying to have a quiet breakfast.

After two beers and the roll, Leo feels more able to carry on with his task. He returns to his room at the hostel and, pouring himself a small measure of Koskenkorva, begins to study a bus timetable and a map of the islands that he'd been given at the bus station, opposite the Marie

Bar. At least there they'd spoken Finnish and Leo was able to tell them where he needed to go.

He glances at his watch and sees it's already past one o'clock. Another beer or two wouldn't go amiss, he thinks, and opens the fridge. It's then that he realizes he didn't get any food and swears under his breath. Thinking back to his walk along the near deserted rainy street, he can't remember seeing a supermarket anywhere, or even an R-Kiosk. Glancing at the window, he sees that the weather has got worse, with the harsh wind accompanied by pouring rain.

Perkele.

Leo uses his favorite Finnish swear word to spur himself on, and once more steps outside. He bends his head against the wind and rain and starts off in the opposite direction from Marie Bar and the temptation of another beer. He has taken the small bottle of Koskenkorva with him, tucked inside his padded jacket, just in case.

ELEVEN

Hilda watches the rain falling onto the surface of the sea. She wonders where the sunny days of spring have gone. She looks at her watch: it's 10am on a Wednesday and she ponders what her daughter is doing right now. She thinks about sending her a note, but decides against it. During the last exchange of messages yesterday, Alicia asked if she and Uffe were alright. When Hilda took some time to compose the appropriate reply, Alicia had rung her with concern in her voice. Hilda missed her daughter terribly, but she didn't want to put demands on her. Alicia was living her new life with a new man in Stockholm and she should be able to do it without worrying about her mother. And really, there isn't anything the matter to bother her with.

Hilda turns away from the kitchen window. Through the open door to the lounge, she can see Uffe has fallen asleep. With that morning's *Ålandsbladet* on his lap, and eyes shut, he looks dead to the world. Hilda waits for the soft snores that usually emanate from her husband's mouth, and gently vibrate his gray mustache. But there's no sound. Or movement. Quickly, Hilda steps close to him and touches Uffe's arm.

'What?' the older man lifts his eyes to Hilda, the look in his watery eyes confused.

'Sorry, you weren't breathing,' Hilda says and goes to sit on one of the other comfy chairs arranged either side of the open fire in the large lounge.

Uffe grunts and lifts his paper up again.

'Why don't we go on a trip? Somewhere warm?'

There's silence, with just the sound of Uffe turning a page of the newspaper.

Hilda exhales again, more loudly this time.

No reaction.

'Uffe!' she says, more forcefully now.

'What?' Uffe's brows are knitted together and he has a stern expression in his eyes.

'Did you even hear what I said?'

Her husband looks blankly at her. He places one hand behind his ear. This infuriates Hilda even more. Last time Uffe had a hearing test, they found absolutely nothing wrong with him. It's a ruse. When he ignores her, which he does daily, he can pretend it's because of his age.

'Don't give me that!' Hilda says and gets up. She's going to drive into Mariehamn and buy herself a dress from a new shop that has just opened inside the Sitkoff shopping center. She cannot stay another second inside this stuffy house with her stuffy husband!

Next morning, Hilda is awake before Uffe. This is so unusual, that she sits up and leans closer toward her husband. He *is* breathing, with his chest going up and down slowly. Hilda exhales in relief. She glances at the clock on her bedside table and sees that it's past eight o'clock. Doesn't Uffe have to oversee something on the farm? It's a Thursday morning, so not even a weekend, although he very rarely sleeps in during holidays either.

'The land doesn't take time off,' he always says.

He's normally gone and out of the house by seven and can be found either in the old milking parlor, which serves as his office, across the yard, or somewhere on the fields, talking to the foreman, Lars Olen.

Hilda places her arm on Uffe's shoulder and gently shakes him, but there's no reaction from her husband. Did he have more to drink last night than usual? Hilda thinks back to what he was like when she returned home and when they were eating dinner. From her memory, he only had a beer and refused a nightcap. She shakes Uffe more forcefully, and eventually gets a reaction.

'What, what is it?' Uffe says as he opens his eyes. They look watery and very gray.

'It's late. You've overslept,' Hilda says.

Uffe stares at her. 'Who are you?'

Hilda glares at her husband of thirty-eight years.

'What do you mean, who am I?' Hilda can feel anger surge inside her. Since Alicia left, she's noticed that Uffe has become much quieter, and often doesn't hear what she says. She knows there is absolutely nothing wrong with his hearing, so it's nothing to do with his health. Being ignored, especially when it is by your husband, is highly frustrating. Hilda decides that she needs to have a serious talk with him.

This will not do!

'Where am I?' Uffe now asks, rising to a sitting position. He looks around the room, seemingly confused. When his gaze returns to Hilda, he smiles, but the expression is one that you'd give to a stranger. Not your wife. Hilda is suddenly conscious of her husband's eyes on her chest. She looks down and realizes her long nightdress is rather revealing at the cleavage. The garment is made out of thin, almost sheer cotton, and is all but see-through.

She lifts her gaze. Uffe has moved closer and is grabbing her waist.

'Isn't this what you want?' he says, with a leery tone. One that Hilda doesn't recognize.

She moves away and gets out of bed, grabbing her velveteen nightgown. Tying the belt firmly, she turns back to Uffe. 'Stop this now. It isn't funny.'

TWELVE

'Look, I'm going to see Mom and Uffe next weekend,' Alicia says.

Patrick lifts his eyes up to her. It was the bright blueness of those eyes that had first attracted Alicia to Patrick, and even now, his direct gaze makes her spine tingle. *I'm becoming a sex addict,* Alicia thinks. They have just got out of bed, after tumbling in after dinner in a nearby restaurant. They are still behaving as if they're on some kind of holiday.

When will reality of the boring everyday kick in?

'But it's a child-free weekend,' Patrick says.

Alicia looks down at her hands. They are sitting on the small balcony overlooking the sea. They both have glasses of red wine in their hands—a post-love-making drink that has become a habit of theirs. The sun has set and darkness envelops them. The air is full of the scent of the recent rain and she has a blanket wrapped around her body to keep warm. She can feel Patrick move an arm around her.

'Is it Mia?'

Alicia rests her head on Patrick's shoulder and strokes the hairs on the back of his hand holding the glass.

'No,' she lies. And then she gives a reason that is not a total lie.

'I'm worried about them. Hilda told me that they had a huge fight this morning and haven't spoken since.'

Patrick places his glass on the small iron table in front of them and lifts her chin up so that she has to face him.

'If you're sure? I'll miss you terribly. Besides, your mom can exaggerate sometimes?'

Alicia is relieved that he's not mentioned Mia again. She nods and leans in to kiss Patrick.

'I need to go. I haven't been back for nearly a month now.'

THIRTEEN

On Saturday morning, Leo wakes up with the habitual fuzzy feeling. His first thought is where to find the bottle of Koskenkorva, but seeing the unfamiliar room around him, he hesitates. He sits up in bed and puts his head in his hands. Today he has to be strong. Alicia and Hilda cannot see him drunk, or hungover. He staggers to the bathroom and fills a mug with water from the tap. He drinks two cupfuls before daring to look in the mirror. What greets him is worse than he feared. His face is lined and gray-looking, with a patchy stubble on his chin. His eyes are bloodshot and his hair stands up in all directions. He runs his hands under the tap, washes his face, and dampens his hair down.

A shower and a shave, breakfast and then a plan for the day.

After standing under the hot stream of water for over fifteen minutes, Leo feels a little better. Wrapping himself in the towel, which is soft and smelling of some kind of flowers, Leo goes back to the bedroom. Ignoring the cans of lager and the half bottle of Koskenkorva on the small desk next to the bed, he opens the curtains and sees the sun is high up in the sky. Its rays sting his eyes, but Leo doesn't flinch. He closes his eyes and lets the light and the warmth of the sun land on his body. He needs it to give him strength. His stomach growls and he decides to go and find some food.

. . .

After two cups of strong coffee and a ham and cheese roll, Leo feels much better, almost human again. He glances at his old watch and sees it's past noon already. He doesn't remember what time he staggered into bed last night, so he doesn't know how long he's been without alcohol. From past experience, he knows that after a binge, the strong need for another drink can start anytime after two to three hours. Over the years, he's learned how to control the desire. Eating is good, as is walking in the fresh air. He's done both now, wandering along the streets of Mariehamn, looking for a place to have breakfast. Perhaps he should walk some more before getting on the bus to Sjoland? He sees a man walk past him with a pint of beer in his hand. He's smiling, talking to a woman behind him. She's holding a large glass of white wine. Leo licks his lips. Surely one pint of low-alcohol beer wouldn't hurt?

No, be strong. She mustn't smell alcohol on your breath.

A memory from when Hilda was pregnant comes to his mind. They had been so young then, barely eighteen and married with a baby on the way. He couldn't cope; his dreams of a career as a pop star crumbling in front of his eyes while Hilda's tummy grew larger. The responsibility of having a family, three mouths to feed, made him feel trapped. But when the baby—Alicia—was born, he immediately felt different. She was so beautiful, so small and vulnerable. He felt like a real man, a father, and just like that the weight was lifted off his shoulders.

But then came the sleepless nights, Hilda's constant complaints about the lack of money, the amount of time he spent away from home, and his apparent inability to look after Alicia. She was a darling, but she needed constant attention and slept badly. Which meant none of them got any rest in the small one-bedroom apartment in Helsinki. And he didn't want to give up his dream of a career in music. Their arguments were terrible. Hilda's tongue had always been sharp, but the things she called Leo, he'd tried to forget over the years.

And then the unthinkable happened. When Alicia was only six months old, Leo came home late. He'd had a gig and he'd stayed out with his friends afterward. He was drunk. When Hilda started shouting at him, waking the sleeping (for once) child, calling him a wastrel and no-good man-child, he lost his temper. He slapped Hilda across the face. A silence followed when Hilda, holding on to her face, straightened herself up and stared at him.

'That's it,' she said.

During the night, which Leo spent lying on a mattress Hilda threw at him in the small living room, Hilda packed all his belongings into a suitcase and told him to leave.

'We'll be better off without you!' she said.

Leo has regretted his actions ever since. He had never hit anyone before, nor since. How did he lose his temper so much that he struck a woman? The mother of his child?

And why didn't he persist? Why didn't he go back to the apartment sooner? After three weeks, which he'd spent sleeping on his parents' sofa, he'd gone back to the apartment in Kallio to ask Hilda's forgiveness. He wished nothing more than for her to take him back. He missed his little girl. He missed the way Alicia would wrap her small fingers around his pinkie, and the way she'd look up at him and smile on the few occasions she'd let him hold her without crying. And he missed Hilda. She was the most wonderful girl he'd ever known, not that he'd gone with many.

But when he got to the apartment it was empty. Completely empty, like someone had wiped his whole life away. He couldn't understand what had happened. Where had Hilda gone?

He'd panicked and phoned the landlord, who wouldn't tell him anything.

Even Hilda's parents wouldn't tell him where to find his wife and child.

Leo had resolved to wait. He was certain that sooner or later Hilda would return, or at least write to him with a forwarding address. He was reassured that she knew the address of his parents, where he'd been living since being chucked out by Hilda.

But months, then years, went by, and even though Leo went looking for Hilda and Alicia each weekend, he couldn't find any trace of them.

He had lost everything.

. . .

Leo watches the young couple, sitting a few tables away from him laugh and flirt with each other. They are wearing jeans and sweaters, and speaking Finnish. Tourists, he thinks. Leo notices that the man's beer is half drunk and fights the desire to go over to the self-service counter and order a pint from the girl with pronounced eyebrows and hair in a long blonde plait. Instead of another drink, Leo makes himself think about what Alicia would look like now. When she was a baby she had light blue eyes and very blonde, almost white, hair, but he'd read somewhere that the coloring babies have at birth often changes. Will she be beautiful like Hilda, with soft curves, or more angular like himself? Not that he's that thin anymore, but he was tall and slim when Hilda last saw him.

Leo shivers. What will she make of him now?

FOURTEEN

'Who is this?'

Hilda is alone in the house. Uffe has, in spite of Hilda's protestations, gone into Mariehamn to talk to his lawyer about his farm accounts. Hilda can't understand what is suddenly so urgent, but he wouldn't be swayed. When the phone rings, Hilda thinks it might be Uffe, asking her to come into town for lunch. Sometimes, when they'd had a bit of a disagreement, he'd treat her to lunch somewhere nice like Indigo, or just at the cafe in Sittkoff's shopping center. They'd eat and perhaps have a glass of wine and, not mentioning the argument, talk about other things, and then go home and make love.

As she listens to the silence at the other end of the line, Hilda tries to remember when they'd last enjoyed each other like that between the sheets. Her thoughts are interrupted when she hears a voice at the other end, speaking in Finnish.

'Hilda, is that you?'

Her breath catches in her throat.

No, it can't be...

Hilda panics and places the receiver back on its hook. For a moment, she stares at the telephone, fixed onto the kitchen wall. She must have been imagining it, surely?

When the ringing starts afresh, Hilda jumps.

For goodness sake, pull yourself together.

She lifts the receiver once more and, trying to sound confident, says, 'Hello.'

'It's me, Leo.'

'What do you want?'

Her hand holding the receiver begins to shake. She leans against the kitchen wall and wraps the fingers of her left hand over her right wrist to steady her grip.

'I just want to talk to you,' Leo says in a quiet voice.

Hilda tries to consider what she should do. She could just put down the phone and not answer if he tries to get hold of her again. He would eventually give up. What if Leo calls when she's not at home? The thought of Leo talking to Uffe makes Hilda's heart race.

His conciliatory tone makes Hilda see another way forward.

'Sorry, it's just a bit of a shock to hear from you after all these years,' she says.

'I bet,' he replies and then carries on, 'Look, I happen to be in Mariehamn at the moment and thought it'd be nice to catch up.'

Hilda stops breathing.

Her ex-husband is in Mariehamn?

'Catch up?' Hilda says incredulously.

'Yes,' Leo replies simply.

'How did you find me?' Hilda asks.

'It isn't much to ask to see you for a coffee, after all these years, is it?'

Hilda is quiet for a moment. The night when Leo came home drunk and hit her comes vividly into her mind.

'You think you deserve that, do you?' she says.

'I looked for you for months and years, you know,' Leo replies.

When Hilda doesn't say anything, Leo adds, 'But now I've found both you and Alicia...'

Hilda shivers. Alicia must not know that her father is alive. She makes a quick decision. 'OK, I can come into town now. But this will just be one coffee, and then we will go our separate ways again. Understood?'

. . .

Hilda agrees to meet Leo in the one cafe in Mariehamn she knows Uffe never goes to. It's a new Italian place, serving food as well as ice creams. The coffee is actually quite good, but in Uffe's mind, a place like that has no place in the islands.

'What's wrong with herring steaks and then pancake for pudding?' he would say.

All of Hilda's arguments about giving tourists what they want have never made an impression on her husband.

'They come to Åland to see the islands as they are, not to eat some foreign rubbish that they can have in Stockholm or Helsinki!' he argues.

The place, called Caffe Bar, is in East Harbor, quite a distance from where the lawyer's offices are on Torggatan, so she's confident they won't bump into Uffe.

That would be disastrous, Hilda thinks as she parks the car outside the cafe.

The new tourist attraction called The Fishing Village is set just beyond the row of jetties of the harbor. The seas beyond the red wooden huts are calm and the storm has passed, leaving lovely sunny weather behind. This area is at the end of a long cove, framed by gently sloping land. It's a sunny but chilly afternoon, with white fluffy clouds hanging high above the water.

She recognizes Leo as soon as she steps inside the bustling cafe. He's sitting in the far corner of the room, stirring a cup of coffee. His light brown hair is as soft as Hilda remembers it, and his frame tall, even though she notices he's filled out in the middle. Her heart begins to beat harder, as she remembers how much she loved this man. She's glad she has a moment before they meet. Reluctantly, she moves her eyes away from Leo.

She's surprised so many people have found their way here from the center of town. They've been tempted no doubt by the delicious smell of coffee. So much for Uffe's theory that tourists don't want an Italian place in Mariehamn!

Hilda scans the room for anyone she knows. She decided before she left Sjoland that if she knew anyone there, she'd ignore Leo and pretend she'd come to buy a couple of Italian cakes. But, to her relief, most of the people sitting at the small round tables seem to be tourists.

FIFTEEN

'You look good,' Leo says as Hilda sits down opposite him in the busy cafe.

Leo is shocked by Hilda's youthful appearance. She's wearing a pair of tight-fitting jeans and a bright red blouse, with a short padded jacket over the top, which she now removes. Her waist is still slim, although, she has filled out a little from when he last saw her, which must be nearly forty years ago. But the added weight suits her. Her face is made up, with red lips, matching her blouse. A few wrinkles here and there around her eyes and mouth reveal that she's no longer young, but my God, she's fared better than most. Better than Leo, that's for sure.

'Well, you look terrible,' Hilda replies.

She looks nervy, but there is a smile hovering around her red lips.

He gives a brief laugh.

There's silence. Leo is madly trying to fill it, but he can't think of anything to say. He can't take his eyes off Hilda.

When she turns her head toward the counter, where two men and a woman are busy with a fancy, steaming coffee maker, he says, 'Would you like a drink? A cappuccino?'

Hilda nods. 'Why not?'

Leo gets up and goes to the counter. As well as the drink, he orders two small, cream-filled cones that the man says are called cannelloni. He remembers them from a visit to Sicily a few years back.

'*Delizioso!*' the man with pitch-black hair and a stripy jumper says, and Leo nods, slightly embarrassed by his effeminate demeanor. He pays, smiles at the man, and takes the cakes and the coffee back to the table.

'So,' he says when Hilda lifts the hot cup to her lips.

Her ice-blue eyes, now slightly faded and showing some gray around the black irises, bore into him, but she doesn't say anything. Instead she takes a bite from the cake and exclaims, 'My, they *are* good!'

Leo smiles. This is how he remembers Hilda. Full of enjoyment for life. That, together with her looks, of course, had attracted him to her all those years ago. She always wanted to try everything, always wanted to enjoy life.

He recalls when once, right after they'd met, they took a picnic to Suomenlinna island outside Helsinki. After they'd eaten their sandwiches and drank the coffee Hilda had brought in a thermos, they got some ice creams from a kiosk by a small swimming beach on the island. Hilda couldn't decide which flavor to choose, so Leo had asked the girl to put all the different flavors onto one cone, filling it as high as she possibly could. Hilda had giggled but managed to eat the whole thing before it melted. She'd told him that it was the best ice cream she'd ever had.

'Do you remember our picnic and your all-flavor ice cream?' Leo says.

'Of course I do,' Hilda replies.

She puts down her half-eaten cannelloni, and looks straight at Leo. 'You didn't come here to reminisce, did you?'

'I want to see her,' Leo says.

He doesn't dare look at Hilda's face. He's sure he'll see nothing but a determination to keep Alicia away from him.

But when another silence settles over their little table, he carefully lifts his eyes toward the woman sitting opposite him. 'I'm ill.'

'I'm sorry to hear that,' Hilda says and there is a softness in her demeanor and voice.

She fiddles with the empty coffee cup in front of her, placing the spoon at an angle on the saucer. Her hands are trembling ever so slightly.

'Alicia is a grown woman, with a life and mind of her own. I can't stop you from contacting her, but I have to tell you that she thinks you are dead,' Hilda says firmly.

Leo feels as if he's been slapped on the face, or worse, as if someone's punched him in the guts.

'Is that how little you thought of me?' he says incredulously.

Hilda isn't looking at him. She moves the spoon around in the saucer. Leo wants to tell her to stop, but he can't.

'You hit me,' she almost whispers.

Leo stretches his hands across the table. He tries to touch the ends of her fingers, but before he can make contact, Hilda pulls them away.

'It was a lifetime ago. And only that one time!' he says, keeping his voice low but forceful enough for Hilda to hear him over the hum of the place.

The coffee house is almost full, and the noise level is high. Many people are having lunch, as well as coffee, and some have glasses of beer or wine in front of them. What Leo would give for a drink! He can taste the hops on his tongue. If Hilda doesn't budge, and let him have Alicia's address or phone number, he's going to go straight to the counter and order himself a beer. Or two.

Hilda puts her padded coat back on and rises from the chair.

'Wait,' Leo says.

He stands up. They face each other.

'As you said, she is a grown-up. Surely she should be able to decide for herself if she wants to see me or not? At least tell me what she's like? Is she married,' here Leo hesitates and adds, 'any children?'

Hilda exhales. She sits down again, but without taking off her coat.

Leo listens while Hilda tells him about how they lost Stefan and how the grief caused Alicia's marriage to break down.

When Hilda has finished, Leo doesn't say anything for a while.

'I'm so sorry,' he then says, almost to himself. 'You know, I never remarried.'

Hilda lifts her pale eyes to Leo and gazes at him for a long time. Surprising him, she smiles. 'No one would have you?'

'Very funny.' For the first time since Hilda sat down in front of him, Leo feels a sense of optimism. Perhaps he will be able to make amends after all? Perhaps Hilda will allow him to make peace with his daughter before he dies?

SIXTEEN

Hilda has no intention of telling Alicia about her real dad. Especially not now, when Uffe is unwell. But she wasn't going to divulge that to Leo. She regrets agreeing to even think about letting him contact Alicia. By the smell and looks of him, he's still a drinker, so no doubt he'll drink himself into oblivion and forget all about his daughter. In any case, why come forward now? He's had nearly forty years to find his family—why do it now when he's at death's door? Meeting her father only to find out that he is seri-ously–terminally–ill would upset Alicia. She's had enough sadness in her life.

And if Uffe died ... But Hilda won't let such thoughts enter her mind. She will get him to the doctor, if it's the last thing she does!

Hilda wonders how much she should tell Alicia about Uffe. Although he's just her stepfather, he's the only dad she has known. And she's very fond of him. Of course, Hilda has nothing concrete to go on Uffe illness, especially as the man won't go and see a doctor. Hilda has a good mind to phone their family physician herself, but she knows what the outcome will be.

'I'm afraid I can't discuss your husband's health issue with you. He has to come and see me,' he will say as he has done so many times before.

It isn't the first time she's worried about her husband. Ten years older than her, Uffe is not far off seventy and needs constant observation. In Hilda's mind, at least.

Doctor Bengtson is known for his gruff disposition, but Hilda knows one way she might be able to get information out of him. The good doctor is very partial to Hilda's baking, particularly her cinnamon buns. So that afternoon after getting home from seeing Leo, Hilda makes a batch of the sweet buns. Still warm from the oven, she takes them to the small island hospital where Bengtson has his practice.

Driving back from the health center, with the smell of cinnamon still lingering in her car, Hilda has a little cry.

'Tell him to come and see me as soon as possible,' Doctor Bengtson had said. Looking at her under his bushy eyebrows, with a grave expression on his tanned face, he added, 'You know how to get your way, Mrs. Ulsson, so use your skills and get Uffe to make an appointment before he has another turn.'

She didn't dare ask what would happen if Uffe didn't follow the doctor's advice.

SEVENTEEN

Arriving in Mariehamn is always emotional for Alicia. Until the previous year, when she'd returned to the islands from England, she hadn't realized how much she'd missed this craggy archipelago. Now watching from the top deck as the ferry moves slowly toward the dock in Mariehamn harbor, she can see the ground beginning to green up after one of the coldest winters she can remember. There are splashes of yellow where buttercups are peeking out on the banks near the old fishing harbor, close to Patrick's island home, and where Alicia's old schoolfriend, Brit, also now lives.

Hilda hugs her hard when they meet outside the terminal building. Alicia had decided on the early ferry from Stockholm so that she'd be able to spend nearly two whole days with her mother and Uffe.

'I thought we might swing by Indigo for a bite to eat?'

Alicia smiles at her mother. She is wearing a very fashionable animal print maxi dress under a jeans jacket and long brown boots. She's got full makeup on and her blonde hair is immaculately styled. She can't believe her mother is in her late fifties; she certainly dresses like someone about twenty years younger.

'You didn't eat on the ferry, did you?' Hilda adds, shooting a concerned look at her daughter over the top of her red sports car.

'Of course not,' Alicia says and laughs. 'You never change!'

Alicia remembers when she used to travel here by ferry with her husband and Stefan, her late son. Whenever Hilda didn't meet them at Stockholm airport to drive them to the ferry and accompany them across the sea to the islands, they would be under strict instructions not to eat on the ship. Eating was only allowed if Hilda was with them. Of course, they'd still spend most of the journey in the onboard restaurant, but both Liam and Stefan knew not to tell her mother.

Alicia's chest aches when she thinks about Stefan, who died too young, only seventeen, but she decides to keep her spirits up.

'Don't think about his death, but celebrate his life.'

The words of her grief counsellor in London still echo in her ears. She is also looking forward to seeing her granddaughter, little Anne Sofia.

Hilda starts the car and Alicia asks if Hilda knows how Frida, Stefan's girlfriend, and the little baby are doing.

'Oh, she's fine. I saw her yesterday in town. The little girl is growing up so fast, she's smiling and making sounds. She'll be speaking soon!'

Alicia smiles as she watches the streets fly past. Hilda drives far too fast, and Alicia decides to stop talking so that she can concentrate on the road. After the tree-lined esplanade park, where Alicia can see the bright green leaves trying to push through on the tips of the bare branches, Hilda turns left and parks the car outside her old fashion boutique. The place is now a trendy men's barbers.

'I never thought that place would be successful,' Alicia says as they step onto the pavement. There are two clients sitting in the luxurious leather chairs, their chins covered in white foam.

As soon as she sees her mother's expression, Alicia regrets her comment. Hilda looks as if she is about to burst into tears. Her chest heaving, she takes out a handkerchief from her designer handbag, which matches the chestnut color of her boots.

Alicia puts her arm around her mother and moves her away from the shop.

'I'm sorry Mom, I didn't mean...'

'I know,' Hilda says, straightening her back. 'It's just seeing it makes me so upset. That man, that Russian, he stole the shop from me.'

Alicia squeezes her mother harder but doesn't comment. Her mom is remembering what happened the previous summer a bit differently from Alicia. Hilda's fashion boutique never made any money, she knows that, having seen her accounts by chance when looking after the shop one day. The Russian loan shark, Alexander Dudnikov, just took advantage of Hilda's vulnerable position by first making large purchases in the shop and lulling her mom into a false sense of security, and then offering her a large loan. With that, he stopped coming to the shop unless it was to intimidate her mother. Dudnikov then increased the interest on the debt, so that it became impossible for Hilda to pay it off. If it hadn't been for Uffe and a sale of some of his land, Alicia's mom would never have got rid of the Russian.

'We'll have a glass of wine, won't we?' Hilda says, interrupting Alicia's thoughts.

'Yes,' she says and nods to the blond boy serving them. They're sitting inside the restaurant, which is nearly empty. Only two other tables are occupied. It's so different from the bustling cafes and bistros she frequents with Patrick in Stockholm, and Alicia is taken aback by the feeling that comes over her. Suddenly, she can breathe again. Walking arm in arm with her mother down Mariehamn's main thoroughfare, they'd said hello to two people they know, even though the town was nearly empty.

'I've missed this,' Alicia now says to her mother.

But instead of smiling as Alicia had expected, Hilda's face crumbles.

'Oh, Alicia, I don't know what to do.'

Hilda's eyes are filled with tears and she dabs at the corner of her eyes with a white napkin that she's dug out of her handbag.

'Please don't cry, Mom. It can't be that bad. Tell me everything,' Alicia says, taking one of her mother's hands.

Hilda looks down at the table.

'Is it this row you've had with Uffe?'

Hilda nods.

Just then, the waiter brings the wine and asks them what they'd like to eat.

Alicia glances at her mother, and is about to ask for some more time, but Hilda is able to keep it together and they both order Cesar salads.

EIGHTEEN

Hilda has decided to say nothing about Uffe to Alicia. Although, Alicia might be able to convince Uffe to go and see Doctor Bengtson...

'What's the matter, Mom?' Alicia says.

'He's ill but he won't go and see the doctor!' Hilda blurts out.

She regrets the words as soon as they've escaped from her mouth. She is hopeless at keeping secrets!

'Uffe?'

'Yes, of course!' Hilda exclaims. She wants to cry but tries to control herself.

'So tell me everything,' Alicia says.

Hilda tells Alicia how Uffe had a turn and how she'd gone to see Doctor Bengtson.

'And the doctor is certain that it's serious?' Alicia asks.

Again Hilda feels frustrated with her daughter and snaps, 'Well, he can't tell, can he, if the stubborn old goat won't go and get examined!'

Hilda feels Alicia's arms around her. She puts her head on her daughter's shoulder, and the tears start flooding.

'Shhh,' Alicia coos, and she gives Hilda a spare napkin from the table. Hilda can feel the eyes of the waiting staff, as well as a young couple, the only other diners, on her. The thought of making an exhibition of herself allows her to control her breathing. She dabs her eyes and blows her nose. Glancing back at the small bar where the waiters are standing, she says, 'Nothing to see here!'

Snapping her head back to face Alicia, she says, 'I'm going to have to tell Uffe I saw Bengtson and let him know what the doctor said. If you're there too, he might actually listen and do something about these turns. Will you support me?'

Now returned back to her own seat opposite Hilda, Alicia nods gravely. 'You said there'd been just the one "turn" as you put it?'

Hilda looks up at her daughter and sighs.

'I didn't want to worry you. As far as I know, he's had three in the last two months, but the one this week was by far the worst.'

Alicia crosses her arms over her chest.

'I wish you'd told me the truth from the beginning, but that seals it. Let's skip lunch and drive straight to Sjoland. If he doesn't agree to phone the doctor today, I'll make him dial the number and drive him there myself.'

Hilda is relieved. Her daughter is going to help her.

'I've missed you,' she whispers and squeezes Alicia's hand over the table. She's afraid of another emotional outburst, but she manages to control herself.

Alicia is not sure what to think. Is Uffe really seriously ill, or is her mother—as she sometimes does—exaggerating the situation? But there was something about the way Hilda acted—angry with her for not understanding without being told that her stepfather had lost consciousness three (or even more?) times during some kind of attack. A cold shiver runs up Alicia's spine when she thinks how serious this could be.

Hilda drives fast, as usual, in the two-seater sports car, speeding around the streets of Mariehamn and the country road to Sjoland. Thankfully, she slows down as she turns into the lane leading up to the three-story white-clad wooden house where Alicia grew up. The early spring sun is low in the sky and its weak rays bounce off the attic window and hit the round flowerbed, bright with lilac, yellow and white crocuses, in the middle of the courtyard. Alicia hasn't realized how much she's missed this place, and even though her worry about Uffe is paramount in her mind, a calm descends upon her as Hilda parks the car outside a large barn that is used as garage.

NINETEEN

L eo is back in the Marie Bar, nursing a beer, trying to make it last. He's decided he is going to have just the one. The meeting with Hilda wasn't great, but he thinks it could have gone worse. The major positive is that she came. She could have not agreed to meet him, or she could have stood him up. He'd been fully prepared for both scenarios. And she'd promised to think about letting him have Alicia's contact details.

He takes out the photo of Alicia that Hilda gave him and gazes at it.

A young woman smiling into the camera, the spitting image of her mother at that age, looks back at him. He strokes the shiny paper, then puts it back in his wallet.

Having drained half the beer in one go, Leo is now convinced that she will let him see his daughter. He looks around him. For a Saturday in the middle of spring, the place is empty. He drinks the rest of his Koff in one slug, the sweet taste of the brown liquid lingering for too short in his mouth. He gets up and decides to go and find a more sociable place.

Walking across the center of the Mariehamn shopping district, something occurs to him. Hilda let it slip that Alicia, after a few months back on the islands, is living in Stockholm, and working for a 'well-known financial newspaper'. She is clearly very proud of her—their—daughter. But this means that it won't be difficult for him to find Alicia's work number. Or her email.

Time for a celebration, surely?

'Vad heter du?'

Leo wakes up to someone shaking his shoulders. At first, he tries to move his body to get away from whoever is trying to attack him, then he opens one eye. What he sees makes him sit up straight. He realizes he's been lying down on a park bench and is freezing cold.

Two policemen in smart dark-blue uniforms and caps are staring down at him.

'What?' he says. He doesn't know how he got here and doesn't understand why the feds are suddenly talking in a foreign language.

'A Finn. Should have guessed,' the younger of the two policemen says to his colleague in English. He grins down at Leo and takes his arm. 'You're coming with us.'

At the police station, Leo tries to convince the officer, an older gray-haired policeman, who's manning the front desk, that he hasn't been drunk and disorderly.

'Look, I have a room in a hostel. I've come here to find my daughter. Yesterday I had lunch with her mother, my estranged wife, but she wouldn't let me see her, so I had a bit too much to drink to drown my sorrows.'

Leo is aware that his breath smells. He's trying to remember what happened the night before, but can only recall his trip to the state-owned alcohol store, where he bought a bottle of extraordinarily expensive Koskenkorva. Had he also drunk the dregs of the bottle of tax-free vodka he had in his room? And why hadn't he gone back there instead of falling asleep on a park bench like a common drunk?

Clearing his throat and straightening his back, he adds, 'It won't happen again.'

'Her name?'

'Alicia Ulsson.'

As Leo utters the name, a tall woman walking across the open office behind the front desk, turns her head in Leo's direction.

She approaches the desk. 'Let me handle this, Andersson.'

The policeman nods and moves along the desk, keeping eye contact with Leo.

'What do you want with Alicia Ulsson?' the female officer asks Leo.

He reads on a tag pinned onto her uniform that the name of the tall policewoman is Ebba Torstensson.

TWENTY

When Hilda and Alicia enter the house it's eerily quiet.

'Uffe?' Hilda shouts and moves from the kitchen to the dining room to the lounge.

There's no reply.

'His car is parked in the barn, so where is he?' Her mother's voice is trembling and Alicia, too, feels a terrible sense of foreboding.

'I'll look upstairs,' she says and touches her mother's arm.

Hilda nods. 'He's probably in the milking parlor.'

The old farm building across the yard is Uffe's office, but without a computer or a telephone, and only an old transistor radio for company, Alicia knows it's where her stepfather hides from his wife, rather than any kind of working space. Besides, he employs a woman in Mariehamn to do his accounts.

Alicia takes the wooden stairs two at a time. She checks Hilda and Uffe's bedroom, but it's empty. The bed is neatly made up with a blue satin coverlet and matching cushions. Next, Alicia checks the small bedroom opposite, and then takes the narrow staircase up to the attic rooms. Memories of summers spent here with Stefan and Liam come flooding back, but Alicia tries to wipe her mind clean. She needs to concentrate on Hilda and Uffe now and forget about herself.

All the rooms are tidy and empty.

Alicia hurries downstairs. She's on top of the main staircase when she hears a scream.

Uffe is slumped in his office chair. His old Nokia cell is lying next to him on the floor and Hilda is on her knees, with her arms around him, rocking back and forth. She's crying hard, a sound Alicia has never heard from her mother before.

With trembling hands, Alicia dials the emergency number and asks for an ambulance.

'Yes, my father is unconscious. No, we don't know what happened, we just arrived home. Thank you.'

'The ambulance will be here in five minutes,' Alicia says, bending down to speak to her mother.

Uffe's eyes are closed and he looks as if he's fallen asleep.

Alicia rubs her mother's back and tries to comfort her.

'They'll be here soon. I'm sure they can do something.'

Hilda quietens down and lifts her eyes to Alicia, 'Do you think so?'

'I don't know, Mom, but let's not think of the worst?'

Alicia puts her fingers to Uffe's neck to see if his heart is beating.

'We need to give him CPR. Here, lay this blanket on the floor,' Alicia says.

She places her hands under Uffe's arms and lifts the old man as carefully as she can from the chair. He's a dead weight and she struggles to move him at first, then Hilda takes hold of his waist and together they manage to place him on the floor.

'Here, you press his chest and I'll blow into his airway,' Alicia says.

The two women start to work on him, but there is no change in Uffe.

'He's not breathing!' Hilda says.

Tears are running down her face.

'Let's not stop,' Alicia says.

Alicia is talking normally and acting as if she's used to reviving Uffe, but it doesn't seem real to her. It's as if she's watching herself as she methodically holds her step-dad's nose and blows air inside his lungs. His lips are almost blue, but she doesn't want to stop. She can remember those lips brushing her cheek as Uffe put his arms around her, but she doesn't think she's ever touched his mouth with her own. Now it seems the most natural thing in the world to give him the kiss of life.

In between Hilda's regular presses on Uffe's chest, her mom is bent down beside her husband. Covering her mouth with her hand, she watches Alicia, and sobs.

It seems an age before they hear the sounds of a siren and a man and a woman wearing green overalls and carrying equipment arrive at the door. The light has gone from outside and Alicia wonders how long they've been trying to revive Uffe.

'We've been doing...'

Crouching next to her step-dad, Alicia tries to speak, but her voice breaks.

'We'll take it from here,' the woman says.

Alicia gets up and places her arms over her mother's shoulders. She tries to comfort her with just her presence. Holding on to each other, they step aside. Alicia watches how the woman with a long dark ponytail examines Uffe with her gloved hands. She glances at the man with her and gives an almost imperceptible shake of the head. The man places a mask over Uffe's face while the woman begins pumping his chest. Hilda looks away and blows her nose, while Alicia's eyes fix on the faces of the two medics. After what again seems like hours, the ponytailed woman removes her hands from Uffe's chest and sits back on her haunches. The man removes the mask from Uffe's face.

The woman stands up and, bringing her eyes toward Alicia and Hilda, says, 'I'm so sorry. My sincere condolences.'

TWENTY-ONE

'May I hug you?' the female and the male medic ask Hilda and Alicia in turn. She's never met these people before, but their embraces and words of condolence warm Alicia's heart. She tries to think if anyone hugged her after Stefan's death, but she can't remember.

'I'll give you a moment with your husband and dad,' the pony-tailed woman says next, moving her eyes from Hilda to Alicia. Her mother is leaning on Alicia, but she's quiet and no longer sobbing.

Alicia nods.

'I'm going to call the duty doctor. She can verify the death.'

At that word, Alicia feels Hilda's body tense. She moves away from Alicia's embrace and goes to kneel next to Uffe. She strokes his cheek, and again Alicia sees tears running down her face.

Alicia glances at the medic, as she addresses Hilda's back, 'Would you like a moment alone with your husband, Mrs. Ulsson?'

Hilda turns around and nods. She looks at Alicia. 'I'll be OK, you go too.'

Outside the milking parlor, in the now darkened yard, the female medic takes Alicia to one side.

'As I said earlier, we can't issue an official death certificate, but I've just sent a message to the duty doctor. You may wish to contact a funeral home. I'd suggest you choose a coffin as soon as possible so that they don't have to move your father more than is necessary. There are two funeral directors in Mariehamn, you probably already know them?'

Alicia can't take all of this in. Things are moving too fast.

'No I don't...I don't live here, I've been in the UK for the past twenty years and now live in Stockholm.'

'Ah, well, just to tell you the procedure in that case. You are obliged to move your father to a holding space until the funeral. If you have no coffin for him, he'll be put into a casket and then moved again once you've chosen a coffin. Naturally, it would be better if he was placed in his own coffin from the start. The funeral director will do that for you and dress him in the clothing that you'd like him to wear for his final journey. And they'll transport your father into the chapel or our central holding space, depending on where and when the funeral will take place.'

At that the medic walks back to the ambulance and returns with something in her hand. She gives Alicia two cards with the names and numbers of funeral directors. But Alicia can't move. She's staring at the cards, both printed on black paper. This is too much; she can't take it all in.

She feels a hand on her arm.

'I'm afraid we have to go now, but the doctor should be here very soon.'

Alicia lifts her eyes.

'Thank you so much.'

For the first time, she notices a name badge on the woman's green overall and adds, 'Thank you, Kati.'

The woman smiles, as does the man, who hasn't actually spoken apart from asking if he could hug her and Hilda. She nods to him too, and the two medics get into the ambulance and drive away. As she watches the yellow and green vehicle turn out of the drive and onto the main road out of Sjoland, she shivers. That's when tears start running down her cheeks. She places a hand on her mouth to muffle the cries that escape from her mouth.

Uffe is gone.

She can't believe that the man who has been the constant pillar in her life is lying in the old milking parlor in front of her. The image of his gray, sunken face and lifeless limbs overwhelm her. Taking deep breaths, she tries to control herself. She must stay strong for her mother.

TWENTY-TWO

'What do you want?'

Down the line, Patrick hears Mia exhale sharply. As if she is surprised by Patrick's reaction to receiving a phone call from her.

'Hello to you too,' she replies.

Instead of the sarcasm Patrick had expected, Mia's voice is soft, almost sexy. He decides he must be imagining it. He places his new AirPods in his ears and waits for the inevitable litany of insults from his ex-wife.

Patrick is walking toward the Skanstull subway station in the center of Stockholm. He has just interviewed a gangly young YouTuber who's become a celebrity after taking part in a popular dance competition on TV. Still technically a teenager at nineteen, Jez now has a stupefying following online, with millions of views of his practical jokes. But he's made some racist comments about the people with an immigrant background living in Sweden, and Patrick's editor had asked him to write an opinion piece on the ensuing media storm. It's not the kind of political story that Patrick likes to write about, but he does find the power these individuals are able to wield fascinating. With no apparent skills, influence, or intelligence, Jez (real name Janne Fredriksson) can make his followers say or do almost anything.

It's early on Saturday afternoon, and Patrick is on his way home to write up the piece, so that he can submit it tomorrow for the weekend edition of the paper.

'So I wondered if we could meet?' Mia says.

She's using the same, soft voice. The tone that reminds Patrick of their first years together. Before the children were born.

He stops walking.

'What do you want, Mia?'

'I told you. I want to meet up and talk about the girls.'

'What's happened?' Patrick is now fully alert. 'Are Sara and Frederica OK?'

Mia gives a little laugh. A flirty laugh.

What is going on?

'They're both fine. Being spoiled to bits by their grandparents as we speak,' she says.

Patrick relaxes. The girls are fine. But being with their grandparents isn't exactly being spoiled. Kurt and Beatrice are both highly competitive people and demand the same from Mia–and now the girls. Their attitude to parenting was one of the reasons Patrick found it difficult to fully belong to the Eriksson family.

'Why aren't they with you? It's your weekend to have them!' Patrick says.

If there's an accusation in his voice, it's fully intended. Mia insisted on custody, so she shouldn't palm the girls off whenever it suits her.

'Relax, I'm in Stockholm on business and I thought I'd stay for the night. Besides, Pappa got the latest Paddington film from one of his mates and they're going to watch it in the home cinema in the country house. They're staying the weekend there. The girls will probably have too much ice cream and soda and fall asleep before the movie finishes. They will not miss me!'

Patrick's thinks of his former in-laws' lavish summer place. Although Mia's parents were difficult to get on with, the large estate on a peninsula just outside Mariehamn is stunning. Patrick remembers, with some shame, sharing his first kiss with Alicia there, right under his in-laws' noses. At the time, he'd been so angry about Mia's affair, and how Kurt and Beatrice were siding with her. Even though she was the one in the wrong, they seemed to blame Patrick for his wife straying. A kiss that was supposed to be a protest had turned into a love affair. How he misses Alicia. He can't wait to FaceTime her later from his apartment.

'Why do you want to talk about the girls?'

'Well, you know, they're growing up and…listen, wouldn't it be better if we meet face to face? I'll buy you dinner at Bakfickan, if you like?'

Mia sits on a swivel chair at the counter in Operabaren, part of the Bakfickan restaurant, sipping a glass of champagne. This is the trendy spot every well-to-do Stockholmer frequents. And the very reason why she chose to meet Patrick here. She knows how much he loves luxury, and how he must miss being able to spend what he likes. Even with the hugely generous divorce settlement, and a free apartment to live in, his lifestyle must have suffered since they parted ways. Mia smiles to herself. The monthly salaries of those two opinionated journalists together must come to less than what she earns in a day.

She scans the room and glances toward the heavy wooden door. He's late as usual, but she makes a conscious effort not to be annoyed. Instead, she enjoys the taste of the vintage Pol Roger and the flirty conversation of the barman, with his long white apron and suggestive smile.

At last, she spots Patrick on the street outside. He waves to her and opens the door to the bar, instinctively ducking. Mia catches her breath. Wearing a pair of pale blue jeans and a light brown suede jacket with a light, almost white shirt and trendy trainers, he looks more handsome than she remembered.

'Hello,' Patrick says as he bends down and brushes Mia's cheek with his lips.

The touch burns into her skin and her heart begins to beat faster.

'We've got a table booked for half past. I thought it would be nice to catch up with a drink first,' Mia says, trying to sound nonchalant and practical.

Patrick looks at her, those eyes of his boring into her. Can he tell she's fibbing? That there is nothing to discuss about Sara and Frederica? That she wants to see him in order to decide whether she wants him back or not? So far, she's veering heavily in one direction...

Keep this up, Patrick, and you'll have your feet under the Eriksson table again.

Patrick orders a beer from the barman, who's wiped the playful smile from his face, and sits down.

Mia tries to calm herself. She admires the high leather seats and the subdued green downlighting of the turn-of-the-century space, in an effort distract herself from Patrick's tight jeans and muscular thighs. She swings on her seat, and her knee touches his leg.

'It's been a while since you and I met here for after-work drinks,' she says and gives him her flirty smile.

His face has surprise edged onto it.

'Yeah, it is,' he says lifting his glass. 'Let's drink to friendship, then,' he adds.

Not if I have anything to do with it, Mia thinks.

She raises her nearly empty flute and smiles into Patrick's cobalt eyes.

TWENTY-THREE

After his beer, Patrick succumbs to Mia's offer of a glass of champagne. Or several. The handsome barman, with whom Mia is openly flirting, flicking her hair back and smiling into his eyes, opens the bottle with a subdued pop. He has to admit, it tastes good. He can't remember when he last had good vintage champagne like this. Not since his separation and divorce from Mia. She always insisted on this make. Patrick can't deny that he's missed the ability to order a glass, or even a bottle, whenever he wants.

A memory of drinking champagne on his yacht with Alicia enters his mind briefly, and he smiles. He takes out his phone and checks his messages. Nothing from her. She promised she'd let him know when she arrives in Sjoland, but he guesses she's been kept busy by Hilda and Uffe. He's going to miss her this weekend. The thought of going back to his empty apartment doesn't appeal.

'She's not replied to you?' Mia says, giving him a playful smile over the top of her glass.

'No, just checking work emails,' Patrick says.

'Liar!' Mia says and laughs.

Mia is wearing a black blazer over a red silky blouse, which is undone to reveal a tiny bit of her black bra. Under her slacks she has bright red stilettos that match her lips. She keeps crossing and uncrossing her legs, showing off her slender ankles.

She looks good.

The barman tops up their glasses and asks if they'd like another bottle. Patrick is about to shake his head, but Mia, cocking her head, says, 'Yes, why not? We're celebrating, aren't we?'

Patrick feels powerless. He knows he's getting drunk, but sitting here in this warm, cozy bar with other after-work drinkers feels right. He's had a tough week. He shrugs his shoulders and lets Mia order.

When the barman leaves the bar in search of a new bottle of Pol Roger, Patrick leans toward Mia and says, 'What are we celebrating, exactly?'

Mia pushes herself closer to him, placing her hand just above his knee. She brings her ruby-red lips close to his ear and says softly, 'Friendship, wasn't it?'

When they've finished the second bottle of champagne, Patrick insists they eat something.

'Good idea,' Mia says, giggling.

Patrick also finds this idea incredibly funny.

The bar is now full to heaving, and there are several people waiting eagerly to get a seat at the counter.

Mia stumbles as she gets down from the high barstool, and Patrick catches her by placing his hand under her arm. They are pushed together by a couple grabbing the now empty seats. For a brief moment, they stand opposite each other, their bodies almost touching. Patrick can smell Mia's perfume, and a memory of their lovemaking enters his mind. He looks into Mia's eyes and smiles. He moves his gaze down and sees Mia's lips, less ruby colored now. Her lipstick must have worn off. Her mouth is slightly open, and suddenly he wonders how it would feel to kiss her.

'Table for two?'

A pretty waitress with pigtails resting either side of her shoulders smiles at Mia and Patrick. They are shown into the small dining room and given menus. Patrick doesn't dare look at his ex-wife. Did she notice what he was about to do? Is that what this is all about? She wants him back? Or just sex? Instead, he takes a piece of bread and devours it in two bites.

'I didn't realize how hungry I was!' he says and smiles sheepishly at Mia.

Mia reaches her hand over the table and places it on Patrick's arm.

'Is that all you're hungry for?'

TWENTY-FOUR

Only a few hours later, Alicia and Hilda are sitting in an undertaker's office in Mariehamn. There's a line of coffins to their right and behind the desk sits an older couple, perhaps the same age as Hilda. Alicia admires their ability to be sympathetic and practical at the same time, asking questions about funeral arrangements, coffin preference and burial plots.

They agree to meet in Sjoland that same evening.

When Hilda and Alicia emerge into the dark Mariehamn afternoon, Alicia says, 'I think I need a drink after that.'

Hilda nods, but to Alicia's surprise says, 'Let's go back. I don't want to leave him alone. And we need to sort out a suit for your dad.'

Since Uffe's death, Hilda has been calling him Alicia's dad, just as the medics did and the funeral directors just now. Something her mother, nor Alicia, ever did when he was alive. But Alicia doesn't correct her, even though all through the years none of them has ever shied away from the fact that Uffe was Alicia's stepfather. Now such distinctions do not seem to matter.

Hilda agrees to let Alicia drive, as she had when they traveled up to town earlier.

'You OK?' Alicia asks when they are about to cross the swing bridge. Hilda has been quiet, watching the dark landscape pass her window. The ground is mostly bare, but in places clumps of bright yellow dandelions are poking through the ground on the side of the road. Spring is on its way.

'We made the right choice of coffin, don't you think?' Alicia asks.

Hilda turns to look at her. She nods and says, 'Yes. They were nice, weren't they? Everyone has been so kind…'

Hilda turns her head away again and Alicia can hear that she's struggling to hold back tears.

'Just let it out, Mom.'

Alicia touches Hilda's shoulder with her free hand.

'No, there's so much to do and organize. And you'll be back to Stockholm tomorrow, so I need to pull myself together.'

Alicia removes her hand and stares at the road ahead of her. She hasn't yet had time to contact Patrick, or think about her job in Stockholm. She was only supposed to stay on the islands for one night, returning to Sweden on the midday ferry tomorrow, Sunday. She makes a quick decision.

'I'm staying on. I'm sure it'll be fine with *Dagens Finans*. There must be something called bereavement leave in Sweden?'

Hilda turns her face back toward Alicia. 'Oh, darling girl, that would be wonderful!'

Alicia sends a message to Patrick, but when he doesn't reply, she tries to phone him. Again, there's no answer. He must be working, she thinks.

Alicia sends two other messages. One to Frida, and one to Liam in London. Both short, with just the sad news. Then, looking at her watch, she suddenly sees it's past seven o'clock. She's supposed to meet Brit in town for a drink in half an hour. She writes another text to her old schoolfriend, who replies immediately.

I'm so sorry. Send my condolences to Hilda. Anything I can do, let me know. Lots of love, Brit.

.   .   .

Alicia gazes at the message from her friend and tears prick the back of her eyelids. Brit's words are so kind. She realizes she needed to talk to Patrick and hear comforting words from him.

When she and Liam lost their precious only son, her ex-husband seemed incapable of showing emotion. Instead, he went off to have a fling with a nurse who worked in his private surgery in West London. It was only after Alicia met Patrick last summer, and Liam found about her affair, that Liam finished with the nurse and told Alicia that the relationship meant nothing. Liam did look after Alicia after Stefan's death, as a doctor should look after his patient, prescribing sleeping tablets and calming medication, and making sure all the practical arrangements were made.

He did what he thought was right, Alicia now supposes. But she wonders if shielding Alicia from seeing their dead boy's tangled body made it harder for her to accept the death? Thinking about the way Hilda was able to say goodbye to Uffe brings another wave of emotion, but Alicia suppresses it and texts her thanks to Brit. She also receives a similar message from Frida. Again, she writes a short reply.

TWENTY-FIVE

L ater on, Hilda comes down the stairs slowly, holding on to Uffe's best suit. It's the one he bought for Stefan's funeral: English tailoring. The outfit was sourced by Hilda via her contacts in the fashion industry. It suited him so perfectly that Hilda wished she had seen him in it more often. Instead of the black tie, which goes with the funeral outfit, Hilda decided on his favorite pale-blue striped one, but she had brought the black one along too, to get Alicia's opinion. Her hands are trembling as she places the jacket, trousers, shirt, and the two ties over Uffe's chair in the lounge.

'I think the blue one, don't you?' Alicia says gently.

Just then Hilda sees the lights of a car pulling up in the drive.

'They're here.' She walks toward the doors and waits for Mr. Hermansson.

Dressed in dark trousers and a brown coat, the undertaker holds Hilda's hands for a long time at the door. He nods to Alicia, who has come to stand behind her, and shakes her hand next. Not taking his coat off, he asks to see where Uffe is, and Hilda grabs her coat and takes the man outside. Alicia follows with Uffe's suit.

The ambulance crew has left Uffe lying on his back with a blanket over him. His eyes are closed and he looks as if he is sleeping. But not really, his face has sunk, and the color of his ruddy cheeks has gone. His face is gray and the skin is dull.

Mr. Hermasson turns around to face Hilda and Alicia. 'Ladies, unless you wish to, you don't need to stay. I can take it from here.'

He takes the suit from Alicia and stretches his hand toward the door of the milking parlor, showing the two women outside. He pulls the door behind him firmly shut.

Hilda looks at Alicia. She doesn't know what to do with her hands and suddenly feels cold. Her mouth is dry and she feels dizzy.

'Mom, let's go inside. We need to eat something.'

The last thing Hilda wants to do is to touch the rye sandwich topped with cheese and pickled cucumbers that Alicia places in front of her. Instead, she takes the glass of white wine to her lips and swallows a mouthful.

'I think I might need something a bit stronger,' she says.

A small smile plays around Alicia's lip. 'I think you're right.'

She goes into the lounge and peers into the drinks cabinet.

'We have some rather fine cognac in there,' Hilda says and takes an exploratory bite of the bread. The piece stays down, so she takes another.

When Alicia returns with two large glasses of brandy, Hilda lifts her glass and says through tears, 'To Uffe, may he rest in peace.'

'To dad,' Alicia says and they both empty their glasses.

'He was as good as your dad, you know,' Hilda says. 'Or better,' she adds.

Alicia places a hand over hers and replies, 'I know, Mom.'

TWENTY-SIX

Brit drops her phone onto the sofa next to her. How awful that Uffe had passed. Since Brit returned to the islands, she's seen him out and about on his tractor when passing through Sjoland on her way to the ferry to visit her dad on Föglö island. But she hasn't talked to him since that eventful Christmas Eve last year. He'd been quiet then, as always. But his warm embrace when she arrived had shown Brit how he felt about seeing her again. There was no need for words.

Even when Brit was at school with Alicia, and the two of them would tumble out of the bus and walk to the Ulsson's house, Uffe never seemed to be at home. Brit wouldn't have known him at all had it not been for the time he came to collect her and Alicia from the center of Mariehamn.

It was a cold May evening and they'd been to an end-of-year school disco at the community center, but had left early because it was just too boring. They were both thirteen at the time and had been stupid enough to go with a couple of Swedish boys who were hanging out in the English Park. The boys had come off the ferry and had a bottle of vodka with them. Alicia and Brit hadn't tasted strong alcohol before. One of the boys looked like River Phoenix, with dirty blond hair that he kept flicking back. The other boy was dark-haired, but both wore leather jackets and were much older than Brit and Alicia. The girls were flattered by the attention.

Brit will never forget the moment when she looked up and saw Uffe standing in front of her.

They were sitting on a small wall next to the marketplace. Brit had been kissing River Phoenix when she heard Alicia shout out her name. As usual, Alicia had been a goody two shoes and had hardly drunk anything, just wetting her lips when the vodka bottle came around. She told Brit later that she didn't fancy the other guy, but Brit knew she was afraid he'd notice that she'd never been kissed. They were too young, and Brit was foolish. Goodness knows what those two guys would have done to them had Uffe not turned up when he did.

In the car back to Sjoland, Uffe stayed quiet until the swing bridge. He'd not spoken a word to the two of them after he'd told them to get off the wall and inside his Volvo. The look he gave the two boys was full of thunder. But as he drove the car over Sjoland Canal, he turned briefly toward the two of them, sitting on the back seat.

'I am going to pretend this never happened. Brit, you can stay over in Alicia's bedroom tonight and I will telephone your father to let him know of the change of plan. I presume you were supposed to go home with someone else?'

Brit nodded. The plan was that after the party had finished, she'd get on the bus with the other kids from the outer archipelago.

'In that case, your dad will be going out of his mind with worry. Do you know what time it is?'

Alicia glanced at Brit. Her eyes were wide and she looked ready to blubber.

Brit looked away from her friend and shook her head.

'It's gone ten at night!' Uffe said, not waiting for a reply.

It wasn't dark, but Brit could tell the sun had set and the sky was the color of steel. Her bus was supposed to leave at 7.30. How had she missed it? She must be very drunk.

Looking straight at the road ahead of him, Uffe continued, 'This will stay between us, but if I ever have to come and get you two from town again, there will be trouble. You hear?'

Both of the girls nodded.

At Sjoland, Brit expected a barrage of accusations from Alicia's mother, but when they got into the house, it was quiet. Hilda was nowhere to be seen.

'Go off to bed,' Uffe said and Brit and Alicia scuttled upstairs.

The next morning, Hilda made the girls breakfast as if nothing had happened. Brit was as polite as she could possibly be. She did, however, want to ask after Uffe, but when she started to say 'And where,' she got such a kick from Alicia under the table that she went quiet.

'Will your dad come to get you or shall I drive you home?'

Brit didn't know, so she glanced at Alicia who said, sweet as pie, 'Could you run her home, Mom? Brit's dad has a lot to do on his farm. He asked me last week if we could do the driving. Sorry, I forgot, like I forgot that I'd asked Brit to stay over.'

Hilda gave Brit and Alicia a long look, and then broke into a smile.

'I'd love to—I haven't been to Föglö for ages and it's such a lovely day.'

Brit remembers now how kind Hilda, and especially Uffe, had been not to drag them over the coals over such a stupid mistake. She's certain nothing like that happened to Alicia again, but for Brit, well, she was a terror at school. She feels sorry for her dad for what she put him through when she was a teenager. At least she's making amends now.

Rolf is becoming more and more frail, and Brit wishes she could convince him to give up living in the house and move into sheltered accommodation in Mariehamn, where Brit could visit him more often. At the moment, she can only manage a trip to Föglö once or twice a week, depending on her sailing schedule. But perhaps he will soon have a stronger reason to consider a move into town, Brit thinks. She glances over to the kitchen table, where several small cardboard packages lie open next to some test kits, and sighs.

She doesn't know what she was thinking. Everything is moving too fast. And she's sure it's all too early in the relationship.

. . .

Jukka and Brit are now on different shifts at Marie Line cruise liners, something he insisted upon. Her new boyfriend is a captain of MS *Sabrina*, where they met on Brit's first day onboard in December.

Jukka had been involved with one of the crew previously, a silly girl who, spurred on by her mother, had afterwards accused him of inappropriate behavior. Luckily, Jukka was completely exonerated, but the incident meant he was super careful not to be put in a similar situation again. So when their relationship became more serious, Brit applied to be transferred to MS *Sabrina*'s sister ship.

The only snag—apart from less time spent with Jukka—is that the mother of the girl now works on the same ferry as Brit. Kerstin is one of the oldest members of the crew and a constant thorn in Brit's side. The otherwise happy restaurant crew welcomed her with open arms, except for the older woman. Oh, well, Brit thinks. Sooner or later she'll have to deal with Kerstin, but now she has a more serious problem.

Brit glances toward the windows where the sun is pale but visible, a hazy blob behind a strip of clouds just above the horizon. The seas are calm, the storm of the week has passed. The rays of the weak sun form a band of light on the surface of the teal-colored water. She looks at her watch. Jukka's ship is due to make its way slowly to the West Harbor just after 4pm.

Brit loves watching how the ferry grows from a tiny red dot into the large cruise liner as it nears her windows. Knowing her new love is onboard makes the progress of the ship all the more compelling. As Brit steps closer to the large floor-to-ceiling windows of the apartment that she rents from an old schoolfriend, and searches the horizon for any signs of the ship, she marvels at the transformation Jukka has made in her.

Gone is the heartbroken, bitter woman who vowed never to fall seriously for a man ever again. The thought of the Italian rat, who for years made her believe that they had a sweet future together, causes her to shiver. For several of those years, Nico was sleeping with not just one, but three, of Brit's fellow crew members on the Caribbean cruise liner. Instead of the promised sweet life together in Puglia, filled with good food and love, Brit had no choice but to return to her home in the islands to lick her wounds.

But as she stepped onboard MS *Sabrina* for the first time, she came face to face with the handsome and intriguing captain of the ship, Jukka. He was so good-looking, he took Brit's breath away.

It was only later, after their first night in his apartment on the other side of the narrow strip of land that formed the capital of the islands, Mariehamn, that she'd realized Jukka was the spitting image of her all-time favorite American film star. With his George Clooney looks and tall frame, Jukka could have had anyone, but instead (after some gentle encouragement), he'd begun making overtures in Brit's direction.

In less than a month, Brit was head-over-heels. Wise it was not, especially as Jukka had a marriage and a questionable love affair with an eighteen-year-old behind him. Naturally, Brit completely believes in Jukka, and his sincere assurances that the teenager had been a one-off, brought about by his unhappy marriage. At the same time, she knows men.

But Brit likes to live dangerously. In the end, she hadn't really believed in a future with the Italian rat, so if Jukka turns out to be another bad mistake, she'll just dust herself off and carry on.

Brit shakes her head. It won't be so easy this time, will it? Now there is the complication that the test kit lying on the kitchen counter adds. Now she hasn't just got herself to think about.

How did I let this happen?

TWENTY-SEVEN

Patrick hears a noise but can't make out what it is. The idea that it is his phone ringing slowly enters his consciousness. He quickly gets up, but then gently lowers himself back down. His head is pounding. Still, the ringing continues and he tries to think. Where did he leave his cell? Jeans pocket!

He grabs it.

'Hello?'

'Hi, it's me. Were you asleep?' Alicia's voice sounds serious.

'Yeah, a late night. What time is it?'

'Oh, just gone eight here. Sorry, I didn't mean to wake you. Of course, it's just seven there. But I wanted to talk to you.'

Patrick hears a sniffle.

'Of course,' Patrick says, panic rising in his stomach. He can taste bile in his mouth. His eyes wander over the room. Seeing his clothes thrown onto the bedroom floor and messy sheets on his bed, he swears to himself.

Alicia must never find out what he's done.

'Oh, Patrick...' Without continuing, Alicia bursts into tears.

· · ·

Alicia is sitting on her bed in the attic room. She was planning to sleep in the sauna cottage, where she usually stays when visiting her parents, but she now wants to be under the same roof as Hilda.

'I'm so sorry, Alicia.' Patrick's voice sounds so warm and lovely that Alicia wishes she could ask him to take the next ferry to Åland. She needs him more now than she could have imagined. But she doesn't want to ask. She knows that his work is important to him and he can't take time off so early in his new stint at the *Journalen*.

'I'm not coming back tonight. I might stop over until next week. There's so much to arrange with the funeral, the farm, letting everyone know.'

There's silence at the other end, so Alicia continues, 'And I can't leave Mom.'

'Of course,' Patrick says.

Alicia can't read from his words or the tone of his voice what he's thinking, but she is too tired to probe him.

Talking to Patrick about Uffe feels like reliving that awful moment when Alicia and her mother found her stepfather slumped on the floor of his office. It was so cold in the room, and his body was equally cold and numb. Alicia keeps wondering whether they could have saved Uffe's life if they'd driven straight home instead of going to the restaurant. Or if she'd come home on Friday night instead, would she and Hilda have been able to get Uffe to see Doctor Bengtson? But how could he have got an appointment so quickly? And neither Hilda nor Alicia would have known that he had taken ill. Uffe would have been in his office while they were in the main house.

Uffe often spent a whole afternoon in the old milking parlor. Alicia smiles when she thinks how Hilda used to complain about the space. He hadn't done any painting or even re-laid a new floor. He'd just moved a desk and a chair into the room. Over the years, her mom tried endlessly to convince him to let her change his office for the better, but Uffe said he liked it just as it was.

'There's still a faint smell of freshly milked cow, which I don't want to give up,' he used to say, winking at Alicia. In one corner of the old milking parlor, he'd placed a side table and a recliner. That's where Alicia can picture him now. Uffe sitting and listening to the local news, and reading *Ålandsbladet*, is one of her fondest childhood memories.

But Alicia knows it's useless thinking like this. Or blaming herself or Hilda. The paramedic, Kati, had said the heart attack was so powerful that Uffe would have died instantly.

Alicia's therapist says, 'Death is part of life, and we can do nothing about that.'

Thinking of Connie, her grief counsellor in London, Alicia makes a mental note to schedule a telephone consultation. She knows she will need help to come to terms with another bereavement so soon after her lovely son was taken away.

She's shaken out of her deep thoughts by Patrick. 'I'm sorry, I can't come over.'

'Oh, Patrick, that's OK. I know work is a priority for you right now. Being back at the paper, you can't afford to take time off so soon. Just come over next weekend, if you can?' Alicia says.

'If you're sure?'

'Liam is coming tomorrow,' Alicia says, then adds quickly, 'And I've got my mom.'

Patrick is quiet over the phone for a few minutes and Alicia curses herself for mentioning her ex-husband. But Liam was part of the family for a long time, so Patrick should really understand that. Surely he's not jealous at a time like this?

He coughs and says, 'I'll call you later? And I am so sorry, Alicia. Uffe was one of a kind.'

The tears start flowing again and Alicia can barely speak to say goodbye to Patrick. She takes deep breaths and dries her eyes and blows her nose. She must stay strong for her mother's sake.

TWENTY-EIGHT

As she watches Liam step off the plane at Mariehamn airport, Alicia thinks how tanned and healthy he looks. His light brown hair is paler, probably bleached by the sun. She smiles bitterly as she thinks of the exotic holidays he's now taking. First, the Caribbean in January, then Cape Verde a week ago. When they were married, Liam had been reluctant to leave his job at the hospital for long. He said his patients needed him. There were always so many of them, and so few staff. And when it came to their annual summer vacation in Åland, he'd rarely stayed the whole two weeks with Alicia and Stefan, preferring to cut his vacation to just a week, or even shorter. But Maria, the nurse he'd had an affair with, seemed to have changed all that. Oh, well, Alicia wants Liam to be happy.

When Liam told her a few weeks after she moved to Stockholm that he'd got back with Maria, she was glad. If he wants to be with her, so be it.

'I'm so sorry for your loss,' Liam says and hugs Alicia tightly.

'Thank you,' she replies and tries to control the sudden urge to burst into tears. The familiarity of Liam's embrace makes her nearly lose it. But she must stay strong.

Smelling alcohol on his breath allows her to think of something other than Uffe and the sadness that envelops her every waking moment—again. She knows Liam hates flying and needs a few drinks to cope. Another reason why his sudden love of foreign travel is so infuriating. He's making an extra effort just to please the nurse.

'Good flight?' she asks as they walk toward Hilda's car. She gives him a sideways glance, smiling.

'I can just about manage the one from London to Helsinki, but these small planes...they give me the heebie-jeebies.'

'Thank you for coming,' Alicia says.

They're sitting in Hilda's bright red sports car. The seats are pale cream leather and the car gives a familiar roar as Alicia starts the engine.

'Still can't quite understand how your mother drives a car like this. At her age,' Liam says, raising his voice over the noise.

'She's always been a petrol head,' Alicia says as she maneuvers the Mercedes out of the parking lot and into the road leading into Mariehamn. 'If only her ability matched her interest in cars.'

They both laugh. Hilda is well known for her bad driving. Alicia often thinks it's a blessing she lives on the islands, where roads are rarely busy. She'd never manage among the busy traffic in London, or Stockholm, for that matter.

'How's Maria?' Alicia asks as they turn into the road leading to Sjoland. She forces herself to say the name out loud. The hurt over the affair is a lesser one than the pain over Uffe.

'Hmm, not sure,' Liam says.

Alicia glances over the gearstick at her ex-husband.

'We broke up.'

Alicia can't detect any emotion in Liam's voice.

'Really?' Alicia can hear that her own voice has risen a few octaves. She swallows hard. That woman wasn't the only reason their marriage failed, but she was a large part of it. And now he's just chucked her aside?

Who Liam dates has nothing to do with me anymore, she reminds herself.

'It was never a real relationship,' Liam says.

Alicia steals another glance at her ex-husband. He doesn't often talk about his feelings, or at least not without Alicia forcibly pulling that kind of a discussion out of him, like extracting a splinter from a child's hand. When they decided to try to patch things up last summer, Liam only once talked about his emotions honestly. His new candor had warmed Alicia's heart and was part of the reason she had wanted to give their marriage another chance. But as it turned out, Alicia had already, without realizing it, fallen for Patrick and there was no going back. Is this another attempt to get Alicia back? At a time like this when they are about to bury her stepfather?

Alicia decides not to rise to the bait, if it was intended as such. Although she's not sure.

Alicia and Liam travel over the Sjoland Canal in silence. The dark water under the bridge flows fast, but there are no yachts or boats waiting to cross on either side. It's too early for sailors. Alicia spots some blue hepatica on the side of the road as she slows down to turn into the large white painted house in the corner of one of the fields. Suddenly the sun peeks out of a cloud, and the sea glimmers, just visible through the dark green pine trees to the right. Summer will be here soon, Alicia thinks.

As she gets out of the car, Alicia looks at the house, heavily reno-vated by Alicia's mother. She scans the neat brown fields, which are ready for the spring planting. She notes the red cottage beyond the largest field in front of the house. Who's going to look after the potato harvest–or the holiday cottages–some of which are rented out to casual workers, now Uffe has gone? It's too soon to raise the issue with Hilda, but at the same time, Alicia knows that the land will not wait for anything. It doesn't pay heed to grief or any other human emotion.

TWENTY-NINE

Brit asked to see Alicia in town. She thought it would be better for Alicia to get out of Hilda's house. The atmosphere must be oppressive there. She's embarrassed that she never contacted Alicia after she heard about her son's passing. She sent a card, but didn't telephone her. At the time, she was too wrapped up in her own life with Nico in the Caribbean. Brit thinks her friend understands, but it isn't something she's proud of.

When her own mother died she was young, barely a teenager. Alicia had been there for her in a way that none of the other girls in her class were. She'd invited Brit over to the farm in Sjoland, and Hilda had fed her *pannkaka* and cinnamon buns. Brit had cried on Alicia's shoulder and her friend hadn't complained. Instead, she'd insisted Brit sleep in her bed while Hilda set a mattress on the floor for Alicia.

Now that Alicia needs her, she will support her friend this time around.

'How are you coping?' she says, trying not to burst into tears herself when she sees Alicia's gaunt face. This is the problem with her, she can't keep her emotions in check when it comes to her friend. With men, and love, she can be as cool as a cucumber. Though she's managed to thaw a little with her latest, Jukka, the sea captain. Just as well really, she thinks.

'I'm OK,' Alicia says and gives her the briefest smile.

'Do you want a cinnamon bun with your coffee?' Brit asks.

They're in Svarta Katten Cafe in town, a favorite of theirs since their school days.

'Thanks, that would be lovely,' Alicia says and lowers herself down to a settee.

'Back in a minute!' Brit says and walks toward a young girl, with rainbow-colored hair standing behind the counter. Brit is glad to have some breathing space. She's so ashamed of her inability to deal with these kinds of situations, but she's worried about her friend. She looks back at Alicia. She's sitting on an intricately curved sofa, with her elbow resting on a round table in front of her, and her hand under her chin, gazing out of the window. She looks so sad.

It's such bad luck, Brit thinks. Her friend had just begun a new life with Patrick in Stockholm, finally able to move on with her life after her son's death, and now this. She wonders if telling Alicia about her own situation would be appropriate, and decides it's not.

When Brit returns to the table, Alicia is on the phone. She looks animated, waving her free hand about, but when Brit is in earshot, she says, 'Got to go, Patrick. Bye.'

'What's up?' Brit says, relieved to have another subject to talk about.

Alicia looks up. She's close to tears and Brit places a hand on her shoulder. Alicia begins to shake and Brit, moving to sit on the sofa beside her friend, pulls Alicia into a tight hug.

'Here,' she says. She hands Alicia a napkin, given to her by the disinterested teenager at the till.

'Is it Uffe?' Brit asks carefully.

She sees Alicia isn't wearing any makeup and that her hair looks dull, the strands of her blonde locks lifeless on her shoulders. Her eyes look paler than usual. And she's lost weight. Brit saw her friend briefly in Stockholm only a couple of weeks ago, but now she's like a different person.

'Yes, and no,' Alicia says. She dries her eyes and takes a sip of the black coffee.

Brit looks around and sees that people are glaring at the two of them. She gives an older man, sitting at a small table with what looks like his wife, a hard stare, which stops his gawking. Sweeping her eyes around the room, she sees that everyone is now concentrating on their own drinks or partners.

Brit moves back to the chair opposite Alicia. 'What is it? Is Patrick not coming over?'

Alicia looks up at her friend.

'I'm not sure. He's acting really funny.'

Alicia wonders if she's overreacting. She knows she's not herself, and that keeping from breaking down in front of Hilda is taking all her strength. She's been with her mother every second of the day since Uffe's passing, apart from the time when she went to fetch Liam from the airport.

Now, sitting here in a cafe with Brit, she feels she's about to come undone.

'I know it must be so hard on you, especially so soon after Stefan...' Brit says, but Alicia stops her.

'Please don't, I'll start bawling again.'

Alicia manages a brief laugh.

She takes a deep breath in. 'I'm not sure it's anything, but Patrick is acting strange. On Sunday morning he was so hungover he could hardy talk to me. Then I tried to get him later that day and I kept missing him. He gave me the usual excuses, low batteries on his phone, busy at work. He said he'd gone to bed early because he was so tired from the night before. On Monday, we just texted, and then today I stopped trying to contact him. He just called now, but he was in a bloody tunnel somewhere and it kept cutting off. I don't know, perhaps I'm just overreacting, but I can't help feeling...'

Alicia looks at her friend's reaction to see if her words make any sense, or if Alicia is going crazy. Brit has always been very good with 'the rules' of a relationship, and although Alicia is skeptical about some of her theories, she trusts Brit's instincts.

'Why? Do you think something is going on? That's he's seeing someone else? Surely not after such a short time. You've only been living together a couple fo months. Besides, he adores you!' Brit says.

'Well, there is Mia and the apartment...'

She takes a bite of the sweet bun.

'What? No, surely not. I know she's a free agent again, but...'

Alicia stops munching.

'What did you say?'

Brit's eyes widen. 'Didn't you know? The love of her life, that Max von Rosengard, dumped her. There's natural justice after all. Serves her right for what she did to Patrick.'

Brit is grinning, but Alicia's heart is pounding so hard in her chest that she can hardly breathe. Since Brit moved back to the islands, Alicia knows she and Mia have been seeing each other for the odd drink or coffee. The three girls were never friends at school, but now Mia is Brit's landlord, which Alicia knows complicates things. However, she knows she can trust her friend.

'What I was going to say was that Mia came to our apartment. She told me it belongs to Eriksson Holdings and that she's effectively my landlord! But Patrick had told me he rents it from a friend. I wouldn't call an ex with whom you fight about every detail of your children's care "a friend", would you?'

Alicia has raised her voice, and again their little conversation seems to be the focal point of the clientele in the cafe.

Leaning closer over the small table and lowering her voice, Brit says, 'What are you saying?'

Alicia shrugs.

'I don't know. It just unsettled me, having her lord it over me like that in my own home. Which turns out to be hers! Its decor and furniture chosen by her. And she was so unpleasant. Dressed up to the nines while I was there in my old worn-out jogging pants and a dirty T-shirt. And why did Patrick have to lie?'

'Because you would never have moved in with him, had you known who the apartment belonged to?'

'Yeah, I guess,' Alicia says. 'Anyway, what did you want to tell me?' she adds smiling.

Brit had asked if Alicia could have coffee with her on the pretext that she had 'earth-shattering news'. She knows her friend is prone to exaggeration, so she doesn't expect Brit to have become a nun or joined the touring circus. All the same, she agreed, even though she had to leave Liam alone in the house with Hilda. He'd been exhausted from the trip, so he said he'd take a nap.

'I'm pregnant!' Brit blurts out.

THIRTY

'Hello, handsome!' Mia is standing outside Patrick's apartment on Monday evening. She's wearing a pair of tight black trousers, high-heeled boots with some kind of tassels on them and a short leather jacket over a roll-neck jumper. She's again wearing very red lipstick, but she has less makeup on, making her look vulnerable in spite of the brightness of the lips.

'Hi,' Patrick says. He's just blown off Alicia, after phoning her just as he stepped onto the subway. He could hear she was getting agitated. They usually talk at least twice a day, sometimes more often. But Patrick is so worried she'll be able to tell from the tone of his voice what he's been up to that he's tried to avoid her. He'd planned to get home, have a shower, and talk to her properly tonight. The last person he wants to see now is Mia. What he really wants to know is what she wants. As if he didn't know.

'You in town again?' he says instead.

He stands a few paces away from her, but Mia moves forward and closes the gap between them. She's so near that he can smell her sweet perfume.

'The girls both have sleepovers and I had a late meeting, so I thought I'd stay on.'

'How convenient,' Patrick says.

He wants to take a step back, but thinks that'll show weakness, so he stays put opposite Mia, inhaling her scent and trying not to look into her dark brown eyes.

'Aren't you going to invite me in? Or is your little bit on the side at home?'

'Alicia is my partner, Mia. It was you who had something on the side, remember?'

'Aww, you still upset? I'm sure we can carry on from where we left off on Saturday and sort things out once and for all?' Mia says and cocks her head.

She threads her hand through Patrick's arm and says, 'I'm getting cold. C'mon let's talk more inside.'

THIRTY-ONE

The church feels cool inside, even though it's absolutely bursting with mourners. Alicia knew Uffe had a lot of friends and acquaintances, but walking behind the coffin, holding Hilda's hand, she is amazed to see that all the pews are full. She nods to a few familiar faces, but seeing tears in their eyes, she tries to focus on Liam's neck. He's agreed to be one of the pall bearers, taking the position at the back. His brown hair is too long and a few strands fall onto the top of the white collar of his shirt. It's so unlike Liam not to worry about appearances. Before, he wouldn't have been caught dead—how apt!—having untidy hair at an important occasion like this. He still looks smart, though, in his well-cut dark suit and polished shoes.

Alicia didn't think she would need him as much as she has done in these past few days. She's delighted he's here, supporting her and Hilda, when she knows he will be needed at the hospital. He's told her he will stay as long as Alicia wants him to. Whereas Patrick...she spots him sitting in a pew at the back. She nods to him and he nods back. Why hasn't he taken a place at the front?

And then she sees the reason. Mia is sitting next to him. She nods to her too, but quickly turns her face away from them and toward the front and the coffin.

What is going on? Is it natural that Patrick and Mia would come to her stepfather's funeral together? Alicia didn't think they were getting on at all well. Is it to do with what Brit told her? Now she's single again, does Mia want Patrick back? Is Mia the reason why Patrick has been so aloof lately? He arrived in Mariehamn with the eleven o'clock ferry last night and stayed in his apartment in town. Alicia didn't want to see him, because they had hardly spoken during the past week. Besides, she wanted to rest. Today would be a long day.

Alicia suddenly realizes that he didn't even ask her to come over. Mia presence could explain why he's been avoiding her. He's been acting so strange, especially now when she needed him most.

Alicia stops her thoughts about what is happening with Patrick.

It's not important now.

As the cortege reaches the altar, Hilda and Alicia slip into the first pew, and Liam takes a seat next to them. He touches Alicia's fingers and envelops her hand in his. The organ starts playing and the pastor, wearing a long white cassock, takes his position in front of the altar.

'Thank you for coming,' Alicia says to Mia and shakes her hand.

Mia is in an expensive-looking black trouser suit, with a lacy white blouse underneath. Her lips are bright red and she wears heavy charcoal-black eyeliner. The makeup is unseemly for a funeral.

'We both wanted to show our respect as a family, didn't we?' Mia replies, looking at Patrick.

He's taken a few steps away from Mia and comes over and hugs Alicia.

'I'm sorry I haven't been here, but work is mad at the moment,' he whispers into her ear.

He leaves his hand resting on her waist, but Alicia moves away, letting his arm drop.

He looks miserable, but then it is a funeral.

Where have you been?

They're standing at the entrance to the old church. Mourners are queuing behind them, waiting to shake hands with Hilda and Alicia, so Mia and Patrick step away. From the corner of her eye, as she tries to keep the tears away, she sees Patrick standing awkwardly a few paces away, next to his ex-wife.

Kindness is the worst, and after she's shaken a few hands and thanked a couple of people for their condolences, Alicia is suddenly overwhelmed by sadness. It's as if her chest is caving in, and she has to take hold of her mother's arm to stay upright. Before she knows what's happening, Liam is holding on to her elbow. He moves his hand around Alicia's waist and holds onto her.

'I've got you,' he says softly into her ear.

Liam begins shaking hands, and lets Alicia lean on him.

The wake is held at Hilda and Uffe's house. On Alicia's insistence, Hilda has got caterers in, with a couple of servers to look after everything. There's coffee, beer, and wine, various salads, cold meats, brought by the caterers, and a cinnamon apple tart made by her mom, but Alicia can't touch any of it.

She's again amazed at the number of people there; the whole of the ground floor of the large house is filled with mourners clad in black. Most of all, she wants to flee upstairs and cry her eyes out in the attic bedroom, but she knows she has to be here to support her mother.

After what seems like an age of making small talk and assuring Liam she is alright, Alicia goes to check on the caterers. The woman in charge has stationed herself by the kitchen sink underneath the window overlooking the sea, where Alicia's mom often stands.

'Everything OK?' the woman, with plaited bright red hair asks. Her name is Ruby. When they first met, Alicia wanted to ask if her parents gave her that name because of the color of her hair, but she'd thought it too personal. Now Ruby smiles in that sorrowful way, which is the worst for Alicia, and it makes her chest contract again.

She swallows hard and replies, 'I just wanted to make sure you've found everything you need in here?'

'No problem. I've got most of my own equipment anyway,' the woman says. She's filling the coffee maker again–for the umpteenth time, Alicia suspects.

A low murmur is coming from the dining room, and the lounge beyond. Alicia moves closer to a serving hatch, where Hilda keeps her decorative jars of coffee and tea, and peers through it. That's when she sees them.

In a corner of the dining room, a place which isn't visible from the lounge, Patrick and Mia are standing close to one another. Mia is speaking animatedly, her face turned up to Patrick. She's at least a foot smaller than him, even in her high heels, but they are so close their upper bodies are almost touching. Patrick is gazing intently at his ex's eyes, but Alicia can't decipher what his expression means. Is he enthralled by what Mia is saying, puzzled, or angry? He's intently watching her and suddenly Alicia can't take anymore. She straightens herself up and turns away from the hatch. Looking at her phone, she sees it's already late, nearly six o'clock. How long are these people going to stay?

'If you like I can start clearing up?' Ruby says, as if she's read Alicia's mind.

When Alicia doesn't say anything, the caterer adds, 'That usually makes them leave.' This time her smile is conspiratorial.

As Alicia turns around to leave the kitchen, she's faced by Liam, who's just stepped in from the lounge.

'Everything OK?' he asks.

His brows are knitted in a worried expression, as he takes hold of Alicia's elbow.

'I'm fine, just tired,' Alicia replies and smiles. 'Thank you for coming, you've been a great support to both my mom and me,' she adds.

'It's the least I could do. For you,' he says.

Alicia looks at Liam's familiar face and his kind eyes. She almost wants to tell him about what she's just seen in the lounge, but suspects Liam also witnessed Mia and Patrick cozying up in the corner of the room. Pride and common decency stops her from complaining about the new life she's chosen for herself to the man she left to make it happen.

'Uffe was always very good to me,' Liam adds.

His face breaks into a wide grin, 'Although I could have done without the trips to the sauna.'

They both start laughing at the memory of Liam's reluctance to go through the island ritual. In all the years Alicia brought her husband and son to the islands for their holidays, Liam never once publicly declared that he disliked sitting naked in a hot room. A room that was sometimes made even more sweltering by the water Uffe threw on the hot stones of the stove, creating an unpleasant scorching steam. The sensation it created on his skin, which most Finns loved, Liam abhorred. Alicia remembers how he once told her he thought sauna bathing was dangerous for your health.

'Just say you don't want to go!' Alicia had told him, but he vowed her to secrecy.

'It's impolite to refuse a national pastime!' he insisted.

At the time, Alicia was annoyed. It was so typically English to carry on doing something one thoroughly hated just for appearances sake, so she let Uffe take Liam into the sauna with him each year. Now she sees what a kind thing it was for him to do. Just for Uffe's sake.

'He was a lovely man,' Alicia says, and holding back the tears pricking her eyelids, she adds, 'He was my father.'

Suddenly she can't hold on anymore. Tears fill her eyes and she brings her hand to her mouth to try to hold the tidal wave of sorrow that hits the pit of her stomach.

Liam puts his arms around Alicia and she leans into him. Rubbing her back with his hand, he says, 'There, there. Just let it out, it's OK.'

How easy it would be to go back to this, Alicia thinks. But she knows it would never work. Not now. Not after everything they've been through. And she loves Patrick, not Liam.

She pulls herself away from her ex-husband and dries her eyes with a tissue from her sleeve. Hilda gave her a small pack just before the funeral, and she's nearly used all of them.

'It's really good of you to have come. But you know we can't go back to how things were, don't you?'

Alicia is gazing at Liam and he nods.

'I know,' he says quietly.

He takes a step back and adds, 'There's a flight back on Tuesday.'

'Of course, you must be missed at the hospital.'

Alicia doesn't mention the nurse. She hasn't commented on the news that they've broken up. It's none of her business, and besides, it's happened before. And she knows Liam is a busy surgeon in an over-stretched health service in London.

'Oh, and by the way, we have an offer on the old house.'

'Really?' Alicia says.

'Yeah, the asking price, so I thought we should accept it?'

Alicia nods. Another chapter of their lives together is closing.

Again, Liam takes hold of her elbow.

'That's what you wanted, isn't it?'

'Yes, it's good,' Alicia replies.

'Actually, I've already accepted. I hope you don't mind?'

Alicia smiles and gives Liam's arm a squeeze. 'Book that flight too. I'll take you to the airport.'

'Thank you, Alicia,' Liam replies.

When Liam has left her, and the caterer comes back from the dining room with a pile of dirty dishes, Alicia excuses herself and heads toward the downstairs bathroom. She needs a moment alone to gather herself.

THIRTY-TWO

When Alicia emerges from the bathroom, she is faced with Brit.

'How are you?' she says and when she sees Alicia's face, she hugs her friend hard.

After a while Alicia remembers Brit's news and says, 'What about you?' She glances toward Brit's belly.

Brit places her hand over her dress, as if to protect the small life growing inside her, even though nothing is showing yet. She's wearing a tight black dress and kitten-heeled boots.

'Oh, you know. Feeling sick all the time, puking day and night, but apart from that...'

Brit gives a quick smile, and Alicia goes and hugs her friend once more. She realizes that Brit has lost weight.

'But you're still eating, right?'

Alicia has heard of women who have morning sickness so bad that they stop eating.

Brit nods, 'Yes, mother.'

'Just trying to look after my friend,' Alicia says with a chuckle.

She stops abruptly. It seems strange to be laughing now, here, today. She feels embarrassed and looks toward the lounge where she can just see the pastor standing with his back to the room and talking to Liam. She momentarily wonders if the clergyman speaks English, but then realizes he must do since Liam is obviously telling him something at length. Perhaps they are discussing theology. Liam is no churchgoer, but she remembers the heated arguments between father and son when Stefan didn't want to be confirmed.

'Alicia,' Brit says gently.

'Sorry, I was miles away.'

'I was just going to say that we are leaving. Jukka is giving me and my dad a lift back.'

'To his or yours?'

'His,' Brit says and looks down at her hands, which are knitted together underneath her belly. 'We'll drop Dad off first and then...'

There is the slightest of little lumps there, but Brit has always had the perfect curvy feminine figure. If you didn't know you wouldn't notice anything different about her. Perhaps, you'd just think she'd slimmed down a little.

'Have you told him yet?' Alicia asks, gazing at her friend.

Brit shakes her head, not looking at Alicia.

She takes a deep breath and adds, 'It's the right time.'

Alicia nods. 'But you do want to keep it, right?'

Brit's eyes widen.

'Of course I do!'

At that moment, Jukka steps into the hall.

'Do what?' he asks and comes to stand next to Brit. Putting his arm around her waist, he adds, 'We'd better be going.'

Turning toward Alicia, he says, 'I'm so sorry about Uffe. He was a nice man.'

Alicia looks at Jukka, the sea captain her schoolfriend fell for just before Christmas. He is tall, with brown hair and a good physique, and Alicia can see how her friend couldn't resist Jukka's charms. But he's divorced with a teenage daughter. She's not sure he will be up for starting again with a new family.

The small group in the hall is joined by Brit's dad. A small man with a pronounced stoop, Rolf Svensson looks even more frail than he did last Christmas when he and Brit had celebrated Christmas with the Ulssons. That day seems a lifetime ago now. Alicia hugs Mr.

Svensson, again aware of how small and thin the man feels under her touch.

Rolf Svensson pats Alicia's hand with his bony palm. 'He was a good man, your dad.'

The old man's eyes fill with tears and Alicia has to battle against breaking down. But she manages to hold it together.

Alicia hugs both Jukka and Brit again and bids them farewell.

Turning toward the lounge, she sees that Mia and Patrick are standing in front of her.

'You leaving?' Alicia asks Patrick. She's purposefully ignoring Mia. She cannot believe the audacity of the woman. It's bad enough that she came to the church, but it's plain rude to attend a wake you haven't been invited to.

'Yeah,' Patrick says. He's shifting on his feet, changing the weight of his body from one leg to the other.

What has he done to make him so nervous?

'Can I talk to you for a moment?' Alicia says.

'Without me, you mean?' Mia says. She's reapplied her lipstick and her bright-red lips lift into a smile.

'Be my guest!' she adds and, pulling her coat from a pile draped over the bannister, she heads toward the kitchen.

'I'm just going to give my respects to your mother, if that's allowed,' she says over her shoulder.

Alicia glances behind her and sees that Hilda is talking to the caterers. Turning back, she doesn't say anything, but just shrugs her shoulders.

'Can we go outside?' she says to Patrick, who's already holding his coat.

Grabbing an old sailing jacket from a hook, Alicia opens the door. She can feel Patrick behind her and she leads him past the front of the house and down a path toward one of Uffe's holiday cottages. She stops in a spot at the corner of the house, away from the large windows of the lounge. Last thing she wants is for everyone in the room to see her have an argument with Patrick. They will be gossiping enough as it is. Although, to her surprise, she realizes she actually doesn't care what people on the island say anymore. But she knows rumors upset her mom. Hilda has to live on these islands, not her.

'What's going on?' she now says, facing Patrick.

She's keeping her eyes on his face, searching for clues, as she waits for a response. She needs to know that whatever he's going to say next, he's telling the truth.

Patrick's eyes hold hers. Before answering, he bites his lower lip.

'What's the matter?' he says.

His voice is defiant. He's got his hands in his pockets, and again he is moving his body, bending and straightening his knees in turn.

'What's going on with you? First, I can't get hold of you for days. While I'm dealing with...with this.' Alicia points her thumb toward the house.

A low murmur, interspersed by the clink of coffee cups being replaced on their saucers is audible from the open lounge window next to them. Briefly, Alicia wonders if their voices will carry inside.

Crossing her arms and lowering her tone, she adds, 'And then you turn up here with your ex! And now you're fidgeting like you've got something to hide!'

Although trying to control it, Alicia is aware that her voice has gone up an octave.

'Nothing is going on,' Patrick says, calmly, standing still now. Like he's showing up her shrill tone.

Alicia releases her arms and lets them hang by her sides. She tries to keep her voice low. 'So Mia and you are best friends now?'

Now Patrick looks down at his shoes.

There is a silence, long enough for Alicia to want to say something, but she controls herself. She knows he won't be pressurized. Whatever this is, she has to give him time to explain.

'The new guy, Max, that Mia left me for, has dumped her, so she's very vulnerable right now. I'm just being a friend to her, that's all.'

'Like she was to you when she wanted rid of you?'

Patrick takes hold of Alicia's hands.

'Look, I know she doesn't seem to be sensitive, but she is suffering right now. As the mother of my children, I need to make sure she's OK.'

Patrick is gazing into Alicia's eyes. He moves closer and lifts her chin up.

'Work is crazy too at the moment. I told you that. You know I want to make a good impression at the paper, so I have to stay and follow every story they give me. With the Brexit deadline, the editor wanted me to cover groups who are calling for Swexit. I just couldn't come over sooner than I did. And I'm really, really sorry I couldn't be here to support you.'

He bends down and kisses Alicia's lips and she's too weak to resist.

'Isn't this cozy!' Mia appears at the corner of the house, a few feet from Patrick and Alicia.

'Mia,' Patrick says, but his ex puts up one of her well-manicured hands and turns on her heels.

'I know when I'm not wanted. I'll let you lovebirds carry on with whatever you were doing. Although, I think you should be ashamed of yourselves. It's your father's funeral for God's sake.'

Mia gives Alicia a dirty look.

'I'll wait in the car.'

She stomps away toward the temporary parking lot that Alicia and Liam had created next to one of the fields surrounding the house.

'You came in the same car?' Alicia says.

'It's not like that,' Patrick says. I told you, I'm just looking after her a bit.'

Patrick kicks stones on the gravel path.

Glancing up at Alicia again, he adds, 'It's good for the girls to see us get on. They hated it when we were fighting all the time.'

THIRTY-THREE

When Jukka and Brit drive away from her father's house in Föglö, Jukka turns toward Brit. 'Is your dad OK? He seems to have got thinner?'

Brit bites her lip. She's noticed the same thing. Rolf has never been fat, but in the past six months he seems to have shrunk. If only she could share her good news with her father. She's certain it would cheer him up and give him a new reason to live. It might even make him agree to move into an assisted living apartment in Mariehamn, something Brit has been talking to him about for ages. It would be wonderful to have him in town, closer to her and Jukka. The drive to Föglö, with the twenty-minute ferry ride in between, is not an issue when her father is well, and the weather is fine. But just last winter, the ferry was out of action for a whole week.

Brit glances sideways at Jukka. She still can't believe that she's found such a good and handsome man. And right here in her home town! He's sexy, kind, and gentle. And he's a sea captain, something that is more important to her father than her. She has butterflies every time she sees him in uniform. They're no longer serving on the same ferry, which means they are often at sea at different times, but that makes their time together even more precious. And exciting. Every time they spend the night together after a long shift on the ferries, it's as if they're making love for the first time.

And now she's pregnant.

Children were never part of the plan for Brit. She loves her job as the restaurant manager on MS *Diane*, even if it means nights spent at sea, long and late hours. A baby wouldn't fit in with her career, so she would either have to give up work altogether or seek a land-based job. Not something that's easy on the islands.

Jukka has a 16-year-old daughter, whom Brit has still to meet, from his fractious first marriage. Jukka rarely mentions the girl, who doesn't want to see her father. During one of their first encounters, after Brit found out that Jukka had been falsely accused of sexual misconduct on a previous ship, he told her the whole sorry affair of his first marriage.

'We were young, and when Leila fell pregnant, I wanted to do the right thing. But we were never well suited. When I went to Gothenburg to study, the whole relationship broke down. It was my fault as much as hers. I didn't come home as often as I could, and poor Leila had to bring up Silja on her own. There were a lot of arguments each time I came home, so in the end I just stayed away. Unforgivable, I know.'

He'd looked at Brit with those kind eyes of his. Brit had kissed him and told him it was OK.

Now pregnant herself, Brit is afraid that Jukka will think the same will happen to them. And would he be right? Will arguments over housework, sleepless nights, and Jukka's inevitable absences make their relationship go the same way as his first marriage? Especially if she is forced to stay at home?

Brit thinks about Alicia, whose career as a journalist was just beginning when she fell pregnant with Stefan. She didn't go back to it until he started school, and even then, she had only part-time jobs. That's the difference between the two friends: for Brit, her career has always come first. How will she be able to give that up now? At her age, pushing forty?

Brit places a hand on her tummy. She has spent nights imagining the small being inside her growing by the day. Soon she will start to show. At eight weeks' pregnant, she's already noticed a pronounced swelling of her belly. Her breasts are also fuller and tender. It's only a matter of time before Jukka, too, will notice.

When they pull onto the ferry and Jukka turns off the engine, he turns to Brit and asks, 'Do you want to walk on the deck or stay inside?'

The weather outside is now unseasonably warm. The storms have cleared the skies and brought on spring. The sun is still high in the sky, and there is only a slight breeze whipping the flag of the ferry.

Brit looks at Jukka and inhales. 'Let's stay in the car. I've got something to tell you.'

THIRTY-FOUR

They drive toward Sjoland and then past Hilda and Uffe's house, visible up on the hill, in silence. Jukka's mind is searching for something to say to make Brit feel better, but he doesn't know what. He should have reacted better to Brit's news. He doesn't know what came over him.

He gives Brit a sideways glance. She's looking away from him, out of the window.

'Hey, I'm sorry,' he says.

At his words, Brit whips her head back toward him.

'No need. At least I now know that I have to deal with this on my own. It's the story of my life. I have shit taste in men.'

Jukka places a hand on her knee and says, 'Honey, come on...'

But Brit moves her leg so that his hand drops away.

'Don't "Honey" me!" she says and turns her head away again.

After a long silence, they reach the turning to Jukka's place in Solberg. 'If it's not too much to ask, can you drop me off at home.'

'Brit, please. We only have tonight together before we're both on duty. And we need to talk about this, don't you think?'

Jukka is trying to appear calm and collected, although his mind is doing somersaults.

He's going to be a father. Again...

At first, the thought of a baby threw him into panic, but now, during this drive, which seems to have taken forever, he is feeling huge love toward the woman sitting next to him. Could it be possible that he can have another chance at fatherhood? Another chance to have a proper family of his own? He needs so desperately to let Brit know that he wants this baby more than anything.

Jukka's next shift on MS *Sabrina* starts tomorrow afternoon, and when he's back on dry land, Brit will be halfway through her stint on the sister ship, MS *Diane*. He can't wait two weeks to try to convince Brit that his first reaction was wrong. That he didn't mean to imply anything when he asked if she was going to keep it. Now he realizes what a terrible thing it was to say.

Brit has always been a career woman, she's told him so herself. Her comments on her classmates and their exes who've had large families have made Jukka believe that children were the last thing she'd want. And to be honest, Jukka hasn't thought about having another baby. He didn't even think it was a possibility.

THIRTY-FIVE

T he Monday after Uffe's funeral, Mia pops into Patrick's office in Stockholm unannounced.

'Surprise,' she says and sits on his desk.

'How did you get in?' Patrick says.

He glances around the large newspaper office, where most people are pretending they haven't seen his ex walk in. As if anyone could have missed her. Mia is wearing a close-fitting red dress with cowboy boots underneath and a tan suede jacket slung over her shoulders. Her lips, again red, match the hue of her robe exactly.

'I told the security guy I was your wife.'

'Which you no longer are,' Patrick says and leans back in his chair.

He cannot but smile at Mia's gumption. *Journalen* is particularly fierce with security. After the terror attacks against several newspapers in Europe and the Stockholm incident in 2017, when a truck driver killed seven people, the management installed bollards on the pavement outside the office and introduced strict vetting requirements for all visitors. Just as well Mia isn't a terrorist, Patrick thinks.

'I wanted to invite you for lunch,' Mia says and leans over to look at his screen.

Patrick moves his computer away from Mia's eyeline and glances at his watch.

'Spoilsport,' Mia says and stands up again. She glances behind her, catching out several people who've been listening in on their conversation.

Patrick sighs and gets up, picking up his jacket from the back of his chair.

'Come on then, where to?'

He knows Mia will have a place lined up. She might have already made a reservation in one of the up-scale eateries in town.

'I don't stand in line,' is one of her favorite sayings.

Now Mia gives him a sparkling smile and slips her arm through his.

Patrick doesn't stop her, but he is aware of the spectacle they are making in the open-plan office.

'I'll be back in an hour,' he says to Jessica, a young intern who looks after the Editor's diary.

She nods and glances quickly at Mia, who gives her a wide smile.

'Make that two,' she says and winks at the girl.

'You're going to get me fired,' Patrick says later when they are sitting next to each other at Sturehov restaurant. It's where they met all those years ago, and as Patrick suspected, Mia had made a reservation. They are seated at a round table meant for four, deep inside the restaurant.

'They've repainted it,' Patrick says.

As soon as the words have left his mouth, he regrets them. The last thing he wants is to start reminiscing about old times. Sleeping with Mia last week was bad enough; he mustn't encourage her. But it's too late.

Mia's face takes on a dreamy expression. She reaches her hand under the table and squeezes Patrick's thigh.

'Do you remember? We went straight to bed after the party. Just like last time,' she purrs.

Patrick looks at his ex-wife. She's made up her face carefully today; there isn't a hint of the tiredness he knows she must feel after all the traveling between the islands and Stockholm. Patrick feels rough if he has to commute more than two or three times a week on the Marie Line ferries. But then he has to get up to go to work at seven, whereas

Mia can keep to her own hours. From the smell of her long sleek hair, she's been to a salon this morning.

The woman studying the menu next to him is full of feminine essence. From her hair and the distinct perfume that is unique to her—a combination of the many creams she uses on her face and body. It's her scent that is most intoxicating to Patrick. It reminds him of the happy times they had together. The first few months when they couldn't get enough of each other, the elation he felt when their two daughters were born, the many summers they spent in Åland.

But he is also reminded of the bad times. When Sara had meningitis, Patrick understood for the first time since they'd had the girls that his love for them wasn't matched by Mia's. His wife, who stayed at home with Frederica while Patrick went to the hospital with Sara, was fast asleep when he returned with the good news that their daughter would be alright.

Different people react differently in a crisis, Patrick had thought at the time, but he was amazed when Mia announced the next day that she had to attend an important meeting. Mia only made it to the hospital once to see Sara. She was only laid up for two days, but Patrick spent the whole time there, sleeping on a folding bed the staff made up for him. He understood that Mia had to look after their youngest, but she also managed to go to work while Frederica was at daycare.

In the end, he accepted that his wife wasn't the loving sort. She was sexy, rich, and clever, and that just had to be enough for him.

'When did you get into town?' Patrick asks to try to move the conversation away from the intimacy they shared.

'Oh, last night,' Mia says, putting down the menu and settling her dark eyes on Patrick.

'And the girls are OK?' Patrick says.

Mia holds his gaze. He can see she's annoyed. The arguments they had in the last year of their marriage were largely about who looked after Sara and Frederica the most. As well as money. Mia worked as a property realtor for her father, a job that she often claimed needed her complete attention 24/7. There were dinners with investors and financiers, networking events three or four times a week, and even weekends away at conferences.

Later, Patrick found out that Mia was seeing another man while Patrick ferried the girls from school to horse riding or swimming classes. But Mia insisted she was making all the money for the family, so she should have a certain amount of freedom. Patrick suspected that Max, the Swedish tycoon, wasn't her first sidestep during their marriage. So how did Patrick get here again? Falling into the same trap with Mia.

The girls, of course.

On the day after Uffe's funeral, he'd been invited to Sunday lunch at Mia's parents' house near the English Park in Mariehamn. Liam was still with Alicia in Sjoland, and neither he nor Alicia wished to relive Christmas last year, when they'd last met at close quarters. It had been awkward, to say the least.

When Mia moved back to the islands, she had settled at her parents' place. It was supposed to be a temporary arrangement, but Patrick suspects it suits Mia well because of the in-house babysitters. On Sunday, Patrick noticed a certain tightening around Beatrice's mouth when Mia talked about her forthcoming meetings in Stockholm.

How long before mother and daughter fall out, he wondered.

But when he said goodbye to the girls after the meal, Frederica had climbed into his lap and whispered into his ear, 'I want you to live here with *Mommo, Moffa*, and *Mamma*.'

It broke his heart when he had to say he couldn't do that, and Frederica lowered her beautiful almond-shaped eyes and began fiddling with the fabric of her cotton dress.

Sara, of course, just hugged him tightly, saying nothing. Patrick wasn't sure if she'd heard what her sister had said. It was Sara that worried him most. She's become so quiet, and grown-up. Far too grown-up for a twelve-year-old.

'Sara and Frederica are absolutely fine. Looked after by my parents,' Mia now replies. A pinched tone has crept into her voice, but when the waiter comes over to the table to ask if they'd like a drink before lunch, she's back to the charming Mia Eriksson again.

THIRTY-SIX

Mia insists on a three-course lunch.

'You work such long hours, taking half a day every now and then can't hurt!' she says and empties her glass of champagne.

Patrick smiles.

'I do have to go back,' he says.

Mia places her hand on his thigh again and whispers, 'What no re-run of last week? I rather enjoyed it.'

Patrick can feel the two glasses of champagne he's already had fuzz his brain. He feels desire for his ex-wife rise again. Sex with her is nothing like it is with Alicia, but it's still satisfying. And it felt safe, comfortable even.

What's the harm in it? For old times' sake...besides, Alicia is fed up with him anyway and he might have already lost her, so why not enjoy the moment?

He takes out his phone and taps a message to the intern, Jessica, saying he won't be back. Not waiting for a reply, he puts his phone back in his pocket. While he's been concentrating on messaging the office, a man has stopped in front of their table.

'Mia Eriksson!' he says.

He's wearing a dark well-cut suit and his fair hair is slicked back.

His face is bronzed in the way you can only tan abroad, and his teeth are gleaming white.

'Oh my God! Justin! How the hell are you?' Mia darts up to hug the guy. They start talking rapidly, exchanging news.

'Island life suits you,' Justin says.

His eyes are devouring Mia's body and his arm is resting on her waist.

Mia giggles and glances down. As she does so, she remembers Patrick.

'Sorry, Justin. This is Patrick.'

Patrick extends his hand to the guy, not getting up.

At that moment, the waiter, carrying their starters, tries to squeeze past the man.

'Are you on your own?' Mia asks, sitting down, while the guy lets the waiter serve the *toast skagen* for Patrick and a green salad for Mia.

At least now the guy looks a little uncomfortable.

'Actually, I am. I was supposed to meet someone but they canceled at the last minute.'

'In that case you must join us!'

'Could you set another place here, please?' Mia directs the waiter who's now pouring the Chablis Mia ordered.

'Of course, Madam,' he says and asks Justin if he'd like to order food.

Neither has checked with Patrick if it's OK for Justin to join them.

For the rest of the lunch, Mia flirts with Justin, barely saying two words to Patrick. At one point, he goes to the restroom, only to return and find Justin and Mia talking in low tones with their heads bent close together. Patrick has a good mind to fetch his jacket and leave them to it.

The leopard can't change her spots.

THIRTY-SEVEN

'I've got something to tell you,' Hilda says.

Alicia and her mother are sitting having coffee at the breakfast table in the kitchen. It's two days after the funeral and the room is bathed in sunlight. It's early, barely 7am, but Alicia is sleeping badly, waking up at 5am most mornings in line with the sunrise. The curtains in the attic room are flimsy and let in the early morning light. Alicia is still used to darkened bedrooms, and now, after Uffe's passing, her sleep is sporadic at best. And she's worried about her mother. As soon as she hears Hilda's steps on the stairs, she gets up and joins her for a coffee, before they start laying out breakfast for Liam.

Alicia raises her eyes from yesterday's newspaper.

'I met someone the week before Uffe...' Hilda wipes her eyes with a tissue and takes a deep intake of breath. 'Someone who'd like to make contact with you.'

Alicia gazes at her mother's face. She is looking at Alicia with an expression she can't interpret. Hilda's hands are fidgeting with the tissue, and without waiting for Alicia's reply, she continues, 'I wanted to tell you before, but then, you know what happened, and I couldn't.'

Hilda starts weeping and Alicia goes over to the other side of the table and takes a seat next to her mother.

'There, there, just let it out. Grief is hard, but it's best not to hold on to tears if they are forcing themselves out.'

'This is not about Uffe.'

Her mom looks at Alicia with such a sad expression that she puts her arms around her and hugs her hard.

'It's OK, whatever it is,' she says, rocking her mom in her arms.

After a while Hilda wipes her eyes and blows her nose.

'I am so sad about him, of course I am. I miss him so much I can't imagine never seeing him come through that door again, but...'

'So, what is it?' Alicia keeps hold of her mother's hands and pulls more tissues from the box on the table.

'You'll be mad at me,' Hilda says and lifts her eyes toward Alicia.

Just then, Alicia hears the door to the middle-floor bedroom open and she recognizes Liam's careful steps on the stairs. Soon, he appears in the doorway to the kitchen.

'*God morgon,*' he says in his accented Swedish and he sits down opposite the two women.

Alicia is grateful for his attempts at speaking Swedish with her mother. She smiles at him and asks, 'Coffee?'

Liam nods, and when he sees Hilda's tearful face, he glances at Alicia, raising his eyebrows.

'Anything I can do?' he says softly, coming to stand behind Alicia while she measures coffee into the percolator.

Alicia shakes her head and says to her mother instead, 'Shall we make breakfast? Did you have something planned?'

With a heavy sigh, Hilda gives both Alicia and Liam a tearful smile.

'I've got American bacon. Can you do the scrambled eggs?'

When Alicia pulls in at the small airport, it seems as if she was here only yesterday. Yet so much had changed. Her stepfather had been buried and she and Liam had come to a new understanding. But she was unsure where she and Patrick stood.

Last night, staying awake in her attic bedroom, listening to the night-time sounds of the island, she'd thought about what she was going to do with her life. The financial newspaper she worked for in Stockholm had given her two weeks' compassionate leave. Her editor had told her that if she needed more time, all she had to do was let her know.

With the news that their house in Crouch End was to be sold, Alicia's options suddenly opened up. The house was mortgage-free, so the proceeds would be split equally. Liam had told her that the buyers wanted to move in as soon as possible, which meant Alicia could get her half of the money in a few weeks.

That morning, fully wakened by the dawn chorus, she had decided to move out of Patrick's (or more accurately Mia's) apartment in Stockholm. She didn't want to go back there at all. As soon as her mother felt a little better, she would take a day trip over the water and collect her things. Patrick had lied to her about the apartment, because he realized she'd never live there with him if she knew it was Mia's.

She looks across to her ex-husband and wonders if he knows what a huge favor he's done her by managing to sell their property.

Liam is getting his baggage from the back seat. He's traveled light, with just a carry-on bag.

'Thank you,' Alicia says when they are standing facing each other outside the small airport building, and she hugs him.

'What for?' Liam asks. The wind suddenly lifts his hair and he looks boyish as he tries to push the brown strands back into place.

'Oh, you know. For coming. And for selling the house.'

'That's nothing. Call me if you need anything,' Liam says.

He steps toward Alicia and kisses her cheek. She lets her lips graze Liam's faint stubble.

Liam smiles and waves as he goes through the automatic door to the security control.

Back in the car, Alicia sees she has a message from Patrick.

Can we talk?

THIRTY-EIGHT

Alicia is surprised to see Patrick is back in Åland. It's the middle of the week, when he should be at work. Lately, she seems to be completely out of the loop when it comes to Patrick's life. Gone are the several messages and phone calls they made to each other every day, along with the intimacy. During the four months they lived in Stockholm, they made love nearly every day.

Something has happened.

Alicia fears that something is Mia. The trouble is, she's not certain she wants to fight for Patrick. If that's what it comes to. She loves him passionately, but if he wants to get back with his ex, there's nothing Alicia can to do about it. A family should stay together, and Sara and Frederica need their mother as well as father. There's a hollow sensation in her gut when she thinks that she'll never be able to be with Patrick again. Not to be touched by his long, sensitive fingers, not to be kissed by him. The intensity of their passion makes Alicia blush. She feels a tingling down her spine. Suddenly, all she wants to do is be taken into Patrick's arms.

Alicia has asked to meet Patrick at a café in town instead of at his apartment. She realizes she can no longer be certain that Patrick received the apartment as part of the divorce settlement. The place also holds precious memories, so she wants to meet on neutral ground.

In view of their fractious conversation at the funeral, and what he might want to tell her today, she wants to be where it will be easier to hold back her emotions.

When Alicia emerges from the underground parking lot at Sittkoff's shopping mall, she spots him straight away. He's slumped in a seat, his long legs stretched underneath the table. He's drinking a beer.

Her tummy somersaults. Patrick, although a little disheveled, looks handsome and sexy. Alicia has to take a slow breath in and out, before beginning to walk toward him. She straightens her V-neck T-shirt, which she pulled in haste from her suitcase that morning. She's wearing her favorite jeans, which have grown a little loose around her waist since she's been on the islands, but she thinks they are flattering. Straightening herself up, she concentrates on each step as if she is on a catwalk.

Be strong, be strong.

Patrick is nervous about seeing Alicia, but he must come clean to her. This island community is so damn small, she'll find out sooner or later. Especially given the mood Mia is in at the moment. She's probably telling everybody she meets. He takes a large swig out of his beer when he spots Alicia in the distance. She's walking up from the far end of the mall.

As she gets nearer, Patrick rises. When he attempts to kiss her, he manages only to just brush his lips on her hair as she hurries to sit down.

'On the beer already?' she says.

The place is almost empty, with only a handful of tables occupied.

Patrick is aware of people clocking their presence. The island's jungle drums will be beating later.

Guess who I saw at Sittkoff's today? And guess what, the love birds were fighting!

If only he could have convinced Alicia to come to the apartment. But she wouldn't budge on that idea.

'It's lunchtime and I've got the day off,' he says, a little too defensively.

'I'm surprised to see you here. I thought you had too much work on to take days off,' Alicia says icily.

She glances at her wristwatch. Patrick knows it's already 3pm, but so what? He *is* on holiday. Besides, he needs the beer in order to have the courage to say what he needs to say.

Patrick knows he wasn't there for her when she needed him most. But death scares him. It always has. He doesn't know why, but he steers away from hospitals, hates funerals, and doesn't enjoy watching violent films. But he knows he should have helped Alicia with her grief.

'Look, Alicia, I'm really sorry. I've been a complete idiot.'

'That's true,' Alicia says.

She lifts her eyes up to his and adds, 'I hear it's over with Mia and her lover.'

Patrick is taken aback. He didn't think Alicia listened to the gossip, especially now she no longer works at the local paper. And Hilda, you'd think she had more important things on her mind than gossip about the Erikssons?

'Oh, you didn't think I knew? Mia knows Brit. Besides, everyone knows she's back living with her parents. At her age, I am surprised.'

'It hasn't taken you long to get back to the island life,' Patrick says, realizing his tone is hostile.

Alicia gives him a look that is full of sadness.

What am I doing?

He reaches out his hand and touches Alicia's fingers.

'I'm sorry. Look, I need to talk to you properly. Couldn't we go back to my place?'

THIRTY-NINE

Leo can't believe his eyes. At first, he's not sure it's who he thinks it is. He digs out the photo Hilda gave him and compares the image with the young woman who's just stepped into the shopping mall through a set of double doors. She's wearing jeans and a T-shirt, with a pair of short boots. Her fair hair is partly pinned up, and she is very pretty.

Leo's heart starts pumping as he watches his daughter walk up to a tall, good-looking man, who is nursing a beer just like himself. They greet awkwardly, half hugging and half kissing. This must be the Swedish news reporter, Leo thinks. The one who's just divorced the daughter of the richest man on these islands. In order to be with Alicia, his daughter. Pride swells inside Leo, and he suddenly feels his heart beating even harder against his chest.

Calm down, calm down. You mustn't keel over now.

Leo watches as Alicia and the newspaperman have some kind of argument. Alicia occasionally glances sideways, at the other people in the bar. Once their eyes meet across the empty tables. She has a defiant look in her face as if to say, 'What you staring at?' so Leo lowers his eyes to his nearly empty beer glass.

What to do?

Leo can see that both Alicia's coffee cup and the man's beer glass are empty, and neither is making any moves to refill their drinks. Leo has an awful feeling that any moment now, the two will get up and disappear though the door and down the stairs. What will he do then? Run after them—as if he could in his condition—or get up right this minute and ask to speak with Alicia. But what will he say? Has Hilda told her anything about him yet?

He read in the local paper that Hilda's husband died last week, which has put a spanner in the works. He's had to extend his stay on the islands because of it. But he's running out of time. His doctor keeps texting him, because he's missed a bunch of appointments at the hospital in Helsinki.

Leo glances over to the tills where another customer is being served a beer and licks his lips. Perhaps he should offer to buy Alicia and her boyfriend some drinks? And then casually start talking to them. But that kind of thing only happens in American movies. No one in Finland, unless they're next to a beautiful woman in a darkened bar, ever offers to buy someone else alcohol. Or coffee for that matter.

No, the best policy is just to go over there and introduce himself.

Gingerly, as if to see if his legs will still carry him, Leo gets up. Keeping an eye on the young couple, who are now in what looks like a full-blown argument, he walks across the cafe toward Alicia. When he gets to their table, they stop talking abruptly. He's acutely aware that this isn't something people in Finland do either. Talk to strangers like this. But then, unbeknown to her, he's not a stranger. Well, not by blood anyway.

Alicia and the man are staring up at him as he stands next to their table.

'Hello,' he says.

'Hello,' the newspaperman says, an amused look on his face.

Alicia says nothing. Close up, Leo can see Hilda as a young woman in Alicia's expression. Her pale eyes and her lanky build are his, though. Leo feels a lump in his throat. After all this time, he is finally face-to-face with his beautiful daughter. All he wants to do now is to hug her and apologize to her. Over and over.

But he must be patient.

'You don't know me,' he says in Finnish, addressing Alicia.

'No,' the newspaperman man says, again speaking first.

Leo gives him a quick stare. He's surprised the Swede speaks Finnish. He has now crossed his arms over his sizable chest and is looking intently at Leo.

'Should we know you?' he adds in English.

Leo ignores the boyfriend and continues to speak to Alicia in Finnish. 'There's no good way to say this, but I'm your father.'

FORTY

Alicia can't quite understand what she's hearing. Perhaps it's her Finnish? She doesn't get to use it as much as she'd like anymore, so she must surely be mistaken. This man didn't just say he was her father, did he?

'Can I sit down?' he now asks, glancing briefly at Patrick, who nods.

The man, who's wearing a worn-out black coat and shabby trainers pulls a chair out and sits down. He keeps staring at Alicia.

'Who are you?' Patrick says in English.

'I am Alicia's father,' the man says and extends his hand to Patrick. 'Leo Tuomainen.'

'My father is dead,' Alicia says.

'Yes, I know that's what your mother told you, but it isn't true. I've been looking for you forever.'

'I don't mean you. I mean Uffe Ulsson. He died last week. I have nothing to say to you.'

Alicia gets up, and as she does so, she feels her feet give away. Patrick is quick and catches her just as she's about to go down.

'I've got you,' he says.

The man calling himself Leo, is scribbling something on a piece of paper.

'Alicia, I know it's a shock, but please, here is my number. I'm leaving tomorrow, and I would so like to talk to you before I go. To explain.'

Alicia stares at the man's hands. There are protruding veins visible on the back, and long, slender fingers. Something about his gestures are familiar. There is a tremor as he holds out the scrap of paper. She lifts her eyes up to his face and sees the pleading in there.

'OK, but I can't promise anything,' Alicia says.

'Thank you,' the man says.

He blows air out of his lungs, his breath laboring. His complexion is very pale and his eyes are yellow around the corneas.

'Are you sick?' Alicia asks.

Leo stares at her for a moment and then nods.

'I'm fine,' Alicia says to Patrick, who's still holding on to her waist. She sits back down.

'Look, my dad, I mean my step-dad, died last week, and I'm not sure. I mean, it's hard...'

She can feel tears welling up, but she manages to hold it together.

The man puts his hand over hers and says in a soft voice, 'I understand. Just seeing you is enough for me. But I would like you to understand what happened when you were a tiny baby. And why I haven't been in touch until now. But if all this is too much for you, I understand.'

Alicia looks at his face. There is a kindness in those yellowing eyes. For a moment she feels an odd sense of calm. Perhaps this strange man is her father after all and not just a nutter? There is something very familiar about him that Alicia cannot put her finger on. She makes a decision.

'I'll meet you tomorrow. Which ferry are you going to take?'

'Oh, the last possible one.'

'Let's meet back here at one o'clock?'

'Do you believe him?' Patrick asks as he's following Alicia down the stairs to the Arkipelag parking lot.

'I don't know,' she replies, not looking at him. She's walking fast, like someone who's trying to get rid of him. Patrick takes hold of

Alicia's arm. The action makes her stop and turn. She's now wearing her large black sunglasses, so Patrick can't gauge the expression in her eyes. Her mouth is a straight line.

'Look, I know you're pissed at me, but what can I do? My income doesn't afford the kind of apartment that I knew we'd need in Stockholm, so the only option was to accept the Eriksson's offer. And I'm sorry I lied to you about that.'

'But you knew I wouldn't come and live with you, had you told me,' Alicia says.

Her tone is calm and calculated. She no longer has the demeanor of a wounded woman that she had upstairs in the cafe.

'Anyway, I can't talk about this anymore. If you want to get back with your ex, I can't—and won't even try to—stop you,' she says. Removing her sunglasses and fixing her pale eyes on his, she adds, 'You must think of Sara and Frederica, I understand that. Choose what's best for them. When you've made a decision, a decision that you can stick to, let me know.'

With that, Alicia turns on her heels and walks up to Hilda's bright red Mercedes.

Patrick stands on the spot, watching Alicia drive out of the parking lot and onto the road skirting the East Harbor. The sun is high in the sky. Its rays reflect on the sea, where a few boats are already moored and bobbing gently in the shimmering water.

Patrick hasn't got his boat out from its winter moorings yet, but suddenly he has a great urge to get onto his yacht and spend the day sailing. He wants to get out into the open and forget all about Mia and Alicia. Could he convince Sara and Frederica to come with him? He's sure he could get the boat out and ready today and they could spend the whole day at sea tomorrow.

What is he thinking? The girls are at school and Mia would never agree to take them out to go sailing with their father on a whim. Plus, getting the boat out means he'd have to pay the winter fees to the boatyard. He's only got away without paying up front because of whom he was married to.

Mia.

What is he to do with his ex? Contrary to what Alicia thinks, he doesn't want to get back with Mia. He loves Alicia, but even though he must have told her that a dozen times before that odd guy interrupted them, she wouldn't believe him. Is he really Alicia's father? If he is, his timing couldn't be worse. He knows Alicia loved Uffe as a father, but at the same time, she has said she's curious about her real dad and that Hilda would never talk about him. All Alicia knew was that he was a 'good for nothing' and that he died when she was a baby. Which doesn't now appear to be true.

A sudden thought comes to him. He turns on his heels and runs back up to the cafe.

As he enters the mall, Patrick can see that the man calling himself Leo is still sitting at the table where he and Alicia were in heated conversation just moments before. Patrick goes to the counter and buys two pints of Koff lager.

'I thought you could do with one of these,' Patrick says in English and settles himself opposite the man.

His clouded eyes lift up to Patrick. Glancing at the beer in front of him, he nods and takes a large swig.

'What do you want?' he says, wiping his mouth on the back of his hand.

'A "Thank you" would be nice.' Patrick grins.

'Thanks,' the man mumbles and takes another large mouthful from his glass.

'So you are Alicia's real father?' Patrick says.

The man nods.

'So what happened?' Patrick asks.

The man gazes at Patrick for a long time.

'You a journalist?' he finally says.

This takes Patrick aback a little. How the hell did he know that?

'Yes,' he says simply.

'You writing a story about this?'

Patrick laughs. 'Sorry to disappoint you but a man connecting with his long-lost daughter is hardly newsworthy. Besides, I work for the *Journalen* in Stockholm.'

Patrick is thinking, however, that *Ålandsbladet* would certainly carry a story like this, but he doesn't mention it to the man sitting opposite him, gloomily but steadily drinking his beer.

'Ah, that sounds important,' Leo says.

Patrick isn't certain whether Leo's words are sincere, or if he's mocking him.

'I wanted to tell you that Alicia is very fragile now,' Patrick says.

Again, the man considers Patrick. His eyes, although far from bright, have an intensity to them he's seen before in Alicia. Perhaps he is her father after all?

'I understand that,' Leo says.

'Why are you here. Now?'

Patrick is leaning toward the man, trying to gauge from his face if he is a swindler or some kind of crazy person.

'That's between me and my daughter,' Leo says and shrugs his shoulders. 'But hear this. If you mess with her, I'll kick your brains in.'

Patrick gives a quick laugh.

'Will you now!'

Leo swallows the last dregs of his beer and gets up.

'You'll find that a man who's only got a few months to live can be quite an opponent.'

With those words, the man turns around and walks out of the cafe onto Torggatan and disappears around the corner.

FORTY-ONE

Alicia is fuming. This is a new sensation and a welcome change from the grief that has clouded every moment since they found Uffe slumped in his chair in the milking parlor. She's angry at everybody. At that man who—although looking seriously unwell—boldly purported to be her dead father, and at Patrick. And at Hilda for telling her lies! Why would you do that? Tell your daughter that her father is dead? How cruel is that!

If the man, Leo, really is her father.

As she approaches the junction where a right turn will take her to Sjoland, she suddenly changes her mind. Switching off her indicator, and lifting her hand in an apology to the driver in a Volvo that was just about to overtake her, Alicia enters the roundabout and turns back toward Mariehamn.

Outside the police headquarters, Alicia takes a moment to gather herself. She needs some information. Ebba is a practical person and doesn't react well to emotional appeals. Usually. Alicia saw her briefly at Uffe's funeral, when she came to the church, but she didn't see her at the wake.

She may not even be at her desk. If the police chief is not available, Alicia plans to visit the newspaper office and ask a former colleague to help find out if her father is still alive. She knows her father is stated as Leo Tuomainen on her own birth certificate, but she can't remember if the online details would include his personal identification number. Through that, she can check if he is still alive. She knows it will be somewhere in the records, and the quickest way to find out is for someone who has access to them to check. Ebba will probably have a photo ID of the man too.

Alicia has to know if the man she's just promised to meet again really is her father.

'Hello, Alicia.'

Ebba gets up and comes in for a hug before Alicia knows what's happening. The woman is so tall that Alicia feels herself being completely enveloped by her friend.

'How are you coping?' Ebba asks.

She indicates with her hand for Alicia to sit on a small sofa at the far end of her office. It's a beautiful space, with large windows overlooking the East Harbor. Alicia sees that Ebba has filled the room with plants and that the sofa where they are sitting is new. There's even a trendy rug on the floor and a small glass coffee table. The office looks a lot more homely than it did just before Christmas when Alicia last visited the police chief. It's as if Ebba's office reflects her happier state of mind.

'I'm OK, but I've had a bit of a shock. Well, two actually, but you can help with one of them.'

'I'm intrigued,' Ebba says, touching a water jug on the table. 'Would you like some water? It's infused with mint.'

Alicia nods and says, 'I met a man today who told me he was my father.'

Her mouth is suddenly very dry. She takes the glass from Ebba and sips the water while she gazes at her friend.

Ebba looks at Alicia as if she's considering what to say.

'Ah, yes, I meant to tell you,' she starts. 'But then Uffe...well, when he passed, the time wasn't quite right. I didn't know whether I should tell you at all.'

'Tell me what?' Alicia says.

'Drunk and disorderly?' Alicia almost shouts the words at her friend.

'We didn't charge him in the end. He didn't cause any harm, he'd just fallen asleep on a park bench. I checked his story out, since he mentioned you,' Ebba says, looking directly at her friend, 'and it seems he is indeed your birth father.'

Alicia has so many questions in her head, but she can't seem to get the words out.

'I'm sorry you had to find out like this. In fact, I rather hoped Hilda would have told you herself.'

'What? My mom knows he's here?'

'Yes, well, I think so,' Ebba says

Again, Alicia is trying to let all this information sink in.

Ebba takes hold of her arm. 'Look, I don't know anything more than what this Leo Tuomainen told me. He'd been on the islands for a couple of days, trying to see you. He told us that he's spoken to your mom and that she told him she'd talk to you. But, I guess, because of what happened to Uffe, she's forgotten, or something.'

'Forgotten! How can you forget to tell your daughter that her dead birth father is alive after all?' Alicia says.

Her mind is whirling. Is everything she knew to be true about her life a lie?

How could Hilda do this to her? All those times when she was younger and she asked about her dad, her mom would clam up, saying it was no use Alicia thinking about him.

'He was no good, but he's gone now anyway,' was Hilda's stock answer.

When she asked about her real dad, Alicia had seen Hilda's expression change, her gestures becoming more concentrated. She never looked at Alicia directly when she brought up her real father. As Alicia got older, she recognized that change in her mom's face as pain, so she hadn't pursued the matter, and at some point she'd stopped asking. And Uffe had always been there, supporting her from a distance. A lump is forming in Alicia's throat, but she takes a deep breath and gathers herself.

The phone on Ebba's desk starts ringing, and the police chief gets up.

'Look, I've got to take this, but—'

Alicia cuts her friend off.

'I'd better leave you to your work.'

She leaves the office before Ebba has time to stop her.

FORTY-TWO

In the middle of the night, Hilda wakes suddenly from a vivid dream in which Uffe was sleeping next to her. Hilda stirred, trying not to wake him, and as she turned toward her husband, he opened his eyes and smiled at her. He put his hand on her cheek, just as he used to do, and kissed her gently.

Hilda can still feel Uffe's lips on hers, but then she sees the empty space next to her and starts sobbing. The dream was so real! She wants to stay in bed and carry on crying, or even howling at the unfairness of losing Uffe so soon. And so suddenly. But she has no strength left for any more tears or wailing. She visits the bathroom and returns to bed, but she can't settle. She lets her thoughts wander, and at about 3.30am, it suddenly occurs to her: she hasn't done anything about Uffe's estate.

The farm needs someone to look after it. Uffe employed a woman in Mariehamn to do his accounts, and there's Lars, the foreman, but he did everything else. Hilda knows that the fall crops will need to be sown soon. But she doesn't know if he made arrangements to employ the seasonal labor for the summer months. She needs to get her head straight, so that she can carry on Uffe's work. A sense of complete helplessness overtakes her and she covers her face with her hands. She knows nothing about running a farm. Uffe wasn't the type of man who talked about work in the evenings. But why didn't she ask? She was so wrapped up in her own shop, which in the end failed spectacularly, leaving Uffe to bail her out. For the past few months, all she has done is feel sorry for herself. She's been so self-centered, she didn't even notice her husband was getting sick. And now she's left with his life's work—his parents' farm—and she has no idea where to begin. How is she supposed to run the place when she knows nothing about farming?

Their solicitor, Staffan Ledin, or Old Ledin, as Uffe called him, even though they'd been in the same class at school, had come to talk to Hilda at the wake. He'd said to give his office a ring.

'We need to look at the estate matters. I have Uffe's will, which he recently updated.' The man, with a pronounced stoop and gray hair had taken Hilda's hands in hers and told her not to forget. Hilda didn't say anything. She didn't want to show her ignorance. If Uffe had made changes to a will, he must have made the original years ago.

But the matter had completely slipped her mind. Determined to make amends, she resolves to go and see Old Ledin first thing. She closes her eyes firmly and wills sleep to come. She must have succeeded because the next time she opens her eyes, it's light outside. Trying not to wake Alicia, she tiptoes to the bathroom, has a quick shower, and dresses in her best suit.

FORTY-THREE

Alicia wakes up with the birds again, after another night of sporadic sleep. She feels tired to her bones, but forces herself up when she hears movement in the kitchen. Sitting at the edge of her bed, she can't think what she's going to say to her mother.

Yesterday afternoon, when she arrived back home, Hilda had hugged her hard.

'There you are! I was getting worried.'

Alicia had seen the tears in her mother's eyes.

'I had coffee with Patrick. We needed to sort out things to do with the apartment.'

Her mom had nodded and given her daughter a brief smile, but she hadn't asked anything about Patrick. Alicia knows that she must have seen him with Mia at the funeral, but Hilda hadn't commented on their obvious closeness. She saw that the presence of both Mia, the heiress of Åland, and Patrick, Kurt Eriksson's former son-in-law and Alicia's lover, attracted discreet attention among the mourners. Especially as the once-married couple spent the whole time huddled in the corner of the dining room, barely saying a word to anyone else. Alicia can only imagine how tongues are wagging at this very moment. It's a testament to how badly Hilda's world has been destroyed by Uffe's sudden passing that she hasn't made the slightest comment on either Mia or Alicia's new partner.

If that's what he is.

Alicia thinks back to the day she left Patrick in Stockholm, and their love-making that morning. It's as if the world since then has been turned upside down. Or the clock turned back.

There is no way Alicia can leave her mother and return to Stockholm in the next week or two. As well as her mental state, there are all the practical matters to consider. Alicia gets up and collects her dressing gown from the chair next to the window, taking a moment to admire the beautiful seaside view in front of her. The sun is high in the sky and behind a very thin layer of cloud. The sea is gray-green, but it's still. Even the reeds are motionless, making the whole scene look unreal, like a picture in a tourist magazine.

'Hello dear, sleep well?' Hilda asks when Alicia comes downstairs.

Looking at her, Hilda already knows the answer. Her daughter's blonde hair is mussed and she has pronounced dark circles under her eyes. She's taking this badly, Hilda thinks. Another matter that she's completely forgotten about enters her mind. She gasps, but manages to hide her reaction with a yawn. She glances sideways at her daughter, who hasn't noticed anything.

How am I going to tell her about Leo now?

'Yeah, fine,' Alicia says, getting herself a cup of coffee.

'Where are you off to this early in the morning?' she asks as she sits on her favorite tall stool in the corner of the kitchen.

Hilda shoots Alicia a glance. She wonders if her daughter is strong enough to deal with Leo, or Uffe's affairs.

Old Mr. Ledin didn't say whether Alicia needed to be present when the will is read, but Hilda knows she should do this on her own. Perhaps after a few days, when Alicia is feeling a bit more settled, she can tell her everything.

'Oh, I'm just off into town to meet Old Ledin,' she says, trying to sound nonchalant.

Alicia looks up and checks the clock on the wall. 'It's a bit early for that, isn't it?'

'I'm meeting him at eight.'

'Oh,' Alicia says and gulps down her coffee. 'Let me get ready and I'll come with you.'

Her daughter doesn't wait for Hilda's reply, but darts upstairs.

'There's no need,' she shouts after Alicia, but her daughter doesn't listen.

Hilda sinks down on the stool vacated by her daughter and sighs.

FORTY-FOUR

Old Ledin has an office in the center of town, in a 1970s office block opposite the library. When Hilda and Alicia enter, a woman in her mid-fifties looks up from a desk and smiles at Hilda. 'Hello Mrs. Ulsson. I'm so sorry for your loss.'

She takes off her spectacles and gets up to hug Hilda.

'Thank you, Marie,' Hilda says and adds, 'You've met my daughter?'

'Yes, yes, I think you took riding lessons with my daughter, Karin?'

'Of course, I remember,' Alicia says. She has a vague memory of a slight girl with red pigtails.

'Karin runs the stables now,' Marie says, lifting herself slightly straighter. She's wearing a cotton dress that is a little too tight around the middle. Then, looking embarrassed, she adds, 'I'm sorry for your loss too.'

'Thank you,' Alicia replies and glances at her mom. Small talk is one of the things Alicia has always found difficult, and now even more so.

'You're living and working in Stockholm now, aren't you?' the woman carries on.

'I wondered if we could see Staffan?' says Hilda suddenly. 'I haven't got an appointment, but I thought...'

'Oh, sorry, here I am chatting, when you...' Marie interrupts her and goes behind her desk. Taking a quick glance at the computer screen, she continues, 'No problem. He's free until ten o'clock. I'll just let him know you're here,' she adds, picking up a telephone on her desk.

'Mrs. and Miss Ulsson are here to see you. Can they come in?'

Marie listens for a moment, then looks back at Hilda and Alicia and nods.

'Go right in,' she says, giving the two women the kind of pitying smile Alicia has got used to.

'Sorry, what did you say?' Alicia says.

Alicia and Hilda are sitting in front of a large leather-topped desk, the kind one sees in old TV series. The desk is almost empty; there is no computer, just one pile of papers inside a light brown folder. One of the papers is in front of Mr. Ledin, or Staffan, as he's begged Alicia to call him. Alicia has met the solicitor, a tall gray-haired man, on only a handful of occasions, but her mother seems to know him well, judging by the hug they gave each other when Hilda and Alicia entered the room.

Alicia is now staring at the man's wrinkled face.

'Uffe has left the entirety of the farm to you, Alicia. Hilda has the right to live in the house until her death,' Ledin nods at Alicia's mother, 'and she has an annuity, which more than covers Hilda's living expenses.'

'But is that even possible..?'

Alicia looks over to her mom, who's staring at the solicitor.

'Besides, I don't know anything about the farm!' Alicia adds. 'I'm a journalist, I have a new post in Stockholm...'

Ledin leans back in his old-fashioned wooden chair, which creaks as his body settles into it. Drawing his fingertips together, and pressing his elbows onto the armrests, he looks at Alicia. Nobody speaks for a moment and Alicia glances sideways at her mother again, who seems to be in shock.

'But...' she starts, but she doesn't continue the sentence.

'This is what your stepfather wanted. In fact, you are legally his daughter. You knew he adopted you when you were a baby, didn't you?'

Alicia snaps her head toward Hilda.

'No,' she says pointedly. 'No, I didn't know that.'

The solicitor shifts uncomfortably in his chair.

'Well, in that case this is good news for you!'

He tries a smile, looking at both of the women in turn.

Hilda is still sitting absolutely still, her back straight.

'It means you don't have an inheritance tax liability, as long as you continue to operate the farm as usual.'

The solicitor is faced with a wall of silence.

'Of course, there will be the usual checks. I will need certificates from both of you, detailing your birth dates, marriages, dependents, divorces, and so on.'

Suddenly Hilda wakes up. 'Is that necessary? You've known Uffe and the family for as long as...'

The solicitor waves his hand. 'A mere formality, I assure you. Unless Uffe had a second wife and children on the side, of course.'

Old Ledin laughs at his own joke.

Alicia glances at her mother, whose face is ashen. She's staring at the solicitor.

'What?' she says.

Ledin's expression grows serious. 'I'm sorry, that was a bad joke. I can assure you, I'd know if there were any irregularities...as I said, these certificates are a mere formality. If you like, I can obtain them from the Population Registry myself?'

'No, that's not necessary, I can order them online,' Hilda says quickly and gets up.

'If that's all, I think...'

Old Ledin appears startled by the sudden end to the meeting. He rises and walks around his large desk, stretching out his hand.

'Thank you for coming to see me. You can either mail me the certificates, or even better, drop them off for Marie. She'll add them to the file, and we can proceed with the probate from there. It should all be very simple since there's a current will and only the two of you sharing the estate. Unless one of you wishes to contest the will.'

The old man is holding Hilda's hands with both of his. He looks from Hilda to Alicia, and proceeds to take Alicia's hand. She tries to raise a smile, but all Alicia manages is a lopsided grin.

FORTY-FIVE

Alicia drives. Again. Hilda hasn't been allowed to drive her own car since Uffe's death. At first, she didn't mind, but now it is beginning to irritate her. She knows Alicia means well, but she's always been an independent woman and she needs to feel that independence now more than ever.

She thinks about the certificates she needs to provide and a cold chill spreads down her spine. And then there's the farm. The shock of finding out that Uffe hadn't trusted her enough to look after it hurts. When she asked what changes Uffe had made to his will lately, Old Ledin had said he wasn't at liberty to say.

'Client privacy,' he'd said and closed his small mouth firmly as if his narrow lips had been glued shut.

'Why mention that the will had been changed if he won't tell me what alterations Uffe made!' Hilda now says, speaking into the silence between them.

They're about to turn into the slip road toward Sjoland. Alicia indicates, and as soon as she's on a straight stretch again, turns toward her mother.

'You left that little detail about me being adopted by Uffe a secret. Another crucial part about my life that you've lied to me about!'

Hilda doesn't say anything. Her breath catches in her throat. She isn't sure she can speak, so she says nothing.

'I can't believe you've done this to me!'

Suddenly Hilda sees that tears are running down Alicia's face.

'Pull over,' she says, placing her hand on Alicia's arm. 'Can we talk about this at home?' she adds, trying to sound gentle, even though her heart is beating ten to the dozen.

Alicia nods and lets Hilda take the driver's seat at a rest area by the Nabben public beach. The small piece of sandy shore is packed in the summer months with both locals and tourists, but now it's deserted, the water lapping at the empty boulders.

They drive in silence until Hilda turns into the lane leading up to the house. Cutting the engine, she glances toward her daughter.

'I did it all for your own good, you know that.'

Alicia doesn't reply. She doesn't even look at Hilda. She gets out of the car and walks toward the house.

Hilda hurries after her. She catches up with her daughter just as she's going through the front door.

She grabs Alicia's arm. 'Please, will you let me explain?'

Alicia gives her a look that is so cold it shocks Hilda enough into letting go and dropping her hand.

'I have no time for you now. I'm seeing my real father in town later. I'll see what he has to say and talk to you later.'

What Alicia found out that morning about Uffe has made her even angrier at her mother. How did she think that she could keep such vital parts of Alicia's life from her? And how did she think she could make those decisions for her? It's cruel, or at best, unthinking.

Alicia is so angry she doesn't dare say anything to her mother. Instead, she runs upstairs like an upset teenager and phones Liam. She tells him everything.

'He what? Left you the farm? How's that going to work?' Liam asks.

Alicia can tell he is busy, and she's grateful he's picked up to talk to her.

It doesn't escape her notice that when they were married, he never took her calls while at work. Of course, later, it was probably because he was with that nurse. Alicia got so used to not being able to talk to him, she became quite good friends with his secretary. Until she realized the woman had been lying to cover Liam's affair.

Alicia decides not to think about the past.

'I've no idea,' she replies. 'I don't know how to run this estate!'

'Well, you could learn. It can't be that hard,' Liam says. He'd always been the practical one in their relationship.

'I guess. I did grow up here,' Alicia says. 'But that's beside the point really. In the past forty-eight hours I found out that the father I thought was dead is alive and that my stepfather had adopted me.'

'What does Hilda say?' Liam asks.

Alicia can hear people talking to her ex-husband. There are the usual echoing hospital noises of beds being moved along corridors and people talking at the same time in the background.

'Oh, I couldn't talk to her. I'm seeing Leo, my father, for lunch. I was thinking that I should see what he has to say and then talk to Hilda.'

'That seems like a sensible idea. You don't want to have an argument with your mother now, do you? You've both been through a lot.'

Suddenly, a lump forms in Alicia's throat.

Liam is right, of course. They are both grieving. The shock of the will must also be hard to bear for Hilda. If Alicia talks to her mother now, she knows she might utter things that she would later regret. With her mother grieving, she just can't upset Hilda anymore. She's already hurting. However angry Alicia is at her.

FORTY-SIX

Leo looks a lot tidier than he did yesterday. His hair is slicked back and he is wearing what looks like a newly pressed suit jacket over a pair of chinos and a neat white shirt.

He's sitting at the very same table she'd been sitting at yesterday. When he sees Alicia, he gets up and waves, slightly awkwardly. This makes Alicia smile. She feels a warmth she hadn't expected.

'What would you like?' Leo asks as soon as Alicia reaches the table. He stretches his arms out, as if to give Alicia a hug. But she holds herself back. It feels wrong to accept that kind of intimacy from a man she has only known for forty-eight hours.

'Coffee would be good,' she replies and sits down opposite Leo.

When he returns, Alicia notices that instead of beer, today Leo is drinking tea. And on the tray are two Danish pastries.

'Thought you might like something sweet?' Leo says, looking carefully at Alicia.

'That's lovely,' she replies. 'My favorite,' she adds.

The man, her father, is trying hard to be nice, so she tells him a white lie.

'It's so good of you to come,' Leo says.

Ever since they've sat down, his eyes haven't left Alicia's face. It's as if he's trying to see something there, or commit her face to memory.

'Can I ask you something?' Alicia says.

Leo opens the palm of his hands and says, 'Anything!'

'Why did you decide to look me up now?'

Leo shifts in his seat and looks down at his hands.

'It's difficult to explain.'

'Try me,' Alicia says and takes a bite of her Danish pastry.

'It's a long and boring story. Why don't you first tell me a little about yourself? Hilda told me you work as a financial journalist in Stockholm? And that you are very clever.'

Alicia laughs, but it's more like a snort.

'Hilda has a huge capacity for exaggerating the truth.'

Leo laughs and his face brightens, with his eyes shimmering.

'Yes, I remember that about her.'

Leo is momentarily lost in thought, looking past Alicia out toward the street, where a few shoppers are milling about. The silence gives Alicia time to study him.

Her father.

Leo has deep lines on his forehead, which is partly covered by fair brown hair. There are grooves either side of his mouth and around his eyes. He must laugh a lot, Alicia thinks. His hands are delicate, with neat, clean fingernails. He doesn't look like a tramp, or an alcoholic, but how would he otherwise have fallen asleep, drunk, on a bench outside the state alcohol shop, ALKO? According to Ebba, there'd been an empty bottle of Koskenkorva vodka on the floor next to the bench. Perhaps it hadn't belonged to Leo at all, but someone else? Perhaps there was another explanation for his behavior? Maybe Ebba and her colleagues hadn't arrested him after all. Alicia is certain that had the man opposite her been very inebriated, the police would have put him in a cell, whether he claimed to be Alicia's dad or not.

'I loved her very much, you know,' Leo says, fixing his eyes on Alicia again.

'So what happened?'

Leo leans back on his seat and looks down at his coffee.

'She was so young. And I was a fool.'

The pain now etched on his face is so visible that Alicia hasn't got the heart to interrogate him further. Instead, she decides to tell Leo about her life in the hope that it will make it easier for him to talk about the past.

'Did Mom tell you that I lived in London for nearly twenty years?'

'She did. And then you decided to move back here?'

Now it's Alicia's turn to grow serious.

'We had a son, Stefan. But he died in a motorcycle accident and I decided to come home.'

Alicia digs in her handbag for a phone and shows Leo a picture of Stefan. It's a photo taken the summer before the accident. Stefan is sitting on the porch of the sauna cottage, wearing a light blue polo shirt. He's smiling directly into the camera. His fair hair is caught in the breeze and he's got a hand out, trying to control it. It's Alicia's favorite picture of him. Looking at him now, she sees a resemblance to the man sitting opposite her. Stefan's long face, the curve of his mouth are unmistakably Leo's.

'Here's your grandson,' Alicia says and hands him the phone.

Leo takes hold of Alicia's phone and gazes at the smiling image of Stefan.

His grandson.

'I'm so sorry,' he says and hands the phone back to Alicia.

She can see tears in Leo's eyes and she has to look away to stop her own eyes welling up.

'He took after you,' Alicia says and puts her hand on Leo's. 'I'm so sorry you never got to meet him.'

Leo is unable to speak. He knew he had a grandson but seeing his youthful, smiling face, so like his own at that age, has made his existence palpable. It's unbearable to think that his grandson has lost his life while Leo himself carries on, 'miraculously still alive,' as the doctor put it.

'I would have given my own life for his,' Leo mutters to himself.

Looking up, he realizes that Alicia has heard him. She's still holding his hands, the softness of her palms soothing against his calloused skin.

She gazes at him kindly.

'Won't you tell me what happened between you and my mother? And why did you decide to look us up now?'

'I wanted to see you, really,' Leo says, removing his hands from underneath Alicia's. He takes a sip of his tea, which has now grown cold.

'What has your mother told you?' he adds.

He's buying time, and seeing the look on Alicia's face, she knows it.

'Not much,' she says, averting her eyes.

'That I'm dead?' Leo says.

'Yes.'

Again, Alicia isn't looking at him and this, in a way, makes it easier for Leo to start his tale.

FORTY-SEVEN

At first, Leo doesn't know where to start. So he decides to take Alicia back to Helsinki in 1980, when he and his friends played in *The Three Lions* band. About their brief success and their gig with Kirka.

'Your mum was in the audience,' Leo says.

When Hilda told him she was pregnant, Leo didn't hesitate to ask her to marry him. They'd only been seeing each other for a couple of months, but both sets of parents were old-fashioned, and a hasty wedding was arranged in the old, imposing Kallio church. Just stepping inside the place made Leo shiver, but when he glanced back at Hilda's smiling face, he felt he was doing the right thing.

Leo, who lived in Eira, the slightly more affluent part of the city, had never visited Kallio before. It was a working-class district. Hilda's parents were proud and wanted to give their only daughter a good send-off. Leo's mother and father were worried about how young they were, but they supported the marriage. They thought a good woman would make Leo settle down and start thinking about a serious career rather than putting all his hopes in a career in pop music. As it turned out, they were right. Leo's ambitions came to nothing. The band broke up when both of his mates found better paying careers, and Leo tried to strike out on his own. He eked out an income as a backing singer, even appearing on a popular TV chat show as part of a studio band, but he was always living hand to mouth. Until his parents died, and left Leo a pile of money.

'Which I intended to drink dry, but it looks like it will kill me before I even achieve that,' Leo says drily.

Alicia's eyes open wide and again she reaches a hand across and wraps her fingers around Leo's palm.

'Please, now I've found you, I can't lose you too!'

Leo is choked. He wants to get up and give Alicia a hug, but he is afraid that will be too much. Instead, he puts his other hand over Alicia's palm.

'You sweet girl,' he mumbles.

While she was with her father, Alicia received a message from Brit.

Are you around? Can we meet?

Driving toward Brit's apartment, Alicia thinks about her father. How she urged him to go back to Helsinki and get the treatment and medication he needs to get better. She wanted to add, 'And stop drinking,' but, then he must know that. They agreed to keep in touch and Alicia promised to go and see him soon.

She also wonders how things might have been if she'd known her mother's parents. Both died before she was seven, and she can hardly remember them at all. Would they have told Alicia the truth about her real father?

FORTY-EIGHT

Alicia finds Brit in her apartment wearing sweatpants and a loose T-shirt. Her dark hair is in a messy ponytail and she's wearing no makeup. Her eyes are puffy and red.

'What's wrong?' Alicia says and puts her arms around her friend.

'Oh, Alicia. He doesn't want the baby!' Brit blurts out.

Her face crumbles and she pulls away, dabbing a tissue at her eyes.

Alicia gazes at her friend. This is what she'd been afraid of. Jukka's previous marriage was a fractious affair, going by what her mother and Brit had told her. He's completely lost touch with his daughter. Now a teenager, she doesn't want anything to do with him. No wonder he doesn't want to risk failing again as a father.

At that moment, Brit's phone rings. She looks at the display, and over her shoulder Alicia sees the caller is Jukka. Brit presses 'Reject' and throws the phone onto the sofa.

'I don't mind if you want to talk with him. I can come back later,' Alicia says.

Brit turns around and says, 'No, you stay. I'm not speaking to him! Coffee?'

She moves toward the modern white kitchen. Alicia follows, admiring the wonderful view of the sea through the floor-to-ceiling windows. It looks like a summer's day outside, although the temperatures are low. The sailing season is still a little way off, but a couple of larger yachts are already trying out their sea legs in the open waters of the Baltic. The sun is shining from a blue-gray sky. Only a few months ago it was dusk by this time in the afternoon. Alicia sits herself down on the sofa. She should be grateful for the onset of spring at least, she thinks.

Every time Alicia visits her friend in Mariehamn, she's reminded of the first time she saw this new apartment block. It's where Patrick lived when they first got together. He still owns the penthouse unit in the luxury development. Unless, it is also rented for free from the Eriksson family. What does Alicia know. It could be yet another one of Patrick's lies. The entire development by the old harbor is part of their property empire.

Carrying two Iittala mugs with trendy blue and white patterns, Brit comes and joins Alicia on the settee.

'I'm on camomile tea. Can't stand coffee now.'

Brit grins.

'Tell me everything,' Alicia says and accepts a chocolate Domino biscuit from a plateful that Brit offers her.

'Oh, Alicia, I'm so upset.'

Alicia stretches her hand over and rubs her friend's arm.

'What happened?'

'I told him in the car on the way home from Uffe's funeral.'

Brit gives her friend a careful look.

'Sorry, I haven't even asked, are you OK?' Brit says.

'Surprisingly, I'm doing fine. I've got some news, too, but you first. Can I just ask, was that the best timing? To tell him in the car after a funeral?'

Brit looks down at her hands.

'I know, it was a bit stupid of me, but I couldn't wait any longer.'

'So what did he say?' Alicia asks.

'At first nothing. We were on the Föglö ferry, on the way back from dropping Dad off. When I told him, he was quiet for such a long time, I didn't know what was going on. And then...' Brit breaks down again and starts sobbing quietly into her tissue.

'Oh, darling,' Alicia says.

Brit sniffles for a while. Alicia rubs her arms and makes soothing noises. She thinks back to when she told Liam about her pregnancy. They'd only been seeing each other for a few months too, but Liam was over the moon. He'd lifted Alicia in his arms and told her he loved her. Alicia had been so incredibly relieved that he was happy. He'd even asked her to marry him on the spot. She's incredibly sorry that her friend's experience with Jukka is the polar opposite of hers.

'He asked me...if I wanted to keep the baby,' Brit finally says between sobs.

'What did you say to him?'

'Nothing!' Brit looks at her friend defiantly.

'I don't want anything to do with him. I'll have the baby on my own and that's that,' she adds.

Alicia looks at her friend and wonders if she's cutting off her nose to spite her face.

'What?' Brit asks, seeing Alicia's doubtful expression. 'You think that's the reaction a future father should have? Is it what Liam said when you told him you were expecting a baby?'

'No,' Alicia replies.

She doesn't want to tell Brit how wonderful Liam was all through her pregnancy. Looking after her like she was a china doll, fulfilling her every whim. Alicia had so many food cravings, and they changed almost daily. He'd go to the ends of the earth to find what she desired. Even though he was working hard as a registrar at the hospital then, with long hours, he'd always come home with whatever she'd asked him to bring. Whether it was Chinese takeaway, strawberries in January, or Swedish meatballs from IKEA.

Alicia takes her friend's hands into hers. 'But for us it was different. We were young and didn't have any emotional baggage.'

'Ah, yes, Jukka's past. But I can't always make excuses for him because of what happened to him previously,' Brit says, and carries on, 'Besides, it's obvious he wants me to have an abortion! This is my last chance to have a baby, I mean I'm already too old, really. But with Jukka, who I thought was in love with me,' here Brit's voice breaks, but she carries on, 'I thought we could make this work.'

'I'm sure he does love you! Perhaps that was just a gut reaction of someone who is afraid? I mean his past experience of family life hasn't been that good, has it?'

'Why are you on his side!' Brit says, but Alicia can see that she's thinking about what Alicia has said.

Of course, Alicia doesn't know Jukka any better than Brit does, but according to Hilda, he didn't have an easy childhood. His father, an alcoholic, beat him and his mother. He eventually left the family and died abroad. Jukka's wife was a bit of a snob, according to Hilda.

'A funny girl,' Hilda had called her.

'I don't know, Brit, but I just think that for the baby's sake, you might want to speak to Jukka? Has he been calling you a lot since your talk?'

Now Alicia can see a small smile forming on her friend's lips.

'Yeah, quite a bit,' Brit admits.

And as if Jukka had been listening to the two friends talking about him, Brit's cell rings again.

Alicia gets up.

'You take the call and we'll talk later.' Alicia picks up her handbag and jacket.

As she closes the door and lets herself out, Alicia hears her friend answer the phone.

Outside, as Alicia is walking toward her mother's car, she sees Jukka park his black Mercedes at the other end of the parking lot. He's wearing his captain's uniform, and as he gets out, Alicia sees he's carrying a vast bunch of pale pink roses. With his cap on, he looks every bit the romantic hero. Alicia waves to him and hopes that he will not let Brit down.

FORTY-NINE

When Alicia turns into her mother's drive in Sjoland, she sees Frida's car parked next to the milking parlor where Uffe had his office. A smile spreads over her face as she anticipates holding her granddaughter, Anne Sofie, in her arms. She hasn't seen Frida or the baby since she's been back on the islands. With Uffe's death, the funeral, and everything that's happened since, she just hasn't had a moment. She completely understood that the girl didn't want to bring an eight-month-old child to a funeral or leave little Anne Sofie with a babysitter while she came on her own.

Frida, her late son's girlfriend, had grown fond of Uffe since the baby was born. And Alicia thinks about her stepfather's fondness for the baby girl and Frida. He'd reveled in the role of great-grandfather, just as he had in the role of grandfather. Childless himself, he had enjoyed seeing Stefan grow up. To have another child, even if Anne Sofie didn't turn out to be Stefan's daughter, gave Uffe—and Hilda—a new chance to be involved in a child's life. Especially after Alicia decided to leave the islands and move to Stockholm. It was easier to go when she knew that Frida and Anne Sofie were close by.

For a few glorious months after Frida told Alicia about her pregnancy, they'd all thought that the child was Stefan's. But it turned out that after Stefan's death Frida, in her grief, had slept with their friend Sebastian and become pregnant. The two had found consolation in one another. Sebastian had then drowned while on a fishing trip, after going too far out to sea.

Since Alicia's move to Stockholm, Frida has become a frequent visitor to the house in Sjoland. Hilda even bought a travel cot, so that Frida and the baby could stay overnight or have daytime naps. Frida has told her that Hilda and Uffe have even babysat Anne Sofie on two occasions, when Frida went to see friends in Mariehamn.

As Alicia walks into the kitchen, she is faced with a lovely family scene, which makes her forget all about the anger she's feeling. Hilda is pretending to throw little Anne Sofie up in the air, and the child's giggles fill the large kitchen. Frida is sitting in the corner of the kitchen, on Alicia's favorite stool. When she sees Alicia, she gets up to hug her warmly.

'I'm so sorry about Uffe,' she says.

Alicia can see tears in the young woman's eyes. She's wearing no makeup and her hair, a shade of pale pink, is short with strands standing up in all directions. She's lost all of her baby weight and looks slim and healthy in her tight jeans and rainbow sweater.

'Thank you, darling,' Alicia replies and pulls away from the embrace.

'Hello, my little pumpkin!' she coos, moving toward her mother and little Anne Sofie.

As soon as she comes near, the girl holds out her hands to Alicia, who takes the baby from Hilda.

'Gosh, you've got heavier!' Alicia says to Anne Sofie, and then to her mother, 'You've got to be careful with your back, Mom!'

'I've been telling Hilda the same, but she wouldn't hear of it!' Frida says, smiling at Alicia's mom.

Alicia is delighted to see both the baby and Frida, but she's also glad because she doesn't have to talk to her mother about her meeting with Leo. She's still angry. Although her fury has abated quite a bit, she needs more time to calm down.

Hilda gives Alicia a look that is full of sorrow. Alicia moves her head away from her mom's gaze and concentrates on the baby. She dances with her and sings her favorite nursery rhyme, 'Små *grodorna, små grodorna är lustiga att se... Little frogs, little frogs, are silly to behold...'*

The little girl's bright eyes shut for a moment and then a small giggle erupts. Alicia swirls the baby around in her arms.

Hilda sighs and sits herself at the kitchen table.

'It's good to hear her laughter,' she says.

Hilda smiles but Alicia can see her eyes are red, as if she's been crying.

Alicia sits down opposite Hilda and asks, 'You OK?'

Hilda nods. Getting up again, she asks, 'Would you like some *pannkaka* with rhubarb jam?'

Alicia's mother lifts a checked cloth covering an oven tray on the kitchen counter and reveals the island specialty.

Both women laugh.

'Of course, *Ålands Pannkaka*! That's what the delicious scent is,' Frida says.

While her mother fusses with the food and fills the coffee maker, Alicia and Frida exchange news.

Frida has moved into her new apartment, occupying the whole of the ground floor in one of the older buildings in Mariehamn. It has an indoor courtyard garden where she'll be able to put a swing and a sandpit for Anne Sofie. There are three bedrooms and a newly remodeled open-plan kitchen.

'You must come and see it before you go back to Stockholm!' Frida says.

Alicia agrees that she will very soon. She's so happy to see Frida settled after all that happened after she fell pregnant. She also tells Frida how the newspaper in Stockholm is allowing her to take as much time off as she needs.

'So you're staying on for a while then?'

Alicia rubs Anne Sofie's back. The baby is still and lets Alicia hug her tight to her body. She looks over to her mom, who's standing a few feet away with her back to them. Preoccupied with the food, she's looking into the kitchen cupboards and getting out some plates. Alicia thinks she should go over and help her, but she knows Hilda would only shoo her away. She wonders how her mom will be able to manage in this big house on her own. And she worries about what she will do with the farm now that it belongs to Alicia. She can't understand why Uffe didn't leave it to Hilda. Is her mother upset about the farm, their argument earlier, or just grieving for Uffe? Probably all three. Alicia doesn't want to unsettle her mom further, but she's still reeling from the deceit. Why would you tell your daughter her father was dead? Was she ever going to tell Alicia the truth?

Alicia thinks of Patrick and how the relationship has suddenly broken down. Even if she wanted to return to Stockholm, she'd have to find a new apartment very soon. Not an easy task in a city where some people write software programs to get the better of the first-come-first-served system for renting accommodation. She knows there is no chance of renting another apartment soon, so she would have to buy something, which will be possible once she gets her share of the money from the house in London. But that would mean making a permanent commitment to a life in Stockholm. With or without Patrick.

'Hi, are you OK?' Frida says when Alicia has been quiet for a while.

'Sorry, deep in my own thoughts. So much has happened in the last few days. I'm not sure when I'll go back to Stockholm,' she says to Frida.

'We found out today that Uffe left the farm to me,' she adds quietly, over the child's head, trying not to let her mom overhear their conversation. The baby starts to wriggle in her arms and suddenly cries, '*Mamma!*'

Alicia hands Anne Sofie back to Frida, who starts rocking the baby.

'She's tired. I'm going to put her down for her nap in a minute,' Frida says gazing down at her daughter, who's stretching her long body over her mother's lap.

Frida adds, 'What are you going to do with the farm? If there's anything I can do, just let me know.'

'It's enough that you're here and bringing little Anne Sofia to see us,' Hilda says coming back to the table, carrying a glass cake stand piled high with slices of *Ålands Pannkaka*.

Alicia gazes at her mother's face, wondering how much of their conversation Hilda has heard.

FIFTY

While Frida is upstairs in the guest bedroom, putting the baby down for her nap, Hilda decides to confront her daughter.

'How was Leo?'

She looks squarely at Alicia.

While waiting for her daughter to come home, she'd made a decision.

'OK,' Alicia says. She's not looking at her, so Hilda takes her daughter's hands in hers.

'I didn't want to tell you what happened because it was so awful. We were young, but that is no excuse.'

Alicia looks up and her eyes are full of tears.

'But to say my father is dead!' she says.

Hilda bites her lower lip.

'I know that was wrong of me, but hear me out.'

She tells Alicia everything. At first, she'd decided not to describe the awful six months when Leo was staying out late after his gigs. When they had no money, and Hilda had to go cap in hand to her parents for money for food and rent. And when they could no longer help the new parents out of their meagre earnings, she'd asked Leo's father.

She will never forget the night Leo came home and saw the wad of money on the kitchen table. He'd woken her up and demanded to know where the cash had come from. When Hilda told him it was from his father, a bitter argument had started. They'd both been shouting insults at each other, and then Leo had struck Hilda across the face. For a moment, they'd both stood there, shocked by the act.

Hilda's face had begun to sting and then Alicia had started crying, filling their small apartment with noise.

'That's it,' Hilda said to Leo, tears running down her cheeks, making the pain even worse.

'Get out!' she shouted and she'd turned on her heels to go and pacify her baby.

While feeding Alicia, she heard the front door to their apartment close.

Early the next morning, or the same day, really, Hilda had packed all their belongings and taken a taxi, using the cash she'd got from Leo's parents. She stayed in her parents' small apartment in Kallio for two weeks, sleeping on the sofa with the baby in a makeshift cot fashioned out of two armchairs.

She refused any telephone calls from Leo and told her parents not to let him in when he pleaded through the door to see her and Alicia. Her parents could see the cut on her lip and the bruise across her face, so she didn't need to convince them that the boy their daughter had married was a violent man. All his phone calls also went unanswered. Hilda didn't want anything to do with a man who strikes his wife. If he does it once, he'll do it again, she thought. And it'll just get worse.

When Hilda saw an advert for a receptionist at Arkipelag Hotel in Mariehamn, she telephoned them and enquired about accommodation. There was a possibility of renting an apartment, and childcare, so Hilda jumped at the chance.

'I was only there for eight months,' Hilda says and smiles. 'I met Uffe on the first day and he asked me to marry him after six months.'

When the baby wakes up and Frida says she needs to get back, Hilda and Alicia exchange looks.

It's been a wonderful afternoon with the young mother and Anna

Sofie. It's the first time since they found Uffe that Alicia has seen her mother laugh. She doesn't want to upset her mom again, but she has to know why Hilda told her that Leo was dead.

Alicia doesn't know what she should think about her new-found father. Striking a woman is unforgivable, and she knows in similar circumstances she would have done what Hilda did. But to lie about Leo all these years? Would she really not have let a father see his child?

Ever?

'Was it the first time Leo hit you?' she asks her mother when they've closed the door after Frida.

Hilda's watery red-rimmed eyes flash with anger.

'Are you saying once isn't enough?'

Alicia goes to hug her mom.

'No, of course not. I'm just trying to understand why you felt you needed to lie about him.'

Hilda pulls herself away from Alicia's embrace and dabs at the corners of her eyes with a tissue. She sits down heavily at the kitchen table.

Not looking at Alicia, she says, 'I know that was wrong. But I wanted to protect you.'

Now Hilda lifts her eyes up to her daughter and adds, 'The thought of having to send you over to the mainland to stay with your real dad was just too scary for me. It would have been different if he had lived closer...'

'But he could have visited me here!' Alicia protests.

'I know,' Hilda says quietly. 'But Uffe...'

'What about Uffe?'

'He was very jealous as a young man. And I didn't think he'd want to adopt you if he knew your real father was alive...'

'So you lied to Uffe too?' Alicia asks.

She's incredulous. She can't believe that her mother, her funny and warm mother, would have been able to lie most of her life about something so important.

'You don't understand, Alicia,' she says, leaning toward Alicia on the other side of the kitchen table.

'Times were different on the islands in those days. People weren't so forgiving. I was a single mother. Being a widow was a whole different thing from being a divorcee.'

Something doesn't add up. Suddenly Alicia thinks of something.

'Wait. You did get a divorce from my real father, didn't you?'

Hilda doesn't look at Alicia, but starts weeping quietly.

'Mom?' Alicia says.

And another thing hits her.

'That's why Uffe left the farm to me. He knew, didn't he?'

Hilda is now wringing her hands. She lifts her gaze toward Alicia. Her tear-filled eyes are pleading.

'I don't know! Perhaps he had found out, but he never said anything to me. The thing was, I couldn't fill in the papers and send them to him because then he would have known where I was. I didn't have a choice. We got married in Sweden, so it was easier. Isn't it best we just leave things as they are? It says in the will that I can live in the house, and if you look after the farm, we'll be fine. Especially as Uffe left me such a generous allowance! No one needs to know now.'

'Oh, Mom. You're forgetting one person. Two people, actually. Leo knows. And Ebba knows that Leo is my real father.'

'How?' Hilda asks, her eyes wide.

'He was picked up drunk and asleep on a park bench outside ALKO. And when he told the arresting officer at the station he was looking for me, Ebba interviewed him. She told me she made an exception and let him go because of my involvement. Which was nice of her.'

Hilda snorts.

'He's not changed then!' she exclaims.

Alicia gets up and puts her hands on her waist.

'Mom, this is serious,' she says, frantically trying to think what they should do.

FIFTY-ONE

'Look, my first thought was that you didn't want a baby. You've said it so many times!'

Jukka is standing in the middle of Brit's living room. She hasn't asked him to sit down and he doesn't dare move in case her anger flares up again.

She took the flowers and let him in. She's now arranging the roses in a large vase. She's got her back to him and Jukka isn't sure if she's even listening.

'Really? You were just thinking of me. That's rich!'

Brit lifts the vase and turns around, but Jukka has anticipated her move and takes it from her.

'You shouldn't be carrying anything,' he says gently.

Brit looks at him and he sees that the expression in her eyes has softened. They are no longer black. The corners of her mouth are lifting a little, with the beginnings of a smile.

They stand there, in the middle of the room, facing each other over the vast bouquet of pink roses.

'Put them on the table, for goodness sake, and sit down. You're making me nervous,' Brit eventually says.

Jukka places the flowers on a wide glass table, set in front of a white sofa. He takes off his uniform jacket, removes his cap, and sits down.

'Can we please start again?' he says.

'Yeah, OK,' Brit says.

Jukka exhales deeply. It feels as if he's been holding his breath for days, ever since Brit got out of his car outside her apartment block. It's been nearly a week. In the end, when she wasn't answering his calls, he asked for a few days' leave and left MS *Sabrina* early so he could come and talk to her.

He scoots up the sofa and puts his arms around Brit. He's relieved that she doesn't resist. He squeezes her gently, then pulls away to look into her eyes.

'I love you, Brit Svensson,' he says and kisses her lips.

Brits accepts all of Jukka's explanations. For now.

He tells her that he was so surprised that he panicked. That he didn't realize how much he wanted this baby with Brit until he thought it wasn't going to happen. That he spent his three-day shift on board MS *Sabrina* worrying that she had done something drastic, and that he had prayed, for the first time in his life, that she would let him explain and would understand how happy, 'ecstatic', he was about the news.

'I'm going to be a father again!' he says and gives her the widest smile she's ever seen from him.

'It's early days,' Brit says, 'I'm not exactly a spring chicken so we mustn't take anything for granted.'

Jukka nods with a severe, concerned expression.

'But you're fine now?' he asks.

Brit smiles.

'Yes, apart from feeling sick nearly all the time.'

They hug and kiss for a long time, until Jukka asks her breathlessly, 'Can we, is it OK if we..?'

'Yes,' Brit says, and they move to her bedroom.

Jukka is so gentle and loving that Brit thinks she's in bed with a new man.

'I'm worried about you at work,' Jukka says afterward, stroking her belly.

They are lying in bed, warm in each other's embrace.

Brit moves onto her side, resting her head on her hand and letting her breasts fall close to Jukka's face.

He puts his nose between them and then kisses her nipples in turn.

'Again?' Brit laughs.

'Why not? We've got some making up to do. I've been in the Sahara for nearly two weeks!'

Jukka kisses Brit's mouth again and they fall back onto the sheets.

Next morning, when they are both wearing the matching dressing gowns that Brit bought on special offer in the ferry's tax-free store, she reopens the conversation about her job.

'What did you mean when you said that you were worried about my work?'

Jukka is munching on a piece of toast while Brit is making tea.

'You're on your feet the whole of the shift. And I know there's always some heavy lifting to be done. Couldn't you apply to work ashore at the ferry terminal?' Jukka says, as he begins to fill the percolator with coffee.

Brit gazes sideways at him. Even in the pale blue cotton gown, which he'd called 'dainty' because it had a tiny bit of embroidery at the sleeves, he looks manly and handsome.

It's nice to hear that Jukka is concerned about her and the baby's health. Brit, too, has been worrying about how she will manage her shifts. But she has always worked. She's always earned her own money ever since she took her first summer job on the ferries when she was sixteen. Besides, the sea is in her blood. Wouldn't she be bored on a shore job? The thought of not watching the ship sail from a restaurant window several decks above the water, or not falling asleep to the clangs and bangs of the ship on a night duty seems unreal. At first, the prospect of being able to sleep in her own bed every night seemed luxurious, but wouldn't it become dull after months and months of pregnancy? Her chest contracts with the pressure of the realization that this is what she'll have to do until the child is old enough to be left alone. When will that be? When she or he is eighteen?

What have I done?

'What's the matter? Are you feeling sick?' Jukka comes over and puts his hand round Brit's waist.

Brit rushes out of the room and just makes it to the bathroom before she throws up.

Sitting on the tiled floor, she wipes her mouth and leans back against the wall. Tears start running down her cheeks. She can't do this! She can't be a mother. She can't even fully take care of herself, let alone another human being. And what if Jukka suddenly panics again and decides he can't have anything to do with Brit or the baby? Can she fully trust him? And how will their fledgling relationship last the stresses and strains of parenthood? The sleepless nights, the worry, the changes to her body?

In the coming months she will become fat and unattractive. Perhaps Jukka will cope with that, but what if she can't shake off the pounds after the baby? She's seen how friends who've become mothers look on Facebook. She cannot remember how many times she's thought that if that's the price of motherhood, she's grateful she's missed the boat.

Since she did the pregnancy test, however, she's been in a haze of happiness about the baby. Even when Jukka said what he said, Brit was determined to keep the baby and looking forward to holding the tiny human being in her arms. She imagined how the baby boy or girl would look, who he or she would take after.

She's already been browsing maternity clothes and baby equipment online, and she even had a quick look in the ship's tax-free shop. She nearly bought organic pregnancy stretch mark oil, but came to her senses when she realized that the staff in the shop would know her secret if she did.

Sitting on the floor of the bathroom, waiting for the nausea to pass, she knows she can't be this person. She's no earth mom, rubbing oil onto her tummy—*organic* oil!—while humming tantric mantras for the foetus inside her. She gets up gingerly, trying to avoid another bout of throwing up. She's going to tell Jukka he was right all along. Her hormones must have been messing with her head. There is no way she can cope with a child in her life. It just isn't her. Luckily, she's only nine weeks gone. There's still enough time to go to her doctor and get a termination.

FIFTY-TWO

Mia is pacing up and down her parents' large dining room in Mariehamn. It's Saturday afternoon and she's alone in the house; her parents, Kurt and Beatrice, have taken the girls out to the small cinema in town to see the latest *Frozen* movie. Although Sara was reluctant to go, saying it was 'commercial capitalist junk aimed at corrupting young people's brains', she was eventually brought around by her sister's pleas. Mia was impressed by her father's restraint when Sara let rip with her newly acquired vocabulary. If she'd done or said something similar when she was Sara's age, there would have been a silence, followed by a punishment. Perhaps a month of no pocket money, and then grounded on top of that. Her girls get away with murder with their *Mofa*. Which is just as well, since her parents have been taking care of the girls quite a bit since she's been back on the islands.

Living with her parents in their large stone house, Villa Havis, has made it easier to look after the girls, but Mia isn't sure their closeness didn't drive Max away in the end. The house is large, three stories tall, but living under the same roof as your wife's family can't have been easy. Especially with two people as opinionated as Kurt and Beatrice. Patrick often whinged about the lack of privacy and independence, but Mia thought he was being ungrateful. Why wouldn't her parents have a say in their lives when they more or less financed their lavish lifestyle?

Villa Havis stands atop a hill near the English Park, with views across the West Harbor. From the dining room windows, where Mia is now standing, she can see the masts of Pommern, the old museum ship, its sails fluttering in the slight wind. Next to the old vessel, the now empty jetties are jutting out to sea. In front of them is the green sloping roof of the Seglarpaviljongen, where Mia and Max often met to have a drink or something to eat, while Kurt and Beatrice babysat the girls. Max had a beautiful yacht, which he parked at the jetty, but Mia refused to board unless it was safely tied up. Unusual for one who'd grown up on the islands, she hated sailing and wouldn't join Max for a day's cruise, however much he begged her.

What is it about sailing and men I love?

Patrick, too, had insisted on getting a yacht in the early days of their marriage. Back when Mia was still infatuated with him, she'd promised to let him teach her how to sail. But it had never happened. Instead, he'd taken that self-important tart out on his boat. The yacht bought with Mia's father's money. When Mia thinks of Alicia, she finds herself imagining ways to humiliate her. To hurt her.

Mia glances at the cell phone in her hand. Patrick promised to call her back as soon as he could. They had agreed to meet while the children and her parents were out of the way, but when she phoned to tell him the coast was clear, he'd said he was in the middle of something and would call her back.

I bet that something is called Alicia.

When the phone goes and Patrick sees it's Mia again, he lets it ring. He can always say he was driving and couldn't pick up. The truth is, Patrick doesn't want to see his ex. Not before he's worked out in his own mind what he wants.

He looks out to sea from the penthouse by the old fishing port. The sea is dark gray. The sun is shining in through the windows, but he can see rain further out in the shipping channel.

Storm clouds are gathering.

Seeing Alicia for coffee had made him even more confused. He knows he loves her and wants to be with her, but she is right. The girls must come first. When he'd spoken to Leo, after Alicia had left, he had been determined to win her back. But then, at home that same evening, he spoke with Frederica on the phone. She asked him when he was going to come over to Villa Havis.

'We could make popcorn and watch a movie together, Sara, you me and Mom,' she'd said in her childish sleepy voice.

It broke his heart to hear his daughter wish that her parents were still together, living in the same house.

Is it selfish of him to want to be happy? Because Alicia makes him happy. She is so unassuming, never worrying about what others think. And she's clever, and far closer to him politically than Mia. The amount of times he had to bite his tongue with the Eriksson family. His father-in-law is utterly right-wing and believes that hard work gets you everywhere. He even thinks that his hard work got him where he is, the richest man in the islands. He doesn't take into account that he was born with a silver spoon in his mouth. His father was a large landowner, who invested in property, so Kurt is far from the poor farmer's boy he purports to be. When he wed Beatrice, he married into more money. She is a famous author, and her parents were well-known artists in Finland.

Money attracts money.

But he'd managed to keep his leftist views to himself all through his marriage. Had it not been for Mia wanting to end it all, he would never have had the affair with Alicia. Or would he? He can't remember feeling the way he does for Alicia with Mia. Mia was an infatuation; he was flattered that someone like her even looked twice at him, a run-of-the-mill reporter. He was poor, his parents were nobodies. Yet, she wanted him!

That elation soon evaporated, but then they had the girls. First it was Sara and then Frederica who were his reasons for keeping it all together. In time, Mia and Patrick fell into a routine. There was little or no sex, but when they made love it was good. Functional, but good. And Patrick was happy with that. He loved being a *hemmapappa*, seeing the girls grow while Mia worked in her father's business and brought home the bacon. Not a little bit of money either. They never wanted for anything and always had the latest gadgets, a large apartment in the center of Stockholm, and nights out whenever and wherever they wanted. When the girls started pre-school, he got a part-time post at his old paper, *Journalen*. Before Mia dropped the divorce bomb, he'd even begun to think that he'd be clever enough and good enough as a reporter.

Would he want to go back to that life with Mia in Stockholm? He certainly wanted to be a family again. He wouldn't have to worry about money ever again, either. He'd make sure that she signed a pre-nup that would properly take care of him this time around.

The thought of having to leave Alicia makes his heart sink. Love-making has never been as good with anyone else. Her sleek body under his, her soft moans and the way she touches him. With her, he doesn't have to try to be someone else, or think about anything. All he needs to do is take her into his arms and go with the flow. And what a flow! He feels himself getting hard just thinking about Alicia's body.

But what if Alicia can't forgive him for what he's done? He knows he should have told her the truth about the apartment in Stockholm. But if he had, she would not have come to live with him. And Mia had solemnly promised that she would never come to the apartment. Like so many promises Mia has made, she broke that one too.

This has to stop. I have to make her stop.

Patrick picks up his leather jacket and car keys and rushes out of the apartment.

FIFTY-THREE

When Mia doesn't hear from Patrick for another ten minutes, she can wait no longer. She leaves the house and gets into her car.

Outside the apartment block in the old fishing harbor, Mia scans the parking lot, but Patrick's BMW is nowhere to be seen. She curses under her breath and checks her phone, but there's no message from him. She puts in another call, but that too, like the one she made from Villa Havis, goes to voice mail.

For a moment, Mia sits in her car, looking at the sea in front of her. The sea glitters as the wind and sun kiss the surface. It's beautiful but Mia can't bring herself to appreciate the view. She glances at the dashboard and sees she still has an hour before the girls and her parents are back from the cinema. If she's lucky they'll take the kids for a pizza afterward.

I might as well make some use of my time.

She rings the intercom downstairs and almost immediately gets Brit's voice at the other end.

'Hi, I was in the neighborhood and thought I'd see if you're home.'

. . .

'It's been such a long time!' Brit says and gives Mia a cursory hug and an air kiss.

'Hasn't it!' Mia replies.

Mia's wearing a stylish denim one-piece that perfectly flatters her slim frame. A pair of tan cowboy boots and a matching bag with tassels complete the look.

Brit feels a prick of jealousy. She wonders if she'll ever get away with wearing something like that. Her skirts and trousers already feel too tight around her belly. Again, she asks herself if she's doing the right thing keeping the baby. Jukka had convinced her yesterday, after a long, protracted conversation ending in more lovemaking, that the baby was the best thing that had happened to him—and them. Seeing his sincere enthusiasm and love both for her and the small blob growing inside her belly made her promise not to do anything rash, at least until they would have time to talk about it again.

'What's up?' Mia asks and flings herself onto Brit's sofa.

'Oh, just tired,' Brit says and adds, 'Coffee, or something stronger?'

'Oh, I'd love something stronger, but I'm driving. And I've got the girls this weekend,' Mia says and makes a face at Brit.

'Don't ever have children whatever you do,' she laughs, as Brit hands her a cup.

Without thinking what she's doing, Brit stares at Mia for a long time.

Too long.

'Oh my God, you're pregnant!' Mia exclaims.

FIFTY-FOUR

'You mustn't tell anyone,' Brit says.

'Of course not!' Mia replies

Mia smiles, gets up and gives Brit a hug. The moment is so surprising, that Brit forgets to stand up and the hug becomes an awkward gesture in which Mia puts her hands loosely around Brit's shoulders. Mia is so stiff and her body so lean that it feels like hugging a slim tree trunk.

After a while, Mia lets go and sits back down on the sofa.

'And there I was thinking I had problems!' she says and takes a sip of her coffee.

Brit doesn't say anything. She's furious with herself. Why didn't she deny it! A panic rises in her gut. Mia is a notorious gossip, which is strange for a woman with so many secrets.

'What's up with you?' Brit says and then realizes that sounded unfriendly. 'You know, problem shared...'

She smiles, trying to cover the awkwardness that fills the space between them.

'I'm not sure I should tell *you*,' Mia says.

Brit knows that Mia needs no invitation to tell her everything, but she encourages her all the same.

'Do go on. I need to take myself out of my own particular crisis just now!'

Brit tries to laugh, but a strange noise comes out of her throat. Like a guffaw, or an aborted giggle.

Aborted! What a word to think about.

'I'll tell you in a second. But you first. Are you going to keep the baby?' Mia asks.

Brit gives Mia a quick glance, and says, honestly, 'I haven't decided yet.'

'Oh,' Mia says. 'Doesn't Jukka want it?'

Brit looks down at her hands. She can't believe this woman. They were friends (of sorts, not like her and Alicia) at school. But they have not seen one another very much since then. Apart from that Caribbean cruise, which Mia and Patrick took without knowing that Brit worked on the ship. Even that was years ago. Like so many times before, Brit regrets her decision to take Mia's offer of an apartment rental in the old fishing port. It had seemed a perfect solution when she needed somewhere to live quickly on her return to the islands last fall, but now she is beholden to her old schoolfriend. Especially as the rent is far below market price. And everything is complicated by the fact that Mia's ex is now living with Brit's best friend.

'Jukka is delighted,' Brit replies.

Mia leans over toward Brit at the other end of the sofa and puts on a kind expression, which frankly doesn't suit her.

'But you don't want to give up your lifestyle? I completely understand.'

Brit doesn't reply to Mia but gets up and says, 'More coffee?'

Mia pouts.

'Oh, don't get all upset with me. You can be honest, I won't tell a soul, not even the baby when it becomes a teenager and wants to hate you!'

Mia gives a short laugh and Brit sees her chance. Coming back with the French coffee press and filling Mia's cup with the dark liquid, she says, 'Yours can't be teenagers already, can they?'

To her relief, Brit has hit the mark. Mia spends the next fifteen minutes talking about her two daughters, and her eldest, Sara, in particular. How ungrateful she is and how she's turned vegan and doesn't want to wear anything made of leather or anything new.

'It's such a bore. I blame the school in Stockholm. They had a particularly militant geography teacher, who was so good-looking that all the girls fell over themselves to please him. It was "Mr. Sorenson thinks this, Mr. Sorenson said that". He didn't give a thought to how difficult all this would be for the parents! I'm just glad there's no one like that in their new school in Mariehamn.'

Brit nods and smiles. She can well imagine that the Övernäs High School Mariehamn hasn't changed much since she attended the yellow brick low-slung building with Mia and Alicia. But she doesn't want to make a comment in case she stops the flow of words and the conversation turns back to her pregnancy again. But her hopes are dashed by Mia's next comment.

'You have all this to come!' she says and pats Brit's knee. 'Or not!' she says and grins. 'At least you have a choice. When I fell pregnant, Patrick was such a drip, wanting to wrap me in cotton wool. When I mentioned how the baby was going to affect my career, and how I hadn't yet decided whether to keep it or not, he cried. Cried! Can you believe it?'

'He wanted kids all along then, did he?' Brit asks, again trying to divert Mia from her own situation.

'Yeah, and it worked out OK, because he could stay at home and look after them. I didn't even have to breastfeed. Which reminds me, if you do go ahead with it, which I would advise against...'

Here Mia cocks her head to one side and gazes sympathetically at Brit and continues, 'Make sure you get a Caesarean. You don't want your bits down there to become like a loose accordion, do you? If you have to push the baby out, they'll never recover. The same with breast-feeding. You'll have a saggy pair for the rest of your life.'

'I'll remember that,' Brit says through her teeth.

'Anyway, that's enough about the horrors. I wanted to talk to you about Patrick,' Mia says. Her eyes have taken on a different kind of expression. They're sharp, as if she doesn't want to miss anything.

'What about him? I never see him now he's over in Stockholm,' Brit says.

'I want your opinion,' Mia says. 'And this is between you and me, just like your little problem,' she adds, nodding her head toward Brit's tummy.

FIFTY-FIVE

'I want him back,' Mia says.

Brit is astounded. The number of times during the past six months that she's heard Mia talk about Patrick with contempt, and now she wants him back?

'But I thought you hated him? And you divorced him!'

'Hate and love are very closely aligned, did you know that?' Mia says, smiling in a way that Brit could only describe as corny.

'Listen, Brit, I know you can't have a drink, but would you mind if I did? I think I need something stronger to talk about all this stuff.'

'Of course!'

Brit gets up and pours Mia a large glass of chilled white wine. As she's standing at the kitchen counter with her back to Mia, she decides to be honest with her. If only for Alicia's sake. The last thing she needs now is Mia making a claim on Patrick.

She hands the glass to Mia. 'You told me the marriage had been on the rocks for ages. I saw it myself when you were together on that cruise. You either ignored each other or argued.'

Mia takes a large swig of her wine. Looking down at the glass, she lifts her eyes quickly up again.

'But I've realized since, that he's the best man I've ever been with.

He's loyal and he loves the girls so much. Just for their sake, it would be best if we were a family again.'

For the first time since Mia entered the apartment, Brit sees vulnerability and honesty in her eyes.

'I can see that, but do you love him. Really?' Brit says gently.

Mia doesn't say anything, but gives a deep sigh.

'I hate being on my own,' she says, and Brit sees that her old schoolfriend is close to tears.

Now it's Brit's turn to get up and give Mia a hug. This time it's a much less awkward affair. Surprising herself, Brit suddenly feels sorry for Mia. It can't be easy for her. Firstly, being in the public eye from the moment she was born, even in such a small community as the Åland Islands, cannot have been straightforward. Having your love life pored over in every home, café, and bar in the islands must have taken its toll. Perhaps she's had to put up a barrier to shield herself from the hurt people's careless talk has caused?

Brit remembers how at school many girls, and even some teachers, would talk behind Mia's back about her father's wealth. And about how Mia should be doing better at school since she had so many more opportunities than her peers.

And now she's seen as a bit of a sad figure, living back with her parents. Only the other day, Brit overheard colleagues on MS *Diane* talk about Mia and the fact that she cannot hold onto a man. "Poor little rich girl", Kerstin called her with a mean tone to her voice. Of course, as soon as Brit came into earshot, the talk stopped. They all knew that Mia and Brit were friends.

'Look, I've been in your shoes more times than I can remember. Either I've left them or they've found they don't want to be with me anymore. But believe me, you will find someone nice soon. Look at you, you're a real catch,' Brit says, sitting back down.

Mia gives her a grateful smile.

'But if I got back together with Patrick again, the family would be united once more. Isn't that best for the girls?'

Brit thinks about how Mia spoke about her daughters just now and wonders if the disdainful tone was just a front. Perhaps all the vile things she's said about Patrick is also a smokescreen? Perhaps she really cares for him? Where is that going to leave Patrick and Alicia? Because there's one thing she knows about Mia. If she wants something, she invariably gets it.

FIFTY-SIX

When Mia has gone, Brit sits alone gazing out to sea. She makes cup after cup of weak camomile tea, the only drink that doesn't make her retch, and lets her mind wander. Usually, when she's faced with a problem she can't solve, she springs into action. When the Italian she was engaged to be married to turned out to be a cheating rat, she quickly resigned her post on the Caribbean cruise line and applied for a position on Marie Line. She escaped the situation and came home. When other relationships have come to an end, she has thrown herself into work, or at another man. But she hadn't loved anyone, or anything, as much as Nico.

Not until Jukka came along.

And now she's pregnant. The ultimate female prison sentence.

What if Jukka turns out to be a cheating bastard, too? They've only known each other for four months, two weeks, and three days. (Not that she's counting.) During this time, she's already found out that he's been married before, has a teenage daughter and slept with a young waitress while still married, and on MS *Sabrina* where he is the captain. Following that incident, he was accused (although acquitted) of sexual harassment at work. All this happened years before Brit and Jukka met, but once a cheat, always a cheat–isn't that how the saying goes?

Jukka has explained to Brit over and over how unhappy he was in his marriage and how unsuited to each other his ex, Leila, and he were. And how the young waitress had come onto him, and that he'd had sex with her in a moment of weakness. Normally, Brit would laugh at an excuse like that, but she believes Jukka was at a low point at the time. Still, he was unfaithful to his wife. That is a fact that Brit comes back to time and time again. Can she really trust him not to be tempted by some young colleague when her belly grows and she looks like a beached whale? How can she be certain that the baby won't leave her fat and ugly? Or that she'll ever regain her figure? She's nearly forty, and she's read that the older you are when you first fall pregnant, the more difficult it is to lose pregnancy fat.

The light has begun to fade and the mug of tea in her hand has grown cold when her phone rings.

'Hello, Brit, how are you doing?'

Brit is delighted to hear Alicia's voice. More than ever, she needs her friend's advice. On the other hand, how is she going to tell Alicia what Mia just revealed to her? She vowed not to breathe a word to anyone, but surely she must tell her best friend?

'I know you can't drink, but would you join me for one in town tonight?'

'Brilliant idea. I'll pick you up, so you don't have to drive,' Brit says.

It'll be easier if they meet somewhere other than her apartment. She knows Alicia is going to be upset and angry when she tells her.

'You sure?'

'Of course,' Brit says. 'I'll be there in about half an hour.'

'Thank you,' Alicia says, 'I knew there was a positive side to you being pregnant!'

'Don't push it,' Brit says and laughs.

'But I thought your birth dad was dead!' Brit says when Alicia tells her the whole story about Leo and her mom.

They're sitting at a corner table in a new pizzeria, which has just opened in the center. While driving into town, they both realized they were hungry. With Brit feeling so ill all the time, she hadn't been able to eat much recently, and as they approached Mariehamn, she remembered her colleagues talking about a new Italian restaurant. She suggested they go there instead of Arkipelag bar, where they'd been heading.

'Well, apparently Hilda has been lying to me all this time.'

Alicia recounts everything that she has learned in the past week, leaving out the fact that her mother is also a bigamist. She doesn't know why, but she can't bring herself to incriminate her mom in front of her friend. She thinks about a wedding picture of Hilda and Uffe that sits in a prime position on a side table in Sjoland. The two smiling faces made her feel warm inside when she was growing up. Later, when married herself, she often thought how lucky her mom had been to fall in love after losing her first husband. Now that was all a lie. It's as if her whole childhood—her whole life—has been built on deceit.

'What are you going to do with the farm?' Brit asks.

Brit is leaning back in her seat. She's managed to eat half of her Margherita pizza, which is a huge feat. She'd been tempted by a seafood one, but at the last minute remembered she shouldn't be eating anything like that.

'Oh, I don't know. But what about you? How did you get on with Jukka?'

Brit smiles. The way she sits makes Alicia think of a satisfied Cheshire cat. She cuts a piece of her Calzone and listens as Brit tells her how loving the sea captain had been and how much he tried to convince her that he wanted the baby.

'And?' Alicia asks, 'You're going to keep it?'

Brit nods.

'I haven't begun to think about how we're going to organize our lives. Jukka thinks I should apply for a shore post, but I don't know...'

Alicia puts down her knife and fork and takes a sip of red wine.

'You may not want to go back to work afterward, you know. I didn't,' Alicia says.

At that moment a large group of men enters the restaurant. They speak loudly in Swedish and one of them, a tall, good-looking guy with a floppy blond fringe, gives Alicia a wide smile. After they pass, Brit leans over the table and says to Alicia in a low tone, 'I think you've scored.'

Alicia blushes. There was something in the look the man gave her that excited her, and she's embarrassed. How could she be so fickle? She's only just separated from her husband and is—officially at least—living with her new boyfriend in Stockholm.

'A stag night, probably,' she says, pretending to look at her cell to hide her embarrassment.

'It's nice to be noticed, isn't it?' Brit says and touches Alicia's hand.

'Yeah,' Alicia says.

'But you and Patrick are good, aren't you?' Brit asks.

Alicia wonders how much of what she is going through with Patrick she can tell her friend.

Brit and Alicia were best friends at school, but lost touch when Alicia moved to London and Brit was traveling the world. After they both returned to the islands, they became very close again. But Alicia knows that Brit is living in an apartment owned by the Eriksson family. Alicia also knows that Mia and Brit meet from time to time for a coffee or a drink. From what Alicia understands, this has been happening more often since Alicia has been in Stockholm and Mia is back living with her parents.

When they were at school, they were hardly friends with Mia, more like frenemies. Brit got on with her better than Alicia did. Mia always wore the latest fashions and had the latest gear, whether that was a Sony Walkman or a Bjorn Borg tennis racket. And she made sure everyone knew about it. She picked up and dropped friends like the clothes she changed, and Alicia had never been admitted to her inner circle.

Now that they're adults, Brit says Mia has changed, but Alicia hasn't seen any evidence of it.

'I think Mia wants him back,' Alicia says, deciding to be brave.

FIFTY-SEVEN

'Alicia!'

When Alicia hears her name being called, she lifts her eyes. Another group of people have entered the pizzeria. She takes a quick intake of breath and puts her hand to her mouth.

Frederica, Patrick's youngest daughter, is running toward their table.

'What are you doing here?' Frederica asks as she stops by their table.

'Hello, you!' Alicia says, forcing her voice to sound normal.

She gets up and gives the girl a hug. She waves to Sara, who's standing next to her grandparents, Kurt and Beatrice Eriksson.

'We've just been to see *Frozen* with *Moffa* and *Mommo*,' Frederica says.

'Really! Was it good?' Alicia asks.

Her smile widens as she thinks about the nicknames the girl has used for the grandparents. She cannot imagine anyone suiting those monikers less well than Kurt and Beatrice.

At her question, Frederica launches into a torrent of words, as she tries to explain the whole plot of the movie. While she's talking, Alicia can see from the corner of her eye that Beatrice is walking toward them.

'Hello Alicia and Brit,' she says stiffly, nodding at the two women.

Alicia greets her, and Brit also gets up and shakes Mrs. Eriksson's hand.

'Come on, Frederica, you mustn't keep Alicia. I'm sure she's not at all interested in the film.'

Alicia watches as the little girl's face crumbles. She looks dejected.

Alicia bends down so that she's on the same level as the girl and takes one of her hands.

'I am really interested! I can't wait to hear all about it another time, though. Now I bet you're hungry for some pizza?'

Frederica's expression changes and she smiles at Alicia, who gets up and says, 'Nice to see you, Beatrice.'

The older woman nods and walks away, holding the girl's hand.

'Friendly lady,' Brit whispers with sarcasm in her voice when they're both sitting down again.

'Yeah, isn't she just? I feel sorry for those girls. They're really good and we got on fine when they stayed with us for the first time a couple of weekends ago. But Beatrice and Kurt are so cold. I can't imagine Beatrice ever being pregnant or nursing a baby, can you?'

Brit shakes her head.

Alicia is pensive as she watches the group in the far corner of the room. The eldest, Sara, keeps glancing toward Alicia, but she doesn't return Alicia's smile.

'I think Mia is just lonely,' Brit says.

She recalls her conversation with Mia earlier that day. She's interrupted by the group of Swedes laughing loudly at a joke one of them must have made. When they see Brit, a couple of them raise their glasses to her. Brit smiles and turns her face toward Alicia again.

'You've spoken to her about this?' Alicia asks, leaning forward over their half-eaten pizzas.

It becomes harder to hear each other talk. Between the Swedish guys and the full restaurant, the noise level is impossible.

'Shall we go back to my place? I can hardly hear myself think,' Brit says.

Alicia nods. Brit notices her friend's eyes moving toward the group of men, who are diagonally behind Brit.

'Unless you want to stay...?' Brit says and gives her friend a wicked smile.

'No!' Alicia says.

'Can you imagine? With Mr. and Mrs. Eriksson looking on?' She catches the eye of a waiter and after insisting she should treat Brit, they leave the restaurant to shouts and whoops from the men behind them. Both Brit and Alicia ignore the catcalls, but fall about laughing on the street outside.

'That hasn't happened for a while!' Alicia says, adding, 'They must have been quite drunk.'

'Or the two of us are quite irresistible!' Brit says, grinning.

Clutching a mug of coffee, Alicia sits wrapped in a fleece blanket on Brit's balcony. She listens to her friend as she recounts what Mia told her about herself.

'She's living with her parents at our age! They are driving her crazy. You can only imagine.'

Alicia nods. She remembers how kind Hilda and Uffe had been to her last summer, taking her in and giving her the sauna cottage to live in. But it wasn't always easy to settle back into home life, even though she wasn't under the same roof as her parents. She wasn't used to accounting for her every move, or being told she was eating too little, looking tired or too thin. She can only imagine what Kurt and Beatrice Eriksson are like as parents and grandparents. She imagines they would have a thing or two to say about everything to do with the girls, and Mia's life.

'Why did she move in with them? It's not as if there's a lack of money. She could quite easily have taken one of the apartments here?'

'And live in the same block as her ex? Run into him in the lift when's she's coming back with a Swede on a stag night?'

Brit laughs at her own joke.

Alicia shrugs her shoulders.

'You know what I mean.'

'Yeah, I guess so, but it's always a matter of convenience. The grandparents can pick up the girls from school and drive them to their various hobbies when Mia is in Stockholm. Otherwise she would have had to hire a live-in nanny, and Patrick was strongly against that.'

Alicia remembers the argument about that back in January.

'And it's not easy to be back here with everyone gossiping about your love life,' Brit adds.

'I know all about that. You should have seen the people ogling me and Patrick at Sitkoff's last week.'

Brit's face brightens.

'So you can understand how she feels?'

'I guess,' Alicia says, adding, 'So Mia's solution is to get back with Patrick?'

Alicia is gauging Brit's reaction. Has she hit the nail on the head? She can't see any change in her friend's expression.

'Well, that's what she *thinks* she wants. But I'm sure she'll change her mind when she sees it's probably the *worst* solution.'

'You think?' Alicia says. She's not convinced it's that simple.

Brit nods enthusiastically.

'Besides, it's not as if Patrick doesn't have a mind of his own. Have you spoken to him about all of this? Properly spoken, I mean.'

'You're the one to say that!' Alicia laughs and adds, 'Look at you and Jukka. He was sending you messages every minute of the day while you were refusing to talk to him.'

'But I did speak with him in the end, didn't I?' Brit says.

FIFTY-EIGHT

In bed that same evening, Alicia replays the conversation with Brit about Mia. Surprising herself, she feels some sympathy toward her old nemesis. It must be horrible to be the subject of people's gossip and jokes. She knows a little of how that is, although she doesn't really care. All the years living in London has made her more open to people's differences and quirks. In the city, you could wear anything, dye your hair the color of a rainbow and no one would bat an eyelid.

Here on the islands, when she sees someone looking at her, and sometimes even prodding their friend and all but pointing a finger at her, Alicia just finds it funny. But she must admit to being more relaxed in Patrick's company in Stockholm. She didn't mind being gossiped about, but she knew Hilda, and to some extent, Uffe, suffered from any negative rumors about her.

Staying with your parents can't be easy after you've lived your own life away from them for so long, either. Alicia should know about that too. She can only imagine what it would have been like if Stefan had lived, and she'd moved back to the islands with him, leaving his dad in London. Alicia cringes when she thinks how Hilda would have expected to have a say in how Stefan should be brought up. From the little she has seen of Kurt Eriksson, she knows he's a man who isn't afraid to express his opinions. No doubt his wife is equally assertive. Alicia shudders when she thinks how oppressive it would be to live under their roof, however massive that roof is.

Alicia peers at her cell and sees there's a message from Patrick. How did she miss it? She's forgotten to take her phone off silent. She opens the app and reads what he has written.

How are you? Can we talk?

The message was written about an hour ago.

Alicia's fingers hover over the keyboard of the iPhone. It's true that they need to talk, but what if Patrick tells her he wants to try again with Mia? Alicia taps on her phone, then erases what she's written. Eventually she sends just a two letter reply.

OK

'Hello, it's me,' Patrick says down the phone and winces at his own words.

It's past midnight and he's just got back to his Stockholm apartment from the newspaper office. There's been some rioting in one of the Stockholm suburbs and Patrick has been interviewing eyewitnesses all evening. He was supposed to stay in Mariehamn for the weekend, but at the last minute he decided to take the story the Editor had offered to him. Most of the people willing to talk to him had been Swedes campaigning against the immigrants in the northern part of the city. The mostly Romanian inhabitants of the suburb had refused to speak. Failing to get a translator to the scene, he had headed back to write up what he'd got so far, which he suspects is a one-sided account of the event.

'Hello,' Alicia says.

'How are things there?' Patrick asks.

Hearing Alicia's voice has an immense effect on him. He misses her so much!

'Fine,' she says.

Is she pissed with him still? He knows she has every right to be. But it's not easy for him either. He has to decide between giving his daughters a family life and what he wants most of all in the world—to be with Alicia.

'Look, I had to cover a disturbance in Rinkeby. I'm sorry I didn't let you know I was here, but you've got so much on...did you meet up with your real dad?' he asks, trying to buy time.

'I did, but I want to talk about something else,' Alicia says.

Patrick is thinking frantically. What can he tell her without making her slam the phone down on him?

'Look, Alicia,' Patrick begins, and then he doesn't know what to say.

'I know what you are going to say,' Alicia replies.

Alicia wants to tell Patrick everything. How Hilda hadn't told anyone she was already married when she wed Uffe, about her meeting with Leo, and that she is now the owner of the farm in Sjoland. But she needs to know first that their relationship hasn't changed. She's still angry with him for lying about the apartment in Stockholm and not being by her side when Uffe died, or afterward. She doesn't understand what was going through Patrick's head. Didn't he know that the truth about the flat would come out sooner or later? And why wasn't he there when she needed him most? Is he really considering getting back with Mia? After everything they went through last year, and long before that, if his stories about his unhappy marriage are true?

'What's that?'

Alicia can hear a smile in Patrick's words and it riles her even further.

'I'm glad you're finding all of this funny,' she says, trying to make her voice as chilling as she can.

There's a brief silence at the other end of the line.

'I'm coming over tomorrow on the first ferry, right after I've written this piece I'm working on. I'm taking a few days off.'

'Really?'

'I should have been with you last week. I'm so sorry,' Patrick says.

Alicia can hear that he is serious, but she needs to be convinced that everything is finished between him and Mia. And is he coming to see her, or Mia and the girls?

'If that's what you want. But I warn you, I've got a lot to sort out, so don't expect me to be able to be with you all the time,' she says firmly, although her heart is beginning to beat faster at the thought of seeing him soon.

'I understand. I'm a big boy, I can look after myself.'

Again, Alicia hears the smile in Patrick's voice and it makes her smile too.

'OK,' she says.

'OK,' Patrick replies.

Shaking her head, Alicia ends the call.

He's impossible.

Patrick gazes at the open laptop in front of him and wonders how he's going to make good his promise to go to the islands tomorrow. The article on the riots is far from finished; it's a piece that has the potential to become an important feature. Is he going to throw it all away to rescue his relationship with Alicia? Of course he is.

When he first heard her voice, he immediately remembered the taste of her lips, and how her soft body felt under his own. How she arched her back when he was pleasuring her and the sounds of her low cries and moans when she was about to climax. He needed to win her back and he needed to be with her. The apartment in Stockholm felt empty without Alicia. He slept badly, and when he woke in the middle of the night he felt despair at the sight of the vacant space next to him.

Again, he reads the last sentence he's written on the screen in front of him. He decides to ditch all but one of the interviews he's done and cut the piece down to a third of what he had planned. He knows his Editor will be happier with a short article anyway—it's Patrick who often insists on long, investigative features in his quest for recognition.

There will be other stories, he decides. He may not have gotten the interviews with the kids who'd been rioting, or their families, but it's a good piece all the same.

He needs to sort his life out. He needs to be firm with Mia and tell her once and for all that they will never make each other happy. If they're not contented as a couple, their daughters will suffer far more than they will if the two of them co-parent successfully, as they have done thus far. Besides, what will happen when Mia falls for some other high-flying Swede? Seeing how she behaved with that Justin who joined them for lunch at Sturehov finally convinced Patrick that she would never love him the way she once did. She was just lonely and hurt after being left by that bastard Max.

Patrick shakes his head. He can't understand how he could have been taken in by Mia again. He looks across the Riddarfjärden sound. Across the black water he can see the green lights on top of *Stadshuset's* turret and the three crowns lit up above it. To the left of the town hall, lower buildings cast their lights against the still, dark water. The waterway is quiet at this time of the night, not like during the day, when it is criss-crossed by ferries and tourist boats. Sometimes he wonders how they manage not to crash into each other, but of course he knows that there is a strict rule of the road at sea that prevents such accidents. He admires the view for a moment and then a thought hits him. He realizes with clarity that if he's ever going to make a complete break from Mia and the Eriksson family, he has to give up this flat. And probably the one in Mariehamn too.

FIFTY-NINE

The next day, Alicia is in the car on her way into town. She's asked to see Ebba for lunch. She wants to find out about the possible charges her mother will face when the fact that she was already married to her real father when she wed Uffe comes out. She's going to have to trust her friend not to report Hilda's crime, if Alicia can find a way around it. And she needs to keep Hilda unaware of the seriousness of her actions.

Since her confession, Hilda's expression has been less pained. That morning at breakfast she even smiled and joked with Alicia about the pointless headline in that mornings *Ålandsbladet*.

Hero cat missing!

The text informed the readers that a cat that had purportedly alerted neighbors to a fire in a wooden house in the outer archipelago a few years ago had now disappeared.

'Can't believe what they think is news these days!' Alicia said.

Hilda had started laughing, which by the time she got her words out had turned into crying.

'You sound just like Uffe,' she said through the tears running down her face.

Alicia went to hug her mom and they had laughed and cried together, until Hilda pulled away.

'That's enough now. Let's have no more tears and another cup coffee. Would you like a cinnamon bun?'

Alicia had nodded and they had spent the rest of the morning reminiscing about the good times with Uffe. Neither had mentioned Leo or Hilda's marriage to him, nor the farm. Alicia had decided not to think about that now.

Lars Olen had come to the house the previous day to inform Hilda and Alicia that he would get the early potatoes in with the help of his son and a nephew.

'I can run things for a couple of weeks until you decide where we're headed,' he said, standing in the middle of Hilda's kitchen, clutching a faded red baseball cap with a Marie Line logo on it.

Alicia had hugged the foreman. She was so grateful for a reprieve from having to make a decision about the farm. He didn't know she now owned it; Hilda had asked Alicia to keep the news to themselves for now, and Alicia had gladly agreed.

'How did you get on with your real dad?' Ebba asks as soon as they sit down at the Seglarpaviljongen cafe at the West Harbor.

It's typical of Ebba to get straight to the point.

Alicia studies the menu to buy time.

'Fine, he's gone back to Helsinki now, but I promised to go and see him,' she says. I think I'll have the fried perch fillets.

Ebba nods.

'A good choice. I'll have the same.'

'How's Jabulani?' Alicia asks when the young male waiter with a mop of messy hair disappears with their menus and orders.

Ebba coughs into her hand. Alicia can see that a faint blush has risen to her friends' cheeks.

'She's coming over tonight,' she says.

Her voice is noticeably softer when she talks about Jabulani.

Alicia raises her eyebrows.

'That's great!' she says.

'We've having lunch with my parents on Sunday.'

Ebba fiddles with the stem of the wine glass. Surprising Alicia, the police chief had suggested they order a glass of white each. Ebba has always been very strict about following the rule book; being under the influence while on duty must surely be one of the regulations she'd never break? Truthfully, Alicia was relived. She was nervous about what she needed to ask Ebba. Besides, a softening of principles played well with what Alicia was going to ask her.

'That's wonderful. I'm really proud of you, Ebba. And good luck,' Alicia says.

She's delighted for her friend. If anyone deserves happiness, it's Ebba.

'I wondered if you and your mom would like to come along,' Ebba says.

'Really?'

Alicia thinks frantically. When did she last set eyes on Ebba's parents? It must have been on graduation day in Uppsala University, which they both attended. Even then, she and Ebba were hardly friends. Ebba studied criminology while Alicia did English. All she can remember of Mr. and Mrs. Torstensson is their height. It was obvious where Ebba got her stature from.

'Won't your mom mind? It's a long time since I met them. And Hilda, she's hardly a friend.'

Alicia doesn't say that the reason Hilda wouldn't go near Ebba's parents is because they are regulars at the Sjoland church. A place where Hilda has only been once or twice in her life. Besides, she's now a bigamist. If that's not a crime against God, what is, Alicia wonders.

Ebba leans across the table and says, 'My parents aren't as narrow-minded as you think.'

'Sorry, I didn't mean...' Alicia tries to think what to say, but is rescued by Ebba.

'Look, I'm going to tell them about me and Jabulani on Saturday. It's not going to be easy, so I thought on Sunday when we're all having lunch, it would be good to have you two there. Besides, Uffe was a great friend of my dad's.'

'Really?' Alicia never heard Uffe mention him.

Alicia wonders if she saw Ebba's parents at the funeral, but she can't remember. So much of the day is a blur to her.

Ebba nods.

'He was part of the gang of school friends who met in town every Tuesday for a beer.'

Alicia remembers the tradition, but she hadn't realized it had carried on. Somehow, the thought of Mr. Torstensson drinking with a bunch of men doesn't seem right. But what does Alicia know? She never thought her mother would have lied to her about her real dad, or have married Uffe when she was already the wife of Leo.

'Of course, we'd love to,' Alicia says.

The blond waiter brings their food and Ebba nods at her empty glass of wine.

'Would you like another one?'

Alicia can't help but ask, 'Aren't you going back to the station this afternoon?'

'No, God, no!' Ebba laughs. 'It's my day off!'

They order two more glasses and when they've finished their buttery white-fleshed fish and potato mash, Alicia finally bucks up the courage to say what she came to say. She glances around her, but luckily the cafe is only half full and the tables near the two women are empty.

'Look Ebba, I need your advice.'

Ebba lifts her eyes to Alicia.

'Go on,' she says.

'If I tell you something, can you keep it to yourself? I mean, do you need to report it, if a crime has been committed?'

Ebba straightens her back.

'I'm afraid I do.'

Her expression is serious as she gazes at Alicia.

Alicia puts her hand on her forehead and leans into it.

'In that case, forget it,' she says and finishes her wine with a large gulp.

'Is this to do with your father?' Ebba asks.

Alicia nods, but she doesn't look at the police chief.

Ebba's professionalism kicks in. In spite of the wine and the fact that Alicia is her friend, she has to know if a crime has been committed.

'What has he done?'

Alicia shakes her head. Eventually, she lifts her eyes to Ebba.

'I can't tell you anything if you have to take it further.'

Her friend presses her lips together.

'Look, it may not be as bad as you think. I know he's got a problem with alcohol, and you saw how I didn't charge him with anything the other day,' Ebba says.

She covers Alicia's hand with her own and squeezes it.

'It's so much easier to have these things out than to keep them a secret. Believe me, I know,' Ebba adds, giving Alicia a smile.

Alicia pulls her hand away and places it on top of her other one on her lap. She takes a breath and says, 'It's Mom.'

'Hilda?' Ebba says.

She can't keep the surprise out of the tone of her voice. She wishes now she hadn't had the wine after all. She'd been so nervous about telling Alicia about Jabulani's visit and how she was planning to come out to her parents at the weekend. It was all Jabulani's idea.

'You can't be yourself if you don't tell your mom and dad,' she'd said.

They were lying in bed facing each other in Jabulani's small studio apartment in the center of Stockholm. Before she replied, Ebba ran her fingers along the side of her hip and thigh. Her perfect brown skin was soft under Ebba's touch. She leant over and kissed her lover's rosy pink lips.

'OK,' she said and cupped Jabulani's small breast. 'Anything for you, my love.'

Alicia bites her lip. The conversation with Ebba isn't going at all as she'd imagined. She feels now as if she's being interrogated rather than getting advice from a friend.

'Look, she says,' opening the palms of her hands upwards. 'I just needed to know if something this person did over thirty-five years ago would still count as a crime. Especially if one of the parties has died.'

Alicia bites her lip and gazes at her friend. She knows she's said too much already. Ebba is smart and it won't take her too long to figure out what Hilda has done. But Alicia hopes that since she hasn't actually told Ebba anything, she will honor their friendship and not take any action.

Her friend's face is serious. Two lines have formed in between her dark eyebrows as she considers what Alicia said. She scratches her short black hair at the side of her head and moves her hand toward her forehead, squeezing it between her thumb and forefinger.

'Are we talking about bigamy?'

Alicia doesn't say anything, but nods. Her chest is tight and there's a hollow sensation in her tummy. She feels she might bring up the food she's just eaten.

What am I doing?

'How long since Uffe and your mother married?'

'Thirty-eight years,' Alicia says.

Her heart is beating so hard that her voice comes out in a whisper. As if she has no breath left in her lungs.

Ebba reaches for her phone, but before she is able to tap in the code to unlock it, Alicia puts her hand over Ebba's fingers.

'Please don't.'

Ebba lifts her face toward Alicia and pulls the hand holding the phone away from Alicia's reach.

'I'm just checking the statute of limitations on cases like these. I'm sure it dissolves with the death of the partner, or within 35 years, whichever is sooner.'

The relief Alicia feels is immense. She thought for a moment that Ebba was going to phone the police station. An image of Hilda being taken away in handcuffs had flashed in front of her eyes.

But she's afraid to say anything until Ebba lifts her gaze from her cell phone and gives Alicia a wide smile.

'As I thought, 35 years of marriage is the limit. By that stage the law decrees that the second marriage is the lawful one, and that the first one has officially dissolved.'

Alicia gets up from her chair and goes to hug her friend.

Ebba pats her back awkwardly and pulls away from Alicia's grip. Laughing, Ebba says, 'I would never have shopped your mom for something like this anyway. It isn't as if anyone has suffered from her misguided actions. Even if she'd been charged, I'm sure there would have been extenuating circumstances. She'd have been either acquitted or given a small fine.'

Alicia sinks into her chair.

'I know we're already had two glasses, but I think I need another one. What about it?'

'Fine by me!' Ebba says and smiles.

SIXTY

When Alicia gets back to Sjoland she immediately tells her mother the good news. Hilda breaks down in tears and hugs her daughter tightly.

'I'm so sorry for everything I've done. Not telling you about Leo was unforgivable, I can see that now.'

'Shh, let's not talk about it anymore,' Alicia says.

She still feels slightly tipsy after the boozy lunch with Ebba. They shared a taxi home and hugged each other for a long time before parting. Alicia can't believe how close she and Ebba have become, but she is so glad of this new-found friendship.

'Do you want coffee?' she asks Hilda. She goes over to the hatch, through which she sees the chair where Uffe used to sit reading *Ålandsbladet*. A stab of pain hits her chest, so strong that she has to gasp for air. She concentrates on the mechanical task of measuring coffee into the percolator and setting the machine. Leaning against the hatch, she remembers how she'd seen Brit and Patrick stand in the corner of the lounge at the wake. And how close their two heads—his blond and weather-worn and hers sleek and dark—had been. What had they been talking about?

Alicia tries to brush thoughts of Patrick away and joins Hilda at the kitchen table. Hilda is sitting opposite her, gazing out of the window at the sea beyond.

'It's calm again today. We've hardly had bad weather since Uffe went. It's as if he's protecting the farm and the newly planted potatoes from up there.'

Hilda's gaze moves up to the ceiling.

Alicia gets up and goes to hug her mom again.

'I forgot to tell you, Ebba has asked us over for Sunday lunch at her parents' place,' she says, trying to change the subject.

'Really? I haven't spoken with Hakan or Gitta for years,' Hilda says.

Alicia considers whether she should tell Hilda the real reason they've been invited. Her mom is old-fashioned and doesn't really understand that people don't choose to be gay. Alicia has often heard her say that it's just a trend that will disappear soon enough.

'Ebba is bringing her girlfriend along,' Alicia says.

Hilda lifts her eyes toward her daughter.

'Oh?' Hilda says.

Alicia gazes at her face. Has she understood the significance of what she's said?

'Jabulani is her lover,' Alicia says. Whether it's the wine she drank at lunchtime, or the giddiness she feels at bringing Hilda the good news about her marriage to Uffe being legal after all, makes Alicia bold. She's prepared to take her mom on if she starts going on about homosexuality.

But to her surprise, Hilda says, 'How wonderful! I didn't think that girl would ever find someone. No one should spend their life without a partner.'

Hilda raises her eyebrows.

'That brings me to you and Patrick. When are you going back to Stockholm? I am OK and I can look after the farm, so there's no need for you to stay.'

The next day, Alicia gets a message from Brit.

'Do you want to come over this evening and stay the night? We'll have a bite to eat and I'll even open a bottle of wine for you? And I'll come and get you too.'

The message ends with two emoji: a smiley face followed by a glass of wine.

Alicia wonders if she can leave her mom alone again, and decides she can. It'll be good to see how she copes. She will have to make a decision about Stockholm too.

As soon as she's replied to Brit, telling her that she'll be ready at six, her phone pings again.

'I'll be on the midday ferry. Can we meet tonight?'

Patrick! How could she have forgotten about Patrick? Without thinking about it too much, she replies,

'Sorry, can't.'

She leaves the cell on her bed and goes downstairs to have breakfast. Her mother will no doubt have been awake for hours already.

When they step into Brit's apartment, Alicia is amazed to see someone sitting on the white sofa. Even though she can see only the back of the head, she recognizes Mia straight away.

'What the hell?' she says, turning to Brit who's standing behind her, holding her keys.

'Look, I think you two need to talk.'

'So you tricked me into coming here?' Alicia says, incredulously.

Hearing their voices, Mia gets up.

'What's she doing here?' she says.

As usual, Mia's appearance is immaculate. Today she's wearing white pants and an animal print silk shirt, tucked into the waistband at the front of her trousers. Her hair rests sleekly on one side of her shoulder. She looks good, slim and smart, but casual at the same time.

Alicia hates her.

'We are all grown-ups here, right?' Brit says, walking past Alicia and Mia into the open-plan kitchen. She takes a bottle of wine out of the fridge and opens it. Grabbing two glasses, she comes over to the sofa.

Looking from Mia, who's still standing by a glass coffee table, to

Alicia at the door, she says, 'You two are at cross purposes. Wouldn't it be so much better for all, for Patrick and the girls, if you two got on?'

Mia sighs dramatically and Alicia shakes her head.

'I can't believe you've done this,' she says.

Alicia considers her options. She could run up to Patrick's apartment, hoping he's at home. But that would mean a loss of face. She's been ignoring his messages; she's still angry with him for his lies and for abandoning her when she needed him most. And for taking Mia to her father's funeral. She hadn't been invited to the church or to the wake in Sjoland.

Or Alicia could just turn on her heels and get a cab at the taxi rank a few streets away. But that would only give Mia the satisfaction of thinking she'd won. It would be immature and childish to dash off like that. She associates that kind of behavior with Mia and doesn't want it to be attributed to herself.

'OK, I'll stay to see what's she has to say,' Alicia says. Grabbing a glass of wine, she sits down at one of the chairs farthest from where Mia had been sitting.

SIXTY-ONE

Patrick is standing in front of the large windows in his penthouse apartment in Mariehamn. He watches a ferry make its way out to the open sea, taking a slow turn to starboard toward Stockholm. Its illuminated portholes are shining bright against the dark sea. The shape of the red and white ship is beautiful against the dull sky. It's just past six o'clock and the light hasn't fully faded. Summer, when there's barely no night at all, just a couple of hours of dusk, is around the corner. Soon, Patrick can take his boat out. He cannot wait to get out to sea himself and feel the breeze against his face. At least he now owns the yacht.

He takes the cell out of his back pocket and looks at the screen. Still no reply from Alicia. She can't be this mad at him, surely? He knows he's messed her about but she must be aware of how much he loves her?

Suddenly he has an idea. He dials the landline number to Sjoland.

'Hello,' Hilda says after the phone has rung a few times and Patrick is about to hang up. He bites his lip. He doesn't want to speak with Hilda. He doesn't know what to say to her about Uffe.

'Hi Hilda, it's Patrick. I'm so sorry for your loss.'

'Thank you,' Hilda says and then, to Patrick's relief, immediately adds, 'Alicia isn't here. She's gone to see Brit in her apartment. I believe she's planning to stay over.'

Patrick can't believe his luck. Alicia is at this moment only two floors below him! He thanks Hilda and ends the call as soon as he can.

Patrick decides to change into a blue chambray shirt that he knows Alicia particularly likes. He brushes his teeth thoroughly, washes his face, shaves and sprays on some Giorgio Armani. He wets his blond hair with his fingers and is satisfied with the man looking back at him in the mirror. The creases around his eyes and forehead have deepened during the past year, but he thinks this makes him look more mature.

Hopefully she won't be able to resist me.

Patrick picks up his keys and takes the stairs two at a time, down to Brit's floor.

When Brit opens the door, she can't believe her eyes.

'Patrick!'

She can feel the eyes of the two women behind her burn into her back.

Patrick has a smile on his face. He brushes back a strand of hair that has flopped over his forehead.

'Brit, how lovely to see you too,' he says and grins.

Patrick steps forward to give Brit a hug, but freezes in mid-motion. His eyes settle on the middle of the room, where Mia is sitting on the sofa and Alicia on an armchair at the far end. There is a silence in the room. He can hear his own heart beating against his chest.

'We were just talking about you,' Mia says.

Brit is panicking. Mia's tone is not a friendly one. It is ice cold.

This is all going wrong, she thinks. Of all the scenarios she had thought of when planning this meeting, Patrick turning up unannounced was not one of them.

Since Mia had confided in her about her loneliness, and Alicia about her love for Patrick, an idea had formed in her head. What if the two women could meet and talk openly to each other? They were friends at school after all! They were grown women with a common problem. After speaking with both of them separately, Brit felt sure they would be able to agree a way froward. With Brit there, as a sort of referee, she felt sure everything would go smoothly.

After half an hour or so, during which Alicia hardly said a word and Mia talked about how she was planning to move back to Stockholm with the girls, Brit realized that she had completely underestimated the hostility between the two women. And now the root of all their hatred toward each other was standing in front of them.

Brit wants to ask them all to leave. She's suddenly tired to her bones.

Why did you have to meddle in something that has nothing to do with you?

Instead, trying to sound cheerful, she asks Patrick if he'd like a drink.

'Why don't you join the girls and sit down. Red or white, or a beer?'

Patrick coughs and walks slowly—the condemned man—toward the sofa. Judging a chair closest to Mia but opposite Alicia to be a neutral spot, he sits down tentatively while the two women stare at him.

'A beer, please, Brit,' Patrick says, noticing his voice sounds weak.

'What no kiss for either of us?' Mia says.

Brit's hands are actually shaking when she flips the top off the beer.

'Glass, or do you want to drink it straight from the bottle?' Brit asks when she returns to where the others are sitting with straight backs, silently regarding each other.

'This is fine, thanks,' Patrick says, taking a large swig.

He gives Brit what she thinks is a pleading look.

With her back to the two women, she widens her eyes. Moving past Mia, she sits herself down on the sofa, out of the line of sight.

The silence is painful. It's as thick as the pea soup her father used to make on Shrove Tuesday. The snow was high outside the window and Brit had just come inside from a day spent sledding down a hill behind their house. The atmosphere in her apartment is as chilly as those childhood days spent outside playing in the snow.

'I'm pregnant,' Brit says into the silence.

Patrick lifts his head and looks at her.

'Congratulations!' he says.

The two other women look at Brit and then each other.

'Yes, you told me,' Mia says, irritably, as if she's annoyed that Brit has brought her own situation to the table.

Alicia stares at Mia.

'How rude you are,' she says. Then, lifting her glass up toward Brit, she adds, 'Congratulations are in order. I'm so happy for you both!'

Mia looks furious.

'Who are you calling rude! I'd call stealing someone else's husband disrespectful.'

Mia's voice has risen, but it remains frosty rather than angry.

'You're incredible. You were the one having the affair. And now that your lover boy has split, you come crawling back to Patrick,' Alicia almost spits out the words, but manages to keep her voice level.

Patrick opens his mouth to speak.

The two women turn at the same time and snap, 'You can shut up!'

Brit leans forward.

Looking at Alicia first, she says, 'Arguing about the past isn't getting us anywhere.'

Turning around to face Mia, she adds, 'Alicia has a point. It was you who broke up with Patrick.'

Seeing Mia ready to protest, she raises her hand to stop her.

'But, as I said before, quarreling about what did and didn't happen is immaterial now. Surely the most important people in this whole mess are the girls? What's best for Sara and Frederica should be foremost in your minds!'

Brit places a hand over her belly and leans back. She lets her gaze run from Mia's face to Patrick.

· · ·

'Mia,' Patrick pauses, waiting for the onslaught. When none comes, he continues, 'You know we can't be together for more than five minutes without arguing. Living in a family where the parents are constantly fighting isn't good for any children. Besides, I love Alicia.'

He lifts his eyes and looks at Alicia.

They are far from each other, on either side of the sofa, but Brit can feel the electricity between them. When she glances at Mia, she can see that Patrick's ex has also noticed the sexual tension between the two lovers.

'So why did you sleep with me last week?' Mia asks.

SIXTY-TWO

The room begins to spin in front of Alicia's eyes. She tries to get up, but feels so dizzy that she has to sit down again. The air is suddenly so stuffy in the apartment that she struggles to breathe.

'Are you OK?'

She sees Patrick is kneeling in front of her. She feels her hands being held between his and pulls them away from his grip.

'Leave me alone,' she says, and this time she manages to get up.

The room spins, but she needs to get away.

And then there's blackness.

Alicia wakes up to the sound of Brit's voice.

She's talking to Patrick in hushed, but angry tones. Alicia catches a few words.

'How could you ...after what she's been through...'

Alicia looks around her and realizes she's lying on the sofa where Brit and Mia were sitting moments ago. She remembers what Mia said.

Was it true?

Now Alicia is fully awake. If Patrick slept with Mia, Alicia can't help but think that it is the worse possible betrayal because she's his ex. She's the mother of his children. The rich mother of his children. Does he want to get back with her, is that it? But hadn't he just told them all he loved Alicia in front of Mia? Had Mia lied?

Alicia sits up gingerly, and her movements cause Brit and Patrick to rush to her side.

'Darling, how are you feeling?' Patrick asks.

Alicia looks into his face but doesn't say anything. Instead, she puts her hand out and gently pushes him away.

'Brit,' she says, lifting her eyes toward her friend. 'Can you get me a glass of water, please?'

She gazes at Patrick, who's on the sofa next to her. His face is full of worry. The lines between his eyebrows are in a deep furrow and his eyes are set on Alicia.

'How could you?' she says.

With her words, Patrick springs into action. He comes to kneel in front of her.

'I am so sorry. You have no idea how sorry! There is no excuse, I know, but I was very drunk.'

Alicia shakes her head, but the moment causes an intense pain in her temples. Brit hands her the water and she takes a few sips.

'Look, perhaps you two need to sort this out privately. I've done enough damage for one evening, don't you think?' Brit says.

Squeezing Alicia's arm, she adds, 'I'm so sorry. I thought it was a good idea to get you two together to talk things out.'

Alicia manages a smile.

'You meant well,' she says.

'Why don't we go up to my place?' Patrick says.

Alicia's first reaction is to say no but seeing how exhausted Brit looks, she nods.

Alicia stands up and finds that she feels OK.

'I'll be down here, if you need me,' Brit says and hugs Alicia.

She picks up her overnight bag and follows Patrick out of the apartment. He tries to take the bag from her, but she holds it tight. Instead, he puts his hand under Alicia's elbow, guiding her inside the elevator. Inside, she shrugs his hand away and moves to the farthest corner of the small space.

SIXTY-THREE

Inside Patrick's apartment, memories of the happier times they've spent there fill Alicia's mind. Last January, before their move to Stockholm, Alicia spent nearly every night here. They made love on the sofa, in his bed, and even in the kitchen when their desire for each other was so strong they didn't make it to the bedroom.

And always in the background was the magnificent view of the sea beyond the entrance to the West Harbor. The outlook tonight is as spectacular as always. She can spot a large container ship, its lights shining brightly into the dark night, move slowly in the shipping lane on the far horizon.

'Sit down,' Patrick says behind her.

'Would you like a cup of coffee?' he asks.

Alicia nods. He knows she can drink coffee any time, without it having any effect on her sleep. But all Alicia wants is to go home to Sjoland. She gazes at Patrick, who's standing with his back to her, spooning coffee into a cafetière. The strong muscles in his back are visible through his shirt, and the rolled up sleeves are straining over the muscles in his arms.

Patrick is tall, fit and handsome. His good looks attract attention wherever he goes. How can she compete for this kind of man? Least of all with Mia.

Alicia knows he loves his daughters above all. It's one of the reasons she was so attracted to him in the first place. She remembers when he told her about rushing Sara into hospital with meningitis, and how close they had come to losing her. His story reflected the anguish Alicia carried—and still does—for her own son. He understood her grief.

Afterward, Alicia could pinpoint that moment as being the one when she'd fallen in love with Patrick, even though she had barely known him then.

However, she also knows that Patrick loves life's little (and large) luxuries. Only Mia and her family can provide him with those. Alicia can never match the kind of fortune that the Eriksson family possess.

As Patrick turns, carrying a tray with two cups, the coffee pot, two glasses, and a bottle of cognac, she wonders what she is really doing here. What does Patrick want with her? To be his mistress while he resumes his married life with Mia? Surely he can't think she'd ever agree to something crazy like that?

But now, sitting here close to him, her resolve is wavering. His closeness has a detrimental effect on her. His scent is intoxicating. He lifts the bottle of cognac and looks at her questioningly.

Alicia nods. She feels better now and needs something strong in order to talk to Patrick without folding herself up in his arms.

Having Alicia inside his apartment is as if the touch paper has been lit inside Patrick. He has a burning desire to take her into his arms. He wants to hold her close and kiss her. He's missed her quiet, confident presence in his apartment in Stockholm in the past few weeks. It's as if his rudder has been removed and he's out at sea, alone.

Alicia, he now realizes, gives his life meaning. Especially now that the girls are growing up and becoming more independent. Patrick and Alicia have a common understanding, which means they don't have to talk to know what the other one is feeling. He has also missed Alicia's bright mind. He can rely on Alicia to give her opinion on whatever he's working on, and he makes her laugh.

How did he think he could live without her? He's got an overwhelming concern that he's blown it. To buy time, he goes to make coffee, and at the last minute adds a bottle of Hennessy XO to the tray. He knows she loves the stuff. His hands tremble, and he has to inhale lungfuls of air before taking hold of the tray and turning to face Alicia.

'Look,' he says when they are sitting down with a glass of cognac in their hands, 'You have no idea how much I wish it hadn't happened. I don't know what I was thinking. Mia was...'

Here Patrick looks at Alicia to see what effect his words are having on her. But he can't read her expression, so he continues.

'Mia was different. Nice. And that's not like her,' he adds drily.

'What are you, her lapdog?' Alicia says. 'Every time she shows a little bit of kindness toward you, you jump into her arms?'

This isn't going at all well.

'No!' he protests and opens his arms with his palms up.

'You must believe me when I say it will never happen again,' he says.

Alicia doesn't reply. Instead, she takes a sip of her drink.

'I couldn't believe it when I saw you two at the funeral. Uffe's last journey and there you were with that, that...'

Alicia's voice breaks and she lowers her eyes.

'She was horrible,' she adds, not looking at Patrick.

He wants to shift closer to her and take her into his arms, but he's ashamed of what he's done. He knows she's right. He's behaved despicably.

'I am so sorry, Alicia,' he says softly, lowering his face to try to meet her eyes.

Alicia looks up at him, and says quietly, 'I love you.'

Patrick moves quickly closer and lifts her chin with his hand.

'And I love you more than you can imagine!'

Alicia shrugs herself free from Patrick's touch.

'I was going to say that I love you very much but I can't understand you. First, I find out you lied about the apartment. Surely you must have realized I'd find out at some point? And that when I did, I wouldn't want to stay in a place owned by Mia of all people? My father dies and you go AWOL, only to turn up with Mia at the funeral. It's as if you only love me when things are going well, but as soon as any difficulties arise, you run into the arms of your ex. How can I trust that the same won't happen again and again?'

Patrick purses his lips, suddenly looking like a schoolboy being scolded by his teacher. Alicia nearly laughs, but she manages to control herself.

What's happening? I'm livid, but I want to smile?

'Alicia, I can't explain myself,' Patrick says.

He opens up his arms and shrugs.

Again.

'I think you should try,' Alicia says matter of factly. She hopes she doesn't betray her true feelings.

Patrick fiddles with the top of the cognac glass. He runs his thumb and finger along the rim.

Alicia cannot help herself: she wishes it was her skin beneath his touch. But she needs to resist him.

'I want you with me so badly in Stockholm. And the apartment was supposed to be part of the divorce settlement. But you know how cunning Mia can be. When I found out the deal was that I could live there rent-free, I'd already asked you to come with me and you'd said 'yes'. Mia was busily organizing her new life with Max, so I didn't think there'd be a problem.'

Patrick's eyes are firmly on Alicia's when he continues. 'As far as your dad...I'm not good with death. When you told me about Uffe, I panicked. I buried my head in my work, and one evening Mia turned up on my doorstep. She wanted to talk about the girls and suggested we get a bite to eat. It was like old times, she was charming...'

Alicia bites her lower lip. She doesn't want to interrupt Patrick, however much she hates hearing the gory details of their liaison.

'The next morning I couldn't believe how stupid I'd been. I left her hotel room as soon as I could. Then when we came to your dad's funeral, she insisted on coming with me. She said she'd tell you what happened if...'

Alicia is shocked.

'You weren't going to tell me?'

Patrick looks down at his hands.

'Of course, I was, but not when you were still grieving for your dad. And then Leo turned up and...I was going to tell you tonight, honestly.'

Alicia wants so desperately to believe Patrick. She wants to go back to normal, the way everything was before she left Stockholm and Uffe died. She feels so alone without Patrick. She needs him. She craves his touch, his lips on hers. She knows she should be furious with him, but all she feels is deep love.

I am mad. Completely and utterly mad.

'It happened just that once?' she asks.

Patrick nods.

'We had lunch yesterday, but that's it.'

Alicia gasps. She shakes her head.

'You're unbelievable,' she says, trying to sound disappointed, but she can hear that her tone is softer.

Patrick comes closer and tries to hug her, but Alicia gets up. He also rises and they stand staring at each other.

'Look, it was just lunch! We were joined by one of her old friends, so it's not what you think.'

Alicia gazes up at Patrick's eyes. Her breathing has become shallow and her heart is pumping hard against her chest. Desire is creeping up inside of her. When Patrick moves even closer and bends down to press his lips onto hers, Alicia lets him. His touch has an electrifying effect on her. He catches her just as she's about to collapse. He lifts her up and continuing to kiss her, carries her to his bed.

SIXTY-FOUR

'I'm going to move back to Stockholm,' Mia tells her parents. The three are in the open-plan kitchen of Villa Havis. Beatrice is frying salmon on the hob, a pan of new potatoes is on the boil, and Mia is making a salad. Kurt is half sitting on one of the stools by the large kitchen island, concentrating on something on his iPad. One of his legs is on the floor, and one is on the stool's footrest. The girls have gone up to their bedrooms. Sara is watching a YouTube channel about the future of the planet on her laptop and Frederica is already fast asleep.

Mia sees her mom glance at her father before replying to her daughter.

'I think that's a good solution,' Beatrice says.

Kurt comes over and gives Mia's hand resting on the table a pat.

'I agree. You don't want to be rotting here on the islands with your old parents.'

This is a reaction Mia hadn't expected. She thought at least her father would try to convince her to stay in Mariehamn. She feels tears welling up.

Even my parents don't want me.

Kurt must have noticed her reaction, because he adds, 'Of course we've loved having you here and would like nothing better than to have you and the girls nearby. But Stockholm isn't that far. I'm thinking of investing in a venture that flies businessmen between Stockholm and Helsinki by helicopter, dropping off in Mariehamn on the way if need be. We can be with you within an hour if we take one of their services.'

He hugs Mia tightly and she smiles up at him.

'OK, *Pappa*,' Mia says

'It'll be better for the girls to be nearer their father too,' her mother says.

Beatrice has turned around to look at Mia.

'Patrick is a good father,' her father says.

'You've changed your tune! I thought you said he was useless and had no ambition!' Mia says. She can't understand why her parents are suddenly talking about Patrick as if he's a saint. Or mentioning him at all.

'We said too much in the heat of the moment. It's true he lacks ambition professionally, but not as a parent,' Beatrice says in a voice that Mia recognizes from her childhood.

Her cool and collected mother never lost her temper but could cut you to pieces with just a few words. As a celebrated author, she now regards the rest of the world, including her family, with condescension. It's as if she's on a higher plane and has to bring herself down to speak with others.

'What are you getting at?' Mia asks.

Her mother's patronizing tone provokes Mia's rebellious side, as it did when she was a teenager. As soon as the words leave her mouth, she regrets them.

Stop behaving like a child.

'Honey, we're just saying that if you wanted to get back with him, that would be fine by us,' her father says.

His hand is still covering Mia's, but now she pulls hers away in a quick movement.

'Are you crazy? Where did you get that idea from?'

Her parents regard her with serious expressions, but neither of them says anything. This infuriates Mia even more, but suddenly she feels too tired to resist.

'He doesn't love me anymore and I don't love him either. I haven't for a long time. I'm not moving back to Stockholm to be near him.'

Mia smiles at her father, and adds, 'Although having him close will help with childcare. And now the girls are nearly teenagers, I'm sure there'll be plenty of times I'll need his support.'

Kurt pats her hand again.

'That's my girl. Very sensible. We'll start thinking about where you can live while we have supper.'

Mia nods and pours herself a second glass of wine.

'I've already chosen the place. I'll be moving in on the second, after the Mayday celebrations.'

Her father's smile broadens.

'Of course, you have,' he says and reaches out his glass, which Mia fills.

'A top up for you, *Mamma?*'

'Why not,' says Beatrice.

She turns off the stove and sets the salmon fillets on a large serving dish.

'Food is nearly ready, but I think we should first toast your new life in Stockholm. Why don't you open a bottle of Pol Roger, Kurt?' she says looking at Mia's father.

Beatrice comes over to Mia and adds, 'You're a strong woman and you will thrive in that city again. You don't need a man to validate you.'

Kurt opens the bottle of champagne and pours three glasses.

He lifts his glass: 'To Mia and her new single girl life!'

SIXTY-FIVE

'I've missed you,' Patrick says when, afterwards, exhausted, they settle onto the bed. Alicia has her head in the crook of Patrick's arm. She runs her fingers along his chest, enjoying the sensation of the contours of his toned body.

'I've been here all along,' she replies.

Patrick lifts himself up on one elbow. His face is so close to Alicia's that she can make out the stubble on his chin. He places one hand on Alicia's cheek and strokes it as if she was a precious bird.

'I will never let you go again,' he says.

'You'd better not,' Alicia replies.

Early next morning, Alicia wakes up next to Patrick. A wide smile spreads across her face as she thinks about the previous night. Their lovemaking was urgent, but at the same time Patrick was gentle and attentive. She gazes at his sleeping face and gets up gently from the bed, trying not to wake him. He stirs, and turns around, but his breathing is still regular.

Wearing Patrick's cotton dressing gown, which she finds in the en suite bathroom, she tiptoes to the kitchen and fills the French press with coffee from a silver tin next to three others on the counter. She pours hot water from the kettle over the black grains.

Alicia sits down on the sofa, holding a hot mug of fresh coffee in her hands.

She needs to think.

She loves Patrick and Patrick loves her. They can't live without each other. A warning voice inside her says she shouldn't trust a man who's been unfaithful, but another one tells her that she has no choice. If she wants to be happy, she needs to be with him.

He explained last night that being with Mia had been like exorcising a demon for him. That he was flattered by her attention after she'd left him for another guy. And he'd let that fool him into thinking that he still wanted her.

'By the time we were in bed, it was too late,' he said.

He looked sincere, and Alicia believed him. She knows how complicated relationships with exes can be. She, too, had tried to rebuild a relationship with Liam last autumn when they thought they were both going to be grandparents. Making love to him was familiar, and easy, but afterward Alicia had realized that she didn't love him anymore. The difference was that she hadn't been with Patrick at the time.

She also knows that she will not be happy living with him in the apartment in Stockholm, owned by Mia. She's not even certain she wants to go back to Stockholm. Her mother has told her that she can look after the farm, but Alicia isn't so sure. Why would Uffe have left the place to her if he didn't want her to run it?

Alicia gazes out of the window. The sea is choppy this morning, with waves forming a white surf as they hit the shore. It's as if the weather reflects her own confused mind. The sky is the color of lead, with dark purple clouds threatening rain. There are no boats or ferries in view. She wonders briefly how Brit is doing. She was due to start a shift onboard one of the Marie Line cruisers early that day, but morning sickness wouldn't be helped by a swelling sea.

Alicia is tapping a quick message to her friend when she hears Patrick's footsteps behind her.

She turns toward the door to his bedroom and smiles when she sees him step out in nothing but his boxer shorts, showing off his muscular body. He takes her breath away.

He comes over and, standing behind the sofa, touches Alicia's breast. She lifts her face up and Patrick leans down to kiss her lips. Desire wells up inside her again.

'Look we need to talk,' she says breathlessly, reluctantly pulling herself out of Patrick's embrace.

'We can talk after,' Patrick says and grins.

He takes one of her hands and places it in on his boxer shorts, which are straining with the hardness of his erection.

Alicia turns around and, kneeling on the sofa, kisses Patrick's stomach, pressing her breasts against his chest.

'Come on, let's get back into bed,' Patrick says hoarsely.

They go out for breakfast. They are both famished and Patrick has no food at all in his apartment. Holding hands, they enter the Bagarstugan Cafe in the center of town. A few faces turn their way when they walk in and Alicia smiles at anyone who catches her eye. The islanders may as well get used to seeing her with Patrick again.

Once they've found a seat and Patrick has fetched coffees and rolls filled with ham and cheese, he gives Alicia a quick kiss on the lips.

'When are you coming back to Stockholm?' he says, taking a large bite of his roll.

'I'm not,' Alicia replies.

Swallowing quickly, Patrick says, 'What?'

'I'm going to run the farm. Uffe left it to me, so I feel duty bound to follow his wishes. Besides, I like the idea,' Alicia says and smiles.

Patrick regards her and continues to eat.

Alicia, too, begins to devour her roll. She realizes she hasn't had anything to eat since yesterday lunchtime.

'You know nothing about running a farm!' Patrick says when he's finished chewing.

'Excuse me,' Alicia replies, 'I grew up on that farm. And we have a foreman. Lars knows what Uffe did.'

'So why not let him run the farm and you carry on being a journalist? Besides, my job is in Stockholm. As is yours,' he says after a while.

There's concern in his blue eyes and deep furrows have formed on his forehead.

'My job...I haven't yet had anything serious to work on since I started at *Dagens Finans*. Reporting on trade figures can be done by a bright college leaver,' Alicia smiles and adds, 'You know how it's been.'

Patrick nods.

'And us...well we can see each other every weekend and holidays. You'll be coming over to see the girls, anyway, I presume.'

Patrick coughs.

'Ah. I meant to tell you. Mia is moving back to Stockholm.'

Alicia places her half-eaten roll back on the plate. To calm herself, she takes a sip of her coffee.

Before she has time to comment, Patrick says, 'I know how it looks, but you have to trust me. I won't go there again. I'm going to give up the apartment and find somewhere else to live.'

Alicia gazes at the man opposite her. She has noticed once again how he draws attention of the café's female customers. There are furtive glances and even some openly flirtatious smiles. Patrick doesn't encourage them, but he's aware of the adoration he draws from the opposite sex. A man like this could be overconfident, even arrogant, but somehow Patrick manages to be neither. It's true that he is self-assured, but the more Alicia gets to know him, the more she realizes that underneath there is a lot of insecurity. Perhaps it's his modest upbringing in northern Sweden, perhaps it's all the years he spent as the son-in-law of Kurt and Beatrice Eriksson. Whatever it is, Alicia finds his vulnerability attractive. And he is trustworthy, Alicia is certain of that.

'I know,' she says.

SIXTY-SIX

'Y ou have made me very happy!' Hilda says.
She's hugging her daughter tightly after hearing that
Alicia is going to stay in Sjoland and take on the running of
the farm.

'You think I can do it?' Alicia asks.

'Of course you can! You grew up here after all.'

Hilda's eyes fill with tears

'Uffe would be so proud of you.'

'Now, Mom, no more crying. This is a joyful day!' Alicia says.

Hilda wipes the corner of her eyes.

'I have some news too.'

She sits down in one of the chairs at the kitchen table.

'I've been thinking about taking in summer visitors. Not into the
cottages, they're often needed for the farm laborers, but into the main
house. There are four bedrooms and an extra bathroom upstairs, in
addition to the one we have off our bedroom. I mentioned my idea to
Uffe last year after the shop failed, but he didn't want strangers in the
house. It would provide me with a little extra money and something
for me to do.'

'That's an excellent idea!' Alicia says.

She's been worrying about what her mom would do. She knows

Hilda will not want to sit at home twiddling her thumbs. With Alicia running the farm, she would invariably get mixed up with it, and that might prove too much for their relationship.

Hilda smiles and says, 'I was thinking of converting Uffe's office and the storage next to it for extra visitor space, but if you are going to stay, how about we turn it into your home instead?'

Hilda rises and takes Alicia by the shoulders. 'Come, I'll show you.'

Across the yard, Hilda explains what she's been planning.

'We can make the office into a large kitchen diner.'

Hilda regards Alicia expectantly.

Alicia grins.

'This is a great idea.'

She knows how much her mother loves a remodeling project. Her mom has been wanting to do something with Uffe's office for ages, but he liked the space as it was and resisted any efforts on Hilda's part even to apply a lick of paint.

Hilda walks past the small space between Uffe's office and a larger barn, which is used as a storage room. She enters the area on the other side of the building. This is at least three times the size of Uffe's office. It's filled with old farm machinery and rusted bicycles. Alicia's tummy flips for a moment when she sees Stefan's old tricycle in the corner.

Her mother walks past all the junk and pulls aside a large plastic sheet at the far wall.

'Look at this. I bet you've forgotten that there's this fantastic view of the sea!'

Alicia gazes at the scene in front of her. The view from the milking parlor is the same as the one from the sauna cottage, where Alicia lived for part of last year. She can see the water's edge beyond a sloping meadow. The reeds are more overgrown here than in front of the cottage, and there is no jetty to swim from. But the view is equally breathtaking, if not more so. It's a windy day and she can see white-topped waves hitting the shore. In the distance there are a couple of rocky outcrops. One is covered in dense forest, but the other is sheer rock face, dropping dramatically into the sea.

Alicia pauses. Living here, where Uffe spent so much of his time, feels right, and not at all mournful as she might have imagined. Before she has time to say anything her mother is talking again, waving her hands in the air and pointing at different parts of the building.

'We could add a mezzanine floor for a bedroom, and a wood burner in the corner there. If we install glazed doors here, you could have a little wooden deck for your morning coffee. Of course, you are always welcome at mine, but I understand you need your privacy. None of this side is visible from the house.'

'Thank you Mom, you've thought of everything,' Alicia says. It's her turn to feel tearful, and even though they are tears of joy, she swallows them back.

She sees her new little house in her mind's eye, just as Hilda has described it.

'If you get a sofa bed, you can even have guests overnight, unless they sleep with you on the mezzanine,' Hilda says, looking carefully at Alicia.

Alicia smiles.

'I expect Patrick will be over quite a few times,' she says.

At that, Hilda comes and hugs her once more.

'Oh, I am so glad you two are back together again! I truly think you are made for each other.'

Alicia laughs and says, 'I think you might be right.'

THE DAY WE MET

Don't forget your free story!

The Day We Met is set at Uppsala University in Sweden where Alicia is studying English. When a migraine is threatening to ruin her day, the last thing she expects is to meet the man of her dreams.

Liam, a British doctor, is in Uppsala attending a medical conference when a beautiful woman chooses to sit at the same table as him in the busy student canteen. There's something beguiling about this young student and Liam cannot take his eyes off her.

Go to **helenahalme.com** to sign up to my Readers' Group and get your free story now!

ALSO BY HELENA HALME

The Nordic Heart Series:
The Young Heart (Prequel)
The English Heart (Book 1)
The Faithful Heart (Book 2)
The Good Heart (Book 3)
The True Heart (Book 4)
The Christmas Heart (Book 5)
The Nordic Heart Boxset Books 1-4
Love on the Island Series:
The Day We Met: Prequel Short Story
The Island Affair (Book 1)
An Island Christmas (Book 2)
The Island Daughter (Book 3)
Other novels:
Coffee and Vodka: A Nordic family drama
The Red King of Helsinki: Lies, Spies and Gymnastics

A NOTE FROM THE AUTHOR

I hope you enjoyed *the Love on the Island Books 1-3!* You may have heard authors talk about reviews and the effect they have on the success of the title. I would be thrilled if you could take a little time to write a review.

Thank you.

ABOUT THE AUTHOR

Helena Halme grew up in Tampere, central Finland, and moved to the UK via Stockholm and Helsinki at the age of 22. She is a former BBC journalist and has also worked as a magazine editor, a bookseller and, until recently, ran a Finnish/British cultural association in London.

Since gaining an MA in Creative Writing at Bath Spa University, Helena has published 12 fiction titles, including six in *The Nordic Heart* and three in *Love on the Island* series.

Helena lives in North London with her ex-Navy husband and an old stubborn terrier, called Jerry. She loves Nordic Noir and sings along to Abba songs when no one is around.

You can read Helena's blog at www.helenahalme.com, where you can also sign up for her *Readers' Group* and receive an exclusive, free short story, *The Day We Met*.

Find Helena Halme online
www.helenahalme.com
hello@helenahalme.com

Printed in Great Britain
by Amazon

52108897R00433